TEXAS! TRILOGY

TEXAS! TRILOGY

Including

- Texas! Lucky
- Texas! Chase
- Texas! Sage

by SANDRA BROWN

DOUBLEDAY

NEW YORK · TORONTO · LONDON · SYDNEY · AUCKLAND

Contents

TEXAS!
LUCKY

Chapter One

There was going to be trouble, and, hell, he just wasn't in the mood for it.

Lucky Tyler, seated on a barstool, was nursing his second whiskey and water. Bothered again by the rough, masculine laughter coming from one corner of the tavern, he glanced irritably over his shoulder to look in that direction.

"Might've known Little Alvin would sniff her out," the bartender said.

Lucky only grunted in response. Turning back to his drink, he hunched his shoulders and sank a little deeper into his slouching position on the barstool. He reasoned that if the broad hadn't wanted the attentions of Little Alvin or any other guy, she wouldn't have come into the lounge alone.

Describing the place as a lounge sure was euphomistic, he thought. The place was a bona fide honky-tonk. It didn't possess a single feature that would elevate it to any higher caliber of drinking hole than that.

It had first opened during the boom, fifty or so years earlier. Before the bar had a flashing neon star out front, before it had indoor plumbing, the place had served bootleg liquor to roughnecks, wildcatters, and the ladies of the night who comforted them when the wells turned up dry or who took their money when they struck black gold.

The highway tavern hadn't had a name then that anybody could remember, and it didn't have one now. It was simply known to locals as "the place," as in, "Meet'chu at the place after work for a drink." Respectable men frequented it alongside those who weren't respectable.

But a respectable woman wouldn't be caught dead inside. If a woman came to the place, she was there for one reason and one reason only. The instant a woman alone darkened the door, hunting season commenced. It was understood.

That's why Lucky wasn't too concerned about the welfare of the woman being hassled by Little Alvin and one of his least savory companions, Jack Ed Patterson.

However, when another burst of laughter erupted from the corner, Lucky swung his gaze around again. Several things struck him as odd. A long-neck beer stood on the chipped Formica table in front of the woman, along with a half-filled glass. A glass? She must have requested it, because at the place long necks weren't usually served with a glass even to a woman. Strange that she had asked for a glass.

She wasn't exactly dolled up either. Oh, she was good-looking, all right, but her makeup was conservative and her clothing upscale and chic. She wasn't your ordinary gal-about-town on the prowl or even a housewife looking for a distraction from the daily grind or revenge on an inattentive husband. He couldn't quite pigeonhole her, and that intrigued him.

"How long's she been here?" he asked the bartender.

"Got here 'bout a half hour 'fore you came in. Know her?"

Lucky shook his head no.

"Then she sure as hell ain't from around here." The bartender guffawed, implying that Lucky kept a more accurate account of the local female population than the Census Bureau. Which was the truth.

"Soon as she came in and ordered her beer, she drew everybody's attention like flies to honey. 'Course, the rest backed off when Little Alvin showed more than a passing interest."

"Yeah, he's a real ladies' man, all right," Lucky said sardonically.

Little Alvin had been so-dubbed merely because he was eighth of the eight offspring born to the Cagneys. Standing 6′ 5″, he weighed about 290, 30 pounds of it put on since he had left the NFL several years earlier.

He'd been playing first-string linebacker for the Denver Broncos when he caused a league controversy. One of his quarterback sacks had left a rookie Dolphins player with blurred vision, stuttering speech, and a retirement pension.

The tackle had been so unnecessarily rough, Little Alvin himself had suffered a dislocated shoulder. The team management had used his injury as its reason for not picking up his contract at the end of that season, but it was speculated that management was glad of the excuse to get rid of him.

Upon his suspension, Little Alvin had returned home to East Texas and picked up where he'd left off years before as Milton Point's meanest bully. He still considered himself a superstud football hero.

Tonight neither his dubious charm nor his fame were working on the woman he'd set his sights on. Even from across the dim, smoky lounge, Lucky could see that she was growing more agitated by the minute.

The George Straight ballad blaring from the jukebox prevented him from hearing the words they exchanged, but when Little Alvin laid a meaty hand on the woman's shoulder, there was no mistaking how she felt about his romantic overtures. She shrugged off his hand and reached for her purse. She attempted to slide out of the booth, but 290 pounds of Little Alvin Cagney, along with his sidekick, Jack Ed Patterson, who had recently done time in Huntsville State Prison for assault with a deadly weapon, blocked her escape.

Lucky sighed. He was going to have to do something about this, and damned if he was in the mood for it. It had been a hell of a week. Business was rotten, and a loan payment was only weeks away from coming due. Susan was dropping hints about a diamond ring for her left hand. The last thing he needed was a run-in with a couple of lowlifes like Little Alvin and Jack Ed.

But what if their quarry had been his kid sister, Sage? He would like to think that some decent guy would come to her aid. Of course, Sage was smart enough not to get herself into a sticky situation like this. But you couldn't decline to protect a woman's virtue just because she was dim-witted.

His daddy had drilled into him and Chase, his older brother by a year and a half, that when a lady said no to a pass, the answer was no. Period. No questions asked. The woman might not be very nice for leading a guy on and then changing her mind at the last minute, but the answer was still, unequivocally, *no*. And his mother expected him to treat every woman chivalrously, no matter how trashy she was.

His ears still rang whenever he recalled the lecture his mother had given him in the ninth grade, when he brought home the delicious gossip that Drucilla Hawkins had "done it" at the drive-in the previous Saturday night. What had gone on in the backseat of her boyfriend's blue Dodge was the talk of the school.

Laurie Tyler wasn't interested in the juicy details of Miss Hawkins's fall from grace. She had sternly warned her younger son that he had better not be overheard defaming any girl's reputation, no matter how reliable the source of the gossip was. He'd been admonished to treat every woman—and her reputation—with respect and dignity. It had been such a scalding lecture that he remembered it to this day, nearly twenty years later, at the ripe old age of thirty-two.

He muttered another foul curse beneath his breath, and tossed back the remainder of his drink. Some things you had to do whether you wanted to or not. Defending a woman from Little Alvin and Jack Ed was one of those things.

One booted foot, then the other, unhooked its heel from the chrome rung encircling the legs of the barstool. Lucky swiveled around on the maroon vinyl seat, worn slick and smooth by too many rear ends to count.

"Careful, Lucky," the bartender warned. "They've been drinking all afternoon. You know how mean Little Alvin gets when he's drunk. Jack Ed's bound to have his knife handy, too."

"I'm not looking for trouble."

"Maybe not, but if you cut in on Little Alvin's action, you'll get trouble."

Apparently everyone else in the place smelled trouble, too, because the moment Lucky left his stool at the bar, bells on the pinball machines fell silent for the first time in hours. The row of video games still beeped and burped and flashed a kaleidoscope of electronic colors, but those playing them turned curiously, instantly attuned to the sudden shift in the atmosphere. It was like the expectant stillness before a tornado struck.

Drinkers at the bar and those occupying booths ceased conversations to follow Lucky's swaggering progress across the room toward the booth where the woman was demanding that an amused Little Alvin get out of her way.

"I'd like to leave now."

Lucky wasn't fooled by the quiet calm in her voice. Her eyes were shifting nervously between the two men. Jack Ed was a fraction of Little Alvin's size, but in his own way he was intimidating. He had a ferret's eyes and the sharp, pointed grin of a jackal. They hadn't fallen for her phony defiance any more than he had.

"How come you're in such a hurry, honey?" Little Alvin cooed. He bent over her so far, she recoiled into the corner of the booth. "We're just startin' to have fun."

Jack Ed giggled at his friend's clever way with words. His laughter broke off when Lucky spoke from behind him.

"I don't think the lady's having any fun a-tall, Alvin."

Little Alvin came around with all the grace, agility and temperament of a bull whose tail had just been given a hard yank. Lucky was standing with one thumb tucked beneath his waistband, the hand casually curled over his tooled-leather belt, and the other braced against the tarnished brass hat rack mounted on the end of the neighboring booth. His feet were crossed at the ankles. He was smiling pleasantly. Only the cocky tilt of his dark blond head and the coldness of his blue eyes belied his friendly tone of voice.

"Bug off, Tyler. This is none of your b'iness."

"Oh, I think it is. Since a dumb slab of meat like you doesn't seem to appeal to the lady, she's still fair game, right?" Lucky looked down at the woman and gave her the warm smile and lazy wink that had coaxed a legion of women out of their better judgment and their clothing. "Hi. How're you doin'?"

Little Alvin growled his disapproval and took two hulking footsteps toward Lucky, whom he championed in size by three inches in height and a hundred pounds. He swung a ham-size fist toward Lucky's head.

Lucky, for all his seeming nonchalance, was braced and ready for the attack. He parried quickly to his left, ducking the blow and simultaneously catching Jack Ed under the chin with his elbow. Everybody in the place heard his lupine teeth smash together. Jack Ed careened into the nearest pinball machine, which set up a chorus of ringing bells.

Having temporarily dispatched Jack Ed, Lucky pivoted in time to place his right eye directly in the path of Alvin's ramming right fist. Lucky had been kicked in the head by a horse when he was twelve. The kick had knocked him cold. It hadn't hurt nearly as much as Alvin's punch.

His whole body shivered with the pain of the impact. If he'd had time to indulge it, his stomach would have rebelled by heaving up two glasses of whiskey and water. As it was, he knew he had to either get back into the fight or die at the enraged hands of Little Alvin Cagney.

Bar patrons were cheering him on, except those who feared reprisal from Alvin. Knowing all he had on his side were dexterity and speed, he lowered his head and drove his shoulder into Alvin's gut, knocking the larger man off balance.

A sudden shout warned him of Jack Ed's recovery. Spinning around, he barely had time to suck in his midsection before Jack Ed took a swipe at it with his infamous knife. He kicked the extended knife out of Jack Ed's hand, then gave him a quick chop in the Adam's apple with the edge of his hand. The ex-con toppled into a table; it crashed to the floor. Jack Ed sprawled beside it unconscious, lying in a puddle of spilled beer and broken glass.

Lucky came around again to confront Alvin. Looking like the provoked giant in a Grimm's tale, the former linebacker was crouched in an attack stance.

"Stop this!"

The woman was out of the booth. Hands on hips, she was furiously addressing both of them, though Lucky seemed the only one aware of her. Little Alvin's eyes were red with fury. His nostrils were receding and expanding like twin bellows.

"Get out of the way or you'll get hurt!" Lucky shouted to her.

"I want this to stop. You're behaving like—"

Little Alvin, giving her no more regard than he would a pesky housefly, flicked his hand at her, catching her lip and drawing blood. She fell backward.

"You son of a bitch," Lucky snarled. Any brute who would strike a woman didn't deserve a clean fight. Swinging up his booted foot, he viciously caught the other man in the crotch.

Instantly Little Alvin was stunned motionless, seemingly held upright by the gasps that rose from the onlookers. Then he clutched the injured area and dropped to his knees, rattling glassware throughout the building. At last, eyes crossing, he went over face first into the puddle of beer beside Jack Ed.

Lucky gulped in several cleansing breaths and tentatively dabbed at his swelling eye. Stiffly he approached the woman, who was attempting to stanch her bleeding lip with a paper napkin.

"You all right?"

She flung her head up and glared at him with vivid green eyes. Lucky, expecting tears, admiration, and gushing gratitude, was startled to see naked enmity on her face.

"Thanks a lot," she said sarcastically. "You were a big help."

"Wha—"

"Lucky," the bartender called to him, "here comes the sheriff."

Lucky blew out a gust of breath as he surveyed the damage the fight had caused. Overturned tables and chairs made the place look as if it had sustained storm damage. Broken glass, spilled beer, and capsized ashtrays had left a disgusting mess on the floor where two battered bodies still lay.

And the ungrateful tart, whose honor he had stupidly defended, was mad at *him*.

Some days, no matter how hard you tried, nothing went right. Placing his hands on his hips, his head dropping forward, he muttered, "Hell."

Chapter Two

Sheriff Patrick Bush shook his head in dismay as he observed Little Alvin and Jack Ed. Alvin was rolling from side to side, groaning and clutching his groin; Jack Ed remained blessedly unconscious.

The sheriff maneuvered the matchstick from one corner of his mouth to the other and looked up at Lucky from beneath the wide brim of his Stetson. "Now, how come you went and did that to these boys, huh?"

"Might've known I'd get blamed for it," Lucky grumbled as he plowed his fingers through his thick hair, raking it off his forehead.

The sheriff pointed toward Lucky's middle. "You hurt?"

Only then did Lucky notice that his shirt had been ripped and was hanging open. Jack Ed's knife had left a thin red arc across his stomach. "It's okay."

"Need an ambulance?"

"Hell, no." He swabbed at the trickle of blood with his tattered shirt.

"Start cleaning up this mess," the sheriff ordered his accompanying deputy. Turning to Lucky, he asked, "What happened?"

"They were coming on to her, and she didn't like it."

Bush looked at the woman, who had been standing nearby, silently fuming. She had tried to leave earlier, but had been instructed to stay put until the sheriff got around to asking her a few questions.

"You okay, ma'am?" The sheriff was looking worriedly at her lip. It was slightly swollen, but no longer bleeding. Despite the unnatural fullness, it was pulled into a tight, narrow grimace.

"I'm perfectly fine. I was perfectly fine when Sir Galahad here took it upon himself to interfere."

"Sorry," Lucky snapped, "I thought I was helping you out."

"Helping? You call this *helping?"* She flung her arms wide to en-

compass the damage done to the place. "All you did was create an unnecessary ruckus."

"That true, Lucky?" the sheriff asked.

Barely controlling his temper as he glared down at the woman, Lucky said, "Ask the witnesses."

The sheriff methodically polled the bystanders. All murmured agreement to Lucky's version of what had taken place. The woman gave each one a disdainful glare. "Am I free to go now?" she asked the sheriff.

"How'd your lip get busted, ma'am?"

"The gorilla did it," she said, nodding down at Little Alvin and corroborating Lucky's account of her injury.

"What was your business here?"

"You didn't ask what *they* were doing here," she argued, gesturing to the men surrounding her.

"I know what they were doing here," Bush replied. "Well?"

"I was having a beer," she answered curtly.

"You didn't lead these men on, did you? You know, wink, flirt, anything like that?"

She didn't deign to answer, and only stared at him with open contempt for even suggesting such a thing. In Pat Bush's estimation she didn't look like a typical bar pickup. During his twenty-year tenure as sheriff he'd broken up enough barroom brawls to recognize a trouble-making broad when he saw one.

This one wasn't typical. Her clothing wasn't provocative. Neither was her demeanor. Rather than inviting male attention, she put out vibes that said *Do Not Touch* and seemed about as approachable as a lady porcupine.

More out of curiosity than anything, he asked, "You from around here?"

"No, from out of town."

"Where 'bouts?"

"I was just passing through Milton Point," she replied evasively, "on my way to the interstate highway."

Sheriff Bush tipped his hat forward so he could scratch the back of his head beneath it. "Well, ma'am, the next time you're just passing through, find another place to have a beer, a place more suitable for ladies."

Lucky made an unflattering snorting sound, implying that he didn't believe she fit the distinction.

"I'll take that into consideration, Sheriff." She gave Lucky another chilling glare. Then, slipping the strap of her handbag over her shoulder, she headed for the door.

"You don't want to press charges for the busted lip?" Sheriff Bush called after her.

"I only want to get out of here." Moving purposefully toward the door, she went out into the waning twilight without looking back.

Every eye in the room followed her departure. "Ungrateful bitch," Lucky muttered.

"What's that?" the sheriff asked, leaning toward Lucky.

"Nothing. Look, I gotta split, too." A glance through the dusty window showed her getting into a red compact car, one of those square, lookalike foreign numbers.

"Hold your horses, Lucky," Sheriff Bush said sternly. "I warned you last time that if you got into any more fights—"

"I didn't start this, Pat."

Though Pat Bush was acting in an official capacity, Lucky addressed him like the family friend he was, one who'd bounced Lucky on his knee when he was still in diapers. So while Lucky respected Pat's uniform, he wasn't intimidated by it.

"Who're you going to believe? Me or them?" he asked, gesturing down to the two injured men.

The red car was pulling onto the two-lane highway, its rear wheels sending up a cloud of dust. Losing his patience, Lucky again confronted Pat, who kept such a watchful eye on the Tylers that very few of their escapades got past him.

He had caught Chase and Lucky pilfering apples from the A&P supermarket when they were kids, and turning over portable toilets at a drilling site one Halloween night, and throwing up their first bottle of whiskey beneath the bleachers at the football stadium. While driving them home, he'd given them a sound lecture on the evils of drinking irresponsibly before turning them over to their daddy for parental "guidance." He'd been a pallbearer at Bud Tyler's funeral two years before, and had cried as hard as any bona fide member of the family.

"Am I under arrest or not?" Lucky asked him now.

"Get on outta here," the sheriff said gruffly. "I'll wait here till these skunks come around." He nudged Little Alvin and Jack Ed with the toe of his lizard boot. "Do something smart for a change, and stay outta their way for a day or two."

"Sure thing."

"And you'd better let your mama take a look at that cut."

"It's fine."

In a hurry, Lucky tossed a five-dollar bill on the bar to cover the cost of his drinks and dashed out the door. He had noted that the red car had turned west onto the highway and remembered the woman saying she was headed for the interstate, which was several miles away. He vaulted into his vintage model Mustang convertible and took out after her in hot pursuit.

Miss Prissy wasn't going to get away with brushing him off like that. He'd risked his life for her. Only good fortune and well-timed quick-stepping had prevented him from getting more than the tip of Jack Ed's knife. His eye was swollen nearly shut now, and his skull felt as if a drilling bit were going through it. He would look like hell for days on account of this ungrateful redheaded chippy.

Redheaded? He thought back. *Yeah, sorta red. Dark reddish-brown. Auburn.*

How was he going to explain his battered face to his mother and Chase, who just this morning had stressed to him the importance of keeping their noses absolutely clean?

Tyler Drilling Company was faced with bankruptcy unless they could persuade the bank to let them pay only the interest on their note and roll over the principal for another six months at least. Lucky shouldn't be seen around town sporting a black eye. Who wanted to extend credit to a brawler?

"Since Daddy died," Chase had said that morning, "everybody's been skeptical that you and I can run Tyler Drilling as well as he did."

"Hell, it's not our fault the price of crude fell drastically and has stayed so damned low."

It was an argument that didn't need voicing. The faltering oil market and its disastrous effect on the Texas economy weren't of their making, but they were suffering the consequences just the same. The equipment Tyler Drilling leased out had been so inactive over the last several months, they had joked about storing it in mothballs.

The brothers were frantically trying to come up with an idea for diversification that would generate business and income. In the meantime the bank was becoming less and less tolerant of any outstanding loans. Though most of the board members were lifelong friends, they couldn't afford to be sympathetic indefinitely when so many banks across the nation, and particularly in Texas, were failing.

"The best we can do," Chase had said, "is show them our intent to pay when we can, try to drum up business, and stay out of trouble."

"That last remark is aimed at me, I guess."

Chase had smiled good-naturedly at his younger brother. "Now that

I'm settled down with a loving wife, you're the tomcat of the family. You're expected to sow a few wild oats."

"Well, those days might be coming to a close," Lucky had remarked unhappily.

His brother, shrewdly picking up on the veiled reference, asked, "How *is* Susan?"

Being reminded of her now made Lucky groan. Or maybe he groaned because, when he turned the Mustang onto the entrance ramp of the interstate highway and pushed it through the forward gears, the cut across his belly pulled apart again and started to ache.

"Damn that woman," he cursed as he floorboarded the convertible in order to close the distance between him and the winking taillights he was following.

He wasn't sure what he was going to do when he actually caught her. Probably nothing more than demand an apology for the snooty way she'd treated him after he'd risked life and limb to protect her from sexual harassment.

However, thinking back on the contemptuous way she'd looked him over, as if he were a piece of bubble gum stuck to the bottom of her shoe, he figured an apology wasn't going to come easily. She didn't seem the simpering type.

Women. They were his bane and his delight. Couldn't live with them. Sure as hell couldn't live without them. He had vowed to abstain numerous times after particularly harrowing love affairs, but he knew it was a vow he'd never keep.

He loved women—their clothes, their paraphernalia, their scent. He liked their giggles and their tears, and, even though it often drove him to distraction, their persistent attention to detail. He liked everything about them that made them different from himself, from their maddening habit of paying with change in favor of breaking a bill to the way their bodies were made. In Lucky's educated opinion, about the best thing God ever created was a woman's skin.

But out of bed they were a royal pain.

Take that young divorcée in Marshall, for instance. She was a complainer, and could whine until the sound of her voice was as offensive as fingernails on a chalkboard. The only time she wasn't griping about something was when they were in bed. There, she purred.

Another of his most recent liaisons had been with a gold digger. If he didn't bring her a gift each time he saw her, any kind of trinket, she swelled up with affront. Only hours of loving could coax her back into a good mood. Then there was the clerk at the drugstore. In bed she was clever and innovative. Out of it, she wasn't as smart as the nearest fence post.

Susan Young was just the opposite. She was smart. Maybe too smart. He suspected that she was withholding sexual favors not because of any moral scruples, but because she wanted him standing at the altar all dressed up in a tuxedo and watching her as she glided down the aisle of First Methodist Church in a long white gown to the tempo of the wedding march from *Lohengrin*.

After his discouraging meeting with Chase that morning, Lucky had kept his lunch date with Susan at the home she shared with her parents. Her father, George, was CEO of the bank that held Tyler Drilling's note. They lived in an impressive home on one-and-a-half perfectly manicured acres in the center of town. As soon as the maid had cleared away the dishes, George had returned to the bank and Mrs. Young had excused herself to go upstairs, leaving Lucky alone with Susan.

He had pulled her into his arms and kissed her. Smacking his lips when they pulled apart, he sighed. "Better than Clara's strawberry shortcake," he said, referring to the sumptuous dessert the housekeeper had served.

"Sometimes I think all you want from me is kisses."

His eyes moved over her, taking in her affected pout and the small, impudent breasts that jutted against her blouse. He covered one with his hand. "That's not all I want."

Susan squirmed away from him. "Lucky Tyler, will you behave? My mama's upstairs, and Clara's in the kitchen."

"Then let's go someplace else," he suggested on a burst of inspiration. Their house was formal and somber and unpleasantly reminded him of a funeral home, which put a damper on romance. In that environment it was little wonder Susan was holding out. "I've got to drive over toward Henderson this afternoon and see a man on business. Why don't you come along?"

She declined with an adamant shake of her head. "You drive too fast. With the top down, my hair gets blown all over the place."

"Honey, with what I have in mind, it'll get messed up anyway," he drawled, pulling her against him again. This time she participated more actively in their kiss. By the time they came up for air, Lucky was hot and ready.

Then Susan had ruined his arousal by mentioning her father.

"Promise not to get mad if I tell you something." Experience had taught him that those words usually prefaced something that was going to make him mad, but he gave her his promise anyway. She didn't meet his eyes as she played with the buttons on his shirt. "Daddy's worried about me spending so much time with you."

"Why's that? He seemed polite enough at lunch."

"He's always polite. But he's still not thrilled about our going out lately."

"Why not?"

"You *do* have a reputation, you know. A reputation that nice girls like me aren't even supposed to know about."

"Oh yeah?" She wasn't so nice that she balked when his hand ventured beneath her full skirt and stroked the back of her thigh. "He asked me what your intentions were, and I had to tell him that I honestly don't know."

He was already bored with the topic of George Young and entranced by the expanse of smooth thigh he was caressing, but the word "intentions" set off alarms inside his head. He withdrew his hand and took several steps away from her. While she had his undivided attention, she drove home her point.

"Of course, Daddy never discusses his banking business with me," she said with a calculated batting of eyelashes, "but I get the distinct impression that he's afraid to extend a loan to a man who isn't settled down. You know, married and all."

Lucky hastily consulted his wristwatch. "Gee, it's getting late. If I can't talk you into going with me, I need to get on the road. Don't want to miss that appointment." He headed for the door.

"Lucky?"

"Hmm?"

Moving to face him and looping her arms around the back of his neck, she arched the front of her body against his. She came up on tiptoe and placed her lips near his ear, whispering, "Daddy would almost have to extend your loan if you were family, wouldn't he?"

He had given her a sick smile and beat a quick retreat, after promising to join them for dinner that evening at seven-thirty. He wasn't ready to get married. Not to Susan. Not to anybody. Not by a long shot.

He liked Susan well enough. He wanted to get her into bed, but mainly because he hadn't yet managed to. She was spoiled and would be hell to live with. Besides, he strongly suspected that she wouldn't be all that great a lover. He believed that for her, sex would be a form of currency, not pleasure.

He liked his women willing, active, and enjoying the tumble as much as he did. Damned if he wanted a wife who swapped him favor for favor, or one who withheld bedroom privileges until she got her way.

No, he hoped Susan Young wasn't holding her breath until he got down on bended knee and asked for her hand in marriage. She would turn blue in the face before that ever happened.

And as soon as he could get to a phone, he would need to call and cancel their dinner date. She would be upset, but he sure as hell couldn't show up at the Youngs' dinner table with his face looking the way it did.

"Women," he muttered with disgust as he took the exit ramp behind the saucy red compact.

Chapter Three

Lucky pulled into the paved parking lot about ninety seconds behind the woman. The roadside complex comprised a U-shaped, two-story motel, a restaurant boasting the best chicken-fried steak in the state—which he seriously doubted—a gas station with dozens of pumps, and a combination liquor and convenience store.

She had gone into the restaurant. Through the plate-glass window Lucky watched a waitress show her to a table. In a short while she was brought what appeared to be a club sandwich. How could she think of food? He felt like hell. Eating was out of the question.

Easing himself out of his car and keeping away from the window so she wouldn't see him, he limped toward the convenience store.

"What happened to you, buddy? Get hit by a Mack truck?"

"Something like that," Lucky replied to the cheerful clerk who rang up his purchases. He bought a pint bottle of whiskey, a tin of aspirin, and a raw steak. Because the gray meat was turning green around the edges, it had been marked down. It was unfit for human consumption, but that wasn't what he had in mind anyway.

"Does the other guy look better or worse?" the curious clerk asked.

Lucky gave him a lopsided grin. "He looks okay, but he feels a hell of a lot worse."

Returning to his car, he slumped in the white leather seat behind the wheel, uncapped the bottle, and washed down three aspirins with his first swig of whiskey. He had just unwrapped the smelly steak when he saw the woman emerge from the restaurant. Because he had been anticipating how good it was going to feel to place the cool meat on his throbbing eye, he was cursing beneath his breath when he reached for the car door handle, prepared to open it.

He paused, however, when she walked down the sidewalk and entered the check-in office of the motel. Within a few minutes she came out with a room key.

Lucky waited until she had backed out and driven her car around the corner before following her. He rounded the building just in time to see her entering a room on the ground floor about midway along the west wing of the motel.

Things were looking up, he thought with satisfaction as he pulled his Mustang into a parking slot. He preferred their confrontation to be private. That was why he hadn't followed her into the restaurant. Unwittingly she was playing right into his hands.

Pocketing his car keys in his jeans, and taking the steak, aspirin, and whiskey with him, he sauntered toward the door she had just closed behind her and knocked.

He could envision her pausing in whatever she was doing and looking curiously at the door before moving toward it cautiously. He grinned into the peephole. "You might just as well open the door. I know you recognize me."

The door was jerked open. She looked as volatile as a rocket about to launch. "What are you doing here?"

"Well," he drawled, "I was following you, and this is where you ended up, so here I am."

"Why were you following me?"

"Because you've got something I want."

At first taken aback, she then regarded him closely. Her wariness was immensely satisfying. She wasn't as tough as she wanted everybody to think. Still, her voice was haughty enough when she asked, "And what might that be?"

"An apology. Can I come in?"

Again his answer threw her off guard, so she didn't initially react when he moved toward the door. However, when his foot stepped on the threshold, she braced a hand against his chest. "No! You cannot come in. Do you think I'm crazy?"

"Could be. Why else would you come into the place all by yourself?"

"What place?"

He glanced down at her hand splayed across his sternum.

She hastily dropped it.

"The *place.* The bar where I courageously defended your honor this afternoon."

"My honor didn't need defending."

"It would have if Little Alvin had got his slimy paws on you."

"That weaselly little man?"

"No, that's Jack Ed. Jack Ed Patterson. Little Alvin is the one you called a gorilla. See, they call him Little Alvin because—"

"This is all very interesting, but I just want to forget it. Rest assured that there wasn't a snowball's chance in hell of them getting their 'slimy paws' on me. I had the situation under control."

"Is that right?" he asked, giving her a smile that said he didn't believe her for a minute, but he admired her spunk.

"That's right. Now, if you'll please excuse—"

"Uh-uh." He flattened his hand against the door she was about to shut in his face. "I don't have my apology yet."

"All right," she said irritably, shoving back a handful of auburn hair he wouldn't mind having a handful of himself. "I apologize for . . . for . . ."

"For not thanking me properly for rescuing you."

Gritting her teeth, she emphasized each word. "For not thanking you properly for rescuing me."

Propping his shoulder against the doorjamb, he squinted at her. "Wonder how come I don't think you really mean that?"

"Oh, I do. I truly do. From the bottom of my little ol' heart." Resting her right hand on the left side of her chest, she fluttered her eyelashes as she made a pledge. "If I ever get hit on in a bar again, you'll be the first one I call to defend me. I'll even recommend you to my fragile, feminine friends. How's that for gratitude?"

Ignoring her sarcasm, he raised his hand and touched the corner of her mouth with the tip of his index finger. "Your lip is bleeding again."

Turning her back on him, she rushed into the room and bent over the dresser top to check her reflection in the mirror. "It is not!" When she turned back around, Lucky was standing inside the closed door with his back to it, grinning like a hungry alley cat who'd just spotted a trapped mouse.

She drew herself up straight and said in an overly calm voice, "You don't want to do this. I'm warning you that I'm capable of defending myself. I'll raise such a hue and cry, I'll bring this building down. I know how to use physical force. I'll—"

Lucky started laughing. "What did you think I had in mind, ravishing you? All I want to do is hear a sincere apology from you, then I'll be on my way. In the meantime I'm going to borrow your bed for a minute."

Setting the whiskey, aspirin, and packaged steak on the nightstand, he hopped on one foot while pulling off his boot, then got rid of the other one the same way. He stretched out on the bed and piled both pillows against the headboard, sighing with relief as his head sank into them.

"If you don't get out of here this instant," she shouted angrily, "I'll call the management! I'll call the police!"

"Will you quiet down, please? My head's pounding. And whatever happened to all that self-defense you were threatening me with?" Removing the steak from its Styrofoam tray, he laid it against his battered eye. "If you'll bring the glasses over, I'll share my whiskey with you."

"I don't want any of your whiskey!"

"Fine. But could you please bring me a glass?"

"All right, if you won't leave, I will."

She marched toward the door and yanked it open. A jangling sound brought her head around. Her car keys were dangling from the end of Lucky's finger. "Not yet, Miss . . . uh, what's your name?"

"Go to hell!" she yelled, slamming the door closed again.

"Hmm. Named after your mother or father?"

"Give me my keys." She thrust out her hand.

"Not until you apologize. While I'm waiting, how about that glass?" He nodded toward the dresser where an ice bucket and two glasses were wrapped in sterile paper.

"If you want a glass, you can get it yourself."

"Okay." He sighed. But when he tried to sit up, the skin across his stomach stretched and the knife wound reopened. Wincing, he fell back onto the pillows. When his hand came away from reflexively touching the area, it was stained with fresh blood.

She gave a soft cry and quickly moved to the side of the bed. "You really are hurt."

"Did you think I was faking it?" Lucky was smiling, but his lips were pale and taut. "And I rarely go around in a shirt that's been sliced to ribbons."

"I . . . I didn't think . . ." she foundered. "Shouldn't you go to the hospital?"

"It'll be okay once it closes and stays closed."

Bending over him, she raised the hem of his ripped shirt. The extent of the cut made her gasp. It wasn't deep, but it arced from beneath his left breast to the waistband of his jeans on his right side. In places his tawny body hair was clotted with dried blood. The thin red line was seeping.

"This might get infected if it's not seen to." The resolution on her face barely had time to register with him before she said, "Better take off your shirt."

He hesitated, because in order to remove his shirt, he'd have to set aside her keys. She sensed the reason for his hesitation and said with asperity, "I wouldn't desert a man who is broken and bleeding."

Lucky dropped her keys on the nightstand, undid his shirt buttons, and eased up far enough to pull the fabric off his wide shoulders. She assisted him, negligently tossing the tattered garment to the floor and focusing only on his wound. "That wretched little man," she said, shuddering.

"Jack Ed? Yeah, he's a real scumbag. I'm relieved to know your flirtation with him wasn't anything serious."

"I wasn't flirting, and you know it," she said crossly. Leaving the bed, she went into the adjoining bathroom. A moment later she was back with a washcloth soaked in warm water. Nudging his hip with hers, she sat down on the bed beside him and applied the cloth to the cut. He sucked in a sharp breath.

"Does it hurt?" she asked in a gentle tone.

"Dumb question."

"I'm sorry, but it really should be cleaned. Lord only knows where that knife has been."

"I wouldn't even want to hazard a guess."

Before, he had been too angry at her to concede what a looker she was. Now he did. She wore her dark auburn hair shoulder length and loose, and probably tried to control its natural tendency to wave. Green eyes were now surveying his wound sympathetically, but he knew firsthand those eyes could be as frigid as a brass doorknob in January.

Her lean face had well-defined cheekbones, but a mouth with a soft, full lower lip. As a connoisseur, with vast experience of lips, he recognized them right off as extremely kissable. Her plush lower lip was a dead giveaway that this was a woman with a sensual nature.

That was probably something else she tried to control. She certainly tried repressing it with tailored clothing that didn't quite conceal a noteworthy figure. Not voluptuous. Not model-skinny either. Somewhere in between. Slender but curved. Spectacular legs. He couldn't wait to see her out of her suit jacket, with nothing covering her breasts except the silk blouse she was wearing beneath the jacket.

First things first, however. He was assured of success, but this woman was going to be an exciting challenge, something rare that didn't come along every day. Hell, he'd never had anybody exactly like her. Rules of the game might have to be adjusted as he went along.

"What's your name?"

She raised deep forest-green eyes to his. "D-D-Dovey."

" 'D-D-Dovey'?"

"That's right," she snapped defensively. "What's wrong with it?"

"Nothing. I just hadn't noticed you stuttering before. Or has the sight of my bare chest made you develop a speech impediment?" He suddenly wanted her face nuzzling in his chest hair. Badly.

"Hardly, Mr.—?"

"Lucky."

"Mr. Lucky?"

"No, I'm Lucky."

"Why is that?"

"I mean my name is Lucky. Lucky Tyler."

"Oh. Well, I assure you the sight of your bare chest leaves me cold, Mr. Tyler."

He didn't believe her, and the smile that tilted up one corner of his mouth said so. "Call me Lucky."

She reached for the bottle of whiskey on the nightstand and raised it in salute. "Well, Lucky, your luck just ran out."

"Huh?"

"Hold your breath." Before he could draw a sufficient one, she tipped the bottle and drizzled the liquor over the cut.

He blasted the four walls with words unfit to be spoken aloud, much less shouted. "Oh God, oh hell, oh—"

"Your language isn't becoming to a gentleman, Mr. Tyler."

"I'm gonna murder you. Stop pouring that stuff— Agh!"

"You're acting like a big baby."

"What the hell are you trying to do, scald me?"

"Kill the germs."

"Damn! It's killing *me*. Do something. Blow on it."

"That only causes germs to spread."

"Blow on it!"

She bent her head over his middle and blew gently along the cut. Her breath fanned his skin and cooled the stinging whiskey in the open wound. Droplets of it had collected in the satiny stripe of hair beneath his navel. Rivulets trickled beneath the waistband of his jeans. She blotted at them with her fingertips; then, without thinking, licked the liquor off her own skin. When she realized what she'd done, she sprang upright. "Better now?" she asked huskily.

When Lucky's blue eyes connected with hers, it was like completing an electric circuit. The atmosphere crackled. Matching her husky tone of voice, he said, "Yeah, much better. But warn me next time, okay?"

"I think that'll be enough to prevent any infection."

"I'd rather have risked infection. Although," he added in a low voice, "having you blow on me was worth it."

Because that flustered her, she raised her militant shield again. "Your eye looks terrible." The steak was now lying on the pillow where it had tumbled when she surprised him with her whiskey disinfectant. She picked it up by her thumb and index finger, holding it at arm's length. "This thing stinks to high heaven." Returning it to the Styrofoam tray, she rewrapped it in its plastic covering and tossed it into the trash can. "Stay where you are. I'll go get some ice."

Taking the plastic bucket with her, she left the room. Lucky liked the rear view of her too. Nice calves, nice bottom. If he didn't feel so bad . . .

But he did. During the fight, a rush of adrenaline had prevented him from feeling every punch. Now he was beginning to bruise in places he didn't even remember getting struck. His head was throbbing. He was feeling woozy, too, probably from the combination of the aspirin and that last shot of whiskey.

So while the thought of thawing Dovey was enthralling, he had to be content to fantasize. He certainly wasn't in any physical condition to take it further.

She returned with a bucket of ice, and filled the center of another washcloth with a scoop of small cubes. Knotting the corners over it, she brought it back to the bed and gently laid the makeshift ice pack on his eye.

"Thanks," he mumbled sleepily, realizing that he might be a little drunk as well as hurt. Her hand felt so comforting and cool, the way his mother's always had whenever he was sick with fever. He captured Dovey's hand with his and pressed it against his hot cheek.

She withdrew it and, in a schoolmarm's voice, said, "You can stay only until the swelling goes down."

A crude comeback sprang into his mind, but he resisted saying it. She wouldn't appreciate the bawdy comment right now. Besides, a reference to another swollen member of his body might be the very thing that would cause her to kick him out.

"I don't think I'll be going anywhere a-tall tonight," he said. "I feel like hell. This is all I want to do. Lie here. Real still and quiet."

"Good idea. You can have this room. I'll get another one."

"No!" he cried, dislodging his ice pack. "I mean, I can't take your room."

"Don't worry about it. It's paid for. It's the least I can do after what you did for me this afternoon."

"I'm not worried about finances," he said sharply. "But at least now you're admitting that I rescued you from Little Alvin and Jack Ed."

"Just so you could put in your bid for me?"

"Huh?"

"You 'rescued' me from them, but you're no better. Your technique simply has more polish."

"You think . . . think . . ." he stammered. "You think I want to share this room so— Come on, lady. Do I look like I'm in any condition to have sex?"

He followed her gaze down the length of his body and realized that he *did* look as if he could have sex. He was shirtless, bootless, and sprawled in the center of a motel bed. His recent vivid fantasies had created a bulge behind his fly that he hoped she wouldn't notice.

Immediately he fell back against the pillows with a great moan, not entirely faked, and replaced the ice pack against his eye. Waving his hand weakly, he said, "Go on. Do whatever you want. I'll be okay."

He watched through slitted eyes as she picked up her purse and headed for the door. "All my injuries are probably external," he mumbled just as she placed her hand on the doorknob.

She turned. "You think you might have internal injuries?"

"How the hell do I know? I'm no doctor." He placed a tentative hand on his side. "I thought I felt some swelling here, but it's probably nothing. Don't let me hold you up any longer."

Putting aside her handbag, she returned to the bed and gingerly sat down on the edge of the mattress. It was difficult for Lucky to look pained rather than give in to a complacent smile. He expected her to murmur sympathetically. Instead, she said nothing.

When he turned his good eye to her, she was staring down at him skeptically. "If you're conning me—"

"I told you to leave. Go on. Get another room. If I need you, I can call you through the motel operator."

She pulled her full lower lip through her teeth several times, which caused Lucky to groan for an entirely different reason. "Where do you feel the swelling?"

She had missed her calling. She could have been a great vaudevillian straight man. She was feeding him cues to which he had terrific punch lines. Again resisting the impulse to say aloud what he was thinking, he took her hand and guided it to his side.

"Around here somewhere. Feel anything out of the ordinary?"

She probed the taut skin for several moments, working her fingers up and down his side from waist to armpit. "No. I don't think so."

"That's a relief." She withdrew her hand. "I just hope no ribs are broken," he said hastily.

"Which side?"

"Same one."

Her fingers walked up his ribs cautiously, gradually feeling their way, until they reached the hair-matted, curved muscle of his chest. It might have been the feel of his chest or of his distended nipple that caused her to pull her hand back quickly.

"You're probably just stiff and sore," she said.

You can say that again, Dovey. "Good."

"But maybe I'd better not leave you alone," she surprised him by saying.

"Oh gee, that's terrific."

"I wouldn't want your death by internal bleeding on my conscience the rest of my life."

He frowned, saying drolly, "I wouldn't be crazy about that either." Removing the dripping ice pack from his eye, he handed it to her. "I'm drowning from this thing."

She took it away, and a few minutes later brought him a replacement. "Maybe by the time this one soaks through, your eye won't hurt so bad."

"Maybe. Could I please have a glass now? I think I'm entitled to a drink."

She poured each of them one. He tossed his back. It made him cough, but the liquor spread an anesthetizing heat through his midsection that made his discomfort more bearable.

Dovey went into the bathroom to add water to her cup, then dropped in a couple of ice cubes and sipped the drink like a lady. He remembered the glass she'd poured her beer into. Classy broad, he concluded muzzily. Not pretty in the soft, cushy, baby-doll sense, but certainly striking. She would turn heads on any sidewalk in the world.

Through a mist of pain and booze, he watched her remove her jacket and drape it over the back of a chair. Just as he'd thought—high, round breasts.

Oh yes, quite a looker was Dovey. But that wasn't all. She looked like a woman who knew her own mind and wasn't afraid to speak it. Levelheaded.

So what the hell had she been doing in the place?

He drifted off while puzzling through the question.

Chapter Four

The room was in total darkness when Lucky awakened. He tentatively opened one eye, after trying to open both reminded him that his right one would be black-and-blue and swollen shut for a day or two.

There was artificial light coming from the parking lot through the crack between the drape and the wall. It was still night, but he didn't care enough about the time to try to check his wristwatch.

His muscles were cramped from lying in one position for so long. He stretched, wincing and moaning slightly, and attempted to turn onto his side. When he did, his knee bumped into another.

He mumbled, "Dovey?"

"Hmm?"

He often awakened in the middle of the night with a woman in bed with him, so he responded as he usually did, by curving his arm across her and pulling her closer. Their knees automatically straightened, bringing their bodies together. Her hair brushed his cheek, and he turned his face into it, inhaling its honeysuckle scent and mindlessly kissing the strands that fell across his lips.

That felt so good, so right, he pressed his lips against her smooth forehead, then let them trail over her brows to her eyelids. Her lashes feathered his lips. He kissed her cheekbone, her nose, then her mouth.

Reflexively she drew back. "Lucky?" she whispered.

"Yes, baby," he whispered back before seeking her mouth again.

Her lips separated slowly. His tongue slipped between them. The inside of her mouth was delicious, but unfamiliar. He didn't remember ever kissing her. He explored deeply, leisurely, thoroughly, before biting gently on her lower lip—*that* he remembered craving to do—and sucking it into his mouth.

Making a small sound, she stirred against him restlessly. Her hands landed softly on his bare chest. As his tongue glided across her lower lip, he felt her fingers combing through his chest hair and her nails gently raking his skin. It struck him as odd that all her responses were so tinged with shyness. Then her fingertips glazed his turgid nipple, and his analysis ended. He had no thoughts beyond the taste and feel of her.

Rolling partially atop her, he lowered his hand to her breast, but became confused when he encountered clothing. It was silk, true, but what was she doing in bed with clothes on? It suddenly occurred to him that he was still wearing his jeans. No wonder he was so uncomfortable.

Befuddled, he reached for the top button of his fly. When it and the others were undone, he eased himself free, sighing with relief. The pressure had been almost painful.

Using his personal system of radar, his lips found her neck in the darkness and began dusting it with kisses as his hand moved to her breast again. The barriers of buttons and her brassiere clasp didn't deter him in the slightest, and soon his hand was filled with warm, malleable woman flesh.

Now we're back on track, he thought.

Everything was as it should be. Her breast was full and soft as his hand gently reshaped it. When he drew his thumb across the tip, it responded as he expected, becoming tight and hard. He sandwiched it between two of his fingers, enjoying the small wanting sounds that issued from her throat each time he applied the merest pressure to her nipple.

Eventually he took it into his mouth. His tongue circled and stroked and teased until her hands were clutching at his shoulders and his own body was burning like a furnace.

"Sweet, sweet," he whispered as he moved aside her garments and hungrily kissed her other breast. "So sweet."

Hose. Pantyhose, he thought miserably when his hand slipped beneath her skirt to caress her knee. He despised the things, and wished he had five minutes alone with the sadist who had invented them.

Moments later, however, he was delighted when his stroking hand discovered satiny smooth skin above her stockings. Apparently she was delighted, too, because at the touch of his hand against her inner bare thighs, her back arched off the bed and she released a staggering sigh of pleasure . . . and mounting need.

He tracked the lacy suspenders up to the V of her thighs. Inside her panties there were myriad textures to explore and fluid heat to drown in—he wanted badly to taste her. But he didn't have the time. His body was compelling him to hurry.

Had he ever had this woman before? No. He couldn't have. Otherwise he wouldn't be experiencing the contradictory urges to hurry and to loiter. He resented the time it took to fumble in his pocket for the foil-wrapped prophylactic and slip it on. The same desire that compelled him to position himself in the cradle of her thighs was prompting him to wait.

But he was already there, hard and hot and pressing toward sweet deliverance. And she was moist and soft and snug and sweet.

He heard himself say hoarsely, "I'm sorry. I'm sorry," but he wasn't even sure why.

All he was sure of was that he could never get enough of this woman. He gathered her beneath him, stroked her expertly, then buried himself deep within the sheath of her body. He wanted to sustain the pleasure, but it was so immense, he was helpless to stop the climax that claimed him, shook him, drained him.

It left him depleted. Totally spent, he laid his head on her breasts, making kissing motions against her nipples with his lips and lightly grinding his stubble-rough cheek against the soft mounds. Tenderly he palmed the nest of damp curls at the top of her thighs.

She touched his hair. Feeling the caress, he smiled. Then he drifted off to sleep again, wondering why, since it had been so damned good, he'd never made love to her before.

No matter how much Lucky drank the night before or how late he caroused, he always woke up at daybreak. His father had had chores for Chase and him to do before school. The habit of waking up early had been ingrained in him.

When he first became conscious, his head felt like a bowling ball stuffed with cotton, which might roll off his shoulders at any moment. It was an effort just to open his one functioning eye. Nevertheless, when he saw through the slit that he was alone in the bed, it came fully open. Stretching out his hand, he touched the imprint her body had left.

Grunting and groaning from the whipping he'd taken from Little Alvin, he sat up, switched on the nightstand lamp, and groggily surveyed the room. No suit jacket. No keys. No purse. No sign that she'd ever been there.

Maybe she'd just gone out for coffee.

He swung his feet to the floor, swearing liberally as pain rocketed up through the soles of his feet straight to the crown of his head. Dizzily he stood up and hobbled toward the window. With as dramatic a flourish as his battered body would allow, he flung back the drapes, startling a middle-aged couple walking down the breezeway.

The woman uttered an astonished gasp and hastily averted her eyes from Lucky's semi-nudity. Her husband gave him a reproving look before taking his offended wife's elbow and ushering her toward their camper parked at the curb.

Lucky automatically began rebuttoning his jeans while staring hard at the empty space where Dovey's red car had been parked the evening before.

"Damn!"

She had made a clean getaway. Sneaked out like a thief. That thought sent his hand plunging into his jeans pockets for his money clip. He found it intact.

She *had* been here, hadn't she? She wasn't just a figment of his imagination? No, of course not. He couldn't have imagined eyes that unusual shade of green. If he had dreamed her, it had been one hell of a dream. One he wished he could have every night and never wake up from.

He limped into the bathroom and switched on the unkind, unflattering fluorescent light. The image the mirror over the basin threw back at him belonged in a monster movie. Not only was his hair a mess and his lower jaw dark with stubble, but, as predicted, his eye was black-and-blue and swollen almost shut. There was a bruise as big as a baseball on his shoulder, probably where he had gouged Little Alvin's middle. The cut across his belly had closed, but was still a bright red line.

Then something incongruent caught his eye, something reflecting the blue-white glare of the fluorescent tube. He pulled a long, dark red strand of hair off his chest. It had become ensnared in his chest hair. Spurred on by that discovery, he returned to the bedroom and checked the wastepaper basket. He found what he was looking for.

Sinking down onto the bed, he held his aching head between both hands. She'd been real, all right. He hadn't imagined her. Nor had their lovemaking been a dream, except in the metaphorical sense.

Unsure whether that made him feel better or worse, he returned to the bathroom and showered. As soon as he was dressed, he left the room and got into his Mustang. He'd been negligent to leave it uncovered and unlocked all night, but thankfully it hadn't been vandalized. He drove it around the building to the office and went in to speak to the motel clerk—not the same one who had been there the evening before.

"Mornin'." His smile was almost as big as his ears. "Have some coffee."

"Good morning. Thanks." Lucky poured himself a cup from the pot brewing on a hot plate. "My name's Lucky Tyler. I spent last night in room one ten. The room was registered to a young woman."

"Yeah?" The clerk propped his elbows on the counter and leaned forward eagerly.

"Yeah. Would you please check your register for her name?"

"You don't know it?"

"Dovey something."

"Must've been some night. She do that to you?" He nodded toward Lucky's black eye and torn shirt.

"What's her name?" Lucky's tone of voice prohibited further speculation or comment.

The clerk wisely checked his files. "Smith, Mary."

"Mary?"

"M-a-r-y."

"Mary Smith?"

"That's right."

"Address?"

"Two hundred three Main Street."

"City?"

"Dallas."

"Dallas?"

"Dallas."

"Two hundred three Main Street, Dallas, Texas?"

"That's what it says."

Lucky was familiar enough with the city to know that the two-hundred block of Main Street was downtown in the heart of the commercial district. He suspected Ms. Smith of duplicity. And Smith! Mary Smith, for crying out loud. Not even very original. Where had "Dovey" come from?

"Did she give a phone number?"

"Nope."

"Car tag?"

"Nope."

"Which credit card did she use?"

"Says here she paid with cash."

Lucky swore. "Driver's license number?"

"Nope."

"Great."

"Sounds to me like the lady was covering her tracks."

"Sounds that way to me too," Lucky mumbled, his mind on where and how he might pick up her trail. "When a guest pays with cash, isn't it procedure to get some form of identification?"

"It's procedure, but, you know," the clerk said, shrugging, "we don't always do it. I mean, people traveling together get the hots, check in for a quickie, things like that. Most times they don't even stay overnight."

Knowing the clerk was right, Lucky combed back his hair with his fingers. He'd washed it with bar soap, and it was drying in a helter-skelter fashion. "What time does the other guy come on duty? The one who works this desk on the evening shift."

"Four."

Lucky tossed his empty disposable coffee cup into the wastepaper basket and ambled toward the door. "Thanks."

"You bet. Come again," the clerk called cheerfully.

Lucky shot him a withering look before he went out into the bright, new East Texas sunlight that was just breaking over the tips of the tall pine trees and spearing through his eyeballs straight into the back of his skull.

He slipped on the sunglasses he'd left on his dashboard the day before and pointed the Mustang toward home. He would start tracing her at the place later this afternoon. Not only did she owe him an apology, but now he was due an explanation as well. In the meantime he couldn't devote the whole day to tracking her. Even though there wasn't much work to do, he and Chase felt better about business if they looked and acted busy.

The drive home would normally have taken an hour, but Lucky was anxious for more coffee and some breakfast, since he hadn't eaten the evening before. He floorboarded the Mustang, and in a little over thirty-five minutes was turning off the farm-to-market road into the lane leading to his family's home.

The narrow blacktop road was lined with pecan trees. In summer, when they were in full leaf, their branches formed a thick green canopy over the road that sunlight could barely penetrate. The only time he didn't appreciate the trees was in the fall, when his mother sent him out to pick up the crop of nuts that covered the ground. Still, the effort became worth it when the pecans showed up in homemade fudge and pies.

They raised only enough cattle to keep them in fresh beef, and stabled a few riding horses. Sage had spoiled them and turned them into pets, and they offered little challenge to hellbent riders like Chase and Lucky. As he sped past, Lucky honked at the small herd grazing on the thick grass that grew on the acreage surrounding the house.

The two-story structure was built of painted white brick, and had black shutters on the windows opening onto the deep front porch. His father had built the house when he and Chase were youngsters, but Lucky never remembered living anywhere else. When Sage came along, quite unexpectedly, another three rooms had been added on to the back side to accommodate the Tylers' growing family.

It was a handsome house, and homey. Lucky knew the day would come when he would marry and move out as his brother had two years earlier, but he dreaded thinking about it. This was home. His fondest memories were directly connected to this house.

He knew every nook and cranny of it. He knew which stairs creaked when someone stepped on them. His initials were carved on every peach tree in the orchard. He'd smoked so much of the grapevine that grew along the fence, it was a wonder there was any of it left.

He could almost recall each individual Christmas, and one particular Easter stood out in his memory because he and Chase had replaced the hard-boiled eggs his mother had dyed for Sage's Easter basket with raw ones, and had got a spanking for ruining her day.

"Oh hell."

This morning he was none to happy to see Chase's car parked in the curved drive in front of the house. It was early for him to be out. Lucky had hoped to give the swelling around his eye a few hours to go down before confronting his older brother.

Resigned to the inevitable interrogation, followed by a lecture about maturity, image, and responsibility, he parked his Mustang and loped up the front steps.

Entering the wide, airy foyer, he followed the smell of fresh coffee toward the kitchen situated in the southeast corner of the house. At this time of day the sun bathed the pale walls with butter-colored light.

"Lucky, is that you?" his mother called through the rooms.

"None other. What's for breakfast?"

He entered the kitchen and was surprised to see Tanya, Chase's wife, sitting with him at the kitchen table. Small and blond, she perfectly complemented his tall, dark brother. Lucky liked Tanya immensely, and often teased her by saying that if she ever got smart and left his brother, he had first dibs on her. That would never happen. She was devoted to Chase, which was one of the main reasons Lucky liked her so much.

When he walked in, she gave him one of her sweet smiles, which turned into open-mouthed gaping when he removed his sunglasses. His smile disfigured his face even more.

Laurie Tyler, attractive even in middle age, flattened her hand against her breasts and fell back a step when she saw Little Alvin Cagney's handiwork on her son's face.

"Good Lord, Lucky, we heard you'd been in another fight, but I didn't expect anything this bad. Did that Cagney brute do that to you?"

"Yeah, but you ought to see him," he quipped as he headed for the coffee maker and poured himself a cup.

"Where the hell have you been?"

Lucky blew on his coffee and looked at his brother through the rising steam. "Are you in another lousy mood today? It's not even time for me to be at work yet, and already you're on my case."

"Lucky, something's happened," Laurie said, laying a hand on his arm. Her eyes were a similar shade of blue, and almost as bright and youthful as her son's. Now, however, they were clouded with concern.

"Happened?"

Just then Sage came barreling through the back door. Here lately, Lucky was startled every time he saw his kid sister. She wasn't a kid any longer. Only a few weeks earlier they'd attended her graduation from the local junior college. Next fall she would be studying at the University of Texas in Austin. She no longer looked like an adolescent. She was a woman. And it seemed she'd become one overnight.

"I was in the stable and saw his car pull in," she said breathlessly as though she'd been running. "Have you told him yet?"

"Told me what? What the hell is going on?"

"We had a fire last night," Chase said grimly.

"A fire?"

"In the main garage." Chase left his chair and went to the coffee maker to pour himself a refill.

"Jeez." Lucky suddenly felt nauseous. "I'm sorry I wasn't available. How bad was it? Nobody was hurt, I hope."

"No, nobody was hurt, but the building burned to the ground. Everything in it was destroyed."

Lucky dropped into a chair and dragged his fingers through his hair again. What Chase had told him was inconceivable, but the grim faces surrounding him confirmed that it was the truth. "How'd it start? What time did all this happen? Did they get it put out?"

"The first alarm came in about two-thirty. They fought the blaze till around four. It's out now. Hell of a mess though."

Chase returned to his chair across from his brother. Once he was seated, Tanya rested her hand on his thigh in a silent, wifely gesture of sympathy and support.

"Thank God we've kept up our insurance premiums," Lucky remarked. "As hard as it's been to rake together the cash for—" He broke off when he intercepted the exchanged looks that went around the kitchen. "There's more?"

Chase sighed and regretfully nodded his head. Laurie approached Lucky's chair as though she might, at a moment's notice, have to render maternal consolation. Tanya stared down at her hands.

Sage was the one who finally spoke up. "There's a whole lot more. Who's going to tell him?"

"Be quiet, Sage."

"But, Mother, he's got to find out sooner or later."

"Sage!"

"You're suspected of setting it, Lucky."

Chapter Five

Lucky's gaze swung toward his brother. "Did she say 'setting it'? The fire was set?"

"It was arson. No question."

"And somebody thinks I set it?" Lucky snorted incredulously. "Why in hell would I do that?"

"For the insurance money."

Lucky's disbelieving gaze moved around the room, lighting briefly on all four faces, which were watching him closely to gauge his reaction. "What is this, April Fool's Day? This is a joke, right?"

"I wish to hell it was."

Chase leaned forward and folded his hands around his coffee mug as though he wanted to strangle it. His light gray eyes shone fervently in his strong face. He was as handsome as his younger brother, but in a different way. While Lucky had the reckless nonchalance of a cowboy of a century ago, Chase had a compelling intensity about him.

"I couldn't believe Pat would even suggest such a thing," he said.

"Pat! Sheriff Pat Bush? Our *friend?*" Lucky exclaimed. "I saw him yesterday evening at the place."

"And that was the last anybody saw of you."

"We heard all about your fight with Little Alvin and that scummy Patterson character," Sage said. "People said you were fighting over a woman."

"Exaggeration. They were moving in on her. She didn't welcome their advances. All I did was step in." He gave them a condensed version of the altercation. "You would have done the same thing, Chase."

"I don't know," he remarked dubiously. "It would take some kind of woman to get me in a tussle with those two."

Lucky sidestepped the reference to Dovey. "Jack Ed got me with his knife. That's how my shirt got ripped."

"He came at you with a knife!"

"Don't worry, Mother, it was nothing. Just a scratch. See?" He raised his bloodstained shirt, but the sight of the long, arcing cut across his middle didn't relieve Laurie.

"Did you have it seen to?"

"In a manner of speaking," he grumbled, remembering how badly it had stung when Dovey poured whiskey along the length of the cut.

"Who was the woman you fought over?" Sage asked. Her brothers' escapades with women had always been a source of fascination to her. "What happened to her?"

"Sage, I don't think that's significant," her mother said sharply. "Don't you have something else to do?"

"Nothing this interesting."

Lucky was unmindful of their conversation. He was watching his brother and gleaning from Chase's somber expression that the situation wasn't only interesting, but critical.

"Pat can't possibly believe that I started a fire, especially in one of our own garages," Lucky said, shaking his head to deny the preposterous allegation.

"No, but he warned me that the feds might."

"The feds? What the hell have the feds got to do with it?"

"Interstate commerce. Over fifty thousand dollars' worth of damage," Chase said, citing the criteria. "A fire at Tyler Drilling qualifies for an investigation by the Bureau of Alcohol, Tobacco and Firearms. Pat stuck his neck out by warning me what to expect. It doesn't look good, Lucky. We're in hock at the bank. Since Grandad Tyler started the company, business has never been as bad as it is now. Each piece of equipment is insured to the hilt." He shrugged. "To their way of thinking, it smells to high heaven."

"But to anybody who knows us, it's crazy."

"I hope so."

"Why me?"

"Because you're the family hothead," Sage supplied, much to the consternation of everyone else present.

"So far," Chase said after directing a stern frown toward his sister, "we can't account for your whereabouts after you left the place last night, Lucky."

"And that automatically makes me a suspect for arson?" he cried.

"It's ridiculous, but that's what we're up against. We've got no problem if we provide ironclad alibis. The first thing they asked me is where I was last night. I was home in bed with Tanya. She confirmed that."

"Do you think they believed me?" she asked.

Chase smiled at her. "You couldn't lie convincingly if you had to." He dropped a light kiss on the tip of her nose. Then, giving his brother his attention again, he said, "You didn't spend the night at home. They're going to ask where you were all night."

Lucky cleared his throat, sat up straighter, and cast a guilty glance toward his mother. Sensing his discomfort, she resorted to her standard cure-all. "Would you like something to eat?"

"Please, ma'am." His mother could make him feel humble and ashamed when no one else could. She turned toward the stove and began preparing him a meal of eggs and bacon.

"Naturally the first person we called this morning was Susan Young," Sage informed him, dropping into a vacant chair at the table.

"Oh terrific," Lucky mumbled.

"She was mighty p.o.'d when—"

"Sage," Laurie said warningly.

"I didn't say it. I just used the initials."

"It still sounds so unladylike."

Rolling her eyes, Sage turned back to her brother. "Susan wasn't too thrilled to find out you'd stood her up at dinner to go tomcatting."

Lucky muttered a curse, careful to prevent his mother from hearing it over the sizzling sound of frying bacon. "I forgot to call her."

"Well," Sage said importantly, twirling a tawny strand of hair around her finger, "you'd better be thinking up a sympathetic story, because she is steamed." Pinching her light brown eyes into narrow slits, she made a sound like steam escaping the tight lid of a kettle.

"We have much more to worry about than Susan's jealousy," Chase said.

"Besides," Laurie added, carrying a plate of food to the table, "Lucky's affairs are no concern of yours, young lady."

Lucky attacked the plate of food. After a moment he realized that the sound of his fork scraping across his plate was the only noise in the kitchen. He raised his head to find them all staring at him expectantly.

"What?" he asked, lifting his shoulders in a slight shrug.

"What?" Chase repeated more loudly. "We're waiting for you to tell us where you were, so that if the badge-toting guys in the dark suits and opaque sunglasses come asking, we'll have something to tell them."

Lucky glanced back down into his plate. The food no longer looked appetizing. "I, uh, spent the night with a lady."

Sage snorted as derisively as Lucky had when Pat Bush had called Dovey that. "A lady. Right."

"What lady?" Chase asked.

"Does it matter?"

"Ordinarily not. This time it does."

Lucky gnawed on his lower lip. "Y'all don't know her."

"Is she from out of town?"

"Yeah. She was the, uh, the one Little Alvin was hitting on."

"You picked up a stranger at the place and spent the night with her?"

"Well, who are you to get so righteous, Chase?" Lucky shouted, suddenly angry. "Before Tanya came along, you weren't above doing the same damned thing."

"But not on the night one of our buildings was torched!" his brother shouted right back.

Tanya intervened. "Chase, Lucky didn't know what was going to happen last night."

"Thanks, Tanya," Lucky said with an injured air.

"Oh, Lucky, that's such a foolhardy thing to do these days."

"I'm not stupid, Mother. I took the necessary precautions."

Sage grinned, her eyes twinkling wickedly. "Aren't you the good Boy Scout. Do they give merit badges for taking 'the necessary precautions'?"

"Shut up, brat," Lucky growled.

Thanks to Tanya, Chase had reined in his temper. Sparks often flew between the two brothers, but the grudges lasted no longer than the temper flare-ups. "Okay, all you need to do to clear yourself is get the woman to vouch for you."

Lucky scratched his stubble-covered jaw. "That might be tricky."

"Why? When she tells the authorities that you spent all night with her, they can eliminate you as a suspect and start tracking down the real arsonist."

Chase, believing their dilemma had been resolved, started to stand. Lucky pointed him back into his chair. "There's a slight problem with that, Chase."

Slowly Chase lowered himself back into his seat. "What problem? How slight?"

"I, uh, don't know her name."

"You don't know her name?"

"No, sir."

This day would go down in Lucky's private annals as one of the worst in his life. His head still felt as though it had a flock of industrious woodpeckers living in it. His vision was blurry in the eye that had connected with Little Alvin's fist. Every muscle in his body was screaming at the abuse it had taken. He was suspected of setting a destructive fire to his place of business. Everybody, including members of his own family, was treating him like a leper because he'd spent the night with a woman he couldn't identify.

And he had thought yesterday was bad.

According to their expressions, neither the sheriff and his deputies nor the federal investigators believed him any more than his family had that morning.

One of the investigators turned to Pat Bush. "You didn't get her name at the scene of the fight?"

Pat harrumphed. "No. It occurred to me later that I had failed to, but there didn't seem any need for it at the time. She wasn't interested in pressing charges."

A skeptical "hmm" was the agent's only response. He turned to Lucky again. "Didn't you think to ask her her name?"

"Sure. She told me it was Dovey, but—"

"Would you spell that please?" The request was made by another agent taking notes in a spiral notebook.

"Spell what?"

"Dovey."

Lucky blew out a breath of exasperation and looked toward Pat Bush for assistance. The sheriff's terse nod merely indicated that Lucky should go along with the ridiculous request. Lucky succinctly spelled the name. "At least I think that's right. She registered at the motel as Mary Smith of Dallas." He snapped his fingers and raised his head hopefully. "Listen, the clerk there will remember me."

"He does. We already checked."

Earlier Lucky had provided the investigators with the name of the motel on the interstate, located about midway between Milton Point and Dallas. "Then why the hell are you still busy with me? If I've been cleared, why aren't you out looking for the guy who burned our building?"

"The clerk could only testify to seeing you this morning," the senior agent informed him. "He didn't see you going into the room last evening. And even if he had, he couldn't vouch for your staying there all night without leaving."

Lucky glanced at his brother, who was leaning against a battered army-green metal filing cabinet in Sheriff Bush's office. Lucky shook his head as though to say that this was a lost cause, and he was tired of playing cops and robbers by their rules.

Meeting the agent's cold stare, he arrogantly asked, "Do you have any physical evidence connecting me with this crime?"

The agent shifted from one wing-tipped shoe to the other. "The exact cause of the fire hasn't yet been ascertained."

"Do you have anything linking me with that fire?" Lucky repeated.

Backed against a wall, the agent replied, "No."

"Then I'm leaving." Lucky came out of his straight chair and headed for the door.

"You'll be under surveillance, so don't even try to leave town."

"Go to hell," Chase told the agent on his way out, following his brother. "Lucky, wait up!" he called as he emerged from the courthouse a few seconds later. Lucky was already at the curb in front of the official building with his hand on the door handle of his car. He waited for Chase to catch up with him.

"Can you believe this crap?" he asked, angrily jutting his chin toward the first-floor office where the interrogation had taken place.

"It's crap, but they're serious."

"You're telling me," Lucky muttered. "The hair on the back of my neck is standing on end. I had enough of jail the night we got arrested for knocking down old man Bledsoe's fence. It was an accident! How the hell were we supposed to know his thoroughbred mare was in that pasture? Or that she was in season?"

Chase peered up at his brother from beneath his heavy brows, and, together, they started laughing. "He went nuts when that jackass raced in there and mounted her. Remember how he was jumping up and down and yelling? Never laughed so hard in my life."

"We stopped laughing the next morning when Daddy came to pick us up. As I recall, he didn't say a single word all the way home."

"The drive from town to home never seemed so long," Chase agreed. "We had all that time to fret about what our punishment was going to be. But you know," he said with a mischievous wink, "that mare's offspring was the ugliest damn mule I've ever seen."

They laughed together for several moments, remembering. Eventually, however, Lucky sighed as he slid his hands into the rear pockets of his jeans and leaned against the fender of his car.

"We've had our brushes with the law, but never anything like this, Chase. They haven't got a damn thing on me, so why am I so scared?"

"Because being accused of a felony like arson is scary. You'd be a fool if you weren't."

"In deference to the ladies in our family, I hope it doesn't become necessary, but a DNA-matching test would prove that I had sex in that motel room."

Chase winced.

"Right, it makes me squeamish too," Lucky said bitterly. "But even though lab tests would prove that *I* was there, they wouldn't prove that *she* was, or that I didn't leave at some point during the night, drive back here, set the fire, then return by daylight and make certain the clerk remembered me."

"The only one who can establish your alibi is the woman." There was an implied question mark at the end of Chase's statement.

Lucky looked chagrined. "It wasn't as sordid as it sounds."

"Sounds pretty sordid, little brother."

"Yeah, I know," he admitted on a sigh. "Look, I chased her down because she hightailed it out of the place without even thanking me for saving her from those two slimeballs. Made me mad as hell. I caught up with her at that motel and talked myself into her room.

"By that time, I was feeling the effects of Little Alvin's punches. A few shots of whiskey had made me woozy. I lay down on the bed. I think she got to feeling sorry for me then, 'cause she cleaned the knife wound and got an ice pack for my eye. I fell asleep."

"I thought you had sex."

Again Lucky looked at something besides his brother's inquisitive face. "Sometime during the night I woke up," he said quietly. "She has this really incredible dark red hair. And her skin is so creamy, translucent, you know." Suddenly he yanked himself out of the self-imposed trance and frowned at his own susceptibility. "She was classy, Chase."

"Then what was she doing causing a stir at the place?"

"Damned if I know. But she wasn't your ordinary barfly, willing to grant sexual favors in exchange for a few drinks. Not a party girl. If anything, she was uptight and . . . and . . . bossy. The kind of woman I usually avoid like the plague."

"You'd have done well to avoid this one."

Lucky was reluctant to agree. For some reason he hadn't yet had time to analyze, he wasn't sorry about the night before. Nor did he think it would be his only encounter with Dovey, or Mary, or whatever her name was.

The consequences of their night together had got him into more trouble than he'd ever been in. That was saying a lot. But inexplicably he didn't regret it. At least not as much as the situation warranted.

"So what's your plan?"

Chase's question pulled him out of his reverie. "To find her."

"How, if you don't even know her name?"

"I'll start at the place and work forward from there."

"Well, good luck."

"Thanks."

"If you need me, you know where to find me."

"I'll be glad to help you and the boys with the cleanup," Lucky offered.

"We can't start until they've finished their investigation. God knows how long that'll take, because they're sifting everything through a fine-tooth comb, looking for evidence. All you could do is what I'm doing, and that's standing around twiddling my thumbs."

"No, your time will be better spent clearing yourself. The insurance company isn't going to pay us one red cent until we've been exonerated." Chase squinted into the sunlight. "Any ideas who might've done this?"

"My first guess would be Little Alvin and Jack Ed."

"Revenge?" Chase chuckled. "From what I've heard, you made Little Alvin sorry he was a man."

"He deserved it."

"Pat thought he might be a suspect, too, but he's got a whole tribe of Cagneys swearing that Little Alvin was playing cards with his brothers all night."

"With an ice pack on his crotch?"

Again Chase laughed. "Remind me never to get you really mad at me." His expression turned serious again. "Which I'm likely to do by saying this."

"What?"

"It might be a good idea to go see Susan Young. Her daddy's already called me twice today demanding to know what's going on."

Lucky swore. "You're right. I'd better get over there and smooth her ruffled feathers. We need to stay in good with the bank now more than ever. Besides, I truly did do Susan dirty by standing her up last night."

"And making it public knowledge that you spent the night with another woman." Chase eyed him speculatively. "She must've been some redhead."

Refusing to be baited, Lucky settled into the driver's seat of his convertible and turned on the motor. "In ten or twenty years we'll be laughing about this the way we did about Bledsoe's mule out of his thoroughbred mare."

She padded into her kitchen and opened the refrigerator. As expected, it was empty. One of the hazards of living alone was a bare cupboard. It was less of a hassle to do without food than to prepare meals for one.

The thought of going grocery shopping on her return to Dallas early that morning hadn't been very appealing. Instead, she'd driven straight to her condo and, after taking a long, hot bath to relieve her soreness, had gone to bed.

There she had stayed most of the day, telling herself she needed the rest after her ordeal. Actually she had dreaded the moment of accountability to her conscience for what she had allowed to happen the night before.

There was about half a cup of skim milk in the bottom of the carton. Sniffing it first to make sure it hadn't soured, she poured it over a bowl of Rice Krispies. They were so old, they barely had any snap, crackle, or pop left in them, but they would line her empty stomach.

She went into the living room, curled into a corner of her sofa, and reached for the TV's remote control. It was too late for the soaps and too early for the evening news. She was left with reruns of syndicated sitcoms.

In one, the male lead had dark blond hair and a mischievous, I'm-up-to-no-good grin. She quickly switched to another channel, unwilling to have anything remind her of the stranger she had spent the night with . . . been intimate with . . . made love with.

The thought of it made her hand shake so badly she had to set the bowl of soggy cereal on the coffee table or risk spilling it. She covered her face with her cupped palms. "Dear Lord," she moaned. What in the world had caused her to behave so irresponsibly?

Sure, she could list a million excuses, starting with her emotional state yesterday and ending with the gifted way that man had kissed her when he drew her out of her dark loneliness and despair into his strong, warm arms.

"Don't think about it," she admonished herself, picking up the transmitter again and vigorously punching through the channel selector.

She had derided women who were susceptible to handsome faces, brawny physiques, and glib come-ons. She had thought she was smarter than that. She was far too intelligent, discerning, and discriminatory to fall for a pelt of gold-tipped chest hair and heavily lashed sky-blue eyes. His charm had melted her morals and feminist resolve. Lucky Tyler had succeeded in touching her where no other man ever had— her heart, her body.

Mortification made her whimper. To stifle the sound, she pressed her fingertips against her lips, then explored them tentatively, feeling the whisker burns. She had discovered those sweetly chafed places on her breasts, too, during her bath. They had brought back tantalizing sensations that swirled through her midsection.

When she had tried to sleep, squeezing her eyes tightly shut, she recalled the tugging motions his mouth had made on her nipples. Her lower body contracted with a pleasurable ache whenever she remembered that first, sweet piercing of her flesh, then the strength and depth of his penetration.

Now she crossed her arms over her lower body and bent at the waist in the hopes of eradicating both the mental and physical recollections. They made her hot. They made her want. They made her ashamed.

Lust for a total stranger? In a cheap roadside motel? What a stupid thing to have done! How reckless! How wrong! How unlike her!

But she hadn't exactly been herself yesterday, had she? Before one could pass judgment on her, one would have to understand the state of mind she'd been in twenty-four hours ago. One would have had to experience the same cruel rejection, traverse the same bleak corridors, feel the lingering sense of suffocation even after escaping those corridors.

One would have to experience the sense of futility and defeat she had felt upon learning that sometimes even making supreme sacrifices wasn't enough. Having reached the devastating realization that someone's love, or even gratitude, couldn't be won, she'd been at her lowest.

Enter Lucky Tyler—as gorgeous as an angel and as delightful as one of the devil's favored children. He'd been funny and sexy and needful.

Perhaps that had been his main attraction. He had needed her, fundamentally and simply, a man needing a woman. She had desperately needed to be needed. She had responded to his need as much as she had to the transporting caresses of his hands and mouth.

"Oh sure. Right," she muttered to herself impatiently. Rationalizations came a dime a dozen, and none was going to be sufficient justification. It had been a foolhardy thing to do, but she had done it. Now she had to come to terms with it.

Thank heaven she had had the foresight to use a phony name and pay in cash when she checked into the motel. He couldn't trace her.

Could he? Had she overlooked something? In her haste to leave that morning had she left behind a clue that would lead him to her if he had a mind to find her?

No, she was almost sure she hadn't. As far as Mr. Lucky Tyler was concerned, she was totally anonymous. Only she would ever know about last night, and she would forget it.

"Starting now," she averred as she left the sofa. Giving the belt of her robe a swift tug, she moved into the spare bedroom that served as her office at home. She switched on the desk lamp and her word processor, slid on a pair of reading glasses, and sat down in front of the terminal.

Work had always been her salvation. Other people relied on alcohol, drugs, sports, sex, to forget their troubles and make life livable. For her —except for last night—nothing worked like work itself. Besides, she had a deadline.

Once she got a clear screen on her computer, she referred to her notes and began typing. Her fingers flew over the keyboard. She wrote well into the night, as though the devil were after her . . . and rapidly closing in.

Chapter Six

Susan Young descended the stairs slowly, looking wounded, her mouth sulky. From her appearance, Lucky guessed that she had been crying most of the day, or at least wanted him to think so. Her eyes were watery and red. The tip of her nose had been rubbed raw by tissues. Her complexion was splotchy.

In lieu of hello she said, "Mama advised me not to speak to you." She halted on the third stair from the bottom.

Seeing a potential way out of this unwelcome encounter, Lucky asked solicitously, "Would another time be better?"

"No, it would not!" she replied tartly. "We've got a lot to talk about, Mr. Tyler."

Drat, he thought.

She descended the last three steps and swept past him into the formal living room. It smelled sickeningly of furniture polish. Afternoon sunlight was shining through the windows, dappling the pale blue carpet with patterns of light and shadow. It was a gorgeous day. Lucky wished he were outside enjoying it. He wished he were anywhere but where he was—in the Youngs' formidable living room being subjected to Susan's hurt, chastising glare.

"Well?" she demanded imperiously the moment she had closed the double doors.

"What can I say? I did something terribly stupid, and got caught."

His demeanor was self-deprecating. He'd learned early on that the only way to handle a woman scorned was to assume all the blame and be as honest as was prudent. There had been those occasions, however, when honesty had been suspended because either castration or his life were at stake. He didn't think Susan's wrath had reached that level of danger . . . yet.

Looking properly contrite, he said, "Can you forgive me for standing you up last night, Susan?"

"Of course I can forgive you for that, although it was a tacky thing to do."

"It certainly was. I owe your parents an apology for it, too."

"We held up dinner for an hour and a half waiting on you. We didn't eat until nine."

That would have been about the time Dovey was blowing on his knife wound, cooling his flesh, and inflaming his passions with her soft breath. Damn, it had felt delicious, stirring his body hair, fanning his skin.

"I have no excuse for what I did."

The apologetic words were beginning to stick in his craw. If not for her father's position at the bank, he'd tell this spoiled brat that he wasn't accountable to her for whom he slept with, and that would be the last she'd see of him.

He was anxious to begin his search for Dovey, and was only going through the motions of stroking Susan because it was politic to do so. He hadn't needed Chase to spell that out to him. However, he rued the day he'd asked Susan for that first date several months ago. He wanted to lash out, reminding her that he'd made her no promises, certainly had made no commitments, and that whoever he slept with, whether it be one woman or a dozen, was no business of hers. Only a reminder of the loan payment coming due forced him to squelch his mounting temper.

Hoping that she wouldn't catch the hopefulness in his voice, he said, "You'd be better off refusing to see me again."

She gazed thoughtfully at the floor for a moment, then raised her shimmering eyes to his. "I've got a more forgiving spirit than that."

Damn! Women loved to be forgiving. It vested them with enormous power over the forgiven. They thrived on the poor sucker's guilt like carrion birds on a carcass, picking it clean.

"I can forgive you for skipping dinner with us," she said. "I can even overlook your engaging in a barroom brawl, because I know you have a volatile nature. I'll admit that's part of the attraction you hold over me.

"What I'm finding very difficult to forgive . . ." Here, her lower lip began to quiver and her voice became tremulous. "You've humiliated me in front of the whole town. They say you couldn't be located when the fire broke out last night because you were with a whore."

"She wasn't a whore." The application of that word to Dovey made him so angry that he was startled by the intensity of his emotion.

"Then who was she?"

"A stranger. I never saw her before last night, but she wasn't a whore." Susan was watching him shrewdly. He softened his tone. "Look, Susan, I didn't set out to sleep with anybody last night. It just sorta happened."

That was the truth. He hadn't wormed his way into Dovey's motel room with the intention of making love to her. He'd only wanted to provoke her as badly as he'd been provoked, get his apology, and then leave.

It wasn't entirely his fault that it hadn't quite worked out that way. He'd been half-asleep when he reached for her. She'd been fragrant and warm and soft and compliant. Her damp lips had been mobile beneath his, her body responsive. He couldn't be blamed for how naturally his body had responded to the sexy stimuli. Of course, it had been conditioned to respond.

". . . understand. You left here yesterday aroused. Right?"

He blinked to clear his vision, and tried to grasp what Susan had been saying. "Uh, right."

She approached him, gazing up at him through spiky, wet lashes. Her mouth looked vulnerable. But for all her tears and sniveling, Lucky knew she was about as helpless as a barracuda.

"So you took your lust for me and spent it on a willing woman," she whispered, laying her hands on his chest. "I guess I should be flattered, though I'm still very hurt. The thought of you in bed with another woman makes me just want to die."

She looked closer to killing than dying. Her eyes, no longer bright with tears, were alight with malice. "But I can understand how when a man gets so aroused, he's got to do something about it or explode."

She came up on tiptoes and brushed a kiss across his lips. "I know the feeling, Lucky. Don't you think I want you, too? Don't you know that the only reason I'm saving myself is so our wedding night will be special? Don't you know how badly I want to make love to you right now?"

True, he had been mildly aroused when he left Susan after lunch the day before, but he had got hotter than that watching certain commercials on TV. His arousal then had been like a mild head cold when compared to the feverish delirium he'd experienced when he'd entered Dovey's giving body.

"Look, Susan," he said irritably, "all this talk about weddings—"

She laid her fingers against his lips. "Shh. I know we can't make an announcement until you get out of the mess you're in. Poor baby." She reached up with the intention of running her fingers through his hair. He snapped his head back and caught her hand before she could touch him.

"Announcement?"

"The announcement of our engagement, silly," she said, playfully tapping his chest. "And just so we can get this misunderstanding about the fire settled quickly, and to prove how much I love you, I'll say that you spent last night with me."

"What?"

"It's all over town that you woke up alone this morning and can't produce your alibi. So I'll say that I was with you. Mama and Daddy will have a fit, of course, but they'll accept our sleeping together as inevitable if I have an engagement ring on my finger. They'll be so happy we're finally making it official, they'll overlook our one night of sin."

She was either downright conniving or entertaining delusions. Either way, she was dangerous and had to be handled with kid gloves.

"What makes you think anyone will believe you if you come forward now and say I was with you last night?"

"I'll say that, at first, you wouldn't let me be your alibi because of what it would mean to my reputation. I insisted until you capitulated."

"Looks like you've got it figured from every angle."

"Ever since I heard you couldn't produce that *woman,* it's all I've thought about. I'll say I sneaked out after Mama and Daddy had gone to bed. Actually I did go out last night."

"What for?"

"I was so upset, I drove around looking for you, searching for your car at all the places you usually go. When I didn't find you, I came home. My parents never knew I went out. I could say that we met and spent the night together, passionately making love." She gave him an impish grin. "Which isn't a bad idea."

"That's not how you felt about it yesterday," he reminded her.

"A girl can change her mind."

She was as easy to see through as the Waterford vase on the mantel. She had turned him down yesterday, so he had slaked his lust with someone else. That was untenable to a conceited woman like Susan, especially when everybody in town knew about it. She had devised a way to save face and, at the same time, lasso him for good. Even though her lie would clear him, it was self-serving.

"You'd be willing to lie to save my hide? You'd do that for me?"

"And for me," she admitted. "I want you, Lucky Tyler. And I mean to have you, no matter what it takes."

Whether I want you or not, he thought.

"I'll call Sheriff Bush right now," she said suddenly, turning toward the phone.

Lucky's arm shot out. He caught her hand. "I can't let you do it, Susan."

Her bright smile dimmed. "Why not?"

"You could get in a lot of trouble by lying to federal investigators. I can't let you do that for me."

"I want to."

"And I appreciate it," he said with what he hoped sounded like sincerity. He could see, however, that she wasn't convinced. "Let me think about it. You know, Susan, perjury is a serious offense. I need to think it through before letting you do it."

Her smile returned, but there was a definite edge to her voice when she said, "Don't mull it over too long. I'm not sure how long my offer will stand."

What a conniving little bitch, he thought. Forcing himself to smile, he said, "You're something, you know that? When I first met you, I had no idea there was so much complexity beneath the surface."

"Whatever I want I go after. It's as simple as that."

God help the man she got her hooks into. Lucky silently vowed then and there that it wasn't going to be him. "Well, I've got a lot of thinking to do, Susan, so I'd better be going."

"Must you?" she whined.

"I must."

"Take this with you." She looped her arms around his neck, pulled his head down, and ground a wet, suggestive kiss upon his mouth. When she eventually pulled back, she whispered, "Maybe that'll make you think twice before going to another woman."

Lucky endured the kiss because he recognized the difference between feminine wiles and real treachery. Susan Young exercised the latter. She would resort even to blackmail to get him to marry her.

As he went down her front walk, having made good a temporary escape, he wiped the remains of her kiss off his lips with the back of his hand.

It hadn't repelled him. It certainly hadn't stirred his ardor. It had left him feeling totally indifferent to it, something that hadn't happened since he first discovered kissing under the tutelage of the preacher's daughter behind the choir loft of the First Baptist Church during vacation Bible school.

Between that first titillating mouth-to-mouth experimentation and Susan's ardent kiss, what had happened to immunize him against the effects?

A taste of Dovey, that's what.

The bartender groaned when he looked up and saw Lucky straddling one of the barstools. "I'd just as soon you take your business somewhere else tonight, Lucky, and give the place a rest."

"Shut up and draw me a beer. I'm not looking for trouble."

"As I recall," the bartender drawled, "that's what you said yesterday." He slid the beer in front of his customer.

Lucky sipped. "I'm in a jam."

"So I hear. It's all over town that you need an alibi for last night."

"Jeez, the grapevine around here is faster and more accurate than a fax machine."

The bartender's face split into a wide grin. "If you don't like the gossip, you shouldn't keep such a—what do they call it?—a high profile. Plain folks are fascinated by the activities of local celebrities."

Lucky cursed and took another sip of his drink. "You remember anything about that woman?"

"Not as much as you do, I'd bet," he chortled. His sappy grin faded beneath Lucky's warning glare. "Uh, well, let's see, natural redhead, wasn't she? And I don't mean anything lewd about that," he added hastily.

"Dark auburn hair, yeah."

" 'Bout so tall." He marked a spot near his shoulder, holding his hand parallel to the ground.

"I don't need a physical description," Lucky said impatiently. "Do you remember anything significant about her?"

"Significant?"

"Did you see her pull into the parking lot?"

The bartender searched his memory. "I think so. Came from the south, I believe."

"The south." Lucky assimilated that. "If you saw which direction she came from, you must've noticed her car."

"Sure did."

"What kind was it?"

"Red," he announced proudly, glad to be of service.

"I know it was red," Lucky growled. "But what kind?"

"Foreign, I think."

"Make?" The bartender shook his head. "Model?" Again Lucky received a negative answer.

"Great," he muttered, his highball glass at his lips.

"Well, you followed her, Lucky. If you didn't notice, how could you expect me to?"

"Don't worry about it. I just thought you might've. You know I don't recognize the make and model of any car manufactured after 1970. Like you, I just remember hers being compact and red. Maybe under hypnosis I could remember the license number, but I've been racking my brain all day, and can't come up with a single digit or letter of it."

"Uh-oh."

"What?" Lucky swiveled around on the stool, following the direction of the bartender's worried gaze. Coming through the door were Little Alvin and Jack Ed. They paused momentarily when they spotted Lucky. An expectant hush fell over the bar. Then the duo ambled toward a corner booth and sat down.

"Two beers each. Right now," Little Alvin bellowed to the bartender.

He uncapped four long necks and set them on a cork-lined tray. "I'll take it," Lucky offered congenially, sliding off his stool.

"Now, look, Lucky, I just got this place—"

"No trouble. Swear." Lucky gave the man his most winning grin. Carrying the tray, he moved across the gritty hardwood floor toward the corner booth. Little Alvin and Jack Ed followed his progress with hooded eyes.

When he reached their booth, he set the tray on the table. "Drink up, boys."

Jack Ed sneered and suggested that Lucky do something to himself that was anatomically impossible.

Ignoring him, Lucky addressed Alvin. "Glad to see you can walk upright today."

Little Alvin glowered at him menacingly. "You'll get yours, you cocky bastard."

"Alvin, Alvin," Lucky said, shaking his head sorrowfully, "is that any way to talk to me after I've brought a peace offering?" He nodded down at the beer Alvin had almost guzzled in one swallow. "I put your drinks on my tab. Felt like it was the least I could do after our misunderstanding yesterday."

"You can't smooth-talk your way past me. Beat it."

The features of Lucky's face pulled taut. "Listen you—"

"Lucky!"

Chase's voice cut through the smoky, dense atmosphere. From the corner of his eye Lucky saw his brother weaving through the tables to join him at the end of Little Alvin's booth.

"Don't start anything else, for godsake," Chase warned him in a terse whisper.

"Well, if it ain't the rodeo star," Jack Ed said snidely, "come to save his little brother from another beatin'."

"That's not the way I heard it, Patterson."

Chase had been a bull rider in his youth. He'd won a considerable amount of prize money, and had made quite a name for himself on the rodeo circuit. But the danger associated with the sport had always worried his parents. They were greatly relieved when he became engaged to Tanya and retired from it with all his faculties and all his body parts still intact.

Chase didn't let Jack Ed provoke him. His unexpected appearance had had a calming effect on Lucky, who said now, "I just wanted to ask them some questions."

"I wouldn't mind asking them a few myself," Chase said.

Feeling expansive, Little Alvin propped his arms, which were as big around as pythons, along the back cushion of the booth. "About what?"

"About the fire last night in our garage," Chase said.

"About the woman who was in here yesterday," Lucky replied tightly.

Alvin responded to Lucky's question. "Heard she ran out on you," he said with a malicious grin. "Too bad. Always suspected that your success with the fairer sex was overrated." Jack Ed thought that was hilarious. His giggle was almost as high-pitched as a woman's.

"I don't believe for a minute you were playing cards with your brothers all night," Chase said.

"Did she ever give you her name?" Lucky asked, miraculously quelling the overwhelming impulse to wipe the gloating grin off Alvin's beefy face.

"You balled her and you don't even know her name?"

Lucky lunged toward the larger man. Chase grabbed him by the shoulders and pulled him back. "Let's get out of here."

"You son—"

"Let's go!" Chase dragged his younger brother backward across the lounge, with Lucky struggling every step of the way. His bootheels thumped along the floor as he dug them in, trying to get traction.

"Too bad you lost the one woman who could keep you out of jail, Tyler," Little Alvin taunted.

Lucky gnashed his teeth and let out a feral sound, straining to get loose from Chase. Chase, however, held tight. "Dammit, I'll knock you out cold myself if you don't settle down. What the hell's the matter with you?"

Once they had made it through the door, Chase slammed Lucky against the exterior wall of the building. Lucky threw off his brother's restraining hands. "You have to ask what the matter is?" he shouted. "They were right. I might go to jail."

"So what does that have to do with what went on in there?" Chase hitched his chin toward the tavern.

"I was looking for information about *her.*"

"Why?"

"Why?"

"Yeah, why?" Chase settled his hands on his hips and confronted his short-tempered brother. "You've been acting just plain weird all day. I think locating this woman means more to you than providing yourself with an alibi."

"You're crazy."

"Don't call me crazy. I'm not the one picking fights with Little Alvin two days straight over the same broad."

Lucky was ready with a vehement denial that she was a "broad" when he caught himself. The protest would confirm Chase's suspicions. Belligerently he said, "Just leave me the hell alone and let me deal with this my way, okay?"

"Not okay. You're my brother. The Tylers stick together. If you're in trouble, we're all in trouble. And since you can't seem to stay out of it, you're stuck with me as your protector."

They looked away from each other, each trying to get hold of his temper. Lucky was the first to come around. "Oh hell, Chase, you know I'm glad you intervened. At least in hindsight I am. I couldn't afford to get my other eye pulverized."

Chase grinned and slapped him between the shoulder blades. "Follow me to our house. Mother's been so upset all day, Tanya offered to cook dinner for everybody."

"Her famous pot roast?" Lucky asked hopefully.

"That's right."

"Hmm," he sighed, smacking his lips. "Tell me—brother to brother —is she as good in the bedroom as she is in the kitchen?"

"You'll die wondering." He shoved Lucky in the direction of his car. "And we'll both die at her hands if we spoil her dinner by being late."

Lucky was tailing Chase's car into town when it occurred to him that his return to the place had gained him nothing. He was no closer to locating Dovey than he'd been when he first woke up that morning, finding her side of their shared bed empty.

Chapter Seven

"Know what Susan Young is spreading all over town?"

In response to his sister's question, Lucky grunted with lack of interest from behind his morning newspaper.

"That y'all are getting married." Sage popped a fat, juicy strawberry into her mouth and chewed with sybaritic enthusiasm. "I've gotta tell you that if you marry the snotty bitch, I'm disowning this family for good."

"Promises, promises." Lucky lowered the newspaper to take a sip of breakfast coffee. "You've been threatening to disown the family ever since Chase and I hid your first bra in the freezer. So far, we've had no such luck." He retreated from her glare by burying his head in the newspaper again.

Sage slathered cream cheese onto a slice of low-calorie whole-wheat toast. "Well, are you?" she mumbled around the first creamy bite.

"Am I what?"

"Marrying Susan Young."

Lucky laid aside the newspaper. "Get serious. While you're at it, get your older brother some more coffee."

"Haven't you ever heard of women's lib?" she asked crossly.

"Sure, I've heard of it."

Picking up his mug, he wagged it back and forth while smiling at her guilelessly. With a theatrical sigh she fetched the carafe from the coffee maker and refilled his mug.

"Thanks, brat."

"You're welcome." She slid back into her chair. "All kidding aside, Lucky, if Susan Young has got it in her head that you're her prospective groom, you'd better be shopping for a diamond ring. When she doesn't get her way, she causes trouble."

"What more can she do? I'm already in trouble up to my gills."

A week had passed since his fight with Little Alvin. It had been the longest week of Lucky's life. The area around his right eye had run the gamut of rainbow colors, and was still a sick, jaundiced yellow. The red line across his abdomen had faded to pink.

Together with Sheriff's Department deputies and insurance investigators, federal agents continued to sift through the debris left by the fire. Due to the unfavorable publicity, Tyler Drilling's client list had dropped drastically. The note payment was coming due in less than a month, and what little revenue had been trickling in had stopped altogether. Bankruptcy seemed unavoidable. There wasn't even a glimmer of light on the dark horizon.

"One good thing," Chase had optimistically remarked the evening before, "they haven't turned up any hard evidence against you. Without something that places you on the scene at the time of the fire, they haven't got a case. It's all circumstantial."

"That's a plus from the legal standpoint," Lucky had said. "But until the insurance company is satisfied that we were victims and not perpetrators, they aren't going to honor our claim. So, while I won't go to jail, we're still in hock."

They desperately needed verification of Lucky's whereabouts that night in order to eliminate him as an arson suspect. They desperately needed Dovey.

Thus far, however, his attempts to track her had led him nowhere except in circles. Daily he polled the patrons of the place, asking everyone who had witnessed the incident with Little Alvin and Jack Ed if he remembered anything about the elusive woman or her car. All the men remembered that she was a good-looking redhead. Beyond that, he had come up empty-handed.

A return trip to the motel to speak with the night clerk hadn't been productive either. The man remembered her, all right, but she had registered as Mary Smith, paid for one night with cash, and that was all he knew. The convenience-store clerk who had sold him the whiskey, steak, and aspirin had never seen him with Dovey.

"She couldn't have just vanished off the face of the earth!" Lucky had exclaimed to his family after his discouraging interview with the motel clerk. "She's somewhere, walking around, breathing, going about her business, eating, sleeping, having no idea of the havoc she's created in my life."

"Maybe not," Tanya had suggested.

He had stopped pacing and looked toward his sister-in-law. "What do you mean?"

"Maybe she's read about the fire in the newspaper and realizes she's your alibi, but hasn't come forward because she doesn't want to become involved."

"That's a possibility," Chase had said.

Because it irked Lucky to think so, he dismissed that worry. "It's only been in the local papers, and she said she wasn't from around here when Pat asked her. I think she was telling the truth when she gave Dallas as her address. She looked like a city girl."

But for the next several days he had logged a lot of miles on his Mustang, driving to neighboring communities and tracking down all the Mary Smiths on the lists of registered voters. He found several. One was eighty-two; one was middle-aged, blind, and living with her elderly parents; one was a coed. All were dead ends.

He considered combing Dallas, seeking out every Mary Smith, but he knew it would be a time-consuming chore and, in the end, an exercise in futility. Tongue-in-cheek, and very cleverly, she had used that fictitious name. Why? She hadn't known then that he would eventually be looking for her to serve as his alibi in a criminal investigation.

"Lucky, are you listening to me?"

Sage's impatient inquiry brought him back to the present. "Hmm? What? You were saying something about Susan?"

"I was saying that she's a spiteful bitch."

"How do you know so much about her? She was several classes ahead of you."

"But her legend lived on even after I got to high school."

"Legend?"

"Her meanness was legendary."

"Example?"

"She was so envious when one of her classmates was named Homecoming queen instead of her that she circulated the rumor that the girl had herpes."

Lucky gave a spontaneous burst of laughter.

"It's not funny!" Sage exclaimed. "The gossip ruined that girl's reputation and made the remainder of her days at high school pure hell. That's not all."

Propping her arm on the edge of the table, she leaned toward him. "Susan was named first alternate on the girls' varsity basketball team. The next morning, when the newly named team was suiting up for practice, a bank of lockers fell over on top of one of the girls and broke her arm. Susan was standing on the other side of the lockers."

"And it's believed that she pushed it over?"

"That's right."

"Sage, that's crazy. It's silly high school back-biting and nothing more."

She shook her head adamantly. "I don't think so. Some of my friends who have stayed in town and know Susan through clubs and such say she's a viper. If she wants to be the president of this or that, she'll do anything to get elected." Her eyes narrowed. "Now she's set her sights on you. She wants to be Mrs. Lucky Tyler."

"I wonder why?" he asked, honestly puzzled by Susan's fixation on him. They'd gone out steadily for the last few months, had shared a few laughs, smooched a little, but he'd never even breathed the word "marriage."

"That's easy," Sage replied to his rhetorically phrased question. "No other woman has had the distinction of marrying you. Those who keep notches on their bedposts prize the one you make. You're the local stud. It would be a feather in Susan's cap to break you."

"Local stud, huh?" he drawled, leaning far back in his chair.

"Will you stop with the conceit," Sage said with annoyance. "A man with gray chest hairs has nothing to be conceited about."

"Gray!" he exclaimed. He bent his head down to investigate the wedge of chest showing through his parted robe. "Those are blond."

"Susan's determination to have you, coupled with this nonsense about the fire, worries me."

"Those lighter hairs are blond, Sage."

"Will you forget the hairs! I was only kidding, for heaven's sake."

His sister's concern touched him, but he couldn't take her warnings about Susan seriously. Granted, the woman was a schemer. She was unquestionably selfish, and could have taught the green-eyed monster a thing or two about jealousy. But he hadn't exactly been born yesterday. Susan would have to practice some mighty refined chicanery to outsmart him.

Reaching across the table, he patted the top of Sage's unruly blond head. "Don't worry, brat. I wrote the book on how to take care of women."

"You don't—"

Her protest was cut short when a knock sounded on the back door. "That'll be Mother," she said, leaving her chair to open the door. "Oh,

Pat!" she said with surprise. "We were expecting Mother back from an early trip to the produce stand down the highway."

"Mornin', Sage, Lucky." Pat stepped into the kitchen and removed his Stetson. "Got an extra cup of coffee?"

"Sure."

He thanked Sage for the cup of black coffee she poured him, blew on it, removed the matchstick from his mouth and sipped it, then stared into it for several silent moments. The coffee was a tactical delay.

If Pat had come in an official capacity to impart bad news, Lucky figured he would make it as easy on him as possible. "Why don't you tell us why you came out this morning, Pat?"

The family friend lowered himself into a chair across the table from Lucky. After glancing uncomfortably around the kitchen, he finally looked directly at the younger man. "Have you bought anything at Talbert's Hardware Store recently?"

"Talbert's Hardware?" he repeated with puzzlement. "Oh wait, yeah. I bought some railroad flares a few weeks back."

Pat Bush blew out a gust of air. "Where were you storing them?"

"In the—" Lucky refocused sharply on the sheriff. "In the garage that burned."

"They, uh, they've determined that the fire was caused by gasoline touched off by railroad flares. Nothing fancy. Simplest thing in the world."

Sage sank into the chair beside her brother and laid her hand on his shoulder. He plowed his fingers through his hair and held it back by settling his forehead in his palm. It was unnecessary for Pat to explain the significance of that find.

"I shouldn't be telling you this, Lucky," Pat said. "I'm here as a friend, not a law officer. Just thought I ought to warn you. They're preparing a case against you. Looks like now they might have enough probable cause to arrest you."

When the sheriff stood to go, Lucky roused himself. "Thanks, Pat. I know you're going out on a limb to tell me."

"When your daddy was dying, I promised him I'd look after Laurie and you kids. That pledge is more important to me than the oath I took when they pinned this badge on me." He moved toward the door. "Sage," he said, replacing his hat before stepping outside and pulling the door closed.

"Lucky," she said miserably, "what are you going to do?"

"Damned if I know."

In a fit of temper he hissed a vile word and banged his fist on the table. The blow rattled every piece of glass in the kitchen, even though it was somewhat cushioned by the newspaper he'd left lying open on the table.

His jaw grinding with aggravation, he stared down at the newsprint sightlessly, periodically spiking his enraged silence with a curse.

Suddenly his whole body tensed. He grabbed up the newspaper and held it close to his face. "I'll be damned," he whispered in awe. He laughed shortly. Then he laughed loudly.

In one motion he dropped the newspaper and stood up, sending his chair over backward and crashing to the floor. He left the kitchen at a run. By the time Sage caught up with him, he was taking the stairs two at a time.

"Lucky, what in the world . . . ?"

He disappeared at the top of the landing. She ran up the stairs after him and flung open the door to his bedroom. He was hiking a pair of jeans up over his hips.

"What's the matter? What are you doing? Where are you going?"

He pushed her aside on his way out of the room, wearing only his jeans, carrying a shirt and his boots with him.

She charged down the stairs after him. "Lucky, slow down! Tell me. What's going on?"

He was already vaulting into his open convertible when she bounded across the front porch after him. "Tell everybody I'll be back by night-fall!" he shouted over the roar of the Mustang's revving engine. "By then I'll be able to clear this whole thing up."

"Here's that reference material you wanted from the morgue." The gofer dumped a mountain of files on her desk.

Holding the last bite of her lunch sandwich between her teeth, she frowned at the extent of the research material and mumbled, "Thanks for nothing."

"Anything else?"

She bit into the sandwich, chewed, swallowed, then blotted her mouth with a paper napkin. "Coffee. From a fresh pot, please," she called after the young man as he dashed off. He was a college student who interned at the newspaper three afternoons a week. He hadn't been there long enough to become jaded. He was still starstruck and eager to please.

Her position as editorial columnist entitled her to a glass cubicle of an office, but the constant noise and hustle from the sprawling city room filtered into it. To anyone unaccustomed to newspaper offices, the incessant noise and motion would have been distracting. She didn't even notice.

That's why she wasn't attuned to the change in the climate that occurred when a man stepped off the elevator and asked for her.

His appearance had an immediate effect on the women in the room. It wasn't only that he was tall, slim-hipped, blond, blue-eyed, and handsome. It was the purposeful way he crossed the city room, as though it were a battlefield on which he'd just won the day and was about to collect the spoils of war. Even the most feminist among them secretly fantasized about being part of those spoils.

He also attracted the curiosity of the men, who, to a man, were glad they didn't have to tangle with him. It wasn't that he was of such an intimidating size, though his shoulders were broad and his chest wide. No, it was the expression on his face that was quelling. His jaw was set with inflexible resolve. His eyes were steady and unblinking; they could have been focused on a target caught in the crosshairs of a rifle sight.

He paused momentarily at the door of the small glass enclosure and stared in at the woman, who was bent over an open file on her desk, absorbed by its contents. A stillness had fallen over the city room. Computer keyboards stood silent. Ringing phones went unanswered.

The woman in the glass office seemed the only one unmindful of his presence as she absently dragged a pencil through her loose dark auburn hair. Without glancing up from her reading matter, she waved her hand to signal him inside.

"Just set it there on the desk," she said. "It needs to cool off anyway."

He moved forward to stand at the edge of her littered desk. She was aware of him, but it was several moments before she realized that he wasn't the college student in the Argyle socks there to deliver a cup of fresh coffee. Raising her head, she gazed up at him through the wide lenses of her eyeglasses.

She dropped the pencil. Her lips parted. She uttered a small gasp.

"My God."

"Not quite," he said. "Lucky Tyler."

Chapter Eight

She swallowed visibly, but said nothing.

"While we're on the subject of names," Lucky said, "what's yours? Dovey? Or Mary Smith? Or is it *Devon Haines?*" He slapped a newspaper, open to her column, onto her desk.

Her eyes lowered to the page, then swung back up to him. "Ordinarily they don't print my picture with my byline. I didn't know they were going to do it with this article, or I would have asked them not to." Her voice was little more than a hoarse croak.

"I'm glad they did. I've been looking for you ever since you skipped out on me. For the second time."

The initial shock of seeing him was wearing off; she was gradually regaining her composure. She assumed the haughty demeanor that set Lucky's teeth on edge. He recognized the expression she had worn while telling him off for interfering with her struggle with Little Alvin.

"If I had wanted you to know my name, I would have given it to you." She threw her shoulders back, shaking her hair off them. "Obviously I preferred to remain anonymous, Mr. Tyler, so if you would be so kind—"

" 'Kind' be damned," he interrupted. "If you want to talk here and let all the spectators in on it, fine." With a jerking motion of his head he indicated the city room behind him. "Or would you rather talk in private? Either way is okay with me . . . Dovey."

He deliberately slurred the last word, letting her know the extent of his anger, and that, if necessary, he had no qualms about discussing in front of an audience what had transpired in the motel room. Obviously she did. Her face paled.

"I suppose I could spare you a moment."

"Smart choice."

He took her arm the minute she rounded the desk and escorted her through the city room, where the onlookers made no pretense of subtlety. Speculative conversation resumed the instant Lucky and Devon cleared the doorway.

"Here are the elevators." She feebly pointed them out when he marched past them without even slowing down.

Propelling her toward the heavy fire door marked STAIRS, he took hold of the knob and pushed it open. "This'll do." He guided her through the doorway and followed closely behind.

She spun around to confront him. "I don't know what you're doing here, or what you expect to gain by—"

"You'll know in good time. First things first."

He shoved his fingers up through her hair and cupped her head. Tipping it back, he captured her surprised lips in a fiery kiss.

Inexorably moving forward, he backed her into the wall without decreasing the pressure of his lips on hers. She strangled on her protests and ground the heels of her hands against his shoulders, trying to push him off.

"Stop!" she managed to rasp out when he came up for air.

Lucky, however, had a week's worth of pent-up frustration to expend, a week's worth of lust to slake, and he couldn't have been budged by a Sherman tank.

"I'm not finished yet."

He sealed their mouths together again, employing the technique he'd begun developing with the preacher's daughter and over the years had mastered to an enviable expertise. The pads of his fingertips pressed into her scalp, while his thumbs met beneath her chin to stroke the smoothest expanse of skin he'd ever felt except for the insides of her thighs.

She never had a chance.

Her protests grew fainter, until they no longer qualified as gargled threats, but sounded more like whimpers of arousal. She stopped resisting the thrusts of his tongue as it hungrily plumbed her mouth again and again.

His first taste of her in more than a week reawakened an appetite that had been whetted but far from satisfied. He angled his body closer to hers, sent his tongue deeper into her mouth, and tilted his hips forward, nudging the cleft of her thighs, wanting, wanting, wanting . . . .

Suddenly coming to his senses, he raised his head and smiled down at her. Gently he flicked his tongue against the corner of her lips, savoring the flavor of her kiss, and whispered, "You're the one, all right. I'd know you anywhere."

"What are you doing?"

"Trying to figure out a convenient way into your blouse." He frowned at the back buttons. "Later."

She raised a hand to her lips and touched them gingerly. "You shouldn't have kissed me like that, Mr. Tyler."

"My mother tells me I've always been guilty of doing things I shouldn't do. My conscience doesn't have a very loud speaking voice. Sometimes I don't hear it." He smiled engagingly and ducked his head for another kiss.

Devon staved him off. "Please don't."

"Why not?"

"Because I don't want you to."

"Liar."

"How dare—"

"You want it as much as I do."

Her eyes flashed like summer lightning, the kind of hot white lightning that brings no rain. She slipped around him and made a beeline for the door leading back into the corridor. Before she could pull it open, he reached beyond her shoulder and flattened his hand against it.

She executed a stiff military about-face. "I don't know what you hoped to gain by finding me, Mr. Tyler, but you're in for a disappointment. What happened last week was a fluke."

"You'll have to be more specific. Are you talking about the barroom brawl or our night together?"

"Our . . . our night together," she repeated, all but choking on the words. "I want to forget it ever happened."

"Sorry. No can do, Dovey."

"Stop calling me Dovey! Now that you know it isn't my real name, it sounds ridiculous."

"Right. I can't believe I ever took you for a woman named something as whimsical as Dovey."

"If you persist in bothering me, I'll have to call—"

"Security? Great, call them. I'm sure they'd love to hear all about my business with you."

The ruse worked. He watched as she obviously considered several options and hastily discarded them all. Finally, crossing her arms over her middle, she looked up at him and demanded, "Well, what do you want?"

"If you're still in doubt, hug me real tight."

Her eyes skittered down the front of his body, then hastily came back up to meet his. "Besides the obvious," she said ungraciously, "what do you want?"

"To talk to you. But not here. Is there someplace we can go?"

"There's a sandwich shop across the street."

"Good. I haven't eaten lunch. Lead the way."

"What'll you have?" Lucky asked, consulting her from across the diner's turquoise tile table.

"Nothing."

To the waitress, he said, "One cheeseburger, cooked medium." He glanced down at Devon, looked pointedly at her mouth, and added, "Cut the onions. French fries, chocolate shake." Politely addressing Devon again, he asked, "Sure you don't want something?"

"I'm sure."

Handing the menus back to the waitress, he said, "Bring us two coffees, too."

"You don't take no for an answer, do you?" Devon asked, after the waitress had withdrawn.

"Rarely from a woman," he admitted.

"I thought as much."

"What makes you think so?"

"You're the overbearing, macho type."

To her irritation, he smiled. "That's me. Caveman Tyler."

Lucky was having the time of his life just looking at her. She was wearing a loose, soft blouse that buttoned down the back. It was primly styled and had full long sleeves, cuffed at her wrists. Beneath the sheer ivory fabric, he could see the outline of quality lingerie. She was wearing the blouse with a plain straight black skirt. For all its practicality and austerity, the outfit was as sexy as hell.

"I suppose sharing a motel bedroom with a stranger is nothing new to you," she remarked.

"It's happened."

"Not to me."

The waitress arrived with their coffees. Lucky watched Devon mindlessly raise hers to her lips and sip at it before she remembered that she had originally declined it. Coffee sloshed over the rim of the cup and into the saucer when she set it down emphatically.

"Now that we're alone, will you please tell me what we have to talk about?"

"What were you doing in the place?" he asked.

"That dive where we happened to meet?"

"Right."

"Did you read my story in this morning's paper?"

He cocked his head to one side, unsure what relevance her question had to his. "No. I didn't get past the picture of you."

"If you had read it, you would have realized I was in the tavern doing research."

He settled his cheek in the palm of his hand, propped his elbow on the table, and regarded her calmly as he silently invited her to elaborate. She took a deep breath.

"My column this week was on the rights still denied women, despite the strides we've taken in the past two decades toward achieving equality."

"You went into the place and bought a drink. What right were you denied?"

"My right to be left alone."

He grunted noncommittally.

She continued, "A woman still can't go into a bar alone without every man in there assuming that she's on the make, to pick up a man or be picked up. The thesis of my article was that there are still bastions of our society that women have yet to infiltrate, much less conquer.

"What took place in the bar proved my point. I did nothing to encourage the attention of those two rednecks. I sat quietly in my booth, drinking my beer, until they came over and started hassling me. It wasn't . . ." She paused and glared at him. "What are you laughing at?"

"I was just thinking that if you were missing a few teeth, and had acne and thick ankles, you probably could have drunk your beer in peace."

The waitress arrived with his food. Once she had set the platters in front of him, Devon picked up her argument.

"In other words, a woman who isn't particularly attractive is *safe* from male attention."

"You look mad," he said, all innocence. "I thought I was being complimentary."

"How much more sexist could you be than to judge a woman's worth —or a man's for that matter—strictly on the basis of looks?"

She brushed locks of her thick, lustrous hair off her shoulders. If she wanted him to judge her on the merits of her mind, Lucky thought, she should stop practicing feminine witchcraft like tossing around that mass of dark red hair and looking so damned seductive.

"Sorry, Devon, it's just not in my genes to think of you as anything but a beautiful, exciting woman."

"Is that spelled g-e-n-e-s or j-e-a-n-s?"

Casually he shook salt and pepper over the patty of the cheeseburger, then placed the top bun on it—all without ever taking his eyes off her. "Both. Better not ask which one makes the most convincing argument." He bit into the cheeseburger and derived satisfaction not only from its taste, but from her obvious discomfiture.

"Tell me, then," she said, making a stab at being composed, "if I had been missing teeth, et cetera, would you still have come to my rescue?"

He reached for the catsup. "Damn right. I would have. But," he said, aiming his finger toward the ceiling to emphasize that he was about to make the most important point of his argument, "I probably wouldn't have followed you afterward. I wouldn't have stretched out on your bed." He lowered his voice and leaned across the table, bringing them nose to nose. "I wouldn't have wanted you to go on blowing on my belly forever, and I wouldn't have woken up later wanting to blow on yours."

For a moment she was too stunned to move. Then she grabbed her purse and scooted toward the opening of the booth. Lucky raised his booted foot beneath the table and propped it on the opposite bench, blocking her escape.

"Hey, you asked, remember? I was just being honest, Devon."

"Spare me your honesty from now on. I want to leave. Now."

"Uh-uh. We've still got a lot to talk about." In no apparent hurry, he took another bite of his cheeseburger and dunked a French fry into the blob of catsup he'd poured into his plate. "Why'd you get mad when I intervened?"

"Because I wanted to handle the situation myself. Part of my research was to see how a woman could get out of a situation like that if forced into one. You took away my opportunity of seeing it through."

"I took away your opportunity of getting to know Little Alvin and Jack Ed better."

"Possibly," she admitted with chagrin. "They were a bit more than I bargained for. I had expected wolf whistles, perhaps a pass or two. I hadn't expected to be manhandled.

"And I'll tell you beforehand," she went on, "that you're mentioned in the article, too. Not by name, of course. You're referred to as a man with the White Knight syndrome."

"What's that?"

"He makes it his personal crusade to rescue damsels in distress."

"Hey, I like that." He sucked on the straw in his milk shake. "Why'd you use the phony name to check into the motel?"

Apparently she hadn't intended him to take the White Knight reference as a compliment. Dropping her forehead into her hand, she began massaging her temples. "I don't know. Whim. Sometimes people recognize my name and want to take issue with one article or another. I didn't feel up to conversation that evening."

He polished off the milk shake and pushed aside the glass, along with his empty plate. The waitress passed with a carafe of fresh coffee and refilled their cups before taking his dishes away.

"You never thought it would matter what name you used," Lucky said softly.

She raised her head. "No. I never thought it would matter. I never expected to see you again."

"That's because you don't know me very well."

His simple statement caused a worried frown to appear between her brows. "What do you want? Why have you come here looking for me?"

"You know what I want, Devon." His eyes slowly moved from the top of her head, over her face and throat, to her breasts. When his eyes reconnected with hers, he said, "I want another night in bed with you. This time we'll both be naked. I'll be looking at you with two clear eyes. And I won't waste any time sleeping."

"That's impossible." Her voice was so husky it was barely audible. "I'm telling you now, so you'll know and won't waste my time or yours. It is impossible. If that's all you came for—"

"It isn't."

"Then what? Hush money? Do you plan to blackmail me now that you know my name means something in this city?"

He ground his teeth in an effort to control his temper. "Don't ever say anything like that to me again, Devon. My name means something in my own town. The Tylers don't need anything or anybody badly enough to resort to blackmail."

"I'm sorry I offended you and your family name."

She said it as if she meant it, as if it was out of character for her to deliver such a low blow unless she was terribly upset. Lucky believed she was. Her original anxiety over seeing him had returned. It showed on her lovely features and in the depth of her green eyes.

"Just please tell me what you want, so I can go back to work and you can leave."

"You weren't just another pickup, Devon."

"Am I supposed to be flattered by that?"

"I'd like for you to be."

She shook her head. "I can't accommodate you. Being a one-night stand made me feel cheap."

"You were more than a one-night stand. My night with you is very significant to my future."

"Oh please," she groaned. "Don't add insult to injury by feeding me juvenile lines like that."

"You are my alibi."

Chapter Nine

"Alibi? Like in a crime?"

"Exactly like in a crime."

Devon shook her head. "I don't understand."

Lucky told her about the fire. "Several pieces of large machinery were destroyed. The damage is estimated at close to seven figures. At this point Tyler Drilling is stuck with the loss."

As always, whenever he thought about it, he became frustrated. "It's crazy. If the local authorities were handling the investigation alone, we, my family and I, would never have fallen under suspicion. But with the feds in on it . . .

"See, apparently a lot of oilmen who are in financial straits are taking desperate measures. I'm sure fraud is rampant. So, the insurance companies are on the alert. Of course their suspicions are unfounded in this case, but we've got to prove them wrong. My brother can verify his whereabouts that night. I can't. Not without you."

She regarded him closely for several moments before averting her head to gaze through the window at the traffic moving along the congested downtown boulevard.

"So you want me to go on record as your alibi. You couldn't have been in Milton Point setting fire to the garage because you were in bed with me all night."

"That sums it up."

She swung her gaze back to him. "I can't do it."

Before he could react, she slid from the booth and headed for the door of the diner. "Hey, what the—" Standing, he worked his hand into the pocket of his jeans and tossed a ten-dollar bill onto the table. "Thanks!" he shouted to the waitress as he bolted through the door in pursuit of Devon Haines.

He caught up with her at the intersection where she was jaywalking. "What the hell do you mean you can't?" He took hold of her upper arm and halted her in the middle of the street. Horns began blaring around them. A beer truck swerved to avoid a collision.

Lucky ushered her to the curb. Once they had reached the sidewalk, he drew her out of the flow of pedestrian traffic and repeated his question. "This time I really can't take no for an answer, Devon."

"You'll have to. I can't vouch for your whereabouts that night."

"The hell you can't," he ground out. Pulling her against him, he lowered his head to within whispering distance of hers. "You know I was lying beside you all night. I fell asleep before you did. You were gone by the time I woke up the following morning. And if you've forgotten what happened in between, I'll be happy to refresh your memory."

She nervously dampened her lips with her tongue. "I don't need to be reminded, thank you."

"At least you're not denying it happened."

"No, it happened, but I wish it hadn't. I'm not proud of it. I'm certainly not going to confess it to the world." She wrestled her arm free. "I'm sorry you're in trouble. Truly I am. But that fire has nothing to do with me."

"Maybe not, but you're the only thing standing between jail and me."

"Oh, I doubt that. A man like you always lands on his feet. I'm sure that before you're formally charged, you'll see a way out." She began backing away from him. "In any event I won't be able to help you."

She turned and entered the newspaper building through the revolving bronze doors. Lucky charged after her. By the time he was disgorged into the lobby by the rapidly turning doors, she was about to step onto the elevator. He raced for it.

Two uniformed guards lunged for him, catching him by the arms from behind. "Hey, buddy, you bothering Ms. Haines?" Apparently they'd been asked to intercept him.

"This won't help, Devon!" Lucky shouted to the closing elevator doors. She refused to meet his eyes as she punched the button for her floor.

He struggled with the security guards. "Let go of me. I'm leaving, I'm leaving." They didn't take his word for it, but pushed him through the revolving doors.

"If you come back, we'll call the police!" one shouted after him.

Lucky yelled back an obscenity, then stood glaring at the front of the

building while pedestrians eddied around him. "Now what?" he muttered. What the hell did she mean by "I can't"?

Using the transmitter, Devon lowered the automatic garage door, then
let herself into the condo through the connecting kitchen door. Once
inside, she ran through the dim, silent rooms until she reached the
living room, where she watched the street through the shutters until
she was satisfied that Lucky Tyler hadn't followed her home. She
wouldn't put it past him to try something like that. She'd driven home
with one eye on the road and the other on her rearview mirror.

The shock of seeing him standing at the edge of her desk this afternoon had affected her more than she wanted to admit. Usually adept at
masking her feelings, she feared she hadn't been successful in hiding
her reaction to his unexpected appearance. Several of her cohorts had
noticed how rattled she was and had teased her about it when she
returned to her office.

"Who's the hunk?"

"Nobody."

"Nobody?"

"Just a man I know."

"Someone out of your murky past, Devon?"

You could say it had been murky, she thought now. But the "past"
had been as recent as last week. None of her coworkers would guess
that.

Finally convinced he hadn't followed her home, she walked toward
the back of her house, where the master suite was located. Shedding
her skirt and blouse, she gazed longingly through the patio door toward the swimming pool. A swim would cool her off. She'd felt feverish ever since she'd looked up expecting to see the gofer's affable face,
and instead had met Lucky Tyler's smoldering blue stare. Several
strenuous laps would relax her. She was as jittery as a kitten, wondering when he would pop up next.

He would. She knew he would.

She stepped into a pair of skimpy swim trunks. After taking a towel
from the lucite rack in the bathroom, she slid open the patio door and
stepped out into her secluded backyard, almost completely taken up by
the pool itself.

There was very little lawn to maintain, only the shrubbery that grew
along the cedar privacy fence which let her indulge in semi-nude swimming. On the deck she had a gas grill and numerous potted plants.
Because her days were spent mostly indoors, she enjoyed spending the

evenings on her deck, tending the plants, even reading research material for her articles. Swimming laps in the pool was also an excellent form of exercise, and about the only one she liked.

Dropping the towel onto a chaise, she dived into the deep end of the pool. The cooling waters closed over her. Serenely she glided along the bottom, swimming from one end to the other in one breath. Only her head cleared the surface in the shallow end, then, taking another deep breath, she executed a surface dive and went under again.

By the time she had swum several laps, her lungs, heart, and limbs felt exercised and were aching pleasurably from the exertion. Peeling her sodden hair back with both hands, she started up the steps in the shallow end. She walked across the deck, head down.

Not until she almost stepped on his boots did she notice him. Then her head snapped up.

Lucky was sprawled in the patio chair beside the chaise. He was half reclining on his spine, his hands folded over his belt buckle, his long legs stretched far out in front of him, ankles crossed. Her towel was draped over one of his thighs. Beneath a shelf of tawny brows, his eyes were riveted on her bare breasts.

Rousing himself, he lifted his gaze to hers. "Towel?" he asked, extending it to her.

She snatched it from him and wound it around her bare torso. "What are you doing here? How did you get in?" She distinctly remembered checking to make sure all the doors were locked and bolted.

"I climbed over the fence. How high is that damn thing anyway? I landed hard. Think I threw my knee out. Old football injury."

His insouciance infuriated her. He acted as though jumping her eight-foot privacy fence was something he did every day at dusk. "You followed me home," she accused him.

"How else would I find out where you live? Since you sicced the guards on me, nobody at the newspaper was going to give me your address. You aren't listed in the telephone directory. I checked.

"See, Devon, the first time I checked the directory, I was looking for Mary Smith. There're dozens of those. But I thought I'd give Devon Haines a try. Sure enough, you aren't there." He ran a glance down her. "Is it heated?"

In the lavender glow of twilight, his eyes shone like twin blue lanterns. They were unsettling. In fact, she hadn't had a coherent thought since he had showed up at her office. The possible effects his reappearance could have on her life filled her with dread. What a fool she had been to lull herself into believing that she could come away unscathed from her earth-shattering experience with him.

Realizing that he was waiting for an answer to a question she couldn't remember, she said, "Pardon?"

"The pool. Is it heated?"

"Why?"

"Because you've got goose bumps as big as mosquito bites, and your lips are turning blue."

She pulled the towel tighter around her. "The air is chilly."

"Then we'd better go inside."

"*I'm* going inside. You're leaving."

"I want a drink, and from the looks of it, you could use one."

He casually slid open the patio door. "After you," he said courteously, stepping aside. Because she was chilled to the bone and because she wanted to put on more clothes as quickly as possible, she swept past him and reentered her bedroom.

"Where's the kitchen?"

"I asked you to leave, Mr. Tyler."

"You don't want a drink?" He dropped into the upholstered easy chair in the corner and crossed an ankle over the opposite knee. "Okay. We'll dispense with the drinks and start our discussion here and now."

It was hard to maintain her dignity, much less her belligerent insistence that he leave, when her teeth were chattering and her hair was dripping icy rivulets of water onto her shoulders and chest. His eyes kept straying to her breasts. Devon was keenly aware that her rigid nipples were making impressions against the thick terry cloth.

"It's a small house," she said scornfully. "I'm sure you can find the kitchen on your own."

Smiling, he rolled out of the chair. Standing only inches from her, he cupped his hand around her shoulder and used his thumb to whisk drops of water off the slope of her breast. In a low, stirring voice he said, "I like you wet."

To demonstrate her immunity to him, she slammed the door in his wake. He would never know that because of his touch her knees were about to liquefy. She dropped the towel, peeled off the swim trunks, and vigorously toweled herself. She dressed in a two-piece velour lounger, because it was quick, convenient, and warm. It also covered her from neck to ankle. Not wanting to take the time to dry her hair, she fashioned a turban out of a towel.

The lamps in the living room had been turned on, and Lucky was surveying her compact-disc library. When he heard her come in, he turned his head.

Their gazes locked. Seconds ticked off ponderously while they continued to stare at each other as if mesmerized.

Devon could remember things about him, small things that only a lover would know, yet he was a complete stranger to her. Suddenly, and with a degree of desperation that shocked her, she realized she was greedy for information. She wanted to know every trivial detail of Lucky Tyler's life.

All she really knew about him was that he adhered to a code of chivalry that had almost disappeared in contemporary America, that he had a keen sense of humor and a pair of startling blue eyes, and that his touch could set her on fire. She couldn't easily dismiss from her mind what had passed between them on their night together . . . even though she had no choice but to try and forget it.

His expression told her that he was also finding it impossible to forget.

At last he said, "All I could find was beer." He was drinking his from the bottle, but on the faux marble block she used as a coffee table, he'd set a cold beer and a glass. She acknowledged her drink with a thank you, but made no move toward it. "Don't you want it?"

"What I want, Mr. Tyler, is to know why you think you can so grossly invade my privacy." She complimented herself on sounding imperious and cool.

"Is that what I've done?"

"What else would you call it? You've harassed me at my office, and trespassed on my private property."

"So why haven't you called the police?"

He was also a cocky bastard, she decided. He knew why she hadn't called the police. His knowing smile grated on her. Forgetting to be cool, she raised her voice. "Why did you follow me home?"

"Because I'm not finished with you."

"Well, that's just too damn bad, Mr. Tyler, because I was finished with you the minute—"

"You left my bed?"

She fell silent.

He took advantage of her speechlessness. "Is that why you stayed with me that night? Were you that hard up for a man? Would any man have done?"

"No, no, and no!"

He responded as though she had said yes. "Then, in the morning, once I'd done stud duty for you, you figured it was all right to sneak out."

"You're wrong," she said, stubbornly shaking her head. "I won't even honor that with a denial."

He set his beer on a shelf in the bookcase and, in two strides, came even with her. His hands bracketed her shoulders, lifting her slightly up and forward. "What else am I supposed to think, huh? Why'd you hightail it out of that motel room?"

"Because I was disgusted."

He was taken aback by her answer. No woman had ever said that to him. "Disgusted? With me?"

"With myself," she lashed out. "With the situation. I didn't want to hash through it again. If you make a habit of sleeping with women you don't know, I'm sure you can understand morning-after awkwardness."

Gnawing on his inner cheek, he assimilated what she'd said and apparently agreed with her. Then, taking another tack, he asked, "Why did you pull that disappearing act this afternoon?"

"Because we had nothing more to talk about."

"Wrong."

"Right."

"Are you going to ask me to spend the night tonight?"

"No!" she said, aghast.

"Then we've got something more to talk about."

"I think that's what's really bothering you," she said heatedly. "You're certain that every woman you meet is panting to go to bed with you. Well, take a good look at the exception, Mr. Tyler. You're only hounding me because I walked out on you and not the other way around. Your ego has been stung."

"Maybe," he admitted grudgingly. "Partially."

"Nurse it someplace else, with someone else. I don't want to see you again. Haven't I made that plain enough?"

"Oh yeah. You've made it plain. But you haven't convinced me, Devon. You haven't even convinced yourself."

He drew her forward with such force that the towel slipped from her head and her hair tumbled out of it. His mouth was damp and demanding as it settled against her lips.

Far from resenting his aggressiveness, she responded to it, reveling in his potency and his blatant hunger for her. Instead of pulling away, as her mind dictated that she should, she treated herself to the heat and urgency of his kisses.

His hands slid beneath her top to splay open across her back and hold her closer to him. She loved his touch on her skin and longed to take the same kind of liberties with him. He was tough, all sinew and muscle. Her curves molded pliantly to his manliness. She loved the rasp of his stubble against her face, the taste of his mouth, the scent of his skin. She was starved for his masculinity.

When he raised the hem of her top, she felt the cold, exciting bite of his metal belt buckle against her bare midriff. Then his hands moved over her breasts—reshaping, stroking, teasing, then gratifying by drawing his thumbs across her nipples.

"Devon," he murmured roughly when he felt their beading reaction through the silk cup of her bra. "Why are you making this so hard?"

She yanked herself away from him, backing up as though he represented something terrifying, which he did. Oddly enough, he was smiling.

"I didn't mean that in a crude or lewd way. I meant 'hard' as in difficult."

"I know what you meant," she said breathlessly, unable to find her full voice. "It's not only difficult, it's impossible. I told you that earlier. Now, please go, and don't bother me again."

"You're bothered all right."

She followed his gaze down to her swollen breasts, defined so well against the soft cloth of her pullover. She would be lying to herself as well as to him to deny that she desired him. On a near-sob she said, "Please go."

"Devon, forget how and where we met. Think only about how it was when we woke up in bed together and turned to each other."

She closed her hands over her ears. "I can't."

"Why?" He forced her hands back down to her sides. "Why, when it was so damn good, won't you let yourself remember?"

"I don't owe you any explanations."

"The hell you don't," he said, his voice low and fierce. "The kiss you just gave me makes a lie out of everything you're saying. You're hungry for me. As hungry as I am for you. I believe that entitles me to an explanation."

His incisive arguments, combined with his sex appeal, were weakening her resolve. Pulling her hands free of his and lashing out defensively, she cried, "I can't see you anymore. Ever. Now, please go away."

Lucky switched tactics. Hooking his thumbs in his belt loops, he assumed a slouching stance, his body thrown slightly off-center. Arrogantly he tilted his head to one side.

"Okay, for the sake of argument, let's say that the kisses we've shared didn't leave us both damned near senseless. Let's say that your blood's not running hot and thick right now. Let's forget all that and focus our attention on my problem—besides the one I have with you, that is. Let's discuss how badly I need you for my alibi."

She was shaking her head long before he finished, first in denial of her physical reactions to him, then to the idea of her testifying to the authorities on his behalf.

"No one can know that I spent the night with you," she said adamantly. "No one. Is that understood? I certainly can't make it a matter of public record." Her previous chill, temporarily dispelled by their embrace, returned. She ran her hands up and down her arms as though to restore circulation.

"You can't just shrug off this arson rap as a frivolous misfortune of mine."

"I'm not. I'm terribly sorry that you're in trouble."

"More than just trouble, Devon. These federal guys are damned serious."

"What kind of case have they got against you?"

"Flimsy and circumstantial," he admitted. "I would never get convicted, but I don't expect we could raise bail. I do not cotton to the idea of going to jail for any length of time, especially for something I didn't do. I don't even like the idea of being charged with a felony. My family, our business, would be irreparably damaged by something like that." Gently he took her by the shoulders again. "Devon, be reasonable about this. You've got to help me."

"No I don't. You can't force me."

"I shouldn't have to. Why won't you just come forward like any decent person would?"

"I can't!"

"Tell me why."

"I *can't!*"

"*Why?*"

"Because I'm married!"

Chapter Ten

"She's married."

Lucky's two glum words echoed as dismally as a death knell. Seated at the bar in Tanya and Chase's small apartment kitchen, he stared forlornly into the cup of coffee his sister-in-law had brewed for him.

He had arrived at their apartment complex before dawn. Ignoring the early hour, he'd knocked on their door and got them out of bed, his unkempt hair and stubble of beard chasing away their annoyance at having been awakened so early.

Besides looking as though he needed a shave, a hot meal, and twelve hours of sleep, Lucky had hair windblown from driving all the way from Dallas, a distance of over a hundred miles, with the top of his convertible down, going at speeds they dared not guess and would rather not know. Strands of dark blond hair were radiating from his head like straw.

His family had been worried about him since yesterday morning. The last one to see him had been Sage. According to her, he had left the house half-dressed, at a dead run, and without a word of explanation.

Now several moments transpired before Chase repeated his brother's bleak report. "Married?"

"Married. You know, matrimony, holy wedlock."

Tanya, having poured her husband and herself another cup of coffee, sat down on one of the barstools. "How do you know, Lucky?"

"She told me." After a lengthy, deep, wet kiss, he thought bitterly.

"You finally tracked her down?"

"Yesterday."

"Where?"

"Dallas."

"What's her name?"

"Devon Haines."

"That sounds familiar."

"You've probably read her newspaper column."

"Sure!" Chase exclaimed, thumping the bar with his fist. "Devon Haines."

"I accidentally stumbled over her byline and picture in yesterday morning's paper."

Lucky recounted the rest of the story to them, leaving out the personal aspects of it and glossing over the tempestuous hours he'd spent in a bowling alley and batting barn—so he'd have something to hit legitimately—after his meeting with her and until he decided to drive home.

"The lady did not want to be found," he said. "When I did find her, she refused to cooperate, said she wouldn't, *couldn't,* be my alibi. Now I know why." The coffee was scalding hot, but he tossed it back as though the mug were a shot glass full of whiskey. Tanya silently rose to get him a refill.

"Did you meet her husband?" Chase wanted to know.

"No."

"Was he there?"

"No."

"Where was he?"

"I don't know."

"What's his name?"

"I don't know."

"If she's married, what was she doing sleeping with you?"

"I don't know that either. Who the hell can figure out what goes on inside a woman's head?"

Angrily Lucky flung himself off the barstool and began to prowl the length of the galley kitchen. "This is one situation I've never run across. I don't have any experience, and I'm stumped." He stopped pacing to address his audience. "Don't get me wrong. I'm not claiming to be an angel. I confess to having done some pretty wild things with women."

"I don't think anyone could dispute that."

"We've done some pretty wild things together."

Chase cast an uncomfortable glance toward his wife. His love for Tanya McDaniel had tamed the former rodeo star considerably. "If it's all the same to you, I'd just as soon not discuss our escapades in front of Tanya."

"Those escapades aren't the point," Lucky said irritably. "Tanya knows you were a hell-raiser before she came along. My point is that for all my carousing, I have never slept with a married woman. I drew the line at that." Mindlessly he rubbed his stomach, as though the very thought of adultery made him queasy.

"I never would even go out with a divorcée until the final, final papers were *final*. So this broad," he said irreverently, aiming his index finger in the general direction of Dallas, "not only duped me with the phony name bit, but tricked me into doing something that, old-fashioned as it sounds, I believe is morally wrong."

He returned to his seat, dejectedly throwing himself onto the padded cushion. Eyes vacant and bleary, he contemplated near space.

"Lucky," Chase ventured after a lengthy period of silence, "what are you going to do?"

"Probably ten to twenty for arson."

"Don't say that!" Tanya cried. "You can't go to prison for something you didn't do."

"You know what I meant, Lucky," Chase said. "You can't let her off the hook that easily. She fooled around, so she can damn well pay the consequences."

"I used that argument."

"And?"

"It got me nowhere."

"Appeal to her basic human decency."

"I did that too. Didn't shake her a smidgen. If she would run around on her husband, I doubt she has a sense of decency. Although," he added on a mumble, "she seemed decent enough at first."

"Well, if worse comes to worst, Pat Bush could subpoena her."

"To appear before a federal grand jury." Lucky sighed and tiredly dug his fingertips into his eye sockets, which were shadowed by fatigue. "I was hoping it wouldn't have to go even that far. With business so bad . . ." He lowered his hands and looked at his brother. "I'm sorry, Chase. I really screwed up this time. And the worst of it is that I'm dragging Tyler Drilling, you, and everybody else down with me."

Chase rose from his barstool and affectionately slapped his younger brother between the shoulder blades. "Your hide is more valuable to me than the business. I'm worried about the guy who actually set the fire. What's the bastard planning to do next?" He consulted the wall clock. "Guess I'd better get on out there and baby-sit those investigators."

"I'll be along later."

"Uh-uh. You're taking the day off."

"Says who?"

"Says me."

"You're not my boss."

"Today I am."

They'd been playing that universal sibling game almost since they were old enough to talk. Lucky gave in much sooner than usual.

Chase said, "You look like hell. Stay home today. Get some sleep." Turning, he headed for the bedroom. "If you're gone by the time I get out of the shower, I'll be in touch later today."

After Chase had withdrawn, Tanya smiled at her brother-in-law. "What would you like for breakfast?"

"Nothing," he replied, getting to his feet. "Thanks, though." At the front door of the apartment, he pulled her into a hug. "I should take a cue from my big brother, find a woman like you, marry her, and quit screwing around for good. Problem is, since you've been taken, there aren't any good broads left."

Laughing, she shoved him away. "Lucky, I seriously doubt you'll sweep a woman off her feet by referring to her as a broad."

He smiled, but there was more chagrin than humor behind it. His blue eyes were tired and dull and puzzled. "Tanya, why would a married woman share a motel room with a total stranger in the first place, then let him make love to her?"

"It happens all the time, Lucky. Don't you read the statistics?"

"I know, but . . ." He gauged her worried frown. "I know you probably feel uncomfortable talking about this with me, but I feel like a jerk discussing it with another man, even Chase. Will you listen? Please?"

"Of course."

He hesitated, but only momentarily. "Devon just wasn't the type to pick up a stranger and go to bed with him. I've been with plenty of women who do it routinely, and she was different."

"How so?"

"In every way. Looks. Attitude. Actions." He shook his head in bafflement. "Why would she take a life-threatening risk like that? For all she knew, I was a psychopath, or had a venereal disease or God knows what else. She's married. She and her husband live well. She's got a successful career. Why would she risk all that? And if she's got the guts to do it, why get squeamish when it's time to 'fess up?"

"I don't know, Lucky," Tanya said, sounding genuinely sorry that she couldn't provide him with an answer. "I can't imagine being un-faithful to Chase. I can't imagine even being tempted."

He squinted his eyes with concentration. "I don't think she planned it to happen. It wasn't like she was on the make. In fact, she tried everything she could to avoid me. She's almost militant in her femi-nism, takes issue with sexual labels, things like that. Real defensive about it." He paused, carefully choosing words to describe Devon Haines to Tanya.

"She's put together well, you know? Dresses professionally. Seems to have every situation under control. I certainly couldn't call her flighty." He blew out a gust of air, indicative of the depth of his confu-sion.

"She's just not whimsical. And it's not like she seduced me, or even vice-versa. I mean, it just sorta happened. We were both half-asleep and kinda rolled toward each other, and I started touching her, kissing her, and she started responding, and before we knew it, we were . . . you know."

During his speech Tanya had been watching him closely. "Lucky," she asked softly, "which bothers you most? The fact that she declines to come forward and clear you? Or the fact that she's married?"

He abruptly pulled his chin back a notch. "What do you mean by that?"

"For the past week you've been obsessed with finding out who this woman is and where she lives."

"Because she's my alibi."

"Are you sure that's the only reason?"

"Yes. Hell yes." He reached for the doorknob and pulled the door open. "Listen, Tanya, I don't want you or anybody else to get any romantic notions about her."

"I see."

"I mean it."

"I understand."

"That's it. She's my alibi. Period." Standing silhouetted in the open doorway, he made an umpire's "safe" motion with his hands. When he did, he rapped his knuckles against the doorframe. "Ouch! Damn!" Sucking on an injured knuckle, he added, "Besides, as it turns out, she's married."

A few moments later Chase, rubbing dry his dark hair with a towel, wearing another around his middle, came to Tanya's side. She was standing in the doorway, watching Lucky's taillights disappear around the nearest corner.

"What was all the shouting about?" he asked.

"That was Lucky," she said, closing the door. "He was adamantly denying that this woman means anything more to him than an alibi."

"Does he think you're hard of hearing?"

She laughed. "No, but I think he is."

"Huh?"

"He's not listening to his heart."

"I don't get your meaning."

"You're not supposed to," she replied coyly. "You're a man."

"You know, that secret little smile of yours drives me crazy." He bent down to nuzzle her neck. "Makes me horny as hell."

"I know," she whispered back, moving against him seductively. "Why do you think I wear it so often?"

Chase dropped both the towels and carried her into their bedroom.

Half an hour later the covers were helplessly tangled around their naked bodies, but neither noticed or cared. They were sated. While Tanya lay on her back, eyes closed, Chase idly caressed her breasts, which bore the faint, rosy markings of recent lovemaking.

"I feel sorry for Lucky," she remarked dreamily.

"So do I. He's got himself in a real jam."

"I'm not talking strictly about the fire. One way or another, he'll be exonerated. This might represent a setback in his life, but that's all it'll be."

"Then why do you feel sorry for him?"

She opened her eyes and looked at her husband, reaching up to lovingly brush damp strands of hair off his forehead. "I think the encounter with this Haines woman has had more of an impact than he's willing to admit. And even if he does admit it, whether publicly or to himself, there's nothing he can do about it. It was finished before it started."

"Define 'it.' "

She shrugged. "A meaningful relationship, I suppose."

"A meaningful relationship? With a woman? My brother?" Laughing, Chase rolled onto his back.

Tanya propped herself up on one elbow. "You think the notion is that ridiculous?"

"As long as there's more than one living, breathing female alive on planet Earth, Lucky will never be faithful to just one."

"I think you're doing him an injustice. He's more sensitive than you think. And he can be very loyal."

"Oh, I agree. He can be very loyal to several women at one time."

Laughter lurked beneath his serious words. "Did I ever tell you how Lucky got his nickname?"

"Come to think of it, no."

"You never wondered why a James Lawrence would be nicknamed Lucky?"

"I took it for granted. For as long as I've known you, that's what you and everyone else has called him."

Stacking both hands behind his head, Chase laughed softly. "I was in tenth grade. He was in ninth, about fourteen, I guess. There was this girl, a woman really, about twenty, who lived in Kilgore. To put it bruntly, she was a tramp. She worked at being a tramp. Real hot-looking. Dressed to display her endowments. She kept all the boys in several counties in a constant state of arousal, but never came across with the goods.

"So one night, me and some of my friends decided to take a car—we couldn't legally drive yet—and go to Kilgore for a look-see at this gal. Lucky begged to come along. We finally agreed after he threatened to squeal our plans to our parents.

"Off we went. After driving around Kilgore for an hour, we found her. She was strutting her stuff at one of the local bowling alleys. All of us ogled until our eyes were bugging out and our tongues were lolling. But Lucky was the only one who worked up the courage to speak to her. Damned if the rascal didn't end up smooth-talking his way into her car, then into her house.

"Positively awestruck, we followed them there. He stayed inside for two hours. The kid who'd sneaked out the family car was in a panic to get back to Milton Point before his folks discovered it missing. He finally started honking the horn. When Lucky came out from around back, he was pulling on his shirt and wearing this very smug grin on his face.

"It made me mad as hell that my little brother had succeeded in doing what so many others had tried to do and failed. I said, 'Quit grinning, you little bastard. You just lucked out, is all.' 'Call me Lucky,' he said, still wearing that complacent grin."

Tanya was trying to look horrified while suppressing a giggle. "You're both incorrigible. How did you explain his new nickname to your parents?"

"I forget now what explanation we came up with. Anyway, from that night forward, the name stuck. He's been Lucky to everybody."

Tanya sighed, resting her head on Chase's hairy chest and sadly recalling what had prompted the story. "I don't think he's feeling very lucky these days."

"No," Chase agreed. Folding his arms around her, he held her close. "But I am."

Devon had reams of research material to read, dozens of periodicals to peruse, and thousands of words to compose, but she couldn't concentrate on anything except her encounter with Lucky the evening before.

In her mind she continued to see his face as it had looked when she told him she was married. His expression had been a mix of incredulity and outrage. His eyes, initially blank with stupefaction, had grown frigid by degrees, until they achieved that hard, cold glare that she shivered beneath even in recollection.

Feeling restless, she left the enclosure of her office and took the long route through the city room to the alcove of vending machines. Desultorily she inserted the required coinage into the refrigerated box. The coins dropped into the concealed bin with a metallic echo that sounded as hollow as she felt. Coworkers spoke to her as she passed their desks on her way back. She pretended not to hear.

"Hey, Devon, what happened with the blond hunk yesterday?"

Ignoring that question, she closed her office door behind her to discourage interruption and returned to her desk, setting aside the cold drink. She hadn't really been thirsty. Getting the drink had merely been a diversion from her haunting thoughts.

"I'm married."

Bending her head over her desk and holding it between her hands, she repeated the words. "I'm married. I'm married."

And yet she wasn't. The license was signed. The judge had pronounced her wed. It was official. As far as the sovereign state of Texas was concerned, she was married.

"But I'm not," she whispered with frustration.

It was a marriage she could easily get out of. She certainly had the grounds to seek an annulment. Anyone who heard her case would sympathize. No one acquainted with the facts would condemn her.

She, Devon Haines alone, was standing in the way of her own freedom from a marriage that amounted to no more than a piece of paper. But it was the right thing to do. She had walked into it with both eyes open. Whether or not it was a bad decision, she had to live with it.

Lucky Tyler didn't know the conditions of her marital status. He probably wouldn't care. He condemned her for being an unfaithful married woman who had duped him into sharing a night of sin and was now unwilling to pay the price. There was no way she could help him without jeopardizing herself and her husband.

She'd seen the contempt in Lucky's eyes. She could have dispelled it with a few simple sentences of explanation, but she had held her silence.

He hadn't realized the truth.

When he entered her, he had mistaken the reason for the sudden tensing of her body. He had obviously taken it for passion, not pain. He had misinterpreted her sharp, gasping breath. His previous kisses had prepared her to receive him too well. She was so moist, he hadn't noticed the snugness.

By the time he was buried deep inside her and moving within, it had been too late to consider the consequences of what she was doing. Like him, she had become oblivious to everything except the undulating, swelling sensations that had engulfed them.

She was glad the alarming truth had been obscured by eroticism. If he knew that she was a virgin, this cloudy situation could turn turbulent. Then again, she wished with all her heart that he knew.

Memories of their lovemaking caused a bittersweet ache in the center of her soul. She marveled over it, exulted in the pleasure, and lamented its brevity.

Her office door was suddenly flung open. "You asked to see this article when the copy editor was finished."

She raised her head and brushed the tears off her cheeks, reaching for the papers. "Oh yes, thanks," she told the gofer.

"Say, are you okay?"

"I'm fine."

"Sure?"

She gave him a watery smile and reassured him before he left. Self-pity was an emotion she refused to surrender to. She had welcomed Lucky's fierce, yet tender loving. Because on that night, above all other nights, she had so desperately needed loving.

But wasn't it poignantly ironic that in the arms of a stranger she had glimpsed what could be—should be—and wasn't?

"Lucky!"

He groaned and covered his tousled head with his pillow. It was immediately wrestled from his grasp. "Go away," he snarled.

"Will you please wake up and tell this woman to stop calling?"

He rolled to his back and blinked his disgruntled sister into focus.

She was standing beside his bed, glaring down at him, her mood as tenuous as the narrow straps of her bikini.

"What woman?" he asked hopefully, reaching for the receiver of the telephone extension on his nightstand.

"Susan Young."

If the telephone had suddenly turned into a cobra ready to strike, he couldn't have snatched his hand back any quicker.

Sage, with supreme exasperation, plugged in the cord he had previously disconnected, lifted the receiver, and, without bothering to cover the mouthpiece, said, "She's been making a nuisance of herself by calling every hour on the hour for two whole days. Will you please talk to her so I can sunbathe in peace?"

She thrust the phone at him. He caught it, juggled it against his bare chest, then mouthed "brat" as he raised it to his ear. "Susan," he said in a voice that would melt butter twenty yards away, "how are you? Thanks for calling. I was just thinking about you."

Sage poked her index finger into her open mouth, mimicking gagging herself, then sat down on the edge of the mattress, unabashedly eavesdropping on her brother's conversation.

His temperament was touchy at best, but she wasn't intimidated by his formidable frown. "What's been going on?" he said into the receiver.

He listened for a moment, but cut into Susan's diatribe. "I know I haven't been around and haven't called. I wanted to protect you from this mess."

"If she falls for that, she's not only devious, she's stupid."

Lucky shot his sister a threatening look. "Until this mess blows over, I didn't think we should see each other. I didn't want to involve you . . . Yeah, I know what you offered to tell them, but—" He listened for another while. "Susan, I can't let you do that. I think too much of you."

"Oh please." Sage groaned. "What's she offering to do? Bed the feds?"

Overriding his sister's sarcastic words, Lucky said, "Give me an hour. . . . Promise. I'll be there in an hour." Thoughtfully he replaced the receiver and continued to stare at it until Sage spoke.

"Well? What was that all about?"

"None of your business. Will you kindly haul yourself off my bed, so I can get up and get dressed?"

"How juvenile. I've seen you in skivvies before."

"For your information, Miss Sophistication, I came to bed straight from the shower, and am buck naked beneath this sheet. Now, unless you want to be educated, get the hell out of here. I told Susan I'd be at her house in an hour."

"Really!" said Sage, taking umbrage. "Do you think I've lived under a rock? Male nudity doesn't shock or offend me. I know what all the parts look like and how they work."

Lucky frowned as he took in her skimpy attire. "Listen here, young lady, I expect you to behave yourself in a manner becoming a lady when it comes to the opposite sex," he said sternly.

"Ha! You're a fine one to talk. Do you behave yourself like a gentleman?"

"Do you run around the wild young studs dressed like that?" he demanded, nodding down at her bikini.

"You gawk at women in bikinis."

"So? Male prerogative."

"Like hell!" Sage exclaimed. "That's a double standard."

A mental image of Devon emerging from the swimming pool, peeling back her wet hair with both hands; buttocks and mound covered by triangles of bronze, metallic fabric; breasts bare, heavy, gleaming, beaded with sparkling drops of water.

Sage was right. He had gawked, and it was a double standard. But that didn't keep his body from reacting to the alluring mental picture.

"You gotta leave now," he said in a voice so low it sounded like a growl.

"Here lately, you're such a grouch." She left the bed and flounced toward the door. However, she pulled up short and turned back, her expression no longer irritable, but sympathetic.

"Chase came by at lunch to check on you. Mother and I told him you were sleeping. He said not to wake you up, that you needed the rest. He, uh, he told us about the Haines woman, Lucky. I'm sorry."

Despite his foul mood, he winked at her. "Thanks, brat. I appreciate your concern."

Once Sage had closed the door, he flung back the sheet and went to his bureau. It took him a long time to dress because he often found himself standing motionless staring into space, or forgetting what he'd gone to the closet for, or wondering why he was searching through a particular drawer. His mind kept straying back to Devon. Damn, he still wanted to see her.

Instead, he had to go see Susan. After avoiding her and her preposterous marriage proposal for more than a week, he acknowledged that he couldn't delay dealing with it any longer.

"Jeez, I dread this," he muttered to himself as he finally left his bedroom and loped down the stairs.

He didn't realize until later just how much his dread had been warranted.

Chapter Eleven

It was almost as though she had expected him.

Devon didn't react with as much surprise as he had anticipated. Her car rolled to a halt beside his where he was parked at the curb in front of her condo. She gazed at him for a moment, her expression revealing little, before she pulled into the driveway.

Lucky stepped out of his Mustang and moved toward the garage door that had opened automatically for Devon's car. They met in the driveway. Obviously she had just come from work. She was dressed in a suit, although she was carrying, not wearing, the jacket. Sunglasses held her hair away from her face. Her other hand held a large, flat pizza box.

"Hi," he said, his expression solemn.

"Hello."

"I, uh . . ." He shuffled and glanced up at the storm clouds darkening the sky. "Is your husband at home?"

"No."

"I don't want to make this any more difficult for you than it has to be."

"Then what are you doing here?"

"I've got to talk to you." He drew his lips tight and said through his teeth, "Dammit, you've got to help me, Devon."

She glanced around worriedly, as though prying eyes might be peeking at them from the other houses on the block. Finally she nodded curtly.

"Come on in." She led him through the garage, lowered the door by depressing the switch on the wall, and asked him to hold the pizza while she unlocked the kitchen door. He followed her inside and deposited the pizza on the white tile countertop.

She flicked another switch. Cold blue fluorescent lighting flickered on. "I'll be back in a minute."

She disappeared through a doorway. Lucky moved to the window overlooking her backyard. It had started to rain. Fat drops bounced on the water in the pool and splattered on the deck. They were such opulent drops, they bent down the leaves of her plants. A jagged streak of lightning divided the sky just above the horizon. Moments later it was followed by a drumroll of thunder.

"Are you hungry?"

He turned. She had come into the kitchen behind him, having changed into a pair of old jeans, a loose pullover, and a pair of soft leather moccasins. Her hair looked freshly brushed. Without the armor of her business suit she looked younger, more vulnerable.

"I guess. Hadn't thought about it."

"Do you like pepperoni pizza?"

"Sure."

"Give me a minute to make a salad."

Lucky was dumbfounded. Was she actually inviting him to stay for supper? He'd expected her to slam the door in his face—if she'd been the one to answer it. If he had encountered her husband on the other side of the threshold, he planned to ask directions or something equally as ludicrous.

When he hadn't got an answer after ringing her doorbell, he had decided to wait and see who turned up first and play it by ear from there. Being invited to dinner hadn't even crossed his mind as a possibility.

She had removed salad greens and tomatoes from the refrigerator and was calmly tearing lettuce into a bowl. He said, "You don't seem surprised to see me."

"I'm not."

He propped his hip against the counter. "How come?"

"You said you never take no for an answer from a woman." She lifted her eyes to his. "I believe you. Excuse me." She nudged him aside, reached into the refrigerator again and took out a bottle of salad dressing, and, to his further astonishment, a bottle of red wine. She passed it to him, along with a corkscrew, which she took from a drawer. "Would you please?"

Mystified by her composure, Lucky peeled the sealing material off the wine bottle and twisted the corkscrew into the cork. He watched her set the table with two place settings. She placed several slices of pizza in the microwave oven to warm.

"Glasses?"

"Beneath the cabinet."

He noticed then that two rows of wineglass stems were hanging up-side down from a rack mounted on the underside of the cabinet. He slid out two and poured each of them a glass of wine. Devon lighted a candle, placed it in the center of the table, and motioned him into a chair.

Lucky approached the table, bringing with him the two glasses of wine, along with the bottle, and sat down in the chair she'd indicated. She sat down across from him and began serving his plate from the large salad bowl. Once both their plates were filled with salad and pizza, he reached across the table and caught her hand in the act of reaching for her wineglass.

"What gives with you?" he asked tautly.

"What do you mean?"

"What happens if your husband comes home and finds us sharing a cozy candlelight dinner?"

"Would that bother you?"

"A whole hell of a lot."

"He won't."

"You're sure?"

"I'm sure. He won't be home tonight." She pulled her hand back, reached for her glass, and sipped the wine.

The mingling, mouth-watering aromas of oregano and mozzarella had reminded Lucky that he hadn't eaten all day. He took a huge bite of pizza and washed it down with a swallow of wine. Wine wasn't his beverage of choice, but it seemed appropriate to drink when the woman he was sharing his meal with had hair the same deep red color.

"It's good," he said politely.

"Thank you."

"Do you do this often?"

She bit into a slice of pizza, pulling on the stringy cheese until it eventually broke off. "What? Bring pizza home for dinner?"

Lucky munched on his own chewy bite, swallowed, and said with a patience he didn't feel, "No, have men over for dinner when your husband is out of town."

"I didn't say he was out of town. I just said he wouldn't be home tonight."

Tired of her word games, he set his fists on either side of his plate and glared at her until she looked up at him. "Do you do this often?"

She held out for a few moments more before answering. Eventually her stubbornness surrendered to his. "You're the first man I've had to dinner in this house. Now, does that salve your ego, or whatever the hell it is that causes you to badger me about things that are none of your business?"

"Yeah, thanks."

"You're welcome."

"I'm flattered."

"Don't be. I just knew you wouldn't go away without first having your 'talk.' I was hungry." She shrugged, letting him draw his own conclusion. "It's certainly not a violation of the marriage vows for two adults to share a pizza."

"Unless those same two adults have shared a pillow."

Her eyes connected with his and reflected the glazed shock of a nocturnal animal caught in headlights bearing down on it.

To increase her astonishment even more, lightning struck nearby. Following a rending sound like the cracking of a bullwhip, all the lights went out except for the steadily burning flame of the candle.

"Are you all right?" Lucky asked, stunned by the sudden absence of the sterile fluorescent lighting.

"Of course. I'm fine." She didn't look fine. The hand that reached for her wineglass was trembling.

"Devon." Acting on instinct, he reached across the table to capture her hand. It was cold. He enfolded it in the warmth of his. After glancing over each of her chilled fingertips with his thumb, he settled it in the cup of her palm, stroking evocatively. "About that, Devon . . ."

"About what?"

"About us sharing a pillow, a bed. You don't have anything to worry about." Her head tilted quizzically. "I mean about birth control or anything. I took care of that. I didn't know if you were aware of—"

"Yes, yes, I was," she stammered. "Thank you. You behaved . . ." She faltered and swallowed with difficulty. "You were a perfect gentleman about that."

His crooked grin was self-deprecating. "If I'd been a perfect gentleman, I wouldn't have tracked you down, tricked my way into your room, and coerced you into letting me stay the night."

"You were injured. By the way, how's the knife wound?" She lowered her gaze to his midsection.

"It's okay. You can barely see it anymore."

"Oh."

He didn't know at exactly what point in the conversation they had started whispering. It was silly, really, but somehow the topic, the setting, and the mood called for soft, confidential voices.

They simultaneously realized that their eyes seemed locked to each other and that he was still stroking her palm. Guiltily she pulled her hand from his grasp, though he was reluctant to let it go. Taking his cue from her, he resumed eating, but his appetite for food had deserted him, to be replaced by hunger for her.

The only sounds in the silent house were those of the rain pelting the windows and of cutlery against their plates. However, if sexual awareness and suppressed longings were capable of generating sound, the noise would have been as blaring as a brass band.

"More pizza?" she asked.

"No thanks."

"Salad?"

He shook his head. As she cleared the dishes from the table, he refilled both their wineglasses. When she returned to the table, he noticed their reflections in the window glass. It was a portrait of intimacy, a man and a woman sharing a candlelight dinner. Devon noticed it too.

"Appearances can be deceiving."

"Yes," she answered softly.

After a moment he said, "Devon, I'm going to shoot straight with you. You don't know me very well, but I assure you that shooting straight is not something I usually do with a woman."

"I don't find that at all hard to believe." She was smiling as she raised her wineglass to her lips.

"No, I guess not," he said ruefully. Leaning back in his chair, he contemplated the candle's flame through the ruby contents of his wineglass. "There's this girl in Milton Point that I've been seeing for a couple of months."

"Rest assured that I don't intend to make trouble between you and your girlfriend."

"That's not what this is about," he said crossly.

"Then why bring it up?"

"Because you need to know about her."

"What makes you think I'm interested in your romances?"

"This isn't about romance. Just hear me out, okay? Then you'll get your turn." She gave him a small nod of concession. "This girl's daddy is a big shot at the bank that's holding a loan on my business."

"Is that why you were dating her?"

He got the impression that she would be disappointed if he said yes.

"No. I started seeing Susan because she was one of the few available women in town that I hadn't been to bed with yet."

She cast her eyes downward. "I see."

"I told you I was going to shoot straight, Devon."

"And I appreciate your honesty," she replied huskily. "Go on."

"Susan is spoiled rotten. Accustomed to winding her daddy and everybody else around her little finger. Selfish. Self-centered." He could go on and on, but felt that he had captured the essence of Susan's personality and didn't want to be accused of overkill. "Anyway, she's made up her mind that she wants to be Mrs. Lucky Tyler."

"Why?"

He shrugged. "My sister says because it would distinguish her."

"That's considered a distinction in Milton Point?"

"By some," he said testily.

"I take it you're not too keen on the idea of marrying her."

"There's no chance in hell that I'm going to marry her."

"Have you told her that?"

"Twice."

"Apparently she doesn't take no for an answer either."

His temper snapped. Scowling, he said, "I'm pouring out my guts here, trying to explain things to you, and all you can do is make these snide little remarks."

"Your romantic intrigues might be fascinating to some women, but I don't see what your problems with this Susan have to do with me."

"I'm getting to that."

"Please do."

"Last week Susan volunteered to lie to the authorities, saying that she had slept with me the night of the fire."

"In exchange for a wedding ring, I suppose."

"Bingo."

"To which you said . . . ?"

"Nothing. I didn't take it seriously. I thought maybe if I ignored her, she'd give up and go away."

"No such luck?"

"No such luck. Today she called and insisted on seeing me."

"What happened?"

"She's threatened to tell another lie. Only this time she says she'll tell them that I outlined to her my plan to torch our garage and use the insurance money to pay off the bank note."

"They would never believe her."

"The hell they wouldn't. To their way of thinking, she would be making an ultimate sacrifice. She's willing to squander her reputation as a Goody Two Shoes by making it public that she's been sleeping with me."

"Has she?"

He could tell that she regretted asking the question almost before she'd completed it. That gave him a glimmer of hope. She cared enough to wonder about his other lovers. Could she also be a tad jealous?

"No, Devon. I've never slept with her. I swear." His eyes bore deeply into hers, trying to impress the truth into her mind. Her next question indicated that she had been persuaded.

"Then what have you got to worry about?"

"Plenty. Susan can be very convincing. Hell, this afternoon, I almost believed her myself when she began to cry and say that she couldn't hold in her ugly secret any longer.

" 'I can't go through the rest of my life with this on my conscience,' she said, or words to that effect. She was talking like it was fact, going on and on about how unhappy I'd made her by confiding my nefarious plan to her."

Devon's fingers absently trailed up and down the stem of her wineglass while she pondered what he'd told her. "I presume that the only way Susan would be happy again is if you proposed marriage, in which case she would conveniently forget that you're an arsonist."

"That was the implication, yeah. If we were formally engaged, she would switch her stories to 'protect' me."

"At the same time protecting your business from bankruptcy."

He nodded grimly. "I dismissed her threats until today. This afternoon I saw just how destructive she could be."

"Hell hath no fury, et cetera."

"Especially since I was supposed to be having dinner with her when I was in bed with you."

Devon's lips parted, but remained speechless.

"When she found out about that, well, that really capped it. My sister, Sage, tried to warn me about Susan. I laughed off her warnings. I shouldn't have. Susan is devious and audacious, willing to go to any lengths to get what she's after.

"Damn my own hide, I made it easy for her to trap me, and at the same time bring down my whole family. Out of pure spite, she's not above making our lives hell. She can and will do it."

"Unless I tell the authorities where you really were the night of the fire," Devon said slowly.

"That's right." With emotional gruffness he added, "Unless you tell them that I was making love to you."

"Don't call it that!" Devon's words were a whisper, but an exclamation just the same. She left her chair so hurriedly that her thigh bumped the rim of the table and rocked the candle.

Lucky left his chair just as quickly. Devon was leaning into the countertop, her hands curled into fists on the tiles along the edge.

He stepped behind her and, for a split second, wrestled with his conscience. He shouldn't touch her. He shouldn't. Even knowing that, he placed one of his hands on the countertop beside hers and curved his other arm around her waist, flattening his hand on her stomach and burying his face in the nape of her neck. He luxuriated in the silky feel of her hair against his lips.

"That's what it was, Devon. Deny it with your dying breath if it soothes your conscience, but that won't ever change what it was."

"Leave me alone," she moaned. "Please."

"Listen to me," he said urgently. "That arson rap isn't the only reason I'm here. You know that. You knew it yesterday. I would have come looking for you whether or not I was in trouble. I had to see you again.

"You wanted to see me again just as badly. I don't care how many times you deny it, I know it's true. You're not only running from involvement in a criminal case and what effects it might have on your life. You're running from this." He lightly ground his hand over her belly, skimmed her mound, the top of her thigh.

"Don't! Don't touch me like that."

"Why?"

"Because . . . because . . ."

"Because it drives you as crazy as it does me."

"Stop."

"Only if you tell me I'm wrong about the way you feel. Tell me I'm wrong, Devon, then I'll stop."

"Please. Just leave me alone."

"I can't." He groaned. "I can't."

She turned her head toward her shoulder. He lowered his. Their mouths met in a greedy kiss. She turned into the circle of his arms, which pulled her against him. Resting his hands on her hips, guiding them, he positioned her against him.

As his passions burned hotter, he also got angrier because he knew she was forbidden to him. Despite his penchant to misbehave during Sunday school, some spiritual training had penetrated his young mind.

That formal religious instruction, plus all the moral lessons drilled into him by his conscientious parents, declared that this was wrong, wrong, wrong.

Yet he couldn't deny himself her kisses, not when her mouth was warm and sweet and eager. He kept telling himself that the next kiss would be the last—forever. But one only made him hungry for more.

"Dammit, Devon, resist me. Stop this. Stop me." He was so obsessed with her, he was seized by a primal urge to fight for her. Pressing her head between his hands, he tilted her head back drastically. "Where is he? Where is the slob you're married to? Where was he when you were traveling around East Texas alone? Is he crazy to give you that kind of freedom? Is he blind? Why isn't the bastard here now, protecting you from me, protecting you from yourself."

Lucky had posed the questions rhetorically. He didn't really expect answers. That's why he was shocked when she cried, "He's in prison!"

The lights suddenly came back on.

Chapter Twelve

Lucky blinked several times. Watching him, Devon realized it was from shock as much as from the sudden glare of the fluorescent tubes overhead. The stark light was offensive and unwelcome. It revealed too much. She edged out from between Lucky and the counter and switched it off. She was more comfortable with only the glow from the single candle on the table. It made her feel less exposed.

"Prison?" He remained in the same spot, as though his boots were nailed to the floor.

"The minimum-security federal prison in East Texas. It's only about fifty miles from—"

"I know where it is."

"I'd been there to see him and was on my way home when I decided to do some research for my article. I figured that a tavern in a less urban area would better prove my theory. As it turned out, I was right."

That was all the explanation he needed. At least, it was all he was going to get. She wasn't going to provide him with a detailed account of her visit with her husband, which had left her terribly upset. It was none of his business to know how shattering that visit had been.

By pure chance Lucky Tyler had happened to be at the right place at the right time—or the wrong place and time, depending on one's point of view—to take advantage of her highly emotional state.

"What's he in the pen for?"

"Insider trading. SEC violations."

"Did he do it?"

"Of course not!" she lied. "Do you think I'd marry a criminal?" At least she'd believed in his innocence when she'd married him.

"How the hell do I know?" He moved then, bearing down on her angrily. "All I really know about you is that you cheat on your husband."

The accusation sounded ugly. Because she couldn't tell him the truth, she pretended to be angry and responded with a quick denial. "I do not!"

"That's not the way I remember it."

Moving to the door, she jerked it open. "You can leave the same way you came in—through the back door. I'll open the garage for you."

"Not that easy, Devon."

"Now that you understand the awkward position you've placed me in, I'm asking you to go."

"I don't understand anything!" he shouted, reaching beyond her shoulder to slam the door closed again. It created a waft of air that disturbed the candle and made it flicker, projecting wavering shadows of them onto the walls. "We're about to have our second night together."

"What are you talking about?"

"I'm not leaving until I have a full explanation from you."

"I don't owe you—"

"Is Haines your name or his?"

"Mine. His name is Shelby. Greg Shelby."

"How long have you been married?"

She was in no mood to be grilled, but he wasn't going to leave without the full picture, and, she admitted, she couldn't blame him. If their positions were reversed, she would be just as frustrated as he. He wouldn't have to know all of it. Just some of it. That would pacify him.

Or would it? When she fell victim to his compelling blue stare, as now, his eyes seemed to see straight through her. It was unsettling, even frightening. What if she accidentally let her guard down and by way of a look, a sigh, prompted him to guess or learn the single most important fact of that night that he didn't seem to remember?

To cover her uneasiness, she politely asked, "Would you like some coffee?"

"No."

"Something?"

"Answers."

"Let's go into the living room."

She cupped her hand behind the candle flame and blew it out. In darkness she navigated the hallway leading into the living room. There, she switched on only one lamp before taking a seat in the corner of an ivory upholstered sofa. Lucky dropped onto the hassock in front of the blue leather chair, spread his knees wide, and loosely clasped his hands between them.

"Shoot," he said.

She began without preamble. "When Greg's trial came up, I asked my editor's permission to do a feature story on him."

"You didn't know him before that?"

"No."

"What piqued your interest enough to want to write about him?"

"Most criminals, from serial killers to petty thieves, fit a particular profile," she said. "White-collar criminals are generally arrogant and condescending toward their prosecutors, whether they're proved guilty or not."

"Go on."

"Well, from what I'd read about Greg, he didn't fit that profile. He was pathetically earnest in his denials of any wrongdoing. That intrigued me. I sold my editor on the idea. He said to go for it. Next, I had to go through Greg's attorney and the D.A.'s Office to get their permission. This took several weeks.

"Greg's lawyer stipulated that he be present during the interviews, which I agreed to. The prosecutor stipulated that the articles would have to be read and approved by someone in the D.A.'s Office before publication. You see, they couldn't lean toward either guilt or innocence, but had to be completely unbiased." Lucky nodded. "When everyone was satisfied, I was finally granted my first interview with Greg."

"Love at first sight?"

"No, but I was attracted."

"Physically?"

"Among other things."

"A man in handcuffs can be a real turn-on."

She ignored his sarcasm. "He wasn't in jail at the time. He had posted bail."

Thinking back on that first meeting in his attorney's office, Devon recalled wondering how anyone could suspect Greg of being guilty of an outstanding parking ticket, much less a felony. He was impeccably dressed in a three-piece, very conservative charcoal-gray suit, white shirt, sedately striped tie. His reddish-brown hair had been carefully combed back from his high, smooth forehead. He could have given Emily Post lessons on courtesy.

"What did you get from that first meeting?" Lucky asked.

"A sense of his background."

"Which was?"

"He was reared in a Pennsylvania steel town by very strict and religious parents from whom he was—and is to this day—estranged."

"Why? I can't imagine willfully cutting myself off from my family."

Devon could have guessed that. Earlier he had expressed regret over causing his family their present difficulties. Apparently what affected one Tyler affected them all, and each took the others' problems to heart.

"Greg wasn't fortunate enough to have the family closeness that you enjoy, Mr. Tyler. Indeed, few people are," she said reflectively, sadly. "Greg's father had worked for the same steel company all his life. He couldn't grasp the concept of playing the stock market, and ridiculed Greg for not holding down a steady job."

"So you've never met his parents?"

"No."

"What about yours? What do they think of having a son-in-law in jail?"

"My parents are dead."

"Oh. I'm sorry. I know how it feels to lose a parent. My dad died a couple of years ago." She acknowledged that with a nod of her head. "How soon after that first meeting did you start dating Shelby?"

"We've never had an actual date." The statement drew a frown of disbelief from Lucky. "It's true. His attorney advised us against being seen together socially. It wouldn't be appropriate for a man on trial to be seen doing the town."

"So the courtship took place under the lawyer's watchful eye? Bet he got a kick out of that," Lucky commented scornfully.

"He isn't a voyeur. After the first couple of meetings he realized he could trust me, that I wasn't there to exploit his client, so he left us alone."

"How convenient."

"Actually it was," she snapped. "We had time to get to know each other."

"I'll bet."

"I realized just how falsely Greg had been accused. He knew that someone in his firm had leaked valuable information to certain clients. Whoever it was had been very clever. He left a trail of evidence pointing directly at Greg. Greg's defense was based solely on his lack of material gain. If he'd committed the crime for profit, where was the profit?"

"Hey," Lucky said, "I'm not the jury. They've already reached a verdict. I'm more interested in you . . . and Greg, of course."

"As time went on, Greg and I became more emotionally involved."

"Hmm."

"It was difficult to maintain an objective viewpoint."

"No doubt."

"I wanted to defend him myself, so I had to give up writing the articles. They created a conflict of interest that no credible journalist can afford. Greg was upset by that. He hadn't wanted our romance to interfere with my career."

"The free publicity couldn't have been all that bad either."

That comment struck a sore spot. "What's that supposed to mean?"

"Nothing, nothing," Lucky said tiredly, as though it didn't matter. "So when Shelby popped the question, you said yes?"

"That's right. He asked me to marry him as soon as the trial was over. But I wanted to get married right then."

"Why?"

Yes, why? What had she been out to prove? That she was smarter than his accusers, that she was right in her estimation of him when everyone else was wrong? Or had it gone back to her mother's death a few years earlier? Her mother's earnest claims of being ill still echoed inside her head. Had they overlapped with Greg's avowals of innocence?

"I'm in pain, Devon. Truly. I can't stand it. Please help me."

"I'm innocent, Devon. I swear it. You've got to help me."

She couldn't turn a deaf ear to a desperate person seeking help. Because of what had happened with her mother, her heart was compelled to believe Greg, even when the facts didn't bear out his claims of innocence.

Only later had she realized she'd been duped. She had bought his entire act, swallowed the bait whole, played right into his hands. It was almost as though Greg had crawled inside her head and heard her mother's feeble voice saying the words that haunted Devon. He had known exactly how to manipulate her to pity.

To admit that to Lucky Tyler was unthinkable, however. She continued to defend Greg adamantly, because there was no graceful way out. Besides, he *was,* legally, her husband. Marriage carried with it responsibilities one didn't just turn one's back on.

In answer to Lucky's question, she perpetuated the myth she had created, even though she knew it to be a justification for her gullibility.

"I married him to demonstrate my confidence in his innocence. We were married in a civil ceremony in his lawyer's office."

"So how long between the nuptials and his conviction?"

"Two days. Greg was the only witness his defense attorney called to the stand," she explained. "He was eloquent and sincere. I couldn't believe my ears when the jury returned a guilty verdict."

She closed her eyes. "I can still see the bailiffs moving toward him to take him into custody. Greg looked stricken."

And furious, she thought. His failure to sway the jurors had enraged him. Those twelve people hadn't been convinced of his sincerity. She was the only one who had been fooled.

"How long ago was that?"

"Eleven months."

"What was his sentence?"

"Two years in prison. Ten years probation. His lawyer says he'll probably serve less than half that."

"So he could be paroled soon."

"He comes up for review in a few weeks."

Lucky stood up and put his back to her. He slid his hands, palms out, into the hip pockets of his jeans. There was a palpable tension in the way he held his shoulders. When he came back around, his expression was fierce and angry.

"How many times in the last eleven months have you cheated on him?"

"None of your business."

"The hell it's not!" Grabbing her hand, he pulled her to her feet. "I don't know if I'm one of dozens, one of an elite few, or the one and only. Frankly I don't know which I prefer, but I damn sure want to know."

"It doesn't make any difference."

"It does to me."

Tears threatened. She wanted to shout the truth at him. *You're the only one. Ever.* Instead, her voice cracking, she whispered, "You're the only one."

His shoulders relaxed marginally, and some of the ferocity in his eyes dimmed. "Guess I'll have to take your word for that."

"Whether you do or not, it's the truth."

"Do you love him?"

"He's my husband."

"That's not what I asked."

"I'm not going to discuss my relationship with my husband with you."

"Why not?"

"Because you have no right to know."

"You shared your body, but you won't share a few facts?"

"I didn't *share* anything." She protested verbally, but the words didn't originate in her heart. "What happened just . . . evolved. It started with a few kisses and went from there. You caught me unaware."

"You were unaware of my tongue on your nipple?"

No, she inwardly groaned. She remembered every touch in vivid detail, but desperately wished she didn't. "I was half-asleep. I merely responded to the stimuli."

He took a menacing step forward. "If you tell me you were pretending that I was your husband, I'll strangle you."

"No," she said tearfully, "I wasn't pretending that."

Unable to meet his stare, she lowered her eyes. The silence in the house pressed in on her suffocatingly. His sheer physicality overwhelmed her.

To put essential space between them, she began to wander restlessly around the room, restacking magazines on the end table, looking for any task that would keep her hands occupied and her eyes off him.

"They used to stone women for doing what you did."

Fluffing the sofa pillows, she sprang erect. "What *we* did, Mr. Tyler. You were in that bed too."

"I remember," he said tightly. "I'm willing to take my share of the responsibility for what happened. You're not."

Placing her hands on her hips, she confronted him belligerently. "What would you suggest I do? Go through the city passing out rocks to everyone? Or start wearing a red letter *A* on my chest? In some cultures, they behead adulterers. Do you think justice would be served then? If so, are you willing to place your head on the same chopping block? Because it sure as hell was on the same pillow."

That reminder abruptly ended the shouting match. She turned her back on him.

"I had a lapse of judgment and made a mistake," she said. "Believe me, my conscience has been punishing me ever since."

He moved in behind her and spoke her name, his voice soft and consoling now. Taking her by the shoulders, he turned her around to face him and tilted her head up with a finger beneath her chin.

"I don't want to punish you. Whether you believe it or not, I blame myself a whole lot more than I blame you. I could confess ten sins to every one of yours, I'm sure. Adultery has *never* been one of them before, but . . ."

As their gazes moved together and locked, his voice dwindled to nothingness.

"Never?" she said hoarsely.

"Never."

"If you had known I was married . . ."

He pondered his answer for several seconds before saying, "I'm not sure it would have mattered."

Then, not only did their stares merge, but their recollections as well. Each remembered the smell and touch and taste of the other. Each had actively participated in what happened in that motel-room bed. Each had to accept his share of the blame, take responsibility for it.

"I have to vouch for you," she whispered. "I really don't have a choice, do I?"

"Yes, you do," he replied, surprising her. "I won't force you to, Devon."

"But if I don't, it'll mean so much more hardship on you and your family. I can't let that happen. Ever since you told me yesterday about the fire, I've known I would eventually have to come forward as your alibi. It's the right thing to do." She gave a wistful little smile. "I guess I was hoping for a miracle that would make it unnecessary."

He touched the corner of her smile with his fingertip. "Your husband will never have to know. We'll keep your identity a secret. I haven't been officially charged. I'm just a prime suspect. Once you've told them that I was with you from dusk to dawn that night, I'll be cleared, and you'll be free to go. It'll never become a matter of public record."

Situations of this magnitude were rarely resolved that easily, she knew. Still, she didn't want to throw a cloak of pessimism over his expectations. "I'll take tomorrow off and come to Milton Point. I want to get it over with as soon as possible."

"I would appreciate that too," he said. "The sooner I'm off the hook, the better."

His mouth split into the same sort of grin he'd first given her from the end of her booth in the bar. It made him dashingly, piratically handsome.

Since the night she had spent with him, she had asked herself a million times how she could have done such a foolhardy thing. The more time she spent with him, the more reasonable the explanations became. What woman, no matter how level-headed and self-reliant, could resist that smile?

Even though she was still suffering the consequences of submitting to it, she felt her body once again growing warm and fluid as a result of it. "Where should I go when I get to Milton Point?" she asked, forcing herself to think pragmatically.

"Why don't you come to the house around noon? I'll call Pat and have him bring out the investigators to take your deposition or whatever they need."

"Who's Pat?"

"The sheriff, Pat Bush. You met him, remember? It's a good thing, too, because he can positively identify you as the woman I picked up in the place."

"You didn't exactly pick me up."

"Figure of speech. No call to get riled."

"Well, I am riled. I've agreed to do what you want, so please leave now." She marched to the front door and pulled it open.

"Don't you need directions to my house?"

"I'll look up the address in the phone book."

"Suit yourself."

"I always do," she retorted, unwilling to let him have the last word.

He got it anyway. Before he stepped across the threshold, his hand shot out and curved around the nape of her neck. He hauled her mouth up to his for a scorching kiss. " 'Night, Dovey," he whispered before releasing her and ambling down the sidewalk.

Chapter Thirteen

She was still miffed when he greeted her at his front door at noon the following day. He had known the goodnight kiss would make her mad. That's why he'd done it. He took mischievous pleasure in provoking her simply because she was so easily and delightfully provoked. He was challenged to see how many different ways he could do it.

Besides, he had wanted to kiss her.

He wanted to now too. But that didn't seem a very good idea, not when she took care not even to let her clothes brush against him as she entered the hallway of his home.

She was dressed for business in a pale yellow linen suit with a straight skirt, the hemline just at her knees, and a tailored jacket decorated with a silver lapel pin. Her matching silver earrings showed up well in her ears, because she had pulled her hair back into a no-nonsense bun. Her expression was just shy of combative.

"Hello," she said coolly.

"Hi." He gave her the cocky grin he knew she found aggravating.

"You failed to mention that you lived outside the city limits in the country."

"I offered to give directions, remember? You wouldn't let me. Did you get lost?"

"I'm here, aren't I?"

"Yeah, you're here, looking more like the preacher's wife come calling than an overnight alibi. Who's gonna believe I tumbled you?" The devil in him was kicking up his heels, goading him to say things he knew damn well would rub her the wrong way. But he felt he was justified in being ornery. He didn't particularly like her attitude either.

"What did you expect me to wear? A negligee?"

"I—"

"Lucky, has our guest arrived?"

Laurie Tyler entered the hallway through an arched opening. "Hello," she said pleasantly, extending her hand to Devon. "I'm Laurie Tyler, Lucky's mother."

"I'm Devon Haines."

"Come in, Ms. Haines. Everybody's out in the kitchen. I don't know why we have so many extra rooms in this house. I think we'd have been better off just building one enormous kitchen. Seems like that's where everybody always ends up."

"Are the investigators here already?" Devon asked with uncertainty, glancing over her shoulder at the cars parked in the semicircular driveway.

"Not yet. Those belong to family," Laurie told her.

"Curious onlookers," Lucky said sardonically. "You've drawn a crowd."

He received a reproving look from his mother before she took Devon by the forearm and led the way. "Lunch is a casual meal around here. Chicken salad is on the menu today. I thought that sounded good since the weather is so muggy. You're hungry, I hope?"

"Well, I, yes, I suppose. I hadn't counted on eating lunch."

Lucky observed the two women as he followed them through the formal dining room, which was reserved for holidays, birthdays, and special parties. His mother's unqualified friendliness had flustered Devon. Laurie often had that effect on strangers. Until given grounds to change her mind, she was always accepting of people, and had a knack for putting them at ease.

She propelled Devon into the kitchen and announced her to the rest as though she *were* a new preacher's wife come calling. "Everybody, this is Devon Haines, who has so unselfishly agreed to help Lucky out of this trouble he's in. Devon, that's Tanya, my daughter-in-law; Sage, my youngest child; and Chase, Lucky's older brother."

They regarded her with unabashed curiosity, but murmured polite hellos, knowing that Laurie would tolerate nothing less.

"Sage, scoot your chair over and let Devon sit there between you and Lucky. Devon, would you like iced tea or lemonade?"

"Uh, iced tea, please."

"Fine, I'll get it. Sugar and lemon are on the table. Lucky, hand her that plate out of the refrigerator. And you can start on your lunch now that she's here." As she passed the glass of iced tea to Devon she added, "He was too nervous to eat before you arrived."

"I wasn't nervous," he remarked crossly. He set the pre-filled plates on the table and threw his leg over the seat of his chair, straddling it. "I was afraid she wouldn't show."

Devon reacted as though she'd been goosed. "I said I would, didn't I?"

"Yeah, but you've been known to skip without giving prior notice."

"Well, she's here and that's the important thing," Chase said, intervening when Tanya gouged him in the ribs with her elbow. "We're all very glad that you agreed to clear Lucky, Ms. Haines. At no small expense to yourself."

"Because you're married and all." Sage, who had remained blessedly silent, could restrain herself no longer. "You sure don't look like what I thought one of Lucky's pickups would."

"Sage!"

"I didn't mean to be rude, Mother. I know you're as surprised as I am that she's not wearing dragon-green eyeshadow and fishnet stockings. I like your suit, by the way," she said, smiling at Devon guilelessly.

"Th-thank you," Devon stammered.

Having wanted to agitate Devon himself a few moments ago, Lucky now wanted to throttle his little sister for being so rude. Devon's cheeks were flushed and her eyes abnormally bright, but her lips looked pale beneath her pearly beige lipstick.

Tanya threw her a lifeline. "How long have you been a journalist, Ms. Haines?"

"Going on five years," Devon replied, giving Tanya a grateful smile. "Ever since I graduated from college. I started out writing obits and fillers for a smaller newspaper in South Texas before getting the job in Dallas."

"I read your columns faithfully. They're very interesting."

"Tactfully put," she said with a soft laugh. "Sometimes my readers take issue with me."

"I don't always agree with your opinion," Tanya admitted with a smile, "but you always give me food for thought."

"I'm glad to hear that."

"Do you write at home, or do you go to the newspaper offices every day?" Sage wanted to know.

"Where do you get your ideas?" Chase asked.

"Y'all hush and let Ms. Haines eat her lunch," Laurie said, then disobeyed her own order and asked, "Do you use one of those word processors?"

Devon laughed. "I don't mind the questions. Really. I enjoy talking about my work."

She answered their questions in turn. Lucky was interested in her answers himself, but tried not to let his interest show as he ate chicken salad that he didn't even taste.

His family was treating her like the Queen of Sheba. Hell, he was the one in trouble, not her. Why weren't they giving her the third degree about sleeping with strangers the way they'd given him?

Even as he posed these disgruntled questions to himself, he knew that if any of them breathed a disparaging word to her, he'd jump right down their throats in her defense.

"Who called Pat?" Laurie asked. She had parted the curtains and was looking through the window over the sink at the approaching patrol car.

"I didn't," Lucky said. "I thought we were going to wait until after lunch, Chase."

"So did I. I didn't call him."

Chase left his chair and moved to stand beside his mother at the window. "He's alone. The agents aren't with him." He had the back door opened before Pat even reached it. The sheriff stepped into the kitchen and removed his hat and sunglasses.

"Hi, everybody." Nodding down at the table, he added, "Sorry to interrupt your lunch."

"Please join us, Pat," Laurie said. "There's plenty."

"I can't, but thanks."

"Something to drink?"

"Nothing, thanks."

So far Pat had avoided looking at any of them directly and was uneasily shifting his weight from one foot to the other while restlessly moving his fingers around the brim of his hat—dead giveaways that this wasn't a social call.

Lucky pushed aside his unfinished plate and stood up. "What is it, Pat?"

Pat Bush looked at him with a beleaguered expression. He removed a folded document from the breast pocket of his uniform shirt. "I have a warrant for your arrest."

Sage and Tanya gasped. Laurie raised a hand to her chest as though someone had just wounded her. Devon's pale lips parted in surprise. Chase's reaction was volatile. He exclaimed, "What the hell?"

Lucky snatched the document from the sheriff, scanned it, then tossed it down onto the table. He muttered words his mother wouldn't normally have allowed spoken in her house. "I have an alibi," he told Pat, pointing down at Devon.

"So I see. Ma'am." After acknowledging her, Pat looked back at Lucky. "Once a warrant has been issued, I haven't got a choice. You'll have to come with me now. Chase can bring the lady in when they start to question you. It'll all be cleared up soon."

"Does he have to be placed under arrest?" Laurie asked.

"I'm sorry about it, Laurie, but, yeah, he does. He can finish his lunch though. I'm in no hurry to get back to town."

"Well, I'm in a hurry to get this mess over with. Let's go." Lucky stamped toward the door.

Pat caught his arm. "We've got to do this by the book. I've got to Mirandize you."

"Fine," Lucky said tautly. "But can we go outside? I don't want my mother to have to listen."

"Don't patronize me, James Lawrence," she said sharply. "I'm not a shrinking violet who needs protection from anything unpleasant. I fought your daddy's cancer for two years before losing him to it. I'm unwilling to give up another member of my family just now, so if they want a fight, they'll get one," she said staunchly.

"Way to go, Mother," said Sage, looking just as determined as Laurie.

Lucky winked at his mother. "Fix something good for supper, because I'll be home way before then." He went through the back door. Pat doffed his hat to the ladies and followed him out.

Pat read him his rights. "Hate like hell having to do this," he mumbled as he clamped the handcuffs around Lucky's wrists.

"Just do it and stop apologizing for it. I understand. It's your duty."

"I'm doubly glad you've got the woman."

"Why?" Lucky asked as he ducked his head and climbed into the backseat of the patrol car. Pat's grim tone of voice sounded discouraging and made him uneasy.

" 'Cause they've got Susan Young, and she, my friend, is saying you did it."

One had to admire Devon's composure as she entered the interrogation room. The two federal agents smoked like chimneys, so the small room was filled with smoke. She was like a breath of fresh air as she entered with Pat.

He directed her to a chair; she sat down without compromising her straight, proud posture. Lucky tried to catch her eye and give her an encouraging nod, but she didn't even glance in his direction. Instead, she gave the agent her undivided attention.

Once the pleasantries were out of the way, he got down to business. "Mr. Tyler claims that he was with you the night his building burned to the ground."

Her green stare was cool and steady. "That's right. He was."

Pat sat down on a corner of the table in front of her. In a far less intimidating voice he said, "Tell us how and when you two met."

"As you know, Sheriff Bush, we met that same afternoon in a lounge on Highway Two Seventy-seven." A frown wrinkled her brow. "I'm not sure about the name."

"It doesn't have a name," Pat said.

"Oh. Then I guess that's why I don't remember it."

"Just tell us what happened," one of the agents interjected impatiently as he lit another cigarette.

Calmly Devon told them about going into the place to do research on her article on sexism. She admitted that it wasn't wise. "However, I was being as unobtrusive as possible. With absolutely no encouragement from me, two men approached my table and offered to buy me a drink. They refused to take no for an answer."

Her eyes suddenly connected with Lucky's. Inadvertently she had used the phrase that they had frequently batted back and forth. He figured that everybody in the room could hear the sizzle of the current that arced between them. Devon quickly averted her head.

She told the rest of the story, perfectly corroborating Pat's and his own account. She verbally led the investigators into the motel room.

"I opened my door to Mr. Tyler because he was hurt." That was a slight distortion of fact, but only he could testify otherwise, and he wasn't going to. "I tended to his wounds," she said. "He was in no condition to drive, so he . . . he stayed there with me all night, and was there when I left the following morning, which was around six o'clock."

Lucky looked up at his two accusers and gave them a gloating smile. "Now, can we cut the rest of this crap?"

They ignored him. One motioned Pat off the corner of the table and assumed that position directly in front of Devon. "Are you a licensed physician, Ms. Haines?"

"What the—"

Devon overrode Lucky's angry exclamation. "Of course not."

"But you felt qualified to take care of a knife wound and a black eye that, by all accounts, came close to blinding him?"

"On the contrary, I didn't feel qualified at all. I advised Mr. Tyler to go to a hospital, but he refused."

"How come?"

"You'll have to ask him."

"I did," the agent replied, frowning. "He, in turn, asked me, given the choice, would I rather spend the night in a hospital emergency room or with you."

Through the pall of tobacco smoke, she gave Lucky an injured, inquisitive, incredulous look. "It was a joke, Devon. A joke."

Paler than she had been only moments before, she turned back to the agent. "I was only concerned about Mr. Tyler's injuries," she said quietly. "He'd received those injuries while protecting me, so I felt somewhat responsible. When he refused to get medical help, I did the best I could to take care of him. I thought that was the least I could do to repay him for coming to my defense."

"Did you sleep with him, too, to pay him back for coming to your defense?"

Lucky was out of his chair before his next heartbeat. "Now just a damn minute. She—" Pat's hand fell heavily on his shoulder and spun him around.

"Sit down and shut up."

Pat looked ready to kill him, but Lucky realized that Pat was acting in his best interests. He flung himself back into his chair, glaring balefully at the agent.

"Well, Ms. Haines?"

"Mr. Tyler appeared to be exhausted. I believe he'd had quite a lot to drink. He certainly shouldn't have been driving. When he asked me to let him stay, I let him stay. He hinted at internal injuries."

The two agents looked at each other and shared an arrogant, just-between-us-boys laugh. "And you believed him?" one asked.

"I'll have to remember to use that line myself," the other chimed in.

Lucky didn't have a chance to come out of his chair this time. The sheriff's hand was on his shoulder, anchoring him in his seat. But he snarled at the two agents who were making this as difficult for Devon as they possibly could. They seemed to enjoy her embarrassment.

"I didn't know if he had internal injuries or not," she said sharply. "And neither do you." Her chin went up a notch. "His eye was battered. He could have had a concussion or any number of head injuries too. I did what I thought was best."

"And you're to be commended for your charity," one drawled,

winking at the other. "You said he was there in the morning when you left around six o'clock."

"That's right," she replied curtly. Her contempt for them was plain. Knowing how she felt about sexism, Lucky realized that their taunts were intolerable to her. Under the circumstances she was holding up well.

"He was still sleeping when you left?"

"Yes. Soundly."

"He'd been that way all night?"

She faltered, but finally answered, "Yes."

"How do you know?"

"I know."

The agent stood up and slid his hands into his pockets. "Couldn't he have slipped out, driven back to town, set a torch to the garage where they kept all that heavily insured equipment, then returned to the room without you ever knowing he was gone?"

"No."

"It wouldn't have taken him more than, hmm, say two hours."

"He didn't leave."

"You're sure?"

"Positive."

"You sound so definite."

"I am."

"There's a fair amount of space in a motel room to move around, Ms. Haines. Couldn't he have—"

"We were sharing not only the room, but the bed," she stated, her eyes flashing. "If you wanted me to admit that, why weren't you man enough to come right out and ask instead of pussyfooting around?"

"Amen," Lucky intoned.

"Mr. Tyler and I were sleeping in the same bed," Devon continued. "A double bed. Very close to each other, out of necessity. And if Mr. Tyler had gotten up and left the room, he would have awakened me. I'm not that sound a sleeper."

God, she was terrific. Lucky wanted to give her a standing ovation. Or a kiss. Or both. She'd cut the s.o.b.'s down to size. But they weren't giving up entirely.

"Did you sleep without waking up through the night?"

Lucky recognized the trap and hoped that Devon did. If she said yes, they could claim that he had sneaked out and returned without her knowledge, planning all along to use her as his alibi. Her alternative was to admit that she had been intimate with a stranger.

"No." At greater risk to herself, she had opted for the latter choice. Lucky admired her spunk, but suffered for her pride. "I woke up once."

"What for?"

Despite Pat's restraint, Lucky shot from the seat of the chair. "What the hell difference does it make?"

Pat shoved him back down, stepped in front of him, and used his own body as a shield between Lucky and the agents, whom Lucky was prepared to tear apart with his bare hands.

With Lucky temporarily quelled, Pat appealed to the agents. "Look, you two, Ms. Haines has volunteered to come here. You know she's married and that this is uncomfortable for her. Take it easy, okay?"

They ignored him. "Answer the question, Ms. Haines."

She glared at the agent, cast Lucky a swift glance, then lowered her head to address her damp, clenched hands lying in her lap. "During the night, Mr. Tyler and I . . . were physically intimate."

"Can you prove it?"

Her head snapped up. "Can you prove we weren't?"

"No," the agent retorted, "but I've got another woman in another room claiming virtually the same thing, except she says that he bragged to her about setting a fire to collect insurance money."

"She's lying."

"Is she?"

"Yes."

"How do we know?"

"Because he was with me all night."

"Screwing?"

It would have taken more than Pat Bush's substantial bulk to stop Lucky then. Roaring like a pouncing lion, he launched himself across the room toward the agent who had practically spat the nasty word in Devon's face.

He threw the agent off balance and into the table, sending it crashing to the floor. Cheap wood splintered. Devon gave a surprised cry, sprang from her chair, and backed toward the door out of harm's way.

But then Chase pulled open the door and came barreling through, nearly mowing her down. He'd been waiting in the squad room, but at the first hint of trouble had come charging in to offer assistance to his younger brother.

The second agent, the one not being pummeled by Lucky's flying fists, charged forward to help his cohort. He was grabbed from behind.

"Not so fast, buddy," Chase growled into the agent's ear as he restrained him.

Pat, recovering from his dismay, dodged Lucky's fists, grabbed him by the collar, and pulled him to his feet. "What the hell's the matter with you?" he shouted. "This isn't going to help."

He slammed the younger man against the wall and pinned him there by splaying one hand open over Lucky's chest. With his other hand he assisted the agent to his feet.

Lucky's torso was heaving from exertion and fury. He aimed his index finger at the agent. "You son of a bitch. Don't you ever talk to her—"

"I'm filing assault charges against you!" the agent shouted. He took a folded white handkerchief from his pocket and tried to stanch the flow of bright red blood from his cut lip.

"You'll do nothing of the sort," Pat declared in a loud voice. "If you do, I'll go to your superiors and lodge a formal complaint against you for the way you've conducted this interrogation. You intentionally badgered and humiliated Ms. Haines, who was doing her best to cooperate with your investigation."

"He's right," Chase said through gritted teeth. He had the agent's hands up between his shoulder blades. He pushed them higher. The man groaned. "Isn't he right? Before you answer, maybe you should know that half a dozen deputies and I were listening through the door to every word said in this room."

"Maybe," the agent gasped, "maybe he did get a little out of hand."

"Chase," Pat barked, "let him go. His eyes are bugging out."

Lucky was virtually unaware of what was going on around him. He had tasted blood and wanted more. Glaring at the agent malevolently, he threatened, "I'm gonna nail you—"

"Lucky, shut up!" Pat called forward a deputy from among those congregated in the doorway. "Take him upstairs and lock him up."

"Huh?" The sobering thought of a jail cell snapped Lucky out of his murderous mood. "What for?"

"Suspected arson, remember?" Pat said calmly, nodding the deputy toward Lucky.

"But I'm innocent!"

"That's how you can plead before the judge later this afternoon. In the meantime I recommend you teach your mouth some manners and cool off your temper."

Lucky was too dumbfounded to resist the deputy's manhandling. Besides, this deputy had played on the same regional championship baseball team with Lucky and had been a friend for years. He looked at Devon. "Take her home, Chase."

"Right," his brother said. "Stay the hell out of trouble, will you?"

"See you in court," Lucky quipped as he was escorted through the door. His smile vanished, however, when the crowd of deputies, clerks, and dispatchers parted for him, and he noticed a spot of color in the otherwise monochromatic gray squad room.

Susan Young was standing against the far wall, twirling a strand of hair around her finger and smiling complacently.

Chapter Fourteen

"That was a damn stupid thing to do."

The pickup truck with Tyler Drilling Co. stenciled onto the doors jounced over a chuckhole. Chase downshifted, giving his brother a fulminating glance across the truck's interior. The upholstery's color was no longer distinguishable. It bore layers of grime from scores of drilling sites.

"Don't you know the penalty for assaulting a federal agent?"

"No, do you?" Lucky shot back.

"You know what I mean."

"Well, I wasn't penalized, so leave me alone, okay?" Lucky slumped lower in his seat as Chase herded the pickup through the twilight evening toward their family home. Then, feeling bad for acting surly toward his brother, he added, "Thanks for posting my bail."

"Thank Tanya. The money came out of her house fund."

"Her what?"

"Her house fund. She wants to buy a house, and has been saving money for a down payment."

Lucky shoved back his dark blond hair. "Jeez. I feel terrible."

"Not as terrible as you'd feel spending the time before your trial in jail. And not as terrible as you'd feel if the judge had listened to the prosecutor and placed your bail higher than we could afford."

The federal agents had convinced the prosecutor that they had enough evidence against James Lawrence Tyler to arraign him on an arson charge. They contended that if one woman would lie on his behalf, another would. Why should they believe Devon over Susan? It would be left to the court to decide the veracity of each woman and determine Lucky's guilt or innocence.

Everyone on Lucky's side believed that the agents were acting out of pique now more than conviction of his guilt, but unfortunately there was nothing they could do about it at this point.

Lucky's attorney had pleaded with the judge to reduce the amount of bail recommended by the prosecutor. He cited how well known Lucky was in the community, and guaranteed that his client had every intention of appearing in court to deny the allegations and clear his name. The judge had known the Tyler boys all their lives. They were rowdy, but hardly criminals. He'd been lenient.

"How's Devon?" Lucky asked now.

"Pretty shaken up. Mother took her under her wing."

"Is there any way we can keep her name out of the newspapers? At least until the actual trial?"

"So far, nobody but the people in that interrogation room know who your alibi is. I doubt the feds will tell anybody. They don't want anyone to know that one of them was overpowered and damn near beat to a pulp." Chase cast his brother another glance of reprimand. "Dumb move, Lucky. If Pat hadn't been there to smooth things over, you'd be in a world of hurt."

Lucky, however, was only interested in Devon's opinion of him. "She probably thinks I'm a hothead."

"You *are* a hothead."

"And you're not?"

"I've got better sense than to attack a federal agent."

"One of them never talked to your woman like that agent did."

"Oh, so now she's 'your woman'?" Chase asked.

"Just an expression."

"Or a Freudian slip."

Lucky stared glumly through the bug-splattered windshield. "Who ever would have thought a fistfight at the place would result in a mess like this?"

Chase offered no reply, but the question had been rhetorical anyway. Broodily Lucky contemplated the scenery what whizzed past. "Anybody seen or heard from Little Alvin and Jack Ed lately?"

"Nope. They're keeping a low profile."

"If you ask me, the feds would do better to lay off us and Devon and go after those two."

"Yeah, but nobody asked you." Chase wheeled the truck into the lane leading to the house, from which mellow golden light was pouring through the windows. "Don't entertain any notions about going after them yourself," Chase warned. "We don't need another assault charge against you."

"Devon's still here."

Lucky was heartened by the sight of her red compact in the driveway. Chase parked the truck beside it. Once out of the pickup, Lucky jogged up the steps and through the front door.

"Hey, everybody, the jailbird is free!"

"That's not funny," Laurie admonished as he entered the living room where she was sitting with Devon, Sage, and Tanya. Chase had phoned ahead and reported the outcome of the arraignment.

"Neither is jail," Lucky said in an appropriately solemn tone. Crossing to where Devon was seated on the sofa, he dropped down beside her and, without compunction, covered her knee with his hand. "You okay?"

"I'm fine."

"Did those bastards give you any grief after I was taken away?"

"No. They allowed me to leave. Chase drove me here." She gave Laurie, Sage, and Tanya smiles. "I've been well looked after, although all the fuss was unnecessary."

"After the dreadful way you were treated?" Laurie stood up. "Of course it was necessary, and then some. My family owes you a debt of gratitude, Devon." She moved toward the arched opening. "Boys, wash up. We've been holding dinner for you."

"I'd like a chance to speak to Devon alone, Mother," Lucky said.

"After dinner. I'm sure she's famished. Chase, stop that smooching and usher everybody into the dining room, please."

Chase reluctantly released Tanya, whose neck he'd been nibbling. Laughing, he remarked, "We should have had Mother in that interrogation room with us today. They wouldn't have dared cross her."

Laurie had heeded Lucky's earlier request and cooked a sumptuous country dinner of fried chicken, mashed potatoes, gravy, corn on the cob, and black-eyed peas. She'd made his favorite banana pudding for dessert. Despite the events of the afternoon, the mood at the dinner table was jolly.

As they were finishing their dessert and coffee, Tanya clinked her fork against her drinking glass. Everyone fell silent and looked at her, surprised because she so rarely called attention to herself.

"I think this family needs a piece of good news." Reaching for her husband's hand, she smiled into his eyes and proclaimed, "There's a new Tyler on the way. I'm pregnant."

Laurie clasped her hands beneath her chin, her eyes immediately growing misty. "Oh, how wonderful! "

Sage gave a raucous, unladylike hoot.

Lucky guffawed. "Don't look now, big brother, but you just dropped a gooey bite of pudding into your lap."

Chase, gaping at his wife, lowered his empty spoon back into his dessert plate. "You . . . you mean it? You're sure?"

Gleefully Tanya bobbed her head up and down. "You're going to be a daddy."

Having reached the white wooden fence that enclosed the peach orchard, Devon rested her forearms on the top rung and took a deep, cleansing breath. Lucky stood beside her. It was the first moment they'd had alone since Chase had brought him back from town. Following Tanya's announcement, everybody had started firing questions at once, which she fielded with poise.

No, she wasn't very far along, but the pregnancy had been positively confirmed.

Yes, she was feeling quite well, thank you.

No, she hadn't had any morning sickness yet.

Yes, she was due around the first of the year.

No, the doctor didn't expect any difficulties.

Discussion of the baby had prolonged dinner. Finally Laurie had stood to clear the table, shooing Devon and Lucky out. The evening was close and warm, the air heavy with humidity and the heady, fertile scents of spring.

Turning her head toward Lucky, Devon asked, "Did you know?"

"What? About Tanya?" He shook his head. "No. But it didn't really surprise me. They've made no secret of wanting kids. It was just a matter of time. I'm glad she chose tonight to announce it."

The top railing of the fence caught him in the middle of his back as he leaned against it and turned to face her. There was a soft breeze blowing, lifting strands of burnished hair out of her restrictive bun. Sage had loaned her some clothes. She had traded her business suit for a casual, long-skirted jumper worn over a T-shirt. She was making it tough on him to decide which way he liked her best. Whether soft or sophisticated, she always looked terrific.

"Your mother is really something," she was saying. "She's strong and yet compassionate. A rare combination."

"Thanks. I think she's special too. I was afraid you'd think the Tylers are all a little crazy. Picking fights one minute. Crying over a coming baby the next."

She plucked a leaf off the nearest peach tree and began to pull it through her fingers. "No, it's nice, the closeness you share."

"You didn't have a close family?"

"Not really. Just my parents and me. No brothers or sisters."

Lucky couldn't imagine such a thing and said so. "Chase and I used to fight like cats and dogs. Still do sometimes. But we're best friends, too, and would do anything for each other."

"That's obvious. I remember the look on his face when he came charging through the door of that interrogation room."

Enough time had elapsed that they could smile about it now. Lucky was the first to turn serious again. "I thought the family bonds might weaken after Dad died. Instead, they're stronger than ever. Mother's held us together admirably."

"Tell me about him."

"My dad? He was strict, but fair. All us kids knew we were loved. He spoiled us and spanked us equally, I guess you could say. To him there were no gray areas where honesty and integrity are concerned. We knew he loved God, his country, and our mother. He was openly affectionate with her, and always respectful."

"So it stands to reason that his son would leap to the defense of a woman in distress."

He gave her a self-deprecating grin and a slight shrug. "Conditioned reflex." Reaching out, he caught a loose strand of her hair and rubbed it between his finger. "What was life like for Devon Haines when she was a little girl?"

"Lonely at times." Her expression became introspective. "Unlike your father, mine wasn't a very warm and giving person. In fact, he was demanding. My mother fetched and carried for him from the moment she said 'I do' until the day he died. Their roles were rigidly defined. He was the domineering breadwinner; she was the obedient good little wife. She spent her days keeping his castle spotless, and her evenings waiting on him hand and foot."

"Hmm. Is that why their little girl turned out to be such a militant feminist?"

"I'm not militant."

Lucky raised his hands in surrender. "I'm unarmed."

"I'm sorry," she said with chagrin. "Maybe I am a trifle defensive."

"That's okay." Then, bending down closer to her, he whispered, "If your eyes keep flashing green fire like that, I'm gonna have to kiss you." He said it teasingly, but his eyes conveyed the message that he meant it.

Devon looked away to stare down the neat, straight row of carefully cultivated peach trees. Their branches were already burdened with un-ripened fruit.

"My mother's whole life revolved around my father. When he died, she was left with nothing to live for."

"What about you?"

"I guess I didn't really count."

"That rejection must have hurt."

"It did." She sighed. "Two miserable years after my father's death, she died too."

"How?"

The ground beneath them held her attention for a moment. When she began speaking, her voice was thick. "For as long as I can remember, my mother was a hypochondriac. She constantly complained of minor aches and pains. They kept her from attending functions throughout my schooling. I couldn't have friends over because she felt bad. That kind of thing."

Lucky muttered something unflattering about the late Mrs. Haines, but Devon shook her head. "I guess the hypochondria was her only means of getting attention from my father. Anyway, I learned early on to dismiss mother's 'illnesses.'

"After my father died, they increased in frequency and severity. Because her life had been so wrapped up in his, she had nothing to occupy her mind except her own body and its many failings. I was just out of college, scrambling to find a job that would subsidize her pension. Frankly, hearing about each stabbing pain and dull ache drove me crazy. I tuned her out as much as possible." She pinched off a piece of the leaf and tossed it into the wind.

"She began to claim that the pains were getting worse. The more she complained about her discomfort, the more stubbornly I ignored her. I thought that honoring the hypochondria would only encourage it."

She rolled her lips inward and pressed on them so hard that the rims turned white. Lucky saw the tears collecting in her eyes. He took her hand and interlaced her fingers with his.

"One day Mother said she was having difficulty in swallowing. She couldn't eat. Everything I gave her came right back up. I . . . I relented and took her to see the doctor." Unable to go on, she pulled her hand from his and covered her face with both hands.

He rubbed her between the shoulder blades. "What happened, Devon?" Instinctively he knew that she had never talked about this with anyone. He was flattered, but it hurt him to see her in such emotional distress.

She pulled in a choppy breath and lowered her hands. "She was dead within two weeks. Inoperable stomach cancer."

"Oh, damn."

She took a clean tissue from the pocket of the jumper and blotted her eyes and nose. Her pretty features were etched with misery and guilt.

"You couldn't have known," he said softly.

"I should have."

"Not based on your past experience."

"I should have listened to her. I should have done something."

"The result would probably have been the same, Devon." His father had died of cancer after fighting it for months.

"Yes, probably," Devon said. "But if I hadn't disregarded her, she wouldn't have suffered. I turned my back on her at a time when she needed someone to believe her."

"From what you said, she had turned her back on you first."

She dusted her hands of the leaf she had shredded. "We weren't tuned in to each other the way you Tylers are. So I can't relate to the camaraderie your family shares, but I think the way you rally together is enviable."

He sensed that the topic of her mother's death was now closed. He wouldn't press. She had opened up to him. It had been too brief a glimpse into Devon's psyche, but he coveted information about her.

He matched her more lighthearted tone. "You don't think we're loud, boisterous, and overwhelming?"

She laughed softly. "A little, perhaps."

"Yeah, we can get pretty rambunctious."

"But it must be nice, knowing you have someone you can count on to stand up for you, no matter what."

"You don't?" He caught her beneath the chin with his fingertip and turned her head to face him. "What about your husband?"

"He's not in a position to rally to my aid now, is he?"

"What if he were in a position to? Would he?"

She lifted her chin off the perch of his finger and turned away again. Lucky dropped his arm to his side. The emotional turmoil on her face was plain. He hated to think he was the one responsible for it.

"You'll have to tell him about us now, won't you?" he asked softly.

"Yes."

"I'm sorry, Devon. I had hoped to prevent that." If he had hoped it badly enough, he would have left her alone, he thought wryly. He wouldn't have asked her to come to Milton Point and counter Susan's lie with the truth. But thinking primarily of himself, he had coerced her to come. He was confident of acquittal; Devon, however, would suffer permanent consequences. "When will you see him?"

"Tomorrow. I don't want him to hear about it from someone else before I've had a chance to explain. That's why I accepted your mother's invitation to spend the night here. Since I'm this close to the prison, it would be silly to drive back to Dallas, only to have to return to East Texas in the morning."

Lucky wasn't as interested in the logistics of travel as he was in what form her explanation would take. "What are you going to say to him?"

Ruefully she shook her head. "I don't know yet."

"What are you going to tell him about me?"

"As little as possible."

"Are you going to tell him how we met?"

"I suppose that'll be a start."

"About Little Alvin, Jack Ed, the fight?"

"I suppose."

"You'll explain why you were in the place."

"He'll understand that part."

"But not the rest. What'll you tell him about the motel?"

"I don't know," she admitted with increasing impatience.

"Well, you'd better think of something."

She turned on him with agitation. "Tell me, Lucky, what should I say? What *can* I say? What words could possibly make this situation easier for him to accept, hmm? Put yourself in his place. He's in prison. How would you react if your roles were reversed? How would you feel if I were your wife and had slept with another man?"

He reached for her and pulled her against him, snarling, "If you were my wife, you wouldn't have slept with another man."

She deflected his kiss. "Don't." He could tell by her tone that she wasn't being coy. He gazed into her eyes. "Don't," she repeated firmly. "Let me go."

He relaxed his embrace; she stepped out of it. "For reasons I can't comprehend, your family has been cordial to me when all I deserve from them is scorn and contempt. I expected to be shunned like a woman of the streets. Instead, they've been inordinately kind. I won't betray their consideration by playing your tramp."

His body was pulled taut, as though he were held back by an invisible leash. "You're not a tramp," he said meaningfully. "I never thought of you that way. I never treated you that way. Didn't I nearly throttle someone today for suggesting that you were?"

Suddenly she ducked her head, and he thought it might be because of the tears that had filled her eyes. "So far," she said in a low, stirring voice, "I've got only one sin to confess to my husband. Please don't make it any worse, Lucky."

"That's the first time you've called me by name," he murmured, taking a step nearer. "That's a beginning."

She raised her head. Their eyes met and held. Eventually she moistened her lips, pulled the lower one through her teeth, and whispered, "We aren't allowed a beginning."

Having said that, she turned and headed for the house.

"My, my. Wonders never cease."

At the sound of his sister's voice, Lucky angrily spun around. "What the hell are you doing out here?"

Sage stepped from behind one of the peach trees. "There's actually a woman who can say no to Lucky Tyler. My faith in womankind has been restored."

"Shut up, brat," he grumbled. "How long have you been there?"

"Long enough to set my heart to palpitating."

"Why were you spying on us?"

"I wasn't. Mother sent me out to tell you that Chase and Tanya are leaving. She thought you'd want to say congratulations one more time. I sensed the nature of your conversation, and decided it would be imprudent to interrupt."

"So you eavesdropped."

Unfazed, she fell into step beside her brother as he stamped toward the house. "Poor Lucky," she sighed theatrically. "He finally finds a woman he really wants, and she turns out to have the loathsome three."

"Loathsome three?"

"A brain, a conscience, and a husband."

Lucky glowered at her. "You know, the day Mother and Dad brought you home from the hospital, Chase and I considered tying you up in a gunnysack and tossing it into the stock pond. Too bad we didn't."

"Lucky looked ready to kill Sage when they came in," Tanya remarked.

Chase and she were driving home in their car. He'd left the truck at the house, unwilling to subject his wife to its rankness, rattles, and rough ride.

"Sage has always been a pain," he said, but with a grudgingly affectionate smile. "She must've said something to him about their houseguest."

"I like her."

"Sage?"

"No." Tanya corrected him indulgently, knowing he had intentionally misunderstood her. "Their houseguest."

"Hmm. She's okay, I guess. She pulled through for us today. Didn't crack under pressure, and stayed as cool as a cucumber. I believed every word she said. A jury will, too."

"Do you think she's attractive?"

Hearing the uncertainty in his wife's voice, Chase parked in their designated space at the apartment complex and turned to face her. "I think *you* are attractive," he avowed softly, stretching across the seat to gently kiss her forehead.

"But Devon's so smart and sophisticated."

"And you're so pregnant with my baby." Working his way inside her clothing, Chase laid his hand on her bare abdomen. "When did you first suspect?"

"Last week. My period was more than two weeks late. I took a home pregnancy test yesterday, but didn't want to trust it entirely, no matter how reliable the guarantee on the box claimed it was. So I called the doctor and made an appointment for this morning. He confirmed it."

"You don't feel any different," he whispered as he caressed her.

Laughing, she ran her fingers through his hair. "I hope not. Not yet."

His caresses increased in intensity. Their kisses became prolonged. Finally Tanya pushed him away. "Maybe we had better go inside."

"Maybe we'd better," he agreed on a suggestive growl.

As soon as they had cleared the door to their apartment, he pulled her toward the living-room sofa. "Chase," she protested, "it's only a few more steps to the bedroom."

"That's too many."

He had already stripped off his shirt. Easing his zipper over his swollen sex, he pulled off his pants and underwear. Impatiently he removed Tanya's clothes, too. It wasn't until he was poised between her thighs that reason penetrated his passion.

"I won't hurt you, will I?"

"No."

"You'll tell me, won't you?"

"Yes, Chase."

"Promise?"

"Promise," she groaned, urging him forward and receiving him fully.

"God, I love you," he whispered into her hair several minutes later as they held each other in the sultry afterglow of their lovemaking.

"I love you too." Snuggling closer to him, she pressed her mouth against his chest. "I feel sorry for anybody who isn't as happy as we are. Especially Devon and Lucky."

Tanya didn't have an envious bone in her body. She was unselfish and generous to a fault. However, she harbored insecurities the same as any other human being. Hers stemmed from her background.

She came from a large, hardworking, but always poor farming family. Schooling beyond high school graduation had been out of the question, and she regarded anyone who had earned a college degree with disproportionate admiration.

It had been Tanya's sweet nature and unpretentiousness that had first attracted Chase. He recognized her insecurities and found them endearing, though he never discussed them with her. It was characteristic of her nature that while being awed by Devon Haines's panache, she could still feel sorry for her.

He said, "You link their names as though they're a pair."

"I think they would be if they could be," she said softly.

"Tanya," he said gruffly, smoothing back her fair hair, "you're going to make a wonderful mother."

"What makes you think so?"

"Because you have such a huge capacity for loving."

Her eyes grew misty as her fingers glided over the strong features of his face. "What a lovely thing to say, Chase."

"It's true."

Before they became too maudlin, she smiled. "You know, one thing that has limited capacity is this apartment. I spoke with a realtor a few weeks ago, before Lucky's troubles started. She said when we were ready to start looking for a house to contact her."

"She?"

"An old friend of yours. Marcie Johns."

"Goosey Johns!" he exclaimed on a laugh.

"Goosey?"

"That's what we used to call her."

"How awful."

"Naw. It was all in fun."

"She's very nice."

"Oh, I know that," he agreed. "She always was. We just goaded her because she was tall and skinny, wore glasses and braces, and studied all the time."

"Apparently she's getting the last laugh. She's a very successful businesswoman."

"So I've heard. She's got her own realty company now, doesn't she?"

"Mm-hmm. And even after robbing the kitty to pay Lucky's bail, I believe we'll have enough for a down payment. Know what?" Tanya said, propping herself up to look down at him. "I think Marcie had a crush on you when you were in school."

"Really?" No longer listening, he cupped one of her breasts and fanned the crest with his thumb. "Lord, that's beautiful."

"She asked a lot of questions about you, was curious to know how you were, that kind of thing."

"Goosey Johns was interested in books, not boys. Especially horny boys like me," he added, pulling Tanya astride his middle. Her body sheathed his hardness again. Breathlessly he asked, "Now can we talk about something else?"

They didn't talk about anything at all.

Chapter Fifteen

It had a tennis court, a nine-hole golf course, a weight room, a jogging track, a library stocked with current best-sellers. For all its amenities, however, it was still a prison.

Using her telephone credit card, Devon had called the warden's office from the Tylers' home the day before and scheduled a meeting with her husband for 9:00 A.M.

She had got up early, dressed, and gone downstairs. Laurie had insisted that she drink a cup of coffee before leaving. Sage was still asleep. She was told, without having asked, that Lucky had left early to return the company truck to headquarters in case it was needed.

A morning drive through the East Texas countryside in early summer should have been a pleasurable experience. Wildflowers dotted the pastures in which dairy and beef cattle grazed. She'd driven with the car windows rolled down. The south wind carried the scent of pine and honeysuckle. The peaceful hour it had required to arrive at those iron gates should have calmed her nerves and prepared her for the dreaded forthcoming visit with her husband.

It hadn't.

Her palms were slick with perspiration as she was led into the room where inmates were allowed to greet their visitors. It was a large, airy room, having unadorned windows that overlooked the flower and vegetable gardens tended by the inmates themselves. The easy chairs and sofas were functional but comfortable. Current magazines were scattered around the various accent tables. There was a coffee maker with a freshly brewed carafe and, this morning, a box of doughnuts nearby.

"He'll be right here," she was told by the prison guard. "Help yourself to coffee and doughnuts while you wait."

"Thank you."

She wanted neither. Her stomach was roiling. Resting her purse on one of the chairs, she clasped her damp hands together and moved toward the windows.

What to say?

Greg, I've had an affair.

It hadn't been an affair. It had been a single night.

Greg, I had a one-night stand.

No, that sounded worse.

Greg, I was swept up in the passion of the moment.

Passion?

Passion.

Whatever else it had been, it had been passionate. How else could it have happened? Reason hadn't entered into it. Not even romance. Common sense had played no part. Morality hadn't been considered. She'd been governed strictly by her passions.

And it had been glorious.

Ever since her night with Lucky, that traitorous thought had been throwing itself against the doors of her consciousness like a deranged beast trying to break down the barriers and get out to celebrate the event.

That's why she felt compelled to confess it to Greg. Whether he was likely to find out or not, she would have eventually told him. If her emotions hadn't got as tangled up as the sheets of the bed she had shared with Lucky Tyler, she might have kept the secret for the rest of her life, never divulging it to anyone.

But her emotions had become involved. Because they were, her conscience was. She felt guilty about it; therefore, she had to discuss it with Greg.

Her marriage to Greg was certainly unorthodox, but the legal document still decreed them husband and wife. She'd freely recited the vows to him, and just as freely she had broken those vows.

What Greg had done or hadn't done, whether or not he was innocent or guilty, whether or not he had used her and her newspaper column—none of that mattered. She was an adulterous wife.

Perhaps if he had given her a wedding night as she had wanted and expected him to . . .

Perhaps if her body hadn't been so starved for the loving attention he had withheld . . .

Perhaps if he hadn't declined his conjugal visits . . .

That had been the crushing blow. Only hours before she had met

Lucky, she had discovered that Greg had been refusing conjugal visits with her. When asked why, he couldn't give her a satisfactory answer.

"Why, Greg, why?" He provided no answers, and only became angry when she persisted.

More than her father's self-absorption, more than her mother's neglect, more than anything in her life, that had been the ultimate rejection. Her self-confidence had been shattered, her self-esteem crushed. Was she so undesirable that even her prisoner husband wouldn't avail himself of her?

While she was in that frame of mind, fate maliciously matched her with Lucky Tyler. He had revived her dying spirit.

Still, no one had forced her at gunpoint to make love with him. Sure, she had needs; everyone had needs. But society would be plunged into chaos if people went around incontinently gratifying their needs.

Down the hallway she heard approaching footsteps and murmured conversation. Turning from the window, she lowered her hands to her sides, but reflexively clasped them together again. She moistened her lips, wondering if she should be smiling when he walked in. She wasn't sure she could even form a smile. Her features felt wooden.

Laurie Tyler had graciously pressed her suit for her. Devon always took special pains with her appearance when she came to see Greg, wanting her visits to be as pleasurable for him as possible. This morning, however, even the quality cosmetics Sage had loaned her didn't conceal the dark circles beneath her eyes, which hours of sleeplessness had left there.

The footsteps became more pronounced and the voices louder. Devon's heart began to thud painfully inside her chest. She swallowed with difficulty, though her mouth was so dry her saliva glands seemed to have been dammed. She tried to hold her lips still, but they quivered around a tentative smile.

Greg and the guard appeared in the doorway. "Have a good visit," the official said before withdrawing.

Greg looked trim and fit. He had told her that he played a lot of tennis during free time. His tanned skin always came as a mild surprise to her. He spent more time out-of-doors now than he had during the days of his trial, when he'd had a pallor.

The inmates here didn't wear prison garb, but their own clothing. Greg was always immaculately dressed, though his three-piece suits had been replaced by casual clothes and his Italian leather loafers by sneakers.

He moved further into the room. The confinement was beginning to tell on him, she noted. It caused a strain on all the inmates of this facility. To a man, they complained of the boredom. Accustomed to being movers and shakers in big business, they found it difficult to adjust to the forced idleness. Worse yet was that they no longer had the privilege of making their own decisions.

Instinctively Devon knew that he wouldn't welcome a broad smile and a cheerful "Good morning," and, fortunately, a subdued greeting coincided with her mood. So she stood stoic and silent in front of the windows as he crossed the room.

He didn't stop until they were within touching distance. It wasn't until then that she noticed he was carrying a newspaper. She glanced down at it curiously, then back up at him. His face was taut with rage. So unexpectedly that it caused her to jump, he slapped the newspaper onto the windowsill, then turned on his heels and strode from the room.

Her arid mouth opened, but she couldn't utter a single sound. She waited until he had cleared the doorway and turned down the hall before retrieving the newspaper.

It had been folded once. She opened it and noted that it was a Dallas paper, a competitor of the one she worked for. Greg had gratuitously underlined in red the pertinent headline.

She slumped against the armrest of the nearest chair and skimmed the incriminating article. For long moments afterward she sat there, clutching the newspaper to her chest, eyes closed, heart tripping, head throbbing.

She had so carefully outlined what she was going to say to him, when, as it turned out, it hadn't been necessary to say anything. The newspaper account was disgustingly accurate.

"Promise me you won't fly off the handle and do something stupid." Chase, casting a tall, dark shadow across the office floor, filled the doorway.

Lucky was angled back in the swivel desk chair their grandfather and father had broken in for them. His boots were resting on the corner of the desk, another relic of oil-boom days. A telephone was cradled between his shoulder and ear. He waved his brother into the room.

"Yeah, we can send a crew out tomorrow to start setting up." He winked at his brother, and made the okay sign with his thumb and fingers. "We didn't lose all that much in the fire, so we're set to go. Just give me directions, and our boys'll be there by daybreak."

Bringing the chair erect, he reached for a pad and pencil and scribbled down the directions. "Route Four, you say? Uh-huh, two miles past the windmill. Got it. Right. Glad to be doing business with you again, Virgil."

He hung up the phone, sprang out of the chair, and gave an Indian whoop. "A contract! A biggie! Remember ol' Virgil Daboe over in Louisiana? He's got four good prospects for wells, and wants us to do the drilling. How 'bout that, big brother? Is that good news or what? Four new wells and a baby on the way! How can you stand that much good news in a twelve-hour period?"

On his way to the coffee maker, he walloped Chase between the shoulder blades. Pouring himself a cup of coffee, he said, "I'll call all the boys and tell them to get their gear—" He broke off as he raised the mug of coffee to his lips and realized that his brother wasn't sharing his jubilation. "What's the matter?"

"It's great about the contract," Chase said.

"Well, you sure as hell can't tell it by looking at you." Lucky set down his coffee. "What's wrong with you? I thought you'd be dancing on the ceiling about this."

"I probably would be, if I wasn't afraid I might have to hog-tie you to keep you out of more trouble."

"What are you talking about?"

"Somebody squealed, Lucky."

"Squealed?"

Chase had folded the front page of the newspaper lengthwise four times so he could slide it into the hip pocket of his jeans. Reluctantly he removed it and passed it to Lucky.

He read the story. The first words out of his mouth were vile. Subsequent words were even viler. Chase watched his brother warily, unsure of what he might do.

Lucky threw himself back into the desk chair. It went rolling back on its creaky casters. Bending at the waist, he plowed all ten fingers through his hair and recited a litany of oaths. When he finally ran out, he straightened up and asked, "Has Devon seen this yet?"

"Mother doesn't think so. She left early for the prison. They had coffee together, but Mother didn't open the paper until after she left."

"Just what the hell does this mean?" Lucky demanded, referring to the copy in the article. " 'According to an unnamed source.' "

"It means that whoever leaked the story is scared of what you might do to him if you ever find out who he is."

"He damned sure better be," Lucky said viciously. "And I'll find out who the bastard is. 'Agents were injured in the fracas that broke out when Tyler's mistress was allegedly insulted,' " he read.

" 'Fracas'? What the hell kind of word is 'fracas'? Devon wasn't 'allegedly insulted,' she *was* insulted. And calling her my mistress!" he shouted. "We were together once. *Once,* dammit."

Lucky flung himself from the chair and began pacing the office in long strides. "This is what I wanted to prevent," he said as he ground his fist into his opposite palm. "I wanted Devon to be protected from scandal."

"She would have lost her anonymity during the trial," Chase reasonably pointed out.

"I figured the case would never go to trial. I counted on something happening first. I thought maybe Susan would—" He stopped his pacing and rounded on Chase. "That's it." As heated and agitated as he'd been only seconds earlier, he was now remarkably calm. The switch was as sudden as closing a door against a fierce storm. "Susan."

"She leaked the story?"

"I'd bet Virgil's contract on it." He told Chase about seeing the banker's daughter in the squad room.

"Yeah, I saw her there too," Chase said. "She was grinning like the Cheshire cat. But would she risk having her name attached to this mess?"

"She lied to those agents, didn't she?" Lucky headed for the door.

Chase, well aware of Lucky's volatile temper, followed him outside. "Where are you going?"

"To see Miss Young."

"Lucky—"

"Hopefully between here and there I'll come up with an alternative to murder."

Clara, the Youngs' housekeeper, demurred when he asked to see Susan. Lucky was persistent, and eventually wore her down. She led him through the house to the backyard, where Susan was enjoying a late breakfast on the stone terrace. Like a hothouse orchid, she was surrounded by giant ferns and flowering plants.

He pinched a sprig of lilac from the fresh flower arrangement on the foyer table and carried it outside with him. As he crossed the lichen-covered stone terrace, he could hear Susan humming beneath her breath while liberally spreading orange marmalade over an English muffin. Lying on the table in front of her was the front page of the Dallas paper.

"You sure do make a pretty picture sitting there, Susan."

At the familiar sound of his voice she dropped her knife. It landed with a clatter on the china plate. She sprang from her chair and rounded it, placing it between them, as though filigree wrought iron could prevent him from snapping her in two.

"Lucky."

Her voice was feeble and airless. There was little color remaining in her face. The fingers gripping the back of her chair were bloodless. She backed up a step as he moved inexorably forward.

When he reached her, he raised his hand. She flinched.

Then her terrified eyes focused on the flower he was extending to her. "Good morning," he whispered, bending down and planting a light kiss on her cheek. She gaped at him wordlessly as he pulled back, then automatically accepted the flower.

"I didn't expect you," she croaked.

"Sorry I'm here so early," he said, nonchalantly pinching off a bite of her English muffin and popping it into his mouth, "but it's been days since I've seen you, and I just couldn't wait any longer. I hope—"

He stopped, made a point of noticing the newspaper, and muttered a curse. The look he gave her then was a mix of sheepishness and exasperation.

"Damn! I wanted to get over here before you saw that." He gestured down to the article. "Susan, honey, I'm sorry."

She stared at him with speechless dismay.

Feigning disgust, he expelled a deep breath. "Some loudmouthed snoop found out who I was with the night of the fire and leaked that story about the Haines woman." Appearing to be supremely exasperated, he plopped down into one of the wrought iron chairs and hung his head.

"One mistake. One lousy mistake," he mumbled in self-castigation. "How was I to know she was married? And to a convict. Jeez!" He swore. "Of course, now you'll have to tell the authorities that you lied to them about being with me the night of the fire."

"I . . . I will?" Her voice had gone from low and faint to high and thin.

"Of course, honey." He rose and took her shoulders between his hands. "I can't let you stick your neck out any further than you already have. Yesterday, when I saw you in that ugly squad room, I nearly died."

He touched her hair, smoothed it away from her neck. "I knew the kind of questions they had put to you. Personal things about us. Lord, how embarrassing that must have been for you. How do you think I felt, knowing you were making that sacrifice for me?"

He laid his hand over his heart. "And then do you know what the bastards told me to throw me off balance? They said that you claimed I had bragged to you about setting that fire. Can you believe that? Sure, you joked with me about it the other night, but you weren't serious, right?"

"Uh, uh, right."

"Don't worry. I didn't fall for the ploy. I knew they were bluffing, trying to trap me into admitting something. You'd never betray me like that. Not when we were planning to get married. The last thing I ever wanted was for you to be dragged into this mess." He pulled her close and spoke into her hair. Astonishment had made her body limp.

"I appreciate everything you did to try and save me from prosecution, but I can't let you do any more. I can't let you be called into that courtroom to perjure yourself."

"Perjure myself?"

"Sure," he said, angling away from her. "If you testify under oath that I was with you the night of the fire, then the Haines woman says under oath that I was with her, I'll have to testify under oath that she's telling the truth. You'll be caught in your lie, sweetheart," he said gently. "That is, unless you recant your story immediately. The sooner, the better."

She pushed away from him, staring up at him whey-faced, on the verge of panic. "I never thought of that."

"I know you didn't. All you thought about was me, us, our marriage. Which, of course," he added regretfully, "can never be."

"Why not?"

He spread his arms at his sides in a gesture of helplessness. "Do you believe your mama and daddy would let you marry me now, a guy who would sleep with a con's wife? Think about it, sweetheart. They wouldn't stand for it. Your daddy would probably cut you out of his will and leave all his money to charity. They'd rather see you dead than married to me. And, frankly, so would I." His voice was laced with so much earnestness that she didn't hear the irony underlying it.

Clasping her against him again, he hugged her tight for several seconds before releasing her abruptly. "Good-bye, Susan. Since all this has come out in the open, I can't ever see you again."

Before she could speak another word, he left her, choosing to take the gravel path around the house rather than going through its sepulchral hallway to reach the front. At the corner of the house he turned and looked back.

"Save yourself while you can, Susan. Don't even give yourself time to think about it. Call Pat."

"Yes, yes. I'll do that today. Right now."

"I can't tell you how much better that'll make me feel." He blew her a kiss. "Good-bye."

Hanging his head, he walked with the measured gait of a self-sacrificing patriot on his way to the guillotine. But he was laughing up his sleeve and felt like kicking up his heels.

Chapter Sixteen

Devon was waiting for him the following morning when he arrived at Tyler Drilling headquarters. Sitting in a straight chair as prim and proper as a finishing-school student, she was talking to Chase and cradling one of their chipped, stained coffee mugs between her hands.

They shared a long stare across a shaft of sunlight in which dust motes danced as crazily as Lucky's pulse was racing at the sight of her.

Chase was the first to break the thick silence. "Devon showed up a few minutes ago," he explained awkwardly. He, too, was evidently at a loss as to why she was there. "We were just having some coffee. Want some, Lucky?"

"No thanks." He hadn't taken his eyes off Devon. Nor had hers strayed from him.

"The, uh, the crew has already left for Louisiana."

"That's good."

Chase's futile attempts at conversation only emphasized the teeming silence. Uneasily he cleared his throat. "Uh, well, I need to be, uh, doing some things outside. See y'all later." As Chase went past Lucky on his way out, he jostled him with his elbow. It was a silent brotherly communique that said, "Snap out of it."

Once Chase had closed the door behind himself, Lucky remarked, "I'm surprised to see you here."

Her smile was swift and unsure. "I surprised myself by coming."

He sat down in a ladder-back chair, his eyes roving hungrily over her face.

"I've been trying to call you since yesterday afternoon, Devon."

"I took my phone off the hook."

"I gathered that. Why?"

"After reading yesterday's newspaper, everybody in the world was trying to call me, it seemed."

Lucky frowned. "I hate like hell that the story came out. I wanted to keep you anonymous for as long as possible. Please believe that."

"I know you had nothing to do with it. Who do you think was responsible?"

He told her about Susan. "She looked guilty as hell when I confronted her. I'm convinced she made it her business to find out who you were and, out of spite, spilled the beans to a reporter."

"Well, it doesn't really matter now how the story got out. The damage is done."

He studied her a moment, noticing that her face was drawn and pale. The last twenty-four hours must have been pure hell for her. She was gripping the coffee mug as though it were a buoy in a turbulent lake.

"Do you really want that coffee?" he asked. Shaking her head, she passed the mug to him. He took it and set it on the desk, then turned back to her. The question uppermost in his mind couldn't be avoided any longer.

"How did things go with your husband yesterday?"

A small shudder went through her, though it was uncomfortably warm in the office. "By the time I arrived, Greg had read the story," she said softly. "He merely dropped the newspaper and walked out."

"Without a word?"

"Words would have been superfluous, wouldn't they?"

"I guess so," Lucky murmured.

He was thinking that if he had a wife whom he loved as much as any husband should love his wife, he would have given her the benefit of the doubt and asked a few questions. He wouldn't have reacted until she either denied or confirmed the newspaper story.

If she had denied it, he would have comforted her, then immediately set out to get a retraction. If she had confirmed it, he probably would have gone nuts and carried on something terrible.

A furious outburst, tears, anguish, teeth-gnashing, threats of retaliation. Those would be the expected jealous reactions. They denoted feeling, passion. Simply stalking out was an almost inhuman response that made Greg Shelby sound cold, unfeeling.

"What did you do?" Lucky wanted to know.

"I read the story through. At first I just sat there, stunned. My character suffered in the translation. Somehow, once they were written down, the facts sounded ugly and shameful. So tawdry." She shivered again.

Lucky reached beyond the back of his chair to take one of her hands. "It wasn't, Devon."

"Wasn't it?" she asked, her eyes brimming.

"No."

The stare they exchanged then was so powerful, she prudently withdrew her hand and used her tears as the excuse. She brushed the back of her hand across her eyes.

"I had the prison guard try to get Greg to see me again, but he refused. Once I returned to Dallas, I called the warden and got permission to speak to him by telephone. I wanted desperately to explain." She shook her head mournfully. "He wouldn't even accept my call."

Lucky mentally called Greg Shelby every dirty name he could think of. "So what now? Do you want me to go with you to see him?"

"No!" Leaving her chair, she began roaming the office restlessly. "I don't believe he'd be willing to see either of us right now. After thinking it over and discussing it with Greg's attorney—who isn't at all pleased with me either—I think it's best to leave him alone for several days. He needs time to cool off and clear his head, so that when we do see each other again, he'll be able to listen calmly to my explanation."

"I don't know, Devon," he said doubtfully. "Given time to think about it, I would just get madder."

"Greg isn't as volatile as you."

"You're right about that." Lucky's concession wasn't intended as a compliment to Greg. "If you were my wife and some guy had messed with you, I'd've busted down the walls of that prison by now and be on my way to tear out his throat."

"Greg's not that . . . physical."

"Do you really think he'll eventually forgive and forget?"

"I hope so. Yes, in time, I believe he will."

The answer didn't cheer Lucky as it should have. Her husband sounded like a sanctimonious creep who could hold a grudge forever. Lucky hated to think of Devon being tied to Shelby for the rest of her life.

Somewhat querulously he asked, "Did you come all the way from Dallas to tell me this?"

"No. There was another reason." She returned to her seat. "This whole thing has blown up in my face. Since I went into that lounge and ordered a beer, I've had nothing but trouble. It's out now that I'm your alibi in an arson case. Until the trial is over, and God only knows when that will be, my life is going to be a three-ring circus. I can't have that. I *won't* have it."

"I don't like the prospect of being a notorious public figure any better than you. But what can we do about it?"

"We can clear you with the investigators."

"We tried, remember? It only got me into deeper Dutch. You too."

"But we didn't present them with the real arsonist."

For the space of several seconds Lucky gave her a blank stare. Then he began to laugh. "You want to play detective?"

"Look, the sooner we get you cleared, the sooner this thing will blow over and we can get on with our lives. It's not going to be easy to make amends to Greg, but it would be a start if he knew we wouldn't be going through a trial together, and that I wouldn't constantly be in your company. I'm sure he would enjoy hearing that I never had to see you again."

She was batting a thousand on dismal thoughts this morning, but since he didn't have a viable alternative, he remained silent.

"I've cleared my calendar," she said. "I told my editor that I'm taking a week's vacation and plan to devote the time to tracking down the arsonist. When I get back, I promised him a terrific story, as well as an article on how interrogators can and do intimidate witnesses. I think— What are you grinning about so idiotically, Mr. Tyler?"

"You."

"You find me amusing?"

"You like having control over things, don't you? Even police matters."

"So far the police haven't done anything to help you. I can't do any worse than they have."

"Granted."

"I don't trust other people to do things for me."

"Um-huh," he said. "You're what we used to call a smarty britches."

Still grinning, he stood up and stretched. He was feeling a million times better than he had been an hour ago. He had been concerned because he hadn't spoken with Devon since the story of her involvement had been leaked. He'd also been dreading an entire day of not seeing her.

Then, lo and behold, she'd showed up and planned to stay for a while. Damn, he was lucky! The dreary reminder of her convict husband was pushed aside. Greg Shelby was a loser, a jerk, and, if Lucky was any judge of women at all—and he considered himself an expert on the fair sex—not that great in the sack.

If Shelby had been the man Devon deserved, no amount of persuasion could have got her into bed with another man. He hadn't even had to persuade. Something about her marriage to this Shelby character wasn't right. Lucky respected her for not discussing her marital troubles with an outsider; on the other hand he wanted to know why she was married to a man who had made her so unhappy. Apparently he was being granted the time and opportunity to find out.

The only thing that clouded his sunny mood was that he wouldn't be able to touch her. They would be spending a lot of time together, but she was still off-limits. That was going to kill him, because wanting her had become his chief occupation. More than worrying about his failing business, more than worrying about the fabricated arson charge against him, his desire for Devon was all-consuming.

But seeing her under adverse circumstances was better than not seeing her at all.

"I always enjoyed playing cops and robbers," he said. "Where do we start?"

"First, I'd better check into a room. Where's the best place to stay?"

"My house."

"I can't, Lucky," she said, shaking her head adamantly. "The reasons should be obvious."

"My mother would skin me alive if I let you check into a motel. Anybody who knows her knows she isn't going to let any extramarital hanky-panky go on beneath her roof. So you're staying with us, and that's settled," he said with finality.

"But—"

"Devon," he said sternly, staving off her protests by holding up both hands, palms out. "No arguments."

She capitulated, but didn't seem too pleased about it. "First, I think we should find out exactly how the fire started."

"Gasoline and railroad flares," he said. "Pat already told me. I had bought some flares recently. That confirmed their suspicions."

"Can we review the official crime report?"

"I don't know. I don't imagine it's a matter of public record."

"I wasn't talking about publicly. Privately. Couldn't your friend Sheriff Bush sneak us a copy?"

Lucky whistled through his teeth. "I'll ask him."

She turned and reached for the phone on the desk.

Lucky snatched the receiver from her hand. "*I'll* ask him. Maybe he'll show us a copy of the report after business hours."

"In the meantime I'd like to see the site of the fire."

"That's easy. It's only half a mile down the road from here." He surveyed her up and down, taking in her dress, high heels, and pale stockings. "The location is only suitable for roughnecks and raccoons. You can't go dressed like that."

"I'll change."

Lucky retrieved her suitcase from her car. She went into the cubicle in the office that was home to a commode and sink. While she was in there, Chase returned. He glanced around and found only Lucky seated behind the desk, speaking into the telephone.

"Where's Devon?"

Lucky cupped his hand over the mouthpiece. "In there," he said, indicating the bathroom door, "taking off her clothes."

When the bathroom door opened, Chase swivcled his head around so fast, his neck popped. Devon emerged, fully dressed in jeans. She was rolling up the sleeves of a casual shirt.

"What's going on?" Chase demanded.

Lucky shushed him and spoke into the phone. "Come on, Pat. I know I acted like a bad boy. Yes, I deserve to be horsewhipped. Now that I've contritely admitted the error of my ways, will you do it or not?"

He listened for a moment while his eyes appreciated the slender shapeliness of Devon's legs and the soft curves of her breasts. "Great. Ten-thirty. Hell no, we won't tell anybody."

"What's going on?" Chase repeated as Lucky hung up the phone.

"Pat's making the crime report available to Devon and me tonight."

"You just promised not to tell anybody," she cried, placing her hands on her hips.

"Chase isn't *anybody*. Pat would expect me to tell him."

"I still don't know what's going on," Chase reminded them.

"We're going to try to find out who set the fire, so I can be cleared of the charge."

"And I can be reconciled with my husband," Devon added.

Lucky declined to comment on her statement. Chase divided his incredulous glance between the two of them. He said, "Devon, would you please give me a minute alone with my brother?"

"I'll wait for you outside, Lucky."

"Be right there."

As soon as she was out of earshot, Chase encircled Lucky's biceps in a death grip. His face close, he said, "Have you lost your friggin' mind? You can't tamper with something like this. Who the hell do you two think you are, Kojak and Nancy Drew?"

"I'm a whole lot better looking than Kojak," Lucky replied cockily.

"I'm not joking," Chase said angrily.

"Neither am I."

"Aren't you?"

Lucky's blue eyes narrowed. "What do you mean by that crack?"

"Isn't this all just a game to you? A game that will keep you in close contact with a woman you have no business being around?"

"Stay out of this," Lucky said tightly, his humor vanishing. "What I do with Devon—"

"You'd better do *nothing* with Devon. She's married."

Lucky, resenting his brother's sermon, though it echoed the one he'd been preaching to himself, jerked his arm free. "I'm a grown-up. I don't need you for a conscience any more, big brother."

"I'm not trying to be your conscience." Chase sighed with chagrin. "Okay, maybe I am. But I'm more worried about her than I am you. She's the real victim here, Lucky. Her life has been turned upside down, and it's your fault."

"I don't need you to remind me of that, either."

"When you're done playing your games, what's she going to be left with, huh? A broken marriage and a broken heart?"

"You're wrong, Chase."

"Am I?"

"Yes! This time it isn't just a game."

Chase stared at him long and hard before stating softly, "That's what really worries me."

All that was left of the machinery garage was a dark area on the ground, covered by ashes that had been sifted through so many times they resembled gray face powder. The remains of the machinery had already been hauled away. What little that could be salvaged had been sold as scrap metal. The revenue from that sale had barely covered the crew's expenses to Louisiana.

Devon sighed as she kicked up a cloud of ashen dust with the toe of her sneaker. "Not much here to look at, is there?"

"I told you." Lucky was squatting; he scooped up handfuls of the ash and let it filter through his fingers.

"The fire was meant to be destructive, not just to serve as a warning of some sort," she observed aloud.

"The agents said that from the beginning. That's one of the reasons they pointed accusing fingers at me. They said it burned quick and hot. The fire trucks never had a chance in hell of putting the thing out. The best they could do was save the woods surrounding it."

Devon moved to an area of green just beyond the perimeter of scorched ground. She sat down on the trunk of a fallen tree. Lucky joined her. They silently contemplated the charred area.

"This is just one of several company buildings, right?" she asked.

"Right. But this is where we kept most of our heavy equipment. This was definitely the place to set the costliest fire and make it look like I did it."

Tilting her head, she looked at him curiously. "Why do you automatically assume that the revenge was directed at you?"

He shrugged. "Who else? Mother? She's got more friends than she can count. Sage? She's just a kid."

"Jealous boyfriend?"

He dismissed that possibility with a curt shake of his head. "She hasn't ever been that seriously involved with any one guy. She scares off even the most determined. Chase has probably cultivated a few enemies, but I feel it here," he said, flattening his palm against his stomach, "in my gut, that it was aimed at me."

"Why?"

Setting her hands behind her, she braced herself up on her arms. The pose drew her shirt tight across her breasts. Lucky had to concentrate on the caterpillar creeping along the tree trunk in order to keep himself from staring at them.

"I'm the one who's always getting into trouble." He lifted his eyes to hers. "Seems I have a knack for getting myself into tight places."

Spiders spinning webs between branches of the nearby trees were making more racket than Lucky and Devon while they peered deeply into one another's eyes. The breeze lifted their hair and flirted with their clothing, but they remained motionless, unblinking, thoroughly absorbed.

After a long moment, Devon roused herself. "Who have you been in trouble with?"

"Why are you curious?"

"Everyone's a suspect."

"Or are you just nosy?" he teased.

She blushed slightly. "Maybe. It's a habit. See, when I do a story on someone, I talk to everyone close to the subject. I gather bits of information from here and there until I can piece together the entire personality of the individual. Sometimes the least likely interview produces the most valuable tidbit, the single element that makes all the other elements click into place."

"Fascinating."

What he found most fascinating wasn't the topic, but her animated way of explaining how she worked. Her eyes weren't one pure hue, but myriad shades of green that sparkled when she was angry or excited about the subject under discussion.

They could also look as deep as wells when she became introspective or sad, as they had done that night in the orchard when she had talked about her parents. He doubted she knew how expressive her eyes were. If she did, she would train them not to give away so much.

Drawing himself back into the discussion, he asked, "But what has your work method got to do with me?"

"To get to the culprit, I have to go through you. So I'll approach it in the same investigative way as if I were writing a story on you. I want to talk to a variety of people with whom Lucky Tyler has had contact. Tell me about everybody you've had trouble with in say, hmm, the last six months."

He laughed. "That'll take all afternoon."

"We've got all afternoon."

"Oh yeah. Right. Chase did say he had that drilling in Louisiana under way, didn't he? Well, let's see." Absently he scratched his neck. "Of course, most recently there was Little Alvin and Jack Ed."

"For the time being, let's set them aside. We'll come back to them. They're almost too obvious to be suspects."

"Okay, for starters, there was this guy in Longview. Owned a club over there."

"A club? Health club? Country club?"

"No, a, uh, you know."

"A nightclub?"

"Yeah. It's a . . . the kind of place where guys hang out. It's got girls. They hustle drinks and, you know, dance a little."

"A topless bar?"

"Sorta like that. Sure. I guess you could call it that."

Rolling her eyes, she said, "Don't spare my sensibilities, Lucky. We'll save time. What about this guy?"

"He accused me of coming on to one of his girls."

"Did you?"

"I bought her a few drinks."

"And for that he got upset?"

"Not exactly," he said, shifting uncomfortably.

"What? Exactly."

"I flirted with her. She read more into it than I intended. When I lost interest and stopped going there, she got depressed."

"How do you know?"

"This guy calls and starts bawling me out. Said she cried all the time, wouldn't work. Said I was bad for his business, 'cause she was a favorite with his customers. He told me to stay away from his club and his girls, this one in particular. I think he had the hots for her and was just jealous."

"Jealous enough to burn down your building?"

"I doubt it."

Devon took a deep breath. "Bears looking into. Who else?"

"There was a farmer."

"Let me guess," she said drolly. "He had a daughter."

"No. He had a cow."

After a moment's wary hesitation she shook her head. "I don't think I want to hear about this one."

Frowning at her lack of faith in him, he explained, "I was driving one of our trucks through a pasture on my way to a drilling site when a cow decided to play chicken with it."

"With what?"

"The truck."

"In other words, you ran over a cow."

"It was an accident! I swear, the dumb animal ran straight for my hood ornament. Anyway, she died."

"Surely you paid the farmer for the cow?"

"Hell, yes. We paid him more than she was worth. But he pitched a conniption fit and threatened to sue us for further damages."

"What happened?"

"Nothing. We never heard from him again, and assumed he had decided he'd come out ahead."

"Maybe not. Although I doubt a poor old farmer would have the moxie to set a fire."

"Poor old farmer, my foot. He was straight out of Texas A&M. You should have heard some of the names he called me."

"Okay, he's a possibility. Remember his name, and we'll check to see if he's bought any flares lately. Who else have you tussled with?"

He squinted into the sunlight. "Hmm. Oh yeah, the Irvings."

"Plural?"

"There's a clan of them over in Van Zandt County."

"Swell. That narrows it down," she muttered. "What did you do to them?"

"Nothing!"

"What did they accuse you of doing?"

He reached for her hands and sandwiched them between his own. "Swear to God, Devon, it wasn't me."

"Who did what?"

"Got Ella Doreen pregnant."

She stared at him in stupefaction for several seconds, then she began to laugh. "Is this a joke?"

"Hardly. You wouldn't have thought it was funny either if an army of shotgun-toting rednecks in overalls had come after you. They surrounded the office one day, demanding I make an honest woman of Ella Doreen and acknowledge her kid as mine."

"Was there any possibility that you were the, uh, donor?"

He shot her a retiring look. "She's just a kid, younger than Sage. I didn't even remember who she was until one of her kinfolk produced her from the back of a flatbed truck. Uncle Somebody shoved her forward to accuse me face-to-face."

"You recognized her then?"

"Sure. We had met a couple of weeks earlier in an office building in Henderson. I was there to see a client. As I was crossing the lobby, I noticed this girl sitting there fanning herself, looking ready to throw up or faint or both. I asked if she needed any help. She told me she'd gotten dizzy and hot. And it *was* hotter than hell in there.

"So I helped her to her feet, escorted her outside, and offered to buy her a can of cola, which I did from one of the vending machines at the nearest filling station. We walked there. I was never even alone with her. The only thing I touched was her elbow.

"During our conversation she asked me what I did for a living, and seemed impressed by the business card I gave her. I remember her running her fingers over the engraving. That's it. After she assured me that she could call someone to come pick her up, I left her there, sitting on a stack of retreads, sipping her coke.

"As it turns out, she had been in Henderson to see a doctor in that building, and was already about four months pregnant. I couldn't possibly have fathered her child. I was just a convenient scapegoat. Eventually she broke down and admitted it."

By the time he finished telling the tale, Devon was shaking her head with amazement. "You attract trouble like a lightning rod."

"Not intentionally."

"And it always centers around women. Even the cow." She looked away from him, adding softly, "And now me."

Laying his palm along her cheek, he turned her face toward him. "You look so sad."

"I am."

"Why? Was it terrible yesterday?"

"Yes. It was awful having to face my husband, both of us knowing that I had betrayed him. Physically. With you."

"And knowing you want to again."

She sucked in a quick little breath. Her eyes widened, and her lips parted. "I didn't say that, Lucky."

"You didn't have to." He brushed his thumb across her lower lip. She whimpered quietly. Glancing down at the peaked centers of her breasts, which were making impressions against her blouse, he whispered, "Just like before, your body says it for you."

Chapter Seventeen

Pat Bush was sitting on a picnic table in Dogwood Park, drinking from a long-neck bottle of beer. It was against the rules to be drinking in uniform, but it was against the rules to hand over official crime reports to civilians, too, so he figured he might just as well be hanged for a sinner as a saint.

Devon scanned the top sheet of the stack of documents. One of the park's halogen security lamps provided her with enough light to read by. She had slipped on her glasses. "What's a trailer?"

"A trail of fuel leading back to the building," Pat explained. "There were several radiating out from the garage like spokes on a wheel. They set the flares to them."

"Then ran like hell," Lucky contributed from the adjacent playground, where he was sitting in a swing.

"Whoever did it was smart," said Pat, playing devil's advocate. "Apparently the perp shut off the ventilation system in the building first. The gasoline fumes collected like air inside a balloon. One spark introduced into those compressed fumes, and *ka-blooy*. You've got yourself an explosion hot enough to melt metal."

"Maybe we'll see something when we've gone over the material more carefully." Devon tried to inject some optimism into her voice, but Lucky knew that her hopes were as faint as his own. He rued the day he'd bought those flares, which the roughnecks sometimes used at night to mark the route to an out-of-the-way drilling site.

Pat finished his beer and conscientiously placed the empty bottle in the trash barrel. "Guess I'd better get home. It's late. If y'all turn up anything, let me know. But for the love of God keep your investigation covert. Don't do anything conspicuous."

"Don't worry, Pat. If we're caught, your name would never enter into an explanation of how we got the crime report."

"You didn't have to tell me that," the older man said to Lucky. He doffed the brim of his hat to Devon and ambled off through the park toward his squad car.

"Ready?" Lucky asked.

Devon pocketed her glasses, picked up the stack of documents, and allowed him to hold her hand as they moved in the opposite direction from Pat, toward Lucky's Mustang.

The house was dark when they arrived. Laurie had already gone to bed. A light shone from beneath Sage's door, and she had a radio on, but for all practical purposes she had retired to her room for the night, too.

At the door of the guest bedroom, which Laurie had hospitably prepared for her, Devon turned to Lucky. "Tomorrow we'll begin again, asking questions about anybody who might be harboring a grudge against you. One by one we'll eliminate them."

"Okay."

"Let me know if you think of anyone else, and I'll add him to my list."

"Okay."

"Are you listening?"

"Of course." Actually he wasn't. "You sleepy?"

"A little."

"I'm not. I've never been so keyed up."

"I started out this morning with a hundred-mile drive, remember?"

He nodded, but his eyes were fastened on her neck with the single-mindedness of a vampire. "Is, uh, is the bedroom okay?" he asked, reluctant to leave her. "Is the bed comfy?"

"I haven't tried it yet, but I'm sure it will be fine."

"Is the room hot?"

"Not at all."

"Too cool?"

"It's just right, Lucky."

"Got everything you need?"

"Yes."

"Towels?"

"Yes."

"Soap?"

"Yes."

"Toilet paper?"

She smiled. "Your mother is a thorough and gracious hostess. I even have a candy dish stocked with little candy bars."

"Oh well, then I guess you've got everything."

"Mm-hmm."

"But if you need anything else . . ."

"I won't."

". . . like extra blankets, pillows . . ." He bent his head and brushed his mouth across hers. "Me."

He kissed her, fluidly, first touching the tip of his tongue to hers, then melding their mouths together. Groaning, he placed his arms around her and drew her against his body, which was full and feverish with a desire he'd studiously kept at bay until now, when he couldn't restrain himself any longer.

Just one taste of her. Only one. Then he might survive the night. But, by the second, his mouth became more possessive, his tongue more intimate, his hands more seductive. She ground protesting fists against his chest. He moaned her name when he finally surrendered and raised his head.

"We can't, Lucky."

"It's just a kiss."

"No it isn't."

"Just one kiss."

"It's wrong."

"I know, I know."

"Then let me go. Please."

He released her but didn't move away. Their eyes met and locked in a searing gaze. It gratified him to hear that she was as breathless as he, and that her protests were without conviction.

She slipped through the guest-room door and closed it behind her, but not before he saw in her eyes pinpoints of confusion and passion that matched those burning in his.

He hardly slept a wink that night, knowing she was only two doors away but unable to do a damn thing about it.

After three days of that he was on the verge of going stark staring mad. One by one the names on their list of possible suspects had fallen through the cracks of logic, reason, and fact. No one who had a recent grievance against him could have set the fire.

His mood was foul, his disposition sour, his language vulgar, his patience depleted, and all because he was desperate for Devon.

Her fourth morning in Milton Point she told him over coffee, "The farmer was our last chance, and he was in Arkansas buying cattle. It seems that the only people in town that night were those who love you. I don't know what else to do."

"Is that right?" He sneered. "I was under the impression that you knew everything. I thought you had a bag of tricks. Don't tell me you've run out."

Furiously she scraped back her chair and stood up, heading for the kitchen door. As she sailed past his chair he put out his arm, encircled her waist, drew her between his wide-spread thighs, and ground his forehead against her stomach.

"I'm sorry, I'm sorry." He butted his head against the soft heaviness of her breasts and rubbed his face in the fabric of her blouse, breathing in her fresh, clean scent. "I know I'm acting like a jerk, but I'm slowly dying, Devon. I'm going to explode if—"

"Somebody's coming."

She backed out of his reach only seconds before Laurie entered the kitchen, followed by Sage. If Laurie noticed the steamy atmosphere and their rosy, guilt-ridden faces, she didn't acknowledge them. Sage, however, split her knowing look between the two of them and winked saucily.

"Well, hello. We're not interrupting anything, are we?"

Lucky snarled at her.

"What's on your agenda today?" Laurie asked.

"Actually we hadn't decided on anything specific," Devon said feebly.

"Well, if you ask me, which I realize you haven't, you're overlooking the obvious."

"What's that, Mother?"

Lucky glanced up at her, curious in spite of his longing to thrash his impudent kid sister. He welcomed his mother's opinion—anything, in fact, that would momentarily distract him from his physical discomfort.

"That Cagney oaf and his unsavory friend."

"Little Alvin and Jack Ed Patterson?"

Laurie gave a delicate shudder at the very mention of their names. "Detestable people, especially Jack Ed. And those Cagney children were hellions from birth."

"But they're *so* obvious," Lucky argued.

"Maybe they figure that's what everyone is thinking and are using it to their benefit."

Devon and Lucky's eyes met as they considered the possibility. "She's got a point," Devon said. "They certainly were peeved at you."

"But they've got ironclad alibis."

"Lies," Sage retorted succinctly. "They've terrorized people into lying for them."

Lucky gnawed his lower lip as he thought it through. "It wouldn't be too smart to confront them. We promised Pat there would be no more trouble. Besides," he said with a grin, "I might not come out alive if I have another fight with Little Alvin."

"So, what are you thinking?" Devon asked.

"Little Alvin is as strong as an ox and meaner than Satan, but he's no mental giant."

"I agree. Jack Ed would have masterminded the fire."

"So let's use Little Alvin's cerebral weakness to our advantage."

"How?" she asked.

Lucky leaned back in his chair and slapped his thighs with satisfaction. "With the thing I do best. A con."

As they pulled up in front of the rusty mobile home, Devon nervously wet her lips and asked, "How do I look?"

"Plumb mouth-watering." Lucky switched off the Mustang's motor.

She tipped up the lenses of her dark glasses. "With this?" Sage had done an excellent job of painting on a black eye, using her vast array of eye shadows and shading crayons.

"Even with that." He was tempted to lean across the car's console and kiss her. But glancing at the windows of the mobile home, he realized Little Alvin could be watching them.

"You'll have to open your own door." He vaulted over the driver's door and headed for the trailer without giving her a backward glance. He knocked loudly on the front door of the trailer, then bawled over his shoulder at her. "Hurry up, will you?"

She moved into place beside him and muttered out the side of her mouth. "Macho pig."

The whispered words were barely out of her mouth when the front door was opened with such impetus, the entire building rocked on its concrete-block platform.

"What the hell do you want, Tyler?"

With admirable aplomb, Lucky stood his ground and growled back. "First off, I want to be invited inside."

"What for?"

"I'll tell you when I get inside."

"When bore hogs grow teats. Get the hell off my porch."

Little Alvin tried to slam the door in their faces, but Lucky caught it before it closed. "We either come in now alone, or come back later with Sheriff Bush. Then the decision won't be left to you."

Alvin regarded Lucky suspiciously, then gave Devon a lecherous leer. "Would the little lady like to come in by herself?"

"The little lady would not," said Lucky, grinding his teeth.

Alvin cursed, then turned inside and indicated with his head that they should follow. Lucky was about to step aside and let Devon go first, when she gave him a slight shove as a reminder that he was supposed to be portraying the role of a heel.

The place was a pigsty. It was furnished cheaply and littered with the debris of numerous meals and a collection of empty liquor bottles and beer cans. The only decorations were centerfolds that had been cut out of the crudest men's magazines and taped to the walls.

One look at those and Lucky felt Devon stiffen beside him. Just to be ornery, he walked over to one and studied it at length, murmuring an "hmm" of approval. He didn't wait for an invitation to sit down, but sprawled on a sofa. Taking Devon's hand, he dragged her down beside him and threw an arrogantly possessive arm around her.

"Whaddaya want?" their host asked.

"A cold beer would be nice. One for me and one for her," Lucky replied, jerking his head down toward Devon.

Scowling, Little Alvin lumbered into the adjacent kitchen and returned several moments later with three beers. After handing them theirs, he sat down across from them in what was apparently "his chair." There was a greasy spot on the headrest and worn spots in the upholstery where his behind fit into the seat and on the cushion where his feet rested when it reclined.

"Well?" he asked belligerently, after taking a sucking swig from his can of beer.

"Pat Bush gave me twenty minutes to make a deal with you."

Little Alvin barked a laugh. "You gotta be crazy, Tyler. I ain't making no deal with you about anything."

"I told you he wouldn't do it," Devon muttered.

"And I told you to keep your mouth shut and let me handle this," Lucky snapped, shooting her a threatening glance. "He may be dumb, but he's not stupid."

"Now just a damn—"

Lucky interrupted. "You want to hear this or not? Because every minute that you sit here shooting off your fat mouth is one minute you come closer to spending time in federal prison."

"For what?"

Devon laughed. Lucky frowned with impatience. "For what?" he repeated scornfully. "Look, Alvin, cut the crap, all right? They've got enough evidence on you guys to send you to jail . . . even without a trial."

They saw a chasm open up then in his armor of insolence. His smug grin faltered. "What do you mean? What evidence?"

"Evidence, okay? There's not enough time to detail it all."

"When are you going to tell him about the paper?" Devon whined.

Lucky cursed, acting as if she had distracted him. "Will you put a lid on it and give me time to get this other business over with first?"

At the prearranged signal Devon removed her sunglasses and revealed her black eye. "I don't care about that stupid fire. You said—"

"What about the evidence the sheriff's got?" Little Alvin asked anxiously, cutting into their lovers' spat.

"Let me handle *my* business with the man first, okay? Then we'll get to yours." Lucky turned back to Alvin and lowered his voice. "She looked so damn good in the place, you know? Now . . ." He flung up his hands in exasperation. "Might have ended up better for everybody if you'd got her that night instead of me. Anyway, where was I?"

"The evidence they've got on me," Alvin squealed.

"Oh yeah, well, they're keeping the files officially closed. All I know is that Pat promised to pick up Jack Ed first, but who knows how long that might take? He could arrive any minute now." For good measure he glanced over his shoulder through the ratty curtains at the window.

"They're picking up Jack Ed?" Sweat popped out on Little Alvin's porcine face.

"As we speak. You know what a weasel that little s.o.b. is. He'd rat on his own mother. Lord only knows what he's gonna tell them about you. Probably that the fire was all your doing."

Little Alvin Cagney made a whimpering sound like a toddler who'd momentarily lost sight of his mother and lunged for the door. Anticipating that, Lucky was right behind him, catching him by the collar and hauling him back.

"We're here to help you, Alvin."

"You think I was born yesterday, Tyler?"

"If you turn state's evidence, you'll get a lighter sentence. Otherwise, you're history."

"Liar." Little Alvin twisted and turned, trying to work himself free. Lucky hung on tenaciously. "Why would you come to warn me, Tyler?"

"I wouldn't. But Pat would. He needs one more piece of evidence to nail Jack Ed. Since he knew we were coming to see you on this other matter, he asked me to offer you a deal. Real decent of him, wasn't it? See, everybody knows that Jack Ed was the brains behind the arson, but they can't prove it."

"Th-that's right," Little Alvin stammered. "Hell, I wasn't even thinking straight that night. You had kicked my nuts up to the back of my throat. But Jack Ed said—"

"Save it," Lucky hissed. "Give all the details to Pat when he gets here, things like where Jack Ed got those flares."

"His sister's garage," he babbled. "Her husband works for the highway department. Jack Ed said they'd think you did it because you carried flares—"

"I said save it. I'm not interested. When they find the flares, they're sure to find the gas cans, too."

"Yeah. We got them out of his brother-in-law's gar—"

"I said save it for Pat." He pushed Little Alvin back into his chair. The football lineman was quivering, a hairy blob of perspiring ectoplasm.

"Now that that's out of the way, will you see to my business?" Devon asked in a petulant tone.

Lucky blew out a breath. "Sure, sure. Get him something to write with."

"Write? Write what?" Alvin's eyes darted warily between Devon and Lucky.

"Did you read in the newspaper about her old man being in prison?" Dumbly, Alvin nodded.

"Well, he accused her of taking up with me long before the night of the fire. He claims we'd been seeing each other even before he went to the pen. If the prison guards hadn't restrained him . . ."

Gesturing toward her black eye, Lucky trailed off ominously. "Anyway, could you just jot down a statement that I picked her up in the place? That it was just an accidental meeting."

"Sure, sure. I can do that."

"Good. I don't give a damn what her old man thinks, but she kept nagging me about it. You know how women are." Devon handed Alvin a piece of paper and a pencil. "While you're doing that, I'll call Pat on his mobile phone. I hope we're not too late. I'll tell him you're ready to talk. Right?"

"Right, right," Little Alvin agreed eagerly. "My folks warned me not to trust Jack Ed."

"They were right," Lucky said sagely. "When it comes to brains, you can't even compare you two." He clapped Alvin on the shoulder as though they were old friends. "His brother-in-law's garage, huh? I don't even want to know where he lives."

"Off Route Four. By that big grain silo."

Lucky looked at Devon over the top of Alvin's head and smiled.

Chapter Eighteen

They laughed so hard that tears streamed down their faces and they kept collapsing against each other. "By the time Pat got there, Little Alvin was blubbering like a baby about the atrocities inflicted on celebrities like him in prison. I always suspected that underneath his meanness he was nothing but a chicken-livered coward. Now I know it's true."

The Tylers were gathered in the living room. Chase, Tanya, Laurie, and Sage were the enthralled audience.

"I actually started feeling sorry for him," Devon said.

"Is that why you brewed him a cup of tea?"

"Tea?" Chase hooted. "Little Alvin sipping tea?"

"She borrowed a tea bag from one of his neighbors in the trailer park, brewed him a cup, and insisted he drink it while Pat and a deputy were waiting for Alvin's attorney to get there so they could take his deposition."

"Well, I think that was a lovely gesture," Laurie said, coming to Devon's defense. "But I can't say that I feel sorry for Alvin. Those Cagney kids were allowed to run roughshod over everybody without any parental supervision. It's a wonder to me they're not all behind bars by now."

"What about Jack Ed?" Chase wanted to know once he had contained his laughter.

"They've got an arrest warrant out for him. Since he thinks he's in the clear, he shouldn't be too hard to find."

"Oh, I'm so glad you're off the hook," Tanya said.

"Hopefully things will get back to normal now," Sage said. "By the way, Lucky, I went into town this morning and saw Susan Young at the dry cleaners. She kept her eyes to the floor. That's the first time since I've known her that she hasn't looked down her nose at me."

"Her dirty, rotten trick almost backfired this time," Chase said. "It put the fear of God into her."

"Or the fear of Lucky," Sage said, grinning at her brother.

Chase stood and extended a hand down to assist Tanya up. "I'm going to the office and call the insurance company. Now that we've been cleared of any criminal charges, they can process our claim."

"What will we do with the money?" Lucky asked him. "Pay back the bank in full, or replace the equipment we lost in the fire?"

"We need to discuss how to allocate it," Chase said.

"Not right now, you don't," Laurie said. "I don't want talk about business to spoil the mood." She took Tanya's arm as she walked with her to the door. "How's the house-hunting? Find anything yet?"

"This morning," Tanya reported with a smile. "Marcie took me to see one I really liked. I want Chase to see it."

"Soon," he promised.

"How are you feeling?" Laurie inquired.

"Fit as a fiddle. A little indigestion in the evenings."

They said their good-byes and left. Celebrating his brother's liberation, Chase honked his car horn as they sped down the lane toward the main road.

"Know what I feel like?" Lucky said. "A good, galloping ride. Who's game?"

"Sage and I have to pass," Laurie said. "We've got dental appointments in town."

"Oh, Mother—"

"I won't cancel it again, Sage. I've canceled three times already."

After an exchange that Sage was destined to lose, she reluctantly followed her mother out the back of the house where Laurie always parked her car. Lucky turned to Devon.

"That leaves you."

"I really should be getting back to Dallas."

"Mother obviously expects you to stay another night."

"How do you know?"

"She didn't say good-bye."

"She did so."

"That? That wasn't one of her formal good-byes. Her formal good-byes take forever. Lots of hugs and Kleenex and stuff."

"There's nothing to keep me here any longer, Lucky."

"Surely you can spare an hour for a horseback ride," he said cajolingly. "Besides, you can't leave the family without first going through the rite of a formal good-bye."

His smile was so disarming, she capitulated after offering only a few more token excuses. "Give me time to wash off my black eye and change clothes," she said, heading for the stairs.

"Meet you in the stable."

Devon reigned in behind Lucky, choking on the dust his mount had kicked up. "No fair," she shouted. "You cheated!"

"Naturally," he admitted breezily as he swung his leg over his saddle and dismounted. "How else could I be guaranteed to win?"

Devon slid from her saddle and jumped to the ground. "Then Lucky is a misnomer. You win by cheating."

Laughing, he took the reins from her and walked both horses into the stable. Its shadows were cool and refreshing in comparison to the sunny heat of the afternoon.

"I've had my share of luck, too," he told her. Skillfully he removed the saddles from the horses, then began walking them up and down the center aisle of the stable to cool them off. Devon walked alongside him.

"Is that how you got your nickname?"

"Sort of."

"Who gave it to you?"

His tanned face broke into a wide grin. "Chase."

"Why?"

"Well, he and some of his buddies . . ." He paused and glanced down at her. "Sure you want to hear this?"

"I'm sure."

"Okay. Just remember you asked."

"It sounds sordid."

"It is. One night when I was about fourteen, I blackmailed Chase and some of his friends into including me when they took out one of the boys' family car. We ended up over in Kilgore at a bowling alley. They'd gone there looking for a woman."

"Just any ol' woman?"

"No. A particular woman."

"Dare I ask why? Here, let me help." She scooped grain into a feed bucket while Lucky rubbed down the gelding she'd been riding. "Tell me about the woman."

His hands, one holding a currycomb, worked efficiently and smoothly over the animal's flesh. "She had a stupefying body, and showed it off to the yokels like us. Got her kicks wearing tight sweaters without a bra. That kind of thing."

They moved to the next stall and began working together on the horse Lucky had been riding. "What happened?" Devon asked as she positioned the feed bucket where the animal could reach it.

"I guess I wanted to prove that I was as much a stud as the rest of them even though I was younger. So I approached her and struck up a conversation."

"About what?"

"My father, who had been falsely accused of being a spy and was imprisoned somewhere behind the Iron Curtain."

Devon's hands fell still. She laughed with disbelief. "And she bought it?"

"I guess so. I never knew. Maybe she was just tired of the bowling alley. Anyway, when I told her I was collecting aluminum cans to re-cycle so I could raise the money to buy his way out of a Communist country, she invited me to her house and said I could have all the cans I could find."

Devon followed him to a deep utility sink at the back of the building where they washed their hands, sharing a bar of soap. "Meanwhile, Chase and his friends don't know what you're telling her," Devon said as she shook water off her hands before pulling a towel from the rack.

"Right. They thought she was taking me to her house for prurient purposes." He bobbed his eyebrows. "Behind her back, I was giving them the high sign, fanning my face, stuff like that, which would indi-cate that she was hot for me and vice versa."

"I've got the picture."

"So I rode with her to her house. I felt like a damn fool fishing soda cans out of her trash and placing them in the grocery sack she had provided. Although the scenery was good."

"Scenery?"

"The body."

"Oh yes, the body."

"She was an adolescent boy's dream. From an adult point of view—my taste has been considerably refined," he said, raking his eyes down Devon's slender shapeliness, "I realize she was a little overblown. Back then, though, I thought she was something.

"So, with my eyes glued to her bosom, I'm riffling through her gar-bage looking for cans, and she's chattering about how admirable it is of me to undertake this dangerous mission and how terrible it must be to be imprisoned in a foreign land. She had a ten-plus body, but a single-digit IQ."

"The type who causes the feminist movement to nosedive."

"Exactly. She was a prototype."

He led Devon into a small room at the back of the stable. In it were a couple of chairs, a double bed with an iron headboard, which at some point in its long life had been painted china blue, and a compact refrigerator.

He pulled the string dangling from the ceiling fan, and it began to hum as it circulated the warm, still air. He took two canned drinks from the refrigerator and handed one to Devon, opening the other for himself.

"She never made a move on you?"

He shook his head with chagrin. "In retrospect I scolded myself for laying it on so thick. I finally worked up enough nerve to embrace her, and she *comforted* me! Saying things like 'Poor baby.'

"In her eyes I was too damn noble to be corruptible, much less horny. When it came time for me to go—when there were no more cans in the house—I told her I'd go out the back. See, I knew Chase and the others would have followed us and were watching her house.

"With this rattling sack of cans in my arms, I went out her back door and hid in the bushes. It was an hour longer before the other guys started honking the car horn for me. I had taken off my shirt, given myself a few scratches across the chest and belly, messed up my hair, all to give the general impression that I'd just been laid by a she-cat."

Devon's expression was a mix of incredulity and hilarity. Groping behind her for the edge of the bed, she sat down. The ancient springs creaked. "I can't believe this. Proving your manhood was that important to you?"

"At that point in time I guess it was. Anyhow, the guys fell for it. By the time I got finished with my breathless, lurid account, they thought she'd taken me to bed and that I had experienced what they'd only dreamed about. That's when they started calling me Lucky. To this day, they don't know any different."

"Not even Chase?"

"No." His brows steepled. "You're not going to tell him, are you?"

Laughing, she flung her arms behind her head and fell back onto the bed. "And spoil the masculine myth? I wouldn't dream of it."

"Good." He sat on the edge of the bed and smiled down at her. "The point would be moot anyway, because it wasn't long after that night that I really became a man with a girl in my algebra class."

Devon's smile faltered; she averted her eyes. "Women have always been easy conquests for you, haven't they?"

She started to sit up, but Lucky slid his palms against hers and exerted enough pressure to keep the backs of her hands lying supine on the cheap bedspread beneath her.

"All but one, Devon. Nothing with you has been easy."

"Let me up."

"Not yet."

"I want to get up."

"So do I," he whispered hoarsely before covering her lips with his. Their mouths came together hungrily and clung. He thrust his tongue between her lips, between her teeth, into her mouth. Their fingers interlocked as he moved his body above hers and used his knee to separate hers.

He released her hands and drove his up through her loose hair. They held her head still while his mouth gently ate hers. All resistance gone, she closed her arms around his torso, hugging him to her tightly. Her hands ran up and down his back, gripping the firm musculature.

Overhead the fan droned, fanning their bodies, which burned hotter by the second. From the stable came an occasional snuffling sound made by horses. But the throaty sounds of want and need were all that echoed through their heads.

He tore his mouth from hers and peered deeply into her eyes. "I want you, Devon. Damn, but I want you. . . ."

He kissed her again, ravenously, while he grappled with the buttons on her plain white shirt. When they were undone, he pushed the fabric aside. The front clasp of her bra fell open at a flick of his fingertips. He caressed her. His eyes adored her. His mouth drew in her sweet flesh and sucked it tenderly.

"Lucky," she breathed, half in anguish, half in ecstasy. Her fingers tunneled through his hair and clasped his head to her chest. Her thighs parted. He nestled his middle in her cleft, moved against it, rubbed it.

He kissed her breasts again and again, using his tongue to excite them. When she thought she couldn't be drawn any tighter, any higher, he brushed her nipples with rapid flicking motions of his tongue until they were tingling.

For weeks he had tried convincing himself that he wanted Devon Haines merely because he couldn't have her. He had told himself that his imagination had run rampant and that their one time together hadn't been as unique as his memory had made it out to be.

One taste of her, however, had shot that theory all to hell. He wanted her. He wanted her right now, and later today, and tomorrow, and the day after that, forever. He wanted the sight and sound and smell of her, the taste and the textures of her.

He wanted her laughter and her temper. He'd grown fond of her feminist defensiveness, her clever, analytical mind, and the delightful and annoying little surprises she constantly pulled on him. He wanted everything and all that Devon comprised.

As his lips kissed their way down her smooth belly, he unfastened her jeans and worked them past her waist. The open wedge fascinated him and he continued to explore it until he felt the softest hair against his lips.

"Devon," he murmured with longing. "Devon."

Pressing deeper, he parted his lips and kissed her earnestly. There was moisture and heat and need, which he wanted to probe.

"No!" Suddenly she shoved him off, rolled away, and drew herself into a ball. "It's wrong. I can't. I can't."

Lucky stared down at her, gasping for breath, trying to clear his head and make sense of a senseless situation. He saw her tears, but even before then he knew this wasn't some trick. She was suffering spiritual torment and emotional hell, and he couldn't bear it.

"It's okay, Devon," he said with soft gruffness, laying a hand on her shoulder. He made ineffectual attempts to draw her blouse together over her breasts, the tips of which were still rosy and moist from his caresses. "I'd never want you to do anything that would make you feel bad about yourself or about me. Never."

She turned her head and gazed up at him through eyes shimmering with tears. "I'm married, Lucky." Her voice trembled with desperation. "I'm married."

"I know."

The ancient bed rocked when he flung himself off it and stamped through the door. He paced the length of the stable a couple of times, cursing fate, gnashing his teeth in an effort to cool his passions and his temper.

However, when Devon appeared, his temper dissipated. Her despair killed it as nothing else could have. There were still tears in her eyes. Her lips, which were swollen from fervent kissing, made her look like a victim. What did that make him? The culprit?

Yes.

"I'll walk you back to the house now," he said gently. She didn't take the hand he extended to her, but fell into step beside him as they moved from the stable to the house.

As soon as they entered, she said, "It won't take me long to pack." Before he could stop her, she ran upstairs.

He wished his mother allowed liquor in the house. If he'd ever needed a whiskey, it was now. The longest ten minutes of his life was spent roaming the rooms of the house, knowing that Devon was upstairs, preparing to walk out of his life forever.

She had reached the bottom stair before he heard her tread and rushed to confront her there. At her side, she was carrying her packed suitcase.

"Devon—"

"Good-bye, Lucky. I'm glad everything worked out well for you. Of course, there was never any doubt in my mind that you would be cleared of the charges. Thank your mother for her hospitality, and say my good-byes to everyone. They're all so kind, so . . ." When her voice cracked, she sidestepped him and headed for the front door.

He caught her arm and spun her around. "You can't just leave like this."

"I have to."

"But you don't want to, Devon. Dammit, I know you don't."

"I'm married."

"To a guy you don't love."

"How do you know?"

He took a step closer. It was time to play hardball. Their futures were at stake. "Because if you did, you wouldn't have let me make love to you that first time. You weren't that sleepy. And you wouldn't have let what just happened, when you were wide awake, go so far.

"Know what else? I don't think he loves you either. If he did, he wouldn't have acted like he did when you went to explain things. He'd be gut-sick, or outraged, or determined to castrate and kill me, but he wouldn't act like a kid whose favorite toy had been damaged."

Her momentary defiance evaporated, and she lowered her head. "Whatever Greg says or does isn't the issue. It's what *we* do that counts. I'm leaving, Lucky. Talking about it won't change my mind."

"I can't let you just go."

"You don't have a choice. Neither do I."

Again she maneuvered around him. He delayed her again. "If you did have a choice—"

"But I don't."

"If you *did*," he repeated stubbornly, "would you want to stay with me?" She did something then that she had avoided doing since coming downstairs—she looked at him directly.

The yearning in her eyes mirrored his own. He exulted in it. Raising his hand, he stroked her cheek. "If you had a choice, would you let me love you like I want to?" he asked in a stirring voice.

The physical and emotional tug-of-war between them was almost palpable. Her eyes cried, *yes, yes!* But aloud she said nothing. Instead, she turned toward the door. "Good-bye, Lucky."

Abysmally dejected, he dropped down onto the bottom stair and listened to her light footsteps cross the porch and crunch in the gravel driveway. He heard her car door being opened, then closed, and the growl of the engine as she turned it on. He sat there long after the motor could no longer be heard and she had had time to put miles between them.

He listened very closely to something else—his own being. He lusted after this woman's body more than all the other bodies he'd ever known put together. His single sexual experience with her stood out above all the rest. He'd had many that were lustier, crazier, faster, slower, but none as heart-piercingly sweet, none that still haunted his mind.

His heart was saying that his craving for her wasn't entirely physical, however. He could no longer even imagine a life without Devon in it. There would be nothing to look forward to. Days would be dreaded rather than anticipated. Years. Decades.

His head was telling him that the situation was hopeless and that he'd known that from the time she had informed him she was married. Their worst enemy wasn't Greg Shelby; it was their own consciences. Neither could engage in an unscrupulous affair, and if they could, they wouldn't be attracted. They would be two different people. What a brutal irony, that the morals they respected in each other made their being together impossible.

But James Lawrence Tyler wasn't only lucky, he was eternally optimistic.

Nothing was impossible. He simply wouldn't accept this situation. Fate couldn't play a bad joke on him like this and get away with it. It couldn't end this way, with Devon just quitting his life and both of them being miserable about it. No way. He wouldn't allow it.

Hell no.

Chapter Nineteen

"Visits are limited to fifteen minutes."

Lucky was shown into the room where, a week earlier, Devon had met briefly with her husband. "I understand," he said to the official. "Thank you for arranging this meeting on such short notice."

During the bleak hours of the night before, it had occurred to Lucky that the manly thing to do would be to confront Devon's husband.

He wasn't yet sure what he was going to say to Greg Shelby. Was he supposed to say that he was sorry for making love to Devon? What an appalling thought. He wasn't sorry for it in the slightest. To say so would be a lie. He supposed he would just come right out and tell the man that he was in love with his wife.

That, too, had occurred to him during the bleak hours of the night.

For all his philandering, he'd always figured that one day there would be a woman who would make sexual fidelity not only an obligation but a pleasure. Devon Haines was that woman. She had made monogamy the only form of sexual activity he wanted to engage in.

As Tanya had done for Chase, Devon had made all other women pale in comparison. She could fulfill his every need and make fulfilling hers a lifetime challenge that he would look forward to meeting.

The idea of his child growing inside Devon gave him goose bumps. It was probably the goose bumps, and the lump that had formed in his throat at the thought of making a baby with her, that convinced him it was love.

Hand in hand with love came honor. That was one lesson the Tyler children had been taught by both their parents. If you loved people, you might hurt them, disappoint them, anger them, but you never, ever, dishonored them.

It was that code of honor that had compelled him to drive through the gates of the country club prison to meet with her husband.

"Are you Tyler?"

At the sound of the voice, Lucky came around and got his first look at Greg Shelby. Mentally he sighed with relief. He'd dreaded meeting a Mel Gibson lookalike garbed in righteous martyrdom and prison stripes.

Instead, facing him was a tanned, nice-looking guy—but not one Sage would deem a hunk. It pleased him to note that Shelby's hair was thinning.

"Mr. Shelby?"

"That's right."

Carrying a chip on his shoulder the size of Mount Rushmore, he moved into the room and sat down on the sofa, laying his arm along the back of it. His nonchalance surprised Lucky. Surprised and provoked. Why wasn't the son of a bitch going for his throat? Didn't Devon deserve that?

Shelby said, "I don't have to ask what you want to see me about, do I?"

"I guess you don't. You read all about it in the newspapers."

"So did everybody else," he remarked bitterly.

Lucky sat down in a chair adjacent to the sofa. The two men squared off and eyed each other. "I'm sorry you found out about it that way," Lucky said, meaning it. "I know it couldn't have been easy on you, but it was a helluva lot worse on Devon."

Shelby snorted. "She's not in prison, though, is she?"

"She didn't commit a crime."

Lucky's bluntness momentarily took Shelby aback. Then he grinned slyly. "Some would think that what she did with you was a crime."

"I don't. And you don't either."

"How do you know what I think, Tyler?"

"If you were torn up over her adultery, we wouldn't be discussing it so casually."

Shelby gave him another wily grin and said sarcastically, "You're right. Devon's a veritable saint. Her only crime was marrying a guy destined for prison."

Lucky leaned back in his chair as though they were discussing the baseball season instead of an issue that, depending on the outcome, could determine his future.

"I wonder why she did that?"

Shelby regarded him shrewdly, then shrugged. He left the sofa and went to pour himself a cup of coffee from the dispenser. "Want some?"

"No thanks."

He blew on his hot coffee, then sipped. "Devon wanted an inside, indepth story on a white-collar crime that most people would merely label good business. Because I claimed to be innocent, the victim of manipulators too smart to get caught, the case made damn good fodder for her column."

"She's got talent."

"She sure as hell does. She had everybody in Dallas rooting for me." He frowned into the Styrofoam cup. "Too bad the judge and jury couldn't read the newspapers. Maybe we should have put her on the stand as a character witness. She might have convinced them of my innocence."

"Like you convinced her?"

Again, Shelby shrugged noncommittally. He was too clever to admit anything or to be caught in a verbal trap. Lucky wanted to pound his complacent smile to mush.

"Devon got out of our marriage what she wanted," Shelby said.

"If you're suggesting that all she wanted out of it was a good column or two, you don't know her at all."

Shelby actually laughed. "Maybe you're right, Tyler. You probably know her at least as well as I do."

Lucky wasn't going to discuss Devon and their relationship with this man, whom he was despising more each minute they spent together.

Shelby finished his coffee and tossed the cup into the wastepaper basket. "I've been a model prisoner, you know," he said conversationally. "I don't complain about the food. I keep my quarters neat. I don't pick quarrels with the other inmates. I had a good chance for an early parole."

He turned a menacing stare on Lucky. "Then you banged Devon, and she didn't even have the good sense to keep it quiet."

Lucky's hands balled into fists, but Shelby was so caught up in his own wrath, he didn't notice that or the flexing motions of Lucky's jaw.

"I didn't want any wrinkles in my plan. My lawyer said I had a good chance to get out the first time I was reviewed for parole, if there wasn't a blemish on my record. Now this," he spat. "Of course, it has nothing to do with me personally, but they're bound to figure that our hasty marriage was a gimmick to try and keep me out of here by swaying public opinion in my favor."

"Which it was."

Lucky was fully enlightened on Shelby's character now. He had manipulated Devon into feeling sorry for him and marrying him on the spur of the moment, as girls marry soldiers on their way to the front trenches. He hadn't thought a man could stoop that low, could use someone so unconscionably, but Shelby didn't have a word of regret for how this scandal had affected Devon. All his concerns were for himself.

He was saying, "I mean, if my wife's bedding other men, it sure as hell doesn't say much for our marriage, does it?"

"No, it doesn't." Lucky came to his feet. "Tell me something. Did you ever love her?"

"Love her?" Shelby repeated scornfully. "That's the real joke on me. There was a possibility that Devon's stirring prose might keep me out of prison, so I milked that for all it was worth. It didn't work.

"Then I married her on the chance that would help, but lost that gamble too. So what have I got? A wife who's no use to me at all. In fact, she's a liability now that she's made her own notorious headlines. And the real kicker is that I haven't even availed myself of the consolation prize, her sweet body."

Lucky's heart slammed against his ribs. Only excellent control kept him from audibly gasping. His ears rang with Shelby's words. A shudder passed through his body.

"Stupid bitch. If she's going to pass it around, the least she could do is keep her affairs secret until I'm released."

Lucky, elated and furious in equal measure, had to get out of there or he was going to ram his fist through Shelby's front teeth. Over the last few weeks he had learned the wisdom of exercising self-control.

He stretched his arm straight out in front of him and aimed an index finger at the center of the prisoner's chest. His eyes were as cold and blue and still as a fjord.

"When you get out of here, I'm gonna beat the hell out of you."

Having made that promise, he pivoted on his bootheels and stalked toward the door. There, he turned and, almost as an afterthought, added, "Before long, it won't matter to you who Devon is sleeping with. She's getting an annulment."

When the office door was pushed open, Chase glanced up from the paper work he'd been doing. He was surprised to see Tanya come in, followed by a tall, attractive woman.

"Goosey!" He stood and rounded his desk to greet his former classmate with a handshake, then a quick, hard hug.

"Hi, Chase," she said, laughing. "It's good to see you."

"Why haven't you been to any of our class reunions?" Smiling down into Marcie Johns's face, he said, "You look fantastic."

"I can't believe you're calling her by that horrid name!" Tanya exclaimed.

"You didn't take any offense, did you?" Chase asked.

"Of course not. If I could bear it as a sensitive, self-conscious adolescent, I can bear it as a mature adult. As for the class reunions, I lived in Houston for several years, and it was never convenient for me to make one."

Chase regarded her approvingly. "You're really looking terrific, Marcie. The years have been more than kind. They've been generous. I hear your business is going great guns, too."

"Thank you, and yes, I've enjoyed being in business for myself. The economy has slowed things down the past year or two, but I'm hanging in there."

"Wish I could say the same," he remarked good-naturedly.

"Oh, I understand you've got something very happy to celebrate."

"I told her about the baby," Tanya informed him. "And she's convinced me that even though our budget is tight, we can afford a house, and that now is an excellent time to buy. It's a buyer's market," she said, repeating Marcie's words.

"Should I be reaching for my checkbook?" he asked teasingly.

"Not yet. Marcie and I want you to come see the house she showed me yesterday. I think it's perfect. Will you come?"

"What, now?"

"Please."

"Sorry, sweetheart, but I can't." Tanya's animated face became crestfallen. "If it was any other time, I would, but I'm expecting a rep from the insurance company. He was supposed to be here right after lunch, but called to say he was running late. I need to be here when he arrives."

"I read in the morning papers that your brother had been cleared of those ridiculous arson charges," Marcie said.

"Is there another problem, Chase?"

"No," he said, reassuringly pressing Tanya's hand between his. "We just need to go over the inventory list of all the equipment we lost and discuss our claim."

She sighed with disappointment. "Well, maybe tomorrow."

"Or even later today," he offered. "Why don't you go look at the house again, and if you're still excited about it, call me. Maybe I can meet you there after he leaves. That is, if you're free, Marcie."

"I blocked out the entire afternoon for Tanya and you."

Tanya was smiling again. She threw her arms around Chase's neck and kissed him soundly on the mouth. "I love you. And you're going to love this house."

With his arms around her waist he hugged her tight. "I probably will, but not as much as I love you. Call me later."

Following them to the doorway, he waved them off.

"I know you're looking at me through the peephole. I'm not going to leave until I see you, even if it means climbing over your fence again. Save us both the trouble, okay?"

Devon unlatched the lock and pulled open the door. "You shouldn't be here, Lucky. You're only making things worse by—"

Her words were stifled by his mouth, which swooped down to claim hers in a scorching kiss. With his arms locked tightly around her, he walked her backward into the nearest wall. Securing her in place by tilting his body forward at the hip, he cupped her head between his hands and held it still for his plundering mouth.

The kiss left her breathless and unable to speak. He used that to his advantage. "I drove straight here from the prison where I had a chat with Greg Shelby." Ignoring her sudden intake of breath, he doggedly continued, "Notice I didn't call him your husband, because in the strictest sense of the word, he isn't, is he, Devon?"

"Yes," she cried mournfully.

"No. I'm more married to you than he is."

He swept her into his arms and carried her into the bedroom, keeping his gaze riveted on hers, which was wide with disbelief. Depositing her gently on the bed, he followed her down.

"I knew there was something odd about that night, something I should remember." He spoke rapidly, the words tripping over each other. "But I could never pinpoint what it was. Now I can. You were a virgin. I was your first and only lover. Not Shelby. Not any man. Me. Right, Devon?"

She closed her eyes. Tears leaked from them and rolled down her cheeks. She nodded. Lucky released a long-held sigh and bent down to rest his forehead on hers.

"Your marriage to him was never consummated?"

She shook her head no.

"Thank God." His breath ghosted over her tear-streaked features.

He sipped a cloudy, salty droplet from the corner of her lips, then whisked them with his tongue.

Their open mouths sought each other. It wasn't as tempestuous a kiss as the previous one, but it was deeper, longer, wetter, more meaningful, their searching tongues conveying unspoken emotions.

Slowly, article by article, he removed her clothing, stopping occasionally to admire, pet, kiss areas of her body that up till now he had only imagined. He had explored them first in darkness and knew them only by touch. Now his eyes had a sensual feast as he marveled over each curve and contour.

Placing her hands above her head, he ran his fingers down the pale undersides of her arms. His hands brushed across her breasts, causing the nipples to peak, then down her belly, over her navel, to her thighs. He caressed the satin texture of each one, delighting in their slender shape. The muscles of her calves perfectly fit his palms. He stroked her slender ankles, the arches of her feet, and ran his thumbs along the pads of her toes.

She was lovely all over, but between her thighs she was so beautifully, wonderfully woman, it made his heart ache. Palming her soft mound, he bent over her and made love to her mouth with his tongue, delving and withdrawing with a tempo that fired their imaginations and their blood.

With anxious longing, she quietly cried his name. He removed his expertly caressing hand and calmed her by dusting her face with light, airy kisses. Leaving the bed, he undressed.

The blinds were open. Afternoon sunlight streamed in, casting alternate strips of light and shadow across his flesh, limning his body hair with gold.

He had never known an ounce of modesty. Yet, standing at the side of Devon's bed, as he stepped free of his jeans and was left naked, he experienced a twinge of uncertainty and self-consciousness. Would his tall, lean body appeal to her? His chest was hairy. Some women didn't like hairy chests.

But when he returned to the bed and stretched out beside her, she allayed his misgivings by imbedding her fingertips in the crinkly pelt on his chest.

To his supreme satisfaction, she explored him with bashful but lustful curiosity. Her deft caresses were driving him slowly mad, but he forced himself to lie still and let her explore to her heart's content. Dying of pleasure wouldn't be a bad way to go.

At last, unable to take any more, he captured her hand. Keeping his eyes on hers, he sucked her fingertips while stroking her palm with his thumb. He then carried her hand down and folded it around his steely erection. He held his breath, wondering if she would accept or reject the gesture.

First with wonder, then with pleasure, then with desire, her hand explored and caressed his sex—the strong root, the smooth length, the head of moisture at its tip.

Groaning his ecstatic misery, he lowered his head to her breasts. They were beautiful, and he told her so as he rubbed his open mouth over one flushed crest, then the other, until they were stiff. Wantonly he kissed her belly and that alluring delta of soft curls.

She murmured a low, throaty "Please."

He said that this time she had to be very ready, very wet.

She said she was.

He tested her to see.

He waited no longer.

As her body closed around him, milking him like a silken fist, he learned the difference between having sex and making love. This wasn't taking, but giving. It wasn't temporal, but lasting. It wasn't just physical, but emotional and cerebral. He was involved with her, totally involved, from the tip of his straining manhood to the outer perimeters of his soul.

They mated eye-to-eye, smile-to-smile, heart-to-heart, body-to-body, moving together with sublime compatibility. She matched his even strokes with a subtle undulation of her hips.

The closer they moved to climax, the tighter she clung, the deeper he penetrated. Gritting his teeth, he held back until he felt the waves of sensation shimmy through her, felt her gentle contractions around his manhood, and saw the lights of ecstasy explode and glimmer in her green eyes.

Only then did he release the rigid control he had imposed on himself. He buried his face in the soft fragrance of her hair and gave himself over to the encompassing pleasure that erupted from within him and into Devon.

"Are you all right?" He felt the affirmative motion of her head where it lay next to his on the pillow. His lips grazed her ear as he whispered, "You're still so small." He kissed her throat. "It's wonderful for me, but I know it can't be very comfortable for you."

He was already becoming aroused again, and there was nothing he could do about it except withdraw, and that was out of the question.

Readjusting their bodies slightly, he heard Devon whimper, but not with pain. With pleasure. He smiled into her neck.

"Did I hurt you that night in the motel?"

"No."

"I must have."

"Not much."

"I remember thinking that something wasn't right. Something was out of sync. But I was so sleepy and so caught up in you that I didn't stop to sort it out. I should have known. You were so tight. So sweet." Of its own accord, his body stirred inside her and her muscles contracted reflexively, leaving them both breathless for a moment.

Panting, Lucky continued, "I didn't remember it later. Not until today when—" He broke off, unwilling to let mention of Shelby spoil the most pleasure he'd ever had in bed. God, it just didn't get any better than this.

"Today, when I realized that you were a virgin that night and that I was the only man you'd ever been with, hell or high water couldn't have kept me away from you, Devon."

Then he groaned her name again and sank deeper into the snug, liquid heat of her body, and they both climaxed. Her throat arched beautifully, and her limbs enfolded him as she experienced her long, sweet release.

Moments later, lying face-to-face, he brushed away the damp strands of hair that clung to her flushed cheeks. Her eyes were limpid and dilated, as though she had been drugged.

"Lucky," she said in a soft, sad rasp, lightly touching his lips with her fingertips.

"That's me." He smiled crookedly.

Without returning his smile, she rolled to the opposite side of the bed and got up. He appreciatively watched as her graceful body moved from bed to closet and she wrapped a robe around her slim nakedness. He was charmed, especially when she used both hands to free her sex-tousled hair from her collar.

But when she turned to face him, his enchantment dissipated.

"What?" he asked with perplexity.

"You've got to go now."

He would have thought he hadn't heard her correctly if her face weren't so pale and blank of all expression. Throwing his legs over the side of the bed, he reached for his jeans, thrust his feet into them, and pulled them on as he stood up. Tamping down his frustration, and a twinge of fear, he approached her calmly.

"That's the craziest statement I've ever heard you say, Devon. What do you mean by it?"

"Just what I said. You'll have to go now. And this time our parting must be final. You can't come back."

"Does the expression 'fat chance' mean anything to you?"

"Don't get angry."

"I'm not angry. I'm incredulous."

"Let's not make this difficult."

He laughed hoarsely. "It started out with a fist-fight, Devon. It was difficult from the beginning, and got more so each time we saw each other. But dammit, we've just proved it's worth fighting for. Tell me you think so, too."

Gnawing her lower lip, she glanced away and began fiddling with the knotted belt of her robe. Her distress was plain. Lucky softened his tone. "Tell me what's wrong."

"I'm married."

"Not to him."

"To *him*," she said with emphasis. "Our names are on the marriage certificate. We signed it. In the eyes of the state—"

"What about the eyes of God? Who's more your husband? Him or me?"

"How dare you drag religion into this," she cried angrily. "Are you suggesting that since you've known me in a biblical sense, you have a greater claim on me than Greg?" She tossed back her hair. Her green eyes were stormy. "If you are spiritually married to every woman you've slept with, then you're a polygamist!"

The barb hit home, and Lucky knew it would be pointless to pursue that line of reasoning. It had been worth a try, however. This was one argument he had to win. He had to pull out all the stops.

"You don't love him," he stated flatly.

"No, I don't. But I'm still married to him."

"And why? Why did you ever marry him? He doesn't love you either."

"At the time it seemed right."

"I applaud your grand gesture, but, Devon, surely you don't plan to throw away your happiness and spend the rest of your life with a jerk like him?"

"I have to stay married to him at least until he gets out of prison."

"He used you."

"I know that."

"He's a felon."

"I know that, too."

"You know he's guilty?" he asked, his jaw dropping open.

She gave a terse bob of her head. "I lied to you before. I'm reasonably certain he did it. At first I believed he was innocent. Later, after he was incarcerated, I began to have my doubts."

"Why?"

"He refused to consummate our marriage. Oh, he told me it was for my benefit. That way, he said, if I wanted to get out of the marriage, I could more easily. I thought he was being self-sacrificing. He might still be."

Lucky was shaking his head. "He was thinking of himself. He wanted to be able to have the marriage annulled when you were no longer useful. I'll bet that even now, he's trying to figure a way to turn the scandal about us to his advantage."

She hung her head. "The afternoon I met you, I learned that he had been declining his conjugal visits, something that I hadn't even known was available until I heard another prisoner's wife talking about it. I confronted Greg. We had a big row. I couldn't understand why he would reject his marital rights."

"Unless he was guilty not only of the crime, but gross manipulation."

"Yes."

It was a tough admission for her to make, but it only frustrated Lucky further. He plowed his hand through his hair. "Why haven't you started divorce—or annulment—proceedings?"

"Because I had used Greg just as much as he had used me. I used his story to help promote my column. That's when the Devon Haines byline really began to mean something to the newspaper. So I, as much as Greg, profited from our marriage."

"Devon, you've got incredible talent. Your column would have succeeded anyway. Why are you staying married?"

"Because I take my responsibilities seriously. I can't just wash my hands of a marriage because it's no longer useful, because it's inconvenient."

He shot down that argument with a curt, "Bullshit. You just don't want to admit that you were duped."

"That's not true!"

He knew by her instantaneous and adamant rebuttal that his guess had been right. "You always have to be in control, calling the shots. It's impossible for you to admit that twice your heart has overruled your head. Greg's sob story got to you, and you can't live with that. Rather than admitting to a mistake in judgment, you'll stubbornly stay married to him just to prove you were right."

"As long as there's the slightest chance that he's innocent, I can't desert him while he's in prison."

Lucky's oaths were vicious. "You don't believe he's innocent any more than I do."

"You said my heart had overruled my head twice."

He glanced at the bed. "You've fought it every step of the way, but you love me and I damn well know it. We connected the first time we laid eyes on each other. What you can't own up to is that you're as vulnerable between the thighs—"

"I won't listen to your lewd—"

"You don't want to be a weak nonentity like your mother was, totally dependent on her husband for everything. Okay. Fine. Guess what, Devon? I don't want to wipe my feet on you. I don't want a silent, submissive partner, in or out of bed."

"I have a husband."

"He's not the issue. He never has been, or so I found out this morning. You're just using him as an escape hatch. This is between you and me."

He gripped her shoulders. "You want a career. Terrific. Have one. I'm all for it. But have me, too. We can have each other and make both our careers worthwhile.

"I want babies. The burden of that responsibility falls on you, I'm afraid. But if you consented to have my babies, I'd put you on a pedestal and make it the most wonderful experience of your life."

He lowered his voice to a compelling, tempting whisper. "I've felt your passion for me, Devon. I've tasted it. I know it's there. Put your arms around my neck. Tell me you need me. Admit you love me."

"Twice you've persuaded me to break my wedding vows. Isn't that enough for you?"

"I want us to exchange our own vows, vows our bodies have already made. Vows you haven't made with Greg or any other man."

"I can't see you again, Lucky."

"Say you love me."

"I can't."

"It's because of the way your mother died, isn't it?" he demanded. Devon fell back a step. "What?"

"You turned a deaf ear to her and she died. You take responsibility for her death."

"Yes!" she cried. "Wouldn't you?"

"Was she incapacitated? Bedridden? Homebound? Unable to drive?"

"What are you getting at?"

"Could she have gone to the doctor alone, Devon?" She hedged, and he knew he was on to something. "She laid that guilt on you because her life had been miserable, and in a warped way she wanted yours to be. She probably wanted to die, and going about it as painfully as possible was her way of guaranteeing your attention for the rest of your life. And in the same damn way, you've shackled yourself to Shelby."

"He might be innocent."

"He isn't."

"But if he is—"

"You will have done all you could do to save him from imprisonment." He clamped down on her shoulders. "Devon, you can't take on responsibility for the whole world. No one's asked you to. You can't sacrifice your present happiness because of what happened in the past or what might happen in the future. Let it go. Let them go. Focus on someone who needs you here and now."

He had never begged a woman for anything. It was difficult for him to do so now. It went against his nature as diametrically as snow in the jungle. But, as he had realized, this was one argument he couldn't lose. His life depended on it.

"Don't throw away the best damn thing that has ever happened to either of us. Not for the sake of pride or principle or anything else. Don't. I'm begging you, Devon, please don't." He bracketed her jaw with his hands and tilted her head back. Enunciating each word, he said, "Tell me you love me."

She stared him down, her features tortured and emotional. Slowly her head began moving from side to side, as far each way as his hands would allow. Then, voice tearing, she said, "I can't. Please don't ask me to again."

Chapter Twenty

Lucky's black mood didn't improve when he got caught in a traffic jam as he approached the outskirts of Milton Point. He cursed the summer heat, the gloriously setting sun, cruel fate. After sitting broiling in his open convertible for several minutes, he got out and flagged down a cattle truck that was driving past in the opposite lane.

"What's caused this snafu?"

"Helluva wreck ahead of you," the teamster shouted down from the cab of his rig. "Two cars. Ambulances. Highway patrol and local cops. The whole shooting match. You might be here for a while, buddy."

"Not likely," Lucky muttered as he climbed back into his Mustang. He was going to the place, where he would drown out all thoughts and memories of Devon Haines and her senseless, stupid stubbornness if it took ten gallons of Jack Daniel's to do it.

He was eventually able to maneuver the Mustang out of the lane and onto the shoulder of the highway. To the fury of other stranded drivers, he breezed along the outside lane, slowing up only when he came even with the site of the wreck and the emergency vehicles.

He was hoping to crawl past without attracting attention, but his legendary luck had deserted him. One of the officers flagged him down and approached his car. Lucky recognized him as a local sheriff's deputy.

"Damn."

"Hey, Lucky, I thought that was you," the deputy called when he was still some distance away. "Stay put," he ordered.

"But—"

"Wait right there." The officer turned and jogged toward a cluster of other officials.

Lucky blew out a gust of breath. Why the hell was he being detained? He had just about decided to disobey the deputy's order when he noticed Pat Bush detaching himself from the huddled group of officers.

"Pat," he called, "get me out of this—"

"Lucky."

Pat's somber expression and hushed tone of voice were out of character under the circumstances. Pat usually commandeered this kind of situation with professional detachment. Lucky's impatience switched to curiosity. "What's going on?"

"Pull your car over there. I need to talk to you."

"What's the matter?" Lucky put on his emergency brake and alighted. Something was very wrong here. Pat was having a hard time looking him in the eye, and Lucky couldn't account for his strange behavior. He was off the hook as far as the arson charge went.

Alarmed, he glanced beyond Pat, toward the tangled wreckage, and slumped with relief because he didn't recognize either car involved in the accident. "Good God, Pat. You had me thinking that one of—"

Pat laid a hand, a consoling hand, on his arm. He and Pat exchanged a meaningful glance. Then Lucky shook off Pat's hand and broke into a run.

"Lucky!" Pat grabbed hold of his shirt.

"Who is it?"

"It's Tanya."

Lucky's chest caved in painfully, his ribs seeming to crack under the pressure of his disbelief. "Tanya?" he croaked. "She's hurt?"

Pat lowered his eyes.

"No," Lucky said in swift denial. What Pat's silent gesture indicated was unthinkable. He ran toward the ambulances, elbowing aside anybody who dared to block his path.

Parting the crowd, he saw that an injured woman was being worked over by paramedics. When he heard her groans, he felt a burst of relief. But as he drew nearer, he saw that her hair color was wrong.

Frantically scanning the area, he spotted another collapsible gurney. It was being lifted into the ambulance. A black zippered bag had been strapped to it. He lunged forward.

Pat stepped into his path and struggled to stop him. "Let go of me!" he shouted.

"It won't do any good to see her now, Lucky."

"Get out of my way!" Bellowing like an enraged bull, he overpowered the older man, shoved him aside, and charged for the back of the ambulance.

The startled paramedics put up token protests as he pushed them aside, but the ferocity of his expression was intimidating, and they fell back. Lucky reached forward and unzipped the black plastic bag.

After one long, disbelieving gaze, Lucky squeezed his eyes shut and spun around. Pat signaled for the paramedics to finish their business. Lucky didn't even respond when the ambulance doors were slammed shut and the vehicle drove off.

"You okay?"

Lucky looked at Pat, but he didn't really see anything except his sister-in-law's still white face. "It's not possible."

Pat nodded his head, as though agreeing. "I was just getting ready to notify Chase of the accident and tell him to meet the ambulance at the hospital."

Lucky's chest heaved. He felt as if a white-hot spike had been driven through his heart. He thought he might vomit. "No. This is a family affair. I'll go. And nobody else tells my mother or sister either, got that?"

"Lucky, this isn't the time to—"

"Got that?"

Pat backed down. "All right. If that's the way you want it."

"That's the way I want it."

"As soon as this is cleared up, I'll come out to the house."

Lucky didn't hear him. He was already headed for his car. It was only a short distance from the accident site to the office of Tyler Drilling. On the one hand, it seemed the longest drive he'd ever made. On the other, he was there far too soon, before he had found the words he must say.

Chase's car was parked out front. Lucky pushed open the door of his Mustang. It felt as though it weighed a ton. On his way into the office he met Chase coming out.

"Hey, where've you been all day? Mother said you struck out first thing this morning and hadn't been seen since." He was obviously in a hurry, and didn't give Lucky time to answer.

"George Young called and wants to know when we plan to make that note payment. That s.o.b. is still putting pressure on us, fire or no fire. I heard from somebody at the courthouse that Little Alvin and Jack Ed both pleaded guilty to arson today and will be sentenced sometime next week. I also met with the guy from the insurance company for two and a half hours. Thank God we kept up those premiums. I'll tell you all about that later. Right now I'm late. I'm supposed to meet Tanya at—"

"Chase, wait a minute." He laid his hand on his brother's shoulder, stopping him halfway down the steps. His lips began to tremble, and Chase's image blurred because of his tears. Lucky's voice faltered. He unsuccessfully cleared his throat. "Chase—"

God, how did one tell a man that the woman he loved and the child she carried were dead?

The following morning Marcie Johns was moved out of intensive care and into a regular room at St. Luke's Methodist Hospital. She had suffered a concussion, a broken arm and collarbone, and trauma, but none of her injuries had been critical.

She was considered fortunate, since the driver of the other vehicle involved in the accident, a Texas Tech student home for the summer, and Marcie's passenger, Tanya Tyler, had been fatalities. The student had run a stop sign and hit Marcie's car broadside. Most considered it a blessing that he and Tanya had died instantly upon impact.

Lucky had wanted to hit anybody he overheard saying such a thing, and was only glad that, so far, nobody had said it to Chase.

His brother wasn't himself. He was acting like a crazy man. A little unreasonableness was justified, but when he had announced that he was going to the hospital to speak with Marcie, the other members of his family had been shocked and had pleaded with him to reconsider. No amount of persuasion could change his mind, however, so Laurie had instructed Lucky to go with his brother and "take care of him."

Together they walked down the corridor of the hospital toward the room assigned to Ms. Johns. "Why are you so bent on seeing her?" Lucky asked quietly, hoping that even now Chase would change his mind. "If anybody catches us with her, they'll throw us out of here. She's still in serious condition, and not supposed to have visitors."

Chase was walking with the determined tread of a prophet on a mission. He pushed open the door and entered the shadowed room. Lucky, after a quick glance over his shoulder, went in behind him. He vaguely remembered Marcie Johns from high school, and knew her now only by sight. She was an attractive woman, but one couldn't tell by looking at her now.

In spite of the fact that she had been wearing her seat belt, she'd been thrown against the windshield with enough force to bruise and abrade her face. Both eyes were ringed with bruises. Her nose and lips were grotesquely swollen. On her shoulder was a cast designed to keep her broken arm elevated.

Lucky was moved to pity. "Chase, for godsake, let's get out of here. We shouldn't bother her."

He had spoken so softly that the words were barely audible, but she heard them and opened her eyes. When she saw Chase, she moaned and made a move as though she wanted to reach out to him.

"Chase, I'm sorry," she wheezed. "So sorry."

Apparently she had been advised that her passenger hadn't survived. She would have had to know sooner or later, of course, but it seemed to Lucky that later would have been preferable. The additional mental anguish couldn't be good for her body's healing process.

"We . . . we never even saw him." Her voice was thin and faint. "It was just . . . a racket . . . and . . ."

Chase lowered himself into the chair beside her bed. His features were distorted by grief. Lines seemed to have been carved into his face overnight. The area beneath his eyes was almost as dark as Marcie's. His dark hair was a mess. He hadn't shaved.

"I want to know about . . . Tanya," he said, his voice tearing on her name. "What kind of mood was she in? What was she saying? What were her last words?"

Lucky groaned, "Chase, don't do this to yourself."

Chase irritably threw off the hand Lucky placed on his shoulder. "Tell me, Marcie, what was she doing, saying, when . . . when that bastard killed her?"

Lucky lowered his forehead into one of his hands and massaged his temples with his thumb and middle finger. His insides were twisted. He couldn't even imagine the hell Chase was going through.

Or maybe he could. What if Devon had been killed yesterday? What if, after he had angrily left her, she had gone out and needlessly been killed by a driver running a stop sign? Wouldn't he be acting just as unbalanced as Chase? Wouldn't he be damning himself for not telling her one more time that he loved her no matter what?

"Tanya was laughing," Marcie whispered. Pain medication had made her speech slow and slurred. Chase clung to every careful word she was able to speak. "We were talking about the house. She . . . she was so excited about . . . about it."

"I'm going to buy that house." Chase glanced up at Lucky, his eyes wild and unfocused. "Buy that house for me. She wanted the house, so she's going to get it."

"Chase—"

"Buy the damn house!" he roared. "Will you just do that much for me, please, without giving me an argument?"

"Okay." Now wasn't the time to cross him, although his brother's request made no sense at all. But was a man who had just lost his family required to be sensible? Hell no.

"Right before we went . . . through the intersection, she asked me what color I thought . . ." Marcie paused, grimacing with discomfort. ". . . what color she should paint the bedroom for the baby."

Chase's head dropped forward into his hands. "Jesus." Tears leaked through his fingers and ran down the backs of his hands.

"Chase," she whispered, "do you blame me?"

Keeping his hands over his eyes, he shook his head. "No, Marcie, no. I blame God. He killed her. He killed my baby. Why? *Why?* I loved her so much. I loved . . ." His voice broke into sobs.

Lucky moved toward him and again laid a comforting hand on his shaking shoulders. Tears marred his own vision. For a long while they were quiet. He realized a few minutes later that Marcie had mercifully lapsed into unconsciousness again.

"Chase, we'd better go now."

At first Chase seemed not to have heard, but he gradually dragged his hands down his wet, ravaged face and stood up. "Order some flowers for Marcie," he told Lucky as they left the room.

"Sure. What do you want me to put on the card? Do you want them to be exclusively from you or from all of—" He came to a dead standstill when he spotted Devon standing at the end of the hospital corridor.

Chase followed his brother's dumbfounded stare. Devon came forward to meet them. Her eyes moved from Lucky to Chase. "Sage called me early this morning," she told him, surprising Lucky. He hadn't known his sister had phoned Devon. "I got here as soon as I could. I can't believe it, Chase." Extending her hand, she took Chase's, pressing it firmly.

"Tanya liked you. She admired you."

Devon's smile was sweet and tearful. "I liked her, too. Very much."

"So did I." Chase didn't apologize for the gruffness of his voice or the tears he continued to shed openly. Indeed, he seemed unaware of them. He addressed the two of them. "I'm going to the apartment now."

"Mother is expecting you back at the house."

"I need to be by myself for a while, among Tanya's things. Tell Mother I'll come out later."

Lucky wasn't so sure that Chase should be alone, but figured he would have to wrestle him to change his mind. He watched him approach the elevator. Moving like an automaton, he punched the button. The doors opened instantly; he stepped into the cubicle. The doors slid closed.

"He looks completely shattered, Lucky. Will he be all right?"

Lucky glanced at Devon, who had been standing quietly at his side. "I doubt it. But there's not a damn thing I can do about it."

"Nothing you're not already doing. I'm sure it's a comfort to him just knowing that he's got your support."

"Maybe. I hope so. He needs to find comfort where he can."

Hungry for the sight of her, he unapologetically stared. Her hair looked a darker, deeper shade of auburn against her black dress and pale face. In the cold glare of fluorescent lighting, her eyes appeared exceptionally green. They were bright with tears.

"It was good of you to come, Devon," he said thickly.

"I wanted to."

"How did you know where to find us?"

"I went to the house first. Sage said that I had just missed you, and that you and Chase were on your way here."

He nodded toward the bank of elevators. "Since Chase took the car, can I bum a ride home?"

"Of course."

They boarded the next available elevator and rode it down in silence. Lucky couldn't take his eyes off her. It seemed like a million years since he'd held her, made fervent love to her, yet it had been only yesterday.

Yesterday. Twenty-four hours. In that amount of time lives had been irrevocably altered, dreams shattered, loves lost. Life was tenuous.

He came to a sudden stop on the plant-lined path that wound through a courtyard connecting the hospital complex with the parking lot.

"Devon." He took her shoulders between his hands and turned her to face him. "I'm going to fight whatever or whoever I must to be with you for the rest of my life, even if it means fighting you first. Life's too damn short and too precious to waste a single day on misery and unhappiness.

"Listen to me. I love you," he vowed, his hands tensing, gripping her tighter. To his consternation, his surging emotions manifested themselves in tears again. Grief over losing Tanya, pain for his brother's suffering, sadness over the Tyler heir who would never know life, love for Devon, all overwhelmed him. He couldn't breathe for the tightness surrounding his swelling heart.

She sighed when she saw his distress, then placed her arms around his waist and laid her head on his chest. "I need you," she whispered earnestly. "I love you."

They came together in a fierce embrace. And after they kissed, they wept.

Epilogue

Lucky entered the house by the front door. "Hello? Anybody home?" He received no answer. His mother was out. Sage was only home on holidays and an occasional weekend, since she was now in Austin at the university. But Devon's red compact was in the driveway, so she should be at home.

Then he heard the familiar click-clack of her word-processor keyboard. Smiling, he following the sound past the stairway to the rear of the house. Laurie's sewing room had been converted into an office for Devon. The conversion had taken place while Lucky and she were away on their honeymoon; Laurie had surprised them with it upon their return.

"I can't sew much anymore because of my arthritis," Laurie had told Devon when she protested the generosity. "The space was being wasted."

Over the last several months Devon had made it her room, filling it with periodicals and books, both fiction and nonfiction, which she used for reference material or pure reading pleasure. Sage's contribution had been a wall calendar featuring a semi-nude hunk-a-month. When Lucky had threatened to take down "the perverted eyesore," Devon had launched into a tirade decrying the double standard, and Sage had threatened to cut off his hand if he tried.

The tragedy of Tanya's death, and Sage's impending move to Austin, had precluded Lucky from even suggesting that Devon and he make their home elsewhere. Following their quiet, private wedding, they moved into the large house with Laurie. Lucky was pleased with the arrangement and, apparently, so was Devon.

The three women in his life got along very well. Devon loved having a younger sister, and Laurie showered on Devon the warmth and affection that her inattentive mother never had.

Lucky knocked on the door to the office, but when he got no answer, he pushed the door open anyway. As he had suspected, she was engrossed in the green letters she was typing onto the black terminal monitor.

Headphones bridged her head, blasting her eardrums with music. Her taste was eclectic; she liked everything from Mozart to Madonna. He thought it was nutty, using music to drown out distracting noise, but that was just one of his wife's idiosyncracies that intrigued him. Her contradictions had attracted him from the beginning.

He waved his hand, so his sudden appearance wouldn't startle her. When she noticed him in her peripheral vision, she turned her head, smiled, and removed the earphones.

"Hi. How long have you been standing there?"

He crossed to her and dropped a kiss on her forehead. "Almost long enough for the rose to wilt." From behind his back he withdrew a single yellow rose. Her eyes lighted up with pleasure as she accepted it and rolled the soft, cool petals over her lips.

"You remembered."

"Six months ago today you became Mrs. Lucky Tyler."

"Only twelve hours after I ceased being Mrs. Greg Shelby."

"Shh! Mother frowns on foul language being spoken in this house."

Lucky didn't have any charitable thoughts toward Devon's first husband. True to his word, the day he learned that Greg Shelby was out on parole, he had driven to Dallas and, following a hunch, located him at Dallas/Fort Worth Airport, covertly about to board an international flight. Lucky engaged him in a fistfight. He had even maneuvered it so that Greg threw the first punch. He hadn't inflicted nearly as much physical damage as he could have or wanted to, but the ruckus had alerted airport security. When they were told Shelby was a parolee about to leave the country, the police were notified, thwarting Greg's plans to retire to Switzerland with the illegally obtained fortune he had banked there.

In the resultant confusion Lucky managed to slip away unidentified. He never told anybody that he'd been instrumental in Greg's second arrest, not even Devon, though he would have liked for her to know he had avenged her. He had to be content with the personal satisfaction he'd derived from drawing Shelby's blood.

Now he pulled Devon from her chair, sat down in it himself, then drew her onto his lap. She asked, "Do you think I'm a brazen hussy for getting a quickie annulment one day and marrying another man the next?"

"Shameful," he growled into her neck.

"Stop that. I'm officially still working."

"What's this column about?" He had encouraged her to continue writing for the newspaper, so she had made arrangements with her editor to work outside the office and mail her columns in on a weekly basis. Lucky squinted into the screen, but the green symbols always looked like Greek to him.

"Bereavement."

Her softly spoken answer brought his eyes back to her. "Well, you've certainly got firsthand experience to base your theories on, don't you?"

"Did you see him today?"

Lucky nodded. They were all preoccupied with Chase and his steady emotional decline since Tanya's death. "He put in an appearance at the office this morning."

"And?"

"He was drunk again."

"Eight months, and he hasn't even made a start at healing," Devon remarked sadly as she studied the petals of her rose. "Do you think he'll ever get over it?"

"No," Lucky said candidly. "I think the best we can hope for is that he can learn to cope with his grief and lead a productive life again."

Her sad expression reflected the regard she had come to have for her brother-in-law. Lucky loved that about her, too. She had absorbed all the concerns of his family. Their sorrows and joys had become her own. She took them to heart. Family life, with all its blessings and drawbacks, was new to her, but she had blossomed within that environment.

Often she cried with Laurie over the loss of her first grandchild. Sage confided secrets to Devon that she kept from the rest of the family.

Devon celebrated with him the day he temporarily staved off the bank by scraping together a loan payment and lent moral support because business was still dismal despite the replacement of the equipment they had lost in the fire. Tyler Drilling Company hadn't had any new contracts since the one in Louisiana.

Chase was useless, immobilized by his grief. Lucky had been left with the responsibility of trying to save a sinking ship. Devon's faith that he could do it boosted his confidence when it flagged.

"It's awful for him to be so unhappy, to waste his life like this," she murmured now. "Awful."

"He's never even been inside that house he had me buy for him. It just stands there empty. He wallows in filth and misery in that apartment he shared with Tanya."

"What can we do to help him?"

"I wish to hell I knew. Criticism and lectures only make him nasty and defensive. Sympathy makes him furious. And he's going to get killed riding those damn bulls. He's too old to rodeo."

"Maybe that's what he wants," Devon said sorrowfully. "To die. Bull riding is just a chancy form of suicide."

"God." Lucky wrapped his arms around her waist and nuzzled her breasts. "I can understand how devastating it must be for him. If I ever lost you—"

"But you won't."

"I lost you after our first night together. I nearly went berserk until I found you again. And that was only for a week."

She leaned back and gave him a quizzical look. "You nearly went berserk? You never told me that."

In spite of his brother's bereavement and the sorry state of their business, Lucky was still a newlywed, and frequently behaved like a groom. That included teasing his bride.

"There's a lot I haven't told you," he drawled.

"Oh yeah?"

"Yeah."

"Like what?" she asked.

"Like how damn sexy you look when you're wearing your glasses."

She crossed her eyes behind the lenses. " 'Boys don't make passes at girls who wear glasses.' "

"I make passes at all the girls."

"So I've heard."

He drew her closer and kissed her with increasing fervency, parting her pliant lips with his tongue. The buttons on her blouse were no match for his nimble fingers. As her breasts filled his gently reshaping hands, she reached between his thighs and caressed him. Freeing him from his jeans, she put the petals of the rose to prurient use.

"Thank you for my flower," she purred as she delicately twirled the stem.

"I taught you too well," he hissed, sucking in a quick breath at the tickling sensation.

"Meaning?"

"Meaning, I don't think we're going to make it upstairs to the bedroom this time."

Leaving his lap, she lay down on the rug and pulled him down on top of her. Moments later they lay panting together amid hopelessly wrinkled clothing, crushed rose petals, and dewy, naked limbs.

Propping himself up on his elbows, he smiled down at her. "Beats writing all to hell, doesn't it?"

Devon took one of his hands, kissed the palm, and laid it against her throbbing left breast. "Feel that? I love you with every beat of my heart, and I don't know what I would do without you in my life."

He gazed down into her eyes, seeing in their green depths the love that mirrored his own. She was intelligent, sensitive, loving, gorgeous, sexy, and hotter than a firecracker in bed. And she freely and generously shared herself with him.

"Damn," he said, sighing with contentment, "no wonder they call me Lucky."

TEXAS!
CHASE

Prologue

"Chase, please, let's get out of here. We shouldn't bother her."

The hushed words had to penetrate pain and narcotics to reach her. Somehow they did. Marcie Johns prized open her swollen eyes. The hospital room was dim, but the scant daylight leaking through the drawn blinds seemed painfully brilliant. It took a moment for her eyes to adjust.

Chase Tyler was standing at the side of her bed. With him was his younger brother, Lucky, whom she recognized though they'd never met. Chase was staring down at her with unstinting intensity. Lucky seemed apprehensive.

Though she couldn't be specific about the time of day, she believed it to be the morning following the fatal auto accident. Earlier, the efficient hospital staff had moved her from an intensive care unit into this standard room at St. Luke's Methodist Hospital.

She had been examined by a team of doctors, each of whom specialized in a different field, and had been informed that her injuries were serious but not critical. She had suffered a concussion, a broken arm and collarbone, and shock.

She was grateful to be alive and relieved that her prognosis for a full recovery was positive. But no one had mentioned Tanya. From the moment she regained consciousness in the intensive care unit, she had frantically asked questions about Tanya. At last they told her: Tanya Tyler had died upon impact in the crash. A Texas Tech student, home for summer vacation, had run a stop sign and hit the car broadside.

Marcie had been wearing her seat belt. Even so, she'd been hurled to the side and momentum had brought her up and forward. Her head had crashed into the windshield. Her face was bruised and abraded. Both eyes had been badly bruised. Her nose and lips were battered and swollen. Her shoulder was in a cast designed to keep her broken arm elevated. The impact that had done so much damage to her had instantly killed Chase's wife.

In less than twenty-four hours, Chase had undergone a physical change as drastic in appearance as Marcie's injuries. His handsome features were now ravaged by grief. He was disheveled, unshaven, bleary-eyed. If she hadn't known him for most of her life, if his face hadn't always been dear to her, Marcie might not have recognized him.

She had been retained as the Tylers' real estate agent, but had been working strictly with Tanya. They had looked at several properties over the course of a few weeks, but Marcie's enthusiasm for one particular house had been contagious. Tanya had fallen in love with it and was eager to see if Chase's opinion would match hers.

Chase Tyler and Marcie Johns had gone through thirteen grades of public schooling together, but hadn't seen each other for years, until yesterday when she and Tanya had unexpectedly called on him at the office of Tyler Drilling Company.

"Goosey!" He had stood and rounded his desk to greet her with a handshake, then a quick, hard hug.

"Hi, Chase," she had said, laughing at the ancient nickname. "It's good to see you."

"Why haven't you been to any of our class reunions?" His smile made her believe him when he added, "You look fantastic."

"I can't believe you're calling her by that horrid name," Tanya had exclaimed.

"You didn't take any offense, did you?" Chase asked.

"Of course not. If I could bear it as a sensitive, self-conscious adolescent, I can bear it as a mature adult. As for the class reunions, I lived in Houston for several years, but it was never convenient for me to make one."

He gave her an approving once-over. "You're really looking terrific, Marcie. The years have been more than kind. They've been generous. I hear your business is going great guns, too."

"Thank you, and yes, I've enjoyed being in business for myself. The economy has slowed things down the past year or two, but I'm hanging in there."

"Wish I could say the same," Chase had remarked good-naturedly.

"Oh, but I understand you've got something *very* special to celebrate."

"I told her about the baby," Tanya informed him. "And she's convinced me that even though our budget is tight, we can afford a house, and that now is an excellent time to buy. It's a buyer's market," she had told him, repeating what Marcie had told her earlier.

"Should I be reaching for my checkbook?" he had asked teasingly.

"Not yet. Marcie and I want you to come see the house she showed me yesterday. I think it's perfect. Will you come?"

"What, now?"

"Please."

"Sorry, sweetheart, but I can't," Chase had said.

Tanya's animated face became crestfallen.

"If it were any other time, I would, but I'm expecting a rep from the insurance company. He was supposed to be here right after lunch, but called to say he was running late. I need to be here when he arrives."

Marcie remembered saying, "I read in the morning papers that your brother has been cleared of those ridiculous arson charges."

"Is there another problem, Chase?"

"No," he had said, reassuringly pressing Tanya's hand between his. "We just need to go over the inventory of all the equipment we lost and discuss our claim."

She sighed with disappointment. "Well, maybe tomorrow."

"Or even later today," he had offered. "Why don't you go look at the house again, and if you're still excited about it, call me. Maybe I can meet you there after he leaves. That is, if you're free, Marcie."

"I blocked out the entire afternoon for Tanya and you."

Tanya, smiling again, had thrown her arms around Chase's neck and kissed him soundly on the mouth. "I love you. And you're going to love this house."

With his arms around her waist, he had hugged her tight. "I probably will, but not as much as I love you. Call me later."

Following them to the doorway, he had waved them off.

That was the last time Tanya and Chase had seen each other, touched, kissed. Marcie and Tanya had gone without him and had spent another hour touring the vacant house.

"Chase is going to love this," Tanya had said as they walked through yet another spacious room. Her excitement had been as keen as that of a child with a secret. Her smile had been so sweet. Her eyes had sparkled with exuberance over life in general.

Now she was dead.

At the sight of her grieving widower, Marcie's sore chest muscles contracted around her heart. "Chase, I'm sorry," she wheezed. "So sorry."

She wanted to reach out and touch him, and she tried to before realizing that her arm and collarbone were unmovable in their cast. Had he come to rebuke her for being a reckless driver? Did he blame the accident on her? *Was* she to blame?

"We . . . we never even saw him." Her voice was thin and faint and unfamiliar to her own ears. "It was just . . . a racket and . . ."

Chase lowered himself into the chair beside her bed. He barely resembled the man he'd been the day before. Always tall, with a commanding presence, he was now stooped. Lines seemed to have been carved into his face overnight. His gray eyes, characteristically intense, were bloodshot. Not only did they look bereaved, there was no life behind them. They reflected no light, as though he were dead too.

"I want to know about Tanya." His voice cracked when he spoke her name. He roughly cleared his throat. "What kind of mood was she in? What was she saying? What were her last words?"

Lucky groaned. "Chase, don't do this to yourself."

Chase irritably threw off the hand Lucky placed on his shoulder. "Tell me, Marcie, what was she doing, saying, when . . . when that bastard killed her?"

Lucky lowered his forehead into one of his hands and massaged his temples with his thumb and middle finger. He was obviously as upset as his brother. The Tylers were a close family, never failing to bolster, defend, and protect each other. Marcie understood the concern they must feel for Chase. But she could also empathize with Chase's need to know about the final moments of his young wife's life.

"Tanya was laughing," Marcie whispered.

Pain medication had slowed and slurred her speech. Her brain had trouble conveying the correct words to her tongue, which felt thick and too large for her mouth. It was a struggle to get the words out, but she tried very hard to make herself understood because she knew Chase would cling to every careful word she managed to speak.

"We were talking about the house. She . . . she was so excited about . . . about it."

"I'm going to buy that house." Chase glanced up at Lucky, his eyes wild and unfocused. "Buy that house for me. She wanted the house, so she's going to have it."

"Chase—"

"Buy the damn house!" he roared. "Will you just do that much for me, please, without giving me an argument?"

"Okay."

His wild and loud outburst was jarring to Marcie's traumatized system. She recoiled from this, another assault, to her injured body. Yet she readily forgave him. In his own way he had been just as traumatized as she by the accident.

To anyone who had seen Chase and Tanya together, it was instantly apparent that they had shared a special love. Tanya had adored him, and he had cherished Tanya, who had been pregnant with their first child. The accident had robbed him of two loved ones.

"Right before we went . . . through the intersection, she asked me what color I thought . . ." A shooting pain went through her arm, causing her to grimace. She badly wanted to close her eyes, surrender to the anesthetizing drugs being dripped into her vein, and blot out consciousness and the anguish that accompanied it.

More than that, however, she wanted to help alleviate Chase's pain. If talking about Tanya would ease his pain, then that was the least she could do. She would continue talking for as long as she could hold out against her own discomfort and the allure of unconsciousness.

"She asked me . . . what color she should paint the bedroom . . . for the baby."

Chase covered his face with his hands. "Jesus." Tears leaked through his fingers and ran down the backs of his hands. This tangible evidence of his grief caused Marcie more agony than the brutal car crash.

"Chase," she whispered raggedly, "do you blame me?"

Keeping his hands over his eyes, he shook his head. "No, Marcie, no. I blame God. He killed her. He killed my baby. Why? *Why?* I loved her so much. I loved—" He broke into sobs.

Lucky moved toward him and again laid a consoling hand on his brother's shaking shoulders. Marcie detected tears in the younger man's eyes also. He seemed to be battling his own heartache. Recently Lucky had made news by being charged with setting fire to a garage at Tyler Drilling. The charges had been dropped and the real culprits were now in custody, but apparently the ordeal had taken its toll on him.

She searched for something more to say, but words of comfort were elusive and abstract. Her befuddled mind couldn't grasp them. It didn't really matter. Anything she said would sound banal.

God, how can I help him?

She was an overachiever to whom helplessness was anathema. Her inability to help him filled her with desperation. She stared at the crown of his bowed head, wanting to touch it, wanting to hold him and absorb his agony into herself.

Just before lapsing into blessed unconsciousness, she vowed that somehow, someday, some way, she would give life back to Chase Tyler.

Chapter One

"We've got a bunch of mean bulls tonight, ladies and gentlemen, but we've also got some cowboys who're rough and ready to ride 'em." The announcer's twangy voice reverberated through the cavernous arena of the Will Roger's Coliseum in Fort Worth, Texas.

"Eight seconds. That's how long a cowboy has to sit on top of that bull. Doesn't sound like much, but it's the longest eight seconds you can imagine. There's not a cowboy here who wouldn't agree to that. Yessiree. In the world of rodeo, this is the most demandin', most dangerous, most excitin' event. That's why we save it till last."

Marcie looked toward her two guests, pleased to see that they were enjoying themselves. Bringing them to the rodeo had been a good idea. What better way to introduce them into pure, undiluted Texana? It was like a baptism of fire.

The announcer said, "Our first bull rider tonight comes from Park City, Utah, and when he's not bull riding, Larry Shafer likes to snow ski. Here's a real thrill-seekin' young man, ladies and gentlemen, coming out of chute number three on Cyclone Charlie! Ride 'im, Larry!"

The couple from Massachusetts watched breathlessly as the Brahman bull charged out of the chute with the cowboy perched precariously atop his bucking back. Within a few seconds, the cowboy/skier from Utah was scrambling in the dirt to avoid the bull's pounding hooves. As soon as he'd gained his footing he ran for the fence, scaled it, and left it up to the two rodeo clowns to distract the bull until it ran through the open gate and out of the arena.

"I never saw anything like that," the woman said, aghast.

"Do these young men train to do this?" her husband wanted to know.

Marcie had only recently become interested in bull riding and her knowledge was still sketchy. "Yes, they do. There's a lot of skill involved, but a lot of chance too."

"Like what?"

"Like which bull a cowboy draws on a particular night."

"Some are more contrary than others?"

Marcie smiled. "All are bred to be rodeo animals, but each has his mood swings and personality traits."

Their attention was drawn to another chute where the bull had already lost patience and was bucking so violently the cowboy was having a difficult time mounting. The woman from Massachusetts fanned her face nervously. Her husband sat enthralled.

"Ladies and gentlemen, it looks like our next cowboy is going to have a time of it tonight," the announcer said. "Anybody here want to take his place?" After a pause he chuckled. "Now, don't all of y'all volunteer at once.

"But this cowboy isn't afraid of a tough bull. In fact, the rougher the ride, the better he seems to like it. He rodeoed for years before retiring from it. Took it up again about a year and a half ago, not the least bit intimidated that he's a decade older than most cowboys who ride bulls.

"He hails from East Texas. Anybody here from over Milton Point way? If so, put your hands together for this young man from your hometown, Chase Tyler, as he comes out of chute number seven on Ellll Do-ra-*do!*"

"Oh, my God!" Unaware of what she was doing, Marcie surged to her feet.

The announcer raised his voice to an eardrum-blasting volume as the gate swung open and the mottled, gray bull charged out, swinging his hindquarters to and fro and, moving in opposition, thrashing his head from side to side.

Marcie watched the cowboy hat sail off Chase's head and land in the dirt beneath the bull's pulverizing hooves. He kept his free left arm high, as required by the rules of the sport. It flopped uncontrollably as the bull bucked. His entire body was tossed high, then landed hard as it came back down onto the bull's back. He kept both knees raised and back, held at right angles to either side of the bull, rocking back and forth, up and down, on his tailbone.

The crowd was wildly cheering, encouraging Chase to hang on. He managed to maintain his seat for about five seconds, though it had seemed like five years to Marcie. Before the horn sounded, the beast ducked his head so far down it almost touched the ground, then flung it up again. The movement had so much raw power behind it, Chase was thrown off.

He dodged the stamping hooves by rolling to one side. A clown, wearing baggy pants held up by suspenders, moved in and batted the bull on the snout with a rubber baseball bat. The bull snorted, stamped, and the clown scampered away, turning to thumb his nose at the animal.

It looked as though it were all in fun and the crowd laughed. The seriousness of the clown's job became instantly apparent, however, when the tactic failed to work.

The bull swung around, slinging great globs of foamy slobber from either side of its mouth, its nostrils flared. Chase, his back to the bull, picked up his hat from the dirt and slapped it against his chaps. A warning was shouted, but not in time. The bull charged him, head lowered, over a ton in impetus behind the attack.

Chase sidestepped quickly enough to keep from being gored by a pair of vicious-looking horns, but the side of the bull's head caught him in the shoulder and he was knocked down. Everyone in the audience gasped when the pair of front hooves landed square on Chase's chest.

Marcie screamed, then covered her mouth with her hands. She watched in horror as Chase lay sprawled in the reddish-brown dirt, obviously unconscious.

Again the clowns moved in, as well as two spotters on horseback. They galloped toward the bull. Each was standing in his stirrups, leaning far over his saddle horn, swinging a lasso. One was successful in getting the noose over the bull's horns and pulling the rope taut. His well-trained mount galloped through the gate, dragging the reluctant bull behind him while one brave clown swatted his rump with a broom. The second clown was kneeling in the dirt beside the injured cowboy.

Marcie scrambled over several pairs of legs and feet in her haste to reach the nearest aisle. Rudely she shoved past anyone who got in her way as she ran down the ramp. When she reached the lower level, she grabbed the arm of the first man she saw.

"Hey, what the—"

"Which way to the . . . the place where the people come out?"

"Say, lady, are you drunk? Let go of my arm."

"The barns. The place where the performers come from. Where the bulls go when they're finished."

"That way." He pointed, then muttered, "Crazy broad."

She plowed her way through the milling crowd buying souvenirs and concessions. Over the public address system she heard the announcer say, "We'll let y'all know Chase Tyler's condition as soon as we hear something, folks."

Disregarding the AUTHORIZED PERSONNEL ONLY sign on a wide, metal, industrial-size door, she barged through it. The scent of hay and manure was strong as she moved down a row of cattle pens. Breathing heavily through her mouth, she almost choked on the dust, but spotting the rotating lights of an ambulance across the barn, she ran even faster through the maze of stalls.

Reaching the central aisle, she elbowed her way through the curious onlookers until she pushed her way free and saw Chase lying unconscious on a stretcher. Two paramedics were working over him. One was slipping a needle into the vein in the crook of his elbow. Chase's face was still and white.

"No!" She dropped to her knees beside the stretcher and reached for his limp hand. "Chase? Chase!"

"Get back, lady!" one of the paramedics ordered.

"But—"

"He'll be fine if you'll get out of our way."

Her arms were grabbed from behind and she was pulled to her feet. Turning, she confronted the grotesque face of one of the rodeo clowns, the one whom she'd last seen bending over Chase.

"Who are you?" he asked.

"A friend. How is he? Have they said what's wrong with him?"

He eyed her suspiciously; she obviously wasn't in her element. "He's prob'ly got a few broken ribs, is all. Had the wind knocked out of him."

"Will he be all right?"

He spat tobacco juice on the hay-strewn concrete floor. "Prob'ly. I reckon he won't feel too good for a day or so."

Marcie was only moderately relieved to hear the clown's diagnosis. It wasn't a professional opinion. How did he know that Chase hadn't sustained internal injuries?

"Shouldn't've been ridin' tonight," the clown was saying as the stretcher was hoisted into the back of the ambulance. "Told him he shouldn't get on a bull in his condition. Course I guess it wouldn't matter. That bull El Dorado is one mean sum'bitch. Last week over in—"

"What condition?" Frustrated when he only gazed at her in puzzlement through his white-rimmed eyes, she clarified her question. "You said 'in his condition.' What condition was Chase in?"

"He was half-lit."

"You mean drunk?"

"Yes, ma'am. We had us a pretty wild party last night. Chase hadn't quite recovered."

Marcie didn't wait to hear any more. She climbed into the back of the ambulance just as the paramedic was about to close the doors.

He reacted with surprise and an air of authority. "Sorry, ma'am. You can't—"

"I am. Now we can stand here and argue about it or you can get this man to the hospital."

"Hey, what's the holdup?" the other paramedic shouted back. He was already in the driver's seat with the motor running.

His assistant gauged Marcie's determination and apparently decided that an argument would only waste valuable time.

"Nothing," he called to his cohort. "Let's go." He slammed the doors and the ambulance peeled out of the coliseum barn.

"Well, I'm glad you made it back to your hotel safely."

Marcie, cradling the receiver of the pay telephone against her ear, massaged her temples while apologizing to the gentleman from Massachusetts. She had probably lost a sale, but when she saw Chase lying unconscious in the dirt, her guests had been the farthest thing from her mind. Indeed, she hadn't even remembered them until a few minutes ago while pacing the corridor of the hospital.

"Mr. Tyler is an old friend of mine," she explained. "I didn't know he was appearing in this rodeo until his name was announced. Since his family isn't here, I felt like I should accompany him to the hospital. I hope you understand."

She didn't give a damn whether they understood or not. If she had been entertaining the President and First Lady tonight, she would have done exactly the same thing.

After hanging up, she returned to the nurses' station and inquired for the umpteenth time if there had been an update on Chase's condition.

The nurse frowned with irritation. "As soon as the doctor— Oh, here he is now." Glancing beyond Marcie's shoulder, she said, "This lady is waiting for word on Mr. Taylor."

"Tyler," Marcie corrected, turning to meet the young resident. "I'm Marcie Johns."

"Phil Montoya." They shook hands. "Are you a relative?"

"Only a good friend. Mr. Tyler doesn't have any family in Fort Worth. They all live in Milton Point."

"Hmm. Well, he's finally come around. Got swatted in the head pretty good, but thankfully no serious damage was done."

"I saw the bull land on his chest."

"Yeah, he's got several broken ribs."

"That can be dangerous, can't it?"

"Only if a jagged rib punctures an internal organ."

Marcie's face went so pale that even the freckles she carefully camouflaged with cosmetics stood out in stark contrast. The doctor hastily reassured her.

"Fortunately that didn't happen either. No bleeding organs. I've taped him up. He'll be all right in a few days, but he's not going to feel very chipper. I certainly don't recommend that he do any bull riding for a while."

"Did you tell him that?"

"Sure did. He cussed me out."

"I'm sorry."

He shrugged and said affably, "I'm used to it. This is a county hospital. We get the psychos, the derelicts, and the victims of drug deals gone awry. We're used to verbal abuse."

"May I see him?"

"For a few minutes. He doesn't need to be talking."

"I won't talk long."

"He's just been given a strong painkiller, so he'll likely be drifting off soon anyway."

"Then if it's all the same to you," Marcie said smoothly, "I'd like to stay the night in his room."

"He'll be well taken care of," the nurse said stiffly from behind her.

Marcie stood firm. "Do I have your permission, Dr. Montoya?"

He tugged on his earlobe. Marcie gave him the direct look that said she wasn't going to budge from her position. Buyers, sellers, and lending agents had had to confront that steady blue stare. Nine times out of ten they yielded to it. Earlier that night, the paramedic had found it hard to argue with.

"I guess it wouldn't hurt," the resident said at last.

"Thank you."

"Keep the conversation to a minimum."

"I promise. Which room is he in?"

Chase had been placed in a semiprivate room, but the other bed was empty. Marcie advanced into the room on tiptoe until she reached his bedside.

For the first time in two years, she gazed into Chase Tyler's face. The last time she had looked into it, their positions had been reversed. She'd been lying semiconscious in a hospital bed and he had been standing beside it, weeping over his wife's accidental death.

By the time Marcie's injuries had healed and she was well enough to leave the hospital, Tanya Tyler had been interred. A few months after that, Chase had left Milton Point for parts unknown. Word around town was that he was running the rodeo circuit, much to the distress of his family.

Not too long ago, Marcie had bumped into Devon, Lucky's bride, in the supermarket. After Marcie had introduced herself, Devon had confirmed the rumors circulating about Chase. Family loyalty had prevented her from openly discussing his personal problems with an outsider, but Marcie had read between the lines of what she actually said. There were hints about his delicate emotional state and a developing drinking problem.

"Laurie is beside herself with worry about him," Devon had said, referring to Chase's mother. "Sage, Chase's sister—"

"Yes, I know."

"She's away at school, so that leaves only Lucky and me at the house with Laurie. She feels that Chase is running away from his grief over Tanya instead of facing it and trying to deal with it."

Chase had also left the foundering family business in the hands of his younger brother, who, if rumors were to be believed, was having a hard time keeping it solvent. The oil business wasn't improving. Since Tyler Drilling depended on a healthy oil economy, the company had been teetering on the brink of bankruptcy for several years.

Marcie put to Devon the question that was never far from her mind. "Does he blame me for the accident?"

Devon had pressed her arm reassuringly. "Never. Don't lay that kind of guilt on yourself. Chase's quarrel is with fate, not you."

But now, as Marcie gazed into his face, which looked tormented even in repose, she wondered if he did in fact hold her responsible for his beloved Tanya's death.

"Chase," she whispered sorrowfully.

He didn't stir, and his breathing was deep and even, indicating that the drug he had been given intravenously was working. Giving in to the desire she'd felt while lying in pain in her own hospital bed, Marcie gingerly ran her fingers through his dark hair, brushing back wavy strands that had fallen over his clammy forehead.

Even though he looked markedly older, he was still the most handsome man she'd ever seen. She had thought so the first day of kindergarten. She distinctly remembered Miss Kincannon's calling on him to introduce himself to the rest of the class and how proudly he had stood up and spoken his name. Marcie had been smitten. In all the years since, nothing had changed.

The mischievous, dark-haired little boy with the light-gray eyes, who had possessed outstanding leadership qualities and athletic prowess, had turned into quite a man. There was strength in his face and a stubborn pride in his square chin that bordered on belligerence, inherent, it seemed, to the Tyler men. They were noted for their quick tempers and willingness to stand up for themselves. Chase's lower jaw bore a dark-purple bruise now. Marcie shuddered to think how close he had come to having his skull crushed.

When he was standing, Chase Tyler topped most men by several inches, even those considered tall by normal standards. His shoulders were broad. Marcie marveled over their breadth now. They were bare, as was his chest. The upper portion of it had been left unshaven, and she was amazed by the abundance of dark, softly curling hair that covered it.

The tape that bound his cracked ribs stopped just shy of his nipples. Marcie caught herself staring at them, entranced because they were distended.

Thinking he must be cold, she reached for the sheet and pulled it up to just beneath his chin.

"Jeez, did he die?"

The screech so startled Marcie that she dropped the sheet and spun around. A young woman was standing just inside the threshold of the door. Her hand, weighted down with costume jewelry and outlandishly long artificial fingernails, was splayed across breasts struggling to be free of a tight, low-cut sweater. A cheap, fake-fur coat was draped over her shoulders. The coat was longer than her skirt, which came only to midthigh.

Chase moaned in his sleep and shifted his legs beneath the sheet. "Be quiet!" Marcie hissed. "You'll disturb him. Who are you? What do you want?"

"He's not dead?" the girl asked. In a manner Marcie thought looked incredibly stupid, the woman rapidly blinked her wide, round eyes several times. That was no small feat considering her eyelashes were gummy with mascara as thick and black as road tar.

"No, he's not dead. Just very badly hurt." She assessed the girl from the top of her teased, silver hair to the toes of her bejeweled, silver boots. "Are you a friend of Chase's?"

"Sort of." She shrugged off the fake fur. "I was supposed to meet him at this bar where everybody goes after the rodeo. I was getting pissed because he didn't show, but then Pete—you know, the clown—said that Chase got trampled by a bull. So I thought I ought to come check on him, see if he's okay, you know."

"I see."

"Did they say what's wrong with him?"

"Several of his ribs are broken, but he'll be all right."

"Oh, gee, that's good." Her eyes moved from the supine figure on the bed to Marcie. "Who're you?"

"I'm his . . . his . . . wife."

Marcie wasn't sure what prompted her to tell such a bold-faced lie. Probably because it was convenient and would swiftly scare off this woman. She was certain that in his more sane and sober days, Chase would have had nothing to do with a tramp like this. His marital status certainly didn't break the girl's heart. It merely provoked her.

She propped a fist on one hip. "That son of a bitch. Look, he never told me he was married, okay? I was out for kicks, that's all. Nothing serious. Even though he is kinda moody, he's good-looking, you know?

"When I first met him, I thought he was a drag. I mean, he never wanted to talk or anything. But then, I figured, 'Hey, what the hell? So he's not a barrel of laughs, at least he's handsome.'

"Swear to God, we only slept together three times, and it was always straight sex. Nothing kinky, you know? I mean, missionary position all the way.

"Between you and me," she added, lowering her voice, "it wasn't very good. He was drunk all three times. As you well know, the equipment is *im*-pressive, but—"

Marcie's mouth was dry. She drew upon reserves of composure she didn't know she had. "I think you'd better go now. Chase needs his rest."

"Sure, I understand," she said pleasantly, pulling her coat back on.

"Please tell his friends that he's going to be okay, though his rodeo days might be over. At least for a while."

"That reminds me," the girl said. "Pete said to tell him that he's leaving in the trailer for Calgary tomorrow. That's where he's from, you know? I think it's somewhere in Canada, but I always thought Calgary had something to do with the Bible." She shrugged, almost lifting her breasts out of the sweater's low neckline. "Anyway, Pete wants to know what to do with Chase's stuff."

Marcie shook her head, trying to make sense of the woman's non-sensical chatter. "I suppose you could mail it to him at home."

"Okay. What's the address? I'll give it to Pete."

"I'm not—" Marcie broke off before she trapped herself in her lie. "On second thought, please ask Pete to leave everything with the officials at the coliseum. I'll pick up Chase's things there tomorrow."

"Okay, I'll tell him. Well, see ya. Oh, wait!" She dug into her purse. "Here's Chase's keys. His pickup is still parked in the lot at the coliseum." She tossed the key ring to Marcie.

"Thank you." Marcie made a diving catch before the keys could land in Chase's vulnerable lap.

"I'm really sorry about, you know, balling your husband. He never told me he was married. Men! They're all bastards, you know?"

Marcie couldn't quite believe the woman had been real and stood staring at the door for several moments after it closed behind her. Was Chase reduced to seeing women like that to ward off his loneliness and despair brought on by Tanya's death? Was he punishing himself for her death by sinking as low as he could go?

Marcie moved to the narrow closet and placed the key ring on the shelf beside the chamois gloves he'd been wearing when he was thrown from the bull. His battered hat was there, too. She noticed a pair of scuffed cowboy boots standing on the closet floor.

His clothes had been hung on the few hangers provided. The light-blue shirt was streaked with dirt. His entry number was still pinned to it. His faded jeans were dusty. So was the cloth bandanna that had been tied around his neck. She touched the leather chaps and remembered their flapping against his legs as they sawed up and down against the bull's heaving sides.

The recollection caused her to shiver. She shut the closet door against the memory of Chase's lying unconscious in the dirt.

Returning to the bed, she noticed his hand moving restlessly over the tight bandage around his rib cage. Afraid he might hurt himself, she captured his hand and drew it down to his side, patting it into place beside his hip and holding it there.

His eyes fluttered open. Obviously disoriented, he blinked several times in an attempt to get his bearings and remember where he was.

Then he seemed to recognize her. Reassuringly, she closed her fingers tightly around his. He tried to speak, but the single word came out as nothing more than a faint croak.

Still, she recognized his pet name for her. Right before drifting back into oblivion he had said, "Goosey?"

Chapter Two

He was giving a nurse hell when Marcie walked into the hospital room the following morning. He suspended the invective long enough to do a double take on Marcie, then resumed his complaining.

"You'll feel so much better after a bath and a shave," the nurse said cajolingly.

"Get your hands off me. Leave that cover where it is. I told you I don't want a bath. When I feel good and ready, I'll shave myself. Now, for the last time, get the hell out of here and leave me alone so I can get dressed."

"Dressed? Mr. Tyler, you can't leave!"

"Oh, yeah? Watch me."

It was time to intervene. Marcie said, "Perhaps after Mr. Tyler has had a cup of coffee he'll feel more like shaving."

The nurse welcomed the subtle suggestion that she leave. With a swish of white polyester and the squeak of rubber soles, she was gone. Marcie was left alone with Chase. His face was as dark as a thundercloud. It had little to do with his stubble or the bruise on his jaw.

"I thought I had dreamed you," he remarked.

"No. As you can see, I'm really here. Flesh and blood."

"But what the hell is your flesh and blood doing here?"

She poured him a cup of coffee from a thermal carafe and scooted it across the portable bed tray toward him, guessing correctly that he drank it black. Absently, he picked up the cup and sipped.

"Well?"

"Well, by a quirk of coincidence," Marcie said, "I was at the rodeo last night when you danced with that bull."

"What were you doing in Fort Worth in the first place?"

"Clients. A couple is moving here from the Northeast. They're going to live in Fort Worth, but have been shopping lake-front property near Milton Point for a weekend retreat. I drove over yesterday to do some stroking. Last night I treated them to a Mexican dinner, then for entertainment, took them to the rodeo. They were exposed to a few more chills and thrills than I bargained for."

"A thrill a minute," he grumbled, wincing as he tried to find a more comfortable position against the pillows stacked behind him.

"Are you still in pain?"

"No. I feel great." The white line encircling his lips said otherwise, but she didn't argue. "That explains what you were doing at the rodeo. What were you doing here? In the hospital?"

"I've known you for a long time, Chase. There was no one else around to see about you. Your family would never have forgiven me if I hadn't come with you to the hospital. I would never have forgiven myself."

He set aside his empty coffee cup. "That was you last night, squeezing my hand?" She nodded. Chase looked away. "I thought . . . thought . . ." He drew a deep sigh, which caused him to grimace again. "Crazy stuff."

"You thought it was Tanya?"

At the mention of her name his eyes sprang back to Marcie's. She was relieved. She no longer had to dread speaking his late wife's name aloud for the first time. It was out now. Just like going off the high-diving board, the first time was the hardest. It got easier after that.

But seeing the pain in his eyes, as though he had been poked with a deadly needle, Marcie wondered if Chase would ever get over Tanya's tragic death.

"Would you like some more coffee?"

"No. What I would like," he enunciated, "is a drink."

Though it was no laughing matter, Marcie treated it as a joke. "At eight o'clock in the morning?"

"I've started earlier," he muttered. "Will you drive me somewhere to get a bottle?"

"Certainly not!"

"Then I'll have to call somebody else." At great expense to his threshold of pain, he reached for the telephone on the nightstand.

"If you're planning to call Pete the clown, it won't do you any good. He's leaving for Calgary today."

Chase lowered his hands and looked at her. "How do you know?"

"A friend of yours told me. She came here last night to see about you when you didn't show up for your postrodeo date. Big hair. Big boobs. I didn't get her name."

"That's okay. I didn't either," he admitted. Marcie said nothing. He studied her calm face for a moment. "What, no sermon?"

"Not from me."

He harrumphed. "Wish you'd talk to my family about preaching. They love to preach. They're all in on the act of saving me from myself. I just want to be left the hell alone."

"They love you."

"It's my life!" he cried angrily. "Where do any of them get off telling me how to live it, huh? Especially Lucky." He snorted in an uncomplimentary way. "Until Devon came along, he had the busiest zipper in East Texas. Nailed anybody who moved and probably a few who didn't. Now he's so bloody righteous it's sickening."

"But I believe his . . . er, zipper is as busy as ever." That brought his eyes up to hers again. "Every time I see Devon, she's smiling."

Her composure was incongruent with the bawdiness of the topic. In light of that, it was difficult for him to remain angry. Although his scowl stayed in place, a fleeting grin lifted one corner of his lips. "You're all right, Goosey. A real good sport."

She rolled her eyes. "Every woman's secret ambition."

"I meant that as a compliment."

"Then thanks."

"While we're still on good terms, why don't you exercise your super brain, do the smart thing, and leave me where you found me?"

"What kind of friend would I be if I deserted you in your time of need?"

"It's because we've always been friends that I'm asking you to leave. If you stick around for long, something really terrible might happen. Something I'd hate."

"Like what?" she asked with a light laugh.

"I'm liable to make us enemies."

Her expression turned serious. "Never, Chase."

He grunted noncommittally. "Pete's heading home, you say?"

"That's right."

"He's got all my stuff in his trailer."

"Taken care of." She took a cup of custard from his bed tray and peeled back the foil seal. "He dropped everything off at the coliseum on his way out of town early this morning. I picked it all up there."

Without realizing he was doing so, he opened his mouth when she foisted a spoonful of custard on him. "You went to all that trouble for me?"

"No trouble."

"Did you call my family?"

"No. I wanted to ask you about that first."

"Don't call them."

"Are you sure that's what you want?"

"Positive."

"They'll want to know, Chase."

"They'll find out soon enough. When they do, they'll make an issue of it."

"Well, they should. You could have been killed."

"And wouldn't that have been a tragedy?" he asked sarcastically.

She stopped spooning in the custard. "Yes. It would have been."

He looked ready to argue the point, but turned his head away instead and with annoyance, pushed back the bed tray. "Look, Marcie, I appreciate—"

"What happened to Goosey?"

He looked her over carefully. The carrot-colored hair she'd had in kindergarten had mellowed to a soft red, shot through with gold. It was still naturally curly and had a mind of its own, but she had learned to arrange it artfully.

For years she had vainly tried to tan. She used to pray that all her freckles would run together. After several severe sunburns and weeks of unsightly peeling, she had eventually given up on that futile endeavor. She had decided that if she couldn't have the sleek, golden tan of beach bunnies, she would go in the opposite direction and play up her fair complexion to its best advantage. It now appeared almost translucent and was often remarked upon with envy by women her age who had basked in the sun for years and were now paying for their gorgeous tans with lines and wrinkles.

Eyeglasses had been replaced by contacts. Years in braces had left her with a perfect smile. The beanstalk body had finally sprouted and filled out. She was still strikingly slender, but it was a fashionable, not an unfortunate, slimness. The curves beneath her expensive and chic clothing weren't abundant, but they were detectable.

Marcie Johns had come a long way from the awkward bookworm all the other kids had called Goosey. While the popular girls in her class had gone out for cheerleader and drum majorette, she had been captain of the debate team and president of the Latin club.

Her more curvaceous classmates had been crowned Homecoming

Queen and Valentine Sweetheart; she had received awards for out-standing scholastic achievements. Her parents had told her that those were much more important than winning popularity contests, but Marcie was smart enough to know better.

She would have traded all her certificates of merit for one rhine-stone-studded tiara and a crowning kiss from the president of the class, Chase Tyler. Few realized that their class valedictorian pined for any-thing other than scholastic recognition. Indeed, who would have even thought about it? Goosey was Goosey, and no one had ever given her a second thought beyond how smart she was.

Chase did now, however. Summing up her appearance, he said, "Somehow the name Goosey doesn't fit a well-put-together lady like you."

"Thank you."

"You're welcome. Now, as I was saying—"

"You were brushing me off."

Chase raked his hand through his unruly hair. "It's not like I don't appreciate all you've done, Marcie. I do."

"It's just that you want to be left alone."

"That's right."

"To wallow in your misery."

"Right again. Now, unless you're prepared to stand there while I come out of this bed with nothing more on than a bandage around my ribs, I suggest you say your farewells and leave."

"You can't be serious about leaving the hospital."

"I am."

"But the doctor hasn't even seen you this morning."

"I don't need him to tell me that I've got a few cracked ribs. Nothing a day or two in bed won't cure. I'd rather pass the time somewhere else, someplace where whiskey isn't so scarce."

He struggled into a sitting position. The pain took his breath. Tears sprang to his eyes. He made a terrible, teeth-gnashing face until the worst of it subsided.

"How are you going to get to this 'place'?" she asked. "You can't drive in your condition."

"I'll manage."

"And probably kill yourself in the process."

He swiveled his head around and speared her with his eyes. "Maybe I should take a safe-driving lesson from you."

He couldn't have done or said anything that would hurt her more.

She almost bent double against the assault of his harsh words. The blood drained from her head so quickly, she felt faint.

The second the words were out of Chase's mouth, his head dropped forward until his bruised chin rested on his chest. He muttered a litany of expletives. Beyond that, the silence in the room was thick enough to cut with a knife.

At last he raised his head. "I'm sorry, Marcie."

She was nervously clasping and unclasping her hands as she stared sightlessly into near space. "I wondered if you blamed me for the accident."

"I don't. I swear I don't."

"Maybe not consciously. But deep down—"

"Not at all. It was a thoughtless, stupid thing to say. I told you I'd make an enemy of you. I can't . . ." He raised his hands helplessly. "Sometimes I get so furious about it, I turn nasty and victimize whoever happens to be around me at the time. That's why I'm not very good company. That's why I just want to be left alone."

His emotional pain was so starkly evident, it was easy to forgive him for lashing out at her. He was like a wounded, cornered animal that wouldn't allow anyone to get close enough to help him. For the two years since Tanya's death he had been licking his wounds. They hadn't healed yet. Left alone they never would. They would only fester and become worse. Chase was no longer capable of helping himself.

"Do you insist on leaving this hospital?"

"Yes," he said. "If I have to crawl out."

"Then let me drive you home. To Milton Point."

"Forget it."

"Be reasonable, Chase. Where will you go? If you were staying with that clown and he's left for Canada, where will you go?"

"There are plenty of other rodeo folks I can stay with."

"Who might or might not take proper care of you." She moved closer and laid her hand on his bare shoulder. "Chase, let me drive you to Milton Point."

Jaw stubbornly set, he said, "I don't want to go home."

What he didn't know was that Marcie could be as stubborn as he. Her personality had an inflexible streak that few ever saw because she only exercised it when given no alternative. "Then I'll call Lucky and discuss with him what I should do with you."

"The hell you will," he roared. He came off the bed, reeling from his weakened condition when his feet hit the floor. "Leave my family out of this. I'll manage just fine by myself."

"Oh, sure. You can barely stand up!"

Gritting his teeth in frustration and pain, he said, "Please go away and leave me alone."

Marcie drew herself up to her full height. "I didn't want to bring up such a delicate subject, Chase, but you leave me no choice. There's the matter of the money."

That took him aback. For a moment he merely stared at her blankly, then, drawing a frown, he growled, "Money? What money?"

"The money it took to admit you to this hospital and get treatment. I didn't think you would want to be admitted as a charity patient, so I paid for everything."

"You what?"

"You had no insurance card in your wallet. We didn't find a significant amount of money there either, so I footed the bill."

He gnawed on his lower lip, his agitation plain. "The entry fee was several hundred dollars, but if I hadn't put it up, I couldn't have ridden in the rodeo. I was low on cash."

"Then it's lucky for you I happened along, isn't it?"

"You'll get your money."

"That's right, I will. As soon as we get to Milton Point you can withdraw it from your bank account or borrow it from your brother."

"Marcie," he said, ready to argue.

"I'm not leaving you to your own devices, Chase. According to sources who know you well, you've been drinking too much. How can your body heal if you take no better care of it than that?"

"I don't give a damn whether it heals or not."

"Well, I do."

"Why?"

"Because I want my five hundred seventy-three dollars and sixty-two cents back." Having said that, she marched to the door and pulled it open. "I'll send a nurse in to help you get dressed." She lowered her eyes pointedly, reminding him that he was indeed naked except for the white swathe of bandaging around his rib cage.

"What about my truck?"

Marcie kept her eyes on the road. Pellets of ice were falling intermittently with the rain. "I took care of it."

"Are we towing it or what?"

He had refused to lie down in the backseat of her car as she had suggested. But ever since leaving the hospital, his head had been reclining on the headrest. Her car was roomy and plush because she used it to drive clients around in. Soft music was playing on the stereo radio. The heater was controlled by a thermostat. Chase was surrounded with as much comfortable luxury as possible. His eyes had remained closed, though he wasn't asleep.

They were only half an hour into a two-and-a-half-hour car trip. Morning rush hour was over, but the weather, deteriorating by the minute, was making driving hazardous. Precipitation had increased, a nasty mix of rain and sleet that frequently plagued north Texas during January and February. The Fort Worth Livestock Show and Rodeo always seemed to herald it in.

Marcie had her eyes glued to the pavement just beyond her hood ornament and kept a death grip on the steering wheel while maintaining minimum speed as she navigated the labyrinth of freeways that encircled downtown Dallas. Unfortunately it fell directly in the path between their starting point and their destination.

"I hired someone to drive your pickup to Milton Point later this week," she said in answer to Chase's question. "By the time you're able to drive, it'll be there."

"*You* hired someone to drive *my* truck?"

"Uh-huh," she replied, concentrating on the eighteen-wheeler whizzing past her at a speed that set her teeth on edge.

"Still competent, aren't you?"

"The way you said that leads me to believe you don't mean it as a compliment."

"Oh, I commend your competency. It's just that most men are intimidated by self-sufficient, overachieving women." He rolled his head against the cushion so he could look at her. "Is that why you never got married? Never could meet your match in the brains department?"

She didn't feel inclined to discuss her private life with him, especially since she detected a derisive quality to his seemingly harmless question.

"You ought to try to sleep, Chase. You're fighting the pain medication they gave you before we left."

"What do they call that?"

"Demerol."

"No, I mean when a woman wants to be a man. Some kind of envy. Oh, yeah, penis envy."

Despite the traffic and glazed highway, she looked across at him. His smug expression was intolerable. She longed to come back with the swift and sure retort.

Marcie turned her full attention back to the road. She swallowed with difficulty. "Actually, Chase, I was engaged to be married once."

His snide smile faltered. "Really? When?"

"Several years ago, while I was living in Houston. He was a realtor, too. We worked out of the same office, although he was in commercial real estate and I was in residential."

"What happened? Who broke it off, you or him?"

She evaded the direct question. "We had dated for several months before becoming engaged. He was very nice, intelligent, had a good sense of humor."

"But you weren't compatible in the sack."

"On the contrary. We were very compatible."

He tilted his head to one side. "It's hard for me to imagine you in the sack."

"What a nice thing to say," she remarked, her tone implying just the opposite.

"I guess because you didn't date much in high school."

"It wasn't because I didn't want to. Nobody asked me."

"All you were interested in was getting straight A's."

"Hardly."

"That's what it looked like."

"Looks can be deceiving. I wanted to be beautiful and popular and go steady with a superjock just like every high school girl."

"Hmm. Back to the guy in Houston, why didn't you marry him?"

She smiled sadly. "I didn't love him. A week before the wedding I was trying on my gown for a final fitting. My mother and the seamstress who was doing the alterations were fussing around me. The room was filled with wedding gifts.

"I looked at myself in the mirror and tried to relate that bride to myself. The gown was gorgeous. My parents had gone all out, but it wasn't *me*.

"I tried to imagine walking down the aisle and pledging undying love and devotion to this man I was engaged to. And in a blinding instant I knew I couldn't do it. I couldn't be that dishonest. I was fond of him. I liked him very much. But I didn't love him.

"So I calmly stepped out of the white satin creation and informed my mother and the flabbergasted seamstress that the wedding wasn't going to take place after all. As you can imagine, my announcement created quite a commotion. The next few days were a nightmare. All the arrangements, flowers, caterer, everything had to be canceled. The gifts had to be returned to their senders with notes of apology."

"What about him? How'd he take it?"

"Very well. Oh, at first he argued and tried to talk me out of it, passing off my reservations as prewedding jitters. But after we had discussed it at length, he agreed that it was the right thing to do. I think he realized all along that . . . well, that I didn't love him as I should."

"That was a helluva thing to do, Marcie."

"I know," she said with chagrin. "I'm certainly not proud of it."

"No, I mean it *was* a helluva thing to do. It took real guts to break it off at the eleventh hour like that."

She shook her head. "No, Chase. If I'd had any guts, I would have admitted to myself, before involving an innocent man, that it just wasn't destined for me to get married."

They were silent for a while, which suited Marcie fine since the road had gone a stage beyond being glazed and was now like the surface of an ice rink.

Before long, however, Chase moaned and laid a hand against his ribs. "This is hurting like a son of a bitch."

"Take another pill. The doctor said you could have one every two hours."

"That's nothing but glorified aspirin. Stop and let me buy a bottle of whiskey."

"Absolutely not. I'm not stopping this car until I get to your place in Milton Point."

"If I wash the pill down with whiskey, it'll go to work faster."

"You can't bargain with me. Besides, it's stupid to mix alcohol and drugs."

"For godsake, don't get preachy on me. Pull off at the next exit. There's a liquor store there. It won't take a sec for me to go in—"

"I'm not letting you buy any liquor while you're with me."

"Well, I didn't ask to be with you, did I?" he shouted. "You ramrodded your way into my business. Now I want a drink and I want it now."

Marcie eased her foot off the accelerator and let the car coast toward the shoulder of the highway. Gradually she applied the brake until it came to a full stop. She uncurled her stiff, white fingers from around the padded-leather steering wheel and turned to face him.

He wasn't expecting the slap. Her cold palm cracked across his bristled cheek.

"Damn you!" Her whole body was trembling. Unshed tears shimmered in her eyes. "Damn you, Chase Tyler, for being the most selfish, self-absorbed jerk ever to be born. Look at my hands."

She held them inches in front of his nose, palms forward. "They're wringing wet. I'm scared to death. Haven't you realized that it isn't easy for me to drive under any circumstances, but especially under conditions like this?" She gestured wildly toward the inclement weather beyond the windshield.

"I'm afraid that every car we meet is going to hit us. I live in terror of that happening to me again. Even more so when I have a passenger sitting where Tanya was sitting.

"I was in that car, too, Chase, when that kid ran the stop sign. To this day I have nightmares where I experience the sound of squealing tires and feel the impact and taste the fear of dying all over again. I had to undergo weeks of therapy before I could even get behind the steering wheel of a car again.

"If you didn't need to get home immediately, I would be holed up in my hotel room in Fort Worth until the next sunny, dry day. I wouldn't think of risking my life or anyone else's by driving in this ice storm."

She paused and drew in a shuddering breath. "You're right, you didn't ask for my help, but I felt I owed you this much, to get you safely home to your family where you can properly recuperate."

She doubled up her fist and shook it at him. "But by God, the least you could do is shut up and stop your infernal bellyaching!"

Chapter Three

". . . still don't think we should wake him up. If he didn't wake up when we came barging in, as much noise as we were making, he needs this sleep."

Marcie, with both arms curled around loaded supermarket sacks, paused outside the door of Chase's apartment. Through it, she could hear voices.

"But how else are we going to find out how he got here, Mother? And how do we know how many of those pills he's taken? That could be the reason he's sleeping like a dead man."

"Lucky, relax," a third voice said, "the pill bottle was almost full. He couldn't have taken many. Laurie's right. For the time being, he's better off asleep."

"That's a wicked-looking bandage around his chest," Laurie Tyler said. "Obviously he needs bed rest. We can wait until he wakes up on his own to find out who brought him home."

"Probably his current squeeze," Lucky muttered.

Marcie had heard enough. She managed to grip the doorknob and turn it, staggering inside under the weight of the grocery sacks. Three heads came around to gape at her with astonishment.

"Ms. Johns!"

"Hello, Mrs. Tyler."

She was flattered that Laurie Tyler knew her. Though she'd been in Chase's class all through school, they hadn't had the same circle of friends. Following her release from the hospital, Marcie had considered going to see Laurie and apologizing for Tanya's death. She had ultimately decided against it, thinking that it would be a difficult meeting each of them could do without.

"Lucky, take those sacks from her," Laurie ordered, shoving her dumbfounded younger son forward.

"Marcie, what the hell are you doing here?" Lucky relieved her of the grocery sacks and set them on the bar, which separated the small kitchen from the living area of the apartment.

Marcie dropped her purse and keys into a chair littered with unopened mail and discarded articles of clothing that had lain there long enough to collect dust. "Let me assure you, I'm not Chase's current squeeze," she remarked as she shrugged off her coat.

Lucky looked chagrined, but only momentarily. "I'm sorry you overheard that, but what's going on? We've had his landlord here on the lookout for him. He was to notify us when and if Chase turned up. He called about half an hour ago and said he'd seen lights on in the apartment although Chase's truck wasn't here. We rushed over and found Chase alone and dead to the world."

"And bandaged," Devon added. "Is he seriously hurt?"

"He's certainly uncomfortable, but the injury isn't serious. He got stamped on by a bull at the rodeo in Fort Worth last night."

Marcie told them about the accident and how she had happened to be there. She avoided telling them that she had spent the night in his hospital room. She had been away from him only long enough to return to the hotel where she was checked in, shower, change clothes, and pack, then drive to the coliseum to pick up his belongings.

"This morning, when I returned to the hospital, he was terrorizing the nursing staff. He refused to be shaved. A bed bath was out of the question. He insisted on leaving."

"He's crazy!"

Devon shot her husband a withering glance. "As if you'd be a more cooperative patient. I can see you submitting to a bed bath." Turning her attention back to Marcie, she asked, "Did he just walk out?"

"He would have, but I called the doctor. He got there in the nick of time. He examined Chase and recommended that he stay in the hospital for a few days. When he realized that he'd as well argue with a brick wall, he signed a release form.

"I volunteered to drive him here and promised the doctor that I would see to it he got into bed. He gave him a prescription for pain medication—the bottle of capsules on the nightstand," she said to Lucky. "He's taken only the prescribed amount."

Obviously relieved, Laurie lowered herself to the sofa. "Thank God you happened to be there, Ms. Johns, and took it upon yourself to look after him for us."

"Please call me Marcie."

"Thank you very much."

"It was the least I could do."

They fell silent then. What had gone unsaid was that Marcie's assistance in this matter was nominal repayment for having been driving when Chase's wife had been killed.

Devon was the first to break the uneasy silence. "What's all that?" She pointed toward the sacks standing on the bar.

"Food. There was nothing but a can of spoiled sardines in the refrigerator. Nothing at all in the pantry. I also bought some cleaning supplies."

Laurie ran her finger over the coffee table, picking up a quarter inch of dust. "I don't think this place has been touched since Tanya died."

"That's right. It hasn't."

As one, they turned to find Chase standing in the doorway. He had pulled on a bathrobe, but sturdy, lean bare legs were sticking out of it. The white bandage showed up in the open wedge of the robe across his chest. His hair still looked like he had run through a wind tunnel, and his stubble had grown darker. It was no darker, however, than his glower.

"It hasn't had any visitors either," he added, "and that's the way I want it. So now that you've had your little discussion about me and my character flaws, you can all clear out and leave me the hell alone."

Laurie, still spry even in her mid-fifties, sprang to her feet. "Now listen here, Chase Nathaniel Tyler, I will not be spoken to in that tone of voice by any of my children, and that includes you. I don't care how big you are." She pushed up the sleeves of her sweater as though ready to engage him in a fistfight if necessary.

"You look so disreputable I'm almost ashamed to claim you as my eldest son. On top of that, you smell. This place is a pigsty, unfit for human habitation. All of that is subject to change. Starting now," she emphasized.

"I'm fed up with your self-pity and your whining and your perpetual frown. I'm tired of walking on thin ice around you. When you were a boy, I gave you what was good for you whether you liked it or not. Well, you're grown, and supposedly able to take care of yourself, but I think it's time for me to exercise some maternal prerogatives. Whether you like it or not, this is for your own good."

She drew herself up tall. "Go shave and take a bath while I start a pot of homemade chicken-noodle soup."

Chase stood there a moment, gnawing the inside of his jaw. He looked at his brother. "Go get me a bottle, will you?"

"Not bloody likely. I don't want her on my tail, too."

Chase lowered his head, muttering obscenities. When he lifted his head again, his angry eyes connected with Marcie's. "This is all your fault, you know." Having said that, he turned and lumbered down the hallway toward his bedroom. The door was slammed shut behind him.

Marcie had actually fallen back a step as though he had attacked her physically instead of verbally. Unknowingly she had raised a hand to her chest. Devon moved toward her and laid her arm across Marcie's shoulders.

"I'm sure he didn't mean that the way it sounded, Marcie."

"And I'm sure he did," she said shakily.

Lucky tried to reassure her. "He wasn't referring to the accident. He was talking about bringing Mother's wrath down on him."

"He's not himself, Marcie." Laurie's militancy had abated. She was smiling gently. "Deep down he's probably grateful to you for being there last night, forcing him to do something he really wanted to do— come home. You provided a way for him to do it and still save face. We owe you a real debt of gratitude and so does Chase."

Marcie gave them a tremulous smile, then gathered up her coat and purse. "Since you're here to take over, I'll say good-bye."

"I'll walk you to your car."

"There's no need to, Lucky," she said, hastily turning to open the door for herself. She didn't want them to see her tears. "I'll call later to check on him. Good-bye."

What had been falling as sleet a hundred miles west was a cold, miserable, wind-driven rain in East Texas. Marcie drove carefully, her vision impaired by the falling precipitation on her windshield . . . and her own tears.

Chase released a string of curses when someone knocked on his door late that evening. After having been dusted, mopped, scoured, vacuumed, and disinfected, his apartment was finally clean, empty, and silent. With only himself and the nagging pain in his ribs for company, he was finishing his dinner in blessed peace.

He thought of ignoring the knock. Whoever it was might think he was asleep and go away. However, on the outside chance it was Lucky sneaking him a bottle of something stronger than tea or coffee, he left his seat at the bar and padded to the door.

Marcie was standing on the threshold, holding a bouquet of flowers.

He had never seen her in a pair of jeans that he could recall. They made her legs look long and slim—thighs that seemed to go on forever.

Beneath her short, quilted denim jacket, she was wearing a sweatshirt. It was decorated with splatters of metallic paint, but it was still a sweatshirt and a far cry from the business suits she was usually dressed in.

She'd left her hair down too. Instead of the tailored bun she had worn that morning, the flame-colored curls were lying loose on her shoulders. They were beaded with raindrops that glistened like diamond chips in the glow of the porch light. He didn't particularly like red hair, but he noticed that Marcie's looked soft and pretty tonight.

About the only thing that was familiar were her eyeglasses. All through school, Goosey Johns had worn glasses. It occurred to him now that she must have been wearing contacts, even two years ago when they had been reacquainted in his office just before she and Tanya left to look at a house together—the afternoon Tanya died.

"It's a cold night out," she said.

"Oh, sorry." He shuffled out of her path and she slipped past him to come inside.

"Are you alone?"

"Thankfully."

He closed the door and turned to her. Her eyes moved over him in a nervous manner that made him want to smile. To please his mother, he had bathed and shaved and shampooed. But he hadn't dressed and was still wearing only his bathrobe.

An old maid like Marcie probably wasn't used to talking to a barefooted, bare-legged, bare-chested man, although she had demonstrated aplomb when he had come out of his hospital bed wearing nothing more than his bandage.

A hospital room was a safe, uncompromising environment compared to a man's apartment, however. Chase sensed her uneasiness and decided that it served her right for butting in where she wasn't wanted.

"These are for you." She extended him the colorful bouquet.

"Flowers?"

"Is it unmacho for a man to accept flowers?" she asked testily.

"It's not that. They remind me of funerals." He laid the bouquet on the coffee table, which Devon had polished to a high gloss earlier that afternoon. "Thanks for thinking of flowers, but I'd rather have a bottle of whiskey. I'm not particular about brand names."

She shook her head. "Not as long as you're taking painkillers."

"Those pills don't kill the pain."

"If your ribs are hurting that badly, maybe you should go to the emergency room here and check in."

"I wasn't talking about that pain," he mumbled, swinging away and moving to the bar where he had left his dinner. "Want some?"

"Chili?" With distaste she stared down into the bowl of greasy Texas red. "What happened to the chicken soup your mother made for you?"

"I ate it for lunch but couldn't stomach it for two meals in a row."

"I bought the canned chili today thinking it would make a convenient meal in a day or two. Spicy food like that probably isn't the best thing for you right now."

"Don't nag me about my food."

He plopped down on the stool and spooned a few more bites into his mouth. Raising his head, he signaled her toward another of the barstools. She slipped off her jacket and sat down.

After scraping the bowl clean, he pushed it away. Marcie got up and carried it to the sink. She conscientiously rinsed it and placed it in the dishwasher, along with the pan he'd heated it up in. Then she moved to the coffee table, got the flowers, placed them in a large iced-tea glass, and set them down on the bar in front of him.

"No sense in letting them die prematurely just because you're a jerk," she said as she returned to her stool.

He snorted a wiseass laugh. "You're going to waste, Marcie. You'd make some man a good little wife. You're so—" He broke off and peered at her more closely. "What's the matter with your eyes?"

"What do you mean?"

"They're red. Have you been crying?"

"Crying? Of course not. My contacts were bothering me. I had to take them out."

"Contacts. I didn't realize until I saw you in your glasses that you usually wear contacts now. Your looks have improved since high school."

"That's a backhanded compliment, but thanks."

He looked down at her chest. "You're not flat-chested anymore."

"It's still nothing spectacular. Nothing like your ladylove."

The muscles in his face pulled taut. "Ladylove?"

"The woman last night."

He relaxed. "Oh. She had big boobs, huh?"

Marcie cupped her hands in front of her chest. "Out to here. Don't you remember?"

"No. I can't recall a single feature."

"You don't remember the silver hair and magenta fingernails?"

"Nope." Looking her straight in the eye, he added, "She was just an easy lay."

Marcie calmly folded her arms on the bar. Her eyes remained steady as she leaned toward him. "Look, Chase, let me spare you the trouble of trying to insult me. There isn't a single insult I haven't heard from being called Four Eyes and Bird Legs and Carrot-top and Goosey. So you can act like a bastard when I bring you flowers and it's not going to faze me.

"As for off-color comments, I've worked with and around men since I graduated from college. I could match every dirty joke you can think of with one even dirtier. I know all the locker-room phrases. Nothing you say can offend or shock me.

"I realize that your virility didn't die with your wife, though you might have wanted it to. You have physical needs, which you appease with whatever woman is available at the time. I neither commend nor criticize you for that. Sexuality is a human condition. Each of us deals with it in his own way. No, it's not *your* behavior that confounds me, but the women who let you use them.

"You have people who care about you, yet you continue to scorn and abuse their concern. Well, I won't allow you to do that to me any longer. I've got better, eminently more satisfying ways to spend my time."

She stood and reached for her jacket, pulled it on. "You're probably too stupid to realize that the best thing that ever happened to you was that damned bull named El Dorado. It's only unfortunate that he didn't give you a good, swift kick in the head. It might have knocked some sense into it."

She headed for the door, but got no farther than his arm's reach. He caught the hem of her jacket and drew her up short. "I'm sorry." For reasons he couldn't understand, he heard himself say, "Please stay awhile."

Turning around, she glared down at him. "So you can make more snide remarks about my single status? So you can try to shock me with vulgarities?"

"No. So I won't be so damn lonely."

Chase didn't know why he was being so baldly honest with her. Perhaps because she was so honest about herself. In everyone else's eyes, she was a successful, attractive woman. When she looked in the mirror, however, she saw the tall, skinny, carrot-headed bookworm in glasses and braces.

"Please, Marcie."

She put up token resistance when he gave her arm a tug, but eventually she relented and returned to her stool. Her chin was held high, but after their exchanged stare had stretched out for several moments, her lower lip began to quiver.

"You do blame me for Tanya's death, don't you?"

He took both her hands, pressing them between his. "No," he said with quiet insistence. "No. I never wanted to give you that impression. I'm sorry if I have."

"When you came to my hospital room the morning after the accident, I asked you if you blamed me. Remember?"

"No. I was saturated with grief. I don't remember much about those first few weeks after it happened. Lucky told me later that I acted like a nut case.

"But I do remember that I didn't harbor a grudge against you, Marcie. I blame the boy who ran the stop sign. I blame God. Not you. You were a victim, too. I saw that today when you were driving us home."

He stared at their clasped hands, but he didn't really see them. Nor did he feel them as he rubbed the pad of his thumb over the ridge of her knuckles.

"I loved Tanya so much, Marcie."

"I know that."

"But you can't understand . . . nobody can understand how much I loved her. She was kind and caring. She never wanted to make waves, couldn't abide anyone's being upset. She knew how to tease enough to make it fun but not enough to hurt. Never to hurt. We had terrific sex. She made bad days better and good days great."

He pulled in a deep breath and expelled it slowly. "Then she was gone. So suddenly. So irretrievably. There was just this empty place, vapor, where she had been."

He felt an unmanly lump forming in his throat and swallowed it with difficulty. "I told her good-bye. Gave her a hug and a kiss. Waved to her as she left with you. The next time I saw her, she was stretched out on a slab in the morgue. It was cold. Her lips were blue."

"Chase."

"And the baby. My baby. It died inside her." Scalding tears filled his eyes. He withdrew his hands from Marcie's and crammed his fists into his eye sockets. "Christ."

"It's okay to cry."

He felt her hand on his shoulder, kneading gently. "If only I had gone with you like she wanted me to, maybe it wouldn't have happened."

"You don't know that."

"Why didn't I go? What was so damned important that I couldn't get away? If I had, maybe I would have been sitting where she was. Maybe she would have been spared to have our baby, and I would have died. I wish I had. I wanted to."

"No, you didn't." Marcie's harsh tone of voice brought his head up. He lowered his hands from his eyes. "If you say anything like that again, I'll slap you again."

"It's the truth, Marcie."

"It is not," she declared, shaking her head adamantly. "If you really wanted to die, why aren't you buried beside Tanya now? Why haven't you pulled the trigger or driven off the bridge or picked up the razor or swallowed a handful of pills?" She came to her feet, quaking with outrage as she bore down on him.

"There are dozens of ways one can do away with himself, Chase. Booze and easy women and bull riding are among them. But they sure as hell aren't the fastest means of self-destruction. So either you're lying about seriously desiring death or you're grossly inefficient. All you've done effectively is fall apart at the seams and make life miserable for everyone around you."

He came to his feet, too. Grief wasn't paining his injured chest now so much as anger. "Just where the hell do you get off talking to me like this? When you've lost the person you love, when you've lost a child, *then* you'll be at liberty to talk to me about falling apart. Until that time, get out of my life and leave me alone."

"Fine. But not before leaving you with one final thought. You're not honoring Tanya with this kind of bereavement. It's unintelligent and unhealthy. For the brief time I knew her, she impressed me as one of the most life-loving people I'd ever met. She positively idolized you, Chase. In her eyes you could do no wrong. I wonder if she would have the least bit of respect for you if she could see the mess you've made of your life since she's been gone. Would she be pleased to know that you've crumpled? I seriously doubt it."

He ground his teeth so hard it made his jaws ache. "I said to get out."

"I'm going." Hastily she fished in her purse and produced a folded sheet of pink paper. She spread it open on the bar. "That's the itemized receipt from the hospital bill that I paid for you. I'll collect it in full tomorrow."

"You already know I don't have any money."

"Then I suggest you get some. Good night."

She didn't even wait for him to go to the door with her, but crossed his living room, flung open the door, and marched out, seemingly impervious to the rain. She soundly pulled the door closed behind her.

"Bitch," he muttered, sweeping the receipt off the bar with one swipe of his hand. It fluttered to his feet. He gave it a vicious kick that sent a sharp pain through his ribs. Wincing, he hobbled toward the bedroom and the bottle of pills on his nightstand.

He uncapped the prescription bottle and shook out a capsule, then tossed it to the back of his throat and swallowed it without bothering to get a glass of water.

As he was returning the bottle of pills to the nightstand, he paused. Turning the amber plastic bottle end over end, he considered taking all the capsules at one time.

He couldn't even conceive of it.

He lowered himself to the edge of his bed. Was Marcie right then? If he had seriously wanted to end his life when Tanya's ended, why hadn't he? There had been many opportunities when he'd been away from home, on the road, in the company of temporary friends, lonely, broke, drunk, and depressed. Yet he had never even thought of actual suicide.

Somewhere deep inside, he must have felt that life was still worth living. But for what?

He lifted his gaze to the framed photograph of Tanya and him taken on their wedding day. God, she had been lovely. Her smile had come through her eyes straight from her heart. He had known unequivocally that she loved him. He believed to this day that she had died knowing that he loved her. How could she not know? He had dedicated his life to never letting her doubt it.

Marcie was right in another respect—he wasn't honoring Tanya's memory by living the way he presently was. Odd, that an outsider, and not one of his own family, had read him so right and had known just what strings to pull to make him sit up and take notice of his life.

Tanya had been proud of his ambition. Since her death he hadn't had any ambition beyond drinking enough to dull his senses and cloud his memory. At first he had put in token appearances at the office of Tyler Drilling, but one morning when he'd shown up drunk while Lucky was cultivating a potential client, his brother had blown up and told him he'd just as soon not have him around if he was going to jeopardize what little business they had.

That's when he'd gone on the road, following the rodeo circuit, riding bulls in as many rodeos as he could afford to enter. He won just enough prize money to keep him in gasoline and whiskey, and that was all that mattered. One kept him away from home and the other made him temporarily forget the heartache he had left there.

His life had become a nonproductive cycle of whoring, drinking, gambling, fighting, riding bulls. Winning money, spending it. Moving from place to place, roaming aimlessly, never stopping long enough to deal with what he was running from.

The smiling groom in the photograph on the nightstand didn't even resemble him now. In fact it mocked him. How naive he'd been then, to think that life came with a guarantee of unending happiness. He studied Tanya's blond prettiness, touched the corner of her smile, and felt remorse for the shame he'd brought to her memory.

According to his mother's speech, his family's patience with him was finally expended. He had alienated all his friends. He was flat broke. He was bedding women he couldn't even remember in the morning. Like the prodigal in the New Testament, he'd reached rock bottom.

It was time he pulled himself together. Life wasn't going to be fun no matter what he did, but it sure as hell couldn't get any worse than it had been.

Tomorrow he'd talk to Lucky and find out what was going on with their business or even if they still had a business. Tomorrow he'd go see his mother and thank her for the chicken soup. Tomorrow he'd scrape up enough money to repay Marcie. That would be a start. He would take it one day at a time.

But first, he thought, as he raised the picture to his lips and kissed her image, he would cry for Tanya one more time.

Chapter Four

"Damn, Sage!" Chase shouted at his younger sister as she drove straight over a chuckhole. "My ride on that bull was nothing compared to your driving." He tentatively touched his aching ribs.

"Sorry," she said cheekily, smiling at him across the console of her car. "That hole wasn't there the last time I was in town. Nor were you for that matter. The last we had heard, you were in Montana or someplace."

Chase had been glad to see her. She had knocked loudly on his door while he was brewing a pot of coffee after a surprisingly restful night.

"Chase!" she had cried, exuberantly throwing herself against him and hugging him hard before he yelped and set her away.

"Watch the ribs."

She had swiftly apologized and joined him for coffee and toast. Since he was still without transportation, he had asked her to drive him to the company headquarters as soon as he was showered and dressed.

"How often do you come home?" he asked her now.

"Hmm, every other month maybe. But when Mother called last night and said you were home, I dropped everything and drove in."

"In this weather?"

It was still cold and wet. The rain was expected to start freezing later in the day. Weathermen in the whole northern half of the state were warning people not to drive unless it was absolutely necessary.

"I was careful. By now I know the road between here and Austin better than I know the back of my hand."

He looked at her profile, which had matured since the last time he'd really taken notice of her. "You look good, Sage," he remarked truthfully.

"Thanks." She winked at him saucily. "I come from good stock." He harrumphed dismissively. "Don't pretend you don't know we're an unusually attractive family. All my girlfriends used to positively drool over you and Lucky. They begged to sleep over, hoping against hope they'd catch one or both of you in the hallways partially unclothed, like without your shirts. I think you two are the reason I had so many friends. Girlfriends that is. You scared the boys off."

"*You* scared the boys off," he said, chuckling. It had been a long time since he'd laughed, and for a moment it surprised him. "You never learned the art of flirting, Sage."

"If you mean that I never swooned over biceps, you're right. It just wasn't in me to make out like some dolt had invented the wheel. I couldn't gush and simper and keep a straight face. Thank God Travis doesn't expect that from me."

"Travis?"

"You don't know about Travis? Oh, yeah, you haven't been home when he's come with me."

"You're bringing him home? Sounds serious."

"We're not formally engaged, but it's understood that we'll get married."

"Understood by whom? You or him?"

She shot him a fulminating look. "Both. He's going through medical school now. We'll probably wait until he's in his year of residency before we get married. He wants to be a dermatologist and make tons of money."

"By squeezing zits?"

"Hey, somebody's got to do it. His dad is a bone surgeon. Does football knees and stuff. They live in Houston in this gorgeous house that one of the Oilers used to own. It has a pond with ducks and swans in the backyard. Everybody in the family has his own BMW."

"Good. Marry the guy so you'll no longer be a liability to us."

He was on the receiving end of another dirty look. "That's almost exactly what Lucky said."

"Great minds think alike."

Sage had accelerated her academic curriculum enough to graduate a semester ahead of schedule. Chase hadn't made it to her commencement. He apologized for that now.

"Forget it. You didn't miss anything. I looked terrible in a cap and gown. Anyway, I immediately enrolled in graduate school."

"Have you decided what you're going to do with your expensive degree? Or is being Mrs. Doctor Travis whatever going to be enough for you?"

"Heck no. Being Mrs. anybody wouldn't be enough for me. I'm never going to be totally dependent on any man. I want a career like Devon. She's managed to blend her work with a happy marriage. *Very* happy, if the silly grin on Lucky's face is any indication. Even after two years of marriage, our brother is still besotted with his wife."

"I can understand that," Chase said introspectively. Sage either didn't hear him or chose to let his remark pass without comment.

"Anyway, I haven't quite made up my mind yet what I want to do. I majored in business. I'm taking graduate courses that could apply to any field."

"Corn field? Cotton field?"

"Do you want another broken rib?" she threatened.

He chuckled. "Whatever field it is, I hope it makes you rich and self-supporting."

"Amen. I want to become independently wealthy like your friend Marcie Johns."

"Is she?"

"What, wealthy? She must be. She wins all kinds of awards. Realtor of the Year. Businesswoman of the Year. Things like that. Her picture is in the paper just about every month for selling the most houses even in this depression or recession or whatever it is that we're in."

"Business major. Right," he said sarcastically.

Sage ignored that crack. "Mother said Ms. Johns looked positively radiant yesterday."

"Radiant?"

"Which I think is remarkable considering that she had a difficult time recovering from the accident. I think she had to have some plastic surgery done to cover a scar on her forehead. I heard some women in the beauty parlor speculating on whether or not she had had an eye job and a chin tuck while she was at it.

"She's . . . what? Your age, right? Thirty-five? Isn't that about the time everything starts sliding downhill? For women, I mean. Damn you men. Your looks improve with age. That's one of many grievances I'm going to bring up with God when I get to heaven. It isn't fair that y'all get better looking while we go to pot."

"But I don't believe Ms. Johns had cosmetic surgery," Sage continued. "Her self-esteem appears to be well cemented. I doubt it would be shaken by a few character lines in her face. Anyway, why would she bother? She's already gorgeous."

"Gorgeous? Goosey?" Chase was stunned. He would never have

attached that adjective to Goosey Johns, but then women had different criteria for beauty than men did.

"Her hair is to die for."

Chase barked an incredulous laugh. "It looks like a struck match."

"What do you know?" Sage said with scathing condescension. "Other women pay hundreds for hennas that color."

"For what?"

"Here we are. Lucky's here, so I'll just drop you off. I promised Mother I'd run errands for her so she wouldn't have to get out today. Pat called her this morning and advised her to stay indoors."

"How is Pat?"

Pat Bush was the county sheriff. Two years earlier he'd been instrumental in clearing Lucky of a false arson charge, which had eventually brought Lucky and Devon together. For as long as the Tyler siblings could remember, Sheriff Bush had been their family friend.

"Pat never changes," Sage said. "But ever since Tanya died in that car crash, he's skittish about traffic accidents and stays after Mother to be doubly careful when she drives."

Hearing Tanya's name sent a little dart of pain through Chase's heart, but he smiled at his sister and thanked her for the lift.

"Chase," Sage called to him as he ducked under the porch roof to get out of the rain. He looked back. She had rolled down her window and was smiling at him through the opening. "Welcome back."

His sister was more mature and insightful than he had given her credit for. Her words carried a double meaning. He formed a fake pistol with his hand and fired it at her. Laughing, she put her car in reverse and backed out to turn around. They waved to each other as she drove off.

His stomach roiled with the memory of standing on this same porch and watching Tanya and Marcie drive away that fateful afternoon. He had waved good-bye then, too.

Putting aside the unpleasant memory, he stepped into the office. Though he hadn't been there in months, nothing had changed. The company office hadn't been modernized since his grandfather had occupied it. It stayed untidy, cluttered, and unabashedly masculine. Even the smells were the same, from the mustiness of old maps and geological charts to the aroma of fresh coffee. The room's cozy warmth seemed to embrace him like a fond relative he hadn't seen in a while.

Lucky was bent over the scarred wooden desk, the fingers of one hand buried up to the first knuckle in his dark-blond hair and the others drumming out a tattoo on top of the littered desk. He raised his head when Chase walked in, his surprise evident.

"Looks serious," Chase said.

"You don't know how serious." Lucky glanced beyond his brother as though expecting someone to follow him in. "How'd you get here?"

"Sage." Chase removed his shearling jacket and shook the rain off it. "She came by the apartment this morning."

"I nearly paddled her when she showed up last night. I hated to think of her driving all that way alone in this weather."

"I would have hated it, too, if I'd known about it. But I was glad to see her. She's . . ." he searched for the right word and came up short.

"Right," Lucky said. "She's a grown-up, not a kid any longer. But she's still a spoiled brat."

"Who's Travis? Seems I'm the only member of the family who hasn't had the pleasure."

Lucky winced. "Pleasure my ass. He's a preppie wimp. The only reason she likes him is because she can lead him around by the nose."

"If he marries her, he'll have his hands full."

"You can say that again. We played so many tricks on her when she was little, she learned to fight back. I'm about half scared of her myself."

The brothers laughed. Their laughter turned poignant, until both became uncomfortable with their rising emotions.

"God, it's good to have you back," Lucky said huskily. "I missed you, big brother."

"Thanks," Chase said, clearing his throat. "I only hope I can stay. If it gets to be too much . . . what I mean is, I can't promise . . ."

Lucky patted the air with his hand, indicating that he understood. "I don't expect you to jump in with both feet. Test the waters. Take your time." Chase nodded. After a short but awkward silence, Lucky offered him a cup of coffee.

"No thanks."

"How are you feeling this morning?"

He answered dourly, "Like a damn Brahman did the two-step on my chest."

"Which is no better than you deserve for getting on one in the first place." He gestured toward Chase's chest. "Think you're going to be okay?"

"Sure," Chase said dismissively. "They've got me bound up so tight those cracked ribs wouldn't move in an earthquake. I'll be fine." He nodded toward the paperwork scattered across the desk. "How's business?"

"What business?"

"That bad?"

"Worse."

Lucky got up and moved toward one of the windows. He rubbed a circle in the condensation and gazed out at the dripping eaves. Every so often a chip of sleet would land on the porch, then quickly dissolve. Hopefully the temperature would remain above freezing.

He turned back to face the room. "I'm not sure you're in any condition to hear this, Chase."

"Will I ever be?"

"No."

"Then give it to me straight."

Lucky returned to the desk and glumly dropped into the chair behind it. "We'll have to file for Chapter Eleven bankruptcy if a miracle doesn't happen. And I mean soon." Chase's shoulders slumped forward. He looked down at the floor. "I'm sorry, Chase. I just couldn't hold it together. The few projects we had going fell apart after you left."

"Hell, don't apologize. Even in my drunkest days, I kept abreast of the Texas economy. I knew it was bad."

"Our former clients are worse off than we are. Most independent oilmen have already gone belly up. The others are dead in the water, waiting for the lending institutions to pick clean their carcasses.

"I've tried my damnedest to cultivate new clients, people from out of state who still have working capital. No dice. Nobody's doing anything. Zilch."

"So all our equipment that was replaced after the fire . . ."

"Has stood idle most of that time. We might as well have left the price tags on it. That's not the worst of it." Lucky sighed with dread. "I couldn't keep the crew on a regular payroll when they were just standing around doing nothing, so I had to let them go. Hated it like hell, Chase. I know Granddad and Dad were rolling over in their graves. You know how loyal they were to the men who worked for them. But I had no choice but to lay them off."

"It becomes a vicious cycle because that places them in a bind."

"Right. They've got families. Kids to clothe, mouths to feed. It made me feel like hell to give them notice."

"What about our personal finances?"

"We've had to cash in some of Dad's savings. Mother and Devon are good money managers. A few months ago, I sold a colt. That helped. We can go another six months maybe before it becomes critical. Of course the longer Tyler Drilling is insolvent, the more vulnerable our personal situation becomes."

Chase drew a discouraged breath. When he made to leave his chair, Lucky said, "Wait. There's more. You might as well hear all of it." He met his brother's eyes squarely, grimly. "The bank is calling in our loan. George Young telephoned last week and said they couldn't settle for only the interest payments any longer. They need us to make a substantial reduction in the principal."

Lucky spread his hands wide over the desktop. "The funds simply aren't there, Chase. I don't even have enough cash to make the interest payment."

"I don't suppose you'd consider tumbling Susan."

Susan Young, the banker's spoiled daughter, had had designs on Lucky and had tried blackmailing him into marriage. Lucky, a natural con man, had outconned her. So Chase was teasing when he brought Susan's name into the conversation, but Lucky answered him seriously.

"If I thought it would make any headway with her old man, I'd be unbuttoning my jeans even as we speak." Then he laughed. "Like hell I would. Devon would kill me." He spread his arms wide, shrugged helplessly, and grinned like a Cheshire cat. "What can I say? The broad is crazy about me."

Chase wasn't fooled into thinking the love affair was one-sided. His brother had been a ladies' man from the time he discovered the difference between little girls and little boys. His reputation as a stud had been well-founded. However, when he met Devon Haines, she knocked him for a loop. He hadn't recovered from it yet.

"From what I hear and have seen for myself, the attraction is mutual."

Chagrined, Lucky ducked his head. "Yeah. As bad as things have been, I'm happier than I ever dreamed possible."

"Good," Chase said solemnly. "That's good." Another silence fell between them. By an act of will Chase threw off his melancholia again and got down to business.

"One reason I came over this morning was to see if there was any money in the till. I find myself indebted to a certain redhead."

"Devon? What for?"

"Another redhead. Marcie. She paid my hospital bill. God knows how I'll pay her back."

Lucky stood up and moved to a filing cabinet. From the drawer he took out a savings account passbook. "This is yours," he said, handing it to Chase, who looked at it curiously.

"What is it?"

"Chase, I sold that house you had me buy after Tanya was killed."

Everything inside Chase went very still. He had forgotten all about that. He had insisted his brother buy the house Tanya had been viewing the afternoon of the accident. In retrospect he realized it had been a knee-jerk reaction to her untimely death. He hadn't given it another thought. He had never seen the house, never wanted to. He certainly never planned to live in it.

He flipped open the vinyl cover of the passbook. There was only one entry—a deposit. The amount was staggering to a man who had believed himself penniless. "Jesus, where did all this come from?"

"Tanya's life insurance policy."

Chase dropped the passbook as though it had burned his fingers. It landed on the desktop. He shot out of his chair and moved to the same position in front of the window where Lucky had stood earlier. The scenery hadn't improved. It was still a dreary day.

"I didn't know what to do with the insurance check when it finally worked its way through all the red tape and was delivered. You were still around then, but you were drunk all the time and in no condition to discuss it or deal with it, so I endorsed it by forging your name, then used it to buy the house.

"About a year ago, Marcie came to see me. She had a client who was interested in buying the property. She thought you might want to sell the house since you had never occupied it and evidently never intended to.

"You were unavailable, Chase, so I had to make the decision on my own. I decided to unload it while I could, make you a couple of grand, and bank the money until you needed or wanted it."

Lucky paused, but Chase said nothing. Finally Lucky added uncertainly, "I hope I did the right thing."

Coming around, Chase rubbed the back of his neck. "Yeah, you did the right thing. I never wanted the house after Tanya died. The only reason I had you buy it was because she wanted it so damn bad."

"I understand. Anyway," Lucky said, shifting moods, "you've got a little nest egg you didn't know you had."

"We'll use it to pay off our loan."

"Thanks, Chase, but it won't make a dent. It'll cover the interest, but we've got to take care of the principal too. This time, they're getting nasty."

It was too much to deal with all at once. He felt like someone who had suffered a debilitating injury and had to learn to function all over again—walk, talk, cope.

"Let me see what I can do," Chase told his brother. "Maybe if I talk to George, assure him that I'm back and ready to get busy again, we can stave them off another few months."

"Good luck, but don't get your hopes up."

Chase took the keys to one of the company pickups. It hadn't been driven in months and was reluctant to start. The cold weather didn't help any. Finally, however, he got the engine to cooperate.

As he drove away from Tyler Drilling Company headquarters, he couldn't help but wonder if it would be there much longer. As the elder son, could he live with himself if it failed?

Chapter Five

From all appearances she was a kook. She had a pixie haircut that cupped her small head, eyeglasses that covered a large portion of her face, and earrings the size of saucers clipped to her earlobes. The name plate on her desk read ESME.

"I'm sorry, but Ms. Johns has left for the day," she told Chase. "Can I help you?"

"I need to see Marcie."

He supposed he could leave the check with Marcie's secretary, but he wanted the satisfaction of handing it to her in person. She had been so snippy about it last night, he wanted to place it in her greedy little hands and finish their business with each other. He was uncomfortable feeling indebted to her.

He was in a querulous mood. His ribs were aching because he hadn't taken any of the prescribed pain medication that day. His interview with George Young had been as unpleasant as Lucky had predicted. Not only was the banker trying to protect himself from the bank examiners, but Chase suspected him of holding a grudge against the Tylers because Lucky hadn't fallen head over heels in love with his devious daughter.

George had obviously taken Lucky's rejection of Susan as a personal affront. Or, Chase thought uncharitably, maybe he was simply disappointed that Lucky hadn't taken her off his hands. The girl was bad news, and for the time being, George was still stuck with her.

Chase was stuck with a check he wanted badly to get rid of. Finding that Marcie wasn't at her real estate office didn't improve his disposition. "Where does she live?"

"Can your business wait until tomorrow?" Esme asked. "Were you wanting to see Ms. Johns about listing your house or were you interested in seeing one? The weather isn't—"

"This isn't about a house. My business with Ms. Johns is personal."

The secretary's eyes were magnified even larger behind her lenses. "Oh, really?"

"Really. What's her address?"

She eyed him up and down. He obviously passed muster because she reached for a sheet of tasteful, gray stationery with Marcie's letterhead engraved across the top and wrote down an address. "The road is probably muddy," Esme said as she handed him the piece of paper.

"It doesn't matter." The company pickup had navigated creek beds, rocky inclines, thick forests, and cow pastures to reach drilling sites. No terrain was too rough for it.

He glanced at the address, but didn't recognize it, which was unusual since he'd grown up in Milton Point and had spent his youth cruising its streets. "Where is this?"

Esme gave him rudimentary directions and he set out. His windshield wipers had to work double time to keep the rain and sleet clear. There were patches of ice on the bridges, and after skidding a couple of times, he cursed Marcie for living in the boondocks. His family lived outside the city limits, too, but at least he was familiar with that road.

When he reached the turnoff, he almost missed it. The gravel road was narrow and marked only with a crude, hand-lettered sign. "Woodbine Lane," he muttered.

The name was appropriate, because honeysuckle vines grew thickly along the ditches on either side of the road. They were burdened with a glaze of ice now, but in the spring and summer when they bloomed, they would perfume the air.

The road was a cul-de-sac. There were no other houses on it. At the end of it stood an unpainted frame structure nestled in a forest of pine and various hardwoods. The entry was level with the ground, but the house sat on a bluff that dropped away drastically. The back of the house was suspended above the ground, supported on metal beams.

He pulled the pickup to a halt and got out. His boots crunched over the icy spots on the path as he carefully picked his way toward the front door. Slipping and falling on ice wouldn't do his cracked ribs any good.

The northwesterly wind was frigid; he flipped up the collar of his lambskin coat. When he reached the front door, he took off one glove and depressed the button of the doorbell. He heard it chime inside.

In a moment Marcie pulled open the door. She seemed surprised to see him. "Chase?"

"I thought the kook might have called you."

"How did you know about the kook?"

"Pardon?"

Shaking her head in confusion, she stepped aside and motioned him in. "It's gotten worse." She commented on the weather as she closed the door against the gusts of cold wind. "How did you know where I live? Come in by the fire. Would you like some tea?"

She led him into one of the most breathtaking rooms he'd ever seen. He hadn't known there was anything like its contemporary design in Milton Point. The ceiling was two stories high. One wall had a fireplace, in which a fire was burning brightly. Another wall, the one suspended above ground, was solid glass, from the hardwood floor to the ceiling twenty or more feet above it.

An island bar separated the large living area from the kitchen. It was utilitarian; it was also designed for casual dining. A gallery encircled the second story on three sides with what he guessed were bedrooms opening off it.

"There's another room behind the fireplace wall," Marcie explained, obviously noticing his interest. "I use it as an office, although it could be a guest room. There are two bedrooms and two baths upstairs."

"You sound like a realtor."

She smiled. "Habit, I guess."

"Have you lived here long?"

"Awhile."

"Aren't you afraid to live alone in a house this large, this far out?"

"Not really. It has a security system. I'm used to the solitude." Tilting her head to one side, she said reflectively, "I guess it's rather selfish for one person to occupy so much space, but I needed the tax shelter. The property is an investment, and with the mortgage that I—"

He held up both hands. "All that stuff is lost on me. I have never understood it. Suffice it to say you've got a nice place."

"Thank you. Let me take your coat."

He hesitated; he hadn't counted on staying that long. However, the fire did look inviting. After coming all this way, he might as well stay awhile and warm up.

He shrugged out of his coat, removed his other glove, and handed them to Marcie. While she was putting his things away, he moved to the fireplace, placed one foot on the low, stone hearth, and extended both hands toward the friendly flames.

"Feels good," he said when she moved up beside him.

"Hmm. I've been curled up in front of it most of the afternoon. Not too many people are house-shopping today, so I decided it was a perfect time to catch up on paperwork."

The cushions of a sprawling cream-colored leather chair were littered with contracts and property plats, as though she'd left them there when she got up to answer the door. There was a pencil stuck behind her right ear, almost buried in a mass of hair that his sister had said was to die for. She was dressed in a soft, purple suede skirt, a matching sweater, opaque stockings . . . and fuzzy, blue Smurf house shoes that enveloped her feet up to her slender ankles.

She followed his amused gaze down to her feet. "A gag gift from my office assistant."

"The kook."

Marcie laughed. "You met Esme?"

"I stopped by your office. She gave me directions here."

"Her zaniness is a pose, I assure you. She affects it so people won't know how smart she really is. Anyway, I'm always complaining about cold feet."

"Literally or figuratively?"

"Literally for myself, figuratively for buyers who back out at the last minute."

Chase suddenly realized that the conversations he and Marcie had engaged in were the longest conversations he had had with a woman since Tanya died. After asking a woman what she was drinking, few words were exchanged until he said a terse "Thanks" and left her on a tousled bed.

The thought made him wince. Marcie misinterpreted it. "Are your ribs hurting?"

"Some," he conceded. "I've been out and around today, so I haven't taken any painkillers."

"Would you like a drink?"

His eyes sprang up to connect with hers. They held for a moment before moving down to the cup and saucer sitting on the end table next to the leather chair. "Thanks anyway, but tea's not my bag."

"If you meant that as a pun, it's terrible."

"You were the word whiz."

"Instead of tea, what I had in mind was a bourbon and water."

"Thanks, Marcie." He spoke soulfully, thanking her for the vote of confidence she had placed in him, as much as for the drink.

She moved toward the island bar and opened the cabinet beneath it.

Selecting a bottle from the modest stock, she splashed whiskey into two tumblers. "The bourbon can't be any more anesthetizing than one of your pain pills. Besides, you can't sip a pill in front of the fireplace," she added with a smile. "Ice?"

"Just water." He thanked her when she handed him the glass. She stacked together the paperwork she'd been working on and resumed her seat in the leather chair, curling her feet beneath her. Nodding toward the hearth, she suggested he sit there so they could face each other.

"And while you're at it, you can add a log to the fire. That's the price of your drink."

After adding to the logs in the grate, Chase sat down on the hearth, spreading his knees wide, and rolled the tumbler between his hands. "I have a check in my pocket for five hundred seventy-three dollars and sixty-two cents. That's why I came out. I wanted to repay you in person and say thanks for all you did."

She lowered her eyes to her own whiskey and water. "I behaved badly about that. I lost my temper. It made me angry to hear you say you wished you were dead. It was a stupid thing to say, Chase."

"I realize that now."

"So you didn't have to worry about paying me back so soon. Anytime would have been all right."

He laughed mirthlessly. "I might not have the money 'anytime.' If you hadn't sold that house, I wouldn't have a red cent."

"Then you know about that, and it's okay? Lucky was concerned."

He nodded. "I never intended to live there. I'd even forgotten about it until today." He sat up straighter and attempted a smile. "So you can credit your salesmanship for your having a check today." He extracted it from the breast pocket of his shirt and handed it to her.

"Thank you." She didn't even look to see if the amount was correct before adding it to the stack of papers on the end table. "To your speedy recovery." She raised her glass. He tapped it with his. They each sipped from their drinks.

For several moments they were silent, listening to the crackling of the burning logs and the occasional tapping sound of sleet crystals hitting the windows that overlooked the woods. Even bare of foliage, the forest was dense. Tree trunks were lined up evenly, looking as straight and black as charred matchsticks, their edges slightly blurred by rainfall.

"Who told you about my phone calls?"

He turned his head away from his contemplation of the woods and looked at her inquiringly. "What phone calls?"

Then it was her turn to appear confused. "When you came in, you mentioned the kook. I thought you were talking about the kook who keeps calling me."

"I was talking about your secretary, that Esme."

"Oh."

"Somebody keeps calling you?"

"Uh-huh."

"Who?"

"I don't know. If I did, I'd confront him and demand that he stop it."

"What does he say?"

"Oh, he likes to talk dirty and breathe heavily."

"What do you do?"

"Hang up."

"How often does he call?"

"There's no pattern. I might not hear from him for weeks, then he'll call several times in one evening. Sometimes it gets really annoying, so I take the phone off the hook. If Esme tried to call and tell me you were coming over, she couldn't have gotten through."

He followed her gaze to the telephone on the entry-hall table. The receiver was lying next to the cradle. "He called today?"

"Twice," she replied negligently. "It became a nuisance because I was trying to concentrate."

"You're sure casual about this, Marcie. Have you reported it to Pat?"

"The sheriff? No," she exclaimed, as though the suggestion were ridiculous. "It's probably just a teenager who gets his kicks by saying dirty words into a faceless woman's ear. If he had any courage, he would be saying those things to her in person."

"What kind of things does he say?"

"Very unoriginal. He'd like to see me naked, et cetera. He tells me all that he'd like to do with his tongue and . . ." She made a vague gesture. "You get the idea."

When she demurely lowered her lashes over her eyes, Chase noticed that Goosey came close to being gorgeous, as Sage had described her. With the firelight flickering over it, her skin appeared translucent. From her hairline to the vee of her sweater it was as smooth and flawless as the porcelain figurines his grandma used to keep in her china cabinet. Her high cheekbones cast shadows into the hollows of her cheeks.

"Did you have an eye job and a chin tuck?"

"What?" The question took her so by surprise, she almost spilled her drink.

"Sage said the ladies in the beauty parlor were speculating over whether or not you had an eye job thrown in when you had plastic surgery."

"No!" she cried again, truly incredulous. "They must not have much else to gossip about if I'm the hottest topic."

"Well, Lucky got married."

She laughed in earnest then. "Yes, he did keep the gossip mill churning, didn't he?"

"So you didn't have the doctor take an extra tuck or two?"

"No, I did not," she said tartly. "He just had to smooth out one scar right here." She drew an invisible mark along her hairline. "A shard of glass got imbedded there."

The inadvertent reminder of the accident put a pall over their easy dialogue. Chase considered tossing back the entire contents of his highball glass, but remembering the resolution he'd made last night, he decided against it and set it on the hearth instead. He stood up.

"Well, I'd better let you get back to work. I didn't mean to interrupt."

"You don't have to go." Unfolding her long, slender legs, she stood also. "I'm not under any kind of deadline to finish."

He looked beyond her toward the glass wall. "It's getting pretty bad out there. Now that I've done what I came for, I should head back to town."

"Hmm. Oh, by the way, the clients I was entertaining the other night called today and inquired about you. They're still interested in buying property over here."

"So you didn't lose a sale on my account."

"Doesn't look that way."

"Good."

"Do you have plans for dinner?"

He had already turned toward the door when her question brought him back around. "Dinner?"

"Dinner. The evening meal. Had you made plans?"

"Not really."

"Chili or sardines?"

He gave a lopsided grin. "Something like that."

"How does a steak sound?" She made a circle with both hands.

"About this big around. This thick." She held her index finger and thumb an inch and a half apart. "Grilled medium rare."

Dinner with Marcie. Dinner with a woman. Somehow that seemed like much more intimate coupling than having a few drinks followed by a roll in the sack, which had been his only interaction with women since he lost Tanya. No thinking was required. No commitment. No conversation.

Dinner, on the other hand, involved his head. Personalities entered in. And social graces, such as looking into her eyes when you said something to her, such as being expected to say something in the first place. He wasn't sure he was up to that yet.

But this was only Goosey, after all. Hell, he'd known her since he was five years old. She'd been a good friend to him the last couple of days. Apparently she had been looking after his interests for a while, because she had saved him the hassle of getting rid of that house he had bought for Tanya. And he couldn't dismiss how polite she'd been to Tanya, and how much Tanya had liked and respected her.

He could do her this one favor, couldn't he?

"Grill the steak blood rare and you've got yourself a deal."

She broke into a smile that made her face look—what was it his mother had said? Oh, yes. Radiant.

With no coyness whatsoever, Marcie excused herself to change into something more comfortable. She returned from one of the upstairs bedrooms dressed in a sweat suit and her Smurf shoes. The pencil had been removed from behind her ear, and she had swapped her contacts for her glasses.

Once the steaks were sizzling on the indoor grill, she put Chase to work making a green salad while she monitored the potatoes she was baking in the microwave oven.

She asked if he preferred formal or casual surroundings, and when he replied, "Casual," she spread place settings on the island bar instead of on the table in the separate dining room. In no time at all, they were seated, demolishing the simple but delicious food.

"I'm afraid there's no dessert," she said as she removed his empty plate, "but you'll find my stash of chocolate chip cookies in the canister on the counter."

The telephone rang—she had replaced the receiver when she returned downstairs. As she went to answer it she called over her shoulder, "You should feel privileged, Mr. Tyler. I don't share my chocolate chip cookies with just anybody. . . . Hello?"

She was smiling at Chase as she raised the receiver to her ear. He watched her smile collapse seconds after greeting her caller. She hastily turned her back to him. Tossing his napkin down onto the bar, he left his chair and in three long strides, crossed the room.

Before he could pluck the receiver away from her, she used both hands to cram it back onto the cradle of the phone, then braced herself against it as though wanting to hold down a lid over a garbage can full of something vile.

Her head remained lowered and averted, probably out of embarrassment. She wasn't as blasé about this as she wanted him to believe. She was visibly upset, her face leached of all color.

"Was that him?"

"Yes."

"Same kind of stuff?"

"Not quite." Her color returned, spreading over her cheeks like a rosy tide. "This time, instead of telling me what he wanted to do to me, he, uh, told me what he wanted me to, uh, do to myself . . . for his entertainment."

"Damn pervert."

Chase and his brother had been reared to respect women. Both their parents had drilled into them a sense of chivalry and sexual responsibility. Even during his drunkest binges, Chase had been careful to take the necessary precautions with the women he bedded. He had never taken advantage of a woman who didn't welcome him or even one who was reluctant to have him in her bed.

In their youthful, single days Lucky and he had enjoyed plenty of women, but always with the women's consent. They had never had to be coercive, but wouldn't have been anyway. Their father had taught them that no meant no when a lady said it. A gentleman never imposed himself on a woman, no matter what.

In Chase's book, telephone pornography was imposition, and it made him furious that Marcie was being subjected to it. Pillow talk was one thing, when you were whispering naughtily into the ear of a lover whose sexual enjoyment you were heightening. Hearing the same words over the telephone from a faceless stranger was sinister and frightening. He didn't blame her for turning pale with anxiety and revulsion.

"Is that the kind of trash you've been having to listen to?" he demanded of Marcie. She nodded and turned away, returning to the kitchen. He caught her arm and brought her back around. "For how long?"

"A few months," she said quietly.

"You shouldn't put up with that. Have your number changed. Let Pat put a tracer on your line."

He was so caught up in his argument that he didn't initially realize he still had hold of her arm and that he'd drawn her so close their bodies were touching. When he did, he released her and quickly stepped back.

He cleared his throat loudly and tried to sound authoritarian. "I, uh, just think you should do something about this."

She returned to the bar and began clearing the dishes. "I thought that after a while, if I continued simply to hang up, he would get discouraged and stop calling."

"Apparently not."

"No, apparently not." She set a stack of dirty dishes on the counter-top and turned on the hot-water faucet. "You never got your cookies. Help yourself."

"I don't want any cookies," he said irritably. For reasons he couldn't explain, he was angry with her for so blithely dismissing her obscene caller.

"Then why don't you make a pot of coffee while I'm putting these dishes in the dishwasher?" she suggested. "I keep the coffee in the freezer and the coffeemaker is right there."

She nodded toward the corner of the cabinetry. Chase recognized her suggestion for what it was—a conclusion to their discussion about her caller. Obviously she didn't want to talk about it anymore. Either she was too afraid to or too embarrassed to, or hell, maybe she got her kicks by listening to smut over the telephone.

She was, after all, a woman living alone, with no boyfriend on the scene. At least none he'd heard about or seen evidence of. The only man she had mentioned was the ex-fiancé in Houston. Maybe the caller was her no-hassle, nonbinding way of getting turned on. If so, why the hell was he worrying about it?

He started the coffee. It was ready by the time she had finished clearing the dishes. Loading a tray with fresh cups of coffee and a plate of chocolate chip cookies, she asked him to carry it into the living room. They resumed their original places near the fire, which Chase stoked before eating two cookies and washing them down with coffee.

"How are things at Tyler Drilling?"

He glanced across at her. "You're a savvy businesswoman, Marcie. You probably know more about the financial climate in this town than anybody else. Is that your tactful way of asking me how much longer we can hang on before declaring bankruptcy?"

"I wasn't prying. Honestly."

"It doesn't matter," he said with a philosophic shrug. "It's too late for pride. Before long, our financial status will be a matter of public record."

"It's that critical?"

"I'm afraid so." He gazed into the fire as he thoughtlessly poked another cookie into his mouth. "We're getting no new business. The bank has become impatient for us to pay back money we borrowed years ago when the market first started going sour. They've been generous to let it go this long, but our time has finally run out.

"Lucky has done the best he could, with no help from me," he added bitterly. "A couple of years ago we started trying to think of a way to diversify until the oil business picked up, but we never came up with any workable ideas. Then Tanya died and . . ." He shrugged again. The rest didn't need clarification.

"Chase." He raised his head and looked at her. She was running her fingertip around the rim of her coffee cup. When she felt his gaze, she looked up at him. "Let me put some money into your company."

He stared at her blankly for a moment, then gave a harsh, mirthless laugh. "I thought you were a shrewd businesswoman. Why would you want to do a damn fool thing like that?"

"Because I believe in you and Lucky. You're resourceful, bright, diligent. You'll eventually think of something to revive the business. When you do, I'll reap a tremendous profit on my investment."

Before she had finished, he was adamantly shaking his head. "I couldn't let you do it, Marcie. It would be like taking charity, and we haven't stooped that low yet. At this point we can retain a little pride.

"Besides, if we had wanted a partner, we would have considered that option a long time ago. We've even had offers, but always turned them down.

"My grandfather started this business during the thirties boom. My dad continued it. We're third generation. Tyler Drilling Company is a family operation, and we mean to keep it that way."

"I see," she said quietly.

"I appreciate your offer, but there's just no way I can accept it."

"There is one way." Her steady blue gaze locked with his. "You could marry me."

Chapter Six

Lucky replaced the telephone receiver and to his wife said, "He still doesn't answer."

From the doorway that connected their bedroom with the bath, Devon tried to reassure him. "That doesn't mean he's vanished again."

"But it might mean he's out getting blitzed."

"Not necessarily."

"Not *necessarily,* but probably."

"You're not showing much confidence in your older brother," she gently rebuked him.

"Well, in the past two years, name one thing he's done to inspire my confidence."

Devon turned on her bare heels and stamped into the bathroom, closing the door behind her so swiftly that it almost caught the hem of her peignoir.

Lucky went storming after her and threw open the door. Rather than finding her confrontational, she was seated at the dressing table, calmly pulling a hairbrush through her dark-auburn hair. Her loveliness squelched his anger.

She was an expert at igniting and defusing his temper and could do both instantly and effectively. Her reversals always came unexpectedly. That spontaneity made his life interesting and was one of the reasons he had fallen in love with her. Devon's unpredictability appealed to his own volatile nature.

He loved her madly, but hated when she was right. In this instance she was.

"That was a rotten thing for me to say, wasn't it?"

"Hmm," she replied. That was another thing he liked about her—

she never rubbed it in when she'd been right. "He did come home, Lucky."

"Under duress."

"But it couldn't have been easy for him."

"He wasn't exactly dragging his tail between his legs."

"Wasn't he? I believe all his mumbling and grumbling was to cover up how embarrassed he was to show how glad he was to be home, surrounded by people who love him."

"Maybe," Lucky conceded.

"He went to the office today and showed an interest in the business."

"Which might be only a token interest."

"It might be. But I don't think so." She set her hairbrush aside and uncapped a jar of night cream. Extending her arm, she began spreading on the scented cream. "I think we should give Chase the benefit of the doubt. Maybe he's finally beginning to heal."

"I hope so."

Lucky took the jar of cream from her, scooped some out with his fingers, and began smoothing it on where she had left off. He pushed her robe off her shoulders, slipped down the straps of her nightgown, and massaged the cream into skin so smooth it really didn't need extra emollients.

"Well, Laurie is encouraged by his coming home. That in itself makes me glad he's back." Devon bowed her head and moved aside her hair so he could rub her neck.

"But Mother doesn't know that he's out carousing tonight."

"Neither do you. He could be anywhere."

"It's not exactly a good night to take a drive."

"Even if he is out carousing, he's a grown man and accountable only to himself." She looked up at him through her lashes, speaking to his reflection in the mirror. "Just like you used to be."

"Humph," he grunted.

Lucky's attention had been diverted to his wife's alluring image in the mirror. The neckline of her nightgown had caught on the tips of her breasts. A single motion of his hand left the nightgown pooled in her lap, her breasts completely bare.

Both hands reached around to caress her. He watched his hands reshape, lift, stroke, and massage her breasts. When his touch began to have an effect, his own veins expanded with desire. "What did the doctor say today?" he asked in a soft voice.

"Baby and I are doing well," she told him, her lips curving into a madonna's sweet smile. "I'm a full five months."

"How long do you think we can keep it a secret?" His hands smoothed over the convex curve of her abdomen.

"Not much longer. If Laurie hadn't been so preoccupied with Chase, she probably would have noticed my thickening waistline."

"She and Sage are going to be mad as hell that we didn't tell them as soon as we found out."

"Probably. But I still think doing it this way was better. In case something happened."

"Thank God nothing has." He bent his head and kissed her shoulder.

"I don't believe Laurie could have withstood the loss of another grandchild. It was better that we not tell her we were expecting until I was out of the dangerous first trimester."

"But now you're into the second and the doctor doesn't expect any complications." He met her eyes in the mirror and smiled as he splayed his hand over her lower body. "I want to announce to the world that I'm going to be a daddy."

"But think of this, Lucky," she said, her smile gradually fading. "Now that Chase is home, maybe we should put off making an announcement for a while longer."

"Hmm." His eyebrows drew together. "I see what you mean. It's going to be tough on him to hear that we're going to have the first Tyler offspring."

Taking his hand, Devon kissed the palm. "You know how much I want our baby. But my happiness is clouded whenever I think of the child that died with Tanya."

"Don't think about it," Lucky whispered.

He drew her up, turned her around, and kissed her while he rid her of the peignoir. After stepping out of his briefs, he pulled her against him, letting her feel the strength of his erection. She sighed against his lips and suggested that he not waste any more time before taking her to bed.

Reclining together, he opened her thighs and kissed her there, testing her moisture with the tip of his tongue. Then he kissed his way up her body, pausing first to lay kisses across the slight mound of her abdomen, then lightly sucking the tips of her breasts, darkened and enlarged from pregnancy. At last he reached the welcome heat of her mouth and sent his tongue deep even as his sex delved into hers.

Marriage hadn't dimmed their physical passion for each other. It burned hotter than ever. Within minutes they both lay replete and satisfied.

Holding her close, Lucky gently stroked the area of her body where his child was nestled. He whispered, "In light of what he lost, how can I blame Chase for anything he does or doesn't do?"

"You can't," she answered, patting his hand. "You can only be patient until he finds a solution to his heartache."

"If there is a solution." He didn't sound too optimistic.

Devon stirred and said in that stubborn way of hers he found so endearing, "Oh, I have to believe there is."

Chase finally recovered his voice. His disbelieving stare was still fixed on his hostess. "What?"

"Are you going to make me repeat it?" Marcie asked. "All right. I said that you could save your business *and* keep it in the family if you married me. Because then, whatever I had would be yours."

He returned his unfinished cookie to the plate, dusted the crumbs off his fingers, and stood up. Quickly retrieving his coat, he pulled it on and started making his way toward the front door.

"Don't you think it warrants some discussion?" Marcie asked, following him.

"No."

She caught up with him before he could pull open the front door, placing her slim body between it and him. "Chase, please. If I had enough gumption to suggest it, the least you could do is have enough gumption to talk about it."

"Why waste my time and yours?"

"I don't feel like a discussion of my future is a waste of time."

He slapped the pair of chamois gloves against his other palm, trying to figure out how he was going to get away from there without hurting her feelings.

"Marcie, I don't know what prompted you to say such an outlandish thing. I can't imagine what was going through your mind. I'd like to think you were joking."

"I wasn't. I was serious."

"Then you leave me no choice but to say no thanks."

"Without even discussing it?"

"Without anything. It doesn't bear talking about."

"I disagree. I don't go around whimsically proposing marriage to eligible men. If I hadn't thought it was a workable idea, I would never have mentioned it."

"It *isn't* a workable idea."

"Why not?"

"Damn," he muttered with supreme exasperation. "You're forcing me to be unkind."

"If you have something to say, don't worry about sparing my feelings. I told you yesterday that I have a tough veneer when it comes to insults. They bounce right off me."

"Okay," he said, shifting from one foot to the other, but keeping his eyes on hers, "I'll be blunt. I don't want to get married again. Ever."

"Why?"

"Because I had a wife. I had a child. They're lost to me. No one can take Tanya's place. And besides all that, I don't love you."

"I couldn't possibly hope to take Tanya's place. In any event, I wouldn't want to. We are two entirely different individuals. And I certainly never imagined that you love me, Chase. People get married for a variety of reasons, the least of which, I believe, is love."

He stared at her, dumbfounded. "Why in hell would you want that, though? Knowing that I don't love you, that I'm still in love with my wife, why would you make such an offer?"

"Because, as you've pointed out numerous times just over the course of the last couple days, I'm an old maid. And even in this day and age, no matter how progressive our thinking, if you're a single person, you're odd man out. It's still a couples' world. People move through life in pairs. I'm tired of being a party of one."

"That argument doesn't wash, Marcie. You told me yesterday that you almost got married but backed out at the last minute because you didn't love the guy."

"That's true. But that was several years ago. I was still in my twenties."

"So?"

"So now I'm thirty-five. A thirty-five-year-old single who is either divorced or widowed isn't that much of a rarity. Even a thirty-five-year-old bachelor doesn't attract much attention. But a woman who is still unmarried at thirty-five is an old maid, especially if she lives alone and rarely goes out." She cast her eyes downward and added softly, "Especially if she's Goosey Johns."

Chase mumbled another curse. He regretted ever calling her that. He could argue now that the nickname no longer applied, but she would think he was just being kind.

"I know I'm not a raving beauty, Chase. My figure isn't the stuff fantasies and centerfolds are made of. But I can give you what you need most.''

"Money?" he asked scathingly.

"Companionship."

"Get a dog."

"I'm allergic to them. Besides, we're talking about what you need, not what I need," she said. "We're friends, aren't we? We always got along. I believe we'd make a good team."

"If you want to be part of a team, join a bowling league."

His sarcasm didn't faze her. "You've had a year and a half of wandering, and though you haven't admitted it, I think you're sick of being a nomad. I can give you stability. I have a home," she said, spreading her arms to encompass the house. "I love it, but it would be so much nicer if I were sharing it with someone."

"Get a roommate."

"I'm trying."

"I meant another woman."

"I would hate living with another woman." She laughed without humor. "Besides, God only knows what the gossips of Milton Point would say about me if another woman moved in here."

He awarded her that point because she was right. Generally speaking, people were small-minded and always looking for scandal even where there wasn't any. But that was Marcie's problem and he wasn't the solution to it.

Still, chivalry required him to let her down easy. If nothing else, he respected her for having the courage to broach the subject of marriage with him. It couldn't have been an easy thing for her to do. She had had to swallow a hell of a lot of pride.

"Look, Marcie—"

"You're going to say no, aren't you?"

He blew out a gust of air. "Yeah. I'm going to say no."

She lowered her head, but raised it almost immediately. There was challenge in her eyes. "Think about it, Chase."

"There's nothing to think about."

"Tyler Drilling."

He placed his hands on his hips and leaned in close. "Don't you realize what you're doing? You're trying to buy a husband!"

"If I'm not worried about that, why should you be? I've got lots of money. More than I need. What am I going to do with it? Who am I going to leave it to? What good has it done me to work hard and achieve success if I can't share the dividends with someone who needs them?"

Jerking on his gloves, he said, "You won't have to look hard to find somebody. I'm sure there are plenty of men around who'd love a free ride."

She laid her hand on his arm. "Is that what you think this is about? Do you think I'd want you under my roof if you were content to be a kept man? Not on your life, Chase Tyler! I know you'll continue to work as hard as you ever have. I'm not trying to rob you of your masculinity or your pride. I don't want to be the man of the house. If I did, I would be satisfied to leave things as they are."

She softened her tone. "I don't want to grow old alone, Chase. I don't think you want to either. And since you can't marry for love, you'd just as well marry for money."

He contemplated her earnest face for a moment, then shook his head. "I'm not your man, Marcie."

"You are. You're exactly what I want."

"Me? A broken, beaten man? Bad tempered? Bereaved? What could you possibly want me for? I'd make your life miserable."

"You didn't make me miserable tonight. I liked having you here."

She just wasn't going to let him do this gracefully, was she? The only alternative she had left him was to say an abrupt no and get the hell out. "Sorry, Marcie. The answer is no."

He yanked open the door and went out into the storm. After hours of sitting idle, the truck was more reluctant than ever to start. It finally came to life and chugged home. The apartment was dark and cold.

Chase undressed, brushed his teeth, took a pain pill, and climbed between frigid sheets. "Marry Goosey Johns!" he muttered as he socked his pillow several times. It was the craziest notion he'd ever heard of, a ludicrous idea.

Then why wasn't he doubled over laughing?

His brother arrived at his apartment close on the heels of dawn. "Hi. You all right?"

"Why wouldn't I be?" Chase replied crossly.

"No reason. I just wondered how your ribs were feeling this morning."

"Better. Want to come in?"

"Thanks."

Lucky stepped inside. Chase shut the door. He could tell, though Lucky tried to pretend otherwise, that he was under close scrutiny.

Stubbornly Chase refused to make it easy on his brother. After a lengthy silence Lucky finally got to the point of the early visit.

"I called here several times last night, but never got an answer."

"Checking up on me?"

Lucky looked chagrined.

"I was out."

"I gathered that much."

"I had dinner out."

"Oh, dinner."

Chase quickly lost patience with their beating around the bush. "Why don't you come right out and ask, Lucky?"

"Okay, where the hell were you?"

"Over at Marcie's."

"Marcie's?"

"I drove out to repay her for the hospital bill and she invited me to stay for supper."

"Well, if that's all it was, why didn't you just say so?"

"Because it wasn't any of your damn business."

"We were worried about your being out last night."

"I don't need a keeper!"

"Oh, yeah?"

By now they were shouting. Each brother's temper was as short as the other's. Yelling at each other was nothing new. Nor was it uncommon for them to reconcile just as quickly.

Chase shook his head, chuckling. "Maybe I do need a keeper."

"Maybe you *did*. Not any longer."

"Sit down."

Lucky plopped down in a living room easy chair across from his brother and immediately directed the conversation to their common worry. "How'd your meeting at the bank go yesterday?"

"George Young is a son of a bitch."

"Are you just now realizing that?" Lucky asked.

"I don't blame him or the bank for wanting their money. It's that sympathetic expression on his sanctimonious puss that I can't stomach. I think he's actually enjoying our situation."

"I know what you mean. He puts on this woeful, gee-I'm-sorry act, but he's laughing up his sleeve."

"Know what I'd like to do?" Chase said, leaning forward, bracing his forearms on his knees. "I'd like to take a big box of cash in the full amount we owe him and dump it on top of his desk."

"Hell, so would I." Ruefully Lucky smacked his lips. "When pigs fly, huh?"

Nervously, Chase's fingers did push-ups against each other. "You said yesterday it would take a miracle to get us out of this fix."

"Something straight from heaven."

"Well, uh . . ." He loudly cleared his throat. "What if, uh, the angel of mercy looked like, uh, Marcie Johns?" Lucky said nothing. Finally Chase lifted his wary gaze to his brother. "Did you hear me?"

"I heard you. What does it mean?"

"Say, do you want some coffee?" Chase came halfway out of his chair.

"No."

He sat back down.

"What has Marcie got to do with our predicament?" Lucky wanted to know.

"Nothing. Except . . ." Chase forced a laugh. "She offered to help us out."

"Christ, Chase, the last thing we need is another loan to repay."

"She, uh, didn't exactly offer to make us a loan. It was more like an investment."

"You mean she wants to buy an interest in the business? Become a partner?" Lucky left his chair and began to pace. "We don't want another partner, do we? You haven't changed your mind about that, have you?"

"No."

"Well, good, because I haven't either. Granddad and Dad wanted the business to be kept in the family. I'm surprised Marcie even thought of it, and I appreciate her interest, but I hope you explained to her that we didn't want anyone outside the family in on our business."

"Yeah, I explained that, but—"

"Wait a minute," Lucky said, whipping around. "She's not thinking about a hostile takeover, is she? She wouldn't pay off the bank and expect to move in whether we liked it or not, would she? Jeez, I never even thought of that."

"Neither did Marcie. At least I don't think so," Chase said. "That wasn't what she proposed."

Hands on hips, Lucky faced his brother. "What exactly did she propose?"

There was no way around giving Lucky a straight answer now. He reasoned that if Marcie could be blunt, so could he. "She proposed marriage."

"Excuse me?"

"Marriage."

"To whom?"

"To me," he answered querulously. "Who the hell do you think?"

"I don't know what to think."

"Well, she proposed to me."

"Marcie Johns proposed marriage to you?"

"Isn't that what I just said?" Chase shouted.

"I don't believe this!"

"Believe it."

Lucky stared at his brother, aghast. Then his eyes narrowed suspiciously. "Wait a minute. Where were you at the time? What were y'all doing?"

"Not what you're thinking. We were having coffee and chocolate chip cookies."

"You weren't—"

"No!"

Lucky lowered himself into the chair again. A long moment of silence ensued while Lucky stared at Chase and Chase attempted to avoid the stare. Finally Lucky asked, "Was she serious?"

"Seemed to be."

"Son of a gun," Lucky mumbled, still obviously dismayed.

"She had her arguments all lined up. Friendship, stability, stuff like that. And of course, the, uh, money."

Lucky shook his head in amazement, then began to laugh. "I can't believe it. She actually said she would give you money in exchange for marrying her?"

"Well, sort of. Words to that effect."

"Can you beat that? I've heard when it comes to business, she's got brass balls, but who would have thought she'd do something like this? What did you say to her? I mean"—he paused and winked—"I assume you said no."

"That's what I said, yeah."

This time Chase was the one to stand and begin pacing. For some unnamed reason, Lucky's laughter irritated him. He suddenly felt the need to defend and justify Marcie's proposal.

"You shouldn't make fun of her," he said tetchily. "If she had stripped naked in front of me, it couldn't have taken more nerve than doing what she did."

Lucky caught his brother by the arm and drew himself up even with him. "Chase, you can't be thinking what I think you're thinking."

Chase met his brother's disbelieving eyes and surprised himself by saying, "It's a way out of this mess we're in."

Lucky stared at him speechlessly for a moment, then reacted in his characteristic, short-tempered way. He shoved his face to within an inch of Chase's.

"Have you completely lost your mind? Has all that whiskey you've consumed over the last several months pickled your brain? Or did a kick from that bull jell your gray matter?"

"Is this a multiple-choice question?"

"I'm not joking!"

"Neither am I!" Chase slung off his brother's hand and spun away from him. "Think about it. Name one single, productive thing I've done since Tanya died. You can't. No one can. You've told me as much to my face. My lack of initiative has put the family business on the brink of bankruptcy."

"This slump has got nothing to do with your private life," Lucky cried. "Or your lack of initiative or anything else except a collapsed oil market."

"But I'm still the elder son," Chase argued, repeatedly stabbing his chest with his index finger. "I'm the one who's accountable, Lucky. And if Tyler Drilling goes down the tubes, it'll be on my conscience for the rest of my life. I've got to do whatever I can to prevent that from happening."

"Even going so far as to marry a woman you don't love?"

"Yes. Even going that far."

"You wouldn't have let me marry Susan Young two years ago to save us from rack and ruin. Do you think I'd let you do something so foolhardy?"

"You won't have any say in the matter."

It suddenly occurred to him that he was arguing strenuously in favor of Marcie's plan. Since when? His subconscious must have dwelt on it all night. Sometime before he woke up, he had made up his mind that her idea wasn't so unworkable after all.

Lucky let loose a string of obscenities. "You're not over Tanya yet, Chase. How can you think of becoming involved with another woman?"

"I don't intend to become involved. Not emotionally anyway. Marcie knows that. She knows I'm still in love with Tanya, and she's willing to settle for companionship."

"Bull. No woman is willing to settle for companionship."

"Marcie is. She's not the romantic type."

"All right, and why is that? I'll tell you why. Because she's an old maid who—as a last resort—will buy herself a husband."

"She's not an old maid." It made Chase unreasonably furious to hear Lucky verbalize the very thoughts he had entertained twelve hours earlier. "It's not easy for a woman as successful as Marcie to find a man who isn't threatened by her success." That argument popped into his head and he was inordinately pleased with it.

"Okay, forget that for the time being," Lucky said, "and think of this. She's probably buying herself a clear conscience, too. Remember, she was driving when your beloved wife was killed."

Chase's face went white with fury. His gray eyes took on the cold sheen of slate. "The accident wasn't Marcie's fault."

"I know that, Chase," Lucky said patiently. "You know it. Everybody knows it. But does *she?* Has she reconciled that yet? Is she trying to do something charitable to ease her burden of guilt, even though it's self-imposed?"

Chase ruminated on that for a moment before speaking. "So what if she is? We'll still both benefit from the marriage. We'll each be getting what we want. Tyler Drilling will be in the black again and Marcie will have a husband and a clear conscience."

Lucky threw up his hands in a gesture of incredulity and let them fall back to his thighs with a loud slapping sound. "Do you even like this woman, Chase?"

"Yes, very much," he said truthfully. "We were always good pals."

"Good pals. Great." Lucky's disgust was apparent. "Do you want to sleep with her?"

"I haven't thought about it."

"You'd better think about it. I'm sure she has. I'm reasonably sure that sex is part of the bargain." Lucky used Chase's temporary silence to drive home his point. "Sleeping with a tramp one night and moving on the next day is different from sleeping with someone you have to face over the Cheerios."

"Thanks for the lesson on women, little brother," Chase sneered. "I'll make a note of it in case I ever need your words of advice."

"Dammit, Chase, I'm only trying to get you to think this through. You'll pay off the bank loan immediately, but you'll be committed to Marcie for life. Unless you plan to dump her once she's fulfilled her part of the bargain."

"I'd never do that!"

"But you've said you still love Tanya."

"I do."

"So every time you take Marcie to bed, it'll be out of obligation, or worse, pity. It'll be a charity—"

"If you finish that sentence, I'll knock the hell out of you." Chase's index finger was rigid and aimed directly at his brother's lips. "Don't talk about her that way."

Lucky fell back a step and gazed at his brother with disbelief. "You're defending her, Chase. That means you've already made up your mind, haven't you?"

In that moment Chase realized that he had.

Chapter Seven

"Thank you for coming, Pat."

Laurie Tyler ushered Sheriff Pat Bush into her kitchen. He was "back-door company." She would have been insulted if he'd gone to the front door and rung the bell. All her married life, Pat had been a good friend to Bud and her. Bud had died several years earlier of cancer, but Pat had remained a steadfast family friend. He could be relied on in times of need. As now.

"What's going on? You sounded upset when you called." He set his brown felt Stetson on the kitchen table and shrugged off his uniform jacket, draping it over the back of his chair before sitting down. Laurie set a mug of coffee in front of him. "Thanks. What's the matter, Laurie?"

"Chase is getting married."

The rim of the mug was already at Pat's lips. Her stunning announcement gave him a start. He burned his tongue with hot coffee. "Getting married!" he exclaimed.

"That's right. Pat, I'm so upset I don't know what to do."

"Who's he marrying? A gold digger claiming he gave her a kid or something like that?"

"No, no, nothing like that," Laurie told him, sadly shaking her head.

Her hair was pale. Formerly blond, it was now softened to beige by the addition of scattered white strands. It was cut short and fashionably styled. She could pass for ten years younger than she was. Her slim figure was the envy of her peers, and her blue eyes were animated and lively. Now, however, they were dulled by concern for her oldest child.

"He's marrying Marcie Johns."

The startling revelations were coming so quickly one after the other that drinking hot coffee proved hazardous. Pat lowered his mug to the table. "Marcie Johns," he whispered. "Son of a gun. Talk about irony."

"Yes, isn't it?"

"How'd that come about?"

Laurie told him what she knew, beginning with Marcie's driving Chase from Fort Worth after his injury and concluding with a verbatim account of a telephone call she'd had from Chase earlier that afternoon.

"He said they'd decided to get married the day after tomorrow in Judge Walker's chambers. He suggested that Sage stay in town if she wanted to be present and if she could afford to miss her classes. He said Marcie wanted her parents to come up from Houston for the ceremony. They were concerned about the roads being clear between here and there."

"Roads! He's fixin' to get married when he's just come off a two-year drinking binge brought on by the death of his wife, and he's worried about roads?"

"That's my point," she said, her voice cracking emotionally. "I don't think he knows what he's doing."

Pat pulled a large, calloused hand down his face. It was a full face, rather ruddy, but he was considered nice looking. He still had a full head of hair, though it was as much gray as brown.

Dozens of women in Milton Point had pined for him through the years. He had dated a few off and on, but the nature of his work and the commitment it demanded had kept him a bachelor. He had more or less adopted the Tyler kids as his own. That's why he shared Laurie's concern for Chase now. He remembered the extent of the young man's suffering when his wife had been killed.

"You want me to talk to him, Laurie?"

"It wouldn't do any good," she said sorrowfully. "Lucky tried talking sense to him this morning. Lucky said the more he argued the reasons against Chase's marrying right now, the more stubborn Chase became that it was the right thing for him to do.

"Naturally Sage had several firm opinions on the subject when I told her. I had to threaten her to within an inch of her life if she said anything to him. Lord only knows what she would spout off.

"Nobody is taken with the idea, but I don't want this to cause a rift in the family when we've just gotten Chase back. He might close doors on us that would never be opened again." Tears began to shimmer in her eyes.

Pat reached across the table and covered her hand with his. "I didn't realize Chase knew Ms. Johns that well."

Laurie dabbed at her eyes with a tissue. "They were classmates. They didn't see each other after high school graduation because her parents moved to Houston. She and Chase didn't become reacquainted until Tanya started house hunting right before she was killed.

"Don't get me wrong, Pat. It's not Marcie I object to. I think she's perfectly charming. She's turned into a beautiful woman and she's always been smart as a whip." Her pretty face drew into a frown. "That's why I can't understand why she would let herself in for this."

"You lost me on that one."

"Well, according to Lucky, who called right after I spoke with Chase, Marcie asked him to marry her, not the other way around."

"You don't say."

Laurie recounted to Pat everything that Lucky had told her.

"He's marrying her for the money," Pat observed when she was done. "He's doing it to save Tyler Drilling."

"So it seems. That's why I'm so upset. Whether consciously or not, Bud and I instilled that sense of responsibility into Chase. He takes everything to heart, assumes everybody's burdens."

"That's usual for an oldest child, Laurie."

"I know, but Chase takes it to the extreme. After Tanya was killed, he blamed himself for not going with her that afternoon, believing that if he had been there, she wouldn't have died."

"That's crazy."

"Yes, but that's the way he is. He takes everyone's problems onto himself. He probably feels guilty for abdicating his business responsibilities over the last eighteen months. This is his way of making up for that. I had hoped his coming home would mark a new beginning. I didn't count on its taking this form.

"He's committing himself to years of unhappiness in order to save Tyler Drilling. And he's sentencing Marcie to misery, too. I can't imagine what her motivation is. But I know beyond a shadow of a doubt that Chase is still in love with Tanya. Just like with Bud and me. I didn't stop loving him when he died."

Unobtrusively, Pat withdrew his hand from hers. He sat quietly and let her cry for a moment before asking, "What do you want me to do, Laurie?"

She raised her head and gave him a watery smile. "What you're doing. Listening. I needed to talk to somebody. Devon hasn't been feeling well lately—something else that's worrying me. Lucky loses his temper, gets mad, and stamps around cursing under his breath and ramming his fist into his palm. Sage talks off the top of her head and says things that only cause me more distress. I needed someone solid like you to listen."

Smiling ruefully, Pat rubbed his hand over his slight paunch. "That's me. Solid. Glad to be of service though. You know I promised Bud before he died to look after his kids. I've a good mind to yank Chase up by the collar and after I've shaken some sense into him, give him a good thrashing. If for no other reason than for putting you through hell all these months."

"He'd probably thrash you back." She gave a shaky little sigh. "They're not children anymore, Pat. They're grownups. They make their own decisions, and there's little or nothing I can do about it, even when I think they're making a terrible mistake."

Her tenuous smile gradually receded as she gazed into her dear friend's face. "Oh, Pat, what can Chase possibly be thinking to do this?"

Waiting outside Judge Walker's chambers, Chase was wondering what he could possibly be thinking to do this.

The last two days had been so hectic he hadn't really had time to let the reality sink in. Perhaps he had subconsciously made things hectic so he wouldn't have to dwell on it.

Marcie had received his decision with more equanimity than he had anticipated. Shortly after his dispute with Lucky, he had gone to Marcie's real estate office. Esme, wearing a solid green dress with purple tights, announced him. Marcie was in her inner office, thumbing through the biweekly multiple-listings book.

As soon as Esme had withdrawn he said, "I think you had a good idea last night, Marcie. Let's get married."

He hadn't expected her to throw her arms around him, cover his face with ardent kisses, and blubber thank-yous through her streaming tears. He hadn't expected her to prostrate herself at his feet and pledge undying fealty.

But he had expected a little more enthusiasm than a handshake.

"Before we shake on it," he had said, "I have one stipulation." She seemed to catch her breath quickly and hold it, but he might have imagined that because her face remained calm. "I will pay back every cent you put into Tyler Drilling."

"That's not necessary."

"It is to me. And it is to this marriage's taking place. If you can't agree to that, the deal's off. It might take me years to do it, but you'll get your money back."

"It will be our money, Chase, but if that's the way you feel about it, that's how it will be."

They had sealed the agreement with a very unromantic, businesslike handshake. From there, things had snowballed. They notified their families and cleared the date on the judge's calendar.

Although it could have been postponed to a more convenient time, Chase vacated the apartment where he had lived with Tanya from the day they were married. A few weeks after her death, her family had come in and disposed of the things he hadn't wanted to keep, so he was spared having to deal with that.

It hadn't taken long for him to pack his belongings and move them to Marcie's house. In effect, moving had sealed off his escape hatch— the reason, perhaps, why he had done it. There was no backing out.

There was one awkward moment during the move.

"This is my bedroom," Marcie had told him as she opened the door to a large, cozy room. The wall behind the bed was covered with fabric that matched the bedspread and drapes. A chaise lounge in the corner was also upholstered in a complementary fabric. Her bedroom wasn't as starkly contemporary as the rest of the house's decor. It was feminine without being cloying and fussy, a pleasant mix of warmth and spaciousness.

His gaze moved to the bed, and he instantly felt uncomfortable. "Where's my bedroom?"

"There."

She had pointed toward a closed door on the opposite side of the gallery. It was into that room that Chase moved his belongings. Marcie hadn't extended him a specific invitation to share her room. He was relieved. He was spared having to tell her no.

Ever since Lucky had mentioned sleeping with her, Chase had given it a great deal of thought. She hadn't come right out and said it, but she obviously expected them to have a sexual relationship. At first he couldn't imagine writhing naked with Goosey Johns, but once he got used to the idea, he reasoned that it wouldn't be all that bad.

She was an attractive woman. He was a man with a healthy sex drive. Looking at it from a purely pragmatic standpoint, he figured he could have occasional sex with her without too much difficulty.

Sharing a bedroom, however, was an intimacy reserved for his wife. Even though he was about to take vows legally bestowing that title upon Marcie, in his heart Tanya would forever be his wife. He might periodically share a bed with Marcie, but he would sleep in another room.

In addition to moving from the apartment there had been blood tests to take, a license to buy, his brother to argue with, his mother to reassure, his sister to keep from murdering if she shot off her smart mouth about his questionable sanity one more time, and a new dark suit to buy.

Because of a fortunate break in the weather, his in-laws had arrived the night before and taken Marcie, him, and his entire family to dinner at the Milton Point Country Club. The couple were almost giddy over their only child's finally getting married. They seemed so pathetically relieved that she wouldn't end up an old maid, Chase felt embarrassed for Marcie. Theirs were the only two happy faces at the table.

To her credit, Laurie had done her best to make the strained occasion convivial. Pat Bush had been there to lend moral support. Devon, too, had kept the conversation going when it flagged, but had displayed her nervousness with an enormous appetite, which became the butt of several jokes.

Under threat of death, Sage had kept her opinions to herself. At the end of the evening when she hugged her prospective sister-in-law good night, one would have thought Marcie was a woman doomed to the gallows rather than a bride on her way to the altar.

Lucky had kept a civil tongue, but his thoughts had been telegraphed by his perpetual glower. It was obvious that he believed his brother was making a dreadful mistake.

Chase wondered if that was true as he glanced at the woman standing beside him now. Marcie wasn't hard on the eyes at all. In fact, she looked beautiful. She was dressed in a white wool suit that somehow managed to look soft and bridal in spite of its tailored lines. Her hair was pulled up, and she was wearing a small hat with a veil that reached her nose. Behind it her blue eyes were sparkling and smiling.

"Nervous?" she asked him.

"Uncomfortable," he said. "I didn't have time to get the coat of this suit altered. It's snug."

She reached up and ran her hand across his shoulders. "That's the price you pay for having such broad shoulders."

Chase jumped reflexively, but he wasn't sure if it was because of Marcie's unexpected and very wifely touch or because the receptionist chose that moment to tell them the judge was ready for them.

They filed into the hushed, paneled chamber—the bride and groom,

Marcie's parents, all the Tylers, and Pat Bush. It was an austere gathering.

Chase's thoughts were pulled back by tethers of memory to the lovely, candlelight church wedding Tanya and he had had. Her large family had filled up the first several pews. It had been a happy occasion, though both mothers had cried a little into dainty lace handkerchiefs that Tanya had embroidered and given to them as gifts.

No one in attendance could have doubted their love for each other. Tanya had looked breathtakingly beautiful as she glided down the aisle in her white gown. They had pledged each other love and faithfulness until death—

"Will you, Chase, take Marcia Elaine Johns to be your lawfully wedded wife? Will you love her, honor her, protect and keep her for as long as you both shall live?"

The question plucked Chase from his sweet reverie and cruelly thrust him into the present. He stared at the judge, who looked back at him with puzzlement. Then he looked down into Marcie's expectant face.

"I will."

The judge posed the same questions to Marcie. She responded in a soft, solemn voice. They exchanged the simple gold bands they had purchased together yesterday. The judge pronounced them man and wife, then said to Chase, "You may kiss your bride."

And Chase's heart stumbled over its next beat.

He had slept with countless women since Tanya's death, but he hadn't kissed a single one. Somehow that melding of the mouths seemed more intimate and personal than climaxing while inside a female body. Kissing was done face-to-face, eye-to-eye, and required some measure of participation from both parties.

He turned toward his bride and took her shoulders between his hands. He lowered his head a fraction. He paused. Their small congregation seemed collectively to hold its breath.

He couldn't look into Marcie's eyes because he didn't want to see her anxiety or censure. So he concentrated on her lips. Well-shaped lips. The color of peaches in the family orchard when they're ready to be picked. Soft looking and now, slightly tremulous.

He bent his head and touched them with his. They were pliant enough to make him curious and tempting enough to make him cautious. He yielded to the former and pressed against them a trifle more firmly. Then he quickly pulled back. She smiled. So did he. But his smile felt wooden.

Thankfully, he was hastily embraced by Marcie's mother. Mr. Johns enthusiastically pumped his hand, welcoming him into their small family. While saying something appropriate to his new mother-in-law, he reflexively whisked his tongue across his lips . . . and was shocked to taste Marcie there.

Chapter Eight

"When did your folks say they're going back to Houston?"

"In the morning."

Chase helped Marcie out of her fur jacket and hung it on the coat tree just inside her front door . . . *their* front door. "What's their hurry? Why don't they stick around for a few days?"

"Since they retired, all they do is play golf. They don't like to break golf dates. Besides, they felt as if being in town would put a damper on the honeymoon."

"Oh." He slipped out of his suit jacket. Glad to be rid of it, he flexed his arms, rolled his shoulders and loosened the knot of his necktie. "Should we open the champagne?"

"Why not?" Her gaiety sounded forced. She removed her hat and set it on an end table, then went for glasses. "It was thoughtful of Devon and Lucky to give it to us. Especially since he's so against our marriage."

"What makes you say that?" He popped the cork on the champagne and poured it into the stems she held out to him.

"Are you kidding? I'd have to be blind not to see his disapproval. He scowls every time he looks at me."

"It's not you he's scowling at. It's me. His reservations have nothing to do with you. He's afraid that I'm going to make us both very unhappy."

"Are you?"

Their eyes connected. Though her mouth was softly curved into a smile, he could tell that her question wasn't flirtatious or frivolous. "I'm going to try my best not to, Marcie."

"That's enough for me." She clinked her glass against his. Holding their stare, they sipped the cold, biting champagne. "Hungry?" she asked.

"Sort of."

Turning her back on him, she went into the kitchen. As she moved away from him, Chase noticed that the slender skirt of her suit fit her fanny very well. Good legs, too. He loosened his necktie even more and wondered why the heat was turned up so high.

To distract himself from his growing uneasiness he said, "Besides, Lucky has his nerve to criticize me when it comes to choosing a wife. Devon was married when they met."

"I remember. It was quite a scandal at the time. His alibi for the arson crime was a married woman he'd spent the night with."

"There were extenuating circumstances."

"Yes, I know. Seeing them together now, no one could doubt that they're made for each other." When she opened the refrigerator, she exclaimed, "Oh, my! Look, Chase!" She held up a large, cellophane-wrapped basket filled with cheeses, fresh fruit, a box of chocolates, and even a small canned ham.

"There's a card." Opening the white envelope, she read aloud, " 'With love and best wishes for your happiness.' It's from your mother and Sage. Wasn't that sweet?"

He joined her at the island bar where she was unwrapping the cellophane. "It certainly was."

He was feeling unusually benevolent toward his sister because she had saved him from making an unforgivable faux pas. Earlier that day, she had asked him what kind of bouquet he'd arranged for Marcie to have. Shamefaced, he had admitted that a bouquet hadn't even crossed his mind.

In a panic Sage had said she would take care of it. Two hours later, and in the nick of time, she had returned with the bridal bouquet of white roses, white lilacs, and baby's breath, which Marcie had gently laid on the island bar beside the gift basket.

Obviously, going to the florist hadn't been the only errand Sage had run for him. Seeing the pleasure on Marcie's face as she unwrapped the goodies made him grateful to his mother and sister for thinking of it.

"They must have delivered it while my parents were here. I'd gone to the hairdresser. Here, want some cheese?" She held a cube of baby Swiss up to him and he ate it from her fingers. His stomach took a nosedive when he felt her fleeting touch against his lips.

"Thanks."

"You're welcome. Newlyweds usually do this with wedding cake."

"We should have had a cake."

"It doesn't matter. I like doing things untraditionally." She was smiling, but he sensed a tinge of sadness in her voice. It disappeared quickly. She even gave a soft laugh. "You'll stay hungry if I feed you every bite. Why don't you build a fire and I'll fix us each a plate. I was too nervous to eat much lunch."

By the time he had a fire burning brightly, she joined him in the living room, carrying two plates filled with crackers, cheese, wedges of apple and pear, and sliced ham.

She stepped out of her shoes and took off the jacket to her suit, making herself comfy in the leather chair she'd been sitting in seventy-two hours ago just before proposing to him.

In what he hoped was a good omen, the sun had come out that afternoon for the first time in days. By now, however, it had already slipped beneath the horizon, and the sky beyond the wall of windows was a deep lavender. There was a generous moon, but the light it cast looked brittle and cold.

Inside, by contrast, enveloped in the fire's glow, they were warm. Marcie shone as bright as the firelight, Chase noticed as he methodically ate from the plate she had fixed him. Her skirt and blouse were almost the same ivory color as the leather she was cushioned by. The monochromatic background set off the vibrant color of her hair. Her blouse was silk, he guessed, and soft looking. It conformed to her shape in a tantalizing, yet modest, way.

"Chase?"

Her hesitant voice brought his eyes up from her breasts. "Hmm?"

"Are you wondering what I look like without my clothes on?"

His mouth dropped open and stayed that way for several seconds. Then he closed it and smiled with self-derision. "I guess I was, subconsciously. Consciously I was thinking how pretty you look in firelight. Your coloring matches it. Even your eyes. They're the same color as the blue in the flames."

"I wasn't fishing for compliments."

"I know."

She set her plate aside and picked up her glass of champagne, which he had already refilled. She gazed into the bubbly wine as she asked, "Have you ever wondered what I look like without my clothes on?" Before he had a chance to reply, she hastily added, "Never mind. I know you haven't." She took a quick drink of champagne.

"Actually I have."

"You have?"

"Yep."

"When?"

"When we were in eleventh grade, I believe. It was the end of the year. Awards day. You walked across the stage to receive one of your many awards. As class president I was seated on the stage. You walked right in front of the spotlight, which was at the back of the auditorium. For several seconds you were cast in silhouette and I caught your profile. I remember thinking then, as a randy seventeen-year-old boy is wont to do, what you looked like naked."

She laughed a low, throaty laugh. "I wondered if you noticed." His baffled expression made her laugh again. "I knew exactly where you were sitting. As I passed you, I stuck out my chest on purpose."

"No fooling?" She nodded. "Why?"

"I guess I was trying to get your attention. Little good it did me," she remarked, brushing a nonexistent crumb from her skirt. "Your curiosity wasn't strong enough for you to try to find out what I looked like naked."

"Well, I was going steady with somebody else then. I think it was Linda—"

"No. Debbie Aldrich."

"Oh, right, Debbie. We broke up that summer right before our senior year."

"And then you started dating Lorna Fitzwilliams."

He shook his head. "How do you remember that?"

"I remember," she said softly. After draining her champagne, she left the leather chair. "Would you like some chocolates or should we leave them for tomorrow?"

"Tomorrow. I'm full."

She smiled girlishly. "Okay. It'll give us something to look forward to." Leaving her jacket and shoes where she had discarded them, she headed toward the stairs in her stocking feet. "I'll go on up."

"Okay."

"See you in a minute then." There was a trace of inquiry at the end of her sentence.

"Sure. I'll just, uh, bank the fire."

She continued upstairs. When she reached the door to her bedroom, she looked down at him from the gallery and smiled beguilingly before disappearing through the bedroom door and closing it behind her.

Chase rubbed his palms up and down the thighs of his dress slacks. Then he gathered their dishes and carried them into the kitchen. He conscientiously replaced the gift basket in the refrigerator. Dutifully, he checked the doors to make certain they were locked. He set the alarm system. He banked the fire.

When there was nothing left to do, he headed upstairs. About half-way up, he changed his mind. Retracing his steps, he returned to the island bar, took a bottle of whiskey from the cabinet beneath it, and only then went to his room.

In the connecting bath, he filled the toothbrush glass with whiskey and downed it in one swallow. The liquor brought tears to his eyes and stung his esophagus, but spread a welcome heat through his midsection. It did little to relieve his anxiety, however.

How the hell was he going to get through this?

Damn his brother! Lucky had either been dead-center correct or else had planted a self-fulfilling thought in Chase's head. Either way, a one-night stand was altogether different from a wedding night.

The woman waiting for him in the next bedroom wasn't just a warm body. She was a personality, a smile, a heart that didn't deserve to be broken. But he had only so much to give and he feared it wasn't going to be enough.

Dammit, she had known that.

She had asked for this.

She had said that she would take whatever he had to give and expect nothing more.

With that in mind he removed his shirt but left his slacks on. The bandage around his middle showed up very white against his tanned chest and dark trousers. He took off his shoes and socks. He raked a hairbrush through his hair. He brushed his teeth. He splashed on some cologne. For good measure he threw back another shot of whiskey.

Then he sat down on the edge of his bed and stared at the door. It was like when he was a kid, knowing he had to get a shot and waiting in the doctor's reception room. Dreading it was the worst part. That's when the stomach fluttered and the palms sweat. The longer he put it off, the worse it became. Best to get it over with. He got up, left his room, and marched down the gallery. He knocked on her closed door.

"Come in, Chase."

There were burning candles and vases of fresh flowers scattered throughout the room. The combination smelled wonderful, as intoxicating as the whiskey.

His eyes made a wide sweep of the room before stopping abruptly on Marcie. She was an angelic vision where she stood beside the king-size bed, which had already been turned down to reveal satin sheets the pastel color of the inside of a seashell.

Her peignoir was pale and silky. The shape of her body was outlined beneath it. Through it, he easily located the centers of her breasts and the delta of her thighs. She had taken down her hair. With candlelight shining through it, it looked like a halo surrounding her head. But the look in her eyes wasn't innocent. Not by a long shot.

Mentally Chase groaned. She was making this out to be something special, a typical wedding night made for lovers.

"I thought you might like more champagne." She indicated a silver ice bucket on the nightstand. In it was an unopened bottle that she must have brought up ahead of time. There were two tall tulip-shaped crystal glasses standing beside it.

"No thanks," he said gruffly.

"All right."

This was no doubt where the bridegroom was supposed to seize the initiative. Moving stiffly, he crossed the room until he reached her. He knew he was expected to say something nice. "I like your . . . your thing." He gestured down at the nightgown.

"Thank you. I hoped you would."

A kiss was called for. Okay. He could handle that. He'd been kissing girls for decades.

Placing his arms around her, he drew her forward—stopping short of bringing their bodies together—and kissed first her forehead, then her cheek, and finally laid his lips upon hers.

Hers parted invitingly. Her breath was sweet and clean. He experienced a flurry of curiosity. Should he acknowledge it, gratify it? Should he slip his tongue into her mouth? It would be the kind and considerate thing to do.

But no. No sense in taking this thing any further than it was required to go. He kept his lips resolutely closed and after a few seconds, raised his head. It had been about as dry, uninspired, and sterile a kiss as one could bestow. Yet his heart was knocking.

That erratic heartbeat forced him to admit that the emotion keeping him from intimately kissing her was fear—the cold, stark fear that once he started, he wouldn't be able to stop. He'd had one taste of her today, and the essence had lingered on his lips for hours. If he indulged that sudden craving now . . .

Another thought suddenly occurred to him, more terrifying than the previous one. What if he couldn't get an erection? Even at his drunkest he had never failed to perform sexually. Of all the women he had bedded, none could fault him when it came to physical preparedness. Knowing Marcie as a friend might make a difference.

Dear Lord, he hoped not. The fear of failure paralyzed him.

Marcie must have sensed that he was having difficulty of some sort. Smiling tentatively, she crossed her arms over her chest and slowly lowered the thin straps of her nightgown from her shoulders, pulling them down her arms until she was bare to her narrow waist.

Her breasts were high and round and pale. She had possibly the pinkest nipples he had ever seen. And the most sensitive. Because when she removed her nightgown and the air touched them, they shriveled and darkened to an even deeper shade of pink. They became very hard.

Chase's mouth began to water. He swallowed to keep from drowning. His body quickened behind the fly of his slacks and he felt a surge of relief.

Marcie let her nightgown slide to the floor. Gracefully, she stepped out of the circle of fabric and faced him naked. Her feet were high arched and slender. Her long legs were almost coltishly thin, but well shaped. There was a definite flaring curve to her hips, but they weren't voluptuous.

What drew his eyes like a magnet, however, was the cluster of ginger curls between her thighs. It was a lush, wanton, feminine sight. He touched it with the back of his fingers. Springy. Alive. Alluring.

His veins exploded with raw desire. A torrent of blood flowed into his groin. That's when he realized he needed to rush this. Otherwise he was apt to explore every inch of her porcelain skin, take her nipples into his mouth, nuzzle that fiery cloud between her thighs. He was liable to make a damn fool of himself over his good pal, Goosey Johns.

"Lie down, Marcie," he whispered thickly.

Hastily he went around the room blowing out the candles, because if he tried this with the lights on, it might not work—and at that moment he desperately wanted it to work.

He removed his own clothing, fumbling in the dark, and slipped on a condom. When he lay down beside her, she moved into his arms willingly. She felt incredibly dainty and crushable as he moved on top of her and opened her thighs.

His entry was so hard and swift, he thought he might have hurt her, but she made no sound except for a long, serrated sigh when he began to move inside her.

No, dammit, no. I'm not supposed to like it.

He couldn't like it. Couldn't enjoy. Couldn't luxuriate. Had to hurry. Had to get it over with before it became habit-forming. Before he wanted to do it all night. Before he wanted to do it every night for the rest of his life.

He pumped feverishly. Gasping for breath, he ducked his head. His cheek accidentally grazed one of her pointed nipples. Turning his head slightly—just to help him get it over with quickly—he flicked it with his tongue.

That did it. It was over.

As soon as his head had cleared and he had regained his breath, he got up and groped for his clothing. Retrieving it, he headed for the door.

"Chase?" He heard the rustle of the satin sheets and knew she must have sat up.

"My ribs hurt. I'll be tossing and turning all night. Don't want to disturb you," he mumbled.

He ducked out, closing the door behind him, feeling as if he had escaped from the most deadly, most delicious torture a man could endure.

Chapter Nine

Raising her head from the sink after bathing her face in cold water, Marcie gazed at her reflection in the mirror. It was a disheartening sight. Having silently cried most of the night, her eyes were puffy and red. Without the enhancement of cosmetics her skin looked washed-out and sallow. She looked every day of her thirty-five years.

She asked her reflection how she could possibly have hoped to entice a handsome, virile man like Chase who could have any woman he wanted. Even the tramp who had come to see him in the hospital had had a better chance of pleasing him than skinny, freckled Goosey Johns.

Salty tears filled her eyes again, but she refused to submit to them. She lowered her body into the hot bath she had drawn. The soothing water eased the soreness between her thighs. His lovemaking had been quick, but it had also been hard and intense.

As she lathered her body she assessed it critically. Cupping her breasts in her hands, she lifted them, wishing they were heavier, fuller. She even considered surgery to enlarge them, but discarded the idea as rapidly as it formed. Big boobs were not going to make Chase Tyler love her.

She despaired that nothing ever would.

It was a bone-deep despair that she had lived with for almost as long as she could remember.

Leaving the tub, she dried herself and began to dress.

Ever since grade school Chase had been her ideal, to whom none other compared. Along with everybody else he had called her Goosey, but somehow, coming from him it had never sounded cruel. She had imagined that he used her nickname with a degree of affection.

Of course she was someone he would never have thought of dating.

It was an unwritten law that class favorites never dated class geeks. That would have been taking friendliness and kindness too far.

Graduating from Milton Point High School with her love still unrequited, she had entered college with the hope of finding a boy among her classmates who would equal or surpass Chase Tyler. She had actively dated—college men didn't seem as bent on dating the beauty queens as high school boys—but she had entered graduate school without finding anyone to supplant Chase in her heart or mind.

It actually came as a relief when her parents left Milton Point and moved to a retirement community near Houston. No longer was she required to take trips home where she invariably heard about the romantic escapades of Chase and his brother or saw him in town, always squiring a beautiful woman.

When she heard that he had married, she cried for two whole days. Then, pulling herself together and pragmatically charting a course for the rest of her life, she decided that carrying a torch was one thing, but obsession was another. It was mentally unhealthy and emotionally demoralizing to pine for a man who didn't know or care that she was alive.

Soon after reaching that momentous decision, she launched her career in residential real estate. Within her first year she had the third-best sales record in the whole Houston metropolitan area. The following year she was number one and held that position for two more consecutive years.

She met the man to whom she would later become engaged. Following that debacle, she decided to begin her own agency, and to the dismay of her parents and friends, she decided to establish it in Milton Point where her only real competition was a nonaggressive, family-owned firm that had been in business for so long, they'd become complacent.

She had been back in Milton Point for two years before Chase's wife had sought her services. Tanya McDaniel Tyler had been lovely, inside and out. Marcie had been inordinately pleased to meet her. She felt better knowing that Chase was married to someone who so obviously adored him.

She had never seen them together, however. The hardest thing Marcie had ever had to do was go into the office of Tyler Drilling and shake hands with Chase as though he were nothing more than a classmate she hadn't seen in a long while.

He had pulled her into his arms and hugged her. She touched him, smelled him, and her heart had nearly burst. He seemed genuinely glad to see her. But he had kissed his wife and held her lovingly while Marcie's heart was breaking.

Then Tanya had died in the passenger seat of her car. While lying injured in the hospital, Marcie had prayed to God for an explanation. Why had he done that to her? Why had he laid on her conscience the death of the woman whose husband she lusted after and loved?

She had vowed then that she would make up his loss to him.

And now, as she descended the stairs, she made that same pledge. She would do anything to restore Chase to the vital man he'd been before the accident, even if it meant having him make love to her when she knew that only his sex organ was involved, not his mind, certainly not his heart.

He turned when she entered the kitchen. "Morning." His eyes didn't stay on her for more than a millisecond before flickering away.

"Good morning, Chase. Did you sleep well?"

"Fine."

"You're up early."

"Habit."

"If I'd known you were up, I'd have been down sooner."

"It's okay. I've got the coffee started. Shouldn't be more than a few more minutes and it'll be ready."

"How are your ribs?"

"My what?" He turned.

She nodded at the bandage swathing his bare chest. He was dressed only in a pair of old, faded, button-fly Levi's jeans. Looking at them made her knees weak. The soft cloth molded to his shape, defining his sex. "Your ribs. You said last night that they were hurting you."

"Oh, yeah, right." Turning his back, he opened several cabinet doors until he located cups and saucers. "They're better this morning."

So his excuse for leaving her bed last night had been a fabricated one. He simply hadn't wanted to sleep with her. Even though he had moved his things into the extra bedroom, she had hoped that once they had made love . . .

Speaking above the ache in her throat, she asked, "What do you like for breakfast?"

"Coffee."

"I don't mind cooking you something. Just tell me what you want."

"Nothing, really. Only coffee."

"Sit down. I'll pour it."

He sat on a stool at the bar. Several moments later she joined him there. They sipped their coffee in silence. Their eyes connected once, briefly.

Was this how it was going to be? Would they occupy the same house, share rooms, breathe the same air, have periodic sex, but live the lives of quiet desperation that Thoreau had written about?

"The sun's coming out again today," she commented inanely.

"Maybe it'll warm up."

"Maybe." After another teeming silence she asked, "What are your plans today?"

"I told Lucky I'd meet him at the office midmorning. He told me I didn't have to feel obligated to come in on account of its being, well, you know, the day following my wedding, but I told him it didn't matter. . . . Does it?" he asked after a brief pause.

"No, no, of course not." She hoped he wouldn't notice how shaky her smile was. "I intended to go to my office, too."

"Well, then, guess I'd better go finish dressing and get on my way." He set down his cup and stood up.

"Maybe you should go see a doctor today about your ribs."

He touched the bandage. "I might. This thing is bugging me. About time it came off."

While he was upstairs, Marcie sat staring into her cooling coffee and trying not to weep with frustration and disappointment. She had hoped that they would spend the day together, not necessarily in bed, as was customary with newlyweds, but getting to know each other.

She had entertained fantasies of his being so taken with her that he couldn't tear himself away, of their lying in bed all day, exploring each other's nakedness with eyes and hands and mouths, going without food and water for long stretches of time in which they appeased another appetite that was scandalously voracious.

That was a fantasy all right. He was leaving for work. It was business as usual. Just another, ordinary day. To his mind, his part of the bargain had been fulfilled. Reminded of that, she left the bar and went into the room she used as an office.

By the time he returned downstairs, she was waiting for him at the foot of the staircase. She held his sheepskin coat for him as he slid his arms into the sleeves.

"What time will you be home this evening?" she asked as she patted the fleece collar into place.

"About five."

"Is dinner at six okay?"

"That's fine."

Reaching inside his coat, she slipped a white envelope into the breast pocket of his shirt. Leaving her hand lying against his chest, she came up on tiptoe and quickly kissed his lips. "See you then."

He bobbed his head once, abruptly. "Yeah, see you then." He rushed toward the door as though the house were on fire.

Because she never went to the office this early in the day, Marcie sank down onto the hearth, took the poker in hand, and dejectedly stirred the live coals beneath the cold ashes. After she carefully fed them kindling, they ignited.

Watching the new flames devour the logs, Marcie wished she could ignite her husband's passion as quickly and easily. Right now it seemed hopeless, but if there was a way, she was determined to find it. She had overcome the—mostly unintentional—cruelties of her childhood peers. Successfully, she had earned the respect of her colleagues and amassed a fortune. She was no longer looked upon as merely Goosey Johns.

All her other goals, however, paled in comparison to making Chase love her. The money she had bartered with was insignificant. She had gambled much more—her pride, her womanhood, her future happiness. With that much at stake she simply had to make it work.

Chase tapped the white envelope against his opposite palm several times before working his finger beneath the flap and opening it. The check was written on her personal account, made out to him personally. She'd had the sensitivity not to make it directly to the bank, thereby sparing his pride. Leave it to her to handle the transaction in a face-saving manner. The amount of her check was generous, more than he needed. The excess would provide operating capital for several months.

With a trace of irritation he tossed the check onto the desk and moved to the window. He sightlessly stared through the cloudy glass.

He felt like a heel. He *was* a heel.

She hadn't uttered a single word of censure or complaint, but he knew he must have hurt her last night, emotionally for sure, and perhaps even physically.

Unaware of it, she had grimaced slightly when she sat down on the barstool. He had left her tender if not in pain; that made him feel like a brute. It had been on the tip of his tongue to express his concern over her discomfort, but he hadn't wanted to broach the subject of their wedding night. Not in any context.

Because if they talked about her physical pain, they might touch upon her emotional battering, and that would have been too difficult for him to handle. He could promise never to hurt her again physically. But emotionally?

It had been readily apparent that she expected them to spend the day together at home. She had said she planned to go to her office, but since when did she wear silk lounging pajamas and ballet slippers to the office?

He couldn't spend the day alone with her and stay away from the bedroom. No way in hell. So, like a gutless coward, he had left her feeling badly about herself, little knowing that he had run not because last night had been so bad, but because it had been so damn good.

Yeah, Marcie probably thought he'd left her bed last night because he'd been repulsed, when, in fact, the opposite was true.

Shoving his hand through his hair, he cursed. Up to last night he hadn't felt guilty about this marriage. Now he felt guilty as hell. Guilt had made his stomach queasy. Guilt was eating at his entrails like an insidious bacteria.

"Face it," he hissed to himself, "last night you didn't want to leave her bed." That's why he hadn't trusted himself to stay. She'd been so tight, so . . . God, help him. He had wanted to make love to her a second time. A third. That hadn't happened to him since Tanya.

He pressed his forehead against the cold pane of window glass and squeezed his eyes shut, trying not to remember how Marcie had looked wearing nothing except the golden, wavering glow of candlelight. Porcelain and fire.

Inside his jeans he grew stiff, thinking of her impudent nipples. He had wanted to test them against the tip of his tongue, suck them into his mouth, tug . . .

He was so lost in the fantasy, he hadn't seen Lucky's Mustang as it rounded the bend in the road and pulled to a halt outside. Chase jumped when his brother bounded in, shedding his jacket before he was fully inside.

Lucky stared at him stupidly. "What are you doing here?"

"I work here."

"Don't play dumb. What are you doing here today? Where's your bride?"

"Probably at her office by now."

"Kind of a short honeymoon, wasn't it?"

Chase frowned at him in a way that he hoped would quell his curiosity. Lucky, however, had never been daunted by his brother's intimidating frowns. "How'd it go?"

"What?"

"Have you gone dense?" Lucky cried impatiently, resting his hands on his hips. "Last night. How was it?"

"Do you expect a blow-by-blow account?"

Lucky's face broke into a wide grin. "Is that particular choice of words significant?"

"None of your damn business."

Lucky barked a laugh, drawing his own conclusions. The check on the desk caught his eye. He picked it up, read the amount, whistled. "Well, you must have done something the lady liked. And done it real good."

"That's not funny." Chase snatched the check from his brother's hand. "Keep your filthy mind off my wife and out of my personal business."

Still chuckling, Lucky went to the hot plate and poured himself a cup of the coffee Chase had brewed. "Careful, big brother. I'm beginning to think all those rationalizations you piled up for marrying Marcie were just so much crap."

"Go to hell." Chase rounded the desk and sat down. "If you're done with being cute and cocky, read that."

He had previously circled an article in the business section of the morning newspaper. When Lucky had finished reading it, Chase asked, "What do you think?"

"I don't know," Lucky said, his brows steepling. "They're from out of state. They don't know us."

"They don't know any locals. That's why they're soliciting bids for drilling equipment and know-how."

"It says they're operating on a shoestring budget."

"A shoestring is better than nothing. Thanks to Marcie's, uh, loan, we can come in with a low bid. We might not clear much, but it would be something."

For the first time in two years, Chase felt a rising excitement about his work. There was a glimmer of optimism on the horizon. A contract, any contract, would do his tottering ego a world of good. Apparently his excitement was contagious.

Lucky grinned. "Hell, why not? We've got nothing better to do. Let's go for it."

Chapter Ten

Eager to discuss the business prospect with Marcie as soon as he got home, Chase rushed through the front door at five to five, loudly calling out her name.

"Oh, there you are," he said when he spotted her standing near the hall table. He hooked his jacket on the coat tree. "Guess what? Today I was reading about these—" Getting his first good look at her face, he drew up short. "What's the matter?"

"Nothing." Looking stricken, she turned away abruptly. "You sound enthusiastic about something. Come into the kitchen and tell me about it."

At first he was mystified by her strange behavior. Then he noticed the telephone on the table. The receiver was off the hook. "Did you get another call?" She ignored his question, so, as he repeated it, he caught her by the upper arm and pulled her around to face him. "Did he call again?" Swallowing visibly, she nodded yes. "What did he say?"

Lowering her eyes to the open collar of his shirt, she shrugged. "More of the same. Nasty propositions. Lewd scenarios."

"Why didn't you just hang up?"

"Because I thought if I listened, I might be able to place his voice among the men I know."

"Did you?"

"No."

"That's not all, is it?" He tipped his head down until he could read her eyes. "Come on, Marcie. What else?"

"He . . . he said that my being married won't make any difference. He plans to keep calling."

"You told him that you got married?" he asked incredulously.

"Of course not. He already knew."

"Christ." Chase realized now why this particular call had upset her so much. "That means the guy is keeping mighty close tabs on you. He knows what you do and when."

"It doesn't mean anything of the sort. It only means he reads the newspaper. Our wedding announcement was in this morning's issue." She gave him a faltering smile. "Now, let's not let him spoil the rest of our evening. I'll fix you a drink and you can tell me your news."

He followed her into the kitchen. "I'm going to call Pat and have him put a tap on our line."

"I'd rather you wouldn't, Chase."

"Why?"

"Because I don't want all our telephone conversations to be overheard. Clients often talk to me about their personal business and financial affairs. That's privileged information intended for my ears only. Sooner or later, the caller is bound to get discouraged and stop calling."

"In the meantime he scares you spitless every time he calls."

"I'm not scared. Just annoyed."

"Marcie, I saw your face. I know the difference between fright and annoyance. You were scared."

Acting on instinct, he pulled her into his arms. Once again he was impressed by how fragile she felt within his embrace. He rested his chin on the top of her head while his arms slid around her waist and linked at the small of her back.

"I hate to think of some sicko creep jacking off while he's whispering dirty words to you."

A shudder rippled through her. She turned her head so that her cheek was lying against his chest. Raising her hands, she lightly rested them on either side of his waist. "I appreciate your concern."

They stayed that way for several moments. Holding her began to feel so good that Chase warred with himself over whether or not to sweep her into his arms and carry her up to bed.

She needed comforting. Wasn't that the least a husband could do for his wife, comfort her when she needed to feel safe and protected?

The only thing that stopped him was the niggling suspicion that providing comfort might not be his only motivation for wanting to take her to bed. He seriously doubted that once they were lying down they would stay dressed for long or that his caresses would remain entirely noble.

Thankfully Marcie relieved him of having to make the choice. She eased away from him, but left her hands at his waist. She tentatively flexed them, then relaxed them, repositioned them, flexed again.

"Your bandage is gone."

"I went to the doctor today. He stripped off the tape, examined me, and pronounced me well."

"Did it hurt?"

"It didn't feel good. But it didn't hurt as bad as it would have if they hadn't shaved me before they wrapped me."

She winced. "Ouch! I can imagine."

"Oh, yeah?" he asked teasingly. "I didn't notice any chest hair on you last night."

At the inadvertent reminder Chase lowered his gaze to her breasts. She was wearing a thick sweater, but his memory penetrated her clothing like X-ray vision.

In vivid color he envisioned the milky mounds of her breasts and their delicate pink centers, that shallow groove that bisected her rib cage into perfect halves, the smooth slope of her belly, and that beguiling, downy delta between her thighs.

He turned his groan into a loud, unnatural-sounding cough. Marcie moved to the bar and mixed them each a drink. Handing him a whiskey and water, she said, "You seemed excited when you came in. Sit down and tell me what's up."

He doubted she really wanted to know. Or maybe she already did. They had been standing very close. How could she not have felt his arousal pressing against her middle?

He observed her as she went about preparing dinner. Her cheeks looked abnormally rosy, but that might have been caused by the simmering pans on the cooktop. Steam was rising from one of them, causing the tendrils of hair on either side of her face to curl.

Willfully tamping down his misplaced desire, Chase told her about the prospect they had for a drilling contract. "Lucky and I spent all day working up a proposal. We submitted what we think is a rock-bottom bid. All we can do now is wait."

"I'll keep my fingers crossed." She drained the boiling pasta in a colander in the sink.

"Sell any houses today?"

"They don't sell just like that, you know," she said over her shoulder.

"Show any?"

"Unfortunately, yes."

"Unfortunately?"

"I've been working with this couple for months. The Harrisons. They still haven't made a decision. About the only thing they agree on is their penchant to argue. I doubt I'll ever get them to sign a contract on a house. Oh, and I talked with Sage. She called to say good-bye before she left for Austin."

"Good riddance."

"Chase! She adores her big brothers."

"She's a pain in the backside."

Her expression told him that she didn't take his invective seriously. "After Sage said good-bye, Laurie got on the phone. She invited us out to lunch Sunday. I accepted."

"Fine."

"She also said she would love for us to join her at church." She had her back turned, ladling an aromatic sauce over the platter of pasta. When he didn't immediately respond, she swiveled her head around. "Chase?"

"I heard you," he said tersely. "I just don't like the idea of church. I haven't been inside one since Tan . . . since the funeral."

Marcie's posture improved to the point of rigidity. For a moment she was still. Then she set down the ladle, turned, and spoke to him directly.

"It's up to you how you resolve your anger with God, Chase. But I must say this. Your first wife's name was Tanya. She is a fact of our lives. We can't continue to dance around her name. I'm not going to feel sick and grow ghastly pale every time it's spoken out loud."

"But I might."

Marcie recoiled as though he had struck her. She did, in fact, grow ghastly pale. Even her lips lost their color. She spun around and braced herself against the countertop as though she might slide to the floor, unable to support herself.

Instantly regretting what he'd said, Chase left his seat and moved up behind her. "I'm sorry, Marcie," he said hoarsely.

He raised his hands and considered laying them on her shoulders, but he couldn't bring himself to. He thought of planting a conciliatory kiss on the nape of her neck where several curling strands of hair had escaped her ponytail. But he didn't dare do that either.

Lamely he said, "I shouldn't have said that."

She turned to face him. He expected her to be tearful. Instead, her eyes were bright with indignation. "I don't like having to walk on eggshells inside my own house. I don't like having to weigh everything I say before I say it, wondering how you're going to take it."

Her anger sparked his own temper. "You know how I feel about Tanya."

"Indeed, how could I not?"

"Okay, then, you know that the wound is still raw."

"Yes," she said, raising her chin a notch. "You made all that perfectly clear before we got married. If not then, certainly last night left no doubt in my mind."

She tried to step around him, but he blocked her path. "Last night? What about last night?"

"Nothing. Forget it. If you'll step aside, I'll get dinner on the table."

"Screw dinner!" He caught her beneath the chin with his fingers and forced her head up. Their eyes clashed. "What was wrong with last night?"

She lifted her chin off the perch of his fingers and retorted haughtily, "Nothing from your perspective. It was less than thrilling for me, however."

He fell back a step, his jaw going slack. "Huh? Oh, I get it. I hurt your feelings, so you retaliate by castrating me, is that it?"

She rolled her eyes. "Spare me the macho tripe. Believe whatever you want to." She stepped around him then, but instead of setting dinner on the table, she headed for the stairs. "Since you decided to 'screw dinner,' I'm going up to my room. When you want me, you know where to find me. Which shouldn't be too difficult for you," she added sweetly. "You managed to find me in the dark last night."

"Listen," he shouted up at her, "I didn't want to do it at all. I was only doing you a favor."

She halted abruptly, turned around, and glared down at him. One of her arched brows rose a fraction. "Well, Mr. Tyler, for your information, that kind of favor I can do without."

"Terrific. I won't have to go to the effort again. Unless, of course, you want to claim your rights as a wife."

"And get another slam-bam-thank-you-ma'am?" She laughed scoffingly. "I certainly won't be missing much, will I?"

His head felt so hot with rage, he thought steam was probably escaping his ears. He wanted to close the distance between them, strip her naked, crush her beneath him, and show her exactly what she was going to be missing.

But damned if he was going to make the first move, not after her scathing review of his lovemaking. Hell would freeze over first.

"Fine," he snarled. "We'll keep this a marriage in name only."

"Fine." She turned on her heel and marched up the stairs. After entering her bedroom, she slammed the door closed behind her.

Five hours later she knocked on Chase's bedroom door. He was lying in bed, but the lights were still on and he was awake. The sheets were tangled around his restless legs. His head was propped up on pillows. He was staring at the ceiling and gnashing his teeth.

At her unexpected knock his heart stopped for several seconds. His eyes eagerly swung toward the door. But his tone was hardly cordial when he growled, "What?"

She opened the door a crack and peered around it. "May I come in?"

"What for?"

"I think we should talk."

He made an assenting motion with his shoulders and she walked in. His fledgling smugness evaporated when he saw how she was dressed. It wasn't anywhere close to the bridal nightgown she had worn last night, but it was just as sexy in a different way.

The pajama set was pink-striped cotton knit. Boxerlike shorts and a T-shirt top. The wide legs of the boxers made her bare legs look even longer. Her hair was still pulled into a ponytail. She was wearing her eyeglasses. She was barefoot. She looked like a coed at a slumber party.

Except for her breasts. They were making pert, prominent impressions against her shirt, and they jiggled slightly as she moved from door to bed and sat down on the edge of it.

"Chase, I'm sorry I behaved so childishly earlier. I guess the pressure of the last several days built up until I had to blow or burst."

Since she had made the overture, he could be magnanimous. "I guess I've been on edge too," he grumbled.

"I took potshots at your male ego and that was uncalled for. Although, it would be dishonest of me to pretend that I was satisfied with last night."

She glanced at him shyly, then away. "You see, Chase, I expected a little more consideration. I don't think I got any more thought from you than the condom you slipped on. I barely got equal time."

His jaw tensed. He was guilty as charged. That made him that much angrier.

"I expected, wanted, more . . . more . . . I guess the word is involvement. I wanted more *involvement* from you."

"You wanted an orgasm," he said, being intentionally blunt. By God if she could tromp on his masculinity, why should he be skittish about calling a spade a spade?

"That's the least of it, yes," she admitted quietly. "I would have liked more attention and affection, too."

"Then you should have hired yourself a gigolo instead of buying a husband. You could have paid him by the hour, or by the orgasm, instead of making such a sizable investment."

It wouldn't have surprised him if she had hauled off and hit him, which he secretly felt he deserved. If a man had dared talk to Sage like that, she would have gone after him with the garden shears. Devon too.

Instead, when Marcie spoke, her reply was calm and conceding. "After sulking all this time in my room, I reached the same conclusion."

Her unmitigated honesty disarmed him. Instead of getting any satisfaction from shocking her, he felt more rotten than he had before. She was a hell of a lot smarter than either his sister or Devon. Her method of disarmament was more poised, but just as effective.

She took a deep breath, drawing his attention to those damn taut nipples again. "If I had wanted hearts and flowers, I should have hired a gigolo. But I don't regret the decision I made," she told him. "You're legally and physically my husband now. I'll try to be a good wife to you." Raising her eyes to his, she added, "So if you want me tonight—"

"No thanks." It rankled that she didn't appear disappointed.

"Did I wound your ego too terribly?"

"I'll live."

"I suppose if you can survive years of bull riding, you can survive me. Does this itch?" Surprising him, she ran the back of her fingers up the center gully of his torso where the hair was beginning to grow back.

He sucked in a sharp breath and wheezed, "No. Not yet."

"It probably will before too long."

"I'll keep you posted."

"Listen, Chase, the thermostat for the whole upstairs is in this room. My room is cold. Do you mind if I turn the heater up several degrees?" She was already off the bed, moving toward the thermostat mounted on the opposite wall.

"Actually I do," he said contrarily. "I'm hot."

He shoved the sheet down another inch or two, until the thick hair on his lower abdomen was visible. He thrust one long, bare leg from beneath the covers. Only one corner of the sheet kept him decent. He was feeling ornery and wanted more than anything to get a rise out of her.

She didn't even flinch. "Oh, well, I certainly don't want you to be uncomfortable. So in that case, I'll just get another blanket for my bed. I store spares in this closet."

She pulled open the louvered door of the extra closet in his room, went up on tiptoe, and reached for the top shelf where several blankets were folded.

Her pose made Chase's mouth go dry. It emphasized every lean muscle in her long legs. It raised her pajama top, baring a good three inches of midriff. The shorts were raised over twin crescents of derriere that he craved to cup in his palms while lifting her up and against him.

In danger of embarrassing himself, he reached for the covers and pulled them above his waist.

She dragged the blanket down from the shelf and hugged it against her with both arms. "There, that ought to do it."

He could swear that was a double entendre. Sure as hell, she was referring to making him rock hard and throbbing. Her statement had nothing to do with extra blankets. Then again, his warped imagination was probably reading more into her smile than was intended.

"Good night, Chase," she said innocently enough. "Sleep well."

He didn't trust himself to speak.

Chapter Eleven

Chase had very little to say for the entire month that followed.

Few had the courage to engage him in conversation. His sour disposition and perpetual scowl frightened off most who would otherwise have attempted it. Those who dared felt relieved if they escaped with their lives.

On a Friday night, sitting with his brother at the bar in the tavern known by locals merely as The Place, he didn't appear inclined to make conversation.

A half hour after his arrival, he was still nursing his first bourbon and water. He was hunched over it like a stingy dog with a bone who didn't really want the bone but didn't want another dog to have it. He was morosely staring into the drink, which melting ice had turned a light amber.

"Well, there's nothing we can do but wait them out."

Lucky's comment only deepened Chase's frown. "That's what we've been saying for a month."

"They've got to make a decision soon."

"When I called last week, they said they would award a contract by the end of this week. This week they said it will be next week. I think they're giving me the royal runaround."

"Well, if there's oil down there, it's not going anywhere," Lucky said philosophically. "All we can do is wait them out."

Chase banged his fist on the bar. "You sound like a damn broken record. Can't you think of something else to say?"

"Yeah, I can think of something else to say," Lucky replied testily, sliding off the barstool. "Go to hell."

"Wait a minute." Chase reached out and grabbed a handful of Lucky's jacket. "Come back. Have another drink."

Lucky threw off his brother's grip. "I don't want another drink."

"I'll buy."

"Doesn't matter. Your company stinks. I've got better things to do than sit around and take your abuse."

"Like what?"

"Like go home to my wife, that's what. Which is what you should be doing. This is the third time this week you've twisted my arm into coming here and having a drink with you after work."

"So? Now that you're married, you can't go out with the boys anymore?"

"I don't enjoy it as much as I used to."

"And one drink is your limit? Devon put a kink in your drinking habits, too, huh?"

"That's right. I'm so happy with her, I don't need any other kind of high."

"Oh, really? Does sex with her make you drunk?"

Lucky's hands balled into fists at his sides. His deep-blue eyes turned glacial and his nostrils flared. Two years ago he would have already charged his brother and been throwing bloodletting punches. Devon had taught him that discretion is the better part of valor. He no longer fought first and thought about it later. He had learned restraint, but Chase was testing the boundaries of it tonight.

Chase could all but see the numbers ticking across Lucky's forehead as he slowly counted to ten in an effort to control his short temper.

Chase set his elbows on the bar and plowed all ten fingers through his dark hair as he lowered his head. "You don't deserve that. Devon sure as hell doesn't." Holding his head between his hands, he rolled it from side to side. "I'm sorry. Try to forget I said that."

He fully expected his brother to leave. Surprisingly, Lucky returned to the stool beside him and sat down. "Why don't you tell me what's really bothering you?"

"We need that drilling contract."

"Uh-huh. Besides that. Something's eating at you, Chase. Mother and Devon have noticed it too. Every Sunday when you and Marcie are at the house, you're as uptight as a man sitting on top of a keg of dynamite. The fuse is short and it's burning hot. What gives?"

Chase swirled the contents of his glass around several times. "Marcie," he mumbled.

"I figured as much."

His head snapped around, his eyes sharp and demanding. "Why'd you figure that?"

"Marcie's a lot like Devon. She had a life before you came into it. She's been an independent lady for a long time." Lucky tossed back the handful of beer nuts he'd scooped out of the bowl on the bar. "I'm not surprised she found the role of wife uncomfortable. Like a new pair of shoes, it doesn't quite fit her yet."

"What, are you kidding?" Chase grunted scoffingly. "She's so bloody good at being a wife, it's enough to make you sick."

"Huh?"

"Dinner is on the table every night at six sharp. She bakes cookies. God knows when because she's always so busy with other stuff. The house is as neat as a damn palace. I lose something, she knows right where to find it."

"I'm relieved to hear it's working out so well," Lucky said cheerfully. "As you know, I had doubts that it would. Sounds like y'all are getting along great. What have you got to bellyache about?"

Chase swiveled on his stool to face his brother. Now that the spillway had finally been opened, there was a lot he'd held back that needed to be released.

"She's too perfect." Lucky merely stared at him as though he'd gone daft. "I'll give you an example. She told me that she liked to go through the Sunday paper methodically. Last week I deliberately scattered it all over the living room, reading a section, then dropping it and letting it fall wherever."

"Why?"

"Just to be provoking."

Lucky shook his head with bafflement. "Why?"

Because I'm horny as hell! Unappeased horniness was a condition he couldn't admit, especially to a younger brother who had come by his nickname because of his uncanny success with women.

"I wanted to see if I could rile her," Chase said.

"Did you?"

"No. She didn't say a thing. Not even a dirty look. She just went around the living room, calmly collecting the newspaper and restacking it so she could go through it the way she liked to."

"I don't get it. You're complaining about a wife who obviously has the patience of a saint?"

"Have you ever tried living with a saint? With somebody so bloody perfect? I tell you she's just not normal. Why doesn't she get mad?" He blew out a gust of air. "It's nerve-racking. I'm always on guard."

"Look, Chase, if that's all—"

"It's not. She sneaks up on me."

Lucky laughed so hard he almost fell off his stool. "Sneaks up on you? You mean like we used to do with Sage? Does Marcie hide in your closet and then when you open the door, she jumps out and hollers boo?"

"Don't be ridiculous."

"Well, what do you mean?"

Chase felt foolish now. He couldn't tell Lucky about the morning he'd been standing at his bathroom sink shaving, when he happened to notice Marcie's reflection in the mirror. He spun around so quickly, he'd nicked his chin with the razor.

"I'm sorry I startled you, Chase. I knocked but I guess you didn't hear me." She had rushed forward and set the stack of fresh towels on the lid of the toilet. "You're bleeding. Here."

She ripped off a sheet of toilet tissue and pressed it against his bleeding chin . . . and held it there . . . for a long time . . . even though he was standing there buck naked and growing hard from the delicate touch of her fingertips against his face.

And just about the time the tip of his sex grazed her, she whispered, "How does that feel?"

For several seconds the blood had pounded through the veins in his head. He finally gathered enough wherewithal to mutter, "Better." He snatched up one of the towels she had carried in and wrapped it around his middle with the haste of Adam, who'd just been caught red-handed committing the original sin.

No, he couldn't tell Lucky that. Lucky would want to know why he hadn't just taken his wife to bed and made love to her until they were senseless. Chase wouldn't be able to provide an answer, because he wanted to know that himself.

Ignoring his brother's question, he said, "You wouldn't know it to look at her, but she hasn't got a smidgen of modesty. She's brazen. Remember how much stock Grandma used to place on a woman's modesty?" He laughed bitterly. "Good thing she never met Marcie."

"What the hell are you talking about?" Leaning in closer, Lucky peered into Chase's feverish eyes. "You haven't started smoking funny green cigarettes, have you?" Chase gave Lucky's shoulder a shove. Lucky only laughed again. "You're nuts. Marcie behaves like a lady."

"Not at home she doesn't. At home she parades around naked as a jaybird."

Lucky's interest was piqued. He cocked his head to one side. "Oh, yeah?"

Chase didn't notice that his brother's interest had a teasing quality.

He was thinking back to a few days earlier when he had gone into Marcie's room with a shirt that needed a button replaced.

She had answered his decorous knock on her door, "Come in."

He had pushed the door open and walked in, but stumbled on his own two feet when he found himself face-to-face with her pretty, pink nakedness.

He had caught her arranging her hair. Her hands were raised above her head. She stood poised in front of her vanity table, the mirror over it offering him a view of her back so he could see her all over at once.

Her blue eyes challenged him to do something, say something. He wanted to pounce on her and feed on her beautiful flesh, but he wouldn't allow himself to. If she could act so blasé about her nudity, then, by all that was holy, so could he.

Pulse thundering, resolutely keeping his eyes on a spot just above her head, he asked, "Do you have a sewing kit?"

"I'll be glad to mend whatever needs it."

"It's just a button. I can do it. Have you got a needle and thread or not?"

"Sure. Right here."

She lowered her arms. Her hair drifted to her smooth, fair shoulders. The small chest where she kept her sewing kit was behind him. She could have gone around him. She could have excused herself and moved him aside. Instead, she practically walked through him, brushing herself against him. Every cell in his body had become a tongue of flame, licking him into a frenzy of sexual heat.

Just thinking about it now made him yearn to touch her impertinent breasts and stroke her translucent skin and explore the mystery at her beautifully decorated apex.

Lucky waved his hand in front of Chase's face. He drew himself back into the present and querulously growled, "I think she was an old maid for too long. It made her an exhibitionist. What does it sound like to you?"

"Sounds like a fantasy I read in *Playboy* once."

"Dammit, Lucky, I'm serious. She's like a nympho or something."

"Damned shame to be married to one, isn't it? I speak from experience you understand." He winked.

Both Lucky's sarcasm and his gesture escaped Chase, who was still deep in thought. "She brushes up against me all the time. Remember the cat we had that rubbed herself against our legs when a tom wasn't around? Marcie's like that. She can't walk past me without bumping into me. It's like she's in heat."

"Maybe she is."

Lucky's flippant comment goosed Chase out of his erotic trance. "What?"

Lucky vigorously chewed another handful of beer nuts and swallowed. "I said maybe she is. Devon believes that a woman gets pregnant when she wants to, when she has subconsciously made up her mind to."

"Pregnant?" Chase repeated, looking stunned. Then he shook his head adamantly. "She's not going to get pregnant. At least she had better not. I don't want anything to do with a baby. I don't even want to talk about one, think about one."

Lucky's grin gradually receded. Uneasily he glanced beyond his brother's shoulder. Instantly his vision cleared. "Speaking of your lady, she's here."

"Huh?"

Chase followed the direction of Lucky's gaze until he sighted Marcie. She was standing just inside the door of the noisy, smoky tavern, surveying the rowdy Friday-night crowd. When her gaze connected with his, he saw relief break across her features.

As unobtrusively as possible, she wended her way through the largely male crowd until she reached the end of the bar where they were seated. "So you are here." She smiled at Chase breathlessly. "I thought I recognized your truck outside." To his brother she said, "Hi, Lucky."

"Hi. I don't suppose Devon is with you. The Place isn't one of her favorite nightspots."

Marcie laughed. "So I've heard. And with good reason. But don't worry. I understand some of the most lasting love affairs have inauspicious origins."

"At least in our case that's true. It started with a fistfight in this hellhole. Look where it got us. Into a marriage made in heaven." He grinned broadly. "Want a drink?"

"No, thank you."

"What are you doing here?"

Chase's abrupt question cut through their lighthearted exchange like a steel rapier. It sounded accusatory and instantly put Marcie on the defensive.

"Remember the couple from Massachusetts? They're in town today. I was showing them a lake house and had to come by here on my way back to town. As I said, I spotted your pickup outside."

"You were checking up on me," Chase said. "Can't I be a few minutes late coming home without you hunting me down?"

"Hey, Chase, relax."

He ignored his brother. "Or don't you trust me to stop with just one drink? Did you think I had run off and joined the rodeo circuit again?"

"What the hell are you doing?" Lucky asked through his teeth, intentionally keeping his voice low so that they wouldn't attract attention.

"He's trying to humiliate me," Marcie said candidly. "When all he's actually doing is making himself look foolish."

With that, she turned her back on them. Proudly, shoulders back, fiery head held high, she moved toward the door.

Before Lucky could speak the admonishment he had ready, Chase turned to him and warned, "Shut up. I don't need any advice from you." Digging in his jeans pocket for currency, he tossed down enough bills to cover the cost of their drinks and adequately tip the bartender.

He elbowed milling patrons aside as he followed Marcie's light-capturing hair toward the door. One grinning, boozy face blocked his path and stood his ground firmly even when Chase tried to set him aside.

"Better catch that one, Tyler. She's one classy piece."

"So then Chase snarls something to the effect of, 'That's my *wife*, you s.o.b.'. Sorry, Deacon. Then his fist smashes into this guy's face and knocks his nose askew. Another punch landed square on his mouth. His partial plate flew right out. I could see it from where I was standing at the bar. Swear to God—pardon me, Deacon—it did. The teeth got crushed in the stampede. Everybody was trying their damnedest— sorry again, Deacon—to get out of Chase's way. He was like a madman."

After Lucky had finished his account of the fight that had occurred at The Place two nights earlier, everyone in the formal dining room of the Tylers' ranch house was held in speechless suspension for several seconds.

Marcie kept her eyes lowered to her plate, still mortified that she had unwittingly caused a brawl. She now shared Devon's aversion to The Place.

Apparently Chase was just as uncomfortable with the recounting of the one-sided fight. He had remained broodily silent, drawing little valleys through his uneaten mound of mashed potatoes with the tines of his fork.

Laurie, Marcie noticed, was nervously fiddling with the strand of pearls around her neck, possibly because Lucky hadn't censored his language in deference to their additional guest at the midday Sunday meal.

"I wish you boys would stay out of that tavern," Laurie said, finally breaking the awkward silence. "The only good thing that's ever happened there was when Lucky met Devon."

"Thank you, Laurie," Marcie's sister-in-law replied. "Would you like for me to clear the dishes for dessert?"

"That's sweet of you. Is everybody finished? Jess?"

Jess Sawyer blotted his mouth with the same meticulous precision as he had sweetened his tea, cut his meat, and buttered his roll one bite at a time. He was a small, neat man dressed in a stiff white shirt and a well-pressed brown suit. He had thin brown hair and dull brown eyes. If personalities had colors, his would be brown.

"Everything was delicious, Laurie," he said politely. "Thank you for inviting me."

With Lucky's help, Devon stood and began stacking empty dishes on a tray. When the table was cleared, Devon held the door for Lucky as he carried the tray into the kitchen. "We'll bring dessert and coffee in," she said, following her husband out.

"I'm glad I caught you as we left the sanctuary," Laurie was saying to Mr. Sawyer. "I hate to think of anyone's eating a meal alone, but I think eating Sunday dinner alone is a sacrilege. Feel welcome to come anytime," she said, smiling at him. "Pat, was the roast beef too well-done for you?"

Pat Bush, a perennial guest at Sunday dinner, shifted in his chair. "It was fine." Glancing across the table toward Mr. Sawyer, he added, "Just like always."

"You didn't eat but one helping."

"My lack of appetite has nothing to do with the food, Laurie. I'm still thinking about that ruckus out at The Place last Friday night." He cast a baleful glance toward Chase.

Devon and Lucky returned, bringing with them a three-layer chocolate cake and coffee with all the fixings. "I'll serve from the sideboard, if that's all right with you, Laurie."

"That will be fine, dear," Laurie told her daughter-in-law.

From her chair Marcie watched Devon slice the first piece of cake and put it on a plate. Some of the frosting stuck to her fingers. She raised her hand to her mouth to lick it off. Before she could, Lucky grabbed her hand, poked her finger into his mouth, and sucked it clean.

Marcie's stomach did a flip-flop.

She felt Chase go tense beside her.

Devon snatched her hand away from her playful husband and glanced quickly over her shoulder to see if their loveplay had been noticed. Marcie pretended she hadn't seen it. She didn't want to embarrass Devon or, more to the point, have Devon see her jealousy.

"Y'all seem to bust The Place up every time you go in it," the sheriff said to Chase.

"What was I supposed to do, Pat," Chase asked defensively, grumpily, "just stand there and let that guy insult my wife?"

"To my way of thinking, Chase had no choice but to deck the jerk," Lucky commented as he passed around dessert plates.

"Well, your opinion on fighting doesn't count for much, does it?" Pat asked crossly. "You fight at the drop of a hat."

"*Used* to fight at the drop of a hat. Now I'm a lover, not a fighter." He kissed Devon's cheek as she went past him.

Chase's knee reflexively bumped into Marcie's under the table.

"I'm certain that Chase did what he felt like he had to do," Laurie said in her son's defense. "He paid for all the damage done to the bar and took care of that man's medical bills. I just hate to think of his teeth being knocked out. Literally."

Lucky emitted a snicker. Before long, everyone around the table was laughing. All except Jess Sawyer, who was gaping at them with dismay.

"He may end up thanking me," Chase said when the laughter had abated. "Those were the god-awfulest-looking false teeth I've ever—"

"Devon!"

The alarm in Lucky's voice silenced Chase. Lucky shot from his chair and launched himself toward his wife, who was leaning over the sideboard. Her face was pale. She was taking quick, panting breaths. One of Lucky's arms went around her waist to help support her. The other hand cupped her cheek and lifted her bowed head.

"Devon? Honey?"

"I'm fine," she assured him with a feeble smile. "A little dizzy spell. I think I just got too warm. Maybe if we turn down the heat a little, hmm? Or maybe something I ate didn't set well with me."

"Oh, for heaven's sake!" Laurie laid her folded napkin beside her plate, left her chair, and joined the couple at the sideboard. "Why don't y'all stop this foolishness and announce to everybody else what I've known for months?" Taking the initiative, she turned toward the table. "Devon's going to have a baby."

"Oh!" Marcie never remembered giving that glad cry. She, along

with everyone else, even Mr. Sawyer, converged on the beaming couple, who were alternately embracing each other and their well-wishers.

Marcie gave Devon an extended hug. Since her marriage to Chase,
the two women had become good friends. Marcie admired Devon's
intelligence and acerbic wit, which she put to good use in the columns
she wrote for one of the Dallas newspapers. Recently she had told
them she'd been approached by a syndicator.

"I'm so glad for you," Marcie said earnestly. "Are you feeling all
right? Is there anything I can do?"

Devon clutched her hand. "Do you know anything about babies?"

"No!" Marcie laughed.

"Then a big help you'll be."

The two women smiled at each other with mutual admiration and
growing affection. Then Marcie kissed the proud papa's cheek. "Congratulations, Lucky."

"Thanks. One of the little critters finally fought his way upstream."

"James Lawrence!" Laurie cried, aghast. "Remember that we have
a guest. I won't stand for that naughty kind of talk. I don't want Jess
thinking that I've reared a bunch of—"

The shrill, obnoxious scraping sound of chair legs against the hardwood floor brought them all around. Chase dropped his napkin beside
his plate and stamped out.

Before he went through the archway, Marcie got a good look at his
face. It looked like a man's shattered reflection in a broken mirror.

The ax arced through the air, making a whistling sound before it connected with the log. *Thwack!* The log, standing on its end, split down
the middle. Chase bent at the waist and tossed the two pieces aside,
then picked up another log and set it upright on the block.

"What are you doing?"

Thwack!

"Knitting a sweater. What does it look like?"

"That can't be good for your ribs."

"My ribs are fine."

Thwack!

Lucky put his back to the nearby fence. He leaned against it while
hooking the heel of his boot on the lowest rail. He set both elbows on
the top one.

"You know, Chase, you can be the most self-centered s.o.b. I've ever
run across."

Thwack!

Chase glared at his brother before tossing aside the split log and getting another. "What did you expect me to do, pass out cigars?"

"That would have been a start."

"Sorry to disappoint you."

Thwack!

Lucky reached in and wrested the ax handle from his older brother while he was bent down. Chase sprung erect, his face fierce.

"I'm not disappointed," Lucky said, throwing the ax to the ground. "I'm mad. Our mother is disappointed. She was counting on your marriage to turn you around."

"Too bad."

"Damn right it's too bad. Because you've got a wonderful woman who is—for reasons I can't comprehend—in love with you. But you're too damn blind to see it. Or too plain stupid. Or self-pitying. I'm not real sure what your problem is."

"You're mad because I didn't make a big deal over your kid."

"And wasn't that small of you!"

"Why haven't you told me?" Chase shouted. "Why keep it a secret? Building anticipation?"

"No, trying to protect you."

"From what?"

"From the hurt that's tearing your guts out right now."

Chase assumed a combative stance. His breathing was labored, but not from the exertion of splitting firewood. He didn't strike his brother as he appeared ready to do. Instead, he turned his back on him and headed toward the house.

Lucky charged after him, grabbed him by the sleeve, and slung him against the toolshed beside the woodpile. He made a bar of his forearm across Chase's throat.

"I didn't tell you about my baby before now because I knew it was going to hurt you, Chase. I hate that. I hate it like hell. But that's the way the cards fell and there's not a damn thing I or you or anybody else can do about it.

"I didn't ask for my child to be the first Tyler grandbaby. I wish it had been yours, as it should have been. But is that supposed to make me less delighted about my own baby? It can't. I'm sorry. I'm thrilled. I'm bursting with happiness over this kid. I can't wait till it gets here.

"However," he enunciated, thrusting his face closer to his brother's, "that doesn't mean that Devon and I don't still grieve for yours that died with Tanya. We all do. We always will. But life goes on, Chase. At least for most of us it does.

"If you want to live the rest of your life from inside a grave, then do it. I think you're stupid, I think you're sick, but if your misery makes you happy, then by all means be miserable. Just don't expect the rest of us to crawl into that grave with you and pull the dirt over our heads. We're all damned sick and tired of catering to you."

With an abrupt little shove he let go of Chase and turned away. He had taken only a few steps when a heavy hand clamped down on his shoulder. Reflexively, he spun around, expecting a blow.

Instead, Chase extended him his right hand. Lucky saw the tears, which made Chase's gray eyes shimmery. His ordinarily firm lips were unsteady.

"Congratulations, little brother. I'm happy for you."

They shook hands. Then they embraced. Then they walked back to the house together.

Chapter Twelve

"You didn't have an inkling?"

"About what?"

"That Devon was pregnant."

"No."

"I thought Lucky might have told you."

"No."

Chase's mumbled replies were grating on Marcie's nerves. Her nerves were already raw. They always were after one of their Sunday dinners with her in-laws.

Not that she was shunned or made to feel unwelcome. The Tylers had graciously incorporated her into the family. Even Lucky, who had expressed the strongest reservations against her marriage to Chase, now teased and joked with her as if she'd been a member of the family for years. Along with Laurie and Devon, he included her in their warm camaraderie.

Chase's family wasn't at fault. Chase himself was the one who made her edgy and nervous. He was never verbally abusive. The one and only time that had happened was last Friday night in The Place. He had apologized later for it, and she had accepted his apology, knowing how worried he was about the future of Tyler Drilling and attributing his outrageous behavior to that.

No, she didn't have a quarrel with his deportment. While they were with his family, he was courteous to her. He didn't criticize her. He didn't embarrass her. He didn't ignore her by treating her as though she were invisible as she had heard wives complaining that their husbands did when they were in public.

In their case, quite the opposite was true.

"You hadn't guessed?"

She jumped, startled by his abrupt question. "What?"

He was driving her car, with his left wrist crooked over the steering wheel. His right hand was resting on his thigh, within easy reach of the gearshift . . . or her knee, which he'd found several occasions to cover and caress during the course of the afternoon.

"Women seem to have a sixth sense about that stuff," he said, referring to Devon's pregnancy. "I thought maybe you had suspected."

"No. Although I guess I should have read the signs. I remember somebody teasing her at our wedding dinner about eating two desserts."

"I just thought she was putting on a few extra pounds."

Marcie smiled. "I'm sure she is." Chase didn't smile. "She's already six months. I can't believe she hid it so well for so long. Of course, she's tall. And clothing can camouflage a lot. But my goodness, the baby will be here before we know it."

"Hmm."

"And when it gets here, are you going to continue acting like a jerk about it?" Chase's head came around. He opened his mouth to speak, thought better of it, and closed his mouth with an angry little click. "When you stamped out of the house like that, Chase, it broke your mother's heart."

"My heart's been broken too."

"Oh, yes, we all know that. You wear it so well on your sleeve for all the world to see. Well, we've all seen it, and frankly, it's getting old."

"I apologized to Lucky, didn't I? I told him I was happy for him."

"I know, I know. I even saw you giving Devon an obligatory hug. That's the very least you could have done."

"If I had gushed and simpered, it would have been hypocritical."

" 'Hypocritical'? What an odd word for you to use."

"What's that supposed to mean?"

He stopped the car in their driveway. Marcie alighted and headed for the door. She was already inside shrugging off her coat when he caught up with her.

"What's that supposed to mean?" he repeated angrily, tossing his coat in the general direction of the coat tree and missing it by a mile.

Something inside Marcie snapped. For over a month she had been pampering him, humoring his dour disposition and overlooking his provocations, which she knew were deliberate. The harder she tried to make life pleasant, the harder he worked at being a jackass. Well, she had had it with him. Good wife be damned. It was time he got as good as he gave.

Her red hair was bristling. As she closed in on him her eyes narrowed. "What it means, Chase Tyler, is that you are a hypocrite every single Sunday we go out there. It means that your congratulations to them were no more genuine than your phony displays of affection for me."

He shook his head stubbornly. "That's not true. I'm very happy for my bro— Wait a minute. What phony displays of affection for you?"

"Come on, Chase," she cried. "You don't want me to spell it out."

"Like hell I don't. What are you talking about?"

She drew back her shoulders and glared up at him. There was heat radiating out of her cheeks. Every muscle in her body was pulled taut.

"I'm talking about the knee massages. I sit on the sofa, you sit on the sofa. I cross my legs, you cover my knee with your hand. I stand up, you place your arm across my shoulders. I shiver, you offer me your jacket. I look up at you, you touch my hair. I laugh. You laugh."

His jaw was working, the muscles in his face knotting. Marcie knew she was pushing, but she couldn't stop. For a month she had been living with a chameleon. For several hours each Sunday she had endured his sweet, husbandly caresses that she knew meant nothing. She would return home feverish and aroused to the point of agony. And there was never any relief. Because once they were away from his family, he reverted to being broody and remote.

"I'm only trying to be nice," he said defensively. "But if you don't like it, I'll dispense with these courtesies." He turned away and went to the fireplace in the living room, where he began stoking up the fire. All his motions were angry, jerky.

Marcie wasn't finished with him. She joined him at the hearth, catching his arm as he laid aside the poker. "Your family is carefully gauging us, watching to see how we relate to each other. Thanks to your Academy Award performance every Sunday, I'm sure they're convinced that everything is hunky-dory. Little do they know that we're celibates."

"Oh, no, because they're bound to have intercepted some of those smoldering looks you send my way when you know they're watching. I'm sure they saw you twining that strand of my hair around your fingertip while you talked NBA basketball with Lucky. How could they miss it when you nudged my breast with your elbow as you reached for your coffee cup?"

"Don't pretend now that you didn't like it, Marcie," he said in a low, vibrating voice. "Because even through my sleeve I felt your nipple get hard. I heard that little catch in your throat." He used her momentary speechlessness to launch his own attack. "While we're on the subject, I don't like your foreplay any—"

"Foreplay?"

"Foreplay. What else would you call it when you lay your hand on the inside of my thigh and rub it up and down? Oh, you're careful to make it look wifely and casual, but you know it's there and I know it's there and we both know what's going on about four inches up from there.

"And if you don't like having me place my arm across your shoulders, you shouldn't snuggle up against me. If you don't like my offering you my jacket, don't make sure I notice through your blouse that you're chilled. While I've got my hand on your knee, you've got your foot moving against my calf. Now if that's not an invitation, I don't know what is."

The building flames in the grate were reflected in his eyes, flashes of passion and anger that fed each other. "I didn't see you pulling your head back when I was fiddling with your hair. Oh, no. Instead, you nuzzled the palm of my hand. I felt your tongue. It left a damp spot.

"You laughed because I dripped coffee into my lap. And I dripped coffee into my lap because you jostled my elbow with your breast. And I laughed back because you blotted up the drips with your napkin, and then it was either laugh or moan. Now which would you rather I do in my mother's dining room while you're mashing your hand against my crotch, laugh or moan?

"So don't preach to me about how to conduct myself. I'll be more than glad to put a stop to this sexual charade if you will. Because if this playacting we do every Sunday makes you crazy, you can imagine what it does to me!"

After his shouting, the quiet in the room was sudden and intense. Marcie took a step nearer to him and in a sultry voice asked, "What does it do to you, Chase?"

He reached for her hand, yanked it forward, and pressed it open against his distended fly. "That."

Her fingers closed around his steely erection. "Why do you stop with the foreplay, Chase? Why don't you do something with this?" With each slow, milking motion of her hand his breath grew louder, harsher. "Are you afraid you won't like it? Or are you afraid you will?"

She released him and raised both hands to his head, sinking her fingers into his hair and cupping his scalp. "Kiss me. Kiss me right." Stretching up so that her lips were just beneath his, she added in a seductive whisper, "I dare you."

The sound that issued from his throat was feral. The manner in which his lips swooped down on hers was savage. So brutal was his kiss that at first her lips were benumbed by it. Gradually, however, she was able to separate them. Then she felt the swift and sure thrust of his tongue. Madly, rampantly, rapaciously, it swept her mouth.

Like her, he buried his fingers in her abundance of hair and held her head in place for the plundering mastery of his kiss. He drew on her like a man starved, as though he wanted to suck her entire mouth into his. He pulled away to catch his breath. Even then, his tongue was flicking over her lips, tasting her. Unappeased, he came back for more. And more. And more.

Marcie reveled in the carnality of his kiss. She loved the texture of his tongue, the taste of his saliva, the firmness of his lips, the rasp of his beard against her chin and cheeks. Her senses wallowed in the pleasure of smelling his skin and feeling his hair—Chase's skin, Chase's hair, Chase's hardness gouging her middle.

As one, they dropped to their knees on the plush rug in front of the hearth. Their mouths went on feeding frenzies over each other's face, indiscriminately moving their lips over cheeks, chins, eyelids.

When their mouths fused again, he sent his tongue deep, penetrating her mouth and saturating her with desire. His hands smoothed over her back, moved to her sides, rubbed the crescents of her breasts with the heels of them. Then, exercising no subtlety, he covered her derriere and pulled her against him.

Marcie didn't even consider being coy. She allowed him to push suggestively against her cleft. She even gloried in the obvious strength of his desire and ground her middle against it.

Groaning, he wrapped his arms around her so tightly she could no longer move and whispered fiercely, "Stop or it'll be all over."

"Not yet. Not yet."

She put enough space between them to peel his sweater over his head. Next she attacked the buttons of his shirt. When it had been cast aside, her fingertips roved over him in an orgy of discovery, like a blind person who was seeing for the first time.

With a hungry whimper she leaned into his chest and pressed her open mouth upon it. He cupped her head, but allowed it to move freely from spot to spot. Her lips found his nipple in a spiral of dark, crinkly hair. Shyly at first, then more aggressively, she caressed it with her tongue.

Swearing in whispered agony, he set her away from him. "Take off your clothes."

"You take them off," she challenged huskily.

They stared at each other a moment. Marcie held her breath until he took the hem of her sweater in his hands. He removed it over her head. His eyes became fixated on her breasts. Reaching behind her, Marcie unhooked her bra and let it fall. Chase's chest rose and fell in one quick, tortured gasp. She saw his stomach muscles contract, but he didn't touch her. At least not intimately.

Pressing her shoulders, he guided her down to lie on her back on the rug. Without ceremony he unfastened her skirt and pushed it down her legs. He wasn't quite so detached when it came to removing her panties, because he had to reach beneath her garter belt to get hold of the waistband.

Once they were removed, he slid his hand between her thighs. They groaned in unison. The fingers that probed her were thorough, yet gentle. His thumb nimbly separated the folds and found that supersensitive tissue.

He only had to stroke it a few times before her blood began to bubble inside her veins and she saw lightning sparks in her peripheral vision.

"Chase!"

That was all the invitation he needed. He unfastened his fly and shoved his trousers past his hips. Marcie boldly assessed him, but for only a second before he mated their bodies.

She gave one sharp, glad cry. Chase murmured either a profanity or a prayer. They remained like that for several tense moments.

Then, bracing himself above her, he withdrew partially and looked down into her face. Eyes locked with hers, he slowly penetrated her again. She felt him deep, so deep that the immensity of his possession swept over, stealing her breath, seizing control of her senses. His dark hair hung over his forehead, mussed and wild. His eyes glowed with the firelight, adding to his animalistic attractiveness. The muscles of his arms and chest bulged with masculine power.

She wanted to concentrate on how gorgeous he was, but he withdrew and sank into her again. He held her breast in one hand, circled the stiff nipple with his thumb. She shuddered. Her eyes closed involuntarily. Her thighs gripped his hips. He slid his hand between their bodies, stroking her externally even as he pressed ever deeper inside.

And her love for him, which had remained unfulfilled for decades, finally culminated in a splintering, brilliant climax.

He let her savor it, experience all of it, even the shimmering afterglow, before he began moving inside her again. But Marcie surprised herself and Chase by clutching him and raising her hips to meet his thrusts.

By the time his crisis seized him, she had reached another. They clung to each other, gasping, grasping, dying together.

Marcie was grateful for the knock on her inner office door that came around eleven o'clock the following morning. The couple who had arrived at ten sharp for their appointment were about to drive her mad.

Of course, on this particular morning, her threshold of sanity had been lower than usual.

"Come in," she called.

"Pardon the interruption, Marcie," Esme said. "Mr. Tyler is here to see you."

Reflexively Marcie rose from her desk chair. "Mr. Tyler? Which one?"

"The one you're married to. The tall, dark, and handsome one."

Then Marcie saw his hand reach beyond her assistant's head and push open the door. "Can I see you for a minute?"

Chase was the last person she had expected to call on her this morning. Her knees almost buckled. Her mouth was so dry she could barely speak.

"Of . . . of course. I'm sure Mr. and Mrs. Harrison won't mind if I step out for a while. You may continue looking through the listings book," she suggested as she rounded her black lacquered desk.

The man sighed and came to his feet, hiking up his trousers importantly. "We're finished anyway. She's not ever going to find anything she's happy with."

"Me? I liked that four-bedroom on Sunshine Lane," his wife retorted. "You said we didn't need that much space. You said the yard was too big. You turned down a beautiful house because you're too lazy to mow the lawn. Which is just as well, I guess. You wouldn't do it right anyway."

"Chase, this is Mr. and Mrs. Harrison," Marcie said, interrupting. "Ralph, Gladys, meet my husband, Chase Tyler."

"Pleased to meet you." Ralph shook hands with him.

"The same."

"Well, come on, Ralph. Can't you see they want their privacy?" Gladys practically pushed her husband through the door.

Esme, rolling her eyes ceilingward, followed them out and closed the door as she went. Chase and Marcie were left alone. They faced each other awkwardly, but didn't meet each other's eyes.

"Are those the clients you told me about?"

"Real prizes, aren't they? I don't think they'll ever settle on a house. Looking is just a hobby with them. It gives them a break from fighting. Unfortunately it costs me valuable time and more patience than I've got."

"Hmm. Uh, these are for you."

He stuck out a bouquet of pink tulips, and confused by the gesture, Marcie took them. In effect, she caught them. Chase seemed anxious to get rid of the flowers once he had called her attention to them. If Marcie's reflexes had been any slower, the bouquet would have fallen to the floor.

"It's not my birthday."

"No special occasion," he said with a laconic shrug. "I had to go to the grocery store this morning to pick up some supplies for the office. I spotted them there in one of those little water buckets by the checkout. Thought you might like them."

She gazed at him with perplexity. "I . . . I do. Thank you."

"You're welcome." His eyes made a slow survey of the room. "Nice office. Fancy. Nothing like Tyler Drilling Company headquarters."

"Well, we have different needs."

"Right."

"Did you hear anything about your contract?"

"No."

"Oh. I thought maybe the flowers were part of a celebration."

"No."

"Oh."

He coughed. She tucked a strand of hair back into her bun. He sniffed. She fiddled with the green cellophane cone around the tulips.

"Did you come here to talk about offices?" she asked after the lengthy silence.

"No." For the first time that morning his gray eyes connected with hers. He had left the house long before she'd gotten up. "We need to talk, Marcie."

A sharp pain went straight through her heart and she recognized it as fear. He looked and sounded so serious. He had never come to her office before. Unless it was absolutely necessary, he rarely even called her while she was there.

Only something extremely important and imperative would bring about this unprecedented visit. The only thing she could think of was that he wanted to back out of his commitment.

"Sit down, Chase."

She indicated the short sofa recently occupied by Ralph and Gladys Harrison. He dropped to the edge of the boldly striped cushions and sat with his knees spread wide, staring at the glossy white tiles between his boots.

Marcie returned to the chair behind the desk, feeling that she needed something between them to help blunt the blow he was about to deliver. She laid the tulips on the desktop. Getting them into a vase of water wasn't a priority just then.

"What do you want to talk about, Chase?"

"Last night."

"What about it?"

"I didn't say much afterward."

"No, but what little you said was very concise. You certainly got your point across. You said, 'Well, you came twice, so now you've got nothing to complain about.' "

"Yeah," he said, releasing a deep breath around the word. "That's exactly what I said."

He lowered his head again. Around the crown of his head his dark hair grew in swirls. She wanted to touch them, tease him about their boyish charm, play with them. But touching him seemed as remote a possibility now as casual conversation between them had been the night before.

Having delivered his hurtful line, he had gotten up, retrieved his shirt and sweater, and gone straight upstairs to his bedroom. More slowly, Marcie had collected her things, then retreated to her own room. She hadn't seen him again until now.

"Marcie, we can't go on like this anymore."

He raised his head and paused as though expecting her to respond. She remained silent and expressionless. If she tried to speak, she knew that both her control and her voice would crack.

"We're like two animals in a cage, continually competing, constantly tearing at each other. It's not good for me and it's not good for you."

"Don't presume to tell me what's good for me, Chase."

He swore. "Don't get your back up. I'm trying to approach this reasonably. I thought—hoped—we could talk this out without tempers flaring."

She clasped her pale, cold hands on her desktop. "What do you want to do? Just please say what you came to say."

"Sex shouldn't be treated like a contest." Her only response was a slight nod of assent. "Our wedding night, the first time we made love—"

"We didn't make love that night. It was impersonal. If you had rubber-stamped my forehead, it couldn't have felt more official."

"Well, thanks a lot."

"You know it's the truth."

He pushed his fingers through his hair. "I thought you promised not to get riled."

"I promised no such thing." If he was going to dump her, make her a laughingstock in front of a whole town that had always found Goosey Johns amusing, she wished he would stop pussyfooting around and do it.

"Would you just sit quiet and listen?" he said testily. "This isn't easy, you know."

He had his gall. He had come to weasel out of his marriage to her and expected her to make it easy for him. "Just tell me straight out, Chase."

"All right." He opened his mouth. Shut it. Stared hard at her. Looked away. Gnawed on his inner cheek. Moistened his lips. "For starters, I think we should start sleeping together."

If her chair had suddenly bitten her on the behind, she couldn't have been more stunned. Somehow she kept her astonishment from showing. But she held her breath so long that she became dizzy and covertly gripped the edge of her desk to keep from collapsing.

"And I don't mean just sleeping together in the usual sense. I mean, sharing a bedroom, living like a real husband and wife."

He sent her an uncertain glance, then left the sofa and began pacing along the edge of her desk. "I gave this a lot of thought last night, Marcie. Couldn't sleep. What I said after, you know, well, that was a spiteful thing to say. I felt like hell afterward.

"It occurred to me that we've been playing sexual oneupmanship. Driving each other crazy every Sunday afternoon. That's silly. On our wedding night, granted, I took you with no regard to what you were feeling. I think I even hurt you." He stopped pacing and looked down at her. "Did I?"

Lying, she shook her head no.

"Well, good. That's something. But anyway, where was I? Oh, yeah. Then last night when we got home, you seduced me. Pure and simple, I was seduced. You asked for it and . . . and you got it. When you, uh, touched me, I could hardly hide the fact that I wanted you. And

Marcie, you were, well, uh, you were very wet, so I know you wanted me too."

He ran his palms up and down his thighs as though drying the nervous perspiration off them. "We've always gotten along. We were friends in school. Only since we've been married have we been at crossed swords with each other. Sometime last night in the wee hours, I figured out why."

Moving to the window, he slid his hands into the rear pockets of his snug-fitting jeans. "There's this chemistry between us. I feel it. You feel it." He glanced at her over his shoulder. "At least I think you do."

Her mouth was arid. Again she nodded.

He turned back to gaze out the window. "So I figured that we're being dumb by fighting this chemistry. We're consenting adults, living in the same house, legally married, and denying ourselves the main bonus of marriage. I think we should stop that nonsense and give in to it. I mean, why not?

"Okay, so we agreed weeks ago to keep this a chaste, in-name-only marriage. I know that. But hell, it's driving me friggin' nuts, and if last night is any indication, you haven't enjoyed doing without either. I mean, you were as hungry for me as I was for you. I've got the claw marks on my back to prove it."

When he came around, she dodged his incisive gaze. She was glad that she wasn't required to speak because she still wasn't able to. Apparently Chase had memorized what he was going to say, and he intended to say it all before he stopped to get her response.

"You know why I married you, Marcie. I know why you married me. We're both intelligent. I like and respect you. I think you like and respect me. We had some pretty good sex last night."

She raised her eyes to his. This time, he averted his head.

"Okay, some *very* good sex," he amended. "I've been sexually active for a long time. Even since Tanya died. Sometimes that was the only way I could forget . . ."

He paused, rested his hands on his hips, hung his head as though reorganizing his thoughts, and then began again. "Anyway, I don't want to dishonor you by going to another woman. Besides, I was taught that being unfaithful to your wife is about the worst sin you can commit." He looked at her soulfully. "But I can't go for months at a time without it."

She indicated her sympathetic understanding with another nod.

"I don't want it to be a competition, either, where we score points against each other. Our sex life can be an extension of our friendship,

can't it? If we work on being compatible in bed, I think we'll be more
compatible in other areas. We know it doesn't work the way it's been
going. Maybe we should give this other way a try."

He waited a moment, then turned to face her. "Well, what do you
say?"

Chapter Thirteen

"Hi."

"Hi."

With shining eyes and a shy smile Marcie greeted Chase at the front door of their house. She still couldn't believe the turn of events that had taken place in her office earlier that day. Her arms bore bruises where she had pinched herself throughout the day to make sure she hadn't been dreaming.

Apparently she hadn't been because now Chase bent down and kissed her cheek. It was an awkward kiss, more like a bumping of faces together.

After his lengthy speech they had agreed to erase the angst of their first month of marriage and start again, not only as friends, but lovers. There was only one thing he had wanted assurance of, and that was that she was taking contraceptives. Without equivocation she had assured him she was.

"How long have you been home?" he asked as she helped him out of his jacket.

"Awhile. Is it still raining?" She dusted drops of water off the sheepskin as she hung it on the coat tree.

"Sprinkling. Something smells delicious."

"Chicken enchiladas."

"Yum. Did you get another phone call from the kook?"

"No."

"Then why'd you take the phone off the hook?"

Her blue eyes sent him a silent but eloquent message.

He swallowed hard. "Oh."

"Would you like a drink?"

"Sure."

Neither of them moved.

"Are you hungry?" she asked.

"Very."

"Are you ready for dinner?"

"No."

Upstairs—they never remembered getting there—he kissed her repeatedly, with passion and heat. His tongue was questing. He used it to explore. Like a gourmand, he sampled and savored her mouth, as though unable to decide which texture and flavor he liked best.

Articles of clothing seemed to melt away from their bodies. When they were both naked, they embraced long and tightly for the sheer animal pleasure of touching skin to skin, body to body, male to female. She was soft where he was hard and smooth where he was hairy, and the differences enthralled them.

He sat down on the edge of the bed and drew her between his knees. His stare alone aroused her breasts. They crested. They ached to be touched. He didn't.

But with his fingertip he traced the shadows they cast on her belly. Like a child who would be chastised for coloring outside the lines, he carefully followed the curving outline of the silhouette and paid close attention to the projecting shadows the flushed nipples made.

Watching his fingertip move with such precision over her flesh, Marcie moaned. She drew his head forward and pressed her nipple against his lips, which opened to enfold it. The heat, the wetness, the sucking action he applied, was so piercingly sweet it was almost painful.

Parting her thighs with his hand, he gently massaged the swollen, pouting lips of her sex. Marcie gasped in ecstasy as his fingers tunneled into her moist center. Her tummy quickened. An electric tingle shot through the tip of his tongue into her nipple and from there into her womb. She softly cried his name.

He lay back on the bed, pulling her over him, and she managed to impale herself upon him in time for him to feel the gentle contractions that seized her. They rippled through her endlessly it seemed before she realized that some of the surges belonged to him.

Moments later, sated, she lay upon his chest. The upper half of it was hairy. The lower half of his torso was still prickly where the hair hadn't completely grown back. She loved it all.

Her thumb idly fanned his nipple while she listened to the strong beats of his heart as they gradually returned to normal. Then another sound caught her attention—a low grumble from his abdomen.

She raised her head and looked inquiringly into his face.

"*Now* I'm ready for dinner," he said.

Chase did something then that he hadn't done in bed with a woman for over two years. He smiled.

During the weeks that followed, Chase was frequently caught smiling. Some days he completely forgot to be sad, miserable, and bereaved. He still thought of Tanya several times every day, but the memories no longer came at him in stunting, debilitating blows. They were cushioned by his general contentment. If life wasn't as sweet and idyllic and rosy as it had once been, it was at least livable.

A little more than just livable—*pleasantly* livable.

The pleasantness was sometimes hampered by feelings of guilt, because the source of that pleasantness was his second wife. Each time his memory conjured up an image of Tanya's sweet face, he felt constrained to reassure it that she still had his love. Nothing would ever change that.

In his own defense he reminded himself that Tanya was dead and he was alive, and because she had loved him so unselfishly, she wouldn't want or expect him to deprive himself of life's pleasures.

Marcie made his life a pleasure.

She was funny and fun, intelligent and interesting, always thinking up innovative places to go and things to do. They even went to a rodeo together in a neighboring town. It surprised him how much she enjoyed it, although during the bull-riding event she laid her hand on his thigh and told him how glad she was that he was a spectator and not a participant.

"It would be a crying shame if you damaged your beautiful body."

He had taken inordinate pleasure in her simple compliment. She was always saying things like that to him, things that took him by surprise and delighted him. Sometimes she was sweet, sometimes playful, sometimes downright bawdy.

She became a bona fide member of his family. They were considered a unit. It was now "Chase 'n' Marcie" in one breath, not just Chase. Sage had started phoning long distance from Austin to ask Marcie's advice on this or that. Marcie hosted a baby shower for Devon. She went shopping with Laurie and helped her pick out a new dress. Lucky frequently remarked on how wrong he'd been about their marriage.

"I'm glad you didn't listen to me, Chase," Lucky had recently said. "You were right to marry Marcie. She's a prize. Smart. Good-looking.

Ambitious. Sexy." The last word had an implied question mark following it.

"Sexy." Chase tried to stop the grin he felt forming. He wasn't quite successful. His brother laughed out loud.

"That sexy, huh?"

"That sexy."

"I thought so. These redheads . . . ," Lucky had said, shaking his head musingly. "There's something about 'em, isn't there? Like they've got fires smoldering inside them or something."

Chase was prone to agree, but discussing Marcie's internal fires made him uncomfortable for a multitude of reasons. He punched his brother in the gut. "You're a pervert, talking about your pregnant wife like that." He no longer winced when Lucky's coming child was mentioned. He could even talk about it freely, with only a remnant of a pang affecting his heart. "Poor Devon. Are you still going at her hot and heavy?"

Lucky bobbed his eyebrows. "There are more ways than one to do it, big brother. Or don't you know?"

He knew.

Because he and Marcie had tried just about all of them and then had made up a few of their own.

One evening she had brought him a bowl of popcorn while he was lounging in the large leather chair in front of the fireplace, mindlessly watching a detective show on television. Within minutes there was popcorn all over the place, and he and Marcie were tangled up in the chair recovering their breath.

Both had remained dressed. Chase had thought that finding her erogenous zones inside her clothing was about the sexiest time he'd ever had. Until a few mornings later when they'd showered together. Propped against the tile walls, they had made love, as slippery, sleek, and playful as otters.

But whether he was ducking his head beneath her sweater to take her breasts into his mouth or squeezing a soapy sponge down the center of her body and tracking the foamy trail with his eyes, he always had one hell of a good time.

So did she. She never demurred from openly expressing her enjoyment of all they did together. The lady was hot. From her cool, professional mannerisms and clipped practicality, no one would suspect the depth of Marcie's sensuality.

They hadn't reached the bottom of it yet. Just last evening she had turned their hello kiss at the front door into one of the most erotic experiences of his life.

"I just can't wait," she had whispered against his lips as she undid his pants and slid her hand inside.

"Be my guest."

That was the last thing he had expected her to do when he came home from a routine day at work . . . until she knelt in front of him and replaced her caressing hand with her mouth. Before it was over, they were both left on the living room sofa feeling weak and wicked.

And when she smiled up at him, he had said, "God, you're gorgeous."

However, he had lived with her long enough to realize that she still considered herself the same Goosey Johns she had been as an awkward adolescent. She had a good self-image professionally. When it came to her appearance, she still nursed fundamental insecurities.

"I wish I were pretty."

They were lying close together in the king-size bed they now shared. Unlike their wedding night, the lights now remained on until they were exhausted and ready for sleep.

"You are pretty, Marcie."

She shook her head. "No. But I wish I were."

"You're pretty," he had insisted, kissing her soft, pliant lips.

And later when his hands moved to her breasts, she sighed despairingly, "I wish they were larger."

"It doesn't matter. They're so sensitive." The damp brushstrokes of his tongue proved him right.

"But not large."

Chase laid his finger across her lips, stilling them. "If they were any larger, it would be excessive. For that matter, I wish I had twelve inches."

Her eyes had grown huge and round and she exclaimed, "You mean you don't?"

He had hugged her hard and they had laughed. When they made love, neither noticed any deficiency in the other.

Chase's life had been so sensually enriched, he no longer invited Lucky to The Place for drinks after work. He never postponed going home unless it was absolutely necessary. If Marcie wasn't there because of an evening appointment to show a house, he paced impatiently until she arrived.

He always had so many things to tell her, it seemed. It took them a full hour to fill in each other on how their days had gone. She was a surprisingly good cook, an excellent conversationalist on an endless variety of subjects, and an adventurous and imaginative lover. Every evening he looked forward to going home to her.

That's why as he approached the house this evening he was dreading an upcoming business trip to Houston. Maybe he could persuade Marcie to leave her agency in Esme's capable hands and come with him. They could incorporate a visit to her folks. Do some shopping. Yeah, maybe she would come along.

He let himself into the house and called her name, although her car wasn't in the driveway and he assumed she wasn't at home. He disengaged the alarm, sorted through the mail, and brought in the newspapers. He got himself a beer from the refrigerator and checked for a note. She was good about leaving him notes, informing him where she had gone and when he could expect her to return. Tonight there was no note.

He was on his way upstairs to change clothes when the telephone rang. He retraced his steps back to the entry table and answered it.

"Hello?"

"Who is this?"

"Who did you want?"

Marcie's caller hadn't phoned in several weeks. Only a few days ago she had remarked on it. "I told you so," she had said in a singsong voice. "He's given up on me and moved on to another victim. One who doesn't have a sexy husband around to fend off unwelcome suitors."

Chase wondered now if this was the man. Had hearing a masculine voice surprised him into blurting out his question?

"I'm calling for Mrs. Tyler," the caller said.

"This is Mr. Tyler. Can I help you?"

"Uh, well, I'm not sure. I spoke with Mrs. Tyler before."

"Regarding what?"

"Painting."

"Painting?"

"I'm a house painter. She called and asked me for an estimate on doing some interior painting."

Chase relaxed. This wasn't Marcie's caller. "I'm sorry. She hasn't mentioned anything to me about it."

"Well, it was a long time ago. Couple of years in fact. I didn't even think about it till I was out your way today. Drove past Woodbine Lane and remembered talking to her. She never called me back, but I remembered her name 'cause she said you were the Tyler Drilling people. I checked my cross directory and got your phone number. I reckon she got somebody else to do the painting before, but if you ever need—"

"Just a minute, Mr., uh—"

"Jackson."

"Mr. Jackson, you said you heard from my wife a couple of years ago?"

"That's right. It was around the time your building burned down."

"And she was calling about *this* house?"

"Yeah, she said it was the only house on Woodbine Lane. Said y'all hadn't bought it yet, but were thinking about it. Said she needed a room painted for a nursery and wanted to know how much I would charge." After several moments of silence he said, "Mr. Tyler? You still there?"

"We don't need any painting done."

Chase slowly replaced the telephone receiver. For a while he merely stood there, staring into near space. Then he pivoted on his heels and gazed at the large living room with its appealing view of the forest beyond, now tinged with the green promise of spring. He tried looking at the room through different eyes, eyes now dead, forever closed.

The front door flew open behind him and he spun around, almost expecting Tanya's spirit to be hovering in the opening. Instead it was Marcie, gathering her windblown hair in her fist.

"Hi," she said breathlessly. "I thought I might beat you home, but I can see I didn't. I stopped and bought carryout Chinese food for dinner. I hope you don't mind. Everybody wanted to look at houses today," she told him with an excited little laugh.

Setting the aromatic sack of carryout food on the table beside the telephone, she shrugged off the jacket of her suit and stepped out of gray high-heeled pumps.

"In the spring the housing market always picks up. I think some people would rather move than do spring housecleaning. Anyway—"

She ceased her happy chatter abruptly when she noticed that he was standing woodenly beside the hall table and hadn't spoken a word. He was looking at her as though he'd never seen her before, rather like an oddity he couldn't figure out and was therefore highly suspicious of.

"Chase?" When he didn't immediately respond, she touched his arm. "What is it? Is something wrong?"

Using his free hand, he pushed hers off his arm. His eyes were dark, implacable. "Chase, what?" she cried, her voice underlain with panic.

"How long have you lived in this house, Marcie?"

"How . . . how long?"

"How long?"

"I, uh, I don't remember specifically." She picked up the sack of food and headed for the kitchen.

"That's bull." He yanked the sack out of her hand and returned it to the table. Gripping her by both shoulders, his fingers dug into her.

"You remember everything, Marcie. You've got a photographic memory. You were the only kid in Miss Hodges's history class who could remember all the state capitals and the presidents in order." His voice increased in volume and intensity. He shook her slightly. "When did you buy this house?"

"Last summer."

"Why?"

"Because I like it."

"*Why?*"

"*Because I like it.*"

"Who owned it before you bought it?"

"Chase," she said plaintively, almost inaudibly.

He, on the other hand, roared, "Who did you buy it from, Marcie?"

She struggled with tears. She wet her lips. She was in obvious distress. Her lips were so rubbery she could barely form the words. "From you."

"Jesus!" Turning, he slammed his fist into the nearest wall. Then he leaned into the wall and banged his fist against it several times. He kept his head averted.

Extending her hand imploringly, she touched his shoulder. "Chase, please let me explain."

He flinched at her touch, but whirled around to confront her. His features were congested with outrage. "What's to explain? I get the picture. This is Tanya's house."

"It's my house," she protested. "I bought it—"

"From me. Because you think of me as some freaking charity case."

"That's not true. I bought it because I wanted to make a home for you here. This is where you were supposed to live."

"With another wife," he shouted. "The wife I loved. Doesn't that matter to you? Don't you have any more pride than to settle for second place? Are you so willing to settle for second place that you'd resort to tricks?"

"I never tricked you."

"Oh, really? Then why didn't you ever mention that this was the house Tanya was so crazy about? The house that you and she looked at right before she was killed. The house that she wanted me to see with her."

Her gaze fell beneath his accusing stare. He raised her head so that she had to look into his face. "Never mind answering. I know why. Because you knew I'd feel just this way about it."

"Maybe I went about it the wrong way. But I only wanted to make you happy."

"Happy?" he cried. "Happy? I've been balling you in Tanya's house!"

"And liking it very much!" she shouted back.

They glared at each other for the span of several seconds. Then, muttering a litany of vulgarities, Chase started upstairs. By the time Marcie caught up with him, his suitcase was lying open on the bed and he was pitching articles of clothing into it.

"Chase," she cried, her voice tearing, "where are you going?"

"Houston." He didn't deign to look at her, but stamped into the bathroom and began tossing his toiletries into a suede kit.

"Why?"

"I was scheduled to leave tomorrow anyway." He gave her a fulminating glare. "I believe I'll go tonight instead."

"When will you be back?"

Brushing past her where she stood in the connecting door, he placed the kit in the suitcase and slammed it closed, latching it with an angry thrust of his fingers against the metal locks.

"I don't know."

"Chase, wait!"

He stormed downstairs. She clambered after him. At the front door she intercepted him and tenaciously hung on to his sleeve.

"Please don't go."

"I've got to. It's business."

"Don't go like this. Not when you're so angry. Give me a chance to explain. Wait until morning."

"Why? So you can give me another night of sex to dull my memories of Tanya?"

Her whole body went rigid with affront. "How dare you talk to me like that. I'm your wife."

He merely snorted, an uncomplimentary sound. "On paper, Marcie. Only on paper. But never where it really counts."

He yanked his jacket off the coat tree and within seconds was gone.

"Lucky? It's Marcie."

"Hey, my favorite sister-in-law! How are you?"

"I'm fine," she lied.

Chase had been gone for three days. She hadn't heard a word from him. She didn't know where he was staying in Houston or why exactly he had made the trip, so there was no way she could track him there. Unable to bear it any longer, she had swallowed her pride and called his brother to fish for information.

"What's up? Getting lonesome for that brother of mine?"

"A little."

A lot. Loneliness ate at her like a vicious rat. Its sharp, pointed teeth gnawed at her. When awake, she replayed the horrid departure scene in her mind, willing it to be only a nightmare. In her sleep, she yearned for him, reached for him, and awoke startled and bereft when she realized he wasn't lying beside her and that he might never again.

"Devon and I discussed taking you out to dinner one night while Chase is gone," Lucky was saying, "but she hasn't been feeling very well."

"I'm sorry to hear that. Has she told her o.b.?"

"Yes, and he tells her to stay off her feet, rest more, and try to be patient for another seven or eight weeks."

"If there's anything I can do . . ."

"Give her a call. It might improve her disposition. She's a regular bitch these days."

Marcie laughed, as she knew she was expected to. Lucky's criticism of his wife wasn't intended to be taken seriously. "I'll call her later this evening."

"I would appreciate that."

The conversation lagged. He was waiting for her to get to the point of her call. "Uh, Lucky, have you spoken with Chase today?"

"Sure. He called right after the interview."

"The interview?"

"With the oil company execs. That's why he went, you know."

"Yes, I know. I just didn't realize the interview was today." She hoped that her bluff sounded convincing.

"Yeah, they interviewed the three finalists, so to speak. Chase wants that contract so damn bad, Marcie. It's more than the money. It's a pride thing with him. I guess because you, well, you know, you bailed us out. He wants to prove to you and to himself that you didn't make a bad investment."

"Did using my money shatter his pride?"

"No," Lucky said, obviously pondering the response even as he gave it. "But he needs to feel as if he's in charge again."

"He is."

"*We* know that. I'm not sure he's convinced of it."

"Well, if you speak to him—"

"I'm sure he'll call you. He's probably just been busy. He had another appointment this afternoon."

Probably with a divorce lawyer, she thought miserably. "Yes, he'll probably call me tonight. Unless he's already on his way home," she suggested tentatively.

"I wouldn't look for him this soon. He said he wouldn't come home until they announced their decision and awarded the contract."

"Yes, that's what he told me before he left." Since when had she become a liar?

"Course if he gets so hot for your bod he can't stand it, he might hop in his pickup and make the trip in record time," he teased.

Unfortunately, she couldn't tease back. Lamely she said, "Well, give Devon and Laurie my love when you get home. I'll try to call Devon tonight. Have patience with her."

"I'll grin and bear it till the baby gets here. Bye-bye."

Marcie hung up. Without interest she padded into the kitchen and poured herself a glass of milk. Ever since Chase left, she had had very little appetite. She would certainly never want Chinese food again.

Hours later, while lying in bed reviewing the latest property tax laws, the telephone on the nightstand rang. She stared at it suspiciously and decided at first not to answer. But what if it was Chase?

"Hello?"

"I'm coming to you," the whispery voice said. "I want you to see how hard I am for you."

Disobeying all the rules of common sense, she asked, "Who is this? Why don't you stop calling me?"

"I want you to touch me where I'm hard."

"Please stop."

"I know your husband isn't there. You're not getting any, are you, Marcie? You must be real horny. You'll be glad to see me when I get there."

Sobbing, she slammed down the receiver. It rang again immediately. This time she didn't pick it up. She reasoned that if he were calling, he couldn't be trying to break into her house. Nevertheless, she shoved her arms into the sleeves of her robe and ran downstairs.

Frantically she checked all the doors and windows. She monitored the alarm system to see if it was set. She considered calling Lucky, but he had enough to deal with. He didn't need a hysterical sister-in-law on his hands in addition to a cantankerous, pregnant wife.

She had insisted in her conversations with Chase that telephone creeps never actually did anything. They got their kicks by scaring their victims because they were usually terrified of or traumatized by women. So why was she placing any credence in this last call?

Because he had called her the night Chase left and every night since. He was knowledgeable about her comings and goings and seemingly everything else about her. And for the first time, he had started warning her that he was coming after her. He intended to take it a step further than telephone terrorism.

Leaving all the downstairs lights on, inside and out, she returned to her bedroom. She didn't fall asleep for a long time. Every sound in the house was magnified by her fright.

She scolded herself for being so afraid over something as ridiculous as telephone calls. It wasn't like her to cower in fear and tolerate something like this. She always tackled her problems head-on.

Tomorrow, she vowed, she would do something to put a stop to this.

Chapter Fourteen

It wasn't quite dark when Chase arrived at the house on Woodbine Lane six days after leaving it, but the sun had already set and the yard was deeply shadowed beneath the trees.

Marcie's car wasn't there. He was glad. He wasn't sure what he was going to say to her when he saw her. During his absence his anger had abated, but he was still distraught over living in Tanya's house with another woman . . . and liking it so much. Unable to deal with that aspect of it, he dwelt on Marcie's clever maneuvering and how unconscionably she had manipulated him.

He slid his key into the notched slot of the front door lock and tried to turn it. To his annoyance and puzzlement, it wouldn't unlock. After several attempts, he stood back, placed his hands on his hips, cursed impatiently, and tried to figure out another way into the house. All the other exterior doors locked from the inside.

The only immediate solution he saw was to break one of the frosted panes of glass beside the front door, reach in, and unlock it from the inside and then get to the digital alarm pad before it went off.

He scouted around the yard for a stout stick, and finding one, carried it back to the door. The window shattered after his first hard rap. He reached in, groped for the lock and unlatched it, then opened the door. His boots crunched on broken glass as he made for the alarm transmitter. He punched out the required code, but the forty-five-second interim beeping didn't stop.

"Damn!"

Wasn't anything working right tonight? He tried the code again, meticulously depressing the correct digits. The beeping continued. Knowing that the central control box was in the utility-room closet, he started across the living room at a run, hoping to get there and disconnect it before the actual alarm went off.

"Stop right there!"

Chase came to a jarring halt and turned toward the imperative voice. He was struck in the face by a brilliant beam of light and threw up both hands to ward it off.

"Chase!"

"What the hell is going on here? Get that light out of my face."

The light was switched off, but the glare had temporarily blinded him. Several seconds elapsed before he could focus. When he finally located Marcie, she had moved to the alarm pad. After she punched in the correct sequence of numbers, the beeping stopped, making the resultant silence even more pronounced.

It was as shocking as the sight of his wife, who, in one hand, was holding a high-powered flashlight, and in the other, a high-powered pistol.

"Is that loaded?" he asked temperately.

"Yes."

"Do you intend to use it on me?"

"No."

"Then I suggest you lower it."

Marcie seemed unaware that she was still aiming the handgun at his midsection. Her arm came unhinged at the elbow; she dropped the gun to her side. Chase realized the pistol would be extraordinarily heavy in her feminine hand. It would have been hard for many men to tote.

He moved to a lamp, switched on the light, and received his third shock. Marcie's face was ghostly pale, in stark contrast to the black, knit turtleneck pullover she was wearing. Her hair was pulled back sleekly away from her face and wound into a mercilessly tight bun on her nape.

Apprehensively he approached her and lifted the handgun out of her hand. She was staring at him fixedly, drawing his attention to her eyes. They were ringed with violet smudges, looking as though they had both been socked very hard. He remembered seeing them badly bruised when she lay in the hospital bed following her auto accident. She had been pale then, too, but nothing like now.

He clicked on the safety of the pistol and set it on an end table. Then he took the flashlight from her and set it aside also. "Want to tell me what's going on? Have you always had that gun?"

She shook her head no. "I bought it Tuesday."

"Do you know how to use it?"

"The man showed me."

"What man?"

"The pawnbroker."

"Jesus," he muttered. "Have you ever fired the thing?"

Again she shook her head no.

"Good. Because if you had, your shoulder would have probably knocked your ear off when you recoiled. Not that you would have needed an ear any longer because the blast would have deafened you. Who did you intend to shoot?"

She wilted like a starched petticoat on a humid day. One second she was standing, the next she was crumpled into a little heap on the sofa. She buried her face in her hands.

It wasn't like Marcie to have fainting spells or crying fits. Alarmed, Chase sat down beside her. "Marcie, what is happening here? What were you doing with that gun?"

"I wasn't going to shoot anybody. I was only going to frighten him with it."

"Frighten who?"

"The caller." She raised her head then and looked up at him. Her eyes were filled with tears, seeming larger and bleaker than ever. "He's called every night since you've been gone. Sometimes two or three times a night."

Chase's jaw turned to granite. "Go on."

"He knew I was here alone. He kept talking about your being away. He also knows where we live. And . . . and he said he was going to come after me. Chase," she said, her teeth beginning to chatter, "I couldn't stand it anymore. I had to do something. So I had a locksmith change all the locks. I set another code on the alarm. Tonight when I heard you on the porch, and you broke the glass and—"

He put his arms around her and drew her against his chest. "It's okay. I understand now. Shh. Everything's fine."

"Everything is not fine. He's still out there."

"Not for long. We're going to put a stop to this once and for all."

"How?"

"By doing what you should have done in the first place. We're going to see Pat."

"Oh, no, please. I'd feel so foolish making this a police matter."

"You'd feel even more foolish if you had accidentally put a hole through me."

She trembled. "I don't think I could ever bring myself to pull the trigger on that thing," she said, nodding down at the pistol.

"I don't think you could either," he said soberly. "So in effect, that still leaves you defenseless when you're here alone." He picked up the pistol and crammed the barrel of it into his waistband. "Come on, let's go."

"Right now?" She resisted when he tried to pull her to her feet.

"Right now. I've had it with this creep."

They reset the alarm. There wasn't much they could do about the broken window, so they just left it. "Where's your car?" he asked as they went down the front path.

"I started parking it in back."

Chase assisted her into the cab of his pickup and climbed behind the wheel. He'd just spent four hours driving from Houston and had been looking forward to getting out of the truck. Lately, things rarely turned out the way he expected or wanted them to.

"I spoke to Lucky," Marcie said quietly once they were under way. "He told me you'd gone to Houston to see about the contract."

"The decision makers had narrowed it down to three drilling companies that had bid on the job. They wanted to talk with us personally. After costing me five nights in a hotel and a week of eating out, they picked an outfit from Victoria."

It had been a crushing disappointment, which a four-hour drive and two hundred miles hadn't ameliorated. He had invested almost two months' time and a lot of worry and planning in getting this contract and had ended up with nothing to show for it except an exorbitant credit-card bill.

What was worse, he had no other prospects to pursue. Thanks to Marcie's loan, he didn't have to worry from a financial standpoint, but his pride and sense of professional worthiness were still on the critical list.

"I'm sorry, Chase. I know you were counting on that job."

He gave her a brusque nod, glad that they had reached the courthouse and that he wouldn't be required to talk about it any more.

They caught Pat Bush in the corridor on his way out. "Where are you going?" Chase asked him.

"To get a cheeseburger. I haven't had dinner."

"Can we talk to you?"

"Sure. Why don't y'all come with me?"

"It's official."

One look at Marcie apparently convinced the sheriff that the matter was urgent. That and the pistol tucked into Chase's waistband. He retraced his steps to his office and held open the door. "Come in."

Chase ushered Marcie inside. Pat's office hadn't changed since Bud Tyler used to bring his boys in for quick visits. While the two men discussed politics, the ten-point bucks that always got away, all levels of sports, and local happenings, Chase and Lucky would strut around twirling fake pistols and wearing badges Pat had pinned to their shirts.

One time they'd gotten in trouble for drawing mustaches and silly eyeglasses on all the wanted posters while their father and the sheriff weren't looking. Another time they'd gotten whippings for dropping a lighted firecracker into a brass spittoon in the squad room.

Now, Chase laid the pistol on the edge of Pat's desk. Pat regarded it closely, but didn't comment. He waited until they were seated across the desk from him in straight wooden chairs before removing the matchstick from his mouth and asking, "What are y'all up to?"

"Marcie's been getting phone calls."

"Phone calls? You mean obscene?"

"And threatening."

"He hasn't actually threatened my life," she interjected softly. "He just says that he's coming after me to . . . to—"

"To do all the things he's been talking about over the phone?" Pat prompted.

"That's right." After nodding, she left her head bowed.

"So it's definitely a man?"

"Definitely."

"And you don't recognize the voice?"

"No. He always whispers as though he's deliberately trying to disguise it."

"You think you might know him?"

"I have no idea. He might just want to make his voice sound scarier."

"When did this start?"

She raised her pale hand to her temples and massaged them. "Several months ago, I think."

"Before we were married," Chase said.

"Hmm. Does he always say the same thing?"

"No." The question made her curious. She raised her head. "Why?"

"Could be we're not dealing with an individual, but a group of kids. They try to see who can say the nastiest stuff, get the best response, that kind of thing."

With a small shake of her head Marcie said, "I don't think so."

"Neither do I." Chase leaned forward. "When Marcie first told me about this, she passed it off as a prankster who got his jollies by talking dirty. She figured he would eventually grow tired of her and move on to someone else. But he hasn't, Pat. He scares her spitless every time he calls. I think it's more than your average heavy breather.''

Pat picked a fresh wooden match from a box on his desk and put it in his mouth. He'd traded cigarettes for matchsticks years ago. He maneuvered it from one side of his mouth to the other.

"What do you do when he calls, Marcie?"

"At first I just hung up as soon as I realized what it was. But he began calling repeatedly, sometimes several times a night. It got to be such a nuisance, I started listening, hoping I'd recognize his voice. I thought it might be someone I run into frequently—the man who sacks my groceries, the man who pumps my gas, the teller at the bank who always flirts. I wanted to embarrass him by calling him by name, you see. But I never could identify him.''

"Any heartbroken lovers in your past?"

"No."

"What about the fiancé in Houston?"

She looked at Chase with incredulity. "He wouldn't do anything like this!"

"How do you know?"

"There's an ex-lover?" Pat asked, showing interest.

"I assure you, Sheriff Bush, it's not him."

"How can you be so sure?"

"Because he doesn't have the sexual imagination for one thing. I'd suspect Chase before I would suspect him."

When she realized the conclusion that could be drawn from what she had said, her eyes collided with Chase's. His were full of expression. Pat coughed behind his hand. Marcie wet her lips and tried to cover the blunder.

"It's not my ex-fiancé," she said staunchly. "Besides, they sound like local calls. Not long distance."

"Better give me his name anyway."

"Is it really necessary?"

"We'll check his long-distance bill through the phone company. Unless he's our man, he'll never even know about it."

"But the thought of invading his privacy—"

"Do you want to find this creep or not?" Chase asked impatiently.

Marcie glared at her husband defiantly, then reluctantly provided the sheriff with her former fiancé's name. "I promise we'll be discreet," Pat told her. He leaned back in his chair. "Why didn't y'all come tell me about this before now?"

"I wanted to," Chase said. "Marcie insisted that we wait."

"Why?" Pat wanted to know.

"I thought he would eventually stop calling."

"But when he didn't, why didn't you tell me about it?"

She wrung her hands. "I'm not sure. I guess I wanted to solve the problem on my own. In the scheme of things it seemed like such a piddling problem. It really didn't get so bad until this week. He called more frequently, and his voice was different."

"Different? How?"

"It wasn't just sleazy. It was sinister. He kept saying he was coming to fulfill my . . . my . . ." Again she rested her forehead in her hand.

"I know this isn't easy, Marcie," Pat said kindly.

"No, I assure you it's not." In a manner that Chase admired, she pulled herself together. In one long breath she told them, "He said he was prepared to fulfill my sexual appetites while my husband was away. Not in those exact words. But that was the gist of it."

Chase growled, "If I ever get my hands on the slimy sonofabitch—"

Pat pointed a stern finger at him as he interrupted. "You'll stay out of it, is what you'll do. I mean it, Chase. You just had to finance a new set of false teeth for that feller you bashed out at The Place. Don't you boys ever learn?"

"Nobody talks smut to my wife and gets by with it."

"If we catch him, he won't get by with it. This is a police matter."

Chase muttered a blue opinion. Pat ignored his muttering. "Which one of you is going to tell me about that?" He pointed at the pistol.

"I bought it for protection," Marcie told him, her cheeks turning slightly pink with embarrassment.

"Foolish thing to do," Pat said bluntly.

"Oh, I wouldn't actually shoot it at anybody. You didn't think that, did you?"

He looked at her for a moment, then dryly replied, "When somebody packs a .357 magnum, that's the conclusion I have to draw, yes, ma'am."

"She almost shot me." Chase told Pat about his hapless homecoming.

"Well, that kind of craziness is gonna stop," Pat said, coming to his feet. "These callers rarely do anything. They're cowards. Don't get me wrong, Marcie. You should exercise caution. Keep all your doors and windows locked and your alarm set even when you're there. But let's not get paranoid over this thing."

"What are you going to do?"

"Put a tap on your phone first thing tomorrow morning. And a tracer. Probably won't do much good. He probably calls from pay phones and knows just how long to talk before hanging up."

Pat opened the office door and called for a female deputy. "In the meantime, I want Marcie to go with Deputy Davis here and give her some quotes of things he says. Key words are important. Try to remember words that he repeats. We'll send the report to Dallas and have them run it through their computer. If he's got a prior, we'll find him that way."

Chase assisted Marcie to her feet, placing his arm around her waist. He moved with her to the door, passed her off to the buxom woman in uniform, and was about to follow them across the squad room when Pat detained him.

"She might be less self-conscious talking about it if you're not there."

"I'm her husband, for crissake."

"Indulge me. Besides, I want to talk to you."

Chase reentered Pat's office. The sheriff closed the door again and returned to his chair behind the desk. "How'd it go in Houston?"

"The Rockets lost and I came home without a contract."

"Sorry, Chase. But don't worry. You'll eventually pull out of this slump."

"I'm beginning to wonder." He stared into near space for a moment. "Met an interesting guy while I was there, though. Named Harlan Boyd. He works as a troubleshooter in oil-related businesses. Or maybe he's just a con artist with a string of b.s. that sounds convincing. Anyway, he said he might have some ideas for us. Hell, I'd be open to anything."

"Chase?"

"Yeah?" Chase raised his head. The older man's tone of voice had changed. It was hesitant. He got the distinct impression that Pat had something except the suffering oil business on his mind.

"Have you ever answered the phone to this obscene caller?"

"He would hang up, wouldn't he?"

"That ever happen?"

"No. Why?"

Sidestepping that question, Pat posed another. "When did Marcie first tell you about him?"

"Let's see." He thought back. "I believe it was the night I went to her place to repay her for bailing me out of the hospital."

"How soon after that did y'all talk about getting married?"

"What the hell difference does that make?" Chase's eyes sharpened. "What are you leading up to, Pat? These aren't random questions, are they? What are you getting at?"

"How are you and Marcie getting along?"

"None of your damn business."

"When you walked through that door and laid a loaded pistol on my desk, you made it my business."

"Okay, then, get to your point," Chase said crisply. "What does our marital situation have to do with an obscene phone caller?"

"Maybe nothing. Maybe everything." Pat leaned forward and placed his forearms on the edge of his desk. "Doesn't it strike you funny that he's never called when you're there?"

Suddenly, Chase had the complete picture, as though Pat had colored in the last numbered space. Angrily, he threw himself out of his chair and made several pacing tours of the office before glaring down at the sheriff. "You think she's making him up?"

"Is it possible?"

"No! Hell, no! That's laughable."

"But *possible?*"

"Wait!" Chase exclaimed. "I was there once when he called."

"You heard him?"

"No. He hung up before I could get to the phone."

"He hung up? Or did Marcie?"

"Look, Pat, what you're suggesting is way off base. It's nuts. Why would she play out such an elaborate act?"

"To win your sympathy. Get attention, affection."

"Some women have PMS and some have obscene phone calls, is that your theory?"

"It's happened before."

Chase barked a laugh. "Don't ever let my sister-in-law, Devon, hear you say something like that. Not if you value your life."

"All I'm saying is that some women—"

"Some women, maybe. But not Marcie," Chase said with an adamant shake of his head. "Not her. She's the most self-sufficient, well-adjusted, both-feet-on-the-ground, pragmatic person I know."

"Now," Pat said, emphasizing the word. "But I remember her when she was that carrot-topped, skinny kid in braces who the rest of you made fun of. Maybe Marcie remembers those times too."

Pat stood up and rounded his desk. He sat down on a corner of it and pointed Chase back into his chair. Reluctantly he returned to his seat.

"I haven't said much about this hasty marriage of yours," Pat said. "Figured it was none of my business."

"You figured right."

Pat ignored the interruption. "Figured a grown man like you could make his own decisions and be held accountable if he screwed up. But Laurie's filled me in on the facts."

"She told you about the money?"

"Uh-huh." His expression softened. "Chase, everybody knows how you felt about Tanya. Marcie is no exception. And even well-adjusted, pragmatic women want to be loved. They want to be loved exclusively. A woman wants to be the only one her man can see."

"Since when have you, a bachelor, become such an expert on women?"

Pat chuckled, conceding the point. "Maybe I'm not an expert on women per se, but on cases like this I know what I'm talking about. I'm not saying it's a foregone conclusion. All I'm saying is that it's a possibility we've got to consider."

Chase met him eye to eye and firmly stated, "You're wrong, Pat. You're dead wrong."

"I hope so. But if I'm not, why did Marcie refuse to come see me sooner?"

"She's self-reliant. She likes to take care of things on her own. And she's good at it."

"Maybe that self-reliance comes across so strongly, she needs something that makes her look feminine and vulnerable in your eyes."

"Don't quit your day job to become a psychiatrist, Pat."

"I'm only playing devil's advocate. It's my job."

"Well, it's a pain in the backside."

"To me too." Undaunted, he proceeded. "Why hasn't she changed her phone number?"

"That's easy. Clients might make a sudden decision on a house and need to get in touch with her. For that same reason she can't have an unlisted number."

Pat glanced beyond Chase's shoulder. "How's Devon?"

Sensing the reason for Pat's sudden shift in topic, Chase picked up his cue. "The last time I spoke with Lucky from Houston, he said she was giving him fits. Nothing he does or says pleases her."

The door opened behind him. He turned his head. Marcie was alone. "We're finished."

"I know that was tough, Marcie," Pat said. "Thanks for being such a trooper. I'll get that file off to Dallas first thing in the morning. There'll be a man out to install a tap on your phone, too." He grinned at them, but Chase had known him long enough to realize that it was forced. "Be careful what you say into the telephone from now on. Others will be listening."

Chapter Fifteen

"He didn't believe me, did he? He thinks I'm making it up."

In her peripheral vision Marcie saw Chase glance at her before returning his attention to the road. Since leaving the courthouse they'd driven in silence and were now almost home. Treetops merged over the two-lane highway, forming a tunnel lit only by their headlights. It gave her a claustrophobic sensation, like being caught in a grotesque chamber in a fun house.

"Sure Pat believed you."

"Give me some credit, Chase." Wearily she rested her head on the back of the seat. "You're always saying how smart I am. I'm smart enough to see through your friend, the sheriff."

"He's your friend, too."

"Until tonight. Tonight he thinks I'm a hysterical female who invents boogers in the vain hope of holding a husband who married her for money and not for love." She rolled her head to one side so she could see his profile. "Doesn't he?"

Chase fidgeted in his seat. "It's Pat's job to look at every angle. It's uncomfortable for him sometimes, especially if the role of sheriff interferes with the role of friend. He didn't like arresting Lucky for arson, but he did it because it was his sworn duty."

"Then while I was with the deputy, he did express some doubts about my mysterious caller."

"Not doubts exactly."

"Doubts," she countered. "Exactly."

They were silent for the remainder of the trip. When they reached the house, Chase went in ahead of her, switching on lights.

"You look ready to drop," he said.

"I am. As soon as I bathe, I'm going to bed." She was halfway up the staircase when she turned around and said, "Your mail is there on the bar."

"Thanks."

She hadn't known what to expect from Chase when he got home. She'd had no guarantee that he would return at all. When he did, she wouldn't have been surprised if he had told her he was moving out permanently and seeking a divorce.

She couldn't allow herself to feel relieved that he hadn't mentioned a separation. It might be that he simply hadn't had the time or opportunity to discuss it with her yet.

She took a long bath. The hot water helped relax her tight muscles. Just knowing that Chase was in the house soothed her nerves like a balm.

But when the phone rang as she was drying off, the living nightmare began again. On the one hand she resented her caller's ability to shatter her peace of mind every time the telephone rang. On the other, she prayed it was he.

Hastily she finished drying off and pulled on a nightgown. She rushed into the bedroom to find Chase turning down the bed. "Who called?"

"Mother. Pat had called her."

"About me?"

"No. He's more professional than that. He just mentioned to her in passing that I was home. She called to say hello."

"Oh." Her disappointment was keen. "I thought it might be . . . him."

"No. Come on. Get in." Chase was holding back the covers for her. She slid between them and laid her head on the pillow. The nightstand lamp was bright on her face. She reached up and switched it off.

She didn't want Chase to see her looking so unattractive. Without makeup, her hair a mess, pale and fatigued from nights of sleeplessness, she looked a wreck. These days she resembled a redheaded scarecrow.

"It would make sense, wouldn't it?" she asked musingly.

"What?"

"For me to dream up a mystery man. You're too chivalrous to desert a woman when she's in trouble."

"Look, Marcie, if Pat wants to entertain some off-the-wall theories, that's fine. That's his job. But don't foist them on me."

"For all you know, I could be lying."

"You're not."

"We had a fight last week. You walked out without a word about where you would be or when you were coming back. And while you were away, the caller got more aggressive and threatening." She laughed, but its foundation was desperation. "No wonder Pat thinks I'm making him up. It's almost a classic case. Pathetically classic."

"You're about the least pathetic individual I've ever met."

"I'm falling apart. Look at me. I'm trembling." She held her shaking hand parallel to the counterpane. "Hardly a pillar of strength and stability."

"Something like this would be nerve-racking to the best of us. In any case, I'm not going to argue with you about it tonight. You need to go to sleep. I don't think you've slept since I left."

"Not much," she admitted.

"Here, take this." He extended her a capsule and a glass of water to wash it down with.

"What is it?"

"One of the sedatives they gave me when my ribs were cracked. I was supposed to take two at a time to help me rest. Surely taking one won't hurt you."

"No, thanks. I'd better not."

"It'll help you sleep."

She shook her head no. "I'll sleep without it."

"Sure?"

"Sure."

With a small conceding motion of his shoulders he set the tablet and glass on the nightstand. "Good night."

He had almost reached the door before she blurted out, "I bought it for you."

Chase stopped, turned. "What?"

"The house."

"This isn't a good time to go into that, Marcie. You're exhausted."

"But I won't rest until I've made you understand why I did it."

"I understand perfectly. You tricked me into living with you in Tanya's house."

"It's my house!"

"Only because you paid for it. In spirit it belonged to Tanya."

"I discovered this house. I saw it before Tanya ever did." She sat up. The covers slid to her lap. "Tanya wouldn't have even known about it if I hadn't brought her to see it."

"Which brings up a pertinent question. If you wanted it, why did you show it to Tanya? Why not just buy it for yourself then?"

"Because I wanted you to live here."

He gaped at her incredulously and lifted his hands away from his sides. "*Why?*"

Because she had loved the house so much, and because Chase had needed a house then, she had wanted to give it to him. The only way she could do that at the time was through his wife.

After the fatal accident she had wanted him to have it more than ever, as recompense for what he'd lost. When it became apparent that he wasn't going to occupy the house he had bought only days after Tanya's demise, a germ of an idea had begun to form in Marcie's mind.

She had purposefully let Lucky believe that the buyer of the house was someone other than herself. From the day she became the owner, she had moved toward one goal—making this a home for Chase and living here with him. She wanted to give it to him like a gift, but without his ever knowing about it.

She had selected furniture and decor she thought he would like. She had planned everything, except attending the rodeo that night in Fort Worth. That had been a coincidence, one that she viewed as a sanction.

Fate approved of her intentions. The gods smiled upon her plan. Her years of unrequited love were finally going to be rewarded. She had been granted permission to do this. She was being allowed to make up for the accident that had robbed him of his wife.

He, however, didn't see it that way.

Now, while he stood searching her face for a plausible explanation, she considered telling him the simple truth—that everything she'd done, she'd done because she loved him, always had, always would. But it was difficult, if not impossible, to declare undying and unconditional love to someone who looked so patently angry.

"I guess I was trying to make up for your other loss, Chase," she said, her voice faltering. "I wanted to give you back a part of it. Obviously I badly bungled it."

Some of the tension ebbed from him. He bent his head down and rubbed the back of his neck. "I don't believe you did it maliciously."

"Thank you for that." She toyed with the hem of the bedsheets, unable to look at him without nakedly revealing her love. The last thing she wanted to be to him was an object of pity. Garnering all her courage, she asked, "Where do we go from here?"

"Damned if I know, Marcie. The only thing I'm sure of right now is that we're both too tired and upset to think beyond tonight." He went to the door and pulled it open. "I'll be in the next room if you need me."

I need you, her heart cried out. "You won't disturb me if you want to sleep here."

He looked at the empty pillow beside hers, but shook his head. "I think we should sort out the rest of this first, don't you?"

"I suppose," she said, trying valiantly to keep her disappointment from showing. "Good night."

"Good night."

After he left her, Marcie rolled to her side and drew her knees up to her chest. Tears streamed from her eyes, down her cheeks, and into her pillowcase. He would never trust her again. He felt she had duped him, and if she were being painfully honest with herself, she would admit that's exactly what she had done.

But only because she loved him so much.

He had denied believing in Pat Bush's speculations that her obscene calls were only a ploy to get attention, an old maid's last, desperate attempt to keep her man. But could she really blame Chase if he had his doubts?

The calls *were* real. The threats were real. She could sense that they were. And as soon as the man called back and Chase heard a replay of his voice, he would know she was telling him the truth. This time, she wasn't trying to trick him.

"Hello?"

"Hello, Marcie."

At last! It was he! Her heart began to pound. "You've got to stop calling me," she said, trying to keep the elation out of her voice. Finally he had called. Chase would believe her now.

"I won't stop calling till I get what I want. You know what I want," he said in the raspy tone of voice that sent chills up her spine. "I want you under me. Wet and wiggling."

"You're disgusting."

"Are your nipples hard? Touch them for me, Marcie. Hmm, Marcie, that's good. That's good." He moaned.

"They ought to lock you up and throw away the key. You're sick. You're a menace to society."

He laughed, sounding superior and condescending. "I know the sheriff has tapped your phone, but I know how to get around that."

Was he bluffing? How could he know the sheriff's office was now apprised of her calls? He couldn't. It was only a lucky guess.

"I know just how long to talk before hanging up so they can't trace the call."

"I don't know what you're talking about."

"They don't believe you, do they, Marcie? Not the sheriff. And not your husband. They think you're making me up, a figment of your imagination."

"No." Her mouth had gone dry. She gripped the receiver harder, until her knuckles turned white. She tried to swallow, but had no saliva. "Chase believes me."

Again that nasty laugh. "I'm coming for you, Marcie. Soon."

"Leave me alone. I'm warning you—"

"You'll like me, Marcie. I'm a better man than your husband." He cackled. "And he doesn't even believe you. He won't be there to save you when I've got you naked and spread open."

"Stop." She whimpered.

"Good-bye, Marcie. Be seeing you."

"No," she said, suddenly panicked. "Wait! Don't hang up. Please, not yet."

"Good-bye."

His voice was singsong. He was playing with her. She knew better than to cry. Her intellect told her that was what he wanted, but she couldn't stop her tears or hiccupping sobs.

"My husband will kill you when they catch you."

He laughed, with more malice than before. "He doesn't love you."

"He does. He will."

"Never, Marcie. You tricked him," he taunted. "Good-bye. See you soon. Soon, Marcie. Marcie. Marcie . . . Marcie . . ."

The voice changed; it became Chase's voice. Her eyes flew open and she sprang erect. Chase was there, sitting on the edge of the bed, rubbing her shoulders gently and speaking her name, drawing her out of her nightmare.

With a harsh cry she flung herself against his bare chest, despising the feminine weakness that caused her to clutch at him. She had always been contemptuous of women who weakly clung to men and used tears to get attention. But when Chase's strong, warm arms enfolded her, she forgot to be resentful of her own frailty. She nuzzled her face in his chest hair.

"You were having a nightmare," he whispered. "I could hear you crying all the way into the other room. But you're awake now and I'm here."

"Hold me, Chase. Please."

He lay down with her, drawing her even closer against him and pulling the covers over them. He stroked her back, cupped her head, and tucked it beneath his chin.

"He was on the phone."

"Shh. He's not there now."

"But I want him to be," she cried frantically. "It's been two weeks since we went to the sheriff. I want you to hear him. I want you to know. Then you'll believe me."

"I believe you."

"He reads my mind, Chase. It's like he knows that I want him to call. He's not calling on purpose."

"Shh. Just relax. Go back to sleep."

"When he calls, you'll know I'm telling the truth." She was babbling, but she couldn't help it. She was desperate to regain his trust. "When he calls, you'll believe me, Chase."

"I believe you."

"He's got to call."

But another week went by and he didn't call.

Lucky came into the office, stamping the mud off his boots. He inspected the bottom of them, decided they were reasonably clean, then glanced up to find his brother slumped in the chair behind the desk, his feet resting on the corner of it, staring into space.

"I thought you would be on your way home by now."

Chase roused himself and lowered his feet to the floor. "No, not yet."

"It's still coming down in buckets out there."

"Hmm."

Chase had regressed into the strong, silent type again, Lucky thought. For a while there, he'd actually acted like a human being. For the past several weeks, though, he'd been morose, uncommunicative, surly.

"That guy from Houston called again while you were at lunch," Lucky told him. "Harlan Boyd. Did you get the message?"

"Yes."

"Did you return his call?"

"No."

It was on the tip of Lucky's tongue to ask why the hell not, but that would no doubt provoke a quarrel, which would serve no purpose. Or maybe it would. Maybe it would clear the air. He knew, however, that his brother's problem wasn't with him. It wasn't even directly related to Tyler Drilling.

"I take it that Marcie hasn't heard from the creep." Chase's head came around quickly, his expression dark and suspicious. Lucky gave a helpless shrug. "Pat told Mother about it."

"That was nice of him." Chase bolted from his chair. "Dammit! Now I'm sure all of you think she's a nut case."

"No, we're relieved to know what the problem is. We all thought she was sick and dying or something too dreadful for y'all even to tell us about."

Again Lucky was on the receiving end of a glower that demanded explanation. "Do you think we're blind, Chase? She's lost weight. She's pale as a spook. She's as jumpy as a turkey the day before Thanksgiving. None of that characterizes the Marcie we've come to know and love. She's usually in control, unruffled and well balanced. Didn't you think we would notice this personality change?"

"Why go to Pat? Why didn't you ask me?"

"Mother didn't go to Pat specifically. They were just talking, and she expressed her concern over Marcie, and to lay her mind at rest that Marcie didn't have cancer or something, Pat told her about the pond scum that's calling Marcie."

"While he was giving away privileged information, did he also mention that he thinks the caller is a product of Marcie's imagination?"

Lucky looked away guiltily.

"I can see that he did."

"Well, I for one think that's crap. And the strength of my opinion can't even compare to Devon's. She went positively berserk when it was even suggested. To his face she called Pat a redneck conservative and a chauvinistic dinosaur. I'll tell you something, Chase," he said, shaking his head, "if our two ladies ever team up against us, we've had it."

Chase's stern lips cracked a smile, but Lucky could tell his heart wasn't behind it. "How're things otherwise?"

Chase asked testily, "What things?"

"You know, things."

"You mean like our sex life? That kind of *things?* You want to know how many times a week I make love to my wife, is that it?"

Lucky refused to get angry. One man with a rigid stance, balled fists, and red face was about all the small office could accommodate. "For starters. How many?"

"Why, are you keeping score?"

"Something like that."

"None of your damn business."

"Come on, Chase, have a heart," he wheedled. "Devon and I have had to taper off these last few weeks. I've had to resort to voyeurism."

"Are you sure you haven't been making those phone calls to Marcie?"

Lucky laughed, not the least bit offended. But within seconds he grew serious. "I hit it, didn't I? Y'all aren't, uh, sleeping together."

Chase flung himself back into the chair, frustration incarnate, a man whose skin had suddenly shrunk too small to fit him.

"I recognize the symptoms, big brother," Lucky said sympathetically. "Remember how much I wanted Devon but couldn't have her because she was married? I nearly went out of my freaking mind. If being horny was a terminal illness, I wouldn't be here to tell about it."

He dragged a stool across the floor and set it a few feet in front of Chase. "Abstinence was forced on me. What I can't figure," he said, leaning forward from his seat, "is why you're not availing yourself of your very lovely, very sexy wife, who is very much in love with you."

"She's not in love with me," Chase grumbled.

"Bull. And I'm not the only one who thinks so. Mother and Devon agree. So does Sage."

"Oh, well, hell, if Sage thinks so . . ." He let the sarcastic response trail off. "What are we, the constant topic of conversation out there?"

"Actually, y'all are about on equal par with the baby."

Chase muttered a series of curses. Not to be so easily dismissed, Lucky reminded him that he hadn't answered his question.

"No, I haven't," Chase said, "because it's none of your business."

"You're not put off by this pervert who's calling her, are you?" He got a dirty look for an answer. "You don't think Marcie's turned on by it, do you? Or that it's somehow her fault?"

"What do you take me for, an idiot?"

"Well, what else could it be? Did you do something to make her mad?"

"No."

"Did she lock you out?"

"No!"

"So if it's not Marcie, then you're the one who's holding out. Why, Chase?"

Chase made to get up. Lucky shoved him back into the chair. The brothers stared one another down. Finally Chase shrugged indifferently. "Okay, you might as well know. You'll probably find out sooner or later. By accident. Just like I did."

"Find out what?"

Chase told him about the telephone call from the house painter. "It made no sense until I figured out that he wasn't talking about the current Mrs. Tyler, but the late Mrs. Tyler. He was talking about Tanya. The house we're living in now was the house Tanya had picked out, the one I was supposed to be looking at with her the day she died, the one I subsequently had you buy. Marcie told you she had a buyer for it. She was that buyer."

This time when Chase left the chair, Lucky made no attempt to stop him. He was preoccupied by this astounding piece of information. He swore softly. "I had no idea."

"No. Neither did I."

"She told me she would handle everything, the closing and all that. I never would have guessed."

"Startling, isn't it? You can imagine how I felt when I found out."

"To think that she loved you that much, all that time."

Chase caught Lucky by the shoulder and spun him around. "What did you say? What are you talking about? Love? She tricked me. She played the dirtiest, rottenest trick—"

"Man, are you muleheaded!" Lucky shouted, surging to his feet. "You're too stupid to be my brother. They must have mixed up the babies at the hospital."

"Make your point," Chase ground out.

Lucky roughly poked him in the chest with his index finger. "You can't see past Marcie's deception to the reason behind it." Then he peered shrewdly into Chase's gray eyes, which were as turbulent as the low clouds that scuttled across the twilight sky.

"Or maybe you can. Maybe that's what's eating at you. It's not the house that bothers you so much. What you can't accept is that you have been loved so well. Twice."

He placed a hand on each of Chase's shoulders. "What's the single worst thing that could happen to you, Chase? The worst possible thing?"

The following silence was broken by the shrill ringing of the telephone. Chase, grateful for the interruption, snatched up the receiver and growled a hello.

"Chase, is Lucky there?"

Lucky saw the expression on his brother's face change as he passed him the telephone receiver. "It's Devon. It sounds urgent."

Lucky grabbed the phone. "Devon? Is this—"

"Yes. My water just broke. I called the doctor. He said to come to the hospital right away. The pains are coming hard."

"Christ." He pulled his hand down his face. He was a good five miles from home. "Okay, okay. Everything's fine. I'll meet you at the hospital. Hurry. But tell Mother to drive carefully. It's raining and the roads—"

"She's not here."

"*What?*"

"She went out."

"Out? Out where? When?"

"A while ago. I think she was taking some food to a sick friend. Anyway she left with a jar of homemade soup and a pecan pie. Or maybe it was an apple pie."

"Devon, who gives a damn about a pie!" he roared. "Sit down. No, lie down. Yeah, lie down. Stay calm. I'll be right there."

"I am calm. And I'm perfectly capable of driving myself to the hospital."

Every blood vessel in Lucky's head seemed to explode. "Don't pull that feminist crap on me now, Devon!"

"Stop yelling at me! As soon as I shave my legs I'll drive myself."

"*Shave your legs?* If you even attempt to drive, I'll murder you. I mean it, Devon. I'm on my way. Five minutes. Lie down, for crissake!"

He hung up before she had time to respond and raced for the door. Chase followed closely on his brother's heels. He had a fair grasp of the situation even hearing but one side of the conversation.

"We can call an ambulance to go get her," he suggested.

"I'll beat their time."

"That's what I'm afraid of."

Chase jumped into the passenger seat of the Mustang because Lucky took the wheel. They sped off into the rain.

Chapter Sixteen

"Lighten up, Pat, or I'm liable to think you're arresting me."

Sheriff Pat Bush, his hand wrapped firmly around Laurie Tyler's elbow, was almost dragging her down the sidewalk toward his squad car parked at the curb. The twirling emergency lights were painting an electric rainbow across the gloomy dusk.

"Maybe I should."

His mouth was grimly clamped around a matchstick. He pulled open the passenger door of the squad car and practically stuffed her inside, then jogged around the hood and slid behind the steering wheel. He engaged the gears and peeled away from the curb with a screech of tires.

"I don't know why you're so angry with me, Pat. I'm not clairvoyant," she said in her own defense. "How could I know Devon would go into labor today? She's four weeks early."

"Nobody knew where you were. Somebody should always know how to contact you, Laurie, for your own safety. If some pervert had snatched you, we wouldn't know where to start looking. As it is, I've been running all over town trying to find you."

Pat had been in his office when Chase called him from the ranch house. "Lucky's carrying Devon to the car now," he had told him. "We're on our way to the hospital, but we don't know where Mother is."

"I'll find her."

"Thanks, Pat, I was hoping you'd say that. I'd look for her myself except Lucky is demented. We barely made it from the office to here in one piece. I can't let him drive."

"I guess an ambulance is out of the question."

"Totally."

"Okay." Pat sighed. "Soon as I locate Laurie, I'll bring her to the hospital."

For the better part of an hour Pat had been driving the streets of town in search of Laurie's car—on the grocery store parking lot, at the dry cleaners, anyplace he could think of that she patronized routinely. In the meantime he'd kept his mobile telephone busy trying to track her through friends. The fourth call he made proved productive.

"I think she was planning to take some supper over to a sick friend," he was told by one of Laurie's bridge club friends. "When I spoke with her this morning about next week's meeting, she was baking a pie."

"A sick friend? Do you know who?"

"That man she's been seeing. Mr. Sawyer, I believe his name is."

Now Pat took the splintered matchstick out of his mouth and dropped it on the wet floorboard of his car. "How's Mr. Sawyer feeling?"

"Much better," Laurie said stiffly.

"I'll bet."

"I'll tell him you inquired."

"Don't bother."

"Poor man."

"What's the matter with him?"

"He's got a cold."

"Humph."

She turned her head, one brow eloquently arched. "What's that supposed to mean?"

"What?"

"That sound."

"It doesn't mean anything."

"Well, I didn't like it. It sounded derisive."

"The guy's a wimp," Pat declared crossly. "Why would you want to play nursemaid to a puny, skinny little wimp like that?"

"I brought you soup when you had the flu last year. Does that make you a wimp, too?"

Pat hunched over the steering wheel, gripping it tighter. "That was different."

"How so?"

"For one thing Sage was with you when you came to my place." Angrily he addressed her across the interior of the squad car. "For godsake, Laurie, have you stopped to consider what people will think about you going to Sawyer's place alone? In the middle of the afternoon? While he's in bed? Jeez! Heaven only knows what people will think was going on in there between you two."

"What do you think was going on?" She tilted her head to one side and fixed a quelling stare on him through slitted eyes.

Matching her stare, he said, "Frankly, I don't know what to think. He's a Milquetoast, but obviously you're smitten. Though why in hell, I can't imagine."

" 'Smitten' is such an antiquated word."

Pat was too caught up in his own argument to notice her gibe. "He's a regular at Sunday dinner now. One night last week I drove out to see you. You were with him at a party at his lodge. The weekend before that, you spent all day Saturday in Canton together at the flea market. Tuesday night it was the spaghetti supper at church."

"I invited you to go to the spaghetti supper."

"I was working!"

"That's not my fault. Nor Jess's."

Pat brought the squad car to a halt at the hospital's emergency room entrance, got out, and came around to assist her out. Taking her arm, he hustled her through the rain toward the door that was reserved for official personnel.

"I'm only thinking of your reputation, Laurie. I don't want your name dragged through the muck, that's all."

"I doubt Jess and I are a hot item."

"Oh, yeah? Everybody already knows you're seeing him."

"What's wrong with that?"

"What's wrong with that?" Pat repeated, coming to a sudden halt in the deserted hospital hallway. He turned her to face him. "What's wrong with that? Okay, I'll tell you what's wrong with that." He raised his index finger and pointed it toward her face. He opened his mouth. Nothing came out.

Laurie gazed at him inquisitively. "Well? I'm waiting."

He drew her face beneath the dripping brim of his hat and kissed her.

When he finally lifted his lips off hers, she wrapped her arms around his waist and whispered, "Took you long enough, Pat."

With a low, hungry groan he kissed her again.

Chase came barreling through a swinging door at the end of the hallway but pulled up abruptly. Pat jumped as if he'd been shot and instantly released Laurie, who was looking blushingly young and more beautiful than he'd ever seen her, and that was covering four decades.

Chase looked as if he'd just walked into an invisible glass wall and hadn't yet recovered from the shock. "Uh, somebody, uh, noticed the squad car pulling in and said you'd be coming in through this entrance."

Pat could only stand there embarrassed and tongue-tied. Laurie handled the awkward situation with grace. "How's Devon?"

"Doing fine. But you'd better rush upstairs if you don't want to miss the main event."

"It's a girl!" Lucky, grinning from ear to ear, emerged from the delivery room. Draped in a surgical gown, with a green cap on his head, he looked sappy and jubilant. "Hey, Mother, you made it in time after all."

"Thanks to Pat." Chase sidled a glance at them and smiled devilishly.

"God, she's gorgeous! Gorgeous!" Lucky shouted, smacking his fist into his opposite palm.

"How's Devon?" Laurie asked anxiously.

"Came through like a pro. I suggested we start making another one right away. She socked me in the nose."

"How much did the baby weigh?"

"They're doing all that now. She's exactly two and a half minutes old. The doctor let me cut the cord. Then he handed her to me. Squishy, squalling, little red-faced thing. And I handed her to Devon. Made a fool of myself. Started crying. Jeez, it was great!"

Chase smiled, but he couldn't help thinking about the child of his who would have been a toddler by now. Considering that, he applauded himself for holding up very well.

"A girl," Chase said ruefully. Then he boomed a laugh. "A girl! If that's not poetic justice, I don't know what is. A girl! God has a terrific sense of humor."

Pat, catching his drift, began to chuckle. Laurie looked between them, perplexed. Lucky's face turned red.

"The fastest zipper in East Texas now has a daughter," Chase said, laughing and clapping his hands together. "Oh, that's rich."

"That's not funny," Lucky grumbled.

"I don't think so either," Laurie said primly.

"It's hilarious," Chase cried. Throwing back his head, he hooted. "Wait till Sage hears about it. She'll give you grief."

"Sage! Oh, my goodness." Laurie began fishing in her handbag for coins. "She made me promise to call her the instant the baby was born. Pat, do you have some quarters?"

"I need to try Marcie again too," Chase said.

"Y'all excuse me," Lucky said. "I'm going back in to be with Devon. Stick around. They'll bring baby girl Tyler out in a few minutes."

"No name?"

"Not yet."

"We'll be right here." Laurie kissed her younger son on the cheek and gave him a bear hug. "I'm so happy for you, Lucky."

"Be happy for Devon. She did all the work."

He disappeared through doors marked DELIVERY. The three of them moved toward the bank of pay telephones. "Where is Marcie anyway?" Laurie asked Chase.

"I tried calling her when we first got here. Her secretary was about to leave for the day. She said Marcie was showing a house, but was expected to return to the office before heading for home. She promised to leave her a message. On the outside chance they missed connections, I'm going to try calling Marcie at the house. She'll want to be here."

"Speaking of her . . ." From his breast pocket Pat extracted a sheet of computer-generated data. "I just received this list of phone freaks from Dallas this morning. The technicians were thorough. The list covers the whole state and even includes suspects who were never convicted. Course her nut might be a new one who's never been caught at it. Anyway, tell her to look it over and see if she recognizes any of the names."

Marcie's ex-fiancé in Houston had been eliminated as a viable suspect. His telephone bills over the last few months showed only long-distance calls to his mother in Detroit and one to a mail order house in Pittsburgh. He had ordered a pocket calculator. He sounded like a singularly dull nerd, and that had secretly pleased Chase.

He, like any other, could be using a pay phone to make the calls, but Chase tended to agree with Marcie that this guy lacked the imagination.

It had taken longer than they had anticipated to receive the information from Dallas. Chase was pessimistic that it would do any good, but he was heartened to know that Pat was continuing the investigation even though the caller hadn't been heard from since the night they had involved the sheriff's office.

He hoped that something would break soon, and that it wouldn't be Marcie. The more time that passed, the more distraught she became. She was determined to prove to him the calls were real. He had never doubted it for a moment.

He'd seen her fear; he'd held her trembling body after she'd suffered through a nightmare. He hoped to God he never got his hands on the bastard who was putting her through this hell. He couldn't be held responsible for what he might do to him.

"Thanks, Pat." Chase took the paper from him and set it on the shelf beneath the pay phone. He dialed his home number. The tapping sound he now knew to listen for signaled that Pat hadn't stopped monitoring their telephone either.

It rang several times before he hung up and tried Marcie's office telephone. He got a recording saying that the office was closed and asking the caller to try again between nine and six the following day.

At the tone he said, "Marcie, it's me. Are you there?" He waited, but she didn't pick up the receiver as he had hoped.

"Sage is thrilled!" Laurie exclaimed as she hung up after speaking to her daughter. "She's leaving Austin now."

"That won't put her here until midnight," Pat said, consulting his wristwatch.

"I know. I tried talking her into waiting till morning, but she insisted on coming tonight."

Mentioning the time had reminded Chase just how late it was. So much had happened since Lucky had received the call from Devon, he hadn't realized the hour had grown so late. "Who's looking at houses at this time of day?"

"Pardon?" Laurie asked him.

"Nothing. Go on back. Don't miss your granddaughter's debut. I'm going to try again to reach Marcie."

Laurie headed toward the newborns' nursery. Pat hung back. "Chase, anything wrong?"

"No. At least I don't think so." Then he finally shook his head. "No, I'm sure there's not."

"Let me know."

"Sure. Hey, Pat." Pat had taken a few steps when Chase called his name. The sheriff turned around. "That was some kiss."

The older man opened his mouth as though to deny all knowledge of what Chase was referring to. Then he ducked his head with chagrin. "It sure as hell was." He and Chase smiled at each other, then Pat turned and moved down the hallway to rejoin Laurie.

Chase dialed his home number again. No answer. He called the office again. He got the recording. Taking the telephone directory from its slot, he looked up Esme's home phone number.

"Oh, hi. You still haven't talked to Marcie?"

"No. Did you speak with her before you left the office?"

"No. But I left your message on the telephone recorder and a note on her desk just in case there was a glitch with the tape. Whether she calls in or goes back to the office, she can't miss it. Was it a boy or girl?"

"What? Oh, it was a girl," he replied absently. Where the hell could Marcie be? Shopping? Running errands? Still showing a house? "Esme, what time did she leave?"

"Just before six. You only missed her by a few minutes. She'd just walked out when you called the first time."

"Hmm. Who was she with? Buyers or sellers? Was it someone she knew?"

"She wasn't with anybody. She had an appointment to meet Mr. and Mrs. Harrison at a house they're interested in."

"The infamous Harrisons?"

"The very same. Frankly, I think she's wasting her time on them, but she said you never know when clients are going to make up their minds and take the plunge."

Chase muttered his exasperation and shoved his fingers through his hair. "God only knows how long she'll be with them."

"As far as I know, they only asked to see one house tonight. It's a new listing on Sassafras Street."

"Well, thanks, Esme. Good-bye."

"I'm sure she'll be in touch soon."

He hung up. For a moment he stared at the phone, weighing his options. Marcie usually checked in with her office before going home. Surely, one way or the other, she would get his message to come to the hospital. In the meantime he would try at intervals to reach her at home. She would never forgive herself for missing the birth of Devon's baby.

He redialed their home number. After getting no answer, he hung up impatiently, retrieved his quarter, and turned away. When he did, the computer printout Pat had given him drifted to the floor. He bent down and picked it up.

As he made his way toward the nursery, where Pat and Laurie were waiting at the large window for a first glimpse of Lucky's daughter, he scanned the sheet.

It was printed in dot matrix. The fluorescent tubes overhead almost bled the letters out. The names were in alphabetical order. He had almost reached the midway point when his feet came to a standstill.

He gripped both sides of the sheet and raised it closer to his face so that there would be no mistaking the name. Then he crushed the paper between his hands and roared. The feral cry came up through his soul. "No!"

Laurie and Pat whirled around, their faces registering astonishment. The bloodcurdling noise stopped a rushing intern in his tracks. All up and down the corridor, heads turned, sensing disaster.

"Chase?" his mother asked worriedly.

Pat said, "What the hell, boy?"

Chase didn't acknowledge them. He was already tearing down the corridor, knocking aside a metal cart and a nurse's aide who was dispensing fruit juice and Jell-O to the maternity patients.

He didn't even consider taking the elevator. It would be too slow. When he reached the door to the stairwell, he shoved it open with the heels of his hands and clambered down two flights at a run, taking several stairs at a time, hurdling the banister at every landing, his heart racing, his mind refusing to consider that, in spite of his haste, he might already be too late.

Chapter Seventeen

The house on Sassafras Street set well away from the street. Marcie commented on that amenity as she and her client approached the front door via a stone walkway.

"You'll notice some lichen on these stones, but plain laundry bleach kills it. Personally, I like it. Maybe Mrs. Harrison will too," she said hopefully.

"Yeah, maybe."

Because this house had a large yard, Marcie hadn't suggested it to the Harrisons. A few weeks earlier the expansive lawn of another house for sale had prompted a dispute between the couple. When Ralph Harrison had called and asked to see this house, Marcie had cited the yard as a possible drawback. To her surprise he had reversed his previous opinion on taking care of a large yard.

"The yard would be no problem," he had told her.

Now Marcie pointed out that even though the yard was generous, it would require minimal care. "As you can see, there's very little grass to mow. Most of it is ground cover, front and back."

"That's why I noticed the house as I passed it today. I liked it and wanted to see it right away."

"It's a shame Mrs. Harrison couldn't join us."

"She wasn't feeling well. But she was real excited about the house when I described it to her. She told me to go ahead and preview it. If I like it, she'll come see it tomorrow."

Things were looking up, Marcie thought. This was the most cooperative the Harrisons had ever been with each other.

It was dark inside the entry alcove, but it was dry. Marcie shook out her umbrella and propped it against the exterior brick wall. The gloom

was so pervasive, she had to try the key several times before successfully opening the lock.

As soon as she cleared the front door she reached for a light switch.
The chandelier in the front foyer had a bubbled, amber glass globe that
she found distinctly offensive. It cast weird shadows on the walls.

She didn't like showing houses at night. Only rarely did a house
show to its best advantage after the sun went down. For the Harrisons,
however, she had made this exception. So much time had already been
invested in them, she was in so deep, she couldn't afford to stop accom-
modating them now. The law of averages was bound to catch up with
her soon. She *would* sell them a house.

"The living room is spacious," she said. "Nice fireplace. Lots of
windows. Lots of natural light. Of course, you can't tell that now. But
tomorrow when Gladys comes with you, you'll see." She opened the
drapes.

"I liked it better the other way," he said.

You would, she thought. She drew the heavy drapes together again
and led him through a narrow dining room into the kitchen. "The
garage is through that door," she told him. "It has a built-in workbench
I know you'll enjoy."

"I'm not much of a handyman."

"Hmm." She searched for something that would pique his interest.
So far, he'd walked through the rooms, following closely on her heels
as though he were afraid of the shadows in the vacant house, and
displaying little reaction either positive or negative.

Not wanting this to take any longer than necessary, she seized the
initiative and asked him point-blank, "What do you think of the house
so far, Mr. Harrison?"

"I'd like to see the rest of it."

She nodded pleasantly, but she was secretly gritting her teeth. "This
way."

It was the kind of house that Marcie personally abhorred, with long,
dark hallways and small enclosed rooms. But because she had wisely
realized years ago that tastes were as varied as people, and because
Sassafras Street was treelined, gracious, and underpopulated, she had
aggressively gone after this listing for her agency. Maybe for the very
reasons she disliked the house so much, the Harrisons would admire it.

She switched on the overhead light in the master bedroom suite. The
carpeting was covered with canvas drop cloths, which, in Marcie's opinion, were a vast improvement over the maroon carpeting. In the center

of the room were a sawhorse, a bucket to mix plaster in, a sack of plaster mix, another bucket of ceiling white paint, and a pile of rags.

"There was a bad water spot on this ceiling. I've already taken care of the roof repair. As you can see, the inside repair isn't quite finished."

He didn't even glance up to see if the work was being done satisfactorily. He didn't ask a question about it. In fact, he showed no interest in the project at all, which was odd since he was usually such a stickler for detail and always found something wrong with every house.

"There are two closets."

Marcie went about her business, refusing to acknowledge her growing sense of uneasiness. For several months she had been showing houses to Ralph Harrison. His nagging wife had never failed to accompany him. They'd always viewed houses in the daytime. He was a nitpicker. Tonight he was keeping his opinions to himself. Marcie preferred his whining complaints to his unnerving silence.

"One closet is a walk-in. Gladys will like that, I'm sure. The other—" At the small clicking sound, she spun away from the open closet. Harrison was locking the bedroom door. "What in the world are you doing?" Marcie demanded.

He turned around to face her, grinning eerily. In a new, yet alarmingly familiar, voice, he said, "Locking the door. So that you and I can be alone at last."

She fell back a step, her spine coming up hard against the doorjamb of the closet. She didn't notice the pain. Nothing registered except his menacing smile and raspy voice. She wasn't so much afraid as profoundly astonished.

Ralph Harrison was her caller.

"What was that all about?" Laurie put the question to Pat, who was frowning at the exit through which Chase had just disappeared.

"Damned if I know." He walked to the spot where Chase had previously been standing and bent down to pick up the computer printout he'd wadded into a ball then dropped. "Must have something to do with this." Sheriff Bush spread open the sheet again and scanned it. "He must have recognized a name on here himself. Someone that Marcie knows."

"Pat, go after him," Laurie urged, giving his shoulder a push. "Catch him before he has a chance to do something crazy."

"My thoughts exactly. Will you be okay?"

"Of course. Go. Go!" Pat jogged down the hallway toward the stairs, unable to move quite as spryly or as rapidly as Chase had moments earlier. "Be careful," Laurie anxiously called after him.

"You bet."

By the time he reached his squad car outside the emergency entrance of the hospital, Chase had disappeared. But Devon's car was no longer parked where Pat had spotted it when he and Laurie arrived. It made sense that since Chase had driven Lucky and Devon from the Tyler place to the hospital, he would still have the keys.

Peeling out of the hospital parking lot, Pat spoke into the transmitter of his police radio and put out an all-points bulletin for Devon's car, describing it as best as he could remember.

"License plate number?" one of his on-duty officers asked through the crackling airwaves.

"Damned if I know," Pat barked. "Just locate the car. Stop it. Apprehend the driver. White male, dark hair, six four."

"Is he armed and dangerous?" another asked.

"Hell, no!" Then he thought about the .357 he'd returned to Chase about a week ago. "Possibly armed." He thought of the Tyler temper. When riled, especially when it involved their women, it was more fearsome than any firearm. "Consider him dangerous. He'll probably resist arrest. Try not to use bodily force. He's got a couple of cracked ribs."

"Sounds like Chase Tyler."

"It is Chase Tyler," Pat replied to the unofficial remark he had overheard one deputy make to another.

"I don't get it, Sheriff Bush. What are we arresting Chase for?"

"Being a hothead."

"Sir, I didn't copy that."

"Just find the car and stop it!"

"Sassafras Street. Sassafras Street," Chase muttered to himself as he headed for the residential neighborhood where he knew the street was located. Sassafras Street. Was it between Beechnut and Magnolia? Or was he thinking of Sweetgum Street? Where the hell *was* Sassafras Street?

The town he had grown up in seemed suddenly foreign territory to him. He couldn't remember which streets ran parallel and which intersected. Did Sassafras run north and south or east and west?

In his mind he conjured up a map of Milton Point, but it was distorted and became an ever-changing grid of streets he could no longer remember, like a maze in a nightmare that one could never work his way through.

He cursed, banging his fist on the steering wheel of Devon's red compact car. Who would have thought that that little weasel, Harrison, had the nerve to terrorize a woman over the telephone? Chase had only met him once, that day in Marcie's office. Harrison had made little impression on him. He couldn't describe him now if asked to do so at gunpoint. He was that forgettable.

That's probably why he made obscene phone calls, Chase reasoned. The calls were his only power trip, his last-ditch effort to achieve machismo. Over the telephone he could be six feet six and commanding. His sibilant vulgarities made his victims gasp and left a distinct impression on them. To a guy like Harrison, revulsion was better than making no impression at all.

"Slimy s.o.b.," Chase said through his teeth. He remembered how disgusted and devastated Marcie had looked after each call.

Why hadn't they consulted a psychologist instead of a law officer? Someone who understood the workings of the human mind might have provided them with character profiles that would have pointed them to Harrison. It was crystal clear to Chase now why he was their man. He had an overbearing, critical wife and a low self-image. They should have gone to a head doctor. Harrison was a sicko. He wasn't a criminal.

Or was he? Maybe talking about sexual perversions no longer satisfied him. Maybe he'd gone over the edge. Maybe he was ready to make good his threats.

"Dammit." Chase stamped on the accelerator.

Marcie's astonishment quickly receded with the onslaught of panic. By an act of will she tamped it down. He wanted her to be afraid. She was. But damned if she was going to give him the satisfaction of seeing it.

"So, you're the pathetic individual who's been calling me. Are you proud of yourself?"

"Don't try to fool me, Marcie. I've frightened you."

"You haven't frightened me in the slightest. Only disgusted me and made me feel very sorry for you."

"If you weren't frightened, why'd you go to the sheriff?"

She tried to keep her face impassive and not let him see her distress. At the same time she was trying to figure a way out of the room and away from the house. Once outside, she could run down the sidewalk screaming, but she had to get out of there first.

If at all possible, she wanted to avoid any physical contact. The thought of his hands on her made her ill. He didn't have a weapon. He wasn't exceptionally tall or strong. In fact, he was slightly built. If it came down to a wrestling match, she doubted he could completely overpower her, but he could hurt her before she could fight him off and that was a major concern.

Not that he would take it that far, she reassured herself. He wouldn't try to rape her. He only wanted to terrorize her.

"Didn't you think I'd know when they put the taps on your phone?" he asked in the taunting voice of her nightmares. "The first time I called and heard the clicks, I hung up."

"Then you must have done this kind of thing before. To be that familiar with police wiretaps and such."

"Oh, yes. I'm quite good at it. An expert. The best."

She forced a laugh. "I hate to dash your self-esteem," she said, hoping to do exactly that, "but you're not very original. In fact, I've had much more, uh, *interesting* calls than yours."

"Shut up!" Abruptly, his voice rose in pitch and volume, alarming her. His face had become congested with blood and his eyes had narrowed to pinpoints of sinister light. "Take off your blouse."

"No." Maybe if she called his bluff, he would get cold feet and run away.

He took three menacing steps toward her. "Take off your blouse."

The empty closet was behind her. Could she step into it, shut the door, and lock herself in until somebody missed her and came looking? She felt behind her for the doorknob.

"That door doesn't have a lock, if that's what you're thinking," he said with a cackle she recognized. Over the telephone it had never failed to send chills down her spine. She experienced them now.

He was right. The closet door didn't have a lock. She glanced quickly at the window. The sill was painted shut. She could never get it open, and even if she could, she couldn't scramble out without his catching her first.

Her only means of escape was through the doorway leading into the hall. He was blocking her path to it. She would have to draw him across the room, closer to her, and away from the door.

Swallowing her repugnance and her pride, her hand moved to the top button of her blouse. Why hadn't she worn a suit today instead of a skirt and blouse? A jacket would have been another delaying tactic.

"Hurry up," he ordered. "Take it off. I want to see your skin. I want to see your breasts."

Marcie slowly undid all the buttons. "My husband will tear you apart."

"Not before I've seen your nipples, touched them. Hurry up."

"He won't let you get away with this. He'll find you."

"You won't tell him. You'll be too ashamed to tell him."

"I wouldn't count on that if I were you."

"Take off your blouse!" he shouted nervously.

She pulled it from her waistband and peeled it down her shoulders. As she withdrew her arms from the sleeves, he released a sigh and actually shuddered orgasmically. Marcie thought she might be sick, but she couldn't surrender to the nausea. She had to get out of the room.

As she had both hoped and dreaded, Harrison took faltering steps toward her. "Now the brassiere. Hurry." He was clutching at his crotch with one hand and reaching out to her with the other.

"You're so fair. I knew your skin would be fair. Beautiful. Soft." His fingertips glanced her chest just above her bra. She recoiled. He took another lurching step toward her. She could feel his rapid breath landing humid and hot on her skin.

"Fondle yourself," he panted.

"No."

"Do it."

"No."

"I said to do it!"

"If you want me fondled, you do it." Her blue eyes haughtily challenged him. "Or are you man enough?"

As she had hoped, he lunged toward her, his hands and fingers forming a cup to seize her breast. She flung her blouse into his face, parried quickly, and ducked under his arm. She scooped the empty bucket from the floor and threw it up at the overhead light fixture, then clambered toward the door at a crouch to avoid the breaking glass that was raining down.

In the sudden darkness she groped for the doorknob. The darkness was to her advantage because she was more familiar with the house than he. She would know how to find her way back to the front door. But first she had to get past this barrier. Having located the doorknob, her fingers had turned to rubber. She couldn't get it unlocked!

From behind, Harrison grabbed a handful of her hair. Her head snapped back. She screamed. He covered her hand and wrested it off the slippery doorknob. They slapped at each other's hands in a battle over control of the lock.

Marcie heard whimpers of fear and draining energy and realized they were coming from her. She had minimized the real threat he could pose to her safety, but had obviously miscalculated. His breathing was the short, choppy panting of a madman. He was stronger than he appeared. Had insanity imbued him with inordinate strength?

She renewed her efforts to escape him, but he gripped her arm so hard that tears started in her eyes. "Let me go," she screamed.

He flung her away from the door and back toward the center of the room. With so much momentum behind her, she reeled forward, stumbling in the darkness over drop cloths, broken glass, and the sack of plaster mix and falling against the sawhorse. It caught her at waist level, and she doubled over it. It toppled over with her, spilling the bucket of paint.

She blinked away the descending blackness of unconsciousness and struggled to her hands and knees. Harrison, bending over her, with his hand on the back of her neck, held her down.

"Bitch, bitch," he said raspily. "I'll show you how much of a man I am."

"Milton seven?"

Pat responded. "Yeah, come in."

"This is Milton five. I've just sighted a red vehicle, license number and make unknown at this time, traveling west on Sycamore at a high rate of speed."

"Close in and apprehend."

"Not a chance, Milton seven. He's driving like a bat out of hell."

"Then follow him. I'm three minutes away. Keep him in sight and let me know any changes of direction."

"Ten four."

"Other units, please converge on that area."

To a chorus of acknowledgments, Pat dropped the transmitter and concentrated on navigating the dark, rain-slick streets.

Chase took the corner close to fifty. Sassafras Street at last! What number? Leaning over the steering wheel, he peered through the darkness, cursing the driving rain and his inability to see beyond the hood ornament.

He sped right past Marcie's car before noticing it. He braked, skidded, and fishtailed, then shoved the automatic transmission into park and opened the car door. The FOR SALE sign bearing her agency's logo was in the front yard. Chase hurdled it in his dash through the pelting rain toward the front door.

He paused in the entrance hall, his blood freezing in his veins when he heard her pitiful cries. But thank God, she was alive. His moves through the unfamiliar rooms and hallways resembled those of a running back going through a horde of defensive players. For every five yards he gained, he had to backtrack two, until he finally reached the closed and locked bedroom door.

He tested the doorknob only once before putting his boot heel to it and kicking it in. From the hallway behind him, light spilled into the room and across the floor, casting a looming, hulking shadow that alarmed him until he realized it was his own.

He dashed inside. Harrison, still crouched over Marcie on the floor, whipped his head around and stared up at Chase with an animal fear so intense Chase could smell it.

"I'm gonna kill you, Harrison."

Reaching from his towering height, he yanked the man up by his collar and shook him like a dog with a dead rat. Harrison squealed. Chase, enraged and unthinking, slung him against the wall. Harrison would have slid down it but for Chase's fist, which slammed into Harrison's midsection, then pinned him to the wall like a nail through his gut. Nose to nose, his lips peeled back to bare his teeth, Chase glared at his wife's tormentor.

"Chase, let him go!" Pistol drawn, Pat Bush shouted the order from the splintered doorway. "Chase!" He had to repeat his name three times before Chase heard him through a fog of murderous outrage.

Gradually Chase withdrew his fist. Harrison, emitting a wheezing sound like an old accordion, collapsed to the floor. One of Pat's deputies rushed forward to see to Harrison while Chase bent anxiously over Marcie. She was lying on her side, her knees drawn protectively up to her chest.

"Chase?" she said faintly.

He placed his arms around her and lifted her into a sitting position, hugging her close to his rain-soaked chest. "I'm here, Marcie. He can't bother you now. Not anymore. Never."

"Is she all right?" Pat hunkered down beside him.

"I think so. Just scared."

"Is she cut? There's glass all over the place. Apparently she broke out the light."

Chase smiled as he smoothed back strands of red-gold hair from her damp forehead. "That's my girl. Always smart. Always resourceful."

"Chase?"

He bent his head down, bringing his face close to hers. Even pale and disheveled she looked beautiful. "Hmm?"

"Get me to the hospital."

"The hospital?"

"I'm bleeding."

His eyes moved over her face, her chest, her exposed midriff, but he saw no trace of blood.

"She's probably cut her hands and knees on the glass," Pat said.

"No, it's not that. Get me to the hospital now," she said, her anxiety increasing. "Hurry, please."

"Marcie, I know you're scared. You've come through—"

"Chase, I'm bleeding vaginally." Her tearful eyes found his. She pulled her lower lip through her teeth. "I'm pregnant."

Chapter Eighteen

It was still raining. Chase looked beyond his own reflection in the window out into the dark, forlorn night. He saw the reflections of his brother and Pat Bush as they approached him, but he didn't turn away from the window until Pat spoke his name.

"I just got back from the courthouse," the sheriff said. "I thought you'd want to know that Harrison is in jail. He'll be arraigned first thing in the morning."

"For assault?"

"Murder one."

Chase's gut knotted. Was this their way of informing him that Marcie had died? He slowly pivoted on his heels. "What?" he croaked.

"I dispatched some men to his house. They found his wife. She'd been dead for several hours. He strangled her with his bare hands. Allegedly," Pat added, remembering his role as a fair and impartial officer of the law.

Chase dragged his hand down his face, stretching the tired, strained features. "Dear Lord."

"Marcie had good reason to be scared of him," Pat said. "Even over the telephone she sensed he was more than just a casual phone freak. I feel like hell for doubting her."

Chase was still too stunned to speak. Lucky squeezed the older man's shoulder. "Don't worry about that now, Pat. You couldn't guess that he was going to carry out his threats. You were there tonight when Marcie needed you." He glanced over his shoulder toward the waiting room at the opposite end of the corridor. "I think Mother and Sage could use you for moral support right now. And vice versa."

"Sure. Chase, if you need me . . . for anything . . . just holler." Chase nodded. Pat ambled off, leaving the two brothers alone.

For a moment they said nothing. Chase couldn't think of anything appropriate to say. He felt hollow. There were no words inside him.

Lucky broke the silence. "Sage made the trip safely."

"So I see. I'm glad she's here."

"She arrived in a mood to celebrate. We had to break the news about Marcie. She started crying. When you feel up to it, she'd like to say hello. Right now, she thinks you'd rather be left alone. Is she right?"

"I don't feel much like talking."

"Sure."

Lucky turned away, but had only taken a few steps when Chase reached out and touched his arm. "I'm sorry this has put a pall on your daughter's birthday."

"It sure as hell wasn't your fault things turned out the way they did. The culprit is in jail. Blame it on him."

Chase's fists flexed at his sides. "He could have killed her, Lucky."

"But he didn't."

"If I hadn't gotten there—"

"But you did. Everybody's safe now."

They didn't mention the baby that Marcie was carrying. There might yet be another casualty of Ralph Harrison's violent madness. Lucky's first child had been born; Chase's second child might die on the same day. He couldn't bear thinking about it.

"Anyway," he said emotionally, "I hate like hell that this had to happen today of all days."

"Forget that part of it. You've got enough on your mind without worrying about that."

The things on his mind were about to drive him crazy. To stave it off he asked, "How's Devon feeling?"

"How do you think? Like she just had a baby. I told her I knew how she felt. I thought she was going to come out of that bed and slug me." He chuckled in spite of the somber mood.

Chase forced a half smile. "The, uh, baby," he said huskily, "how is she?"

"Fine, even though she was several weeks early. The pediatrician checked her out. He wants to monitor her closely for the next few days, but he says her reflexes are normal, lungs and everything seemed well developed." He broke into a wide grin. "She's squalling loud enough."

"That's good, Lucky. That's real good."

Chase's throat closed tightly around the lump stuck in it. He cleared it self-consciously and blinked gathering tears out of his eyes. Lucky placed a consoling hand on his shoulder.

"Look, Chase, Marcie's going to be okay. And so's the baby. I know it. I feel it. Have I ever steered you wrong?"

"Plenty of times."

Lucky frowned with chagrin. "Well, not this time. You wait and see."

Chase nodded, but he wasn't convinced. Lucky stared at him hard, trying by sheer willpower to inspire optimism and faith. The last couple of years Chase's confidence in good fortune had been shaken. Today's events had merely confirmed his skepticism in the benevolence of fate.

Lucky left him to join the rest of the family huddled in the waiting room. The nursing staff had become well acquainted with the Tylers since dusk that day. They now had two Mrs. Tylers in the obstetric ward. One of the nurses was passing around fresh coffee.

Chase turned his back on the well-lighted corridor, feeling more in harmony with the dismal gloom beyond the window.

I'm pregnant.

At first he had just stared into Marcie's anxious blue eyes. Unable to move, unable to speak, unable to think beyond that word, he had mutely gaped at her. Then Pat's elbow had nudged him into awareness.

"Chase, did you hear her?"

Adrenaline assumed control. He scooped Marcie into his arms and carried her past the shattered bedroom door. Pat put two deputies in charge of Harrison and the house on Sassafras Street. He followed Chase through the vacant rooms. "I'll call an ambulance."

"Screw that. I'll make it faster driving myself."

"Like hell you will. And kill yourself, or innocent people? Forget it. If you won't wait for an ambulance, put her in the patrol car. I'll drive you."

So he had held Marcie on his lap in the backseat of the patrol car behind the wire mesh that separated them from Pat. He turned on all the emergency lights and the siren. At intervals he spoke into his police radio transmitter, informing the emergency room staff that they were on their way. Windshield wipers clacked in vain against the torrential rain. The ride to the hospital had taken on a surreal quality to Chase, as though he were watching it from outside his own body.

Because he hadn't wasted time on getting an umbrella, rain had left Marcie's hair damp. There were drops of it beaded on her face and throat. Pat must have retrieved her blouse because Chase didn't re-member picking it up. He wrapped her torso in it but didn't bother with working her arms into the sleeves or fastening the buttons. He kept touching her hair, her pale cheek, her throat. She continued staring up at him with tearful and wary eyes. They said nothing to each other.

At the entrance to the emergency room she was whisked away on a gurney. "Who's her o.b.?" the resident on duty asked. Everyone looked at Chase expectantly.

"I . . . I don't know."

Admitting her to the hospital was a seemingly endless procedure of questions and forms to be filled out. Once it was done, he returned to the emergency room. There he was informed that Marcie had been transferred upstairs to the maternity ward and that her doctor was on his way.

Before the gyn even examined Marcie, he asked Chase pertinent questions relating to the attack. "To your knowledge was she raped?"

Feeling bereft, numb, he shook his head no.

"Did he even attempt penetration?"

"I don't think so," he said, barely able to get the words out.

The doctor patted his arm reassuringly. "I'm sure she'll be all right, Mr. Tyler."

"What about the baby?"

"I'll let you know."

But he hadn't. And that had been almost two hours ago. Pat had had time to go to the courthouse and deal with Harrison and come back, and still there had been no word on the conditions of Marcie and the baby.

What the hell was taking so long?

Had they had trouble stopping the bleeding? Was there hemorrhaging? Had she been rushed into surgery? Was her life in danger as well as the child's?

"No." Chase didn't realize he had moaned the word out loud until he heard the sound of his own voice, pleading with fate, pleading with God.

Marcie couldn't die. She *couldn't*. She had become too important to him. He couldn't lose her now that he had just come to realize how important she was to him.

He remembered something that Lucky had asked him earlier that afternoon. That afternoon? It seemed eons ago. Lucky had asked, "What's the single worst thing that could happen to you, Chase? The worst possible thing?"

Perhaps he had known the answer to that question then. Devon's phone call had prevented him from having to deal with it at the time, but now he repeated the question to himself.

The answer was full-blown and well-defined in his mind. After losing Tanya, after losing their child, the worst possible thing that could happen to him was to love again.

Almost anything else he could have handled. A drinking problem. Getting seriously hurt by bull riding, perhaps permanently injured, perhaps killed. Professional and personal bankruptcy.

Whatever misfortune fate might have hurled at him, he could take because he had reasoned that he didn't deserve anything better. Partially blaming himself for Tanya's death, he had pursued self-punishment. He had cultivated calamity like a twisted gardener who preferred weeds to flowers. Nothing that could happen to him could be worse than losing his family—nothing except loving another one.

That he couldn't deal with.

He couldn't handle caring about another woman again. He couldn't handle another woman's loving him. He couldn't handle making another baby.

He banged his fist against the cool, tile hospital wall and pressed his forehead against it. Eyes closed, teeth clenched, he battled acknowledging what he knew to be the truth.

He had fallen in love with Marcie. And he couldn't forgive himself for it.

Acting a fool, he had rejected her when she needed him most. He had turned his back on her when she was pregnant and frightened. And why? Pride. No man liked to feel that he'd been manipulated, but the business about the house now seemed more an act of love than manipulation. He'd just been too muleheaded to accept what was so plain and simple. Marcie loved him. He loved her.

If that was his worst crime, was it so terrible?

He examined the sin from all angles, even from Tanya's viewpoint. She wouldn't have wanted it any differently. Her capacity to love had been so enormous that she would have been the first one to encourage him to love again if she had seen what their fate was to be.

Why was he fighting it? What had he done that was so despicable? Why was he continuing to punish himself? He had fallen in love with a wonderful woman who, miraculously, loved him. What was so bad about that?

Nothing.

He raised his head and turned. At the end of the corridor the obstetrician was coming out of Marcie's room. Chase moved toward him, his long strides eating up the distance between them, gaining speed and momentum as he went.

"Listen, you," he said harshly before the doctor had a chance to speak, "save her life. Hear me?" He backed the startled physician into the wall. "I don't care if it costs ten million dollars, do whatever is necessary to make her live. You got that, Doc? Even if it means . . ." He stopped, swallowed with an effort, then continued in a rougher voice, "Even if it means destroying the baby, save my wife."

"That won't be necessary, Mr. Tyler. Your wife is going to be fine."

Chase stared at him, unwilling to believe it. The fortunate twist of fate took him totally by surprise. "She is?"

"And so is the baby. When she fell over the sawhorse, a vaginal blood vessel burst. It was weakened and under unusual pressure due to her pregnancy. There wasn't much bleeding, but enough to alarm Mrs. Tyler. Rightfully so.

"We've cauterized it. I did a sonogram just to make certain that everything was okay, and it is. The fetus wasn't affected in any way." He hitched his thumb over his shoulder toward the room from which he'd just emerged. "She insisted on taking a shower. A nurse is helping her with that now. When she's done, you can go in and see her. I recommend a few days of bed rest. After that, she should experience a perfectly normal pregnancy."

Chase mumbled his thanks for the information. The doctor moved to the nurses' station and left instructions, then departed. Chase's family surrounded him. Laurie was weeping copiously. Sage was doing her share of sniveling. Pat was wiping nervous perspiration off his forehead with a handkerchief and mercilessly chewing a matchstick.

Lucky slapped Chase soundly on the back. "Didn't I tell you? Huh? When are you gonna start trusting me?"

Chase fielded their expressions of relief with what he hoped were the correct responses, but his eyes were trained on the hospital room door. As soon as the nurse came out, he excused himself and rushed inside.

The single, faint night-light behind the bed shone through Marcie's hair, making it the only spot of vibrancy in the shadowed room. Its magnetism drew him across the floor until he stood at her bedside.

"History repeats itself," she said. "I remember another time when you came to see me in the hospital."

"You look better now than you did then."

"Not much."

"Much."

"Thank you."

She averted her eyes and blinked several times, but it did no good. Twin tears, one as fat as the other, slipped over her lower lids and rolled down her cheeks.

"Are you in pain, Marcie?" Chase asked, bending closer. "Did that bastard hurt you?"

"No," she gulped. "You got there just in time."

"He's behind bars." He thought it best not to inform her of Gladys Harrison's murder. "Don't waste your tears on him."

"That's not why I'm crying." Her lower lip began to tremble. She clamped her teeth over it in an attempt to prevent that.

After a moment or two she said, "I know how you feel about having another baby, Chase. I didn't mean to trick you. I swear I didn't. It's true, I should have been more honest about the house, but I didn't lie to you about contraceptives.

"I started taking birth control pills as soon as we agreed to get married, but I guess they hadn't had time to take effect. It had only been a couple of days. It happened on our wedding night."

"But I used something, too."

"It must have broken."

"Oh."

"That happens sometimes. Or so I've been told."

"Yeah, I've heard that too."

"Has it ever happened to you before?"

"No."

"Do you think I'm lying about it?"

"No. I, uh, I was pretty potent that night when I, you know . . ." She swung her eyes up to his. "It must have happened then."

"Hmm."

"I'm sorry, Chase." Her lip began to tremble again.

"It wasn't your fault."

"No, I mean about the baby. About making you feel trapped. I know that's how you feel. You think I bound you to me first with money, now with a baby you said you never wanted." She licked the collecting tears from the corners of her mouth.

"You should have told me you were pregnant, Marcie."

"I couldn't."

"You've never lacked the courage to tell me anything else."

"I've never felt so vulnerable before. I found out while you were in Houston. That's why I had no appetite and lost so much weight. That's why I wouldn't take the pill you tried to give me. I knew then and should have told you, but you were so angry about the house. And then that mess with Harrison came up."

She clutched the border of the sheet. "I want you to know that I won't bind you. You're free to go, Chase. I won't hold you to any bargains if you want out of the marriage."

"Are you trying to get rid of me?"

"Of course not."

"Then be quiet. I want to tell you how much I love you." He smiled at her blank, incredulous expression, then lowered his face to hers and sipped the tears off her cheeks. "I love you, Marcie. Swear to God, I do. He blessed me with you."

"I thought you didn't believe in Him anymore."

"I always believed. I was just mad at Him."

"Chase," she sighed. "You mean this?"

"From the bottom of my heart."

Her fingers roamed over his face, his hair, his lips. "I have loved you since I can remember. Since we were kids."

"I know," he said softly. "I realize that now. I'm not as smart as you. It takes me a while to grasp these things. For instance, I still haven't figured out why you didn't tell me about the baby. I could have helped you through this nightmare."

"Could you?"

"Couldn't I?"

"Remember that night I took you home to your apartment, then came back and you were eating chili? We got into an argument when I told you to snap out of your bereavement, that it was self-destructive. You said, 'When you've lost the person you love, when you've lost a child, *then* you'll be at liberty to talk to me about falling apart.'

"I didn't realize until I was at risk of losing you how immobilizing heartache can be, how one does fall apart. I internalized my agony just as you had done then, Chase. I fully understand now how you must have felt following Tanya's death. It's almost self-preservation, isn't it, the way we draw into ourselves when we think no one cares?"

"We won't have that problem anymore."

A radiant smile broke through her tears. "No. We won't."

He kissed her, deeply but tenderly, and wondered why, until now, he'd never recognized the special taste of her kiss as being love. He knew he'd never get enough of it.

"Maybe you were wise not to tell me about the baby, Marcie," he whispered. "I don't think I was prepared to hear about it until today."

"But now that you know, it's all right?"

"All right?" His splayed hand was large enough to cover the entire area between her pelvic bones. "I love the idea of us making a baby. Hurry up and get well so the three of us can go home."

"Home?"

"Home."

Epilogue

"All this fecundity is positively nauseating," Sage commented drolly.

"What the hell's 'fecundity'?" Lucky wanted to know.

"Oh, that's rich," his sister remarked. "Especially coming from you."

All the Tylers had gathered at the ranch house to celebrate little Lauren's three-week birthday. Everyone else had gorged on German chocolate cake. The baby was greedily sucking her mother's breast behind the screen of a receiving blanket. The proud papa looked on, ready to assist at a moment's notice.

"Know what I can't wait for?"

"Careful, Sage." Chase, who'd been twirling a strand of Marcie's hair around his finger while whispering bawdy things into her ear, paused in those pleasurable pursuits to caution his sister. "You never learned when to quit."

Ignoring Chase, she continued goading her other brother. "I can't wait till some guy makes a pass at Lauren. I want to be there. I want to rub your nose in it, Lucky."

Lucky took the infant from Devon so she could close her blouse. He glowered at his sister. "I'll kill any s.o.b. who even thinks of laying a hand on my daughter. I'll kill anyone who even looks like he's thinking of laying a hand on her."

"How're you going to explain the origin of your nickname to Lauren?" Chase asked, joining in.

Devon burst out laughing. Lucky stopped cooing to Lauren long enough to consign his brother and sister to hell.

"Lucky, please watch your language," his mother said with a long-suffering sigh. "Remember we have a guest."

Travis Belcher, Sage's beau, had accompanied her home for a weekend visit. He had been sitting quietly, either repulsed or dumbfounded by the frankness with which the Tylers spoke to one another.

Chase had noticed the young man registering shock when he had put his hand over Marcie's tummy and patted it affectionately. His estimation of Sage's Travis coincided with Lucky's. The guy was a wimp. Just for the hell of shocking him further, he had leaned over and kissed Marcie's lips.

He got his own shock when she slipped her tongue into his mouth. "Stop that," he had moaned into her ear. "I'm already hard."

Then he had had the pleasure of watching a blush spill into her fair cheeks.

Laurie was jealous of anyone who got to hold her granddaughter longer than she did. Once Lauren had finished nursing, she crossed the living room, plucked the baby from her father's arms, and carried her back to the rocking chair, recently taken out of storage in the attic. It was the chair Laurie had rocked her three children in.

Lucky had offered to buy her a new one, but she wouldn't hear of it. She had said that the squeaks and groans of the wood in this one were familiar and brought back precious memories.

"My goodness, you're getting fat, Lauren!" she exclaimed to the child.

"No wonder," Lucky said. He placed his arm around Devon, who cuddled against him. "She's getting some delicious meals."

"How do you know how delicious they are?" Chase asked with a bawdy wink.

Lucky, not to be outdone, came right back with, "You don't think I'd let my daughter eat something I hadn't sampled first, do you?"

"Lucky!" Devon exclaimed, horrified.

"Lawrence! Chase!" Laurie remonstrated.

Chase threw back his head and roared with laughter, causing baby Lauren to flinch.

Lucky assumed an innocent pose. "But Devon, you begged me to."

"Agh!" Sage jumped to her feet. "You two are *so* disgusting. Come on, Travis. I can't take any more of this. Let's go horseback riding."

She took his hand and pulled him from his chair. "Again?" Obviously the suggestion didn't appeal to him.

"Don't be a spoilsport. I'll saddle a more docile horse for you this time." As Sage dragged Travis through the front door, she called back, "Bye, Marcie. Bye, Devon. See y'all later." While at any given time Sage could strangle either of her brothers, she adored their wives.

"Bye-bye, Lauren. I love you. Too bad you've got a reprobate for a father."

"You're a brat, Sage," Lucky hollered after her.

Moments after Sage and Travis's departure, Pat Bush stepped into the living room. "Hi, everybody. I saw Sage outside. She said to come on in."

He was offered cake and coffee and had just taken his first bite when Chase began sniffing the air. "What's that smell?"

He sniffed in Pat's direction. "Why, Pat, I believe it's you!" he said, feigning surprise. "What are you all spruced up for?"

Pat choked on his bite of cake and shot Chase a drop-dead look. Laurie's cheeks blossomed with flattering color. Chase hadn't spoken a word to anyone, not even Lucky, about seeing his mother and Pat in a heated embrace. But the temptation to tease them about it was too strong to resist.

Coming to his feet, Chase pulled Marcie up beside him. Ever since the night following Lauren's birth, he'd slept in the same bed with her, holding her close, verbally vowing his love, but prohibited from expressing it physically.

They'd resumed their torturous game of unfulfilled foreplay. It was making him crazy, but it was a delicious craziness. His body was constantly abuzz with desire. He moved around in a rosy haze of euphoria that made his nights magic and his workdays more tolerable.

Apparently the troubleshooter, Harlan Boyd, had given up on him. Once Marcie was out of danger and he'd gotten around to contacting him, the man had moved on, without leaving word of his whereabouts. It was probably just as well, but that meant he and Lucky needed to get real creative if they were going to save their business.

When he got discouraged, Marcie was his staunchest supporter and cheerleader. Placing his arm around her now, he said, "Well, we'd better be going on home."

"What for?" Lucky's countenance was as guileless as a cherub's. He batted his eyelashes. "Nap time?"

Ignoring him, Chase leaned over his mother where she sat rocking his new niece and kissed her cheek. "Bye. Thanks for the cake. It was delicious."

"Good-bye, son." Their eyes caught and held. He knew she was searching for the pain that had resided in his eyes for so long. Finding none, she gave him a beautiful smile, then turned it on the woman who was responsible for his newfound happiness. "Marcie, how are you feeling?"

"Perfectly wonderful, thanks. Chase takes very good care of me. He will hardly let me lift a fork to feed myself."

Once they were in their car and headed home, she said, "They thought I was joking about your not letting me do anything for myself."

"I've got to protect you and baby. I almost slipped up once." He gave her a meaningful look. "Never again, Marcie, will anyone come close to hurting you."

"You're the only one who could hurt me, Chase."

"How?"

"If you ever decided you didn't love me."

He reached for her hand, laid it on his thigh, and covered it with his own. "That's not going to happen."

The woods surrounding their house bore the virgin and varied greens of spring. Blooming dogwood trees decorated the forest like patches of white lace. The tulip bulbs that Marcie had planted the year before were blooming along the path leading to the front door.

Once inside, Chase moved to the wall of windows and contemplated the view. "I love this house."

"I always knew you would."

He turned around to embrace his wife. "I love it almost as much as I love you."

"Almost?"

He unbuttoned her blouse and pushed the fabric aside. His hands moved over the silk covering her breasts. "You've got a few amenities that are hard to beat."

After a lengthy, wet, deep kiss, she murmured, "I got the go-ahead from the doctor this morning."

Chase's head snapped back. "You mean he said we could—"

"If we're careful."

He swept her into his arms and took the stairs two at a time. "Why didn't you tell me sooner?"

"Because we were invited to Lauren's party."

"We wasted two hours over there!"

Once he had deposited her at the side of their bed, he began tearing off his clothes. Laughing, she helped him. When he was naked, she reached out and stroked him.

He moaned. "You're killing me."

Frantically he removed her skirt and blouse. She was still in her slip when he lowered her to the bed, laid his head on her belly, and nuzzled her through the silk.

"How's my baby?" he whispered.

"Fine. Healthy. Growing inside me."

"How are you?"

"Deliriously happy, so much in love."

"Lord, so am I." He planted a damp kiss into the giving softness.

"Hmm," she sighed, tilting herself up against his face.

He raised his head and smiled down at her. "You like that?"

"Uh-huh."

"Hot redhead that you are." He pulled her slip up by the lace hem, over her middle, over her breasts, over her head. Bra and panties and stockings were quickly discarded. Seconds later, he was gazing at her with loving approval of all he saw.

"They change color a little more every day," he remarked, brushing his fingertips across her nipples.

"They do not. You just enjoy inspecting them."

"That's not all I enjoy."

He bent his head and kissed her breasts, raking his tongue back and forth across the delicate peaks until her tummy quivered with arousal. "Chase?"

"Not yet. We've had to wait weeks for this."

He kissed his way down her body, paused to relish the texture and scent of the glossy curls covering her mound, then parted her thighs and kissed her between them.

She sighed his name and clutched handfuls of his hair, but he didn't temper his ardency until his agile tongue had drawn from her a sweet, undulating climax.

Then he rose above her and slowly, considerately, buried himself within the snug, moist sheath of her body. Mindful of her condition, his strokes were long and smooth, which only heightened the eroticism and prolonged the pleasure.

The pleasure was immense. Overwhelming. Ecstasy eddied around him in shimmering waves that matched the tempo of her gentle contractions.

Yet he couldn't totally immerse himself in it. Because in the back of his mind, behind the physical bliss, he was thinking how marvelous life was, how much he loved living it . . . how much he loved Marcie, his wife.

TEXAS!
SAGE

Chapter One

Her lips were soft and inviting against his as she sighed, then whispered, "Merry Christmas."

"Merry Christmas to you, too, Sage."

Smiling, she folded her arms around his neck and placed her lips on his again, putting more passion into their kiss . . . or trying to. "Travis!"

"What?"

"Kiss me."

"I did."

"I mean, really kiss me," she said and growled sexily. "You're allowed to kiss sexy, you know, even though it is Christmas."

"Sage, please." Nervously the young man glanced toward the windows. A party was underway inside the house. "Somebody might see us."

She removed her arms from around his neck and blew out a gust of air. "Oh, for heaven's sake, Travis, you're so damn proper! Nobody is looking. And if anyone is, who would care if we're out here necking?"

"Mother would care. Do you like your bracelet?"

Temporarily distracted, she replied, "Of course I like the bracelet. What woman wouldn't? It's beautiful."

Raising her arm, she shook the heavy gold bangle around her wrist. "I'm glad you let me open my present tonight instead of waiting for Christmas Day."

"This way you can enjoy it over the whole holiday."

"That was very thoughtful of you. Thank you."

"I still sense that you're disappointed."

Sage Tyler looked up at him through her dense lashes and made a softly spoken confession. "I thought you might give me my engagement ring for Christmas."

Before he could say anything, she rushed on. "But it's not as though we've already picked out rings. Who knows? I might not even want a traditional engagement ring. I'll probably flaunt convention and choose something radically different. Maybe a colored stone instead of a diamond."

Travis cast his eyes down to the white leather pants she was wearing. Her sweater was appropriate enough—white angora with a tasteful amount of glittering studs and rhinestones sprinkled over the shoulders and upper bodice. The pants, however, were definitely a fashion risk.

He smiled weakly. "Nobody ever accused you of being conventional, Sage."

"Thank heaven for that." A movement of her head sent her mane of dark blond hair swinging over her shoulders. "I thought your mother was going to have heart failure when I came downstairs and joined the party wearing these pants."

"Well, she, uh, associates leather clothes with Hell's Angels and rock stars, I guess."

"Hmm. Maybe I should have worn something in a nice pastel taffeta."

He frowned in disapproval of her sarcasm. "Mother is Mother. She and her friends are more or less alike. They do the same things, go to the same places, wear basically the same kind of clothes. She's accustomed to certain things."

"If I'm going to be her daughter-in-law, she had better get accustomed to me, hadn't she? I hope she doesn't expect me to start wearing long plaid skirts and respectable navy flats when I become your wife. All I'll be changing the day we get married is my last name. Speaking of which," she added on a burst of inspiration, "Valentine's Day would be such a romantic date to get officially engaged. Even better than Christmas."

Sage had dragged Travis outside for a breath of fresh air on the long, wide veranda of the Belcher home. The redbrick Georgian structure was strung with twinkling Christmas lights. In the living room behind them, an enormous Christmas tree, arranged by a decorator who favored lace, pearls, and butterflies, commanded attention from one of the wide windows overlooking the veranda.

Three evergreens had been temporarily transplanted in the front lawn and decorated for the benefit of passersby who came from all points of Harris County to view the elaborate Christmas displays the residents of this affluent Houston neighborhood put up each year. A trail of bumper-to-bumper cars snaked along the street, their headlights blurred by the mist.

Though the temperature was relatively mild, Travis hunched deeper into the collar of his dark suit coat and slid his hands into his pants pockets. This belligerent stance never failed to irritate Sage who thought it made him look like a sulky rich kid. It usually meant he had something unpleasant on his mind that he dreaded discussing.

"The fact is, Sage, I'm wondering if we're not jumping the gun to announce our engagement."

The statement caught her off guard, but instantly captured her full attention. "What do you mean?"

Travis cleared his throat. "Well, after the spring semester, I've still got internship and my year of residency ahead of me. After that, there's all the specialty courses in dermatology to get through."

"I know exactly what's required before you can open a practice, Travis. We'll be all right. Now that I've got my master's degree, I'll find a good job."

"I'm not worried about money. My parents will support me until I set up a practice."

"Then what are you worried about? Lighten up. It's Christmas!"

He glanced at the line of cars crawling past the house. "I don't think you understand what I'm trying to tell you, Sage."

Her wide smile faltered. "Apparently not, but it must be something terrible. You look like you're about to throw up. Don't torture yourself any longer or keep me in suspense. If you've got something to say, let's hear it."

He scratched his head, he coughed behind his fist, he shuffled his feet. "I've given this a lot of thought lately, and . . ."

"And?"

"And I don't think . . . It's not that you're . . . Sage, we're just not . . ."

"Not what?"

He floundered, opening and closing his mouth several times before blurting out, "Suited. We're just not suited to each other."

Having said that, his shoulders relaxed. He exhaled a deep breath. By all appearances, he had relieved himself of a tremendous burden.

Dumbfounded, Sage stared at him. She couldn't believe her ears. She had been dating Travis exclusively for more than a year. It had been understood that they would get married when she earned her master's degree. The semester was ending, and she had been expecting an engagement ring and a formal announcement of their impending marriage during the holiday season. It was preposterous to think he was dumping her. Her! *Sage Tyler!* Surely she had misunderstood.

"You can't mean you're breaking our engagement?"

He cleared his throat again. "I think we ought to think about it some more."

"Don't beat around the bush, Travis," she said testily. "If you're dumping me, at least have the guts to come right out and say so."

"I'm not dumping you. Exactly. Mother thinks—"

"Oh, 'Mother thinks . . .' Mother thinks that I'm not good enough for her little boy."

"Don't put words in my mouth, Sage."

"Then spit it out."

"Mother thinks, and I agree, that you're, well, a little too rowdy for me."

"Rowdy?"

"Showy."

"Showy?"

"Flamboyant."

"Because I wear leather pants?"

"Sage, be fair," he protested.

"Fair be damned. I'm mad."

"You've got no right to be."

"No right?"

"If you'll think back, I never officially asked you to marry me. Did I?" he asked uncertainly.

"Of course you did!" she cried. "We talked about it all the time. My family—"

"Will be delighted if it never comes off," he interrupted. "Your brothers think I'm a wimp. Your mother only tolerates me because she's nice to everybody. That sheriff who's always hanging around harrumphs and shakes his head with what appears to be disapproval every time he looks at me."

"You're imagining all of that," she averred, though she knew he wasn't.

"Well, whatever," he said impatiently, "I think we need a rest from each other."

Her anger gave way to hurt. "I thought you loved me."

"I do."

"Then why are we having this conversation? I love you, too."

He looked earnestly miserable. "I love you, Sage. You're beautiful and sexy. You're the most unpredictable, fascinating woman I've ever met. You make my head spin. You're exuberant. You like pushing people around, bending them to your will."

"You make me sound like a longshoreman!"

"I don't intend to. You've got a zest for life that I can't match. I'm tired of trying. You're spontaneous and impetuous. I'm methodical and careful. Your politics are liberal. Mine, conservative. You believe wholeheartedly in a personal God. I have my doubts. All things considered, I'd say our differences are irreconcilable."

"Opposites attract."

"I'm beginning to think not."

"This is all crap, Travis. You're trying to sugarcoat it, aren't you? You're lining up your justifications. If you're going to jilt me, at least dignify it by not being so mealymouthed."

"Don't make this harder for me than it is," he complained.

Hard on him? Sage formed a fist as though preparing to sock him. "You don't love me anymore. Isn't that what this is really about?"

"No. Everything I said before is true. I do love you, Sage. But, damn, it takes so much of my energy just keeping up." He gave a helpless laugh. "You're like a playful puppy. You require constant attention and affection."

"I haven't noticed you complaining about my affectionate nature before," she said coolly. "In fact you've begged for more on numerous occasions."

He had the grace to look chagrined. "I deserved that. The fact is, Sage," he said, sounding dispirited, "I've run out of steam. You've drained me. I can't keep up with you and devote the time and attention to my studies that they demand. I think we should take a break from each other and give ourselves time to reassess the situation before we jump into marriage."

He touched her for the first time, placing his hands lightly on her shoulders. "When you've had time to think about it, I'm sure you'll agree with me. I'm no more right for you than you are for me. You might believe you love me, but I think you've only talked yourself into it."

She jerked her shoulders free. "Don't start doing my thinking and believing for me, Travis." This must be a bad dream, a nightmare, she thought. Soon she would wake up, call Travis, and tell him about the bizarre dream she had had and warn him never to make it come true.

It was too real, however, to be a dream. Holiday lights twinkled all around her. She could smell evergreen boughs and hear carols playing over the stereo system inside the house. She could feel the pressure of tears behind her eyelids. Humiliation had a brassy taste. She had always been the one who told admirers when it was over. If there was any breaking off to be done, she was the one to do it.

Travis, even tempered and ambitious, had been positively crazy about her. She couldn't believe he was dumping her. Why several months ago, he had pleaded with her to share an apartment with him, which she had declined to do. After sulking for a few days, he claimed to love her all the more for her strong moral fiber.

They rarely quarreled. He had his moments of pique when he could stubbornly take a position and refuse to give way. Like now. When backed into a corner, however, he usually surrendered to her stronger will.

"To tell you the truth, Travis, I'm not big on postponements. Either you love me and want to marry me, or you don't." She tossed back her hair and confronted him challengingly. "Make up your mind. It's now or never."

He looked pained as he studied her determined expression and the belligerent angle of her chin. Finally, he said, "If you put it that way, I guess it's never, Sage."

That knocked the wind out of her, though she managed to maintain a proud posture. Such bald rejection was inconceivable. He couldn't do this to her!

When he had time to think about it, he would regret it. He would come crawling back on hands and knees, begging her to share his bright future as a successful dermatologist. Until then, she'd be damned before she would show him how much he had hurt her. Not a single tear would he see.

Mrs. Belcher was no doubt behind his unheralded decision. His mother could cow Travis with one imperious glance, but Sage wasn't afraid of her. Her hauteur only made Sage want to provoke her further —by doing things like wearing leather pants to her dinner party. When Travis finally came to his senses and crawled back, she would marry him and have six children, evenly spaced ten months apart.

In the meantime, she wasn't going to let Travis off easily. Defiantly she said, "That's finc with me. I'll get out of your life as soon as I pack my things."

"Now?" he exclaimed. "But you can't go now, Sage. Your car's in Austin. Where will you go?"

"I'll manage."

He shook his head with diminishing patience, as though he were dealing with a willful child. "You can't leave now."

"The hell I can't," she fired back, knowing that Laurie Tyler would cringe if she could hear her daughter's language.

"Look, Sage, there's no reason why we can't enjoy the holidays together as we planned. As friends. I still want to be friends."

"Go to hell."

"If you don't come back inside, it'll spoil Mother's party. There'll be an odd number at dinner."

"I don't give a damn about your mother's dinner!" she shouted. "Those stupid little chickens she serves every year are always stringy and tough. I wouldn't go back in there if my life depended on it. It was a stifling, dull, boring party to begin with. I should thank you for giving me a good excuse to get out of it."

Uneasy with the volume of her voice, he glanced over his shoulder. Formally attired guests were milling around the opulent living room, nibbling canapés served by white-coated waiters and toasting the season and each other with highballs and spiked eggnog.

"Sage, be reasonable. I . . . I wasn't going to discuss this with you until after the holidays, but you, well, you sort of forced the issue tonight. I don't want you to feel badly."

"Badly?" she scoffed. "I feel marvelous. Now I can enjoy Christmas without wondering if a society grande dame is going to approve of my wardrobe. Not that I give a fig."

"Don't behave this way," he pleaded.

One of her brows arched malevolently. "What way?"

"Like a high-strung brat."

"First you make me sound as pushy as a Roller Derby queen, then you compare me to an annoying pet, then a simpleton who doesn't know her own mind, and now I'm a high-strung brat. And you claimed to love me!"

"There's no reasoning with you when you get like this." Travis cursed beneath his breath and turned away from her. "Mother will start missing us. I'll see you inside after you've thrown your little temper tantrum." Righteously indignant, he went through the front door.

"Don't hold your breath," she called after him.

The door was decorated with a wreath that in Sage's opinion was extravagant to the point of vulgarity. So was the Christmas tree in the living room. Where were the Santas and candy canes and tinsel they decorated with at her home?

She glared at the gaudy artificial tree through the sparkling windowpanes. The lights placed at precise intervals along its perfect branches began to blur. The tears that had threatened before, now filled her eyes, making the shiny decorations look crystalline.

As her initial anger abated, she began to feel the impact of what Travis had done. Someone whom she loved, whom she believed had loved her, had rejected her.

All that he'd said could be paraphrased in four simple words: "I don't want you." She might be cute and cuddly and capricious, but the bottom line was, he didn't want her. Her zest for life, as he had called it, was irksome to him.

She placed her arms around one of the six fluted white columns supporting the balcony over the veranda. Hugging it, she laid her cheek against its cold, ridged surface. What was she going to tell everybody? How could she hold her head up when word of this got around? What would her own family think? About the only thing they expected of her was to marry someone who loved her as much as she loved him. Well, she had blown that. Like everything else.

How could Travis do this? She loved him. They were perfectly compatible. Couldn't he see that? She liked to maneuver; he would rather be maneuvered. He plodded; she was good at prodding. He was so stolid, he needed someone exuberant in his life—to quote him.

He must be suffering from temporary insanity, she decided. He would come around. Eventually. Her guess was that it wouldn't take too long. He would miss her terribly. Without her, his life would be like his parents', tepid and colorless.

When he did come slinking back with his tail tucked between his legs, and his pride a big goose egg caught in his throat, she would be slow to forgive him for hurting her this way. He had ruined her holiday. They were supposed to be celebrating her earning her master's degree, something neither of her brothers had done. Travis had put a blight on that as well. She would never forgive him.

Stepping away from the column, she wiped the tears off her face, refusing to indulge in them. As a child, whenever her feelings were hurt she had brazened out the situation rather than let her real emotions show. That only tended to invite more ridicule. If she had been a crybaby in front of her brothers, she never would have survived childhood. Not that they would have harmed her; she would have died of her own shame over crying.

Now, she had no choice but to tough it out until Travis realized how foolish he was being. It was absolutely unthinkable that she run home to her family, a jilted woman, tearful and dejected.

First on the agenda was finding a way out of this place. Hell would freeze over before she'd return to the Belchers' party. Nor would she ask for their help, although she knew Mrs. Belcher would gladly see her on her way. Taking a deep breath of determination, she turned toward the corner of the veranda.

She took only one step before drawing up short.

He was loitering against the ivy-covered wall, partially hidden in the shadow thrown by a potted evergreen. There was, however, enough light spilling through the windows for Sage to see him well. Too well.

He was tall and lanky, even thinner than her brother Lucky. Although much of his hair was hidden beneath a damp, black felt cowboy hat pulled low over his brows, Sage could see that the hair above his ears was dark blond, shot through with streaks of pale ivory. Long exposure to the outdoors had left him with a deeply baked-on tan and sunbursts radiating from the outer corners of electric blue eyes, which were regarding her with unconcealed amusement.

He had a firm, square jaw that suggested he wasn't to be messed with, and a lean, wiry musculature that justified the arrogant tilt of his head and his insolent stance.

He was wearing a pale blue western shirt, with round, pearl snap buttons. His jeans had a ragged hem. The faded, stringy fringe curled over the instep of his scuffed boots, the toes of which were wet and muddy. His only concession to the chilly evening was a quilted, black vest. It was spread open over his shirt because he had the thumbs of both hands hooked into the hip pockets of his jeans.

He was about six feet four inches of broad-shouldered, long-legged, slim-hipped Texan. Bad-boy Texan. Sage despised him on sight, particularly because he seemed on the verge of a burst of laughter at her expense. He didn't laugh, but what he said communicated the same thing.

"Ho-ho-ho. Merry Christmas."

Chapter Two

In an attempt to hide her mortification, Sage angrily demanded, "Who the hell are you?"

"Santy Claus. I sent out my red suit to be dry cleaned."

She didn't find that at all amusing. "How long have you been standing there?"

"Long enough," he replied with a grin of the Cheshire cat variety.

"You were eavesdropping."

"Couldn't help it. It would have been rude to bust up such a tender scene."

Her spine stiffened and she gave him an intentionally condescending once-over. "Are you a guest?"

He finally released the laugh that had been threatening. "Are you serious?"

"Then are you part of that?" She indicated the sight-seeing traffic. "Did your car break down or something?"

While shaking his head no, he sized her up and down. "Is that guy queer or what?"

Sage wouldn't deign to retort.

The stranger smacked his lips, making a regretful sound. "The thing is, it'd be a damn shame if you ever got rid of those leather britches, the way they fit you and all."

"How dare—"

"And if you'd squirmed against me the way you were squirming against him, I would have given you the sexiest kiss on record, and to hell with whoever might be looking."

No one, not even her most ardent admirers, had ever had the gall to speak to her like that. If she hadn't shot them herself, her brothers would have. Cheeks flaming, eyes flashing, she told him, "I'm calling the police."

"Now why would you want to go and do that, Miss Sage?" His usage of her name stopped her before she could take more than two steps toward the door. "That's right," he said, reading her mind, "I know your name."

"That's easily explainable," she said with more equanimity than she felt. "While rudely eavesdropping on a conversation that obviously went way over your head, you heard Travis call me by name."

"Oh, I understood everything that was said, all right. Y'all were speaking English. Mama's Boy dumped you, plain and simple. I thought I'd politely wait until he finished before delivering my message to you."

She glared at him with smoldering anger and keen suspicion. "You're here to see *me?*"

"Now you're catching on."

"What for?"

"I was sent to fetch you."

"To fetch me?"

"Fetch you home."

"To Milton Point?"

"That's home, isn't it?" he asked, flashing her a white smile. "Your brother sent me."

"Which one?"

"Lucky."

"Why?"

"Because your sister-in-law, Chase's wife, went into labor this afternoon."

Up to that point, she'd been playing along with him. She didn't believe a word he said, but she was curious to learn just how creative a criminal mind like his could get. To her surprise, he was privy to family insider information.

"She's in labor?"

"As of two o'clock this afternoon."

"She's not due until after the first of the year."

"The baby made other plans. Didn't want to miss Christmas, I guess. She might have had it by now, but she hadn't when I left."

Her wariness remained intact. "Why would Lucky send you after me? Why didn't he just call?"

"He tried. One of your roommates in Austin told him you'd already left for Houston with Loverboy." He nodded toward the windows behind which the guests were being ushered into the dining room.

"All things considered," he continued, "Lucky reckoned it would take me less time if I just scooted down here to pick you up." He pushed himself away from the wall, gave the dripping skies a disparaging glance and asked, "You ready?"

"I'm not going anywhere with you," she exclaimed, scornful of his assumption that she would. "I've been driving to and from Milton Point since I was eighteen. If I'm needed at home, my family will contact me and—"

"He said you'd probably be a pain in the butt about this." Muttering and shaking his head with aggravation, he fished into the breast pocket of his shirt and came up with a slip of paper. He handed it to her. "Lucky wrote that for me to give you in case you gave me any guff."

She unfolded the piece of paper and scanned the lines that had obviously been written in a hurry. She could barely read the handwriting, but then no one could read Lucky's handwriting. Lucky had identified the man as Tyler Drilling's new employee, Harlan Boyd.

"Mr. Boyd?"

One corner of his lips tilted up. "After all we've been through together, you can call me Harlan."

"I'm not going to call you anything," she snapped. His grin only deepened.

Her brother had instructed her to accompany this man back to Milton Point without any arguments. The last two words had been underlined . . . for all the good that would do.

"You could have forged this," she said accusingly.

"Why would I do that?" he asked, giving her that taunting grin again.

"To kidnap me."

"What for?"

"Ransom."

"That wouldn't be too smart. Your family's broke."

That much was true. Tyler Drilling Company was barely making expenses and then only because Marcie Johns had made Sage's older brother Chase a loan when they got married. Because of the sagging oil industry, drilling contracts were few and far between. Presently, the Tylers were among the genteel impoverished. These days that was almost like wearing a badge of honor.

It stung her pride, however, that this reprobate knew about her family's financial difficulties. Her light brown eyes narrowed. "If the company is in such bad financial shape, why did Chase and Lucky put you on the payroll?"

"They didn't. I'm working strictly on commission. Occasionally I get a bonus. Like tonight. Lucky offered me fifty bucks to come fetch you."

"Fifty dollars?" she exclaimed.

He tipped back his cowboy hat. "You sound surprised. Do you figure that's too much or too little?"

"All I know is that I'm not going anywhere with you. I'll drive myself to Milton Point."

"You can't, remember? You left your car in Austin and drove down here with Hot Lips." The lines around his eyes crinkled when he smiled. "I guess you could ask him to take you home. Although his mama would probably have a conniption fit if her little boy wasn't home at Christmastime. But you're not going to ask him, are you, Miss Sage?"

He knew the answer to that before he asked it, and she hated him for it.

While a group of carolers strolled down the sidewalk, harmonizing about peace on earth, Sage stewed. She weighed her options and considered the advisability of leaving the relative security of the Belchers' veranda with a man who looked as though committing felonies was his favorite pastime.

On the other hand, her family was the most important thing in the world to her. If she was wanted at home . . . The note from Lucky looked authentic, but if a crook were clever enough to track her to her fiancé's house . . . .

"What time did you say Sarah went into labor?"

His slow, easy grin could have basted the Christmas turkey better than melting butter. "This is one of those trick questions, right? To see if I'm legit."

Unruffled, she folded her arms across her middle and stared back at him as though waiting.

"Okay, I'll play," he said. "Chase's wife's name isn't Sarah, it's Marcie. Maiden name, Johns. She's a realtor and, every once in a while, Chase affectionately calls her Goosey, his nickname for her when they were in school."

Throwing his body weight slightly off-center and relaxing one knee, he assumed a stance that was both arrogant and pugnacious. His thumbs found a resting place in his hip pockets once again. "Now, Miss

Sage, are you coming peaceably, or are you going to make me work for my fifty dollars?"

She gnawed on her lip. He was correct on several points, chiefly that she was stranded at Travis Belcher's house. She wasn't about to throw herself upon Travis's mercy. Even though Harlan Boyd was a lowlife and her brothers had consigned her to spend time with him—something she intended to take up with them at her earliest possible opportunity—her pride wouldn't allow her to turn to a single soul in that house.

"I guess you don't leave me much choice, do you, Mr. Boyd?"

"I don't leave you any choice. Let's go."

"I've got to get my things."

She tried to go around him, but he sidestepped and blocked her path. Tilting back her head, she glared up at him. It was a long way up. She had inherited the Tyler height from her daddy, just like her brothers. There were few men she could really look up to. It was disquieting. So was the heat radiating from his eyes. So was his voice, which was soft, yet tinged with masculine roughness and grit.

"Given the chance you gave Loverboy, I'd've lapped you up like a tomcat with a bowl of fresh, sweet cream."

She swallowed with difficulty, telling herself it was because her head was tilted back so far. "My sister-in-law once had a phone freak who called her and talked dirty. Now I know just how disgusted she must have felt."

"You're not disgusted. You're scared."

"Scared?"

"Scared that you'd like it if I kissed you."

She scoffed. "I'd like to see you try."

"I was hoping you'd say that."

Her face was still taut with the dire warning she had issued when he cupped the back of her head and drew her up to his mouth for a searing kiss. In less time than it took for her brain to register what was happening, his tongue was inside her mouth, exploring inquisitively.

Bug-eyed with astonishment, she could see beyond his shoulder through the window into the formal dining room. The waiters were moving around the long, elegantly set table, serving Rock Cornish game hens and candied yams to the Belchers' guests while their former-future daughter-in-law's mouth was being scandalously ravaged out on the veranda by a man with a larcenous grin and muddy boots.

If she hadn't been frozen with shock, she would have been laughing hysterically.

Within seconds, however, she regained her senses. Giving his chest a push with all her strength behind it, she shoved him away. Breathing didn't come easily. She gulped oxygen and swallowed air several times before wheezing, "You try another trick like that and you'll wish you hadn't."

"I seriously doubt that, Miss Sage. And so do you." He gave the skies another worried glance. "Before the weather gets any worse, we'd better skeedaddle. Go get your stuff. I'll be waiting for you right here when you come back."

Too infuriated to speak, she marched off.

"This is the lowest, sneakiest trick you've ever played on me," Sage said into the telephone receiver. It stank of tobacco breath and was sticky with God-only-knew-what.

"Sage, is that you? Devon's got her tongue in my ear. You'll have to speak up."

"I know you can hear me, Lucky," she shouted. "I also know my sister-in-law wouldn't neck with you in a hospital corridor. By the way, has the baby come yet?"

"No. Can't be long now though. Better not be. Chase is driving us all crazy."

While her brother apprised her of Marcie's condition and Chase's expectant-father antics, something dark and furry scuttled among the packing crates only a few yards away from the pay telephone. Sage shivered and would have raised her feet off the concrete floor, but there was nowhere to go.

This had to be the worst night of her life. First her fiancé had dumped her, then she was "fetched" home by a smart aleck whose manners were intolerable.

The Belchers' maid had accompanied her up the back staircase to the guest room, where she had helped to pack Sage's belongings. As he had said, Harlan Boyd was waiting for her when she returned. He had placed her in the passenger seat of a car that was surprisingly clean and reasonably new.

However, no sooner had she become resigned to making the long car trip with him, than he took an exit off the interstate highway and turned onto a narrow road that was virtually unmarked and totally unlighted.

"Where are we going?"

She wouldn't panic, she had told herself. These people could sometimes be talked out of their misdeeds if only the victim kept cool. She promised herself she wouldn't reach for the door handle, open it, and hurl herself into the gloomy night until she was certain that his plan was to demand from her family a high ransom in exchange for the whereabouts of her brutally beaten body.

Sounding far more sane than her own thoughts, he replied, "This is the road to the airstrip."

"Airstrip?"

"Where I landed the plane."

"Plane?"

"Are you hard of hearing or what? Stop repeating me."

"You mean we're flying home?"

"Sure. What'd you think? That we were going to drive?"

"Exactly."

"Just goes to show how wrong a person can be. Kinda the way you were about Casanova back there."

She had let that remark pass without further comment and lapsed into hostile silence for the remainder of the trip. It was quite a come-down from the earlier part of the evening when she'd been rubbing elbows with the upper crust of Houston society.

Now she found herself standing in a drafty, damp, rodent-infested airplane hangar, waiting for a man who kissed like he made his living from it and who teased and insulted her every chance he got. He was currently outside, putting the aircraft through a preflight check.

She took out her frustration on her brother, whom she had had paged at the hospital in Milton Point. "Lucky, what were you thinking of to send this . . . this person . . ."

"Are y'all about to leave?"

"Yes, we're about to leave, but I'm furious with you. How could you send a person like him after me?"

"What's wrong with Harlan?"

"What's wrong with Harlan?" She was repeating herself again. "This is a long distance call," she said, trying to massage the headache out of her temples, "and it would take too long to enumerate his bad quali-ties. Why did you send him? Why didn't you just call the Belchers' house and tell me to come home?"

" 'Cause I knew you'd taken Travis's car to Houston and left yours in Austin. Your roommate told me. You had said that Travis's folks weren't too pleased that y'all were coming up here early Christmas morning, so I knew they wouldn't want him to bring you two days early and miss Christmas Eve at home, too. So—"

"Okay, okay, but you could have warned me that I was going to have an escort."

"I'm sorry, Sage, but there hasn't been time. Chase is tearing his hair out and gnashing his teeth. He's worried because Marcie's thirty-six and this is her first baby."

"She's all right, isn't she?" Sage asked, instantly concerned for the woman she admired.

"Basically, yeah. But she's not having an easy time of it. It's all Mother can do to keep Chase civilized, much less calm. You know what this baby means to him. Lauren's fussy because she's cutting a tooth."

"Oh! Her first?"

"Right. Smart little dickens can already bite with it, too. Anyway, Devon's got her hands full with our baby, so it's been kinda wild and hairy."

Sage could imagine the scene at the hospital. Nobody could keep the Tylers away when one of their own was in need. She recalled the night Devon had given birth to Lauren. It had been chaotic. Of course, there had been extenuating circumstances. That night, one of Marcie's clients had assaulted her. Sage had arrived after Marcie had been rescued and hospitalized, but she had empathized with Marcie's terror. It was crises like that that bonded families.

A lump formed in her throat. For all the pandemonium, she longed to be there with them now. "I could have rented a car," Sage said sulkily.

"We didn't want you to. The cold front hasn't reached Houston yet, but it blew through here around noon and it's cold. Wet, too. We didn't want you driving in the bad weather and knew you'd argue about it. So we decided not to give you the opportunity and sent Harlan after you."

"I'd be safer with the weather than with Harlan."

"What was that? I didn't hear it. A cart was wheeled by."

"Never mind." She didn't want to malign Harlan to her brother, who obviously trusted him. It would serve no purpose now but to worry everybody until she arrived safely in Milton Point. Once there, however, she intended to give them a full account of his outrageous behavior. "I'll see you when I get there. Give everyone my love. Especially Marcie."

"Will do. See ya, brat."

Wistfully she replaced the receiver. She was trying to wipe the yuck off her hand when Harlan sauntered up. "Has the baby come yet?"

"Not yet. Soon, Lucky said."

"Plane's ready whenever you are."

"Is there a place I could wash my hands first?"

"This way. Better take care of any other necessities before we leave, too. This is a nonstop flight."

She didn't find him in the least amusing and showed it by sweeping past him when he pushed open the restroom door. When he switched on the light, she drew up short, her back coming into contact with his chest.

"Good Lord." It was a disgusting facility that hadn't been tended to in ages.

"Everything you need," Harlan said, laughter underlying his words.

Sage, tamping down her revulsion, marched into the room and slammed the door in his face. She did only what was necessary, being careful not to touch anything. After washing her hands in the rusty sink, she shook them dry.

Emerging from the corrugated tin building, she found Harlan waiting for her on the tarmac. "Where are my suitcases?"

"Already stowed, ma'am. May I see your boarding pass, please?"

She shot him a drop-dead look. "Can we please get on with it?"

"Don Juan shot your sense of humor straight to hell, you know that?"

Taking her elbow, he ushered her toward a single engine plane. The closer she got to it, the more dismayed she became. It was a wreck, a relic of years gone by. The skin of the fuselage had been patched and repainted so many times, it looked like a quilt. The propeller was whirling, but the engine knocked, whined, and rattled. She pulled her arm free of his grasp and turned to confront him.

"Did you build this heap yourself?"

"It's not mine. I only borrowed it."

"You don't really expect me to fly in it, do you?"

"Unless you've sprouted wings."

"Well, forget it. I've heard ancient sewing machines that ran smoother than that motor. Did my brothers know what you were flying in?"

"They trust my judgment."

"Then I mistrust theirs."

"It's perfectly safe." Taking her arm again, he all but dragged her across the cracked runway. When they reached the passenger side of the aircraft, he palmed her fanny and gave her a boost up to the step on the wing. "Up you go."

She clambered into the tiny cockpit. When he was seated in his pilot's chair, he reached across her chest and made sure the door on her side was fastened securely. His arm slid over her breast. It could have been an accident, but she didn't risk looking at him to find out. She stared stonily through the windshield and pretended that she wasn't tingling all over.

"Seat belt fastened?"

"Hmm."

"Comfy?"

"Fine."

"You might want to take off your jacket," he said, nodding at the short, fitted jacket that matched her pants. The outfit had been her Christmas present to herself. It had been in layaway since August. So far, Harlan Boyd was the only one besides herself who had liked it. That didn't say much for her taste.

"Will you please hurry and take off so I can stop dreading it?" she said crossly.

For the next several minutes, Harlan was busy clearing his takeoff with the "tower," a room on the second story of the large building. He taxied to the end of the runway, waited for clearance, then rolled forward. Sage was tempted to pedal her feet in an attempt to help out.

Long before it seemed to her they had sufficient ground speed, the small craft lifted into the air. Harlan put it into a steep climb that had her reclining in her seat like it was a dental chair.

Gripping the edge of her seat cushion, she risked looking out the window. "I can't see the ground anymore!"

" 'Course not. We're in the clouds."

"What are we doing in the clouds?"

"Will you relax? I flew choppers out to oil rigs in the Gulf for a year or two. This is duck soup."

"This is pea soup. You can't see a thing. How do you know you won't run into something?"

"I know, okay? Once we get above this low ceiling, it'll be smooth flying straight into Milton Point."

"Are you sure you'll know where to find it?"

"I hit the right spot every time. I've got a fail-safe instrument." He glanced at her and grinned.

"Cute," she said shortly. "If you value your job, you'd better cut that out."

"What?"

"The sexual innuendoes."

"Why? Are you going to tattle to Chase and Lucky?"

"They won't think you're near as clever as you obviously consider yourself to be."

He eased back in his seat and stretched his long legs as far as they would go in the tight confines of the cockpit. "Bet you don't tell them a damn thing about tonight."

"Why not?"

"Because I know a better story. The one about you and Hot Lips." His eyes caught the reflection of the instrument-panel lights. "I don't think you're going to give them that story straight, are you?"

"Whatever happened between Travis and me is my personal business," she said indignantly. "How I deal with it, what I tell my family about it, is private. Certainly no concern of yours, Mr. Boyd."

He chuckled. "Nope, you're not going to tell it to them straight. You're not going to tell them that he dumped you. That's okay, Miss Sage." He winked at her. "It'll be our little secret."

She muttered something wholly unladylike and turned her head to gaze out the window. All she could see below the plane was a ghostly, gray blanket of clouds. Looking down made her nervous, so she rested her head on the top of her seat and closed her eyes.

"How long will it take?"

"An hour. There 'bouts. Depending on the turbulence."

Her head sprang up. "Turbulence?"

"Just kidding, to see if you were really asleep. Want some coffee?" He reached between his knees to the floor and came up with a shiny chrome thermos. He passed it to Sage. "Sandwich?" He let go of the wheel in order to open a brown paper sack and peer inside.

At the mention of food, her stomach growled indelicately, reminding her that she'd missed Mrs. Belcher's Rock Cornish game hens. "You concentrate on flying. I'll unwrap the sandwiches."

He handed her the sack. She placed the thermos between her thighs. "Bologna and cheese with mustard," she said, investigating the contents of the first sandwich. She unwrapped the second and lifted the top slice of bread. "Two bologna and cheese with mustard."

She handed him one and bit into the other. Around vigorous chewing, she said, "Mother is usually more creative when she packs a lunch."

"Laurie?" he mumbled around his first bite. "She didn't fix these."

"Where'd you get them?"

"Catering by Moe."

"Who's Moe?"

Harlan swallowed and pulled off another big bite. "Moe. I took his car to the Belchers' house. Guess you didn't meet him. That's right, when he came downstairs, you were in the john. Moe runs the landing strip back there. I asked him to throw together whatever he had handy."

Sage spat the bite of food into her palm. "You're kidding, aren't you?"

"Nope. Say, if you don't want the rest of your sandwich, I'll take it."

She practically threw the remainder of her sandwich at him. It landed in his lap, directly over the faded fly of his jeans. "You don't like Moe's cooking?"

"No! You knew I wouldn't eat anything that came out of that rat motel."

Her fury amused him. "You would if you got hungry enough. Pour me some coffee into the lid of that thermos, will you?"

"Pour your own coffee."

"Fine. But I'll have to let go of the wheel. And I'll have to reach for the thermos."

The thermos was still held securely between her thighs. Harlan smiled at her guilelessly, one of his eyebrows raised into an eloquent question mark.

Sage poured his coffee.

Chapter Three

Ten minutes after Sage's arrival at the hospital, Marcie delivered her baby. Sage had barely had time to hug everybody when Chase barged through the double swinging doors.

"It's a boy!" His face was drawn and haggard, his hair was standing on end, and he looked silly wearing the blue scrubs, but he was beaming a thousand-watt smile.

He had suffered tremendously after the death of his first wife, Tanya. His unborn child had died with her in an auto accident, which had also involved Marcie Johns. Last year, to everyone's surprise, he'd married Marcie.

The details of their courtship and sudden decision to marry remained a mystery to Sage. It wasn't until several months after the civil ceremony that she became convinced they were in love and that the marriage was going to work.

By all appearances it was working exceptionally well. Chase had never look so tired, or so happy. "The baby's perfect," he proudly told them. "Nine pounds seven ounces. Marcie's fine. Real tired though."

"Nine pounds plus? Hmm? Pretty big for a preemie," Lucky said, digging his elbow into his brother's ribs.

"James Lawrence, behave," his mother remonstrated.

"Before y'all go counting it up, I'll admit that Marcie got pregnant on our wedding night."

"You didn't waste any time, big brother."

"I sure as hell didn't," Chase said to Lucky, winking. "By the way, my son's named after you. We decided on James Chase."

"Damn," Lucky said, swallowing hard. "I don't know what to say."

"That's a switch." Chase slapped his brother on the shoulder; both looked embarrassingly close to tears. To prevent that from happening,

Chase quickly looked elsewhere and spotted Sage. "Hey, brat, glad you made it in time."

Chase was ten years older than Sage. He and Lucky were barely two years apart. Her two rowdy brothers had been her tormentors when she was growing up, but she had always adored them. She wanted to believe her affection was reciprocated.

She derived a lot of comfort from Chase's strong hug. "Yes, I made it. Barely," she added, shooting Harlan a dirty look.

"Congratulations, Chase," he said, stepping forward and extending his hand.

"Thanks." After they shook hands, Chase said, "Y'all excuse me now. I want to get back to Marcie."

"Do you want to stay at the house with us tonight?" Laurie offered.

"No thanks. I'll be here as late as they'll let me stay, then I'll go on home."

He began backing toward the swinging doors. Even though he had been eager to share the news of his son's birth with them, Sage could tell he would rather be at his wife's side. She felt a pang of envy at their happiness. No one else was as important to them as they were to each other.

Sage doubted she would ever be so essential to another person, so much the center of someone's universe, a source of light and love. Travis's rejection had reinforced her doubt.

Within a few minutes, a nurse carried James Chase Tyler to the nursery window and held him up for their inspection. "He's dark like Chase," Laurie said, her eyes misting. "He looks like Chase did when he was born. Remember, Pat?"

Pat Bush, the county sheriff, was a lifelong friend of the family. Sage didn't remember a time when Pat wasn't around to lend support if the Tylers needed him. When her father had died several years earlier, he'd been indispensable to them. In Bud Tyler's absence, he'd been a staunch ally, protector, guardian, and friend.

He nodded down at Laurie now. "Sure do. Young Jamie here looks the spittin' image of his daddy."

"Jamie!" she exclaimed. "Oh, I like that. Pat, I think you've just nicknamed my first grandson."

Shortly the nurse withdrew with the squalling newborn. "Guess that's our signal to go home," Lucky said. "Besides, Lauren needs her own bed."

His seven-month-old daughter was asleep in her mother's arms, but the excitement had partially awakened her. She was beginning to fret.

"I need my own bed, too," Devon said with a weak smile. "I've been wrestling her for hours."

"Let me hold her." Sage reached for her niece, whom she didn't get to see often enough. It was just as well. Devon had said that if Sage had her way, Lauren would be spoiled rotten. "You take a break," she said to her sister-in-law. "I'll hold her on the way home—that is, if you don't mind giving me a ride."

She refused to travel another step with Harlan Boyd, especially since the pickup truck waiting for them at Milton Point's small landing strip had been in no better condition than the airplane they'd flown in from Houston.

It wasn't that she was snobbish about the make and model of vehicles she rode in. Her brothers drove company trucks that looked like they'd come through a war. Travis teased her about her car because it rattled. She was driving the same one she'd taken to Austin her freshman year at U.T. She did, however, expect a few small frills, like windows and ignition keys. Harlan had started his pickup by touching two bare wires together. For all Sage knew, it could have been stolen. The passenger-side window was gone. The opening had been plugged up with a square piece of cardboard, which hadn't kept out the cold, damp wind.

Harlan didn't appear to be offended because she chose not to ride with him again. "See y'all," he said, and moved toward the elevators.

Sage was annoyed to notice that as he passed the nurses' station, several pairs of female eyes were distracted from business. They watched his loose-jointed swagger all the way down the corridor. Sage conceded that his hair was an attractive mix of brown, blond, and platinum shades, and that his eyes were spectacular, and that ordinary Levi's did extraordinary things for his rear end, but she hated herself for thinking so.

"I'll take Laurie home," Pat offered.

"We've got plenty of room in our car, Pat," Lucky said. "Save yourself the trip."

"No problem."

They left the hospital en masse. As Lucky pulled out of the parking lot, Sage glanced through the rear window of his car to see Harlan climbing into the cab of his pickup.

"I hope he remembers to deliver my suitcases to the house," she remarked. At the landing strip he'd placed them in the bed of the truck and slung a tarpaulin over them. It was still raining. Hopefully the covering hadn't blown off.

"Who? Harlan? You can count on him."

"Apparently you do."

Lucky glanced up at her through the rearview mirror. "Do I detect a note of snideness?"

He'd given her a golden opportunity to express her opinion of his new employee, and she was going to give it to him. "Either you have an inexplicably high regard for him, or no regard at all for your little sister."

"I hold Harlan in high regard. And you're okay," he said, deliberately trying to get a rise out of her.

In the rearview mirror, she could see the mischief twinkling in his eyes—which she had always thought were the bluest in the world until she met Harlan. Lucky's charm failed him this time, though. Sage had had all the ribbing she could take for one evening.

"Who is this person, Lucky?" she demanded. "He appears out of nowhere, I've never heard of him, you give him a job in the company business, and entrust him with your only sister's life. What's the matter with you?"

"In the first place," Lucky began, curbing his famously short temper, "he didn't appear out of nowhere. Chase met him last year in Houston."

"Oh, well, why didn't you say so?" she asked sarcastically. She shot him a fulminating glare in the mirror. "Houston's crawling with criminals and cutthroats. Don't you read the newspapers? Having met him in Houston hardly makes him instantly trustworthy."

"Chase trusted him."

"Based on what?"

"Gut instinct."

"Then I'm beginning to doubt Chase's judgment. Did Harlan just show up here one day unannounced?"

"About six weeks ago."

Because she'd been studying so hard, she hadn't come home at Thanksgiving. Otherwise she would have met him then. In recent weeks there had been little time to spare on anything except writing her thesis. Her phone calls home had been brief and to the point. During those short conversations, no one had mentioned the new hired hand, by name or otherwise.

"He wanted to sponge off Chase, I suppose," she said.

"Not sponge. He was looking for work. His last job had run out."

"I'll bet. He looks like a vagrant. A sly, shifty no-account who'll probably abscond with the company's profits."

"There aren't any profits," Lucky said dismally.

Devon, who had wisely stayed out of the quarrel, now placed a reassuring hand on her husband's shoulder. "They're hoping some of Harlan's ideas will save the business, Sage."

Sage divided her gaping stare between them. "What? Are you kidding me? *Him? His* ideas? Did I miss something? Did he drop out of the sky? Hatch from a golden egg?"

"Enough, Sage," Lucky said tetchily. "We get your drift. Apparently Harlan didn't make a very good first impression on you."

"That's putting it mildly."

"What did he do that was so terrible, track mud into the Belchers' marble foyer?"

"Much worse than that. He—"

He had eavesdropped on a conversation she didn't want her brothers to know had taken place.

He had said things to her she didn't want to repeat to her brothers because there might be bloodshed.

He had kissed her with a carnality that had stolen her breath. She wanted to pretend that both the kiss and her surprising reaction had never happened.

"Well?" Lucky prompted from the front seat. "He what?"

Quashing every word she had been about to say, she substituted, "He's rude and obnoxious."

"Harlan?" Devon asked, sounding surprised. "He's usually very polite."

Having hoped that at least Devon would share her impressions of him, Sage now felt abandoned. Curtly she said, "I don't like him."

"Well, just steer clear of him, then," Lucky said. "You've got nothing to do with the business, so what do you care who works for it? Soon you'll be married and outta here anyway. Speaking of which, how's the future zit doctor?"

The insult to Travis went unnoticed. Sage's attention had snagged on Lucky's reference to her disassociation from the family business. His offhand, but painfully correct, remark cut deeper than he or anyone else would ever guess.

Naturally she had nothing to do with Tyler Drilling. She was the baby girl of the family. An afterthought. Probably an accident. A hanger-on. Hadn't she come along eight years after her parents' second strong, healthy, overachieving son? The boys were a team, a pair. Whenever anyone in town mentioned the Tyler boys, there was no doubt who they were talking about. She was the Tyler boys' little sister.

Her brothers hadn't been too crazy about the idea of having a baby sister. For as far back as she could remember, they had teased her unmercifully. Oh, she knew they loved her. They would protect her from any and all harm and give her anything she asked of them.

But they were very close to each other, best friends and confidants, as well as brothers. She had never been a part of that special male bonding and was always secretly jealous and resentful of it. It was something she hadn't outgrown.

Quelling her deep-seated hurt, she moodily responded to Lucky's question. "Travis is fine."

"Is he coming up Christmas Day as planned?"

"Uh, I doubt it. He's . . . he's bogged down with his studies. It was going to be inconvenient for him to make the trip in the first place. Now, with Jamie's arrival, Christmas is going to be so hectic. . . ."

At the risk of painting herself into a corner, or telling an outright lie, she let her explanation trail off. The unvarnished truth was that Travis wouldn't be joining them on Christmas Day, period. They didn't need to know anything beyond that.

Once Travis and she were reconciled, she might tell them about the "spell" he'd taken at Christmas, but probably not. It would be a long time before his rejection would qualify as one of those episodes in life that one could look back on and laugh about.

"Damn shame he won't be here," Lucky said with affected sincerity. Devon gave his shoulder a hard nudge.

Any other time, Sage would have lit into Lucky for poking fun at Travis, but, again, his comment went virtually unnoticed. She was experiencing a twinge of conscience and arguing with herself that she hadn't actually told a lie.

Lucky hadn't asked her point-blank, "Are you still engaged to Travis, or did he break it off earlier tonight?" Sage reasoned. She had avoided mentioning it, that's all.

Then why was she haunted by Harlan's gloating grin? Why could she hear the echo of him saying, "I don't think you're going to give them that story straight, are you?"

All her life she'd managed to hide her hurt feelings and screen her disappointments by bluffing. It was unsettling that an imperfect stranger, a tramp like Harlan, had seen straight through her bluff.

Laurie Tyler was never happier than when bustling around her kitchen, the house full of family. She had been a housewife since marrying Bud Tyler when she was eighteen. She made no apology for never having had a career outside the home. It would never occur to her to regret her life because she had always been blissfully happy with all the choices she had made.

She was active in civic and church work and could be depended on to handle either a leadership position or the most menial and thankless task. She was quite comfortable in either capacity.

But in her kitchen, with her noisy, rambunctious family seated around the large table, she was in her element. Tonight she was especially happy because she had been blessed with another grandchild . . . and Sage was home.

Sage had been conceived long after Bud and she had thought their family was complete. The baby girl was an added bonus, like a gorgeous gift wrap on a very special present. Her blond prettiness had dressed up the family. Her personality had given it spiciness.

Laurie entertained no illusions about her daughter, anymore than she did her sons. Sage had many attributes. She also had flaws. She was headstrong and stubborn and had the same trait as Chase of being very hard on herself. Like Lucky, she had inherited the Tyler temper.

She wasn't demure and soft-spoken, qualities some might use to typify the ideal daughter. Not Laurie, who was glad that Sage was more passionate than proper. She preferred vivacity to vapidity, and Sage had plenty of the former.

Laurie loved her daughter in a special way, even though Sage herself sometimes made loving her difficult. She didn't accept or express love easily. As though fearing a rebuff, she always kept a part of herself protected. In that way, too, she was much like Chase and very unlike Lucky, who often let his emotions run away with him.

"Would you like something to eat, dear?" Laurie asked her daughter, unable to resist the impulse of lovingly smoothing her hand over Sage's mane of hair.

"Please, Mother, if it's not too much trouble." Momentarily she rested her cheek on the back of Laurie's hand. Then, as though embarrassed by the childish gesture, she pulled away. "Hmm, Christmas cookies."

"Yes," Laurie replied, laughing as she surveyed the mess on the kitchen countertop. "Marcie went into labor while I was right in the middle of frosting them. As you can see, I dropped everything and ran. We'll finish them tomorrow."

"I'd like that," Sage said, giving her a swift hug before taking a chair at the table.

"I'm so sorry we had to interrupt your holiday plans with Travis."

Laurie dropped a pat of butter into a hot iron skillet and began building a cheese sandwich.

"Don't worry about it."

"Secretly I'm glad you're going to be home tomorrow."

"Me, too."

"Christmas Eve just wouldn't be the same without you here, snooping around all the presents."

"I never snooped!"

"Like hell." Lucky sauntered in and dropped into a chair. "Remember the Christmas that Chase and I unwrapped your presents and replaced what was inside with dead crickets? You wished you hadn't snooped that Christmas."

"Infidel." Sage threw a Frito at him. Grinning, he caught it and ate it.

"I remember that," Pat said. He was leaning against the countertop, snitching raw cookie dough and sipping the coffee Laurie had poured for him. "Bud had to paddle you both on Christmas Eve. Hated like hell to do it. Laurie, you tried to talk him out of it."

"Though Lord knows they needed it for that stunt. Where's Devon, Lucky?"

"She said to tell everybody good-night. She was exhausted."

"For all the tricks you and Chase played on me, it's a wonder I'm not psychotic," Sage remarked.

"I think you are."

She threw another Frito at her brother. This one he threw back. She threw another one. He threw it back too. Soon corn chips were flying.

"Children! I swear, you're worse than three-year-olds."

They were all still laughing when Harlan came through the back door, carrying Sage's suitcases, one in each hand. Whenever Laurie saw him, no matter how briefly or how long it had been since the last time, she was always a little surprised by how handsome a young man Harlan Boyd was.

Quite objectively, she thought her sons were the handsomest men around. That opinion was borne out by the number of ladies they had squired before falling in love and getting married. For his age, Pat, too, was a heartthrob. Plenty of women in and around Milton Point were jealous of his devotion to Laurie.

Harlan, however, was movie-star handsome. Some matinee idols might even envy the angular bone structure of his face and the provocative shape of his mouth. And his eyes . . . One look into those eyes could steal the breath of even an old woman like herself, Laurie thought.

"Thank you, Harlan," she said to him now. "Set those suitcases down there. We can take them up later. Would you like something to eat?"

"No thanks." He removed his damp hat and raked his hand through his thick, tousled hair. "Just some coffee, please."

Laurie poured him a cup. When she turned around to hand it to him, she caught Sage looking at him with such disdain, he could have been one of the crickets her brothers had replaced her Christmas presents with.

Granted, Harlan was a little rough around the edges, but she was disappointed that Sage couldn't feel more charitable toward him.

Then she saw Harlan smile at Sage and wink. No wonder Sage was in a snit. Laurie could barely suppress her smile. He was barking up the wrong tree if he was trying to flirt with Sage. Unless her strong-willed daughter could lead a man around by the nose, the way she did Travis, she wasn't interested.

Harlan, however, seemed unfazed by her condescension. To Laurie's amusement, he continued to stare at Sage while she methodically ate her grilled cheese sandwich and drank two glasses of milk. About the time she finished, Lucky stood up and stretched.

"Guess I'd better check and see if Devon got Lauren to bed okay." He said his good-nights and left the kitchen for upstairs.

"I'm beat, too," Sage said, coming to her feet. "I had a harrowing trip," she added, looking pointedly at Harlan who continued to nonchalantly sip his coffee, though a betraying grin played around his mouth. "Good night, Mother. We'll get on those cookies first thing in the morning." She kissed Laurie's cheek. "Good night, Pat."

Harlan stood up when she went for her suitcases. She waved him back into his chair. "I can get them."

"No problem," he said, lifting the suitcases off the floor.

Sage wrested the handles from his hands and marched from the kitchen without another word. Pat looked at Laurie inquisitively. She shrugged with puzzlement. Harlan returned to the table to finish his coffee.

"It's late. I need to get back to town," Pat said.

"I'll walk you out." Laurie reached for her jacket hanging on the rack just inside the back door and threw it around her shoulders.

Once Pat and she were out of earshot and away from the pools of light coming from the windows, he pulled her into his arms and kissed her. His mouth was warm and mobile over hers. Their kiss was giving, loving, and sexy. He drew her closer, and, for a moment, she submitted to having his hands on her hips before self-consciously stepping back, her cheeks flushed.

"You sure as hell don't kiss like a grandma," he teased.

"You make me behave in a scandalous way," she murmured, nuzzling his neck.

They nibbled on each other before falling into another deep, lasting kiss. Pat placed his large hand inside her jacket and rested it lightly on her ribcage, just beneath her breast. She moved enticingly, letting him know she longed for his touch as much as he longed to touch her. He covered her breast, massaging it gently through her clothing.

Moments later, he released her, making a low groan in his throat. "Laurie, have you thought about it some more?"

She didn't have to ask what he was talking about. Most of their evenings together ended on this subject. "It's all I ever think about, Pat."

"Don't you want to?"

"You know I do."

"You asked me to give you until the holidays. Well, the holidays are here."

"But I didn't know that Jamie was going to arrive early."

"What difference can that make? That's no excuse," he said shortly. "Look, I'm getting fed up with all this sneaking around, stealing kisses, and groping in the dark like a couple of kids. I'm too old for this."

"I don't like it any better than you do."

"Then let's go ahead and do it. Nobody's going to be shocked. Chase already knows about us. They all probably suspect."

"I don't know, Pat," she said uncertainly.

"Laurie, I'm dying," he said, then groaned again. "I want to sleep with you, dammit. I've wanted to for forty years. Why are you making me wait any longer?"

"Sage, for one thing."

"Sage?"

She could tell by his tone that she'd surprised him. "Soon she'll be making wedding plans. I don't want my romance to take any gilt off hers. That would be awfully selfish of me, wouldn't it?"

"It's about time you were selfish. You've spoiled those kids rotten."

"And you've helped me spoil them," she fired back.

"Sage is a modern-thinking young lady. She'll understand."

Indecisively, Laurie gnawed her lower lip. "I'm not sure how she'll take the idea of us being together. She was Bud's sweetheart, a real daddy's girl."

"She was no more devoted to Bud than you or I were." His mouth turned grim. "I want an answer, Laurie. Soon. I won't go on like this indefinitely."

His harsh tone of voice didn't intimidate her. It didn't fool her either. She placed her arms around his neck. "Are you issuing an ultimatum, Sheriff Bush?"

"Take it any way you like."

She moved closer to him. "Don't even think of leaving me, Pat. If you ever leave me, I'll hunt you down and shoot you."

"Damn. I believe you might."

"I would. Count on it."

A smile tugged at his lips for several seconds before he gave into it. "Aw, hell. I ain't going to leave you and you damn well know it." He lowered his head again and kissed her meaningfully. They finally parted reluctantly. He ambled toward his squad car. "I'll be out tomorrow evening to drive you to church."

Laurie waved him off and dreamily moved back toward the house. She had just made it through the kitchen door when a terrible, crashing racket came from upstairs.

"What in the world?" she exclaimed. Her first concern was for Lauren in her crib.

"Sounds like the house is falling down."

Harlan bolted from his chair at the table and ran out of the kitchen, headed for the staircase in the hall. Laurie was right behind him. They scrambled upstairs. Lucky and Devon stumbled from their bedroom. Lucky was in his briefs. Devon was pulling on a robe over her nightgown.

Across the hallway from their room, Lauren had set up a howl from the nursery. Devon went in to calm the baby and get her back to sleep. Lucky scratched his chest and glared darkly, asking, "What the hell was that?"

"*That,*" Sage enunciated, "was your baby sister entering her room and finding that it's been taken over by somebody else." At the end of the hallway, she was standing with both hands on her hips, tapping her foot and bristling with rage.

"Oh, dear," Laurie said with a sigh. "I forgot."

"I reckon there's going to be hell to pay," Harlan said.

"Let me handle it."

"Be my guest," he muttered.

"Sage, dear—"

"Mother, what is this *person*'s stuff doing in *my* room?" she pointed her finger at the center of Harlan's chest.

"That's what I was about to explain," Laurie said calmly. "We invited Harlan to stay with us. He lives here now."

Chapter Four

"Lives here? He lives here? In my room? You took in a vagabond and gave him *my* room?"

"Sage, if you'll calm down—"

"I can't believe this!" Sage cried, cutting Laurie off in midsentence. "Has everyone in this family except me gone daft?"

Devon slipped out of the nursery and quietly closed the door behind her. "Lauren's gone back to sleep."

"Good," Lucky said. "Pipe down, will you, Sage? That shrieking could wake the dead."

He shackled Devon's wrist with his long fingers and drew her across the hallway and into their bedroom, giving her bottom an affectionate pat. "But I sure do appreciate your waking Devon up." Lecherously bobbing his eyebrows, he closed their bedroom door behind him.

Sage glowered at the closed door and muttered, "Animal." Then she returned her attention to her mother and the man who had not only intruded into her life, but had apparently seized control of her home and family. She had never heard of him before tonight, now he was the bane of her existence. What was more, he seemed to be enjoying it.

"What's his stuff doing in my room?" She had lowered her voice only a few decibels in deference to the sleeping baby. "Where are my things, Mother? I can't believe you just moved me out and moved him in without even consulting me."

"Sage, that's enough! Calm down this instant."

When her mother used that tone of voice, it was time to hush up and listen. By an act of sheer willpower, Sage reined in her anger. The way things were going, if she didn't mind her p's and q's, she'd be kicked out into the cold while Harlan Boyd basked in the warmth of her family's love and adoration.

"I *did* ask your permission to rearrange the rooms," Laurie said. "Remember, several weeks ago, I called and asked if I could move some of your things into the guest bedroom?"

"Oh." Reminded of that particular conversation, Sage's accusatory gaze lost some of its angry sheen. "I vaguely remember something like that. I was working on my thesis. I barely listened. But I'm sure you didn't tell me that you had taken in a boarder who was going to reside in my room."

"I sensed your distraction," Laurie explained. "I ended the conversation because I knew your mind was on your studies. I didn't think it was necessary to tell you about Harlan at that time."

"You didn't think I'd want to know that somebody had taken over my room?"

"Sage, you haven't lived in that room since you went away to college almost seven years ago!" Laurie's maternal patience had finally been expended. "You have an apartment in Austin. Soon you'll be married. You and Travis will have a home of your own."

Harlan noisily cleared his throat. Folding his arms over his chest and crossing his ankles, he braced himself at a slant against the wall. Sage saw his struggle to keep a straight face and could have murdered him with her bare hands.

"Married or not, I thought I'd always have a room in the house where I grew up." In spite of her best efforts not to, she sounded wounded and plaintive. Well why not? Without her knowledge, somebody must have declared this Let's-kick-the-slats-out-from-under-Sage Day.

Laurie's expression softened and she drew Sage into an embrace. "Of course you have a room in this house," she told her gently. "You always will. And when you're married and bring your family here, I'll find room to sleep everybody.

"But from now on, Sage, this house will be a stopover for you. You'll be in and out. I transferred your things into the guest room so Harlan could have more space. Otherwise, all that roominess was going to waste. Doesn't that make sense?"

It made perfect sense, but it still wasn't acceptable. The reason was Harlan. If someone else were sleeping in her bed, she wouldn't have minded so much. The fact that it was *him* made her want to chew nails.

In that frame of mind, she said, "One might ask where Harlan planned to stay if he hadn't imposed upon your hospitality."

"In the first place, he didn't impose. I offered him the room. I saw no need for him to stay in that trailer alone."

"Trailer?"

"The Streamline I pulled behind my pickup," he supplied, speaking for the first time.

"No offense, Harlan," Laurie said, laying her hand on his arm, "but it's seen better days. It's probably drafty," she told Sage. "I'm sure he's much more comfortable here."

"Oh, I'm sure he is, too." Sage gushed so sweetly it could have caused tooth decay. "I'm sure he's as contented as a pig in the sunshine. My room has always been very comfortable. At least I've always thought so. Ever since I was a little girl, I've thought it was comfortable."

Laurie frowned a silent but stern reprimand.

"Look," Harlan said, pushing himself away from the wall, "I don't want to be the cause of a ruckus. I'll move my things back to the trailer tonight, so you can have your room back."

"Don't do me any favors," she said tightly, her lips barely moving to form the words. "As Mother said, this house is only a stopover for me."

"Is that right?" His drawl suggested that he knew better.

"That's right," she retorted crisply. "Now, if you'll both excuse me, I'm going to shower and go to bed." She struck off down the hallway, clumsily toting her suitcases, which she felt were about to pull her arms from their sockets. She stopped midway to the guest bedroom and turned back. "I *do* still have bathroom privileges, don't I?"

"That's not funny, Sage," her mother said.

"You're damn right it isn't."

She disappeared into the guest bedroom and slammed the door behind her. Harlan whistled. "I sure as hell didn't mean to cause a family dispute. Sorry, Laurie."

"Don't worry about it tonight. I'll smooth things out with her tomorrow."

"If it would make things easier, I'm more than willing to move back into the trailer. Probably should have stayed there in the first place."

"That won't be necessary," she assured him, patting his hand. "I'm delighted to have you here. You've given Chase and Lucky new hope for the business. In return, providing you with a room while you're here is the least I can do." She glanced down the hallway. "I apologize for Sage's rudeness. She's . . . well, she's rather high-strung."

"Yeah, I noticed that." His grin cancelled any hint of rancor.

"Good night, Harlan."

" 'Night."

Harlan went into the bedroom formerly belonging to Sage Tyler. He felt badly about this. She'd been fun to tease, but he hadn't wanted to really hurt her feelings. Not after what had happened to her earlier in the evening. Strange. She seemed more upset over the room situation than she had been over her breakup with Belcher.

"What a dumb sonofabitch," he said beneath his breath as he pulled off his cowboy boots, hopping on alternate feet while tugging them off.

Sage didn't know it yet, Harlan thought, but she was well rid of Belcher. It might take her a while to realize it, but one of these days she was going to wake up to the fact that she'd been rescued from the maws of unhappiness.

Sure, right now her pride was stung. Her self-esteem had taken a beating tonight. But deep down she was relieved. A smart woman like her had to know she'd been spared making a big mistake.

Life with a dreary wimp like Belcher would make her miserable, Harlan reasoned. She had more spirit, more spunk, more vibrancy in the pad of her little finger than Belcher had in his whole pale body. She shivered with vitality from the top of her head to the soles of her feet. That mama's boy couldn't have satisfied her or made her happy in ten million years.

Especially in bed.

If Belcher had been satisfying her, giving her all her healthy young body craved and then some, she would have protested the breakup more strenuously. She would have cried and kicked and carried on something terrible. She hadn't. Not really. He'd seen women shed more tears over a broken fingernail than Sage had over Belcher.

Getting cold feet might be something Belcher did routinely and she knew it would pass. She could think she had a surefire plan for winning him back . . . or perhaps in her heart she knew she wasn't missing much for having him out of her life.

If the last were the case—and Harlan hoped it was—her sex life with Hot Lips couldn't have been all that great. She had taken it too well for good, satisfying sex to be lying on the sacrificial altar.

Linking Sage Tyler and sex in Harlan's thoughts painted a provocative image in his mind, one which brought a smile to his lips. Damn. In bed, she would be as untamed as a lioness, all tawny and supple and savage.

He sobered instantly.

It wasn't right for him to be envisioning her sprawled across satin sheets as smooth as her skin, hair spread out behind her head, tangled and wild, like her nature.

What the hell do you know about her nature? he asked himself derisively.

A lot. Instinctively he knew that Sage's sensuality had never been tapped—a seductive thought he had no business entertaining. It was wrong. It was also downright dangerous.

The Tylers had been good to him. They'd taken him under their collective wing. He had won their trust. But he knew they'd draw the line at him lusting after their sister. Hell, yes, they would. They wouldn't tolerate that. Nor should they.

He couldn't shake his thoughts though.

His heart had gone out to Sage when he watched her hugging the pillar and crying over that rich nerd. None of the photos of her that he'd seen around the house had prepared him for his first glimpse of her in the flesh. When she moved toward him, her long thighs encased in those leather pants, desire had slammed into his groin like a punch from a prize fighter. Ever since then, he'd been struggling to keep it under control.

Reminded of his discomfort, he unsnapped his jeans and unbuttoned the top button of the fly. He shrugged off his vest and hung it in the spacious closet, then peeled off his shirt, balled it up, and tossed it into the wicker hamper Laurie had provided him. His socks followed the shirt.

He flung back the covers of the bed and lay down, stacking his hands behind his head and staring at the ceiling. This was the position he usually assumed when he needed to think.

Tonight his thoughts centered on Chase and Lucky's kid sister. He wasn't surprised that she was attractive. The two men were attractive, each in his own way. Laurie Tyler didn't look anywhere near her age and could turn the heads of men much younger. She sure had turned the sheriff inside out, Harlan mused, smiling at the thought of the moony-eyed gazes they exchanged when they thought no one was looking.

So, he had it figured that Sage would be as good-looking as the rest of her family. What he hadn't expected was the impact she would have on him. Women were easy to come by. They were just as easy to leave behind when it came time to move on.

This one wouldn't be easy to say good-bye to. Sage would be a bottomless bag of surprises that would be hard to give up. Her roller-coaster range of emotions had captivated his attention as it had never been captivated before.

She had been so prissy when she caught him eavesdropping, he couldn't resist teasing her. She had been so sassy, he'd really had no choice except to kiss her smart mouth into silence. And the kiss had been so damn good, he'd wanted to carry her to bed and have her right then and there.

Recollections of their kiss made his lower body even more uncomfortable, so he unbuttoned another button of his fly. He wasn't proud of this desire. He was ashamed of it. The Tylers trusted him and he would never betray their trust.

On the other hand, they couldn't read his mind. And a man couldn't hang for what he was thinking. He'd been around Lucky and Chase long enough to know that each was madly in love and in lust with his wife. They were virile men who would understand desire.

Still, it wouldn't be too smart to—

His eyes sprang to the door when it suddenly flew open. Sage was silhouetted against the light in the hallway. It was difficult to take her militant expression seriously since she was wearing a bathrobe and her wet hair had been combed back from a recently scrubbed face.

"I want my blanket."

"Pardon?"

He could neither sit up nor stand. Currently it was a physical impossibility. The only activity his body was primed to do was out of the question—he gauged by her expression that Sage wasn't there seeking romance—so he lay as he was.

She marched into the room, not halting until she reached the foot of his bed. "My electric blanket," she said. "It's been mine since I can remember. I always sleep under it in the wintertime. I want it."

"Don't you ever knock before you come barging into a man's bedroom?"

"I was raised with two brothers. I'm used to seeing men in their skivvies."

"Lover-boy, too?" he couldn't stop himself from asking. For one thing, he was honestly curious about her sex life with Belcher. For another, he wanted to provoke her. "Somehow I can't quite picture him in his drawers. Bet he's got knobby knees."

She gave him a look that would have withered a dozen fresh roses in a matter of seconds. "Can I have my blanket, please?"

Harlan cast his eyes down the length of his body toward his bare feet. When his gaze moved back up to her, he said, "Anything you see that you want, help yourself right to it, Miss Sage."

She didn't like that. Not a bit. Her lips narrowed into a straight line of pique. She flung the bedspread to the floor and tugged on the electric blanket until it came free from its military fold between the mattresses. Turning on her bare heels, she stalked toward the open doorway, only to be brought up short when the electric cord ran out. She barely caught herself from falling backward and landing flat on the floor.

"Unless you've got a mighty long extension cord, I reckon you'd better unplug it," he drolly observed.

From where she stood, she yanked the cord from the wall socket. Gathering the blanket against her chest, she glared at him. "You might have buffaloed my whole family, but I'm not fooled. I'm onto you, mister. I don't trust you as far as I could throw you."

"Now that's an interesting thought."

Ignoring him, she continued. "It's amazing to me that my brothers, usually intelligent and intuitive men, have placed any confidence whatsoever in you, much less embraced you as one of the family.

"And don't be flattered by my mother's kindness. She'd feel sorry for a rabid dog, and I consider you much more dangerous. Mother loves everybody unless they proved to be totally wretched, which I fully expect you to prove yourself to be any day now.

"You're very good at your game. I'll hand you that. Even Pat's been fooled, and he can usually spot a con man a mile away. He's fallen for your act, too.

"Well not me," she said, thumping her chest with a small fist. "You might have hoodwinked everyone else, but I've seen you at your worst. I've seen how you operate when you're not turning on the sickening, hokey, phony, good ol' boy charm.

"It's my moral obligation to expose you as a fake and a fraud to my gullible family, and that's exactly what I'm going to do the first chance I get."

"And get me out of your life at the same time," he said smoothly. "Won't that be convenient? Because I'm the only one who knows you're living a lie, right? That's the real reason you don't want me around. I make you nervous. You're afraid I'll let them in on our secret."

Quivering with rage, she headed for the door again, this time reaching it successfully. Windowpanes rattled when she slammed it behind her.

Harlan laughed. She had a hell of a temper when she got riled. Experience had taught him that when a woman's temper was hot, her other passions burned hot, too.

At the thought, he groaned with pleasure and pain. "Oh, to hell with it."

Rather than unbuttoning another button on his fly, he got up and pulled his jeans off altogether. While he was at it, he took off his underwear too. He straightened the bed linens, replaced the bedspread and climbed back in, assuming his original position, but pulling the covers up to his chest in case Miss Sage decided to make another unannounced entrance. Not that what he was sporting could be well hidden beneath the covers, he thought wryly, glancing toward his lap.

She was wrong, of course. She wasn't onto him. Nobody was. Nobody had been for the fourteen years he'd been on his own. A few people might understand his reasons for drifting and living the way he did, but he never gave anybody a chance to form an opinion. He didn't discuss his former life with anyone. Knowing his background might change an individual's opinion of him. At the very least, it would color an opinion.

He wanted to be accepted for what he was today. Now. He wanted to be appreciated for his sharp mind, and innovative ideas, and easygoing manner. He wanted to be judged on what stood in his size eleven boots and nothing more.

He was at peace with the decision he'd made fourteen years ago, but few women would be, not with their natural nesting instincts. Especially not a woman like Sage whose roots went deep and to whom family meant everything. She would never understand his need to roam. Of course, he would never have a reason to ask her to understand his lifestyle. Hell, no.

The sooner she was out of sight and out of mind, the better. Concentrating on the work at hand was going to be difficult, if not impossible, with her on the scene. Hopefully she wouldn't prolong her Christmas vacation. If luck were with him, she would leave as soon as the turkey leftovers ran out.

But until she did, he was going to have one hell of a time keeping his head on straight, his eyes off her, and the fly of his pants feeling comfortable.

Sage woke up to the tantalizing aroma of cooking pork. She grinned into her pillow, feeling warm, snugly, and content in the knowledge that her mother was downstairs preparing biscuits and sausage gravy.

Travis had called her favorite breakfast "country food" and made fun of it.

The thought of Travis brought with it all the unpleasant memories of the night before. They crowded against her contentment and dispelled it.

Her eyes came open. Hanging on the wall she was facing were familiar framed photographs—Sage as captain of the Milton Point High School cheerleading squad, Sage in cap and gown receiving her high school diploma, Sage in a similar photograph accepting her college degree from the dean of the business school at the University of Texas, Sage with her brothers and daddy in Yellowstone National Park, taken during the family vacation when she was seven. Beloved photographs.

Wrong wallpaper. Wrong room.

Then it really hadn't all been a bad dream. This wasn't her room. *He* was residing in her room, using her furniture, sleeping in her bed, wallowing in her sheets. That was the most disturbing thought of all.

She had been eagerly looking forward to Christmas, the burden of school finally having been lifted. Then Travis had started whining about having to divide their time between his family and hers, and she'd had to make concessions to spending the entire holiday at home. He had his nerve, breaking their engagement after getting her to compromise on the time she would be able to spend with her family.

He had his nerve, breaking their engagement, period.

For this, he was going to have to work for her forgiveness. He would find her stingy with it. When he came crawling back, she planned to let him know in no uncertain terms how churlish he'd been to pull this stunt during Christmas and ruin her holiday.

For the past year, they'd constantly talked marriage. They had made plans. They agreed that marriages should be well blueprinted and based on common goals rather than strictly romance. Sexual heat was a shaky foundation to build a life on.

Sage had decided long ago that she would never depend on a man for her happiness. Travis understood that. Likewise, he wanted his wife to be committed to the success of his medical practice. She loved Travis. Hadn't he admitted last night that he loved her? But they were more practical about love than some couples.

Travis could be driven to passion, just like any man. They'd had their steamy moments together. But it wasn't as though his center of gravity was in his loins. He didn't possess that raw, animal sexuality like her brothers. Not like—

Her mind snapped closed around the traitorous thought. She would not allow that man to spoil another minute of her holiday. She would put him out of her mind.

Unfortunately, her mind had a will of its own. Emblazoned upon it was the image of Harlan Boyd lying in the middle of her bed. It was almost too short for him. The crown of his blond head had been touching the headboard; his long legs had reached nearly to the foot of it.

He hadn't attempted to make himself more decent, but had just lain there, one knee bent and slightly raised. She'd seen layouts of naked men in *Playgirl* that didn't come close to being that sexy. It was sexier than being naked, lying there with the top snap and two buttons of his fly undone.

It disturbed her that she remembered it in such vivid detail, but she was absolutely certain that she was right. Two buttons had been undone. She had seen the elastic waistband of his shorts.

She had a clear mental image of his chest, wide and muscular and covered with fuzzy, brown hair. His stomach and belly were well muscled. She could have bounced a quarter off his abdomen, it was so tight. He hadn't even had the decency to take his hands from behind his head. Instead, he had exposed his underarms, which were lined with patches of soft hair.

He'd known all those nurses at the hospital were gawking at him. The jerk was well aware of his good looks. And he *was* good-looking, if the scoundrel type appealed to you. He was a conceited exhibitionist. When she went into the room, had he stammered apologies for being caught without his shirt? No. Had he clambered to cover himself? No.

Instead, he had lain there with that insufferably complacent smile on his face, looking like he was either thinking about having sex, or had just had sex, or—she recalled the smoldering heat in his eyes—was waiting to have sex.

His thoughts might have been dirty, but at least he wasn't. The bedroom had been as neat as she had ever kept it, neater in fact. She'd noticed at the kitchen table, while she'd eaten her sandwich under his steady blue stare, that his nails were clean and trimmed. He didn't smell bad. In fact, in the cockpit of the airplane she'd caught a whiff of her favorite men's fragrance. His clothes certainly made no fashion statement, but they were right at home in Milton Point. He spoke with a Texas twang but sounded quite literate. He hadn't made any blatant grammatical errors.

However, his limited virtues hardly made up for his gross character flaws. How dare he kiss her like that? It had been a kiss straight out of an X-rated movie, which was probably the only kind of movie he went to see. She'd never been kissed like that. Not even Travis—

Judiciously she didn't carry the comparison of Harlan to Travis any farther. Loyally, she told herself the comparison wouldn't be fair to Travis, but she didn't delve into precisely why it wouldn't be.

All she knew was that Mr. Harlan Boyd was the most annoying, aggravating, and arrogant individual she'd ever had the misfortune to meet, and he'd witnessed her most humiliating moment.

No way on earth could she live with that. It was untenable. Since he had bamboozled her family and made himself indispensable to Tyler Drilling, she could eliminate hopes of his disappearing any time soon.

Her only alternative was to get Travis back quickly. "Then we'll see who laughs last, Mr. Boyd."

Chapter Five

Single file, the Tylers paraded down the center aisle of the church for the midnight candlelight service. Attending was a Christmas Eve tradition that hadn't been broken for decades. Everyone in the family was expected to be there. This year, for obvious reasons, Chase and Marcie had been excused.

"But we have Harlan with us to take up the slack," Laurie had said happily as she slid her arms into the coat Pat had held for her.

Sage had patently ignored Harlan as the family gathered in the entry hall of the ranch house before leaving for town. He'd been away from the house all day, so she hadn't seen him since the night before.

That morning, she had visited Marcie in the hospital and taken another look at her nephew Jamie. The rest of the day she had been occupied with baking cookies and eleventh hour shopping. The prevailing Christmas spirit had lightened her dark thoughts of Travis.

Her holiday mood was squelched, however, when Harlan came loping down the stairs as they were preparing to leave for church. Failing to take the hint that she didn't want to acknowledge him, he sidled up to her as they were crossing the front porch.

"You don't mind if I go to church with y'all, do you, Miss Sage?"

"I do indeed. You're not family." She gave him a condescending onceover. He wasn't dressed up by any means, but he had on black slacks and a white shirt under a brown leather bomber jacket that looked battle-scarred. "But I suppose I should be glad that you won't disgrace us."

Grinning in the manner that made her grind her teeth, he lunged forward and opened the car door for her. Before he had a chance to get in beside her, she soundly closed it.

It was well known by the rest of the congregation that the third pew from the front was tacitly reserved for the Tylers. They had occupied it for as long as Sage could remember. Their processional down the aisle created quite a commotion. They were carrying the candles each of them had been issued at the church door, their programs, their coats, and baby Lauren and her paraphernalia.

Pat Bush stood aside and let Laurie precede him into the pew. She had taken only a few steps when she backed into the aisle again and whispered, "I'd like to sit beside Sage. You go ahead." Pat went in first and moved to the end of the pew, followed by Laurie and Sage.

Glancing over her shoulder, she was relieved to see Devon moving in behind her. Lucky came next. Then Harlan. Thank heaven she had avoided having to sit beside him.

She looked toward the front of the church and let the ambiance seep into her. The altar and choir loft were decorated with bright red poinsettias. The organist and pianist were playing a Christmas medley. The atmosphere was hushed and reverent.

". . . but if she starts crying, we might need to slip out."

Sage was distracted by Devon's whispering.

"Good idea. We'll swap places with Harlan." Lucky didn't know how to whisper. His voice could be heard throughout the sanctuary. The pastor, sitting near the podium, frowned down at him, as he had been doing from the pulpit every Sunday of Lucky's life since graduating from the nursery.

Harlan stood up, Lucky scooted to the aisle seat, and Devon moved next to him, leaving a vacant space beside Sage. Harlan shuffled between the pews, trying to avoid feet and knees, and dropped into the space beside her.

Her back stiffened and she groaned audibly.

Leaning toward her, he whispered, "Did I step on your toes?"

"No."

"Did I bump your knee?"

"No."

"Were you groaning because I didn't?"

Her head whipped around in time to see him turn his attention to the podium and assume a righteous countenance. Steaming, Sage moved as close to her mother as she could get, so that even her clothes wouldn't be touching Harlan.

The yuletide medley ended on a crescendo. The pastor stood in the pulpit. The service always began promptly at eleven-thirty so that it could conclude at midnight.

"Hi, everybody."

Chase whispered to them from the outside aisle, leaning in over Pat's shoulder. His smile was for all of them seated along the pew.

"Oh, you got to come!" Laurie gladly exclaimed in a stage whisper.

"Marcie insisted that I not miss it on her account."

"How's Jamie?"

Chase grinned like only a new father can. "Wonderful." He cast an apologetic glance toward the pastor, who seemed to be waiting for the Tylers to get situated before starting the service. "I'll just sit up here," he whispered, and moved to take a seat in the row in front of them.

"You'll do no such thing. We can make room," Laurie said. "I want all of us to sit together. Scoot in, Pat."

They shifted again, barely making room for Chase and getting settled before the minister asked them to bow their heads for the opening prayer.

Sage's mood was hardly spiritual. She was crammed against Harlan's side. Her thigh was pressing his from hip to knee. Their shoulders battled over the forward position until Laurie nudged her and admonished her to be still. She had no choice but to relent and place her arm and shoulder behind his.

He stared forward, seemingly enraptured with the reading of the scriptures. Sage knew better. The soft lighting reflected the mirth in his blue eyes. He placed unnecessary pressure on her arm with the back of his. When he reached for the hymnal, she was sure the brush his arm gave her breast was no accident.

The thirty-minute service seemed to drag on interminably. At last the lights were turned off and ushers moved down the aisles with candles, lighting those of the people sitting on the aisles.

When Lucky's was lit, he turned to Devon and, after touching the flame of his to the wick of hers, kissed her softly. Devon, being careful of the baby, held her candle to Harlan's.

Sage held up her candle as he turned toward her. He didn't look at their touching wicks, but at her. Feigning indifference, she lifted her eyes to meet his gaze. Just as her wick ignited, something leaped inside her chest, as hot and spontaneous as the flame at the top of her candle. For a moment, she was held captive by his blue stare. Then quickly, shakily, she turned to light her mother's candle.

She refused to look at Harlan again during the candle lighting process. She sat with head bowed, staring at the burning candle held between her perspiring, unsteady hands. She tried to convey a picture of piety. Surely everyone would think that she was at prayer and not riotous with confused emotions.

Her insides churned. Her mouth was dry one minute and profusely salivating the next. It took all the self-discipline she possessed not to look at Harlan again. She was distinctly aware of every place her body was touching his. She felt lightheaded.

She had never felt this way before, and it was frightening. Maybe she was coming down with the flu. She felt uncomfortably warm and unaccountably flustered.

Her knees were weak and would barely support her when the pastor signaled for the congregation to stand. A cappella, they sang "Silent Night," before extinguishing the candles and filing out of the church while the chimes tolled midnight.

This had always been a reviving, uplifting moment for Sage. But tonight, as she moved toward the exit, the pounding of her heart had nothing to do with the spirituality of the moment. She had a guilty notion that it was carnal in nature.

"I'll have to skip the cider and cookies tonight, Mother," Chase told Laurie when they reached the parking lot. "This is our first Christmas together. I want to spend as much of it with Marcie as possible."

"I understand," Laurie said, hugging him. "We'll miss you. Give Marcie our love."

"See you tomorrow."

"Then you are coming for dinner?"

"I wouldn't miss that," he called back as he jogged toward his car.

Sage rode home with Pat and Laurie, while Harlan rode with Lucky's family. During the drive, they discussed the church service and Jamie and plans for Christmas Day, but Sage was uncharacteristically subdued.

It distressed her that Harlan Boyd had sparked such a drastic physical response in her. She had never been so sexually aware of a man in her life, not even the man she'd been planning to marry. Nor did she believe she could have been that tuned into him, to the point of being aware of each breath he took, if he hadn't been equally tuned into her.

Nonsense. It was the season. Christmas did crazy things to people's minds, made them believe in Santa Claus and such.

To be on the safe side, however, she avoided Harlan as she helped her mother set the table. Earlier they had prepared sandwiches and dips. A kettle of wassail was simmering on the stove. In deference to the occasion, they used the dining room, but Christmas Eve was always casual.

"Did you hear from Travis today?"

Sage choked on the cookie she'd been chewing when Laurie asked the unexpected question. "Uh, no, but he, uh, his family had plans for most of the day and tonight. I didn't expect to hear from him. Pat, another sandwich? You've only eaten two."

She teased the sheriff in an effort to divert attention away from herself. Only one person at the table wasn't fooled by her bluff. When she risked looking at Harlan, he winked at her.

Later, carrying a tray of dirty dishes into the kitchen, she met Harlan coming through the back door, his arms loaded with Christmas presents. She didn't even acknowledge him.

However, as he passed her, he leaned down and, placing his lips directly against her ear, whispered, "You lie real well, Miss Sage. They don't suspect a thing."

The shock of feeling his lips and breath on her ear nearly made her drop the tray. She slammed it down onto the counter. Dishes rattled. "I did not lie! I didn't expect Travis to call me today. And while I've got you alone, I want you to know that I didn't appreciate what you were doing to me in church."

"Probably not. But you *liked* it."

Before she could refute him, he slipped through the door.

Laurie, Devon, and Sage were in the kitchen by seven o'clock the following morning, preparing Christmas dinner. Laurie fretted over the turkey, which she was afraid would either be undercooked or over-done.

Sitting at the kitchen table, Harlan ate a light breakfast and then volunteered to carry in firewood and build a fire in the living room fireplace. Laurie blessed him with one of her special smiles. Sage pretended he was vapor.

Lucky came in, saying to Devon, "Lauren's been fed, bathed, and is down for her nap."

Sage dropped the celery stick she'd been chopping and turned away from the counter, her jaw hanging slack. "You're kidding!"

"What?" he grumbled as he poured himself a cup of coffee and opened the Dallas newspaper.

"The former stud of Milton Point, ladies' man extraordinaire, gives his baby daughter baths?"

"Yeah, and I'd better be the only man who ever bathes her."

"Why, Lucky, what a strange thing for *you* to say," Devon cooed, batting her eyelashes in mock surprise. He snarled at her, then buried his head in the newspaper, coming up several minutes later to exclaim,

"Hey, Devon, this is your best article yet. No wonder you're syndicated statewide. Have you read it, Mother, Sage?"

They both answered that, yes, they had read her Christmas editorial about the homeless in America and that it was both insightful and poignant.

Midmorning, Pat arrived bearing gifts. Lucky took them from him to place beneath the tree in the living room.

"When can we open our presents?" Sage asked.

"After dinner."

"Aw, Mother. *After* dinner?"

"Yes, after dinner."

Plans changed, however, with the unexpected arrival of Chase and his family. Laurie burst into tears when he laid her first grandson in her arms. She immediately forgot the turkey and retreated to the rocking chair in the living room with the newborn. Chase solicitously helped Marcie into an easy chair, though in Sage's opinion she seemed perfectly capable of moving under her own power.

"I hope you'll have enough room for us at the table," Marcie said, laughing. "I know you weren't counting on my being here, but when the doctor released me this morning, Chase and I decided we'd come out for a while."

"Just until she gets tired." He laid his arm across her shoulders. "Doesn't she look great?"

She did. Her red hair was falling loose and full on her shoulders. If anything, her gorgeous complexion had improved with pregnancy. Her figure was fuller, too.

"This really made my Christmas," Laurie said, nuzzling Jamie's sweet-smelling neck.

Everyone clustered around to admire the newborn. Sage suggested that since everyone was already there, they might just as well open their presents. She was indulged.

Pat played Santa Claus, removing the gifts from beneath the tree that was decorated, in Sage's opinion, as a Christmas tree should be. Among the candy canes and tinsel were ornaments that her brothers and she had made in school. Not even the most amateurish efforts had ever been destroyed, but were proudly displayed each year.

She was delighted with all her gifts, but especially with the new riding quirt from Chase and Marcie. "I know you'd never touch it to animal flesh," he said, affectionately tugging a lock of her hair, "but it looks good."

"Here's one more for you, Sage," Pat said, handing her a gift-wrapped box. "This is from . . ." Pat consulted the gift tag. "From Harlan."

"Harlan!" Her tone suggested that he was a descendent of Attila the Hun. Ameliorating it somewhat, she glanced at him and mumbled, "We only met night before last. You really shouldn't have."

"Oh, I wanted to."

His earnestness set her teeth on edge.

"What is it, Sage?" Laurie asked.

She unwrapped the package. "It's a bookmarker."

"There's a quotation on it," he said, making certain everybody's attention was called to it.

Sage scanned the swirling calligraphy, then scowled at him.

"What does it say, Sage?" Chase wanted to know.

"Read it to us."

"It's just a quote from H. L. Mencken," she told them all, hoping that would suffice. It didn't. They all looked at her expectantly. She was in the spotlight and on the spot, which was exactly where Harlan had wanted to place her. With absolutely no inflection, she read, " 'Conscience is the inner voice which warns us that someone may be looking.' "

Lucky laughed. "You should have given that to me."

"What have you done to have a guilty conscience about?" Devon asked, her eyes narrowing.

Everyone's attention moved to them. Sage, glaring at Harlan, stuffed the bookmarker back into the shallow box and stood. "I'll go check the turkey." Feeling his laughing eyes boring a hole into the center of her back, she retreated.

In spite of Harlan's presence at the table, Sage enjoyed Christmas dinner enormously. It was so good to be at home, surrounded by the people she loved. During the meal, she realized that she was more relaxed than she'd been in a long time, and it was because Travis wasn't there.

He had always annoyed her brothers, and their wisecracks had always annoyed him. Sage had been caught in the middle, trying to pacify all of them and to reassure Travis that teasing was a Tyler family tradition. Today, it was a relief not to have to pander to his supersensitivity.

As though her thoughts had conjured him up, the telephone rang just as they were clearing the table. Laurie went to answer. "Sage, it's for you. Travis."

As she left the dining room for the hall telephone, she shot Harlan a smug glance over her shoulder. Taking the receiver from her mother, she raised it to her ear and, loud enough for everyone in the adjoining room to hear, said, "Merry Christmas, darling."

"Uh, Merry Christmas." It was obvious he was taken aback. He hadn't expected her to sound so joyful. "I just called to make sure you'd gotten home all right."

"You shouldn't have worried about me. I made it fine."

"Well, uh, that's good. I'm relieved."

He didn't ask how she had made it. Didn't he care? Wasn't he curious? For all he knew she could have hitchhiked and been picked up by a sexual deviate . . . which, when she considered some of the things Harlan had said and the way he had kissed her, wasn't far from what had happened.

"Marcie's baby was a boy," she told Travis. "He's been nicknamed Jamie."

"Really? That's nice."

"Wait till you see him, Travis. He's so cute."

"Sage, I . . . What I mean to say is that nothing's changed. The only reason I called was to see that you were safe. You weren't in a very stable frame of mind when you left. The maid found the bracelet I gave you lying on the end table in the guest bedroom."

"That's right."

"I wanted you to have it, Sage."

"Why?"

"Well, you know, I felt so rotten about having to tell you that we were off. It hit you hard. I could see that. Now that you've had time to adjust, how are you taking it? I don't want you to be too upset."

So, he wasn't calling with reconciliation in mind. He wasn't offering her apologies and an olive branch, only condolences and a gold bangle bracelet to salve his conscience.

By the tone of his voice, she realized that he never was going to come crawling back. Over the last couple of days, she had been deceiving herself into thinking that he might. This was for real. It was final. What she heard in his voice wasn't contrition and appeal, but pity.

How dare he be that conceited! Had he expected her to jump off a bridge? Or, having made it home, be prostrate in bed with cold compresses over her tear-bloated eyes? Apparently so.

Not bloody likely, she thought angrily. And she would rather have a shackle around her wrist than the bracelet he had given her as a consolation prize. She wished she had the opportunity to cram the thing down his throat.

Ever mindful of eavesdroppers, she said cheerfully, "Well I must run, Travis. Thanks for calling. Merry Christmas."

Replacing the receiver, she gripped it hard for several seconds, as though wanting to extract bravado from it. She still didn't intend to spoil everyone's holiday by announcing that Travis and she were no longer getting married. Until she could figure out a graceful way to break the news to her family and save face, she planned to brazen it out.

But she needed a moment to collect herself. Rather than returning to the dining room, she rushed upstairs. As she approached the door of the room she was now sleeping in, she heard voices coming from the other side.

Marcie was lying on the bed. Jamie was at her breast, sucking greedily. Chase was adoring both. "Oh, I'm sorry, Sage," Marcie said when she saw her standing in the doorway. "We'll go someplace else."

Masking her distress behind a smile, Sage breezed in. "Don't be silly. I just came in to repair my lipstick."

She moved to the vanity table and checked the mirror for signs of discomposure on her face. None were visible. She used a tube of lipstick, then crossed to the bed and sat down on the opposite side from Chase, who couldn't take his eyes off his wife and child.

The threesome embodied familial bliss. Tears threatened again, but they were easily explained. Everyone got emotional over babies. "Jamie is beautiful, you two," she said gruffly. "Truly beautiful."

"Thank you. We think so too." When Marcie and Chase's eyes met, they looked at each other with such naked love and devotion that Sage felt like an intruder. After a moment, Chase said, "I've barely had a chance to say hello, brat. We're damned proud of you for getting that master's degree."

"Thank you."

"It's a shame Travis couldn't be here to celebrate Christmas with us," Marcie said with commiseration. "I think Jamie and I ruined your plans."

"It doesn't matter. We—"

If she could tell anybody that her engagement was off, it would be Chase and Marcie. Marcie was extremely sensitive to other people's feelings. Chase had always been more serious than Lucky, who would either demand to know how dare the sonofabitch jilt his sister or tease her until she couldn't stand it.

But Sage couldn't bring herself to admit her failure yet. They would offer condolences, too. Their pity, like Travis's, would be intolerable.

To spare them all an awkward scene, she perpetuated the myth that she was still engaged.

"We had changed plans so many times already, once more didn't matter."

"Hey, Chase." Lucky knocked on the door. "Can you tear yourself away from your wife and kid long enough to watch the Cowboys kick the Redskins' butts?"

Chase looked at Marcie inquiringly. She laughed. "I couldn't possibly ask you to miss that."

"I could watch the game at home."

"No. Enjoy the day. I'm fine. After Jamie's finished here, I'll stay and rest for a while."

"Sure?"

"Sure."

He bent down and kissed her lips before leaving the room. Marcie's eyes followed him from the room, before they returned to Jamie. He had stopped sucking. She cupped her breast and moved it aside, her nipple popping from his mouth.

Sage extended her arms. "Do you mind if I hold him?"

"Not at all." Sage had learned how to handle an infant when Lauren was born, but she lifted the baby gingerly. Observing her, Marcie said, "You're getting a lot of practice before having one of your own, which shouldn't be too much longer."

Sage shook her head emphatically. "No, I don't think so."

"Haven't Travis and you talked about having children?"

"Oh, sure. But we planned to postpone it for five years at least."

"You've been that specific?" Sage nodded, and Marcie laughed softly as she settled against the pillows behind her. "Sometimes it doesn't work out that way."

"Chase said you got pregnant on your wedding night."

"That's right, even though we thought we were protected against it. Thank God we weren't," she said, gazing at her son lovingly.

Sage bent her head over the infant sleeping in her arms and rubbed her cheek against his soft, warm head. "Amen to that. He's an angel."

After a while, she returned the child to his mother. Marcie seemed content to lie there and watch him as he slept. She was perfectly serene, secure in the knowledge that she loved and was loved, where before she had been so career-driven.

"What about your business?" Sage asked.

"I'm taking a leave of absence, at least until Jamie is weaned and goes on a bottle. I have two agents selling for me now. Esme runs the office like a boot camp. Things are well in hand."

Sage felt a stab of envy for Marcie, just as she had for Devon earlier that day. She wasn't that much younger than either of them, yet she had accomplished so little. She didn't have a career. She wasn't diligently pursuing one. She didn't have a child who depended on her for its very existence. She didn't have a man who worshiped and adored her and wanted her forever as his partner in life.

Suddenly the walls of the room closed in on her, as suffocating as her own sense of worthlessness. "I think I'll try out my new riding quirt." With no more explanation than that, she virtually ran from the room.

She had dressed in her leather pants that morning, so she didn't have to change clothes. Within minutes of leaving the house via the back door, she was saddled and galloping across the open pasture.

It was a glorious day. The sky was so clear and blue, it hurt the eyes to look at it. The sun was warm on her face, but the wind was cold. As it tore through her hair, it brought tears to her eyes. At least that's how she explained them to herself.

What did her life amount to? Nothing. Where was she going? Nowhere.

Marrying Travis Belcher had seemed like the ideal thing to do when they began dating. Now she acknowledged that he had been right—she had only talked herself into believing she loved him. They had had a risk-free relationship. It had been safe because she didn't love him enough for him to hurt her. His *rejection* hurt, yes, but not because she was emotionally bonded with him.

There, she had admitted it. She hadn't been as much in love with Travis as she had been with the ideal that he represented. So losing Travis, the person, was no great loss, except that it left a gaping hole in her future where marriage to him had previously been scheduled. That was the loss that hurt. That's what she was crying over. What was she going to do with the rest of her life?

If she told her family what she really wanted, they would be flabbergasted. They would pat her on the head and tell her that it was an amusing notion. None would take the "brat" seriously. They never had.

Her horse grew tired long before she had decided what action she should take next. All she had resolved was that she couldn't withstand another grievous disappointment right now. So, for the time being, her secret ambition would remain a secret.

She walked the gelding back to the stable, rubbed him down, and gave him a bucket of oats. Leaving his stall, she saw movement from the corner of her eye and turned to find Harlan lounging against one of the double doors.

"What do you want?" she asked crossly, hoping that her mascara hadn't left muddy tracks on her cheeks.

"Just getting some fresh air and stretching my legs."

"I thought you were watching the football game."

"It's halftime."

"Who's winning?"

"Redskins."

"Figures."

"You're not in a very festive mood. I thought Hot Lips's telephone call would cheer you up."

"It did."

"Did he beg for your hand back?"

"He made some overtures," she said coyly. "I told you he would come around." She lied brazenly. Her conscience didn't apply when it came to Harlan. "Every bridegroom gets premarital jitters and tries to back out at least once before the wedding."

"Not every bridegroom."

"Have you ever been one?" she demanded, planting her hands on her hips.

"Can't say that I have."

"Then how in hell do you know what they do or don't do?"

He whistled. "Cussing, too. We really ought to do something about this blue funk you're in."

"I lost the Christmas spirit the moment I opened that stupid present you gave me."

He grinned unrepentantly. "You didn't like it? When I saw it, it cried out, 'Buy me for Sage.' "

"You should have saved your money."

"Well, now I really feel responsible for your lack of holiday merriment." He glanced above his head. "Maybe that would help."

She looked up. A fresh sprig of mistletoe was hanging from the doorjamb. "Who put that there? It wasn't there earlier." She leveled a gaze on him. "Oh, that's cute."

"Call it charity. I figured you'd be missing Travis. Since he's not here to give you a Christmas kiss . . ." He raised his arms at his sides as though offering himself to her service.

"Are you serious?" she exclaimed.

"Never more so."

"You expect me to kiss you?"

Sliding his hands into the back pockets of his jeans, he tilted his head to one side. "Why not? It won't be the first time."

"I didn't kiss you before."

"That's not how I remember it."

"You forced it on me by rubbing our mouths together."

"Fun, wasn't it?"

"Hardly."

He laughed as he sauntered toward her. "Come on, what do you say?"

"No."

"How come?" He had moved so close they were almost touching. His eyes were heavy lidded, impelling. "Scared you might like it again, even more than you did the first time?"

His challenge was as brassy as a trumpet. No Tyler, particularly Sage, had ever backed down from a dare. She had picked up every gauntlet her brothers had ever tossed down. If she hadn't, she would have been called a chicken and a crybaby. Harlan had probably guessed that and was using it to goad her. Even so, Sage couldn't back down from such a flagrant challenge.

"Oh, what the hell? One kiss under the mistletoe. What's the big deal?"

Chapter Six

The big deal was that he knew how to kiss.

The big deal was that if a panel of expert kissers were ever asked to appear on "Donahue," Harlan Boyd would serve as chairman.

The big deal was that she felt the kiss straight through her body to her toes.

She had planned to call his bluff but keep the kiss short and chaste, to show him that she wasn't intimidated by his dare. Even when he cupped her head between his hands and tilted it back like he meant business, she hadn't panicked. She could handle this. He was only a man. This was just a kiss.

But before she realized quite how he had accomplished it, her lips had been seduced to separate and she was receiving his tongue. Receiving was the appropriate word. He hadn't forced his way inside her mouth with brutal thrusts. He didn't make hit or miss stabs at the seam of her lips like some of her less talented boyfriends had done in their vain attempts to thaw her.

His tongue entered nonaggressively, stroked lazily, explored leisurely, tasted thoroughly. The only thing abrupt and shocking was her response. His lips were firm, not loose and floppy. He applied just the right amount of pressure and a delightful degree of suction. His mastery was startling, but too marvelous to stop. it would be like cutting off the hands of a gifted magician.

Harlan spun his own kind of spell. Her stomach fluttered weightlessly, yet her limbs felt heavy. She was lightheaded, but her earlobes throbbed with an infusion of pressure. Her breasts tingled, especially her nipples. Between her thighs she experienced a dull, feverish ache.

Without releasing her mouth, he moved his hands from her head to

her shoulders. They slid down her back, then over her derriere. He
pulled her against the front of his body.

Feeling his hardness, Sage whimpered. Her knees went weak, much
as they had the night before in church. Her bones seemed to have
liquified, so she leaned into him for support. Her mouth clung to his.
She laid her hands on his shirt, her fingers involuntarily curling into his
sturdy chest.

"Damn, Sage," he muttered, momentarily lifting his lips off hers and
gazing down at her.

Her eyelids were afflicted with the same lassitude as the rest of her
body. She could barely lift them. Later, she knew she would bitterly
regret this, but right now, she thought she would die if he didn't go on
kissing her.

Apparently he was of the same mind because he walked her backward into the barn, out of the doorway where they could be spotted by
anyone inside the house who might glance out a window. He didn't
stop until her back came up against the slats of the first stall.

Barn smells filled her nostrils. Animal flesh and fresh hay and old
leather . . . and Harlan. His smell was a mix of man and cologne and
outdoors and sunshine. Healthy. Sexy. Masculine.

As his head lowered to hers again, she reached for his lips with her
own. When his tongue slid into her sweetly receptive mouth, he made a
low, wanting sound and angled his body against hers, pressing into her
softness. She reached up and sank her fingers in his hair.

By the time they broke apart for breath, they were panting. Their
faces were flushed, their bodies on fire with yearning, their loins
pounding with lust.

"Damn," he murmured again, burying his face in her neck.

He kissed it hungrily, with an open mouth, drawing her skin against
his teeth. She had threatened to murder the last man who had left a
mark on her. Now, she ran her hands up and down the rippling muscles
of Harlan's back, dropping her head back and giving him access to her
throat.

At first he only nudged aside her collar with his nose. Then he undid
the first button of her blouse and kissed the hollow of her throat. She
moaned, arching her back and sliding her middle across his. He undid
the second button of her blouse, then the third. As they came undone,
he tracked the fragrant opening with hungry lips.

Finally he raised his head so he could see her breasts. They were
rising and falling rapidly, nearly tumbling out of the sheer, lacy cups of

her low-cut brassiere. Her nipples, raised and pointed, strained against the weblike lace.

"Damn, Sage," Harlan hissed through his teeth. He laid a hand over each breast.

Her eyelids closed and she released a long, staggering sigh. "Yes."

He ground the stiff centers of her breasts with his palms.

"Hmm, yes." She moaned, swaying slightly.

Suddenly, not only were his hands withdrawn, but his warmth as well. Sage struggled to open her eyes and pull him into focus. He was standing several feet away from her. The hands that had been gently caressing her, were now planted firmly in the hip pockets of his pants, as though he didn't trust them. His eyes were trained on her breasts. He was gnawing his lips and cursing beneath his breath.

Sage came to her senses, as though she'd been snapped out of an hypnotic trance. If she had discovered herself prancing naked in front of a sideshow audience, she couldn't have been more furious with her hypnotist. She closed the distance between them in two short strides and slapped Harlan across the face as hard as she could.

To her consternation, she privately acknowledged that she wasn't slapping him for what he'd done, but because he had stopped doing it.

Rubbing his cheek, he said, "Well, it almost worked."

"It didn't even come close." Her voice was low, vibrating with outrage. "You've got nothing to pat yourself on the back for." Clumsily she began rebuttoning her blouse, then gave up on that tricky endeavor and pulled her jacket together over her exposed chest. "I didn't feel a thing."

"I wasn't referring to my efforts," Harlan calmly remarked. "I was referring to yours."

He wasn't making sense. Either that or she was too angry to piece the words together to form a cohesive thought. She shoved back her mussed hair. "What are you talking about? Not that I really care."

"I'm talking about your unsuccessful attempt to get rid of me." Sage stared at him, blinking stupidly. Her incomprehension seemed to annoy him. He pulled his lower lip through his teeth several times. "It's obvious what you were up to, Sage."

"I wasn't up to anything."

He snorted scoffingly. "I wasn't born yesterday, you know." Then, moving in closer and leaning down to her, he added, "A woman doesn't go from icicle to sexpot in that short a time, unless she's got a real good motive."

"Icicle? Sexpot! Motive?" She was uncertain which offensive word to take issue with first.

"With good reason, you want me out of your life. So you figured you'd get me to try something with you, then run screaming to your brothers, didn't you?"

"What?" she gasped.

"That's right. You thought that if I messed with you, they'd kick my butt right outta here. You're probably right. Only it didn't work." He glanced down at her breasts. "It came close, but I regained my head in the nick of time." Having said that, he turned and sauntered toward the door.

For the space of several seconds Sage stared at his back. Then she launched herself at him, grabbed his sleeve, and whipped him around. "In all my life, I've never been accused of anything so low, so demeaning, so—What kind of woman do you think I am?"

"You're a liar."

"I am not!"

"Could've fooled me. You haven't told your family that Casanova dumped you."

"No one's asked."

"So he *has* dumped you. When he called a while ago, it wasn't to kiss and make up."

Sage stood accused guilty as charged. Harlan laughed. "Okay, so I lied to you," she shouted. "I haven't lied to my family."

"But you haven't volunteered the information anytime Travis's name comes up."

"What business is that of yours?"

"None, I guess. I'd like to keep it that way. Don't make it my business by trying to manipulate me the way you do everybody else."

"I didn't try any such thing."

One of his eyebrows rose sharply. "Is that right?"

"Yes," she said defiantly. "That's right."

"Then why'd you kiss me like that?"

She opened her mouth to make a sharp retort, but suddenly realized she didn't have one. She closed her mouth quickly and looked away.

"Say," he said slowly, advancing on her until she had to back up a few steps, "you didn't by chance really lose your head over our kisses, did you? I thought you were faking all that moaning and groaning, that grasping and clawing. Are you saying it was for real? Was that begging and pleading, that 'yes, yes' genuine?"

"Shut up. You're disgusting."

"Disgusting huh?" He laughed, repeating the word several times as though he found it more amusing each time he said it. "Yeah, that's probably why you took to my tongue the way a baby does a pacifier."

His self-assurance was unbearable. She had had a momentary lapse in common sense, that's all. Mark it up to her recent rejection, or the pervasive love and good will of the season, or an inexplicable hormonal imbalance. For whatever reason, she had experienced temporary insanity.

Not only had she allowed him to take liberties, she had convinced herself that she was enjoying them, even craving them. If he ever realized that, he would utilize it to make her life miserable. Better to let him think she was a heartless schemer.

She tossed back her hair and looked down her nose at him. "Well, it was worth a try, wasn't it? If you'd gone any further, I'd have exposed you to my brothers for the lowlife you are. I still might."

"They'd probably believe you too," he said, scanning her from head to foot. "You look like you've just been well smooched. Lips all red and pouty. Hair a mess. Eyes dilated. Yeah, looking as sexy as you do, if you told them I'd tumbled you, they'd no doubt come after me with a loaded shotgun."

He grinned cockily and closed one eye. "But you aren't going to tell them, are you? 'Cause then I'd have to tell them that you kissed me back and moved against me like we were lying down. And because they're fair men who understand lust, they'd ask how you could lead one man on like that while being engaged to another. Then that whole business about Hot Lips's rejection would have to come out in the open and . . ."

Smacking his lips and shaking his head, he looked at her regretfully. "That'd ruin Christmas Day for everybody, wouldn't it? They'd miss the last quarter of the football game. Laurie would probably start crying because she couldn't believe her little girl would toy with a man like that. Marcie might get so upset her milk would go bad, and then baby Jamie would get sick and—"

"You're scum." She drew the word out, straining it through her teeth, saying it like she meant it with her whole heart and soul. Seething, she pushed past him and headed for the wide doors.

"Hey, Sage?"

She spun around. "What?"

"Did you ever kiss Mama's Boy like that?"

"Ha!" Striking a defiant pose, she declared, "Much better than that."

"Then he's no more than a damn fool you're well rid of, is he?"

"What's the matter, Marcie, can't you sleep?"

Chase reached for the lamp on the nightstand and switched it on. His wife was lying beside him on her back, gazing at the ceiling. She was rubbing her hand back and forth across her abdomen. Chase was instantly alarmed.

"Is there something wrong?"

"No," she said, smiling over his concern.

"You did too much today. We should have come straight home from the hospital. I shouldn't have let the doctor convince me that you were ready to leave. He probably wanted to take Christmas Day off."

"Will you relax? I'm fine. I'm just not used to having a flat tummy again. It feels good. I'm glad he's where he is now instead of where he was." She glanced toward the bassinet across the room where their son lay sleeping.

"Your flat tummy isn't what's keeping you awake." Chase propped himself up on his elbow and looked down at her.

"It's almost time for Jamie to nurse again. Mothers have this sixth sense, you see."

"Ah." He studied her teasing grin for a moment. "Something else is on your mind. What is it?" Taking her hand, he raised it to his lips and kissed the backs of her fingers. "What?"

"Sage."

He stared at her with perplexity. "Sage? What about her?"

"I don't know. That's why she's on my mind. Something wasn't right with her today, but I couldn't put my finger on what it was."

"She was piqued because Travis wasn't spending Christmas with her."

"Maybe," Marcie mused.

"You don't think so? You think it was something more than that?"

"I got the feeling that she's going through a difficult time. She was restless."

"She's always restless."

"Unusually so today. She didn't light for more than a few minutes at a time."

He thought for a moment. "She's probably still keyed up from her exams."

"That could be it, but somehow I don't think it's so simple. It goes deeper."

"Any theories?"

"Hmm. I remember how I felt when I left college. I suddenly realized that I was officially a grownup. It was scary, like being on a cliff about to take a plunge into life."

He chuckled. "You can hardly compare Sage with you. You're a brain. She's an airhead."

"Is she?" she asked tartly, snatching her hand from his. "Have you ever really talked to her, paid any attention to what she was saying, considered her opinion as something worth listening to?"

"Hey, Marcie, I—"

"No you haven't," she said, answering her own questions. "Lucky and you treat her like she's still your kid sister. Well, she's not. She's a woman. A well-educated woman."

"I hope so. Her education cost enough."

"And that's another thing," Marcie said, sitting up. "Every time her education is mentioned, it's in the context of how much it cost you. Have you told her how proud you are of her?"

"Well sure," he said. "Today, in fact. You were sitting right there."

"It sounded obligatory to me. Your education and Lucky's cost just as much as Sage's. Are you afraid that because she's a woman you won't get a return on your investment?"

"Possibly, especially if she marries that wimp Belcher."

"So you don't think she's even capable of choosing her own mate."

"I didn't say that."

"That's what you intimated. What's worse, you've let her know how you feel about him. Don't you rather imagine that hurts her feelings?"

"Sage never gets her feelings hurt."

"Of course she does!"

Chase plowed his fingers through his hair and blew out a gust of air. "I can't believe that we're lying here in the middle of the night having an argument about my kid—my *younger* sister."

"We're not arguing. I'm just pointing out a few things that have previously escaped your notice." She paused, and he indicated with a nod of his head that she should proceed. "First of all, she's no longer a child. She's an adult, equal to Lucky and you in every way."

"I'm not a caveman, Marcie. I believe in the equality of the sexes."

Ignoring him, she continued. "She's highly intelligent. She's sensitive." He raised his brows skeptically. "She is, Chase. She just doesn't show it because she's afraid her two brothers would mock her. Which you would."

"Okay, so we tease her. But we acknowledged a long time ago that she had grown up."

"But you still exclude her, the same way you did when she was little and wanted to tag along with you." He grudgingly admitted that her point was well taken. "I think she feels left out. Lucky, Devon, and Lauren are a unit, the same way you, Jamie, and I are. Laurie's wrapped up in Pat and her grandbabies. Can you see how Sage might feel alienated?"

"I guess so."

She reached across the pillows and laid her hand against his cheek, a gesture of forgiveness. "Treat her with a little more understanding and respect."

He nodded. "I promise to be more aware of it."

"Thank you, honey. I'm sure Sage will appreciate a shift in your attitude."

"Speaking of Mother and Pat, when do you think they're going to stop their silly game?"

Chase had told Marcie about seeing Pat kissing his mother the day Lauren was born. He knew their secret would be safe with her.

"I don't know, but I wish they would hurry and do something about it." Marcie looped her arms around his neck. "I want everyone in the world to be deliriously in love, so they'll understand how happy I am every time I look at you."

He closed his arms around her and drew her close, kissing her with passion and love. "How long before—"

"Eight weeks. At least," she breathed against his lips.

"It's going to be a long, tortuous two months."

Reaching beneath the covers, Marcie caressed him. "It doesn't have to be. Not for you anyway."

At the touch of her hand, he groaned with pleasure. "If every new mother was as sexy as you, men all over the world would be impregnating their wives."

Jamie chose that moment to wake up. Rather than resenting the interruption, Chase got out of bed and pulled on a robe. He changed the diaper, then lifted his son out of the bassinet and carried him back to Marcie, who had already lowered her nightgown, preparing to feed him.

Chase laid the crying infant in her arms and watched with wonder and love as Jamie found and latched onto Marcie's nipple. "Greedy little cuss," he said, chuckling.

"He takes after his father." Marcie looked up at her husband through her lashes and smiled.

"He takes after me if he loves you." His throat grew thick with emotion as he watched his son nursing. "I never would have thought it was possible to love you—or anyone—the way I love you, Marcie. Only you could have made it possible for me to love again after Tanya died."

Her own eyes misted. "Lie beside me," she whispered. He dropped his robe and slid between the covers again. Marcie curved her hand around his head and drew it to her other breast.

Each year, Sage was stricken with postholiday blues. This year they were so dark they were almost black. For the first few days after Christmas, she managed to stay busy by helping Laurie take down the decorations, repack them, and store them in the attic until next year.

They prepared meals for Chase and Marcie, making numerous trips back and forth to their house on Woodbine Lane. Sage even offered to sleep there and help out with Jamie, but Marcie's parents came up from Houston to spend several days, so her offer was graciously declined.

She made the rounds of her friends who still lived in Milton Point, but that was depressing to her. Most were either involved in their careers or with husbands and young families. She had little in common with them anymore.

Although she avoided Harlan whenever possible, he was at the dinner table each evening. To her vast relief, he paid no more attention to her than she did to him, but spent most of his time discussing business with Lucky. Laurie passed along his offer to vacate her room. She refused. The damage had been done. The beloved room was tainted now, and she never wanted to occupy it again. The subject was dropped.

She adroitly dodged talking about Travis with either members of her family or close friends who inquired about her wedding plans. One evening when Pat dropped by, Sage overheard Laurie speculating to him that Travis and she must have had a lovers' spat.

"To the best of my knowledge, he hasn't called her since Christmas Day, and then their conversation was short," Laurie had said. "They must have had a quarrel. What do you make of it?"

Sage could envision Pat rolling a matchstick from one side of his mouth to the other while he ruminated. "Damned if I know. Boys are sometimes hard to figure out, but girls are impossible."

Because she didn't discuss any immediate plans with them, their curiosity increased a little each day. No one asked questions, but she could sense their concern.

Her time was running out. She had to tell them the marriage to Travis was off. But how could she do that and save face? For the time being, she could only bide her time until something happened that would take care of the problem for her.

Something did happen, but it wasn't quite what she expected.

Early one morning, while she was dressing, someone tapped lightly on her bedroom door. Grabbing a robe and holding it against her like a shield, she padded across the floor and opened the door a crack.

"What do you want?"

Harlan wasn't put off by her rudeness. Instead he held up a newspaper clipping. "This was in this morning's society section of the Houston paper. I cut it out before anyone else got to it."

Puzzled, she scanned the society page headline.

New Year's Eve Gala To Be Held in Honor of Engagement.

There was a subheadline that read, "Childhood sweethearts announce plans to marry."

Beneath that was a picture of Dr. and Mrs. Belcher, Travis, and his new fiancé.

Chapter Seven

". . . and when I walked into the room to check on him, he was holding his head up and looking around at all the ducks and stuff on his blanket."

Lucky glanced at Harlan, his skepticism plain. Harlan gave a noncommittal shrug.

Chase intercepted the exchange. "I'm not lying. I swear. He was holding his head up. And that's nothing. Listen to this—"

"How long is it going to take?" Lucky asked. He had the desk chair tilted back as far as it would go. His boots were propped on the corner of the desk.

"Why?"

"Because you've been going on about Jamie for the last fifteen minutes. He's a cute kid, but give us a break, will ya?"

"Do you remember when Lauren was born? I had to sit and listen to you carry on about every little accomplishment. Well, it got boring after a while."

Lucky sprang erect. "You took the words right out of my mouth."

Chase signaled his brother back into his chair. "But I listened anyway."

"Jeez." Groaning, Lucky once again sought help from Harlan.

He had a straight chair angled back and precariously propped against the wall. The atmosphere in the office of Tyler Drilling Company was always casual. He liked it that way. He also enjoyed the affectionate bantering between the two brothers who, he knew without any qualification, would die for each other.

Trying to remain impartial, he said, "He's plumb dotty over that baby, Lucky."

Encouraged, Chase leaned forward in his chair. "Jamie's hung, too. I mean h-u-n-g."

"He's just a baby!" Lucky cried incredulously.

"I know, but you can tell he's going to make the ladies mighty happy when he's grown up." Chase grinned smugly. "He takes after his old man."

"You mean his uncle Lucky." The younger brother looked over at Harlan and winked. Harlan chuckled.

"Go to hell," Chase told his brother. "Anyway, he's smart as a whip. Did I tell you about—"

"Yes!" Lucky cried.

Chase glowered at him with exasperation, but before he could say anything more, Sage walked in. Silently, Harlan caught his breath and held it. His gut always drew up tightly whenever he saw her, and that was the least of his physical responses.

That's why he'd been keeping his distance the last couple of days. He had had a close call with trouble in the barn on Christmas Day. From now on he intended to stay out of harm's way.

This morning, of course, he'd had to break his own resolution. When she had opened her bedroom door to his knock, her shoulders had been bare except for the satin straps of her bra. She had bunched a robe against her front; he couldn't see anything but his imagination had gone into overdrive.

Only half of her makeup had been applied and her hair was still damp, but she had looked fantastic. She looked even better now. There was tension around her smile, but considering the news he had brought her earlier, he had to give her credit for pulling herself together so well. He shouldn't be surprised. He had already seen her bounce back after receiving a felling blow. That kind of gumption he had to admire.

They made eye contact, but it didn't last as long as a blink before she looked away. He couldn't blame her. She was embarrassed about what he knew, although she shouldn't be. Travis Belcher was the fool, not her.

"Hey, Sage," Chase said, "did I tell you about Jamie—"

"Yes," she said quickly. "Twice."

"You don't even know what I was going to say."

"Whatever it was, I've heard it. Can't you say hello first?"

"Sure. Hi. Want some coffee?"

"No thanks. I just finished breakfast."

"What brings you out, brat?" Lucky asked. His question was obviously rhetorical. Before giving her time to answer it, he picked up the morning newspaper and opened it.

Sage moved to the desk and snatched it from his hands. Smart girl, Harlan thought. She'd got to him before Lucky had a chance to see the society section. Not that he was likely to read that anyway. It had been pure chance that Harlan had run across that article about Belcher.

"I want to talk to you."

"To me?" Lucky asked.

"To both of you."

She included Chase, then turned and looked pointedly at Harlan. Behind her imperious expression, he detected nervousness, near desperation.

The front legs of his chair hit the floor as he rolled off his spine to stand up. "I've got some work to do over in the garage. See y'all later."

He put on his vest and cowboy hat, pulling it low on his brows. Meeting Sage's eyes again, he touched the brim with the tips of two fingers before opening the door and stepping outside. As he pulled the door closed behind him, he wondered what she wanted to talk to her brothers about. Whatever it was, he sensed that she was dreading it.

Thankfully Harlan left the office without giving away, either by word or sign, that they had seen each other earlier that morning. After handing her the newspaper clipping, he had tactfully withdrawn, closing her bedroom door as he went.

The last thing she wanted from him was pity. She almost preferred his teasing and taunting to sympathetic silence. He was behaving as though someone—or something inside her—had died. However, she now had more to worry about than Harlan Boyd and his opinion of her.

She had spent a tumultuous hour in her room, pacing, brainstorming, trying to make up her mind what to do. Should she return to Austin and look for work there? Should she stay in Milton Point and twiddle her thumbs while waiting for inspiration? Or should she do the courageous thing and seize control of a bad situation and try and make it better?

Once she had decided her next course of action, she wasted no time, but dressed quickly and left the house. When Travis's engagement to another woman became a well-known fact, no one would find Sage Tyler huddled in a dark corner licking her wounds. She would already have alternate plans in place.

As soon as the office door closed behind Harlan, Lucky asked, "What's up?"

Since time was of the essence, Sage saw no point in beating around the bush. "I want a career."

The two stunned men looked at her for a moment, then at each other, then at her again. "A career?" Chase repeated.

"I didn't stutter."

"You've got a career," Lucky said. "You'll soon be getting married."

"Marriage isn't a career!"

"Being married to Travis Belcher will be the most demanding job anybody could ask for."

"Lucky." Chase sighed retiringly.

Sage gripped the back of the nearest chair in an effort to control her temper. It would serve no purpose now to spar with Lucky. She had to plead her case convincingly. Flying off the handle would accomplish nothing except make her look immature and unprofessional.

"I'm not sure when I'll be getting married," she said, evading a bald lie yet skirting the truth. "In the meantime, I need a job, something challenging to keep me occupied and interested. I want to earn my own living."

"Well, hey, I'm sure there are lots of jobs to be had in Houston," Lucky said, breaking into the charming grin that had earned him a reputation with women. "Or do you plan to stay in Austin until you and Travis tie the knot?"

"I . . . I thought I'd stay in Milton Point for a while. That is, if it won't be too much of an imposition on you and Devon for me to live at home."

"Hell, no. That's your house, too, Sage. It belongs to all of us. What the hell do you mean about being an imposition?"

"Lucky," Chase said, intervening again, "let's hear her out first, okay? Then open it up for discussion."

"Wasn't that what I was doing?"

Chase, ignoring his brother, turned his intense gray eyes onto Sage. "Are you asking us to run interference for you, Sage? Grease the skids? Put in a good word with a prospective employer? Write you a letter of recommendation? We'd be glad to, wouldn't we, Lucky? Give us a name, we'll do what we can. Where would you like to work?"

They still didn't get it. To them she was their kid sister, useless except as an object to play practical jokes on. It crushed her to know that what she wanted to do would never have even occurred to them.

She couldn't afford the time to indulge her disappointment, however. So much more than hurt feelings was at stake. Squaring her shoulders and holding her head up proudly, she stated, "Here. I want to work for Tyler Drilling."

Again, they stared back at her with stupefaction. Chase managed to speak first. "Here? Well, hey, Sage, that's, uh, that's terrific."

"What the hell are you—" Lucky clamped his jaws shut when Chase shot him a warning glance. "Uh, yeah, Sage, that's great."

She released a deep breath. The band of tension around her ribcage relaxed. A soft laugh erupted from her mouth. "Really? You mean it?"

"Sure," Lucky drawled expansively. "Why not? There's always something to do around here. We're always behind on our filing. Even in these hard times, bookkeeping is a bitch that Chase and I both hate dealing with. Neither one of us is very good at it. And, as you can see, we're not very good housekeepers either."

Sage, seeing red, turned on her heels and marched toward the door. Chase went after her and caught her wrist. "Let me go." She struggled to be released.

"No, and if you bite me the way you did when you were a kid, I'll slug you. Now, be still." He rounded on Lucky. "The next time you're tempted to shoot off your big, dumb mouth, do the world a favor and keep it shut."

Lucky spread his arms wide in a gesture of total confusion. "What'd I do? What'd I say?"

Sage managed to wrest her arm free. Rather than leaving, however, she forgot about her resolve to control her temper and confronted them with the ferocity of a brave, young lioness, fangs bared, claws extended. She was, after all, fighting for her life.

"I wasn't looking for work as a file clerk, or a gofer, or a maid, Lucky," she shouted. "When it comes right down to it, I'm as qualified as either of you to operate a business. Maybe not in practical, hands-on experience, but I've got more education.

"I was weaned on discussions about the oil industry, every single aspect of it. By osmosis, I've absorbed a lot of knowledge. This business is currently failing. I'm not blaming that on either of you, but it sure as hell can't hurt to bring another person into the company. A member of the family, that is," she added, thinking of Harlan.

"No one has thought to ask, but I just might have some fresh ideas. Besides, even if I don't, I've got as much right to be here as the two of you. The only difference between us is that I've got ovaries instead of balls. If I had been born male, you would have expected me to join the company straight out of college.

"And before you go labeling me an aggressive feminist, let me set you straight on that. I love being a woman. I wouldn't want to be anything else. But I want to be treated fairly and equally when it comes to a career, the way both your wives are treated in their professional fields. I don't think either of you doubts their femininity.

"I want you to start thinking of me as an intelligent adult and not the child in pigtails you used to torment for recreation. I'm not merely precocious, I'm intelligent. I've been grown up for a long time, though obviously you haven't noticed.

"Well, it's time you did. I refuse to be patted on the head and then pushed aside and overlooked as though I were invisible. I won't be shut out any longer."

A long silence followed her speech. Her breasts heaved with indignation and her golden brown eyes flashed with remnant anger.

Finally Lucky said, "Whew! That was some lecture, br . . . uh, Sage."

"Thanks."

"Did Devon coach you?"

"I did it all myself."

Chase spoke for the first time. "We didn't intentionally exclude you from the family business, Sage. But since you've been grown, you've been away at school. We assumed that you wouldn't be working at all after you got married, certainly not here in Milton Point." He frowned. "I assume you've discussed this with Travis. What does he think about it?"

"It doesn't matter. I never have been, nor will I ever be, his chattel." Never had she been more truthful. "Until I get married I want to be productive."

"What did you have in mind doing for the company?"

She looked at them uneasily, then cast her eyes downward. This was a weak link in her argument. "I'm not sure. I know that for several years you've been trying to think of ways to diversify. Maybe I could help there by providing a fresh perspective.

"Or maybe I could try to cultivate new clients, since most of our old ones are currently out of business. I think if I had access to the figures, I could put together deals that would be profitable, but provide good incentive to potential clients."

"We couldn't pay you much," Lucky said grimly.

"You don't have to pay me at all." They looked surprised. She hastened to add, "I could work on commission. You wouldn't have to pay me anything until I generated some business, and then I'd take an agreed-on percentage of the net."

"What'll you live on?"

"I didn't use all the money you gave me for that last semester of school. It's still in savings. Besides, if I'm living at home, I won't need much beyond gasoline money. I'm accustomed to making do with what clothes I've got and stretching my wardrobe."

Chase looked chagrined. "I'm sorry about that, Sage. We haven't been able to lavish material things on you the last several years. You've been damned understanding about it."

"You never asked for much either, and we appreciate that," Lucky added.

Her heart melted and she moved toward them, wrapping an arm around each. "We're all in this crisis together, aren't we? From now on, I want to do my part to get us out. Is it settled?"

"Fine with me," Lucky said.

Chase looked down at her. "Okay, you're in. But don't thank us too soon. It might only mean that you sink right along with us."

Hearing only his consent, she threw herself against him and hugged him hard before turning to Lucky and hugging him with equal exuberance. "You won't be disappointed in me. I swear. Thank you for giving me this chance."

"You don't have to prove yourself to us, Sage," Chase said.

"Maybe not. But I have to prove myself to me."

"You know, Chase," Lucky said, "she might be able to sell Harlan's idea to somebody better than we could."

"Harlan," she muttered. Her burst of elation dissipated at the mention of his name. In her excitement, she had almost forgotten him. "Exactly what *is* Harlan's idea?"

Taking her arm, Chase steered her toward the door. "Come on, we'll show you."

Situated a short distance from the office, the garage was a large, cavernous building. Several years earlier, it had burned to the ground. Lucky had been accused of setting the fire, but Devon Haines, with whom he had spent that night, had provided him with an alibi. Alvin Cagney and Jack Ed Patterson, local no-accounts, were still in prison serving time for the crime.

The building had been reconstructed on its original site and all the equipment destroyed in the fire had been replaced. For all that, the garage wasn't what it had been in its heyday. Sage remembered it from her childhood as a dirty place, smelling of oil and mud and hardworking men, a place ringing with the racket of machinery and the salty language of the roughnecks.

It hadn't been a proper environment for a young lady, and for that reason it had been generally off-limits to her when she was growing up. She had envied her brothers their freedom to come and go at will, to mix with the men who worked for their father. Many times, she had wanted to visit the drilling sites and take part in the celebration when a well came in.

She was sad to note, when Chase drove his pickup through the wide double doors, that the garage had changed. It was too clean. The equipment stood silent and dusty. There were no roughnecks milling around wiping their dirty faces with grimy bandannas while cursing bad weather, rotten luck, and dry holes. The laughter and tall tales of the good ol' days in the East Texas oilfields had disappeared.

There was only one man in the garage now and he was bent over a drafting table, studying a mechanical drawing. At the sound of the pickup pulling in, he stood upright and shoved a yellow school pencil into the thick blond hair behind his ear. He looked at Sage inquiringly as she approached him with her brothers walking on each side of her.

"Any progress, Harlan?"

He shook his head. "Not much. I just don't see a way to make it any cheaper."

"Make what?" Sage asked.

Harlan stepped aside and waved his hand over the drawing. She studied it for a moment but couldn't make heads or tails out of it. She hated to show her ignorance, but had no choice.

"It's not a surrealistic still life of a bowl of fruit is it?"

The men chuckled. "You explain it to her, Harlan," Chase suggested. "It's your idea."

"Well, it's like this," he began. "I figured that with some adaptations, an oil well pump could be converted into a pump for something else, namely water."

"Sometimes water is pumped into an oil well."

"Very good," Lucky said, patting her on the head. Then, as though remembering her earlier words, drew his hand back. "Meaning no offense."

"None taken," she said automatically. Harlan was holding her attention with his dynamic blue eyes, which weren't only insolent and mocking when he wanted them to be, but clearly the windows into a clever mind as well. "What application did you have in mind?"

He hesitated. Chase said, "Sage is part of the company now. You can tell her what we've been working on."

"Oh, I'm sure she can keep a secret," he remarked with just a trace of laughter behind his words. "The application would be irrigation, Sage. With a little ingenuity, and some working capital," he added, giving Chase and Lucky a grim smile, "we could adapt the drilling equipment into an irrigation system."

She digested that a moment. "For whom?"

"That's where you might enter in, Sage," Lucky told her. "Once we get a prototype, we'll need to do some marketing."

"Farmers," she said.

"That would be a good start."

"And the citrus growers down in the valley." The wheels of her mind began turning, but before she carried her ideas too far, she saw the immediate and pressing problem. "You said you needed working capital."

Chase sighed. "Harlan's almost finished with the prototype, but we had to stop him because we haven't got any cash to invest."

"But you can't let that stop you!" she cried. "Before you can do anything, you've got to have a prototype."

"Tell us about it," Lucky muttered.

"Surely you could borrow—"

"Forget it. There isn't a bank in Texas that's loaning any money to anyone in the oil business."

"Outside the state," she suggested.

"Once they hear your Texas twang, they all but hang up on you. Being from the Lone Star State is the kiss of death if you're looking for financing," Lucky said.

"We're dead in the water," Chase told her.

"No pun intended," Harlan said.

"We've got literally miles of pipe stacked up behind this building ready to be put to use," Chase said. "But for right now, we have to leave it there."

"What do you need?" she asked Harlan.

"Minicomputer," he told her.

"What for?"

"Automatic timing."

"I see. It wouldn't work without one?"

"It would, but it wouldn't be state of the art."

"And we need it to be high tech."

"Right."

For a moment they silently considered their frustrating situation, then Lucky glanced at his wristwatch. "I need to get back to the office, Chase. Even though this is the week between the holidays, some people are still doing business, and I've got some calls out. I should be there if they call back."

"Sage, why don't you stay here with Harlan till suppertime," Chase suggested. "He can bring you home. Let him explain how this thing is going to work. If you're going to be selling it, you've got to know all the answers."

"A-all right," she faltered.

She would rather be strung up by her thumbs than pass the rest of the afternoon in Harlan's company, but she couldn't very well refuse her first official assignment as an employee of Tyler Drilling Company.

Chapter Eight

After her brothers had departed, she glanced around the silent building, folding her arms across her chest against the chill.

"Cold?" Harlan asked.

"A little."

"Scoot over here closer to the heater."

There was a small, electric space-heater on the floor near his feet.
She moved toward its directional heat rays and extended her hands to
capitalize on the warmth. The fisherman's sweater she was wearing
over her slacks had been sufficient outside, but the building seemed
colder.

"I guess I owe you my thanks for not telling them about Travis's
engagement."

Their eyes connected and held for a moment. He looked vaguely
disappointed in her. "You don't owe me anything. Hand me that ruler,
please."

She reached behind her into the tray of drafting tools he indicated.
He took the narrow metal ruler from her and used it to add a line to his
drawing.

She leaned forward for a closer inspection, but the schematic still
looked to her like nothing more than an odd arrangement of lines and
arcs. "Are you sure you know what you're doing?"

"I've got an engineering degree from Texas A&M that says I do."

"*You* have a college degree?"

Her incredulity didn't insult him, as it might have. Instead, he
grinned and turned his head toward her. "If he pays his tuition and
completes the required courses, they'll give a degree to just about anybody."

"I'm sorry I sounded . . . well, I'm surprised, that's all. Where'd you graduate from high school?"

"I didn't." He made an erasure and readjusted the length of a line, measuring it precisely. "I got my high school diploma by correspondence."

"Why, for heaven's sake?"

"I was working in a refinery. That was the only way I could get an education and earn a living at the same time."

"You were working full time while you were in high school?"

"That's right."

"Supporting yourself?"

"Hmm. No football games, no homecoming pep rallies, no proms. I worked the graveyard shift and studied during the day when I wasn't sleeping."

Sage felt incredibly sad for him and had to stop herself from laying a consoling hand on his shoulder. "What about your parents?"

He dropped his pencil and faced her again. "You sure ask a lot of questions, you know that?"

"If we're going to be working together, we should know something about each other."

"I don't think that's necessary."

"I do."

He studied the stubborn angle of her jaw and apparently saw the advisability of humoring her. "What do you want to know?"

"What about your family? Why were you working in a refinery to support yourself when you should have been enjoying high school?"

"I left home when I was fifteen."

"Why?"

"I just split, okay? I've been on my own ever since. As soon as I got my high school diploma, I enrolled at A&M and went through in three years. By the time I was twenty, I was educated and accountable to no one except myself." He tapped her chin with his fingertip. "That includes you."

"I can't imagine being so adrift."

He shrugged laconically. "You get used to it. Wanna see this thing or not?"

Whether she liked it or not, he had brought the discussion to a close. She regretted not having learned more about him. What little he had told her had left her more intrigued than pacified. For the time being, it seemed, he would remain an enigma.

He ushered her toward a large tarpaulin and pulled it back, uncovering a piece of machinery that looked to her like any other oil well pump. "This is as far as we've got," he said. "It still needs—"

"Were you a runaway?"

He dropped his head forward and studied the concrete floor for several moments. Finally he looked up and said resignedly, "I guess you could call me that, yeah."

"Fifteen," she murmured. At fifteen the biggest crisis in her life had been if she woke up with a new zit. During her adolescence, her brothers had teased her incessantly about her budding figure and any yokel who became smitten with her. Home life hadn't always been grand, but she couldn't imagine leaving her family at that age, walking away from everything familiar and dear. She told Harlan so.

"Well, Sage, consider yourself lucky. Not every kid had it as good as you."

"Was your home life and childhood that terrible?"

"I thought you wanted to know about the irrigation system."

"You're not going to tell me about your past, are you?"

"No."

Now it was Sage's turn to sigh with resignation. She had met her match in being obstinate. She could tell by the determination in his expression that he had divulged all he was going to.

Turning away, she critically examined the pump. "A machine is a machine. They all look alike to me."

"If you're going to sell folks on this idea, you'll have to know what it's capable of doing."

"I only want to know what's absolutely necessary. Keep the explanations simple and in layman's terms. I don't understand the mechanics behind a hair dryer."

A smile spread across his features. "You've got moxie, I'll say that." She tilted her head inquiringly, so he expounded. "Without any prior experience, you convinced your brothers to let you work for them."

"*With* them," she corrected.

"That took guts. Or desperation." He eyed her keenly. "Do you think that working for Tyler Drilling will get you over Lover-boy?"

"I'm already over Lover-boy."

"Just like that?" he asked skeptically.

"What you fail to understand," she said loftily, "is that my involvement with Travis wasn't based on passion. We weren't like Chase and Marcie or Lucky and Devon. Those are love affairs of the heart, mind, body, and soul. One would be devastated if anything happened to the other because they depend so much on each other. That kind of marriage rarely works."

"Theirs seem to be rock solid."

"They are, but they're the exception. I would never have thought that Lucky could remain faithful to one woman or that Chase could love again after losing his first wife. Logically, neither of their marriages should have worked. From the outset of our relationship, Travis and I took a more pragmatic approach to matrimony."

"And look where that landed you."

She swiftly gave him her back and stalked away. Reaching far, he grabbed her by the seat of her pants. "Hold on. Hold on. I was just kidding."

"You're not funny," she said slapping his hand off her fanny.

"Sometimes life isn't either."

"Your point?"

"Well, life's full of unpleasantness," he said. "Backed-up plumbing, crabgrass in the lawn, sick kids, bills you can't pay. If you're going to share all those hassles with somebody, it seems to me that the passion you're downplaying could go a long way to make the bad stuff more bearable." Eyes crinkling at the corners, he added, "And it's damn good fun."

She kept a straight face. "Your point is moot because I'm not marrying Travis."

"Did you tell Chase and Lucky?"

"No. I didn't want them hiring me out of pity. I told them that I wasn't sure when I would be getting married, which is the truth. I even used the singular pronoun and not we, as in Travis and I. I told them that, in the interim, I wanted to be productive and work in the family business. By the time they learn my engagement is off, they'll think that the breakup was gradual and mutual, that Travis and I merely grew apart. Mother already suspects that we're embroiled in a lovers' quarrel. No one will be surprised."

"I see you've got it all figured out."

"I do."

He shook his head with misgiving. "You know what they say about well-laid plans. They usually backfire. I'll bet you ten to one that before it's all over, they'll find out that Hot Lips dumped you."

Her temper snapped. "Why is it that every time—"

Laughing, he grasped her by the upper arms and lifted her off the ground, dangling her body so close to his, she could feel each hard muscle in stark detail. Her face was level with his. She feared, and half hoped, that he was going to stop her angry outburst with another bone-melting kiss.

"They'll probably quiz you on all you learned today," he said. "You have a bad habit of talking too much. If you want to impress them, sit down, keep your mouth shut, your eyes open, and listen."

He pivoted on the heels of his boots and deposited her on a high stool. Then, shoving up the sleeves of his faded denim jacket, he began to explain the workings of his invention.

"So it could be programmed to irrigate certain areas at certain times on certain days, very much like an ordinary home sprinkler system."

Harlan grinned at Sage's basic understanding. "Except it could cover acres. It could be pumped from a reservoir or through a normal water source."

"That would require a lot of pipe."

"Laying the pipe will be a piece of cake. This is what counts," he said, patting the piece of machinery. "The whole system would be controlled from this computerized pump."

"Only you need a computer before you can even lay some pipe and try it out."

"Yeah, at least some kind of timing device. And the company till is empty."

After two hours of intense indoctrination, Sage believed that she had a decent grasp on his idea. She had listened carefully to every word Harlan had said—and not to just what he said, but how he said it.

His vocabulary was extensive. He was articulate. She began to believe that maybe he did have a college degree. Certainly there was more to him than what one saw on the surface. He camouflaged his intelligence with his good ol' boy demeanor. Why? As a defense mechanism?

Possibly. She could understand that. Hadn't she sometimes assumed a bratty posture as a defense mechanism to cover feelings of insecurity and inferiority?

What did Harlan have to be defensive about?

He glanced toward the wide doors. There was a cloudy sky, and it would be growing dark soon. "We'd better close up shop for the day. You've got a lot to absorb. Your mama'll get worried about you if you're not home by dark."

"Did your mama worry about you when you split?"

His eyes cut to hers sharply. "No. She didn't."

That's all he said before clamming up. Sage waited for him inside his pickup truck while he closed the garage, checking everything meticulously before padlocking the door. Her brothers had entrusted him with securing their building, a responsibility he took seriously.

"Mind if I stop at my trailer for a minute?" he asked as the truck chugged down the narrow road that led to the main highway.

Instantly suspicious, she asked, "What for?"

"I'm gonna ravish you." He laughed when she jumped reflexively and turned her head so quickly her neck popped. "Don't get your hopes up, Sage. I need to pick up a book."

"You have a warped sense of humor, Mr. Boyd."

"It may be warped, but at least I have one."

He was justified in putting her down. Even to her own ears, she sounded prissy and prim. Why couldn't she just laugh off his jokes? He continued teasing her only because her reactions were always so violent. Hadn't her mother advised her to ignore her brothers when they became their most obnoxious? It was a lesson she had never learned and, therefore, couldn't exercise now.

"My sense of humor is one of the many things you don't like about me," he said. Looking at her across the ramshackle interior of the pickup, he added, "One of these days, I'm going to get you to admit all the things you do like." His voice was soft, the words spoken like a warning. Sage was the first to look away.

His trailer was parked in a vacant, uncultivated field not too far from the Tyler Drilling Company office. They reached it within a few minutes of leaving the garage. Sage wasn't surprised that the Streamline looked like it was barely holding together at the seams. A coughing generator provided it with electricity.

"You can stay put or get out. Suit yourself." He got out and jogged up two concrete blocks serving as steps. The doors weren't even locked. He opened them and disappeared inside. Through the curtains hanging over the narrow windows, Sage saw a light come on.

Her curiosity got the best of her. She left the truck and moved up the steps. The screen door squeaked when she pulled it open. She winced, but pushed on the metal door and stepped inside.

She expected it to be a disaster, littered with girlie magazines and empty beer cans. Instead it was rather cozy and very neat. The furnishings were tacky and cheap, but everything was clean. He did have some reading matter, quite a lot in fact, but it ran more toward news periodicals and current fiction paperbacks, bestsellers mostly. There was one respectable copy of *Playboy*.

Without being obvious, she nosed around, looking for family photographs, mail with return addresses, anything that might give her clues about his background. There was nothing. She had no inkling of what he'd been doing before he came to Milton Point.

She sensed his presence before she heard him and turned to face him. She didn't think before she spoke, but asked the question at the forefront of her mind. "Have you always lived alone?"

"Yes."

"Have you ever been married?"

"You asked me that already."

"I asked if you'd ever been a bridegroom."

"That's splitting hairs, isn't it?" Seeing her ill-concealed annoyance, he said, "I've never been married."

"Children?"

His lips twitched with the effort of suppressing a smile. "No."

"How old are you?"

"Twenty-nine. Going on thirty soon."

He looked older, as old as Lucky who was in his early thirties. "Where's your family?"

"I don't have a family."

"You have a mother. You said she hadn't worried about you when you left, so you must have had one."

He laid aside the book he'd brought from the back room and took a step closer. By doing so he seemed to reduce the size of the trailer by half. "Why are you so curious, Sage?"

"I don't know. I just am."

"Besides my family, what else are you curious about?"

"Where you came from. What you did before you met Chase in Houston. Why you don't bother locking your doors. Why, since you're college educated and intelligent, you choose to live like this."

He gave the dim surroundings an assessing glance. "What's wrong with the way I live?"

She floundered, not wanting to state the obvious at the risk of sounding unkind.

"I like the way I live, Sage. Very much. I don't lock my doors because I don't own anything anybody would want. When you don't possess anything, you can't be possessed by things either. You don't have to worry about somebody taking something valuable from you. I like being free from all that."

He took another step, closing the distance between them. The toes of his boots grazed the toes of her shoes before he widened his stance and placed his feet on either side of hers, a stance that tilted his hips slightly forward.

His nearness in the quiet, still trailer overwhelmed her. Because he was looking down at her so intently with those laser-beam blue eyes, she was a little afraid of him. Or was she afraid of the marshy feeling she got in the pit of her stomach every time he stood this close to her?

"Ask me something else, Sage."

"You answered all my questions," she said breathlessly. "There's nothing else I need or want to know."

"Yes, there is."

"What?"

"You want to know when I'm going to kiss you again."

"I want to know no such thing! What gave you that idea?"

He wasn't the least bit fazed by her hasty rebuttal. "You're like a cat, aren't you, Sage? Always scratching and clawing and hissing in self-defense. Every time anybody gets close to the real Sage, you arch your back." His eyes moved down to her mouth. "If you gave yourself half a chance, you'd purr."

She swallowed with difficulty, wanting to move away, but unable to, wanting to look away, but incapable of it. "You'll never know. I'll never let you kiss me again."

"Yes you will. You liked it too much."

"I didn't like it at all."

His hands came up and framed her face. His thumbs took turns sweeping across her lips. "We both know you're a liar, Sage. A lousy one at that."

Then his mouth settled on hers. It was warm, soft, undemanding, fluid. She allowed the contact for several seconds, but when the tip of his tongue touched the tip of hers, she recoiled and turned her head away.

"Harlan—"

"That's it. Say my name."

His lips captured hers again. Her whimper of protest was feeble and thoroughly disregarded. When he introduced his tongue this time, she obliged him, greeting it with a stroke of her own.

He slipped his arms around her waist and drew her up against him as he angled his head to one side and deepened the kiss. Sage's ears rang with a cacophony of sound, and she realized it was the pounding of her own heart and the rushing-wind sound of consuming lust. She had never heard it before, yet she recognized it immediately. A tide of heat rivered through her body, pooling between her thighs.

He tasted her again and again, sending his tongue deep into her mouth for samples. When they had to either breathe or die, he buried his face in her neck, kissing it madly. He worked his way to her ear. Sage felt the warm, damp stroke of his tongue and gave a soft cry. Her knees buckled and she stumbled backward onto the sofa.

He followed her down, partially covering her body with his. She plowed her fingers into his hair and pulled his head down to her. She needed this. She needed a man's weight crushing her, his desire hot and hard for her, his mouth stealing her breath.

She kissed Harlan as though she were starving for his love. She bent one knee up and pressed the inside of her thigh against his hip. It felt so right, so good. His erection was firm against her cleft. She moved her hips, rubbing against it, wanting more.

Harlan slid his hand inside her sweater to caress her breast. "Sage, do you want me to touch you like this?"

She raggedly sighed an affirmative answer while randomly kissing the features of his face, which, she now admitted, had mightily appealed to her from the first time she'd laid eyes on him.

His hand scooped her breast from the cup of her bra. He caressed the raised nipple with his fingertips. Sage moaned and arched her back, begging for more.

"Honey, baby, Sage." Sighing miserably, he withdrew his hand and tried to stave off her ardently seeking lips.

At last she realized that he was no longer fondling her and wanted her attention. Her thrashing head came to rest between his palms as she gazed up at him through wide, golden eyes cloudy with passion. "What's wrong?"

"Not a damn thing," he replied thickly. "You're perfect. You look perfect. You feel perfect. You taste perfect."

"Then why'd you stop?" she asked, her voice husky.

"I like your brothers, Sage. They like and trust me. I don't want to do anything to betray their trust."

Still restless, she shifted slightly, lodging him more comfortably between her thighs. He closed his eyes and groaned softly. When he opened his eyes again, they were exceptionally bright. The lines on either side of his mouth were tense. His breath was short and shallow.

"I never should have kissed you again. I didn't think it would go . . . I didn't think you would be so . . . Aw, hell." He grimaced as though in pain. "Believe me, Sage, I'd love nothing better than to have my mouth all over you right now. You know where I want to be. Inside you. Deep inside you." Again, he shut his eyes briefly and sucked in an uneven breath.

"But before we go any farther, I've got to know that you know what you're doing and want it as much as I do. I don't want to be used to salve a spoiled little girl's ego."

She wouldn't have believed that any emotion could override the desire pumping through her. However, when his words registered, she discovered that outrage could conquer anything. With a growl of pure fury, she pushed him off her, almost dumping him onto the speckled linoleum floor of the trailer.

She scrambled off the sofa and shoved her disheveled hair out of her eyes. "You won't have to worry about any retribution from my brothers," she shouted. "One day I'm going to kill you myself."

Having issued the threat, she threw open the door, jumped over the steps and marched off into the darkness. She'd gone about a quarter of a mile on foot when he pulled the pickup along side her.

"Get in," he said through the open window.

"Take a flying leap straight into hell."

"What are we going to do, swap invectives? Stop acting like a brat and get in. It's starting to sprinkle."

She came to an abrupt halt and confronted him. "I'll walk. I'd walk a hundred miles through a torrent to keep from riding with you."

"What'll you tell your family when you show up hours late for supper?" She paused to consider that. Harlan pressed his advantage. "Are you prepared to tell them what held us up?"

She glared at him through the gloomy dusk. He looked away from her, toward the horizon. His regret was evident. When he looked at her again, all traces of his characteristic arrogance were absent.

"I take full responsibility for starting something today that shouldn't have got started, Sage. I apologize for ever laying a hand on you. After what happened in the barn on Christmas Day, I should have known better than to touch you again. But," he continued softly, "you've got to accept part of the blame for where it went from that first kiss, and where it would have gone if I hadn't stopped it."

Sage, remembering how wantonly she had writhed against him, privately acknowledged that he was right, though she would rather have her tongue cut out than admit it. Her present behavior only demonstrated to him how upset she was that he had called off their lovemaking. That was untenable. Besides, Chase had asked him to bring her home. If he didn't, her family would want to know why.

Walking stiffly, she rounded the hood of the truck, opened the passenger door, then climbed inside the cab. The window hadn't been replaced, the opening was still patched with cardboard. Since that didn't offer a view, she stared stonily out the front windshield.

Feeling the sting of tears in her eyes, she blinked them away, unwilling to let him see them. She would rather have him think that she was a spoiled little girl than a woman whose raging desire for him had been thwarted.

And she did desire him.

If she hadn't been totally honest with everyone else the last several days, she should at least be honest with herself now. As aggravating as he was, she desired him.

Whatever brand of magic he weaved, it was none she had encountered before. With his loose cowboy's gait, lean body, piercing blue eyes, shaggy blond hair, aura of mystery, and insufferable arrogance, he had made her want him in a way she had never wanted another man.

She was acting like an ingenue in the throes of puppy love. Her girlfriends used to go positively ga-ga over her brothers, and she had scoffed at such silliness. It was beneath her dignity to respond to a man that way, to get all warm and dewy and feverish every time he looked at her.

But Harlan wasn't like other men. He possessed secret powers. He hadn't merely kissed her—he'd made love to her mouth. Travis's kisses had certainly never weakened her to the point of losing her balance. She had never lost her head in his embrace.

Harlan also coaxed more than physical responses from her. He tapped into her emotions. Apparently he'd been deprived as a child. His telling of missing high school had touched a cord in her, made her somehow want to make up for his deprivations.

She had wanted him to make up for hers too. She had wanted his touch, his fervent kisses. What he'd said about having his mouth all over her had been outrageous, yet the very thought of his lips on her skin made her body tremble even now.

She sneaked a glimpse of his profile from the corner of her eye. He would die without knowing how he had affected her. He would never know how much his rejection had wounded her, no matter how honorable his motives had been. He had rebuffed her when she was feeling more vulnerable than she had in her entire life.

Travis had raked her self-esteem over the coals. Now, while it was still seared and blistered, Harlan had drawn her back into the fire.

What bothered her most, however, was that this man had the capability of hurting her so badly. She couldn't figure out why.

Chase and Lucky were sitting together on the porch, sipping beer, when Harlan parked his truck in the driveway. What would they think of her if they learned that, on her first day on the job, she had made out with the hired help?

She glanced uneasily at Harlan. "What happened in the trailer was strictly between us."

"Right."

"So don't make any heartfelt confessions."

"Right."

"Forget it happened."

"Wrong."

She swung her gaze up to his. It had such impact, she had difficulty recovering her breath as she alighted and shakily made her way toward the house. "Hi."

"Where've you been?" Chase wanted to know.

"What difference does it make?"

"We've been waiting for you," Lucky said. "Chase didn't want to leave for home until you got here."

"Well, I'm here," she said testily.

"There's no call to get your dander up," her older brother said. "We had a brainstorm and wanted to discuss it with you."

"What kind of brainstorm?"

She moved beneath the porch covering to get out of the cold, gray drizzle. In her peripheral vision, she noticed that Harlan propped himself against one of the support posts, just as he'd been leaning against the corner of the Belchers' ivy-covered wall the first time she saw him.

"How'd she do, Harlan?" Lucky asked.

He cleared his throat. "She, uh, she did fine. Just fine. She's got a real feel for it."

Sage felt her cheeks growing warm. She didn't dare look at him, but tried to put him and his sexy kisses out of her mind and concentrate on what her brothers were saying.

Lucky was speaking excitedly. "The final say-so is up to you, of course."

"Say-so about what?"

"We wouldn't want you to approach him if you didn't feel absolutely comfortable about it," Chase said.

"Approach whom?"

"And he might say no," Lucky said.

"In which case," Chase butted in, "there would be no hard feelings."

"But he's got an inside track. He knows people with money who might be willing to invest in our new enterprise."

"All you have to do, Sage, is sell him on the idea."

Sage had been dividing her puzzled gaze between them. Now, holding up both hands in a gesture of surrender, she laughed. "*Who?*" she cried. "Would one of you please tell me what and who you're talking about?"

"Dr. Belcher," Chase replied with a grin. "Travis's dad. Your future father-in-law."

Chapter Nine

"Hi, Lucky. I'm sorry I'm calling so late."

"Harlan? What time is it?"

Harlan checked his wristwatch. "Just after two. Jeez, I'm sorry. I lost track of time."

"It's all right. I asked you to call me. Well?"

Harlan heard the sleepiness fading from Lucky's voice. He hated like hell waking him up from a dead sleep to tell him bad news. "Now I know why the school board was willing to sell me that computer so cheaply."

For days he had been scavenging the town for a secondhand computer and had finally heard of one the public school system was willing to part with for a nominal price.

"It doesn't work," was Lucky's dismal guess.

"Not so far."

"Damn."

"Ditto."

The silence between the two telephone terminals was rife with disappointment. "Well, come on home," Lucky told him. "You shouldn't have stayed with it this long."

"No, I'm going to try one more thing before calling it a night. Should I telephone Chase?"

"Naw. I know he asked you to, but why wake him up if the news is bad?"

"My thoughts exactly."

"Damn," Lucky repeated, "I wish Sage would call and report in, so we'd know where we stood with Belcher."

Harlan concentrated on a hangnail as he picked at it. Trying to sound casual, he asked, "Nothing yet?"

"Not a word. I guess she didn't want to talk business over New Year's Eve. She and Travis probably had plans."

Though he knew better, Harlan went along with Lucky's theory. "Yeah, probably."

"I'm sure the Belchers were either entertaining or being entertained on New Year's Day, so I guess in light of the holiday, Sage hasn't had a chance to talk to Dr. Belcher. Still, you'd think she could call and tell us that much."

"I'm sure she has her reasons," Harlan said lamely.

"Who the hell knows what goes on in a woman's mind? Ouch, Devon, that hurt!" he exclaimed. Harlan heard him speak softly, "I thought you were asleep." After a pause, he spoke into the receiver again. "Come on home to bed, Harlan."

"I won't be much longer."

"See you in the morning."

Harlan hung up, feeling bereft and jealous of his friend for having a bed partner he could curl up with and go back to sleep. Harlan not only didn't have a partner, he really didn't have a bed, unless one counted the lumpy, narrow bed in the trailer.

The bed he was sleeping in was borrowed. When he was in it at night, he couldn't sleep for thinking about the woman who had slept in it prior to him.

"What's she doing tonight?" he wondered out loud as he picked up a small screwdriver and began tinkering again.

He had worked on the prototype almost around the clock. He never minded hard work, but he was especially glad he had this challenging project to occupy his mind and keep it off Sage.

She had guts, that lady. She had showed the stuff she was made of when Chase and Lucky suggested that she contact Travis's father as a potential source of financing. Placed in that kind of compromising position, any other woman might have fainted. Or burst into tears. Or begun stammering explanations.

Sage had foundered for only a heartbeat or two before smiling brightly and saying, "That's a great idea!"

Harlan had watched and listened with disbelief. She was indefatigable. At the risk of letting her brothers down, she perpetuated her original lie.

One had to admire her tenacity and unselfishness. Because she wasn't lying now to save her own skin. In fact, just the opposite. No matter how much pride she had to swallow, she would go see Dr. Belcher for her brothers' sake.

She had maintained the pretense all through dinner, babbling on about how much influence Belcher wielded and how certain she was that he would be the solution to their problem.

"I know he's invested in other ventures and has been very successful," she had told them over homemade enchiladas. By the time they'd got to the orange sherbet and Oreos, she was saying, "I'll leave first thing in the morning."

That's when she had looked him straight in the eye, something she had avoided doing up to that point. Her eyes dared him to expose her. He wouldn't, of course. This was her gig. She had to play her part as she saw fit without any direction from him.

"Excuse me now," she had said, leaving the table. "I'll go upstairs and pack." Her voice was high and light, her eyes unnaturally bright, but he seemed to be the only one who noticed.

He'd sat there mute, dipping his spoon into melting orange sherbet, and watched her climb the stairs, knowing that going to Houston and having to face the father of the man who had jilted her would be the hardest thing she'd ever had to do. He doubted he would have the courage to do something like that.

Sage did. She was the damnedest woman he'd ever met.

By the time he came downstairs the following morning, Laurie informed him that Sage was already on her way. "I hate for her to be driving on a holiday weekend, but I couldn't talk her into postponing her trip. She's so headstrong."

That was an understatement. Sage Tyler was about the stubbornest individual he'd ever come across, inordinately obstinate and proud and courageous. She was also the most desirable woman he'd ever had any contact with, and there had been no small number of them.

From that mane of blond hair to the tips of her toes, Sage Tyler was sixty-some-odd inches of fascinating female. He liked the way she tossed her head with impertinence and the way she tapped her foot with impatience. He liked her sauciness. He admired her spunk. And he positively loved the way she kissed.

She was a compact package of vibrant femininity.

The sad thing was, he didn't think Sage knew just how feminine and desirable she was. She had been so busy proving that she was as important to the family as her brothers, that she hadn't realized no one except her doubted it. She saw her femininity as a weakness, not a strength.

It wasn't going to be easy to convince her of the contrary either. Anything Laurie said, Sage dismissed as the words of a loving mother, blinded by bias. She thought she was merely tolerated and patronized by her brothers.

What she needed to convince her of her value was the right man.

"And you ain't him," he said, jabbing the screwdriver to emphasize each grammatically incorrect word. "So put that thought right out of your head."

When he kissed her, he could tell instinctively that the power of her passion was unknown to her. Once she made up her mind to kiss, she poured her all into it. Her mouth became the soft core of her world. If that were true of a kiss, Lord only knew what it would be like to—

He snapped his wandering thoughts away from treacherous territory.

The strength of her sensuality had probably scared off a lot of men because it posed a threat to their masculinity. Belcher, no doubt, was among them. But some lucky man would eventually acknowledge it, welcome it, and seize it. He would be a charmed sonofabitch. He would spend the rest of his life satisfying the hungry lioness he had unleashed.

In the course of the last few minutes, Harlan's jeans had grown uncomfortably tight. Just thinking about Sage prompted a physical response. That had to stop. Twice he'd come close to showing her what she was capable of, and where had it got him? She hated him.

He couldn't afford that. Not if she was going to be working with him at Tyler Drilling. He knew the Tylers. They liked him and believed in his ideas, but if it came down to a choice between Sage and him, he would be out in no time flat.

Of course, leaving at some point in the future was inevitable. He never stayed anywhere long. But he always liked to finish what he'd started before moving on. He had never walked out on a project, except one time when he'd discovered the man he was working for was a gangster.

Sage Tyler, with her fiery temper, tempting body and cream-center mouth, posed a far more serious danger than that temporary alliance with the mob. He'd do well to stay the hell away from her.

But as he tinkered with the insides of the machine, his thoughts kept drifting back to her. He wondered where she was, what she was doing, and if she felt as lonely as he.

"This was a hell of an idea," Pat grumbled as he nudged Laurie forward. They were standing in the breakfast line at Milton Point's new McDonald's restaurant, waiting to place their order. "I feel like a damn fool, Laurie."

"Why should you?"

"Because I've never eaten a breakfast wrapped in paper with a goofus clown printed all over it."

"I explained the reason I wanted to meet here," she whispered over her shoulder. "You've been out to the house for breakfast every morning this week."

"So?"

"Two Egg McMuffins, two orange juices, two coffees," she told the smiling hostess. Then to Pat she said, "I'm afraid the children are going to think you're sneaking in to spend the night with me."

"Which isn't a bad idea."

She shot him a withering glance over her shoulder, then moved aside so he could get their tray. They found a vacant table near the windows. Highway traffic sped past. Pat squeezed himself between the bright orange banquette and the small table. Muttering swear words beneath his breath, he removed his Stetson and placed it on the padded seat beside him.

"You're acting like a big baby."

"Babies don't get horny," he mumbled around the first bite of his sandwich.

Laurie blushed and tried to look annoyed. "Watch your language in front of me, Pat Bush. I swear, I don't know what to make of you lately. You've been so ornery."

"I'm tired of all this. I'm tired of having to beg. New Year's is over. What's your next deadline, Easter? Memorial Day?"

Into his argument, he leaned across the table. "Listen, Laurie, it's not like we don't know each other. It's not like you doubt I love you. I've loved you for almost forty years. If Bud had lived, I'd have gone on loving you in my own silent way.

"Even after he died, I bided my time. I didn't want to offend you or have you thinking I was trying to take advantage of your loneliness. The day Lucky's baby was born and I kissed you in the hospital corridor, well, that was about the happiest day of my life.

"But stealing a few kisses now and then isn't enough. Sitting beside you in church, having meals at your house, and escorting you to this and that doesn't cut it anymore. Neither one of us is getting any younger." She opened her mouth to speak, but he shook his head sternly and continued.

"I don't want to waste any more time. I want us to live together. I want to see you naked. I want to make love to you."

"Shh, Pat! People will hear you."

"Let 'em. I don't give a damn. I want you, Laurie. All of you. All the time. Through my entire adult life, I've had to share you with my best friend, and your children, and everybody else you take under your wing. Well, dammit, I'm feeling real selfish all of a sudden. I want to be the center of your attention, or I don't want your attention a'tall."

After a moment of combative staring, she said, "That was some speech."

He gnawed off a bite of his cold and nearly forgotten sandwich. "That's how I feel."

"So now I know."

"So now you know."

She pinched a crumb off her biscuit and rolled it between her fingers. "Pat?"

"What?" he asked crossly.

"I was just wondering."

"What?"

She looked up at him through her lashes. "Is your bed large enough for the two of us?"

Sage hummed in tune with the radio as she approached the Milton Point city limits. It was a cold morning. A raw north wind was blowing, but the skies were clear.

Her mood was just as sunny.

She passed the town's new McDonald's restaurant and considered stopping for breakfast, but decided against it. She was so eager to tell her brothers her good news, she would go straight to the office. After hearing what she had to report, they would probably want to take her out for an elaborate, celebration lunch.

Long before dawn she had checked out of the budget motel where she'd been staying the last few days—including New Year's Eve and New Year's Day—and headed north. Luckily she had beaten Houston's rush hour traffic and had made good time. Devon's car, which she had borrowed since hers was still in Austin, was newer than hers and much sleeker. The miles had ticked by.

Or maybe time had only seemed to fly because her spirits were soaring. Her meeting with Dr. Belcher couldn't have gone better. He'd been surprised, no *shocked*, to hear from her when she finally worked up enough nerve to phone his office. She had asked to speak to him personally about a nonmedical matter. He had expressed reservations, but had finally agreed to an appointment yesterday afternoon.

It had gone splendidly.

Still on the outskirts of town, she exited the major highway and jounced along the rough road that led to Tyler Drilling. Both Lucky and Chase's vehicles were parked in front of the building, signaling that they were already there. She checked her hair and makeup in the visor mirror before hopping out of the car and heading for the door.

The mood inside the office was sepulchral. Lucky was desultorily tossing a baseball toward the ceiling and catching it. Chase was contemplating the contents of his coffee cup. They raised grim faces to her when she came bouncing in, smiling and rosy-cheeked.

"Hello, Sage."

"Hi, Sage."

"Hi! Why so glum? I've got great news."

"We heard it already."

"You heard about Belcher?"

Lucky's lips drew thin with dislike. "Yeah."

"I don't get it." Their lack of enthusiasm rubbed the gilt off her brilliant smile. "Didn't he tell you that he agreed to finance the prototype?"

"That's what he said," Chase remarked.

"Then—"

Lucky interrupted her, but not before sending the baseball crashing into the farthest wall. "We told the pompous sonofabitch to shove his money where the sun don't shine."

She fell back a step and wheezed, "What?" All her anxiety, the hard sell, the pride she'd had to swallow! For nothing? "*Why?*"

"You don't have to pretend with us any longer, Sage. We know about Travis and you. We heard about the way he just dumped you and announced his engagement to another girl at the big New Year's Eve bash."

"You . . . you . . ." She couldn't form a coherent thought, much less vocalize it.

"If our sister isn't good enough for that slimy, wimpy bastard, then we don't want any part of his ol' man's damn money!" Lucky stood up so fast, he knocked over the chair he'd been slouching in. "To think of him leading you on all this time and then jilting you right before Christmas." He slammed his fist into his other palm. "I'd like to get my hands around his scrawny neck. Harlan said—"

"Harlan?" *Harlan!* "Where is he?"

"He's sleeping late this morning in his trailer," Chase told her. "He called a while ago and said he'd been up all night and that—Hey, Sage, where are you going?"

She bolted out the door and clambered down the steps to the car. She jammed the key into the ignition, shoved the transmission into gear, and floored the accelerator. The chuckholes went unnoticed as she sped toward the trailer. Her rear wheels skidded on the loose soil and sent up a shower of pebbles when she braked in front of the Streamline.

As before, the doors were unlocked. She didn't bother to knock, but stamped inside and turned left, storming through the tiny galley into the narrow hallway that led to the sleeping area.

He was lying diagonally across the bed on his stomach, all four limbs extended. The covers were twisted around him. Sage picked up the extra pillow and hit him on the head with it.

"You bastard! You scum! You lowlife creep!"

Harlan rolled to his side and brought up one arm to protect his head from the raining blows. "What the—"

"I'm going to kill you!" She raised and lowered the pillow in rapid succession. "How could you do this to me? You ruin everything. You've ruined my life. Ever since I met you—"

The breath whooshed from her body when Harlan grabbed one of her arms and yanked her down onto the bed. He wrestled the pillow away from her and tossed it aside. It fell against a red lava lamp on the nightstand and sent it crashing to the floor.

"What the hell's the matter with you?"

"Let me up!"

She began to buck and kick and flail her arms. He anchored her legs to the bed by throwing one of his across her thighs. She tried to knee him in the groin. He managed to avoid emasculation, but barely.

"Stop that! Dammit, Sage, calm down. What the hell brought this on?"

"You told them. How long did you wait after I left town to go blabbing everything? The minute my back was turned you betrayed my confidence."

"I don't know what the hell—Ouch!"

Astonished, he gazed down at the four thin lines of blood oozing from his chest. Cussing elaborately, he manacled her wrists together and pulled them over her head, stapling them to the mattress with his own hard fingers.

"If you scratch me again, I swear, I'll cut off every one of your fingernails at the quick."

"I don't care. I don't care if you shave my head. I don't care what you do to me. You couldn't humiliate me any more than you already have."

"Just what did I do that was so horrible? Huh? I haven't even seen you for almost a week." He secured her by lying across her.

She squirmed beneath him, trying to get away. Eyes narrowed with loathing, she said, "You waited until I got out of town, then, like a sneaky coward, you told them."

"Told who what?"

"You let me go through the humiliation of begging that old buzzard for an appointment. I had to sit there and listen to his patronizing explanation for Travis's seemingly sudden engagement. 'She's been his friend and companion since they were children, Sage. I'm sure you understand these things, Sage. Travis honestly didn't want to hurt you, Sage. It has always been more or less understood that he and this other young lady would marry one day, Sage.' On and on he went until I wanted to throw up all over his desk.

"But for the sake of Tyler Drilling's future, I sat there with my eyes lowered and my mouth zipped and took every condescending word he uttered. I wanted to tell him how glad I was to be away from his weak-willed son and his overdressed, overbearing, overweight wife. Instead, I acted demure and properly heartbroken."

She glared up at Harlan, whose face was bent low over hers. "But it was worth eating humble pie because I came away with his promise to finance the prototype. I got what I wanted out of the old codger.

"Then you ruined everything by telling Chase and Lucky about Travis. Didn't you realize how they would react? Didn't you know that their family pride wouldn't tolerate his rejection of me? Are you sure you didn't forget any titillating details? Did you tell them every heart-rending word he said when he jilted me?"

"I didn't tell them."

His firm but quiet denial only made her more furious. She renewed her efforts to get away from him. "You did! I know you did. You're the only one who knew."

"Belcher knew."

She ceased struggling and gaped at him. "What?"

"Belcher knew. If someone told your brothers, it was Dr. Belcher. Not me. I swear it, Sage."

He didn't look like a lying man. His blue eyes were still puffy from lack of sleep, but they were steady as they probed hers. She moistened her upper lip with her tongue and was surprised to taste perspiration there. Or had that saltiness come from tears?

"But Lucky said that you said . . . something." She hadn't waited to hear the quotation. Was it possible he was telling her the truth?

"The only thing I've said about Travis in Lucky's presence was that my opinion of the guy coincided with his. He asked me if I'd met him when I went to Houston to get you. I told him that, no, I hadn't had the pleasure. I said I had only seen Travis from a distance, but that to me he looked like a guy who was more interested in a woman's position on the social register than her favorite position in bed.

"After a few off-color remarks, which I doubt you'd enjoy hearing repeated, I told him that when I arrived, Travis and you were having a serious discussion. He asked me if I knew what the discussion had been about. I hate lying, Sage, but for your sake, I told him no.

"That conversation took place on Christmas Day, long before you even thought about returning to Houston and asking Belcher for money. So if Lucky and Chase know about your broken engagement, the news came from somebody else."

She pulled her lower lip through her teeth and tried unsuccessfully to stem the flow of tears. They fell anyway, rolling down her temples into her hair.

"I've made a fool of myself in front of you again. I hate you," she whispered earnestly.

"Right now, the only one you hate is yourself." He shook his head sadly, as though he deeply regretted the agony her stubborn pride continually put her through. "Don't be so hard on yourself. Everybody makes mistakes."

One of his hands still had her wrists pinned to the mattress. The fingers of the other sank into her hair and settled against her scalp. "Shave your head, huh?" Laughing softly, he dipped his head and caught one of her tears on the tip of his tongue, then brushed his lips across her damp cheekbone.

"Stop that. What are you doing?"

"Giving you what you've been asking for all along."

"I don't know what you mean. You always talk to me in riddles. You—"

"Sage, be still and shut up."

"I said to, uh, stop. Harlan . . . Harlan, don't. I mean it now. Hmm . . ."

His mouth settled firmly on hers, and when he parted her lips with his agile tongue and delved into her mouth, she was all too willing to keep quiet. Only small sighs of gratification escaped her throat. Her anger dissipated like morning fog after sunrise.

She purred.

He released her hands but she didn't even realize it until he slid both his beneath her sweater and, after unfastening her brassiere, laid them on her breasts. He tenderly squeezed her, reshaping her flesh to fit his strong, yet gentle, hands.

With her hands free, she could have pushed him away or scratched him again. Instead she laid one arm across his bare back and cupped his head with her other hand. Her mouth became his to explore and penetrate. She did some exploring of her own, slipping her tongue into the sweet heat of his mouth, tasting him, and sipping at his lips when they had to pause for breath.

His caresses grew bolder and more impatient. She moved restlessly beneath him. Tacitly they agreed that she had on too many clothes. When he angled her up to peel off her sweater, she obliged him.

That's when she noticed that he was naked. She sucked in a quick breath of surprise. He shrugged. "Never sleep in anything."

The muscles of his long arms were well defined, as was each strong vein. His chest was wide and hairy. The swirling pattern of hair tapered at his narrow waist, then flared again, dark and abundant, around his full sex. He was quite beautifully made.

A small, airless exclamation of excitement escaped her before she could stop it.

The sheets felt cool against the skin of her back when she lay down. They smelled like Harlan. She wanted to wallow in them but wasn't given the opportunity.

He lowered his rumpled, blond head over her breasts and flicked her nipples with his tongue, catching them briefly between his lips, bringing an ache of longing to her lower body and a sense of euphoria to her soul.

When he drew one raised crest into his mouth, her back arched off the bed and she moaned with shameless need. He laid his fingertips against her lips; she kissed them while his mouth tugged on her with exquisite finesse. Mindlessly, she clutched him, raking her nails through the pelt of golden hair on his chest.

"Before you draw blood again, we'd better get you out of these clothes." He spoke jokingly, but his eyes were concentrated points of vivid light. Much as hers must look, she thought.

When she lay beside him naked, he gazed at her, cursing softly beneath his breath. "Lord, but you're something to look at, Miss Sage."

His lips drew hers into another entrancing kiss. Only the introduction of his fingers into her soft, vulnerable flesh could have jolted her out of the golden haze spinning around her.

"Harlan, don't hurt me," she whispered breathlessly.

He raised his head and looked down at her inquisitively. "Hurt you? What do you take me for? I wouldn't dream of hurting you." Smiling at her gently, he bent down to kiss her again as he positioned himself between her thighs.

She felt the velvety smooth tip of his penis separate, enter, stretch, penetrate her.

She gave a soft cry.

Harlan went rigid. His head snapped up. Bridging her with stiff arms, he pushed himself up and looked searchingly into her face. In the space of seconds, a thousand questions were telegraphed from the depths of his eyes. Then he pinched them shut, bared his clenched teeth, and swore lavishly.

He didn't move, didn't say anything for so long, that Sage became anxious. She raised her hands to his armpits and slid them down his corrugated sides.

His breath hissed through his teeth. "Don't. Please don't move." His eyes came open. "See, baby, you're just so . . . tight," he grated. "So . . . ah . . . so small." He ducked his head, his eyes fastening on her breasts beneath his chest. "So beautiful," he added huskily.

He palmed her breast and stroked the dainty pink nipple with his thumb. When he did, her body reacted by closing around him reflexively.

"Aw, Sage," he groaned, lowering himself on top of her again. One arm curved around her waist and lifted her lower body up against his. He buried his face in her neck and closed his teeth over a bite of her flesh.

Sage felt his spasms deep inside her. It was a thrilling sensation, but she wasn't sure what he expected of her. Her recent mistakes had made her self-conscious and unsure. The feelings rioting inside her were so new and transporting, she didn't want to spoil them by doing something foolish, so she tried to lie still.

Her body, however, countered the commands of her brain. Her hips lifted and ground against his in a circular pattern. She clasped his taut buttocks between her thighs. Grasping hands kneaded the supple muscles of his back.

For several moments after his climax, Harlan didn't move. Gradually, he unsnarled his fingers from her hair and disengaged their bodies. He rolled away from her to sit on the edge of the bed, elbows propped on his knees, his head held between his hands. Staring at the floor, he muttered self-deprecations.

Now that it was over, the enormity of what she had done hit Sage. She hastily gathered her clothes and slipped into the closet-sized bathroom.

Chapter Ten

There wasn't much she could do about the whisker burns around her mouth or on her neck. The ones on her breasts wouldn't show. She rinsed her face with cold water. She washed all over with a washcloth, redressed, and raked her hands through her hair, trying to restore it to some semblance of order. In her enraged haste, she had left her purse in the car. With the resources that were available, she'd done as well as she could.

She gripped the doorknob for several moments, garnering all the courage possible before returning to the bedroom. There was no more than twelve inches of space on either side of the bed, so she instantly came face-to-face with Harlan.

Or rather belly to face, as he was still sitting on the edge of the bed. He had, however, pulled on a pair of jeans. Sage thought she must be the most wanton woman in the history of the species because—with his touseled hair, whisker bristle, bare chest and feet—Harlan looked mouth-watering. Her tummy fluttered, and, though she hadn't even begun to chastise herself for what had just happened, she wanted it to happen again.

"Sage," he began, raising his hands in a gesture of helplessness, "I don't know what to say."

"Good. Because I don't want to talk about it. I've got to go. G'bye."

She slipped through the narrow door and hastened down the passageway. He caught up with her in the galley and turned her to face him.

"We've got to talk about it."

She stubbornly shook her head no.

"Why didn't you tell me that you were . . . that you hadn't . . . that I was the first?"

"It wasn't any of your business."

"Maybe not until ten minutes ago. Then it became my business."

"That's where it ended, too."

"Like hell it did. Did I hurt you?" He reached up and touched the corner of her whisker-burned lips. "Christ, Sage, I could have hurt you."

"Well, you didn't, so stop acting guilty."

"Are you . . ." He paused to swallow hard. "Bleeding?"

Embarrassed and exasperated, she lowered her eyes. "You're the one who's bleeding." There were still four distinct red lines on his chest. "I'm sorry I did that to you."

He made a negligent motion with his hand, dismissing the scratches. "I've got to know if you're all right."

"Yes!" she cried, her voice cracking. Rather than show him how emotional she felt, she resorted to anger. "I thought you'd be crowing. Now I've really given you something to gloat about, haven't I?"

She freed her arm from his grasp and left the trailer. She was tempted to run but didn't, wanting to maintain a shred of dignity. On the other hand, she didn't dawdle. From the open doorway, Harlan watched her leave, the expression on his unshaven face grave. She avoided meeting his eyes as she backed the car away before turning into the road. She hadn't gone far when she met Chase driving toward her in one of the company trucks.

"Sage," he called from the open window. Extending his arm, he flagged her down. "What's going on? Why'd you hightail it out of the office like that?"

Her choices were limited to two. She could either burst into tears and confess to her older brother that she was afraid she had fallen in love with the wrong man. Or she could brazen it out.

Since the former was unacceptable, even to herself, she forced a smile. "I lost my temper."

"Over Belcher?"

"Indirectly. See, I thought Harlan was the one who'd told you about Travis and me."

"Why would you think that?"

"He overheard my conversation with Travis the night he came to Houston for me." Nervously, she wet her lips and tasted Harlan. Was his taste visible, like a milk mustache? "I confronted Harlan about it. He . . . he claimed he hadn't said anything."

"No, we didn't hear it from Harlan. Dr. Belcher called this morning to say how glad he was that we could work together on a business venture despite what had recently happened between you and Travis. I was in the dark as to what he meant. When I asked him for an explanation, it all came out."

"I'm sure he painted me as the wounded loser in a love triangle."

"Something like that."

"Well, he's wrong."

Chase hesitated a moment, studying her, as though gauging the veracity of her statement. "Then why didn't you tell us, Sage? Why put on an act this last couple of weeks?"

"Because I didn't want to involve the rest of the family with my problem. It would have put a pall over Jamie's arrival. The holiday would have been spoiled. What purpose would it have served except to make everyone uncomfortable and uptight?"

"You still should have confided in us, Sage," he said gently. "That's what this family is about. If one of us is suffering, we all take it to heart. You know that." He grinned. "Ever since Belcher's call, Lucky has been threatening to go to Houston and pound Travis to mush."

She rolled her eyes. "And wouldn't that be dandy?"

"Say the word and we'll both go."

Heart swelling with love, smiling her gratitude, she shook her head no. "But thanks for the thought."

"Mother's gonna have a conniption fit."

"Oh, Lord, you're right, Chase. I dread having to tell her. She'll want to ply me with hot tea and extra food."

"Humor her. It'll make her feel better to fuss over you." He reached across the space that separated his truck from her car. She extended her hand and took his through the open window. "Sure you're okay?"

"Don't worry about me. I wasn't as brokenhearted as everyone might presume."

"I'm glad to hear you say that, Sage. Travis is no big loss."

"True. The other loss is much greater—Dr. Belcher's contacts in the business community."

He shook his head with a stubbornness she recognized. "No way. We'll survive without the Belchers' help, thank you."

It was gratifying to know that her brothers felt that strongly about it, although it wasn't the wisest stand for them to take. It demonstrated their loyalty and formed a family bond that included her.

She squeezed Chase's hand before releasing it. "I was on my way home. I left Houston awfully early. I'm ready for a nap."

"You do look a little ragged around the edges. Marcie's a good listener if you'd like to talk to another woman about the breakup."

"I don't want to dwell on it. I'd rather mark it up as a bad experience in my past and go forward from here."

His expression was still full of misgiving. He sensed that something was bothering her, but couldn't isolate it. "Go home and get some sleep."

"I intend to. Bye."

She raised her car window, waved at him, and drove away. Arriving home, she was glad to see that no one was there. Laurie and Devon were probably out running errands. She climbed the stairs, one hand trailing wearily along the polished bannister as she lugged her suitcase with the other. Instinctively, she headed for her former room before remembering that someone else now occupied it. Retracing her steps, she went into the guest room.

After her bath, she examined her body in the long mirror mounted on the back of the bathroom door. She looked remarkably the same. It didn't seem possible. She felt so drastically different, it was a mystery to her why the changes were invisible.

More mysterious than that, however, was why she had allowed "it" to happen with Harlan Boyd. Countless young men had tried to woo her in a variety of ways ranging from the ridiculous to the romantic. She flung herself on to her bed.

Harlan. Expending very little effort, he had accomplished what so many had tried to do and failed.

It had never seemed right or natural before. Travis had asked, of course. At one time, he had even suggested that they get an apartment together. He wanted to elevate the intimacy of their relationship, he had said. Her reasons for not wanting to were vague, even to herself, so for months she had hedged. Finally, he'd stopped pressing her.

Then this blue-eyed, slim-hipped drifter had come along, and she melted when he looked at her. It made no sense. Harlan represented everything she did *not* want in a mate. She wanted at least a promise of future prosperity. He had no visible means of support. She wanted big-city slick. He was country scruffy.

In the last thirty-six hours, she had groveled to Dr. Belcher, failed in her first endeavor for Tyler Drilling, and had had sex with the hired hand.

"You're doing great, Sage," she muttered sarcastically into her pillow.

Maybe Harlan was right about her being too hard on herself. To err was human. Perhaps she was just more human than most. There was a positive side to everything negative.

Even though she had swallowed a great deal of pride in order to go to Dr. Belcher, he had been impressed with her courage to face him so soon after Travis's rejection. She must have convinced him that their irrigation system was marketable. Her sales presentation had sold him on the idea. He had enthusiastically pledged to invest in it. The reason for the deal falling through had been circumstantial, not poor salesmanship.

Only Harlan and she would know what had happened between them this morning. He wasn't going to tell because he didn't want to sacrifice his job or his friendship with her brothers.

She'd just have to grit her teeth and bear his smugness, which shouldn't be too difficult to do because, if things went well, she would be traveling for the company. They wouldn't be spending that much time together.

She snuggled deeper into the covers, nursing the kernel of optimism that was germinating. Now that everyone knew about her broken engagement—her brothers were certain to tell her mother and their wives —she could relax. The deception would no longer be a dark cloud hanging over her head.

As she had told Chase, she wanted to leave the past behind her and move forward. She now had specific career goals, which would not only serve her self-esteem, but also benefit the family business.

During the years spent at the university, she had missed living at home, surrounded by her family. Now she had a niece and a nephew to spoil. Her mother would be delighted to have her back. They could spend much more time together. It would be like old times. Her mother loved to baby and indulge her.

Comforted by the thought, she drifted off to sleep.

She woke up to the delicious aroma of roasting meat. Her stomach growled, reminding her that she hadn't eaten in almost twenty-four hours. As she dressed, she noted that the sun was setting. She had slept nearly the entire day. Feeling fresh and rested, despite the incident that morning, she opened the door to the bedroom and skipped downstairs.

She met Harlan coming up. Sage froze. He stopped. Their gazes locked. Sage might have stayed petrified beneath the power of his gaze had he not lowered it to encompass the rest of her body. When he did, a surging fever took the path of his eyes, engulfing her.

She forced herself to move. With both of them living under one roof, this was likely to happen often. She wouldn't let his presence intimidate her into being a prisoner of her bedroom. Whose house was this anyway, his or hers?

Her intention was to brush past him with a mumbled word of greeting. Nothing more. She didn't quite succeed. When she reached the step immediately above him, he raised his hands and bracketed her hips, stopping her in midflight. The heels of his hands settled on the knobs of her pelvic bones. His fingers followed the curve of her hips toward her back.

"Sage?" He looked up at her entreatingly. "You okay, baby?"

His voice was so soft and compelling, it alone was almost capable of stopping her in her tracks without the use of his hands. She was extremely conscious of their position on her body because it was reminiscent of that morning. She might have moved into his arms and begged him to hold her if she hadn't seen the one emotion in his eyes which was anathema to her—pity.

"Excuse me," she said coldly. She pushed away his hands and went around him, jogging down the remainder of the stairs without looking back. "Mother?"

"In here," Laurie called from the kitchen.

Her cheeks were flushed from the heat of the stove. An old apron covered her flannel slacks and sweater, but she'd never looked prettier to Sage.

"I'm so glad you're back, dear."

She held out her arms, and Sage moved into her maternal hug. "It's good to be back, Mother."

They prolonged the embrace, each sensing that the other needed to. Sage inhaled Laurie's familiar fragrance and felt like a child again, in search of comfort and getting it where it could always be found.

When at last they pulled apart, she said, "I know that by now Chase and Lucky have told you about Travis."

"Yes."

"I want to assure you that I'm fine. I was mildly disappointed at first, but that didn't last long."

"I'll bet you were more mad than disappointed. You didn't mind the breakup so much as the fact that he was the one who did it."

"You know me too well, Mother."

"I am very pleased by the outcome," Laurie said staunchly, stabbing a boiling potato to test its tenderness. She replaced the lid on the pot and turned back to Sage. "It'll take a stronger man than Travis Belcher to satisfy you."

Sage's insides took a free-fall. She had a clear recollection of how strong Harlan was, yet how tender. How greedy, yet giving. Every time she thought about him stretching and pulsing inside her, she grew weak. She had entertained a foolish notion earlier today that what she had felt for him was love, when, in fact, he was just particularly gifted at sexual stimulation.

She turned away before her mother could notice that her own cheeks were turning rosy. She couldn't use cooking as an excuse. "What's all this food for?" she asked.

"I invited Chase and Marcie over for dinner."

Sage groaned. "We aren't going to have a wake for my dead romance, are we?"

"Nothing of the sort."

"I really don't want anyone's condolences, Mother."

"Chase made that clear to everybody. Now stop fussing about it and help me set the table."

By the time they were finished, Devon had brought Lauren downstairs and set her in her high chair to watch while they dished up the food. Lucky returned home from work, kissed his wife and daughter, then excused himself to go wash up. On his way through the kitchen door, he paused.

"Are you surviving, brat?" Sage stuck out her tongue at him. He grinned broadly. "She seems perfectly normal."

Pat arrived at the same time Chase's family did. In the ensuing confusion, Sage didn't notice precisely the minute Harlan came down from upstairs. But she knew the instant she backed into a solid body that it was his. Her bottom bumped against his middle.

With a grunt of pleasure and surprise, he raised his hands to rest lightly on her ribcage. "Careful there."

"Sorry."

"No problem."

Her hands were occupied with the heavy platter of food she was carrying. Quickly, she moved away from him and scurried into the dining room. His touch had left her jumpy. She could still feel the hot impressions of his fingers through her clothing. The low, confidential tone of his voice reminded her of everything he'd said while their bodies had been joined.

They all gathered around the dining table. To her consternation, Sage was relegated to a place next to Harlan. Amidst the aromas of roast beef, steamy, buttery vegetables, and Laurie's homemade yeast rolls, she picked up whiffs of his cologne.

Keeping up with the mealtime conversation was difficult. Harlan's nearness proved to be a constant distraction. They bumped knees numerous times. When they reached for the salt shaker at the same time, their fingers collided.

She covertly watched him handle his silverware. Those were the same hands that had elicited chills and heat waves from her skin. When he blotted his lips with his napkin, she recalled those lips repeatedly kissing her nipples until they were raised and aching, then sucking them into the damp heat of his mouth.

Everyone behaved normally, but Sage sensed that her family was closely observing her, as though her indifference to being jilted might be a facade and that at any moment she was going to succumb to emotional collapse.

She might, but not for the reason they believed. Little did they know that the reason for her strained expression, insincere smile, and uncharacteristic nervousness wasn't Travis, but the man sitting right beside her.

With a gusto she didn't feel, she ate food she couldn't taste with an appetite that was counterfeit. What she felt was arousal. All she wanted to taste was Harlan. The only thing she had an appetite for was the weight of his naked body upon hers.

While they were demolishing a chocolate layer cake and drinking coffee, Pat surprised them by rising from his chair and clinking his fork against his water glass. Everyone fell silent and looked toward him curiously.

"Uh, Laurie figured that I ought to be the one to, uh, tell y'all."

"Jeez, Pat," Lucky remarked, "the last time you looked this sickly, you were telling us that I was being formally charged with arson."

Laughter went around the table. Pat didn't laugh. In fact he looked ready to throw up. He ran his finger round the inside of his collar. "No, it's nothing like that this time. It's . . . well, you see . . . we, Laurie and me that is, uh . . . ."

Laurie left her chair and moved to stand beside him. She slid her arm around his waist. "What Pat is trying to tell you, and doing a poor job of it, is that he's asked me to marry him and I have accepted."

"If y'all don't mind," Pat interjected.

"Mind?" Lucky was the first out of his seat. "I'm relieved. I was afraid she'd get a reputation as a loose lady before you got around to marrying her."

"James Lawrence!"

He silenced his mother's admonitions with a bear hug. He was moved aside by Chase who also enveloped her in a hug. Devon and

Marcie were kissing Pat's ruddy cheeks and dabbing happy tears from
their eyes. Harlan added his hearty congratulations by pumping Pat's
hand and unself-consciously hugging Laurie.

Sage stood up slowly and moved toward the middle-aged couple,
who were smiling as giddily as children. No one could doubt or begrudge the love between them.

Sage hugged Pat first. "I'm so happy you're finally becoming an
official member of this family. We're all slightly nutty. Are you sure
you know what you're getting into?"

"Damn sure," he said, affectionately tugging on a lock of her hair.

When Sage turned to Laurie, the older woman gazed anxiously into
her daughter's face. "I know this isn't the best time to spring this on
you, Sage."

"It's the best time for you and Pat. That makes it the right time. He's
waited years for you."

"You knew?"

"How could I not?" she exclaimed. "You didn't raise any dimwitted
children. Except for Lucky."

"I heard that," he shouted over Lauren's crying.

Sage gave her mother a sustained hug, squeezing her eyes tightly
shut, holding in the stinging tears. Not for anything in the world would
she have them know that another rug had been yanked out from under
her. She wondered how many were stacked beneath her. Which one
would be the last one, the one that sent her plunging into a black abyss
of despair?

Chapter Eleven

The wedding took place two Saturdays later, although the sisters-in-law complained that such short notice barely gave them time to prepare.

"Give the guy a break," Chase had said in response to their protests.

Lucky had agreed. "From the looks of him, poor Pat's about to burst."

Despite the joke he had cracked directly following Pat's announcement, Lucky and the rest of them knew that their mother would never sleep with a man, even one she loved as much as she loved Pat, until she was married to him.

"Laurie, Pat, you've asked your family and friends to gather here today to witness your exchange of wedding vows and to celebrate your love for each other."

The officiating pastor had known the bride and groom for years. He seemed as happy about the marriage as the other guests who filled the first several rows of the church.

Sage, serving as her mother's attendant, tried to concentrate on every word coming from the pastor's lips, but her eyes strayed beyond Pat's shoulder to the man seated in the second pew.

Harlan wasn't attentive to the ceremony either. He was watching Sage. Every time she turned around, she fell victim to his eyes, which seemed to follow her everywhere, even into her dreams.

They no longer gloated or provoked her with their know-it-all smugness. The intensity that had replaced it, however, was even more disturbing. She was afraid he would see too much, perceive things she didn't want him to know.

For the last two weeks, she had avoided him whenever she could.

Along with her sisters-in-law, she'd been terribly busy making arrangements for the wedding.

Harlan spent most of his time at the garage working on the prototype, which even the prenuptial chaos hadn't deterred. He began to look thin and drawn. At first Sage thought it was her imagination, then she heard Laurie nagging him about his lack of rest, overwork, and poor appetite.

There were lines making deep parentheses around his mouth today, but he looked extremely handsome. His hair was combed, somewhat. He had dressed up, somewhat. He was wearing boots, but they were shined. His dark slacks were pressed, and, though he had on his bomber jacket instead of a suit coat, he had compromised by wearing a necktie. His shirt was starched and showed up starkly white against his tanned face.

During the brief ceremony, against her will, Sage's gaze was drawn again and again to his electric-blue stare. The magnetic power of it made her angora sweater-dress feel uncomfortably warm and snug. The padded, beaded shoulders felt like football pads weighing her down. The butterscotch color was one of her most flattering.

She knew she looked good. But the last thing she wanted to do was look good to Harlan. She would rather die than have him think she was trying to attract him. According to the single-minded way he was staring at her, however, he liked not only what he saw on the outside, but what was underneath too.

"You may now kiss your bride, Pat."

Tears collected in Sage's eyes as she watched the big, burly sheriff, his own eyes glistening suspiciously, draw Laurie into his arms and kiss her. Sage remembered how much her mother had suffered through her father's lengthy illness and eventual death. She deserved this happiness. Apparently she was flourishing in Pat's love. Looking incandescent, she turned and faced the congregation.

Sage had hostess duties to attend to at the house, so she and Devon left the church as quickly as possible. They had decorated the house with flowers, greenery, and candles and had prepared all the food with the exception of the tiered wedding cake.

The guests complimented them effusively. The rooms of the house rang with laughter and echoed genial conversations. It was a joyous day.

The party passed in a blur for Sage, who welcomed the tasks that occupied her. They kept her away from Harlan and gave her something else to think about.

Before she realized how much time had elapsed, everyone gathered on the front porch to see off the newlyweds. Laurie went to each of her children individually and hugged them, then she drew Chase, Lucky, and Sage into one giant hug. Pools of tears collected in her eyes as she said her final good-byes.

"I love you all so much. Thank you for being such wonderful children. Thank you for being happy for me."

"Better get her away from here, Pat," Chase quipped. "She's beginning to leak."

Amidst laughter and a barrage of good wishes, Pat escorted his bride to her car—they couldn't very well take his squad car on their honeymoon—and drove off beneath a shower of rice.

The guests began to disperse until only the family was left. While both babies were asleep upstairs, the men pitched in to help with the unpleasant chore of cleaning up.

When everything was done, they convened around the kitchen table for sandwiches. "Wedding cake and canapés just doesn't do it," Chase said, stacking sliced ham and Swiss cheese onto a piece of rye bread.

"Maybe we should have packed Laurie and Pat a lunch to take with them," Devon said. "They ate less than anyone and have a long drive ahead of them."

Their plans were to drive to the New Mexico mountains, where there was snow in the higher elevations. Neither had any desire to ski, merely to enjoy each other and the scenery from their cozy suite at a ritzy lodge.

"Are you kidding?" Lucky chortled. "They've probably already stopped for the night not ten miles from here. I'll bet Pat made it no farther than one of those motels on the interstate."

"I understand they can be very romantic," Marcie said, glancing teasingly at Devon and Lucky.

Lucky reached over and squeezed his wife's shoulder. "Damned if you're not right, Marcie."

Devon was known to give as good as she got. With no compunction whatsoever, she hooked her hand around Lucky's neck and kissed him long and hard on the mouth. When she finally released him, he gasped for breath. "I love weddings. They make the womenfolk horny as hell."

Sage cast a nervous glance toward Harlan. He was observing her with the motionless concentration of a jungle cat. She left her chair and carried her empty glass to the refrigerator to get a refill of her drink. A moving target was harder to hit, she thought, feeling like prey caught in the fine cross-hairs.

Chase groaned. "Little good it does me for Marcie to be horny."

"That's the only bad thing about having a baby. How much longer?" Lucky asked sympathetically.

"Two more weeks and counting," Marcie replied, laying a consoling arm across her husband's shoulders. He lowered his head and laid it on her chest.

"The thing about weddings and women," he said dreamily, "is the organ music. It reminds them of the sounds they make when they make love."

Sage dropped her glass. It crashed to the floor and shattered. Milk splashed up on her shoes and stockings.

Marcie shoved Chase's head away. "You should be ashamed of yourself! You embarrassed your sister, and I don't blame her one bit."

Lucky was laughing so hard, he was clutching his waist. "That was a good one, big brother. Wish I'd've thought of it myself."

Devon was trying as hard as Marcie to stifle her own laughter.

Sage didn't dare look toward Harlan. This conversation was for happily married couples who were comfortable with jests about sex. It was torture for two people who had a guilty secret to hide.

She mopped up the spilled milk with a dishtowel, and, in the process, cut her hand on a piece of broken glass. As she was bent over the sticky mess, a familiar pair of boots moved into her field of vision.

Harlan squatted down beside her and began picking up the larger chunks of glass. "Let me help with this."

"No thanks."

He caught her hand. "You're bleeding."

"It's nothing," she said, pulling her hand from his grasp. "I'm going upstairs to change."

She darted upstairs, shimmied out of her dress, kicked off her suede shoes and peeled off her hosiery. She replaced the finery with her oldest pair of jeans, riding boots, and a heavy jacket. In the bathroom medicine cabinet, she located a Band-Aid and placed it over the cut before working her hands into tight leather gloves. Within minutes, she was on her way down the stairs, carrying the new quirt she'd been given for Christmas.

"I'm going riding," she announced as she sailed through the kitchen without even slowing down.

"Now?" Chase glanced through the kitchen window. "It's almost dark."

"I won't be gone long."

Before they could stop her, she bolted through the back door and ran toward the barn. She saddled her favorite horse in record time. As soon as they cleared the yard, she nudged the gelding into a gallop.

The wind tore at her hair. It felt icy on her cheeks when it connected with the wet patches her tears had left. She had ridden quite a distance before it no longer felt as though her chest was going to crack from internal pressure.

She sucked in the cold air. It hurt her lungs and brought new tears to her eyes, but at least it was a new pain. For two weeks, ever since learning of her mother's intention to marry, she'd been coping with her sense of loss.

It was selfish of her, she knew. She wouldn't begrudge either her mother or Pat their happiness together. But their marriage only compounded her feelings of alienation.

What was she going to do? Where was she going to live? With whom did she belong?

Laurie had told them of their plans to live in Pat's small house. Lucky had objected.

"This is your house, Mother."

"It's *our* house," she had corrected. "It belongs to all of us. But Devon and you are using it to raise your family in, and I couldn't be happier about that. I love this house. I loved the man who built it. But now I love another man. I want to live in his house, with him, as a newlywed."

Sage knew she would always be welcome in the ranch house. It was her home, too. As Laurie had said, it belonged to all of them. Devon and Lucky wouldn't boot her out.

Even so, she would feel like an intruder now. The house should be home to a nuclear family. She wasn't part of that anymore. She didn't belong there any longer. She didn't belong with Laurie and Pat. She didn't belong . . . period.

There were hundreds of thousands of career women who lived alone. That wasn't what bothered her. It was that she felt so cut off from everything familiar and dear. Laurie's first priority would be Pat now. That was as it should be. Chase and Lucky had their families.

What did she have? Nothing. No real home. No real career. No one.

She reined in her horse and dismounted. Laying her cheek against his muzzle, she admitted to him that she was indulging in a bad case of self-pity. Sympathetically, he nudged her shoulder.

"I'm no use to anybody. What am I going to do with the rest of my life?"

The gelding, his short supply of sympathy expended, dipped his head and began to graze.

Sage's swift departure left a vacuum in the kitchen. Lucky was the first to speak. "What got into her?"

Harlan reached for his jacket on the wall rack and pulled open the door. "I'll go after her." He left almost as hastily as Sage had.

"I haven't wanted to bring it up, but Sage has been acting peculiarly," Marcie said.

"How can you tell?" They all shot Lucky a dirty look. "Well, she's always been a little off the wall, hasn't she?" he said defensively.

Chase said to Marcie, "You've mentioned this before. I've gone out of my way to be nice to her. You don't think it's helped?"

Marcie shrugged. "Something's still bothering her."

"I've noticed it too," Devon said. "She hasn't confided anything to me though."

"Me either," Marcie said.

"Could it be Belcher?"

Devon's brows puckered. "I really don't believe so, Lucky. I never was convinced she was madly in love with him. I think I would recognize the signs." She exchanged a tender look with her husband.

"I agree, Devon," Marcie said. "All I know is that she hasn't been herself since she came home for Christmas."

"You don't think she could be jealous of Pat, do you?" Chase suggested. "Taking her mommy away, his becoming more important to her than Sage is."

They silently pondered that for a moment, then Marcie said, "Their marriage might have contributed to the problem, but I don't think that's at the base of it. Sage is too emotionally well-grounded for the marriage to throw her for such a loop."

Worriedly, she glanced toward the door. "I feel badly saying this, but, I'm not sure Harlan is the right one to go after her."

"You think Sage's weirdness might have something to do with Harlan?" Lucky asked.

"I don't know," Marcie hedged. "There seems to be a lot of latent hostility between them." Almost as soon as the words were out, she negated them with a wave of her hand. "I'm probably imagining it."

"You're not," Devon remarked. "The other day I saw them meet on the stairs. He tried to engage her in conversation. She moved right past him with barely a civil word. I didn't think too much of it then, but, now that you mention it, on more than one occasion I've seen her snub him."

"Well, I'll be damned," Lucky muttered. "He's such a likable guy." He looked across the table at Chase. "What do you make of it?"

"Hell if I know. Maybe she's sore because we brought him into the company. It's always been strictly family before. In any event, I'd better find her before he does."

"I'll come too."

Minutes later, the brothers were in Chase's pickup, following the dirt path across the pasture.

At the sound of approaching hooves, Sage raised her head from her horse's neck. The twilight had turned so deep that at first the rider appeared only as a dark, moving shadow. He slowed his mount to a walk and clip-clopped toward her.

Recognizing the shape of his hat and breadth of his shoulders, she warred over being irritated or overjoyed that he had followed her. Harlan threw his leg over the saddle and dropped to the ground.

"What are you doing here?"

He hitched his head in the direction from which he had come. "They were worried about you. The way you tore out, we were scared you'd break your neck. Or the gelding's."

"I appreciate your concern, but, as you can see, the horse and I are fine and don't need any assistance. Especially yours."

"I'm just relieved we won't have to shoot either him or you."

Sage, her expression thunderous, moved to the animal's side and placed her boot in the stirrup. Before she could boost herself up, Harlan caught her arm and pulled her around.

"How long did you figure on avoiding me?"

"Forever."

"After what happened between us?"

"I told you I didn't want to talk about it."

"Well, I do," he said, raising his voice to a near shout. "I've got plenty to say on the subject. And since I risked my own neck galloping out across this prairie after dark, you're damned well going to stand there and listen until I'm finished."

With the grip he was keeping on her arm, she couldn't very well leave. Not that she wouldn't fight for her freedom if she really wanted it. In spite of herself, she wanted to hear everything that was obviously pressing on his mind.

"Okay. You've got me," she said tersely. "What's so important that I've just got to hear it?"

"You were a virgin, Sage."

"I know that better than you."

"So now I've got to wonder whether or not you were taking birth control pills."

She inhaled a short, little breath. When she opened her mouth to speak, she discovered she was temporarily mute. She shook her head no.

He removed his hat and slapped it against his thigh. "Christ."

"Well, don't worry about it, Mr. Boyd," she said acidly. "If there's a *problem,* I'll take care of it. I absolve you of any and all responsibility."

"Guess again, Miss Sage," he said, pushing the words through clenched teeth. "I didn't ask to be absolved. I just wanted to know everything we're up against. What the hell were you thinking about to go to bed with a man who didn't protect himself and didn't protect you? You ought to be horsewhipped for such criminal disregard for yourself. For all you know I could be carrying a disease."

She swayed and placed her hand upon the gelding's flank for support.

"I'm not." His voice gentled a bit. "I've always taken the proper precautions before. As you'll recall, I didn't have any pockets on me when you came barging into my bedroom."

The memory of his beautiful nakedness left her cheeks warm. "Is that all you have to say?" she asked huskily.

"No. Hell no." He released her arm and slid both hands into his back pockets. He stared into the dark distance for a moment, before looking at her again. When he spoke, his breath vaporized in the cold air, creating a cloud between them.

"I didn't want anything bad to happen to you, Sage. You've got to believe that. It blew my mind when I realized you were a virgin. By the time I did, it was too late. I was in solid." Their eyes collided. Sage's fell away quickly. His voice had dropped an octave when he continued. "I planned to just, uh, you know, pull out."

She swallowed hard and stared fixedly at the point of his shirt collar.

"But, you were . . . It was . . . Hell, I don't have to tell you how it was." He blew out a gust of air and muttered a swear word. "You moved a little, baby, and I was lost."

His breathy words brought back all the sensations that had assailed her as it happened. His voice and the intensity with which he spoke made it real again. Feeling dizzy, she instinctively reached for support.

He captured her shoulders and drew her against him, then tightly wrapped his arms around her. His lips moved through her hair.

"Tell me you're all right. Reassure me, Sage."

"I'm all right. I promise. I'm fine."

"I didn't hurt you?"

"No."

"Swear?"

"Swear."

"I couldn't have lived with myself if I had hurt you, but, damn, you felt good, Sage. Did you, uh, get any pleasure at all out of it?"

She nodded against his chest.

"A little?"

"Some," she murmured shyly.

"You mean more than a little?"

Again she nodded.

Sighing "Ah, Sage," he used a fistful of her hair to pull her head back. His parted lips sought hers. The cold night only made his mouth feel hotter, wetter, softer. They kissed hungrily until he pulled away and pressed her face into his open collar, where she could smell his clean skin, feel his strong heartbeat in his neck.

"Listen, I know you haven't had time to know if there's a baby or not. With the wedding and all that's been going on, you might not have even thought about it."

She hadn't. The act itself had so overwhelmed her that she hadn't had room in her brain to consider anything else, even the consequences.

"What I'm saying," he went on, "is that if you skip a period, I want to know about it right away. I'd want to do the right thing, Sage. I'd marry you."

The warmth of his body, the security of his embrace, the low tone of his voice had lulled her into a false sense of tranquility. The edges of cold reality had been blunted by his caresses, his deep kiss, and the feel of his breath in her hair.

But when the meaning of his words finally penetrated this lovely haze, it dispelled it completely and instantly. Immediately replacing the rosy fog of romanticism was a red mist of rage.

Sage shoved him away from her at the same time the toe of her boot connected with his shin. "You bastard!" She doubled her fists and aimed blows at his head, most of which he succeeded in dodging. "I don't need your charity. I can take care of myself. Who would want your help? I wouldn't marry you—"

"Sage, calm down. I didn't say it right. What I meant—"

"I know what you meant." She flew into him again.

"Stop that. Dammit! Stop. I don't want to have to hurt you."

"Hurt me!" she shrieked. "All you've done since I met you is hurt me in one way or another," she said, belying her previous assurances.

He managed to grab both her wrists, which infuriated her. She struggled and kicked and curled her fingers into claws that, if ever freed, would scratch his eyes out.

It startled them when a pair of headlights cut a swathe through the darkness and landed on them like a spotlight. Seconds later, Chase and Lucky stood silhouetted against the bright lights.

"What the hell is going on here?" Chase demanded.

"You'd better have a damn good reason for holding her like that, Harlan," Lucky barked.

"I do. If I let her go, she's liable to kill me."

"I will!" Sage threw her shoulder into his ribs. He grunted and bent at the waist.

Wheezing, he said, "She . . . she might be—"

"No!" She froze, ceasing all her struggles, and gazed up at Harlan imploringly.

"I've got to tell them, Sage." He gave her a look full of regret, then faced her brothers again. "She might be pregnant with my baby."

For a moment the atmosphere crackled with expectation, like the suspension of time between a close lightning flash and the clap of thunder.

"You sneaky sonofabitch!"

Lucky launched himself at Harlan. Harlan pushed Sage out of the way just in time. Lucky's fist caught him in the gut. He doubled over only to be brought upright by a crunching uppercut to his chin.

"Lucky, I don't want to fight you. I want to—"

Whatever appeal Harlan was about to make was cut short by another punch that glanced his shoulder. Dodging it caused him to lose his balance. He landed on his bottom in the dirt.

He flung his head up and glared at her brother. Sage recoiled from the fury in his eyes. "Dammit, I said I didn't want to fight you, but you give me no choice." Then he pulled himself to his feet, ducked his head, and charged Lucky.

"Chase," she shouted, "do something!"

Chase wasn't as short-tempered as his younger brother, but he was as powerful, strong, and quick. He had never backed down from a fight, especially one where the family's honor was at stake.

But, although Sage had threatened to kill Harlan herself moments earlier, she was relieved to see that it wasn't going to be a two-against-one fight. Rather than joining in, Chase tried to break it up.

Lucky and Harlan were having none of it, however. They were slugging it out ferociously. Both men fought off Chase's peacemaking overtures. He got a bloody nose for his efforts. Sage wasn't sure whose fist had landed the blow.

For a while Lucky had the upper hand. Harlan was on the defensive. Then the tables turned. Harlan became the aggressor. He pummeled Lucky's middle, paused, and then sent one vicious fist into his chin. It was a solid punch. Lucky's head snapped back. He stumbled backward, turned, and careened into the grill of the pickup.

Even from where Sage was standing, she heard the bone in his forearm snap. He seemed to hang in suspension for an agonizing eternity before sliding to the ground. Cradling his right arm against his stomach, he collapsed into the dirt.

Chapter Twelve

Sage had thought she understood the definition of misery.

As thorough as *Webster's* was, however, the definition fell far short of comprehensive explanation. Until tonight Sage hadn't realized misery's total dimensions, its height and breadth. Misery went bone-deep. Like a severe chill, it could cause one to huddle beneath layers of blankets without any hope of ever getting warm. Misery caused one's teeth to chatter. It cramped muscles until they ached.

She stared wide-eyed into the darkness beyond her bed, reviewing the bizarre events that had taken place in the last several hours.

If she closed her eyes, she could still see Harlan and Lucky fighting in the unworldly glare of the pickup's headlights, raising clouds of dust that swirled dizzily in the twin beams. She heard again the sickening sounds of splitting skin and snapping bone. She vividly recalled seeing her brother's face, grimacing in agony, his lips white with pain.

Chase had hustled her and Lucky into the cab of the truck and then driven like a bat out of hell to the ranch house. It had been a rough ride. Lucky had cursed elaborately with every jolting motion of the truck.

Their arrival had created panic and pandemonium throughout the house. All their clothes were bloodstained, though exactly whose blood it was remained uncertain. In addition to his broken arm, Lucky's jaw was bruised, one of his eyes was swelling shut, and there was a nasty cut on his lip. Within minutes he was on his way to the hospital accompanied by Devon and Chase. Marcie and Sage stayed with the children, who were already down for the night.

It was a while before Sage remembered the horses that had been deserted in the pasture. She ran to the stable. The horses had been returned to their stalls, unsaddled, and rubbed down. Obviously

Harlan had done it, but he was no longer around and his truck was gone.

Near midnight, Chase and Devon returned home without Lucky. The break in his arm had been clean and would heal without complications, but the doctor advised that he spend the night in the hospital for observation.

"He didn't want to," Devon had told them. "But I insisted. Could I prevail on you to spend the night here? If I was needed at the hospital or something . . ." she finished lamely.

Chase and Marcie agreed to spend the night. Sage showered and got ready for bed, executing each task routinely. Her body and mind were numb. No one had pointed a finger and specifically blamed her for what had happened, but the silent consensus must be that it was her fault.

Chase knocked on her door just as she was turning out the light. "Is there any possibility of truth to what Harlan said about you being pregnant with his child?"

"A possibility, Chase," she answered meekly, unable to look at him directly, "but very little likelihood."

"Did he rape you, Sage? Because if he did, I'm not going to bother calling the police. I'm going after the sonofabitch myself."

"No! Don't do anything, Chase." She couldn't bear the thought of causing her family more grief, worry, and difficulty. "He didn't force me. It wasn't like that at all."

"Did he coerce you in any way?"

"No. It was . . . mutual."

He stood on her threshold for several moments more. She could almost feel his eyes boring into the crown of her bowed head in search of the truth. "All right," he said at last. "Good night."

"Good night. Oh, Chase," she said, calling him back. "You're not going to try and notify Mother and Pat, are you?"

"We discussed it on the way to the hospital and decided not to ruin their honeymoon."

Vastly relieved, she said, "That was my thinking, too. Good night."

That conversation had taken place hours ago, and she still couldn't sleep. Lucky was in the hospital on account of her. Chase was threatening to hunt down Harlan and inflict bodily harm or worse. Her sisters-in-law had been told the reason for the fight. They kept their eyes lowered when speaking to her, either out of pity or scorn. She couldn't be sure.

Her whole family was in an uproar, and it was her fault. How had things become such a jumble? The week before Christmas she had thought she had her life under control. When it began to topple, it had come crashing down and now lay around her feet in shambles.

She had made some bad decisions which had affected not only her, but everyone around her and the family business. Thinking of that, she groaned and buried her head in her pillow.

Chase and Lucky were so optimistic about this irrigation system. They saw it as a means of getting them in the black again. What possible future did it have now? As things stood, their working with Harlan again wasn't even within the realm of possibility. The business would sink until it hit bottom. The blame would rest on her shoulders.

The chill in her bones suddenly vanished. She grew uncomfortably warm and kicked off her electric blanket. Leaving the bed, she began to aimlessly prowl around the room.

She couldn't allow the family business to fail. If it did as a result of her poor judgment, she would never recover her self-respect. Her Grandpa Tyler had started that business. Damned if it was going to be said that it had collapsed because his only granddaughter had had hormones that made her succumb to the allure of sexy blue eyes and a well-fitting pair of old Levi's.

"I'll be damned first," she vowed into the darkness.

She had to do something, anything, to prevent that from happening. But what? She was almost afraid to do anything except stand still. Recently, every step she'd taken had been a wrong one. If she wanted to prove herself worthy of the Tyler name, she couldn't afford any more errors.

But, no pain, no gain.

No guts, no glory.

The T-shirt philosophies echoed through her head. Some of them began to carry weight and make sense. That was probably dangerous thinking, because the idea that was jiggling the lock on the back door of her mind was risky to say the very least. Should she invite it in to take a look around?

All she knew for certain was that she couldn't return to bed and pull the covers over her head. She had to make a move now, before the light of day and the dawn of reason stopped her to reconsider.

Before she could talk herself out of it, she hurried to the closet, took out her suitcase, and began to pack.

"Hellfire and damnation!"

Harlan stuck his injured thumb into his mouth and sucked on it hard.

While trying to attach the trailer to his pickup, he'd mashed his thumb between two immovable objects of metal. The trailer hitch was being uncooperative. He could hardly expect anything to go smoothly after the evening he had spent.

"Just goes to show what being honest and open with folks can get you," he said to the trailer hitch, which finally connected.

He heard the approaching car before he saw the headlights slicing through the trunks of the surrounding pine trees. He eased himself into an upright position, although standing perfectly straight caused some parts of his battered body to ache and throb. Of course, a few cuts and bruises wouldn't matter if the Tyler boys were toting shotguns this time.

Resigned to having another fight, he braced himself for it, mentally and physically. He didn't relax one iota when he saw Sage, not her brothers, alight from the car. If anything, he tensed up tighter.

"Before you say anything, hear me out," she stated for openers.

"You'd better get out of here, Sage, before they catch you with me. Or did they send you in as bait to see if I'd bite?"

"I told you to hear me out," she snapped. "I'm alone. Chase is at home asleep and Lucky is in the hospital."

"Jesus." He dragged his hand over his face. He hadn't intended to hit him that hard. The sound of the breaking bone had turned his stomach. He had wanted to go with them and help out, but knew his help wouldn't be welcome.

"Don't look so stricken," Sage said. "It could have easily been you instead. The doctor's only keeping him there overnight for observation." She pulled her coat tighter around her. "It's cold out here. Can we talk inside?"

"No way. Besides, in case you haven't noticed, I'm clearing out. Five minutes more and you would have missed me."

"Then you'd have missed a golden opportunity."

"To do what? Get beaten to a pulp by one of your irate brothers? No thanks. I'll pass. Right now the only option open to me is to leave."

He pointed his finger at her. "But I swear to God, Sage, I'm coming back. When I do, if you're carrying my baby, I'm laying claim to it if I have to hogtie you and carry you off. I'll keep you and my baby, and I don't care if your brothers come after me with all the bloodhounds of hell."

"There won't be a baby," she said with annoyance. "I'm going inside."

She sashayed past him and stepped into the trailer. Knowing it was a bad idea that he would surely regret, Harlan followed her. The door slapped shut behind them. It wasn't much warmer inside the trailer. He'd already disconnected the generator and turned off the heat.

Sage was rubbing her hands up and down her arms, but he sensed the action was more from restlessness than cold. She was keyed up, moving around like a high-strung filly at the starting gate of her first race.

"Say what you've come to say and then scram," he said. "You're a peck of bad news."

"I have a proposition to make you."

"Isn't that usually left up to the man?"

"Not that kind of proposition."

His eyes narrowed suspiciously. "Then what kind?"

"Answer a question first."

"Conditions already, and I haven't even heard the proposition."

She frowned, but didn't address his sarcasm. "How far are you from finishing the prototype?"

He folded his arms across his chest and leaned against the door. "Why?"

"I want to sell it."

"That's no surprise. That's been the goal all along, hasn't it?"

"No, I mean sell it now. You and I. Together. We start making calls and sell clients on the idea. If they want to see the prototype, will we have something to show them? Before we get to that point, I need a guarantee from you that the damn thing will work."

Several thoughts sprang immediately to his mind, but uppermost was that this was the damnedest woman he'd ever met. Knock her down, she bounced back for more. Fighting or making love, she was fascinating. Her ideas, however, were a little harebrained.

"You want to just strike out and start selling irrigation systems door-to-door?"

"Don't make fun of me, Harlan. I'm serious. I'm committed to this."

"Yeah, well I think you ought to be committed, all right. To the state hospital."

"Damn you, I'm fighting for my future and for the future of my family's business. Stop cracking stupid jokes and answer my simple question. Can you get it to work?"

"It does work."

"It does?" Her mouth hung open for several seconds. Her eyes were wide with disbelief. "It really does?"

"Yep. While everybody else has been in a tailspin doing wedding stuff, I managed to acquire a used computer."

"Acquire?"

"Don't ask."

"Okay, I won't. Go on."

"It didn't fit inside the casing I'd built, but I hooked it up. I tried out the system day before yesterday. If it had been attached to a pipeline, this whole field would be well-watered by now."

Her voice was high and shrill with excitement. "Why didn't you tell anybody? Why keep it to yourself?"

"I was waiting for all the excitement over the wedding to die down. Besides, I wanted to make some adjustments and try it several more times before I broadcast it."

"But there's no doubt in your mind?"

He grinned, unable to contain his own excitement over his success. "No doubt. It'll work."

Sage clasped her hands beneath her chin. "Oh, Harlan, that's great news! That's wonderful!" Galvanized, she shoved him away from the door and reached for the latch. "Let's not waste any more time. We'll take your truck as far as Austin and pick up my car there."

"Whoa! Hold it. Stop right there." He barred her exit. She turned to face him, her expression quizzical. "Correct me if I'm wrong, Miss Sage, but I don't think you discussed this idea of yours with anybody. You sneaked off in the middle of the night with this wild notion and figured to surprise them later, right?"

"Of course I didn't discuss it with anybody. After tonight, they wouldn't let me go away with you."

"Um-huh. So what makes you think I'm going to take you anywhere with me? I'd have to be crazy to take you out for coffee, much less leave the city limits for parts unknown. I don't want every law officer in this state out looking for me with an arrest warrant in one hand and a loaded pistol in the other."

"Don't worry about it."

"Well, I do worry about it. When it comes to my hide, I'm funny like that."

She sighed with exasperation. "I left them a note. I told them that I was with you by choice and asked them not to come after me. I promised to call periodically and let them know that I was safe."

"But you don't intend to tell them what you're up to."

She adamantly shook her head. "Not until I can bring them a contract. I won't come back without one."

"You're forgetting something, Sage." He bent in closer. "You've got nothing to sell."

"That's where you come in. I want you to bring all your blueprints and drawings of the machinery. First we'll sell potential customers on Tyler Drilling's excellent reputation, which they should already know is the best in the oil business. Then we'll show them your designs for adapting drilling pumps to an irrigation system and give the impression that the machinery is already in production and that they'd better get in line if they want one any time soon."

"Which constitutes fraud."

"I wouldn't commit a crime!" She seemed incensed at the very thought. "As soon as we get a contract, we'll rush the machinery into production. In the meantime, you can be working on a solution to the computer problem."

He stared at the floor between his boots, shaking his head and chuckling. "Damnedest, craziest plan I ever heard of."

"It'll work."

"That's what's really scary."

"Harlan," she said, moving forward and laying her hand on his arm. "I know you don't want to disappoint my brothers any more than I do. You told me that you didn't want to betray their trust. What happened between us," she said, her voice thickening, "was as much my fault as yours. I'm not blaming you, but Chase and Lucky, with their outdated code of chivalry, might.

"Doing this provides each of us a way to win back their respect and confidence." She pulled her lower lip through her teeth and looked at him imploringly. "Anyway, I think it's worth a try, don't you?"

"What about this thing that happened between us, Sage?"

"It was an isolated incident, nothing more."

"You think so?" he asked softly. She didn't answer, but he could tell that her own affirmation hadn't convinced her. "We'll be traveling together, in each other's company day . . . and night."

"We're adults," she said hoarsely. "From now on, we're strictly business partners. Agreed, Harlan? Please?"

He studied the face that had already gotten him into trouble with two men he respected more than any men he'd met in a long time. Before it was all over, he'd probably dig himself in deeper, but damned if he seemed to be able to help himself.

She had a way of worming her way beneath his skin, burrowing down into his gut, and curling around his heart. He doubted he could deny her anything when she looked up at him like that, entreating him with eyes the color of smooth whiskey. He'd gotten drunk and done foolish things on whiskey a whole lot less intoxicating than those eyes.

What the hell? He didn't have any particular destination in mind when he left here. He hadn't figured on leaving this soon, so he hadn't made plans. Besides, he hated leaving a job unfinished. He always tidied up after himself before moving on. That had always been important to him. He had never left anyone disappointed in his association with Harlan Boyd.

"Okay, Miss Sage," he conceded on a sigh. "Haul your buns into the cab of my truck. *But,* one derogatory word about it, and you walk."

Lucky hobbled into the kitchen under his own muscle power, but Chase hovered nearby in case his brother needed additional support. Lucky had been discharged from the hospital early that morning and had called asking Chase to come drive him home. As soon as they cleared the back door, Devon raised a hand to her mouth to cover her gasp.

"It's worse than last night," she murmured sympathetically. Hugging him gently, she kissed an undamaged spot on his forehead and led him toward a chair at the kitchen table.

"Yeah, but you ought to see the other guy," he joked through swollen lips.

He had earned a reputation as a hotheaded fighter during his youth and had maintained it up until he met Devon. It had been several years since he'd had a split lip and swollen eye. Wincing, he lowered himself into the chair.

"Does your arm hurt?" Devon asked solicitously.

"I'll live."

"Can you eat?"

"Just coffee, please, for now." He removed something from his jacket. "They gave me this at the hospital." He held up an elbow-shaped straw. "It sucks."

His joke didn't spark much laughter. What little there was sounded forced. The mood around the kitchen table was somber. Marcie glanced warily at Chase as she rocked Jamie. Lauren was taking her morning nap upstairs. Devon kept herself busy pouring coffee for everyone.

While they drank it, Chase told the women the doctor's report. "Lucky'll have to wear that splint for six to eight weeks. He'll look like hell for several days—"

"Thanks," Lucky threw in.

"But then he'll be his usual handsome self."

"Hopefully before your mother and Pat get back," Marcie commented.

Devon reached up to ruffle Lucky's hair, which the hospital pillow had flattened to his head. "I doubt they would be too shocked. From what I understand, he used to look like this frequently."

"Not since I met you." He reached for her hand and squeezed it, then took a sip of his coffee through the straw. "Is Sage up yet? I'd like to talk to her."

For several moments, no one said anything. The other three avoided making eye contact with Lucky. At last Chase cleared his throat and said, "She's gone."

"Gone? Gone where?"

"We're not sure. Just gone."

Lucky's eyes darted around the circle of averted faces. "You're leaving something out, and whatever it is, it's already eating a hole in my gut."

"She left with Harlan."

Lucky swore and banged his bruised fist against the edge of the table, then cursed because it hurt. "And you let her go?"

"I didn't *let* her go." Angrily Chase left his chair and began to pace the width of the kitchen. "She didn't exactly ask my permission, Lucky. She packed her suitcase and sneaked out, leaving a note saying not to worry and that she would call in occasionally and for us not even to think about coming after her.

"I checked, and Harlan's trailer is gone. So are all his schematics of the prototype. By the way, did you know he had a computer attached to it?" he asked out of context.

Lucky plowed his fingers through his hair. "I can't believe you let her waltz out of here with that womanizing bum. Are they eloping or what?"

"Damned if I know. Maybe they took the drawings so he could peddle the idea to some other company."

"I don't believe what I'm hearing!" Marcie exclaimed, surging to her feet.

"Neither do I," Devon said. "Listen to yourselves." She included her brother-in-law and husband in her critical glare. "All we've heard for months is how smart and wonderful Harlan Boyd is. 'He's got terrific ideas.' 'This idea of his is great.' 'If it works, we'll have all our people back on the payroll soon.' 'This is going to save us.' "

"Devon's right," Marcie said. "That's exactly what we've heard.

Chase, just a few nights ago you were telling me how you planned to take over the manufacturing while Lucky handled installation."

"You said the same thing," Devon reminded her husband. "You were so excited about the prospect of working hard again. You took Harlan's idea and ran with it. I haven't seen you so optimistic and full of energy about your business since I met you."

Marcie again picked up the argument. "And all because Harlan figured out a way to adapt your equipment and know-how to do another job. Now, all of a sudden, he's persona non grata. Yesterday, he was a hero. He could work miracles."

"A hero who, behind our back," Lucky mumbled through his swollen lips, "seduced our baby sister."

"So what?"

"So what?" he incredulously repeated.

"Yes, so what?" Marcie said. "She's *not* your baby sister. She's a grown woman. If she wanted to sleep with Harlan and vice versa, it was none of your business. Or yours," she said, making a jabbing motion toward Chase's chest.

"By jumping to conclusions, you're doing Sage, as well as Harlan, a grave disservice," Devon said. "I'm appalled by your lack of confidence in them, particularly your own sister. On top of all that, you're making yourselves look like a couple of fools."

"How's that?" Chase asked.

"I see exactly what she means," Marcie said. "Don't you trust your own judgment of people? You had every confidence in this man twenty-four hours ago."

"Twenty-four hours ago I didn't know he'd taken advantage of Sage."

"You still don't," Marcie shouted at her husband. "Maybe Sage took advantage of him. Did you ever think of that?"

"You, Lucky Tyler," Devon said angrily, "are a fine one to be accusing any man of taking advantage of a woman!"

"Aw, come on, Devon." He spoke hastily in self-defense and winced when the cut on his lip reopened. Nursing it, he muttered, "You can't compare them with what happened between you and me the night we met."

"All I know," Chase shouted over everyone else, "is that Sage is vulnerable right now on account of the breakup with Travis. She's probably feeling bereft over Mother's marriage too. Otherwise, she would never fall for a guy like Harlan."

"Why not? Harlan's gorgeous and sexy."

Lucky's discolored jaw fell open. He was stunned by his wife's comment. "Well now, that's a fine way for a married lady with a baby to be talking about a man."

"I'm married, not blind," she snapped. "And he *is* gorgeous and sexy. Even Laurie thinks so."

"My mother?" Lucky shrieked.

"Yes, your mother. She told me so."

"What makes you an expert on the kind of man Sage would fall for?" Marcie demanded of Chase. Lucky and Devon, occupied with shooting each other fulminating glances, subsided and gave the other couple the floor. They squared off chin-to-chin.

"I know her," Chase said. "I've known her a hell of a lot longer than you have. Harlan, with his lack of polish and breeding, is the last man Sage would go to bed with if her head were on straight."

"Well, love does that sort of thing to people," Marcie said loftily. "It spins their heads around."

"Love? Who said anything about love? At best, we're talking lust here."

"Whatever it is, it has a powerful effect on people. It makes them do crazy, out-of-the-ordinary things."

"Crazy things like running off in the middle of the night with no explanation?"

"Crazy things like making Chase Tyler marry Goosey Johns," she shouted. "What do you figure were the odds against that?" Reining in her redhead's temper, she eyed her husband coolly. "Before you and Lucky get up a posse to go rescue Sage, you'd be wise to consider that she might not want to be rescued." She sniffed sanctimoniously. "You'd better come upstairs with me, Devon. I think I hear Lauren crying."

Carrying Jamie with her, Marcie swept from the room. Devon was right behind her.

Lucky raised his one good eye to his brother and said dejectedly, "I warned you that if they ever teamed up against us we'd be sunk."

"Well," Chase said, then sighed, dropping into the nearest chair, "we're sunk."

Chapter Thirteen

Harlan's pickup didn't even make it as far as Austin.

About thirty miles north of the capital city, the engine began to wheeze. After another ten miles, white smoke started curling from beneath the battered hood.

Sage opened her mouth to speak, but, remembering his threat to make her walk, closed it again. She glanced at him. He was wearing a smug grin.

"I see you're taking my warning to heart," he said, sounding pleased.

Testily, she asked, "Are you going to let it blow up and take us with it?"

"I'm looking for a convenient place to stop."

A quarter of a mile farther, he took an exit to a roadside park. The choking, coughing truck was a laughingstock to the other motorists using the facility. Sage wanted to crouch down in the seat and cover her head.

Harlan, however, didn't appear to be the least bit self-conscious as he got out and ambled toward the front of the pickup. The rusty metal hood screeched in protest when he raised it. A cloud of white smoke billowed out.

He waited, waving most of it away, before ducking his head and bending over the motor. After a few minutes, he came around to the passenger side. Since Sage had no window to roll down, she put her shoulder to the door and shoved it open.

"What's the diagnosis?"

"Busted water hose," he reported. "The radiator has boiled dry."

"Is that bad?"

He propped one elbow on the corner of the door and looked at her with amusement. "It is unless you want to burn up your engine."

That sounded like an attractive way of dispensing with the detestable vehicle. "I don't suppose this heap is insured."

He shook his head. "Don't believe in it."

"Triple A?" she asked hopefully.

"Nope."

"Then what do you suggest?"

He began unbuttoning his flannel shirt. When the buttons were undone, he tugged the shirttail from the waistband of his jeans and peeled it off. "Hold this."

She took the shirt he thrust at her and watched speechlessly as he crossed his arms over his chest and pulled up the hem of his plain, white T-shirt. He took it off over his head, leaving his torso bare.

It bore bruises from last night's fist fight. Morning sunlight glistened on his chest hair. The chilly wind shrank his nipples.

Sage's tummy did a flip-flop.

With both hands, he ripped his T-shirt down the middle, then tore off the sleeves. He moved to the front of the pickup again, giving Sage a good view of his shirtless back, which was almost as tantalizing as the front. His pale blond hair curled down over his nape. His skin was stretched smooth over supple muscles.

Curious, she leaned out the door so she could see what he was doing beneath the raised hood. Dry-mouthed and fascinated, she watched the muscles of his lean arms flex and relax as he wrapped the strips of cotton around the leak in the hose. His veins stood out. His hands looked strong and capable as they tied a hard knot in the cloth. From a nearby hydrant, he replaced the water that had leaked out.

He slammed the hood cover and headed for the square brick structure that housed the public toilets. "Be right back," he said over his shoulder. "Got to wash my hands."

Sage hastily turned the rearview mirror toward her. The image it reflected came as an unpleasant shock. Not only did she feel like she had been up all night, she looked it. Since getting eight hours of sleep was currently out of the question, she did the best she could with the cosmetics in her handbag.

As Harlan had improvised to repair the pickup, she improvised to repair her face, working quickly so he wouldn't think her vanity had anything to do with him. Just as he rounded the corner of the building, she crammed her hairbrush back into her purse and tried to appear impatient and bored over the delay.

Moments after he climbed into the cab, he sniffed the air. "Do I smell perfume?"

"I wanted to freshen up a little. Is that all right with you?"

"Sure, it's fine with me. You looked like hell before." Miffed, she pushed his shirt toward him. He caught it and began to laugh. "You can't take a joke, can you?"

Resting his forearms on the unfashionably large steering wheel, he turned his head and gazed at her. "If it makes your ego feel any better, Sage, I've had a hard time keeping both hands on the wheel."

The stare they exchanged became uncomfortably long. During it, Sage reminded herself that theirs was a business-only relationship. That had been her rule. She had decreed it, so she couldn't be the first one to break it. Besides, she couldn't let anything distract her from her ultimate goal. Harlan didn't even have to try very hard to be a distraction. In fact, he didn't have to try at all.

She finally pulled her eyes away from his stare and nodded toward the hood. "Is it, uh, working now?"

"Oh, it's working all right," he replied huskily.

"Do you think it will explode?"

He swallowed hard. "It might. I've just got to make sure it doesn't get too hot."

Having the distinct impression that they were talking about two different engines, she nervously moistened her lips. "Aren't you going to put your shirt back on?"

"Why? Does looking at my bare chest bother you?"

"Not at all."

He grinned in that knowing way that made her feel transparent. As he connected the two bare wires that started the motor, he added, "Miss Sage, you're no better at lying than you are at taking a joke."

"This is really fun. I feel a sense of freedom, don't you?"

"I've been free since I was fifteen, remember?"

They were speeding down the six-lane divided highway that bisected the Texas map from the Red River, south to the Mexican border.

"Well, being completely unencumbered might be nothing new to you, but it is to me," Sage said. "I feel as carefree as a gypsy."

From Austin she had insisted that they travel in her car, which had been left parked at her apartment since the day Travis had picked her up and driven her to Houston for the holidays.

Over the last several months of her college career, she had gradually been moving things from the apartment which had been home for three years. Her two roommates were pleased to purchase her share of the furniture and household items since they planned to continue living there. What few personal items that remained, they promised to store in a spare closet until a convenient time for her to take them.

At the bank, she emptied her savings and checking accounts. It wasn't a sizable sum, but she wouldn't soon starve. While she had been settling her affairs, Harlan had gone off alone and returned to the apartment on foot.

Within a matter of hours, they were heading south from Austin, traveling lean. She had asked him to drive because she was too excited and nervous to concentrate. Now that old ties were severed, her mission well defined in her mind, her plan in full swing, she was bursting with energy and enthusiasm.

They had gone several miles before she thought to ask him about his Streamline trailer. It had been necessary for them to leave it behind since her car didn't have a trailer hitch.

"I left it with a friend," he told her. "He owns a filling station. Said I could park it behind his building."

"Are you sure it'll be there when you come back for it?"

He frowned at her. "I said he's a friend. We worked on the same offshore rig for a time. That's like going through a war together."

"What about your truck? Did you just desert it on the side of the road?"

"That would've been a waste, wouldn't it? I sold it for two hundred dollars."

"Two hundred dollars! What idiot gave you two hundred dollars for that piece of junk?"

"A junk dealer."

"Oh." They smiled at each other. His eyes returned to the road. Sage asked, "Have you always worked in oil-related industries?"

"Mostly."

She waited for him to elaborate. He didn't. His reticence aggravated her, so she probed. "If you had to fill out a form of some sort, what would you write down as your occupation?"

"I never fill out forms," he said.

"But if you had to."

"I don't."

"Harlan!" she cried in frustration. "Just suppose you did."

He heaved a sigh. "Okay. I guess I'd say I was a professional troubleshooter. If somebody has a problem, I go in and try to fix it."

"Somebody? You mean anybody?"

"If I like them and they like me, and if I believe I can do them some good."

"So you scout out people with problems?"

Clearly uncomfortable talking about it, he shrugged. "Yeah, I guess you could say that. Like when I met Chase in Houston last year, I liked him immediately. It was mutual. He told me his company had bottomed out. I wasn't available to help at the time, but I didn't forget him. As soon as I was free, I went to Milton Point."

"Once a problem is solved—"

"To everybody's satisfaction . . ."

"You—"

"Move on to another one."

"No attachments."

"That's right."

"Ever?"

"Ever."

"Hmm."

She pondered the stretch of highway for a moment, suddenly feeling lonely and dejected. He disposed of things—trailers, pickup trucks—easily and with no remorse. When it was time to move on, he left people behind, too, without looking back. Sage wondered how many women he had left behind, women who had been in love with him.

The thought took the fizzle out of her effervescent mood. For the next few miles, she said nothing.

"There's a Dairy Queen up ahead." Sage pointed to the familiar red and white sign. "Let's stop. I'm starving."

"Sage, we stopped an hour ago because you had to go to the bathroom. Thirty minutes before that you had to have a Snickers bar or die."

"It's suppertime. Let's stop and eat, then drive all night."

"Okay. But with your stomach and bladder along for the ride, I'm afraid we'll never get to the valley."

They had made the Rio Grande Valley their general destination because there was so much agriculture in that region. They reasoned that cotton and citrus growers would be potential customers for their irrigation system.

The Dairy Queen was doing a thriving dinner business. They had to wait in line to place their order.

"I'm so hungry, I could eat a horse," she murmured while perusing the menu.

"Sorry. Not on the menu."

Undaunted by his teasing, she said, "I want a cheeseburger with everything. A large order of fries. A chocolate shake. And an order of nachos."

"With peppers?"

"Of course with peppers. What're nachos without peppers? Lots and lots of peppers."

That's when he kissed her. One second she was smiling up at him, smacking her lips in greedy anticipation of the spicy food, and the next, he was curving his hand around her nape and drawing her mouth up to his for a long, deep kiss that blocked out the racket of the restaurant. She tentatively rested her hands at the sides of his waist, then slid her arms around him and hugged him tight.

Harlan ended the kiss long before she was ready for him to. He gazed into her face for a moment, telling her with his eyes that propriety and not desire had prompted him to end it.

He draped his arm across her shoulders and pulled her close. She left one arm around his waist and reached up with the other to clasp his hand where it dangled over her shoulder. Sage thought that, to everyone else, they must look like a couple in love out on a casual date.

At that moment, she desperately wanted them to be.

When it came their turn to order, Harlan smiled down at her as he spoke to the waitress. "The lady wants an order of nachos with peppers. Lots and lots of peppers."

Sage gorged indelicately on the fast food. Food hadn't tasted this good to her in . . . She couldn't remember when food had ever tasted this good and wondered if Harlan's kiss had, in some mystical way, seasoned it.

"Want another cheeseburger?" he asked as she polished off the last bite.

Laughing, she blotted her mouth with the paper napkin. "No thanks, but it was delicious. It's been ages since I've had one."

"Didn't Don Juan ever take you to a Dairy Queen?"

"Travis?" Even saying his name sounded odd now, as though he had belonged to another lifetime. In a very real sense, he had. "The future Dr. Belcher wouldn't be caught dead in a fast food restaurant. For a while, he got on a health food craze and tried force-feeding me stuff like bean curd and tofu."

"Tofu? Is that a cousin to toe jam?"

She laughed until she was weak . . . and Harlan didn't even seem to mind that she was making a public spectacle of herself. In fact, he seemed to enjoy her laughter.

It was getting dark by the time they got underway once again. Her full stomach, general sense of well-being, and the monotonous growl of the car's engine made her sleepy. Before long, she was having a hard time keeping her head upright and her eyes open.

"Here," Harlan said, patting his right thigh. "Lay your head here and stop fighting it."

Warily, Sage stared at the notch of his thighs where his jeans were soft and faded and far from roomy. "I'd better not," she said uneasily. "You might fall asleep while you're driving."

He chuckled. "Having your head in my lap is one surefire way of keeping me wide awake." He laughed out loud at her startled expression. "I was only kidding. Come on." He patted his thigh again, and she couldn't resist. She lay down along the seat and gingerly laid her head on his thigh.

He swept her hair off her neck, exposing it briefly before covering it with his hand. His thumb stroked her jaw. "Nighty-night, Miss Sage."

"I won't sleep. I'll just rest my eyes for a minute or two."

He continued to idly stroke her neck, jaw, and earlobe.

The next thing she knew, he was nudging her awake. "Come on, Sage, sit up. My leg's gone to sleep."

Woozy, she sat up but seemed unable to open her eyes. "What time is it?" she mumbled. "Why are we stopped?"

"It's going on midnight. I stopped because the center strip was blurring into two. I'm sleepy and didn't want us to become a highway statistic. By the way, did you know you snore?"

"Shut up," she said grouchily, rolling her shoulders and rubbing her neck. "Where are we?"

"A nice, clean motel."

Because clean was an amenity, she was instantly suspicious. She forced her eyes open and looked around. The individual bungalows were limned with pink neon tubes. In the central courtyard, some prickly pear and a few oleander bushes struggled for survival around a swimming pool so murky a person could walk across it. The office of the complex looked sinister and dim behind a blinking blue star. A pair of longhorns were mounted above the door.

"Great. Texas's rendition of the Bates Motel. Norman Billy Bob Bates and his dead mother, proprietors."

"This is a nice place. I've stayed here before."

"Somehow that doesn't surprise me."

"Sit tight. I'll see if they've got a vacancy."

"What, are you kidding?"

Moments later, he came back wagging a key. On the short drive from the office to the cabin they'd been assigned, she said, "Couldn't we stay in something luxurious, like a Motel Six?"

"We'll only be here for a few hours' sleep. All we'll be using are the beds."

"You're right about that. I'm sure not going to take a shower. From what I could see of him, the clerk was a dead ringer for Anthony Perkins."

The room had twin beds with a tiny, spindly table between them, and a chest of drawers. No telephone. No T.V. It was, however, warm and clean. Sage sniffed the sheets of the bed and, satisfied that they were sanitary, slid between them fully dressed.

She was too sleepy to take off her clothes. It was the first night of her life she had gone to bed without brushing her teeth, but she didn't care. All she wanted to do was sleep.

Harlan went into the bathroom. Seconds later she heard the water in the shower running. He was showering to spite her, she thought acidly. But there was a smile on her face. She was permeated with contentment. Strange, when she considered how inauspiciously this day had begun.

She'd left home with a man she'd known less than a month, riding in a broken-down pickup truck that had sold for scrap metal.

She'd cleaned out her bank accounts, which represented every cent she possessed, and it was a woefully meager amount.

She'd gorged on fast food without giving a thought to the high calories or low nutritional value.

She'd deserted everything safe and familiar and had embarked upon a quest that might yield her nothing except humiliation and animosity from her beloved family.

And she was spending the night in a sleazy motel room that had probably been the scene of countless illicit trysts.

Despite all that, her mind was at ease and she was smiling as she snuggled beneath the covers and plumped up the pillow beneath her head.

Harlan was still in the shower, singing a Rod Stewart song, slightly off-key. When he came out, would he lie down beside her and place his arms around her, or would he use the other bed?

She wouldn't mind if the other bed stood empty all night.

She had never felt happier.

"Sage, will you cut it out please? That's not helping our situation."

"I don't care," she blubbered, holding a damp tissue to her leaking nose. "I feel like crying, so I'm going to cry. Now leave me alone and let me do it in peace."

"We could have irrigated every parcel of land in south Texas with the tears you've cried. Maybe we should have tried to market them."

She glared at him through red, swollen eyes. "I'm really tired of your jokes about it, Harlan."

"Well, joking's better than bawling."

Two weeks on the road together without anything to show for it had strained their tempers to the limit. As they headed back on the same highway they had so optimistically traveled fourteen days earlier, Harlan's knuckles were white with tension as he gripped the steering wheel.

If he had a destination in mind, he hadn't informed her. She felt indifferent toward it anyway. They were just driving aimlessly, mile after mile, while she wept and he simmered. He seemed to be spoiling for a fight. Sage, feeling fractious herself, was prepared to give him one.

"You can't imagine how important the success of this trip was to me."

"I can guess," he shouted back. "You wanted to come home triumphant. You wanted your family's love and adulation."

"What do you know about family love?"

She saw a spark leap in his eyes, but he didn't acknowledge the question. Instead he counterattacked. "You think you've got the whole damn world fooled, but I can see clean through you, Sage. You don't think anybody respects you. Well, you're wrong. You should have heard your family bragging to me about how hard and diligently you worked to earn your master's degree. Long before I met you, I was sick of hearing about you."

"They may talk about me, but they don't take me seriously. They never have."

"Maybe because you're always flouncing around and shooting off your mouth."

"Oh, thanks. I'm beginning to feel a whole lot better now that we've had this little talk."

He took his eyes off the road to study her for a moment. "You're in competition with your brothers, aren't you?"

"Of course not!"

"The hell you're not. Somewhere deep inside you, you're afraid you don't measure up to them, that compared to them you're second-rate."

"You're crazy."

"No, I'm right. Listen, Sage, you're a Tyler through and through. You've got the same rugged stuff inside you that Chase and Lucky do. It's just packaged differently. You've got grit and guts and integrity. You're a decent human being, and you're certainly not lacking in looks, personality, or intelligence."

"Then why did I fail to get one measly contract? Only a few people would even talk to me. Several laughed in my face when I explained why I wanted an appointment."

"You didn't fail," he said with emphasis. "You did everything you could. You left every morning dressed up fit to kill, looking professional but still feminine. You practiced your presentation until you got it letter-perfect. Hell, every time I listened to you deliver it, I was ready to sign on the dotted line myself."

"Then why didn't one of those prospects we called on sign?"

"Bad luck. Bad economy. Neither of which reflects on anything you did or didn't do. Even the best fishermen using the best bait can't catch a fish if the fish simply refuse to bite."

She derived some comfort from everything he said. Secretly, she was persuaded that she had done her best. Through co-ops and agricultural associations she had gleaned a list of prospective clients. Together Harlan and she had systematically called on them. Their efforts had produced nothing, not even a prospect with good potential. She had done everything she had known to do.

She couldn't blame their lack of success on Harlan either. He had surprised her by wearing a necktie everyday. His explanation of the mechanism was articulate and thorough. He easily won the confidence of everyone they spoke to. People seemed instinctively to trust his opinion on a variety of subjects. He was a good ol' boy with a lot of smarts and a charm that wasn't cloying.

People liked him and he liked people. Very much like Laurie, he accepted people as they were and expected them to do the same regarding him. He made friends wherever they went. His need to develop friendships no doubt arose from his lack of a family.

But for all Harlan's affability, they were still leaving the valley empty-handed. It was their rotten luck that the farmers and fruit growers were suffering their own setback due to unseasonable freezes the previous year. The agricultural business was no healthier than the oil industry. The growers were worried about making ends meet this year. None was inclined to make an investment and increase his overhead, no matter how receptive he was to the product.

"Everybody agreed that we've got a terrific idea," Harlan reminded her now.

"Try paying bills with a terrific idea."

He hissed a curse. "So what do you want me to do? Take the next exit and head for east Texas? Are you giving up?"

"No. Absolutely not. That's the Harlan Boyd method of doing things. When the situation gets tough, simply disappear. Wash your hands of it and walk away."

"What the hell do you know about Harlan Boyd's method of doing anything?"

"Well, isn't that so?" she shouted, rounding on him. "Why does putting down roots and making a home like a normal person scare you so much?" It was a rhetorical question, so she didn't even wait for a reply. "I'm different from you. I don't slink away from my problems."

"No, you either avoid them by telling half-truths or hide them behind a smart mouth and highfalutin manner."

She glowered at him, then turned her head and stared out her window. The fields they passed were lying fallow. The dried, dead stubble of last year's crops lay in the furrows, waiting to be plowed under in spring.

Cultivation reminded her of irrigation, and irrigation reminded her of Harlan's invention, which could be the salvation of Tyler Drilling, at least until the oil business recovered. When it did—and she believed that it would—her brothers might turn the entire irrigation business over to her. It could be a subsidiary of the original company.

Before her imagination could run away with her, she bitterly reminded herself that their money was about to run out. Then she would have to return home not only defeated but penniless as well.

How long could Harlan and she stay together without murdering each other? The alternative was to make love again, and that was just as prohibitive. Some of her tears, she acknowledged now, stemmed from sexual frustration.

The closer their quarters, the more standoffish they were. The smaller the room, the wider the berth they gave each other. That avoidance hadn't been her choice. She'd taken her cues from him.

He hadn't kissed her since that night at the Dairy Queen. He didn't even hint that he might like to waste one of the beds in their double rooms. Their conversations revolved around the business at hand and lacked the double entendre teasing she had thought she despised but now missed. She was confused and disappointed.

Why hadn't he made one single pass in two weeks? Was he already preparing her for the day he would walk out of her life as unexpectedly as he had stepped into it?

Miserable over the thought, Sage propped her elbow on the ledge of the window and supported her chin with her palm as she gazed through the window at the passing landscape.

On the outskirts of Waco, they passed an extremely green, well-manicured field. There was pedestrian traffic on it and little white carts scurrying about. Triangular flags on skinny, swaying poles seemed to wave at her to get her attention.

She sat bolt upright. "Golf."

Chapter Fourteen

"Pardon?"

"Golf. Golf. *Golf.*"

Harlan looked beyond her toward the golf course. "You want to stop and play a few holes?"

"Harlan, we've been fishing in the wrong fishing hole." In her excitement, she reached across the seat and gripped his thigh. "We've got the right bait, but we're not casting it in the right waters."

His blue eyes lit up with sudden understanding. "Golf courses."

"Yes. And . . . and planned communities where there's a golf course and homesites and lots of landscaped grounds."

"Upscale retirement communities."

"Health care facilities."

"Multidimensional industrial parks."

"Yes!" Unbuckling her seat belt, she launched herself against him, throwing her arms around his neck and noisily kissing his cheek. "We should be calling on property developers, not farmers. We need to see investors and contractors, movers and shakers."

"Do you want to head back to Houston?"

"Not particularly. Why?"

"Belcher. He would be a source."

She contemplated the suggestion for a moment, before vetoing it. "He's on the fringes. I want to go to the sources. Besides, I don't want to risk bumping into him after Lucky and Chase said their piece. My gut instinct tells me it was profane."

"I imagine your gut instinct is right. Then, where to?"

"Dallas."

"Why Dallas?"

"Because it's an expanding city with lots of areas just like we've been talking about."

"So's San Antonio. And Austin."

"But we're closer to Dallas, and it's closest to Milton Point. We can be there in a couple of hours."

Her excitement was contagious. With his easy grin, he said, "Buckle your seat belt," and depressed the accelerator.

He got them to Dallas in under two hours. While she was admiring the silver, mirrored skyline, he shocked her by pulling into the porte cochere of a hotel that outclassed the ones they'd been staying in by a million miles.

"What are we doing here?"

"I think we need to treat ourselves."

"You mean by staying here?"

"You're the treasurer. Can we afford it?"

"Probably not, but let's splurge," she said, her eyes dancing at the prospect.

"Let's eat at a fancy restaurant tonight. Cloth napkins, matching silverware, the works. Maybe go to the movies or something."

"Oh, yes, Harlan, yes. I can't wait."

"But tomorrow it's back to the salt mines, Cinderella," he cautioned.

"Now that we have a new plan of attack, I can't wait for that either."

"So I guess I grew up believing that I meant no more to my brothers than one of their sports balls, something to play with and kick around."

Her mood was reflective as Sage stared into the candle burning in the center of the small portable table. The hotel room was a palace compared to some they had recently occupied. In-room movies were available on the television set. The room-service menu was extensive.

The quarters had offered so many amenities that they opted to stay in. They were road-weary. Relaxing in the room had held much more appeal than dressing up and going out. They'd eaten a four course dinner served in their room. Now they were lingering over chocolates and coffee.

"I don't really feel competitive with them, Harlan. I just want them to recognize me as an essential part of the family and our business. I want to be more than their kid sister, the brat."

"I can understand your point." He peeled the gold foil off a disk of semisweet chocolate and placed it in his mouth to melt slowly. "But you've got to realize, Sage, that you'll always be the baby of the family, just like Chase will always be the oldest."

"This sounds like first year psychology."

"It is," he admitted on a short laugh. "I took it as an elective at A&M."

"Then your observations aren't based on personal experience?"

"No."

"No brothers or sisters?"

"No."

She fiddled with the slivers of bright foil she had removed from her own chocolates. She weighed the advisability of prying, but knew that if she didn't, he wouldn't voluntarily divulge anything about his past.

"I know your home life must have been rough, Harlan." She glanced at him across the candle's flame. His face remained impassive. "You don't have to tell me about it if you don't want to." She paused again, providing him an opportunity he didn't capitalize on.

"I don't want to."

She was disappointed that she hadn't yet won his confidence, but covered it by saying, "I'm sorry you had to bear the brunt of it alone. My family is my foundation. I can't imagine a childhood without my parents and boisterous brothers."

"You drew a lucky lot."

"I know," she conceded softly. "As aggravating as they can be, I love them very much."

"They love you too." Propping his forearms on the edge of the table, he leaned forward and drawled, "What's not to love?"

By the time she had finally left her long, hot bubble bath, their dinner had arrived. Rather than let it get cold, Harlan had insisted that she come to the table with her hair still wet, sans makeup, and wrapped in her no-frills terrycloth robe.

Now, as his eyes took a leisurely tour of her, he reached for her hand and pulled her to her feet, drawing her around the table toward him. He spread his knees wide and maneuvered her to stand between them.

Loosely clasping her hands at her sides, he nuzzled the spot where the lapels of her robe overlapped. "You smell good."

Her insides began to hum. After two weeks without so much as a mild flirtation, his touch was as shocking as an electric current. Still, she didn't want him to believe he could have her easily. Did he think all he had to do was crook his finger and she would come running?

"Harlan, what are you doing?"

"If you'd shut up long enough, I'd like to seduce you."

"That's not a good idea. You agreed to keep our relationship strictly

business. And about what happened before, Harlan, I don't want you
to think—"

" 'Bout the only thing wrong with you is that you talk too damn
much."

He didn't stop her mouth with a kiss, but with a signal from his eyes
that was just as potent. When she stared down into that smoldering
gaze, the protests died on her lips, her insides turned to marshmallow,
and her carefully arranged resolves scattered. He continued holding
the stare as he untied the knot at her waist and parted the robe.

"Damn, Sage," he said when his hands slipped inside, "if I'd've
known you were naked underneath this, I wouldn't have dawdled over
my supper."

With his hands at her waist, he drew her forward and planted his
open mouth in the very center of her torso. Her flesh jumped beneath
the damp contact with his tongue. Reflexively, she rested her hands on
his shoulders for support. She gripped them hard when he kissed first
one nipple, then the other, idly flicking them with the tip of his tongue.

Sage moaned and almost lost her balance. He came to his feet and
caught her, holding her against his chest. "Unfasten my jeans."

His whispered urgency didn't induce her to hurry. Rather, she hesitated before timidly reaching for his fly. The top snap was easy. The
buttons gave her some difficulty, especially since he was kneading her
breasts and making love to her mouth with his chocolate-flavored
tongue. He grunted with pleasure whenever her knuckles bumped
against the rigid flesh behind the soft denim. Finally the last button was
undone. She withdrew her hands.

"Thanks," he said, sighing his relief. "Will you take my shirt off, too,
please?"

He had showered before she claimed the bathroom for her bubble
bath. He had emerged dressed in the worn jeans that his lean body
seemed made for and a white cotton T-shirt, stretched tight across his
broad chest and shoulders.

Now, through the cloth, she could see that his nipples were distended. The sight of his bare chest never failed to elicit a response from
deep inside her. She took hold of the bottom of his T-shirt and worked
it up over the firm muscles, over the pelt of tawny hair, and pulled it
over his head. His hair fell back into place, looking sexily mussed.
Several strands dipped low over his brows.

"That's much better," he whispered as he drew her into an embrace
that brought their bare torsos together.

The kiss lasted an eternity and gave Sage a mighty appetite for more of him. She moved against his chest, delighting in the tickling sensation of his body hair against her smooth skin. The contact aroused her nipples. He noticed it immediately and caressed them lightly, first with his fingertips, then with his lips, which continued to wander down her body.

He sat down in the chair again and kissed her belly, her navel, each prominent hipbone. Pulling back, he studied the patch of down between her thighs for several moments before letting his fingers play with it.

Sage's breathing and heart rate escalated. Everything grew dark around her, as though her peripheral vision were shrinking in scope until all that was highlighted were Harlan and her and the glow of the single candle.

When his lips touched that springy nest, she uttered a low groan and dug her fingers into his hair. The pleasure she derived from his sweet kisses was so exquisite it was almost unbearable.

Harlan dropped to his knees. Gently he separated the soft flesh with the pads of his thumbs, then did something wonderful to her with his mouth.

Her soft cry was one of desire mixed with doubt. Sensations, unlike any she'd felt before, skyrocketed up through her body into her head. And while they made her wildly ecstatic, the magnitude of the ecstasy frightened her.

She backed away from him and threw herself facedown across one of the double beds, burying her face in the pillow. Her fingers gripped the bedding because the sensations wouldn't stop. One by one, the aftershocks rippled through her. She couldn't stop making that breathy, choppy sound.

The mattress sank beneath Harlan's weight as he lay down beside her. He laid his hand on the back of her head. "What's wrong, Sage? What are you afraid of?"

She rolled to her back, still breathless, still flushed, still overwhelmed. But her pride was at stake. "I'm not afraid of anything."

"Then why didn't you let yourself climax?"

Embarrassed, she turned her head away. He caught her beneath the chin and brought it back around. "You were shimmering. You were on the brink. I could feel it. Why didn't you go with it?" His eyes demanded an answer.

"It startled me," she replied huskily.

"Didn't you and Travis ever make love like that?"

The thought was as appalling as it was unappealing. Vehemently, she shook her head no.

"That man's either an idiot or a fairy," he mumbled. "Why didn't you ever make love with Travis, Sage? With any man? I'm sure plenty have tried."

"Yes, plenty have tried."

"Then why?"

"I don't know, Harlan. Don't badger me about it."

He cupped her head between his hands. "Listen to me. I've been struggling to keep myself decent around you for two weeks. It hasn't been easy. Just about everything you do, everything you say, each toss of your head and smile and expression makes me hard as all get out. Now, dammit, I think that entitles me to the answer to one simple question."

Sage was still very aroused herself. His erotic words didn't help her arousal subside. "It's not a *simple* question, Harlan. It's complex. I don't even know the answer myself."

"I've got a good guess. You didn't give a guy a chance to make love to you because you were afraid of being disappointing to your partner and disappointed yourself."

She gaped at him incredulously. "Where do you come up with this stuff?"

"You'd heard all the tales about your brothers' successes with women. You knew you couldn't compete in the romance department unless you turned into a bonafide slut."

"Talk about a double standard!"

"You're right. It stinks. But that's the way it is. So you decided that sex was one arena in which you wouldn't even try and be as good as they are."

"I have never even thought such drivel."

"I'm sure you haven't. It's all subconscious, but it's there. Well, listen to me." His hands increased their pressure around her head. He leaned over her, sliding one leg between hers, the denim feeling—impossibly—rough and soft at the same time.

"There's no one here but you and me, Sage. I haven't got a score card. You don't have to prove one damn thing to me. I already know you're sexy. I already know you make me hot and hard. I already know you'd burn, too, if you'd only let yourself.

"But if you say no, that's okay, too. I won't make any judgments one way or the other. You know I want you in the worst way, but it's up to you. What's it going to be? What do you want?"

"I want—" She faltered, unable to continue.

"What? Say what you were thinking. For once just be Sage, the woman, without worrying about what is expected of Sage Tyler, daughter to Bud and Laurie, and younger sister to Chase and Lucky."

She took several hard breaths, then said in a rush, "I want you to touch me."

"Where?"

"Everywhere."

"Be specific."

"You mean say the words?"

"I mean say the words."

She did. His eyes turned dark with sexual intensity.

"And?" he rasped.

"When you kiss me . . ."

"Yeah?"

"Be thorough with my mouth. Eat it up like it was your last meal."

"Sounds good so far," he whispered thickly. "Go on."

Sensuality pumped through her veins like a powerful narcotic. Her nerves were exposed and tingling deliciously. She felt high, exuberant, and marvelously alive.

"I want to run my hands all over your beautiful body. I want to hold you against me and squeeze the breath out of you. I want you to be inside me again, Harlan."

He whistled softly. "For a beginner, you talk damn good sex, Miss Sage."

Their first fiery kiss prompted her to put her brave words into action. She slid her hands into the seat of his jeans and cupped his buttocks.

Making a low, hungry sound, Harlan rolled to his side and shoved down his jeans, then kicked them off. His chest was rapidly rising and falling with each breath, but he left the next move to her.

Her eyes detailed his body. Curiously she touched his nipple with her fingernail. Harlan sucked in a sharp breath and held it but still didn't rush her.

She lowered her head to his chest and pressed her mouth over the projected bud, then pushed her tongue against it. He murmured her name and buried his fingers in her hair. She surrendered to every whim and brought to life the fantasies that she had been secretly entertaining for weeks. Her mouth danced across his chest, kissing randomly, nipping playfully, licking lightly, sucking softly.

The more she tasted, the greedier she became. Kneeling beside him, she rested her hands on the tops of his thighs and kissed her way over his ribs. She dipped her tongue into the fuzzy mystery of his navel.

He gasped her name repeatedly and knotted her hair around his fingers.

She nuzzled her face in the musky warmth surrounding his sex and glanced the smooth tip with her lips, then returned several times.

"I'm dying, baby," he moaned, dragging her up and sealing their mouths together around a wild, ravenous kiss. She ground her hips against his hardness. He lifted his head and hung it low over hers. "We've got to slow it down. We don't have to go this fast unless the hotel catches on fire. I don't want to hurt you again."

"You won't. Please, Harlan. Now."

For all her urgency, his entry was slow and gentle, yet firm. "You're so wet." He sighed, sinking into her. "Lord, you feel good."

"So do you."

They smiled at each other as he pressed even deeper. "Can you feel that?"

"Hmm, yes."

"And that?"

Closing her eyes, she murmured an incoherent yes.

"Good. Good. Now, draw your knees back. That's it. Ah, Sage."

In moments, he forgot to take his own advice against unnecessary haste. Sage didn't remind him, but eagerly met each of his thrusts. Emptying her mind of all else, she reveled in the thrilling sensations, returned them, relished each new one.

She drew him into her with her body and mind and soul until she couldn't tell that they were separate individuals.

When her extremities began to tingle in a way she now recognized, she didn't fight it, but clasped Harlan tighter. All her concentration centered on their joined bodies, on the friction and the heat and his pulsing, giving motions, until she dissolved in the sweetness and light of their mutual release.

Several minutes later, he would have slipped away from her. She whispered, "Don't go."

Without compromising their intimacy, he rolled to his side, bringing her with him until they lay face-to-face. "You talked me into staying."

Their smiling lips came together in a chaste, soft kiss before she nestled her face in his neck.

"Harlan?"

"Hmm?"

"Thanks."

"My pleasure."

She smiled against his warm skin. "Harlan?"

"Hmm?"

"Nothing. I was just saying your name out loud."

Drawing a deep, contented sigh, she closed her eyes and drifted to sleep.

The following morning when she came bustling through the door, he was lying on his back in bed with his hands stacked beneath his head.

"Well, you're finally awake," she said with a happy smile.

"Where'd you go? I was getting worried."

"I woke up early, simply bursting with energy. I waited for you to wake up, but when you didn't, I went out for donuts and scalding, black coffee just the way you like it."

She set the two white paper sacks on the table that was still littered with their dinner dishes and the candle which had burned down sometime during their night of lovemaking. They had napped and reawakened to make love so many times, Sage had lost count.

Moving to the bed now, she bent over him and kissed his forehead, where strands of pale hair lay, then his lips. Taking a corner of the sheet between her thumb and fingertip, she raised it and took a peek underneath. "Why, Harlan, you're naked! How uncouth."

"Is that a fifty-cent word for horny?"

"You went to college. You know what uncouth means."

"And you know what horny means. Come here." Snarling playfully, he grabbed her wrists and pulled her down over him. She put up only token resistance before melting on top of him, letting her body's softness conform to the hard strength of his.

"Again?" she whispered seductively. "I thought doing it too much could make you go blind."

"You only go blind if you don't do it enough."

"Oh, my. Well, we can't let that happen, can we?" she said, meshing her mouth with his.

Between fervent kisses, she wrestled out of her clothing until she lay stretched atop him, touching skin to skin, hairy to smooth, male to female. She registered momentary surprise when he slid his hands over her derriere onto the backs of her thighs and parted them, lifting her up slightly to straddle his lap.

"I don't know what to do," she told him with genuine anxiety.

"Yes, you do."

"Like this?" She executed a movement that made his eyes glaze.

"Yeah," he struggled to say, "exactly like that."

When it was over, she lay upon his chest, panting like the victim of a shipwreck washed ashore.

He folded his arms across the small of her back. His expression was soft and full of affection. "Who needs fantasies with you around, Sage?"

"You've fulfilled all of mine, too."

"All?"

"Well, there is one . . ."

He grabbed a double handful of her hair and lifted her head off his chest. "Well?"

"Can I wash your back in the shower?"

A slow grin spread across his sexy face. "Miss Sage, you can wash whatever your little heart desires."

Sage emerged from the bathroom first, leaving him to shave. Humming to herself, she collected her discarded clothes from around the bed and dressed again. She was removing the lids from Styrofoam cups of coffee when Harlan came out of the bathroom, hiking his jeans up over his hips.

"I'm afraid the coffee got cold," she apologized, handing him a cup.

"It was worth it. I'd rather have hot sex than hot coffee anytime."

She purred coyly. "I do believe you would."

He kissed her before taking a sip of the lukewarm coffee.

"The donuts are still fresh," she told him. "Have one."

She poked one into his mouth. He took a bite, then used the donut to gesture toward a pile of papers scattered across the table. "What's all that?"

"Before I went out, I skimmed the local business magazine we picked up in the lobby when we checked in. There were some impressive success stories in it, so I started compiling a list of potential clients."

"Very good," he said with approval as his eyes ran down her handwritten list.

With something close to idolatry, Sage was dreamily assessing his face when she saw his eyes fix on one of the names. He stopped his vigorous chewing and held the bite of donut in his mouth for several seconds before swallowing it.

"Strike the next to the last name." Abruptly, he tossed down the sheet of paper.

Sage picked up the sheet and read the name. "What have you got against Hardtack and Associates?"

"What difference does one name make? You've got another dozen companies listed there."

She looked at him with perplexity. Having set aside his coffee and the remainder of the donut, he was moving around the room restlessly, snatching things up, then setting them down just as quickly. She had never seen him behave this way. He was acting as testy as a caged animal.

"Harlan? Why has that one name upset you so much?"

"I'm not upset."

"Don't lie to me," she cried. "I can see that you are. Do you know something about Grayson Hardtack that I should be aware of?"

"Drop it, okay? Scratch his name off your list and everything will be all right. Just omit his name."

"Without a full explanation of why I should? Not hardly. According to the article about him, he's got a finger in every juicy pie in this city. He's exactly the kind of client we need."

He spun around to face her, his hands on his hips, his features taut and belligerent. "Save yourself the trouble. Hardtack wouldn't give you the time of day if he knew I was working with you. Believe it."

"Why?"

"That's my business."

"Do you two have an ax to grind?"

"You could say that."

"What kind of ax? What was the quarrel over?"

"Drop it, Sage."

"What kind of quarrel did you have with Hardtack?" she repeated insistently.

He gnawed on his lower lip for a moment. When he made up his mind to answer her, he spoke tersely. "For a while, I had something that belonged to him."

She gave the words plenty of time to sink in, but their meaning remained unclear. "You mean you stole something from him?"

Supremely agitated over her persistence, he raked his fingers through his hair. "I asked you to drop it."

"Not until I get an answer from you, Harlan. What did you have that belonged to Hardtack?"

His blue eyes turned brittle and cold. "His wife."

Chapter Fifteen

Sage nervously thumbed through the magazine without retaining a single word printed on any of the glossy pages. The suite of executive offices at Hardtack and Associates, Incorporated, was austere and ultramodern, decorated mostly in black and gray, with touches of maroon.

She glanced at Grayson Hardtack's secretary. The woman gave her another plastic smile. "I'm sure it won't be much longer, Ms. Tyler."

Her carefully outlined magenta lips barely moved. A gale wind wouldn't have disturbed a single lacquered strand of hair, which perfectly matched the color of the gray wall behind her.

"Thank you."

Sage was as jumpy as a cat. At any second she expected Harlan to come crashing through the black-lacquered doors and accuse her of double-crossing him. Because that was exactly what she was doing, she was all the jumpier.

After their argument two days before when he had dropped his bombshell about Hardtack's wife, they checked out of the luxury hotel and moved to one within their budget. Even though that budget was almost exhausted, Sage had rented her own room. She'd spent most of that day locked inside it, alone.

Hours of self-flagellation were behind the decision she had finally reached: She must put her personal feelings aside. The task she had chosen for herself had to take priority. Having arrived at that conclusion, she had marched to the door of Harlan's room and knocked.

He hadn't rushed to open it. In fact, he'd been deliberately slow about it. He pulled the door open, braced himself against the doorjamb, and waited her out, forcing her to speak first.

"I made some calls," she began coldly. "We have appointments with these people tomorrow morning." She slapped a list of names into his hand. He glanced through the list. Hardtack and Associates wasn't on it.

"Fine."

"Then you're still interested in working with me on this project?" she asked stiffly.

"You're the one who has spent hours sulking, not me."

"It just came as a shock that you had been involved with another man's wife."

He rolled his eyes and gave her a retiring look that made her furious. How dare he put her on the defensive? She wasn't the one who had an unsavory and suspicious past.

"That has no bearing on the here and now, on us," he said.

"You're wrong, Harlan. Everything in one's background is vitally important and relevant. Our pasts are what make us what we are."

He sadly shook his head. "If you believe that, then I'm not the guy for you, Sage."

In a matter of seconds, she recalled everything they had done together in bed, everything he had taught her to do, his coaching on how to draw the maximum pleasure from them both. The heat of embarrassment had made her face red, but she kept her eyes cool.

"How convenient for you to realize that now that I've already gone to bed with you."

She had stalked away and spent the night alone and miserable in her room, already missing him in her bed and hating herself and him because of it. During their appointments over the next couple of days, they behaved civilly toward each other and successfully suppressed the animosity between them. Each performed his part of the presentation as before.

From most of the vice presidents in charge of this or that, they received a polite brush-off. They agreed to keep Tyler Drilling in mind and contact them at some unspecified point in the future, which would doubtfully ever come.

After another disappointing meeting that morning, they had returned to the motel at noon feeling disheartened and dejected. She had told Harlan, "Unless you need to go somewhere, I'd like to take the car this afternoon and see if I can find a place to have my hair and nails done."

He was instantly alert. "You always do them yourself."

"They're beginning to look like it." His eyes were as sharp as rapiers. She tried to keep her expression bland.

"Fine with me," he said at last. Before he left the car, however, he reached into the back seat and retrieved the portfolio carrying all his designs.

"G'bye."

"Bye."

Sage was blocks away before she reached beneath the front seat and removed the folder of copies she had made a week earlier while she'd had access to his portfolio. The drawings had to be greatly reduced in size, but were still legible. If Harlan decided to split, she didn't want to be left with nothing. Due to the most recent development, she was glad she had taken the precaution.

Luckily that hadn't been the only precaution taken that she now felt relief over. Harlan had been efficient and unobtrusive, but each time they'd made love, he'd protected her from getting pregnant.

Thinking about his sweet, passionate lovemaking brought tears to her eyes, which she blinked away before Hardtack's formidable secretary could see them.

It had come as no surprise to Sage that Harlan had been involved with other women. He received more than his share of smoldering come-ons and nonverbal invitations.

Everywhere they went, Sage was aware of the restless attention he generated in females. One of his disarming smiles could fluster an efficient cashier. One penetrating look could turn a cantankerous waitress into Miss Congeniality. One flirtatious wink could make even the most average-looking woman smile as radiantly as a beauty queen. Harlan Boyd definitely had an effect on the ladies.

Apparently Mrs. Grayson Hardtack was no exception.

Harlan had had an affair with her, probably while he was working for Hardtack. Hardtack had found out about it and all hell had broken loose. Sage was surmising, of course, but she was confident that his involvement with them was something like that.

What really hurt was that Harlan still felt hostile about it. Whatever had brewed between Mrs. Hardtack and him was still brewing as far as he was concerned.

Did he still care for the woman? If he didn't, why had he become so vexed? He could have laughed and said, "You'd better go on that appointment alone, Sage. See, Mrs. Hardtack wasn't very discreet about her infidelities. Hardtack got sore and, well, you understand these things."

But he hadn't dismissed it as a fleeting affair without emotional entanglements. He had paced and flapped around like a marionette worked by an uncoordinated puppeteer. His personality had undergone a drastic change. For him to have behaved that irrationally, the affair must have been left unresolved.

How many affairs of the heart did Harlan have in his past that had been left unresolved? Dozens? Scores? Whatever the number, add one, Sage thought with biting self-criticism.

He had said he was a professional troubleshooter. She was just another problem he had spotted. She was a frustrated virgin whose ego had been badly bruised and was in desperate need of sexual awakening. If she had taken out a personal ad, she couldn't have publicized her problem more clearly.

Harlan, having the equipment and skill to solve her problem, had responded to her silent advertisement. He had introduced her to her own sexuality and released her from being uptight about expressing it. Now that she had demonstrated just how unrestrained she could be in bed, he would consider her problem solved and go on his merry way, ready to tackle another's dilemma.

She wondered if he would tell her good-bye, notify her of his leaving. Or would she just wake up one morning and find him gone? Probably the latter. She couldn't envision him in a sad, tearful farewell scene. However it happened, it was going to break her heart.

She had fallen in love with the jerk.

"Ms. Tyler?"

She jumped and snapped to attention. "Yes?"

"Mr. Hardtack will see you now."

"Thank you."

She gathered her handbag and folder from the sofa and followed the secretary across an acre of polished marble floor, through a floor-to-ceiling door, into Hardtack's inner sanctum.

Its austerity was marginally relieved by Oriental rugs forming islands of pricelessness on the floor. A wall of windows afforded a spectacular view of the Dallas skyline. Having done her homework, Sage knew which of the buildings belonged to Hardtack. The immensity of his wealth and power intimidated her for a moment. What was she doing in this temple of commerce?

Well why not, a small voice argued back. Family pride asserted itself. She was a Tyler. The Tylers were as good as anybody.

Squaring her shoulders, she approached his desk and extended her hand. A graying, robust man, impeccably dressed in a business suit, partially rose from his chair and shook her hand across his desk.

"Hello, Mr. Hardtack. I'm Sage Tyler. Thank you for seeing me this afternoon on such short notice."

"Sit down, Ms. Tyler." While Sage was taking her seat, his secretary passed him a note card. He referred to it, then nodded at her. She soundlessly withdrew. "You told my assistant that you had to see me about something urgent and personal."

Hardtack was a man in his late fifties, with a wide chest and expansive belly, although it was more muscle than fat. His nose was large and bulbous and had the ruddiness of a man who enjoyed several bourbons spaced at intervals throughout the day. He had a quelling habit of peering from beneath his bushy gray eyebrows.

Sage, shocked by her own temerity, stated boldly, "I lied, Mr. Hardtack. I came here to sell you something."

He was taken aback by her candor. He studied her for a moment. Then he readjusted himself in his leather chair and, folding his hands over his stomach, chuckled softly. "Well, you've got guts, Ms. Tyler, I'll say that. What are you peddling? Has my subscription to *TV Guide* run out?"

Unsure how long his good humor would last, she gave him a tentative smile and spread open the folder on the edge of his desk.

"I want to acquaint you with a new sprinkler and irrigation system. I have the designs here."

He didn't even glance at Harlan's drawings. He didn't look at anything except the space between her eyes. "Ms. Tyler, I'm a busy man. I've got an army of employees who handles that kind of thing for me."

"I'm well aware of that," she said quickly, sensing that he was about to toss her out. "But I've been seeing vice presidents and young executives for weeks. They're much more interested in staying within their present budgets than making an investment. None wants to rock the corporate boat in these troubled times, so no decisions are made.

"This time I thought I'd come straight to the top man, the one who signs the checks and ultimately makes the decisions anyway. I'm tired of being shunted from one subordinate to another."

For several ponderous moments, he stared at her, then he checked his wristwatch and said, "You've got five minutes." She pushed the folder toward him while hyping the sterling reputation of Tyler Drilling. A few seconds into her spiel, he interrupted her. "I'm familiar with your family's reputation in the oil business. Tell me what you're selling and why I should buy it."

"Have you awarded a contract for the sprinkler and irrigation system at Shadow Hills?"

Land-clearing had just gotten underway for the planned community several miles north of Dallas. Sage had read that, when it was completed, it would encompass several square miles, would have one eighteen-hole golf course, a nine-hole course, a polo field, a landing strip, a shopping area, a ritzy country club, as well as obscenely expensive homesites.

"Not to my knowledge," he told her.

"I would appreciate the chance to bid on the contract. We've got precisely what you need."

"Do you have references? Who else is using your system?"

"No one. If you buy it, you'll be our first customer."

She didn't want to commence her career with a lie. Even if she were so inclined, Hardtack would find out. She met him eye-to-eye, waiting for him to say he wasn't interested and signal for his secretary to usher her out.

Instead, he said, "I'm still listening."

Swiftly regurgitating everything she had heard Harlan tell their prospective clients, she explained the mechanics. "We can install aboveground sprinklers as well as lay underground systems. And we can do it a lot cheaper than any competitor because we've got the supplies, the pipes and pumps that went out of use when the oil market collapsed."

He studied the drawings for much longer than she would have dared hope. In fact, he studied each one at length. Without raising his head, he addressed her from beneath his brows. "Who did these drawings?"

"Our designer," she replied evasively. "My brothers will be in charge of all the installation and operation."

"Hmm."

Although she was curious to know if Hardtack would react as violently to the mention of Harlan's name as Harlan had to his, she didn't dare risk it. Hardtack was too excellent a prospect to take the gamble. A single contract with him could lead to many. He could lend Tyler Drilling's new enterprise more credibility than anyone.

That had been her primary reason for wanting to meet with him personally. The other had been that she wanted to see the betrayed husband.

"I'm keeping these," he said abruptly, stacking the drawings together.

"F-fine," she stammered. She would have to see that Harlan filed for a patent immediately.

"I'd like to look them over more carefully and speak with the project supervisor."

"Certainly."

"How can I get in touch with you?"

Her heart was knocking. After so many dismissals, she didn't trust her ears. "Then you're interested?"

"I'll be honest with you. A sprinkler system for Shadow Hills isn't one of the pressing problems on my mind right now. Someone within this corporation, an employee I don't even know by name, could buy one from a thousand different sources—"

"But none with our unique—"

"Save the sales pitch. I've heard it." He aimed his index finger at her. "I'm offering you a piece of free advice. Learn when to keep your mouth shut, Ms. Tyler."

"Yes, sir," she said meekly. Someone else had told her recently that she talked too much.

"What I'm saying is that I'm not as interested in your products as I am in you. It took guts for you to walk in here today. I like to reward people who take chances. I also admire people who don't sling bull, but tell it straight the first time." He checked his watch. "You're thirty seconds over your time limit. Leave your phone number with my secretary. Good-bye."

"Good-bye and thank you."

She stood up and confidently shook his hand. But as she turned to leave, she drew up short. Mounted on the far wall, the one she had been sitting with her back to, was a photographic portrait of a beautiful woman.

Deep waves of blond hair framed her lovely face. She was dressed in a sapphire sequin ball gown that looked tailor-made for her perfect figure. She was standing in the curve of a winding staircase, her bejeweled hand resting negligently on the carved bannister. Precious stones twinkled at her ears and throat. She looked extremely well kept.

"Who is that?"

From behind her, Hardtack replied, "My wife Marian."

Marian. "She's beautiful."

"Yes, she is."

Sage gave him a shaky smile, then hastened from the office. After stopping at the secretary's desk and providing her with the company telephone number in Milton Point, she departed.

On her way to the elevators, she would have been skipping down the corridor, singing at the top of her voice, doing a gleeful little jig, if Marian Hardtack hadn't been one of the most beautiful women she'd ever laid eyes on.

Grayson Hardtack watched the young woman leave his office. He allowed time for her exchange with his secretary before speaking to the secretary himself from the intercom system on his desk.

"Get me Harry downstairs, please."

"Yes, sir. You're three-thirty appointment is here. Shall I send him in?"

"Give me five minutes."

"Yes, sir."

While he waited, he stared fixedly at the portrait across the room. He wasn't kept waiting long. The caller identified himself as Harry, one of the plainclothes security guards who patrolled the high-tech headquarters of Hardtack and Associates.

"Harry, there should be a young woman coming down any minute. Blond. Black suit. Pretty. Good legs."

"I see her, sir. She just stepped off the elevator."

"Follow her for a few days. I'll get someone to cover your shifts here. I want to know where she goes, who she sees, and any background information you can dig up. Report back to me within seventy-two hours."

"Yes, sir."

He paid his people well and hired only the best. Confident that his directive would be carried out thoroughly and with utmost secrecy, Hardtack resumed his study of the designs. He could swear they had been drawn by a draftsman whose work he knew.

When his secretary escorted in his next appointment, he was still frowning over the sheets scattered across his otherwise immaculate desk.

Chapter Sixteen

"Sage is coming home tomorrow," Chase said.

Marcie glanced up from her unfinished plate of lasagna. She and Chase were having a quiet dinner at home. Jamie was sleeping in a portable bassinet nearby. "Did you hear from her?"

"She called this afternoon from Dallas."

"I thought they were in south Texas, somewhere in the valley."

"Nothing happened there. They made a U-turn and went to Dallas with a different marketing strategy in mind."

He recounted to Marcie what Sage had told him. "She's excited about it. After being there for several days, she's compiled a list of six potential clients that are more than 'maybes.' "

"Then she's done some great work!"

"I told her so."

Marcie gave him a wide smile. "Good, Chase. She needs to hear that from you. Did she mention Harlan?"

"She's called us—what?—three or four times since she's been gone. This is the first time she's brought his name into the conversation. She asked if Lucky and I were going to beat him up if he came back with her."

"All things considered, I believe that was a fair question."

Chase frowned. There had been disharmony between them ever since their argument two weeks earlier. "You can't blame us for defending our sister, Marcie. We would have done it for any female member of our family."

"I admire you for feeling protective of us. But that's not the point. The point is that if Sage went to bed with Harlan, she did it of her own free will and doesn't need 'defending.' Lucky didn't ask anyone's permission before he fell in love with Devon, even though she was married at the time, legally if not technically.

"Lucky was appalled when you told him you were going to marry me. At the time, you were in a fragile state of mind and still very much in love with Tanya. From his perspective, he was giving you a sound piece of advice. Instead, you followed your heart and married me anyway. You trusted your instincts over his.

"Hell or high water or your own stubborn pride couldn't have kept either of you from falling in love with the women you fell in love with. Why should Sage be any different? She's a Tyler, too. She knows her heart and mind better than anyone else does. You have no right to interfere."

"We just don't want her to be hurt."

"Neither do I. But if she is, you couldn't have prevented it no matter what you did." She pondered the contents of her wineglass for a moment. "Do you think the incident with Harlan was isolated, or are they still sleeping together?"

"I got the feeling today that they haven't been. She referred to 'Harlan's room.' Whenever she mentioned him, it was in a business context."

"Hmm."

"You sound disappointed. Do you really think anything could come of that, Marcie?"

"Stranger things have happened."

"Spoken like a woman," he muttered with exasperation. "What does your woman's intuition tell you about him?"

"That he's very intelligent, more than he lets on. He's not afraid of hard work."

"I mean where women are concerned."

"Ah, where women are concerned." She steepled her index fingers and tapped her lips. "Well, as Devon said, much to Lucky's aggravation, he's sexy and gorgeous." Her eyes wandered to Chase's glowering face. "But not as sexy and gorgeous as you."

"Go on," he muttered, somewhat mollified.

"I think he must have lived through something very painful. He's still running away from it. Something or someone hurt him terribly. That's why he always stays on the fringes of any close group. He's personable, but guarded. An observer, but not an actual participant."

"I've noticed that too. Do you think a woman hurt him?"

"One can only guess."

"What would you guess?"

"I'd guess a woman."

"I thought so," he said unhappily. "I hope he's not punishing the entire female population, including Sage Tyler, for what one rotten female did to him."

"It could go either way." Chase looked at her quizzically, so she expounded on her theory. "That kind of emotional pain can either result in extraordinary cruelty or extraordinary sensitivity. I can't imagine Harlan being cruel, can you?"

"No. But who knows? We might not have seen him at his worst."

"Possibly, but you're overlooking a clue into his character."

"What?"

"He was the one worried about making Sage pregnant, right? Didn't you tell me that he admitted sleeping with her before anyone even accused him of it? That doesn't sound like a man without scruples who's out to break a woman's heart."

"No, it doesn't. Jeez," he said, running a hand down his face, "I guess we can't do anything more than sit back and watch the cards fall."

"Now you're catching on."

"So anyway, back to business. Where was I? Oh yeah, Sage said today that Harlan wants to come back and actually install a system. He wants to work out all the bugs before we get an order. My little sister must be quite a saleswoman," he said, smiling fondly. "Who would have ever thought she could take off like that and pull it all together?"

"I did," Marcie remarked staunchly.

"It appears that our first sale is imminent. I hope to hell it is. For everybody's sake." He set aside his empty plate and picked up his glass of red wine. "I haven't forgotten our deal, Marcie."

"What deal is that?"

He wasn't fooled by her nonchalance. "The deal we made when we got married."

"Oh, that deal."

Whenever he brought up this subject, she craftily maneuvered the conversation around it. He wasn't going to let her do that this time. "You bailed us out, Marcie, and I haven't forgotten it. Without your money—"

"*Our* money. It became yours when we got married."

"It was your money. Money you worked hard to earn. I told you when we got married that I intended to pay back every red cent. So far, I haven't been able to. But if we land one of these big contracts that Sage was prattling about today, you'll get your money back."

Leaving her chair, she circled the table and sat down in his lap. "Do you think I care, Chase?"

"*I* care."

"Your integrity is admirable. It's just one of the millions of reasons why I love you. And always have. Ever since kindergarten."

She bent her head and kissed him meaningfully. When they finally pulled apart, she said softly, "The payoff on my investment has been tremendous, Chase. Look at all I got in return. A healthy, beautiful baby boy and a husband who loves me."

"Well, I'm your husband and I love you. Though sometimes I'm intimidated by your computer brain and totally baffled by your quirky logic."

"Think how bored you'd be otherwise."

"Bored? With you? Never." He slid his hands beneath her sweater. "Hmm. You always feel so warm and soft." Her breasts were heavy with milk. He fondled them gently. She kissed his ear, following the rim of it with the tip of her tongue. "Please, Marcie," he groaned. "Have pity. Cut it out."

"Are you getting hard?" she whispered teasingly.

"*Getting* hard? I've been miserable for weeks."

"Then don't you think it's time we did something about that?" She reached for his fly and unfastened it.

His eyes swung up to hers. "You mean . . . ?"

"Um-huh."

"Green light?"

She closed her hand around him and smiled seductively. "It doesn't get any greener than this."

"You look like the cat that just swallowed the canary," Lucky commented as his brother entered the office the following morning.

Chase was humming. His step was springy. He poured himself a cup of coffee from the automatic maker and turned with the cup raised in a toast. "To love and marriage."

Lucky laughed and raised his own coffee mug.

They hadn't yet finished their coffee when they heard a car pull up outside. Chase glanced through the window. "It's Sage and Harlan." He gave his younger brother a stern warning. "Stay cool."

Sage came in first, followed by Harlan, who looked reluctant and unsure. Sage gave Chase a hard hug. "It's so good to be home! Milton Point never looked so wonderful. I got a lump in my throat when we drove through downtown."

All her remarks so far had been addressed to Chase. She turned. "Hi, Lucky." Smiling and forgiving, she crossed the office and hugged him too. "How's your arm?"

"It's okay," he said laconically. His arm was still riding in a sling. "Good to have you back, brat."

Chase stepped forward and shook hands with Harlan who was still standing near the door. "Have some coffee."

"No thanks. We stopped a couple of times between here and Dallas." Warily, he looked at Lucky, then moved toward him. "I'm sorry as hell about your arm. I didn't want anything like that to happen."

"I threw the first punch, but I figured you had it coming."

"Well you figured wrong," Sage said, intervening before tempers began to fly again. "Can we please forget all about it? We've got much more to deal with than my personal relationship with Harlan and whatever ramifications it might have." Bashfully, she added, "You'll all be greatly relieved to know that I'm not pregnant. Now, shall we talk shop?"

"Sounds like a good idea," Chase said, drawing up a chair for her. "Show us what you've got."

For the next hour, she filled them in on the results of their trip, detailing their failures as well as their successes.

"Harlan and I are convinced that this is our market."

"These are the people with the money," he contributed. "Even if they don't have it, they know how to get it from people who put together deals."

Glancing over the list of potential clients, Lucky whistled. "These are the head hogs at the trough, all right. I'm impressed."

"For a while there, it was looking grim," Harlan admitted. "We weren't getting anywhere with anybody. Then, the day before yesterday—wasn't it, Sage?—things started turning around. The folks we contacted began listening and were much more receptive."

She tugged on a strand of her hair. "It was getting rid of the split ends that did it."

"You lost me," Chase said, looking befuddled.

"Inside joke." She waved her hand as though clearing the air. "All the companies on this list are ripe for a follow-up call. Our next step is to have a lawyer draw up a standard contract, so that if we do get a call, we'll be prepared to negotiate. Before leaving Dallas, I had Harlan file a patent application."

"Under whose name?"

Harlan's spine stiffened as he aimed a hard look at Lucky. "Tyler

Drilling Company. I may be a despoiler of young women, but I'm not an embezzler."

"Just checking."

Chase held up his right hand in a gesture of peace. "Relax, you two." He turned to Harlan. "How do we stand on the machinery itself?"

"I'd like to lay some pipe and give it several run-throughs. I know that pump will work, but we should have one setup in case somebody wants to see it in operation. 'Course it still needs a timer that can be computed—"

"Lucky can help you with that," Chase said. "Tell him, Lucky."

"While you were gone, I scouted out several possibilities. Turns out that an old buddy of mine just got into the computer business. He's real hungry right now and eating his overhead. I think we can swing a good deal with him if we buy in volume."

"Fantastic!" Sage exclaimed.

"Meanwhile," Chase said to Harlan, "several of the old crew are on standby and chomping at the bit to go to work. We've got a few cleared acres out at the ranch you can play on. Just tell us when you're ready, and I'll show you where to dig."

"I'm ready, but I need transportation."

"Where's your pickup?"

"It expired in Austin," Sage told them as she stood up, zipping her portfolio closed. "We gave it a proper burial. Come on, Harlan, I'll drop you in town. Chase, who's Marcie's business attorney? I'd like to consult with him about a contract as soon as possible."

Chase wrote down the lawyer's name for Sage. They gave Harlan several tips on where he might find a dependable, but inexpensive, used pickup and warned him against the dealerships where he was certain to get ripped off. Then the brothers stood on the office porch and watched the couple drive away.

"She seems all right," Lucky remarked.

"Yeah, she seems fine."

"It took guts for him to come back with her."

"Hmm."

"You've gotta respect a man with that much character."

"As Marcie pointed out last night," Chase said, "we would never have known he'd slept with Sage if he hadn't told us himself."

"Unless she had gotten pregnant."

"Thank God that didn't happen."

"Thank God," Lucky repeated.

"They're talking strictly business now."

"Strictly business."

"I guess that whatever was between them is all over."

"Guess so."

They watched the car round the bend and drive out of sight.

"So," Lucky asked, "what do you really think?"

"I think they've got the hots for each other and are fighting it for all they're worth."

"Yeah," Lucky bleakly agreed, "that's what I think, too."

Harry, the security guard, entered Hardtack's office unannounced. It was early in the morning, before anyone else's business day had begun. His boss habitually arrived well before daylight, working at his desk while there was no one around to interrupt him. This was one interruption he wouldn't mind.

"What have you got?" Hardtack asked. He extended his hand to receive the envelope he expected the guard to have, which he did.

Hardtack pried open the metal brads and dumped the contents onto his desk. The guard was a lousy photographer, but the people he had captured on film were clearly identifiable. He had caught the couple several times, always together. Hardtack wasn't surprised by what he saw, but he was careful to screen his reaction from his employee.

"Are they lovers?" he asked.

"Tough to say, Mr. Hardtack. They shared a room at one hotel, then moved the next morning to another one. They had separate rooms there."

"Interesting. Go on."

"She paid their bills at both places in cash."

"Where are they now?"

"They left town yesterday morning. I followed them to Milton Point. They're both staying at the family home there."

"So she's legit?"

"Very." He summarized for his boss all the information he had gleaned about Tyler Drilling. It coincided with what Hardtack already knew.

"They've been having a rough time the last few years, but their reputation is above reproach. The number two son—they call him Lucky—had a run-in with federal agents a few years back. An arson charge."

Hardtack's head came up quickly. He glared at his employee from beneath his brows, demanding specifics. "Turned out to be a bum rap.

The arsonists are in prison. Oldest son's first wife died in a car crash. It was an accident. Currently both are married with families.

"The girl in the picture has just earned a master's degree from the University of Texas, Austin. Never married. Involved for a while with a Travis Belcher from Houston. Affluent medical family. Nothing shady. Laurie Tyler, their mother, a widow for more than five years, recently married the county sheriff, an old family friend."

"Can't get much more respectable than that," Hardtack said with finality. The guard took his cue and began backing out of the room. "Thank you, Harry. I'm sure you made all your inquiries with discretion."

"Absolutely, sir."

"You'll be compensated and reimbursed for your expenses. See my secretary later in the day. As usual, I'll depend on your confidentiality."

"Sure thing, Mr. Hardtack."

Once the security guard had withdrawn, Grayson Hardtack studied the pictures more closely, spending several minutes pondering each one.

It was Harlan Boyd, all right, no mistaking that.

Had he sent the Tyler girl? Or was it a contrivance she had conceived? Was her intention to sell him a sprinkler system or blackmail him? What? Or was it all merely a bizarre coincidence? Was she totally innocent of the hornet's nest she had stirred up?

He raised his head and gazed at his wife's portrait across the stately chamber. These unsettling questions needed answers he had to hear for himself. He couldn't send an emissary in his place. He would have to find out what was afloat, even if it resulted in an unpleasant confrontation.

Depressing a button on his panel telephone, he got an outside line and punched in a sequence of numbers. When the telephone on the other end was answered, he barked an order.

"I want the Learjet ready to fly to Milton Point first thing tomorrow morning."

Hanging up, he went back to studying the fuzzy photographs, particularly the handsome visage of the man who had broken his wife's heart.

Chapter Seventeen

Sage's horse limped toward the parked pickup. "Hi." She threw her leg over the saddle and dropped to the ground.

Harlan was sitting on his heels studying a connection in the pipe that had recently been laid. He pushed his hat back on his head and looked up at her. "What's up?"

"I was sent to get you. Somewhere along the way, I think my horse picked up a pebble." Using the caution she'd been taught, she stepped behind the gelding and raised his right rear hoof, securing it between her knees. "Hmm. Sure enough."

A small rock was caught between his hoof and the horseshoe. "I don't think I can get it out without the proper tool." She patted the horse's rump consolingly. "You'll have to give me a ride back," she told Harlan.

"No problem. It's quitting time anyway. Getting dark. I'll only be a minute."

While he applied a wrench to the faulty connection, she walked around the pickup, kicking the tires as she'd seen her brothers do, but having absolutely no idea what purpose was served by that strange, masculine maneuver.

"This wreck looks as bad as its predecessor," she observed out loud.

"Beats walking."

After tying her horse's rein to the bumper, she let down the rusty tailgate and hopped up on it to sit down and wait. It was a moderately mild evening. The sky had already turned dark enough to see the moon.

She removed her riding gloves and unbuttoned her jean jacket. Her horseback ride had loosened her ponytail. Wispy strands of hair drifted across her face with the merest hint of wind.

"Who sent you to get me?" Harlan stood up, peeled off his leather work gloves and slapped them against his thigh to knock the dirt off before tucking them into the hip pocket of his jeans. When he smiled at her, she was glad he didn't know about her secret interview with Hardtack.

Because his trailer was still parked behind a filling station in Austin, he was staying in the house. He and Lucky weren't yet to the backslapping stage, but were working at being friends again. Everyone's focus was on their common goal. Personal feelings had been temporarily suspended.

Well, not all personal feelings, she mentally amended. Harlan and she kept up a pretense of pure professionalism, but she remembered their lovemaking all too well. At night she tossed restlessly and sleeplessly and wondered if he found it just as impossible to sleep.

She hadn't deluded herself. He wouldn't be staying much longer. Once he drew his commission from their first contract, he would leave. Money meant nothing to Harlan. He wouldn't stick around, waiting to profit on bigger and better contracts.

He would have achieved his goals. Tyler Drilling would be back on its feet and prospering. Although she was no longer sexually repressed, she wouldn't be included in any of Harlan's plans for the future. The sooner she started getting over him, the better.

That didn't stop her from loving him. The sight of him in his hat and boots and vest, looking just as he had the first time she saw him on the Belchers' veranda, had painfully increased her yearning and completely obliterated the reason for her being there until he reminded her of it.

"Oh, yes, Mother and Pat called from town," she blurted out. "They're due home any minute."

"No kidding? How do they sound?"

"They were jabbering like magpies, neither making much sense. Like newlyweds, I guess."

Harlan chuckled. "That's good."

"Devon insisted on having everybody out to supper to hear all about their trip."

"All about it?"

"The stuff they can tell." Her insides responded warmly to his naughty inflection. "The boys are picking up babyback ribs from Sammy's Smokehouse. Marcie's bringing baked beans. Devon's making potato salad. I baked a batch of brownies before I left."

"I'm impressed."

"Don't be. I used a packaged mix and prechopped nuts."

"What can I bring to supper?"

"Just yourself. Devon was afraid you'd stay out here working and miss the party altogether, so she sent me to get you."

He sauntered forward, moving to stand directly in front of her. "I'm glad she did."

Her resolution to begin withdrawal procedures evaporated in the heat of his gaze. She missed being with him day and night. She even missed his annoying penchant to tease. She missed his kiss, his touch, and ached to have them again.

Damned if she'd let him know that though.

"Well," she said, scooting forward so she could jump from the tailgate, "I guess we'd better get on our way."

Before she could deflect his hand, he pulled the loose rubber band from her ponytail and plowed his fingers through her tumbling hair. His mouth was hot and masterful as it covered hers. She returned the kiss for several seconds before pushing him away.

"Harlan, I'm still mad at you."

"And the madder you get, the better you look. Put that energy to good use and kiss me like you mean it."

She did. For one thing, she couldn't resist meeting the challenge in his eyes. For the other, she was dying to gobble him up. She threw her arms round his neck and arched her body into his.

Awkwardly, keeping their mouths cemented, he climbed into the pickup's bed, dragging Sage with him. Once he was sitting against the cab, she lay on her back across his lap and reached for his mouth with her own.

"Damn, Sage, I gotta breathe sometime," he said, finally tearing his lips free.

"You said for me to kiss you like I meant it. I only did as I was told."

"That's a switch." Grinning, he whisked his thumb over her moist lips. "You're the damnedest woman I ever met."

"Half the time I don't know whether to slap you or kiss you."

Chuckling, he parted her faded Levi's jacket and lowered his head to nuzzle her breasts. She tugged his shirttail from his waistband far enough to get her hands underneath it and onto his bare skin.

His lips caressed her breasts through the weave of her sweater. Breathlessly she said, "I could kill you for doing this to me."

"What, this?" He rubbed his open mouth over her nipples.

"No," she sighed raggedly, "for making me want you when I can't have you."

He continued kissing her through her sweater while he unfastened her jeans. He pulled down the zipper and slid his hand inside. "I almost wish there was."

"What? You almost wish there was what?"

He placed his hand low on her abdomen. "A baby."

She drew a sudden breath of chilly air and lay very still within his embrace. "Don't lie to me like that, Harlan Boyd. You'd run like a jackrabbit."

He squinted one eye, as though considering it. "No, I think that might give me a damn good reason to stick around." He gazed down at her tousled sexiness. "Not that you're not reason enough, Sage," he added hoarsely.

"I know you've had lots of women. You've left them by the dozens." Beneath his shirt, her fingers curled into his chest hair and pulled tight. "Sage Tyler is going to be the one you find hard to leave and even harder to forget."

"You're right about that." His fingers probed her intimately, finding her soft and moist. Gruffly he added, "You're going to be hell to leave and impossible to forget."

Looking flushed, flustered, and windblown, they arrived at the ranch house just as everyone was convening in the dining room. Sage was immediately smothered in Laurie's embrace.

"Oh, I'm glad to see you looking so well. Doesn't she look wonderful, Pat?"

"Sure does. Like her old self."

Laurie set her daughter away from her and gazed into her face. "You finally got the sparkle back in your eyes and the color back in your cheeks. Whatever you're doing has been very good for you."

"I, uh, well, I've been working very hard. And I went riding out to get Harlan. M-my horse picked up a pebble, so I rode back with him in his truck. We, uh, we left the windows down. Then when we got back, we had to take care of the horse before coming inside." She paused for breath. "Welcome home, Mother, Pat. How was your honeymoon?"

Chase, who had been closely observing his sister and Harlan, cut his eyes toward Lucky, who was also watching the new arrivals with ill-concealed suspicion.

"We put the ribs in the oven to keep them warm," Chase said. "I'll get them."

"I'll help." Lucky instructed Devon to get everybody seated, then followed his brother from the dining room.

When they were alone in the kitchen, Chase posed a silent question with one arched eyebrow.

Lucky nodded soberly.

"I love you, Sage."

Her eyes flew open as a hand closed over her mouth. She panicked for an instant before recognizing Harlan who was bending low above her.

Beneath his hand she tried to ask what in the world he was doing sneaking into her room in the middle of the night. The words came out a garbled mass of unformed syllables.

"Shh! If Lucky catches me in here with my hand over your mouth, he'll skin me alive and ask questions later." She frantically bobbed her head up and down. "Okay, so lie still and listen." He lay down beside her, but kept his hand cupped firmly over her mouth.

"Did you hear what I said? I love you, Sage. You're exasperating as hell. Bullheaded. Impetuous. A spoiled brat. A frequent liar." She glared at him murderously. His white smile showed up in the darkness. "But you're also a hell of a lot of fun, as exciting and unpredictable as whitewater. You kiss like a high-priced call girl, and those brownies you baked for supper weren't the worst I've had.

"What I'm leading up to is, if—and that's a big if—if I asked you to marry me, would you say yes?"

Lying perfectly still, she stared up at him over the back of his hand. Someday, she thought irrationally, she would be able to tell her grandchildren the crazy manner in which their grandpa had proposed to her.

Slowly, she nodded her head.

"Aw, *damn!*" he cursed. "I was hoping you'd say no. Then I could just thank you kindly for your time and a couple of terrific rolls in the hay and be outta here once Tyler Drilling was turned around.

"Now . . ." He made a regretful sound and shook his head. "Since you've said yes, that means we've each got some heavy thinking to do. I guess you love me, too, huh?"

She nodded.

"I'm not what you want, Sage."

She nodded, making guttural protests.

"I'm not ever going to be a society doctor who drives a fancy car. I'll never be city slick. What you see is what you get."

She nodded vigorously.

"But you wanted the other and all the trappings that went with it."

She shook her head no.

"You know how I live. I mean, I wouldn't ask you to live in the trailer. We'd get a house around here somewhere, but it wouldn't be a mansion like Belcher's." His eyes probed hers. "I wouldn't stock our house with things we didn't need just to impress the neighbors."

She shrugged.

"But I promise you this." He scooted closer, half covering her body with his. His voice turned soft and sexy. "I'd be faithful to you, Sage. I'd make good love to you every night. And sometimes during the daytime, too. I'm not squeamish when it comes to making love. I do it all, baby. Whatever you want. There's nothing I wouldn't do if it made you feel good."

She swallowed visibly.

"When I left for work every morning, you'd know that you were the most important thing on my mind. Not making a buck, not chasing a dollar, not getting ahead of the next guy."

The fingers of his free hand slid up into her hair, then closed into a fist next to her head on the pillow. "You'd better give this careful consideration, Sage. You're an executive in a company that's on the brink of busting wide open. You would be marrying the hired help."

She rolled her eyes as though saying, "Oh, please."

"What the hell do you know? You're just a bratty kid."

She shook her head.

"You're smarter than I am."

She shook her head again.

"Prettier."

Another shake of her head.

"Sexier."

A vehement no.

"Yeah?" he asked, pleased. "Well, softer, anyway."

He ducked his head and used it to work the covers off her shoulders. He kissed her there, then on her collarbone, then lower, moving the linens down as he went. When his lips reached the top curve of her breast, he raised his head.

"Are you naked under there?"

She nodded her head yes.

"Lordy." He paused as though weighing his options. To help him make up his mind, she shimmied her shoulders until the covers slipped down to reveal her breasts.

Groaning, he asked, "Do you think they'd know if we—"

She shook her head.

"Okay, then. But you've got to promise not to make those little hiccupping noises you usually make."

Using only one hand, he stripped off his jeans, his only article of clothing, and slid between the sheets beside her. Sighing, he curved his arm around her waist and drew her against him. His sex was pressed full and strong between their bellies.

Sage shuddered at the sensations that coursed through her. Her heart overflowed with love and happiness. She rocked her body against his invitingly. Bracing himself above her, he leaned over for a kiss. Only then did he remove his hand.

"You can open your mouth now," he whispered.

She did . . . in order to receive his tongue. As they kissed, he gathered her beneath him. Effortlessly, he slipped into her warm center. The loving was smooth and easy, creating no more havoc than butter melting, with the smallest motions and minimal sounds, only the rustling of their naked bodies among the linens. He stretched into her, reaching higher than before because love propelled him.

His hands covered her breasts, rubbed them, petted them. He stroked her thighs. When the momentum reached the breaking point, they clasped hands on either side of her head and held onto each other until long after the climax had subsided.

Finally he eased off her and brushed his lips across her dewy forehead. "I don't want to say good-night, but I've got to."

"Don't go," she whispered, ensnaring her fingers in his hair.

Tenderly, he kissed her lips. "You know I have to."

"Don't go." Her hands slid beneath his waist.

"Ah, Sage, baby . . ."

"Don't go."

He didn't go until dawn when she finally slept peacefully beside him. Then he slipped from the room as silently as he had come in.

"Good morning," Sage chirped as she entered the kitchen the following morning. Though the weather was inclement, her mood was positively sunny.

"Hi." Devon was spooning baby oatmeal into her eager daughter's rosebud mouth. "Coffee's ready. Help yourself."

"Thanks. Where is everybody?" Sage asked casually.

"He left about thirty minutes ago."

Sage turned away from the counter and gave her sister-in-law a sharp glance. There were teasing green glints in Devon's eyes. "He said he'd be working on the system all day."

"In this weather?"

"That's what he said." Sage joined her at the table. "Sleep well?" Devon asked with phony innocence. She was barely suppressing her laughter.

"I take it you know."

"Um-huh."

"Does Lucky?"

"No. I wasn't spying on you, Sage. I swear. I happened to wake up and went across the hall to check on Lauren."

Swamped with embarrassment, Sage cast her eyes downward.

Devon reached for her hand and squeezed it. "You love him, don't you?"

"So much it hurts."

"I know what it's like."

"Do you?"

"Absolutely."

"Then you don't think I'm cheap or trashy for letting him sneak down the hall and climb into my bed?"

Devon gave her a smile that was tinged with sadness. "How can you even ask me if I judge you? The first night I met your brother we made love."

The two women smiled at each other with complete understanding. "When people find out," Sage said, "they're going to think I'm crazy. I just came out of a near engagement to Travis."

"If I had let public opinion bother me, I would have stayed married to a convicted felon, ruining my life and Lucky's in the process. Marcie would tell you herself that people were shocked when Chase married her. She didn't let that stop her."

Devon tightened her grip on Sage's hand. "You have to go with your instincts, Sage. Follow your own heart. Do what's best for you and Harlan. To hell with what an outsider thinks about it."

Sage laid her hand over Devon's. "Thanks." Before they could yield to the tears that threatened, the telephone rang. Sage sprung up to answer it.

"Hi, Lucky. Devon's right here. Need to talk to her?"

"No, actually I'm calling you." His voice was laced with excitement. "One of your prospects came through. He's on his way now to talk terms. Chase said for you to haul tail over here to the office. Is Harlan around?"

"He told Devon he was going to work in the field all day."

"Too bad. Chase wanted him here, too, but said for you not to waste time rounding him up."

"Who is it, Lucky? What's the client's name?"

"Hardtack and Associates. Big, bad Grayson Hardtack himself flew in to negotiate the deal."

Chapter Eighteen

The silver Mercedes limousine looked odd parked outside Tyler Drilling Company between a company truck and a pickup. To keep out of the rain, the uniformed chauffeur was sitting behind the wheel. Disinterested, he barely gave Sage a glance when she alighted from her car.

There was no sign of Harlan. She sent up a little prayer of thanksgiving that he had been unavailable when Grayson Hardtack put in this unexpected appearance. It was still a close call, however. She prayed they could conclude their business quickly, and she could contrive some sort of explanation before she saw Harlan. Her legs were rubbery as she went up the steps and pushed open the door.

From across the room, Hardtack said, "Hello, Ms. Tyler."

Sage froze on the threshold. The blood drained from her face. Her brothers, expecting her to be effusively glad to see their guest, looked at her with puzzlement, but she simply could not move or speak.

Her eyes had immediately been drawn to the woman. Sitting quietly in a scarred, scratched straightback chair, she looked as out of place as a masterpiece in a paint-by-number box.

Her clothes, makeup, hair, and the way she held herself were impeccably correct. The back of the chair had been draped with a white mink coat, its pastel satin lining facing out. A pair of kid gloves, which perfectly matched her mauve shoes and suit, were lying in her lap along with a matching handbag.

The breathtaking portrait in Hardtack's office hadn't even done her justice. She was more than beautiful; she was exquisite. Although, Sage thought with a tiny grain of gratification, Marian Hardtack was older than she had expected her to be.

Sage finally regained her composure. She moved inside and extended her unsteady right hand to her client. "Good morning, Mr. Hardtack. It's so nice to see you again."

"Likewise. This is my wife, Marian. Marian, Sage Tyler."

"Hello, Mrs. Hardtack." The woman raised her well-manicured hand. Surprisingly, it felt soft and warm. Sage would have expected it to feel cool. Mrs. Hardtack was so immaculately groomed that, by comparison, Sage felt tacky and disheveled, though there was certainly nothing wrong with her own grooming and attire.

Mrs. Hardtack's smile was warm, too, and that came as another surprise. Her expression was gracious, a tad curious, and as gentle as her voice. "It's a pleasure to meet you, Ms. Tyler."

Sage wondered if she would think so if she knew who she'd been sleeping with the night before.

Remembering her manners, she asked, "Did my brothers offer you coffee?"

"They did, but we drank several cups on the flight over," Hardtack said.

"Oh, you flew from Dallas. I thought . . ." She gestured toward the door.

"The limo? It's only hired for the day to get us around Milton Point." Hardtack resumed his seat. "Let's get down to business."

"While we were waiting on you," Chase said to Sage, "we showed Mr. Hardtack the contract our attorney drew up."

"I think you'll find it's standard," she said.

Hardtack grunted noncommittally. His wife said nothing, but Sage was uncomfortably aware of her unwavering stare as she sat down in the chair Lucky brought for her.

"We guarantee all the parts on the machinery for five years."

"That's at least three years longer than most companies guarantee either their equipment or their work," Lucky said. "We firmly stand behind both and are willing to put our reputations on the line to guarantee them."

Sage had never seen her brothers looking so intense or well behaved. They realized the importance of making a sale to Hardtack. Using his name as a reference would give them instant credibility. Additionally, because he had so many business interests, one job with him could lead to several.

"As I told your sister the other day," he said, speaking to Chase and Lucky, "I can get a sprinkler system anywhere. She sold me on herself. She piqued my interest in your small company. I wanted to come over and personally meet the rest of the family."

He leaned back in his chair. "You know, not everybody in the oil industry is suffering these days. If you know where to get operating capital, there's still money to be made."

Chase's Adam's apple slid up and down. Sage could tell that Lucky was having a hard time keeping his exuberance in check. She hoped he wouldn't leap up and execute one of his infamous backward flips.

Chase said, "We've got a crew standing by, and every man in it likes hard work." Sage was proud of him. He was showing his interest without groveling.

"Glad to hear that," Hardtack said. "I like knowing where I can find expert drillers." He slapped his thighs. "I think this visit has been well worthwhile for everybody, hasn't it?" Looking toward Sage, he said, "I'll have my project supervisor for Shadow Hills contact you. You'll be working directly with him from here on."

He was halfway out of his chair when she asked, "When can we expect the deposit?"

He dropped back down and peered up at her through his eyebrows. Chase and Lucky looked as though lightning had just struck them. They gaped at her, their expressions a mix of incredulity and anger.

"Deposit?"

"That clause is on page three of the contract, Mr. Hardtack. We require a ten thousand dollar deposit, payable immediately upon retention." Her heart was making a racket against her ribs, but she didn't flinch from Hardtack's intimidating stare.

"I'll send you a check by messenger tomorrow. Will that do, Ms. Tyler?"

"Splendidly."

Her brothers slumped with visible relief. Sage, trying to maintain a cool, professional demeanor, glanced at them. Chase gave her a subtle thumbs-up signal. Lucky winked.

"Thank you for taking such a personal interest in this, Mr. Hardtack," she said with a big smile. "Working together will be—"

"Before we shake on it," he said, interrupting her and ignoring her extended hand, "there's one thing I want to know."

Her heady, jubilant flight had been short-lived. Her ego-boosting success stalled, then went into a spiraling nosedive. She lost oxygen on the descent. She awaited the inevitable crash.

"The drawings you left with me had distinctive traits I believe I recognize," Hardtack said. "Was the draftsman Harlan Boyd?"

For a moment her ears roared. She was certain that, had she been standing up, her knees would have buckled. She might have fainted.

The realization of all her aspirations came down to one simple question. Success or failure hinged on her answer. Equivocating would mean an enormous contract with one of the most influential men in the state. It would mean the end to Tyler Drilling's years-long financial struggle and virtually guarantee future prosperity for her family and their employees.

Her ingenuity would get partial credit for bringing it about. She would have won the admiration and confidence of her brothers, proved herself to be a knowledgeable and capable businesswoman, not just their kid sister.

She was a master at avoiding the truth. She didn't lie, exactly, she merely skirted the truth when it wasn't convenient. Hardtack had asked her a pointblank question that required either a yes or no answer. This was one question she couldn't dodge. Somewhat to her surprise, she found she didn't want to.

Even if Lucky and Chase hadn't been looking at her strangely, wondering why the cat had suddenly got her tongue, surely ready to correct her if she told a fib, she confronted Grayson Hardtack, prepared to tell the truth.

Gazing up at her from beneath his shelf of heavy brows, he was an intimidating presence, but she faced him squarely and opened her mouth to speak.

"Yes, I did the drawings. You knew that before you asked her."

Heads turned in the direction of the open doorway. Harlan was standing on the threshold, rain water dripping off the brim of his hat. He was wearing a bright yellow slicker, but his boots and his jeans from the knees down were wet and muddy.

Lucky and Chase seemed baffled, as though they had missed the first two acts of a mystery play and were getting in on the denouement.

Sage recoiled from Harlan's expression. It matched the one he'd assumed when he first saw Hardtack's name on the client list she had compiled. She wanted to go to him with a sound explanation for why she had betrayed his wishes, but his belligerent face and stance kept her rooted where she was.

It was impossible to gauge what Hardtack was thinking.

The woman's reaction, however, was swift and baldly honest. She shot up from her chair. Her gloves and expensive handbag slid from her lap and fell unheeded to the floor. One pale hand, decorated by Tiffany's, found its way to her chest, which was rising and falling rapidly.

"Harlan." His name was expelled on a faint breath. Then she repeated it with more stamina. Finally she cried it joyfully. "Harlan, darling!" She rushed across the room, throwing herself against him, regardless of what his wet slicker was doing to her fine, designer clothing.

He fell back a step to regain his balance and awkwardly placed his arm around her. "Hello, Mother."

"The bottom line is, Harlan is loaded with a capital *L.*"

The entire Tyler clan was gathered in the kitchen, as if tom-toms had notified all members of the family that there was a crisis afoot.

Sage, chopping onions for the pot of chili simmering on the stove, kept her back to them. Since Lucky was the best storyteller, he held the others in thrall.

"We're talking rich. Learjet rich. Limousine-and-driver rich. College-grants and museum-loans and getting-hospital-wings-named-after-you rich." He shook his head in disbelief. "To look at him, you never would guess, would you?"

"I'm confused," Laurie said. "Does the wealth belong to Harlan or Mr. Hardtack?"

"Both. See, Harlan's father Daniel Boyd and Hardtack were business partners. They made millions in commercial real estate and went from there. Daniel died of a heart attack like that," Lucky said, snapping his fingers. "Hardtack bought his interests from the widow, Marian. About a year later, he married her."

"How do you know all this?" Marcie wanted to know. She switched Jamie to her other shoulder. Chase, seeing that she was getting tired, took his son onto his own shoulder.

"It all came out during the shouting match," he said. "At first we weren't able to keep up. Gradually, the more they said, the more we were able to piece together."

Sage raked the chopped onions off the cutting board into the chili pot. With her sleeve, she blotted tears from her eyes and wiped her runny nose. The onions gave her a good excuse to cry.

She had felt so smart, so smug. She thought she had pulled together a big deal, a granddaddy of a deal, a Mount Everest of a deal. Instead, all she had really done was alert Hardtack to Harlan's whereabouts.

That was the only reason he'd flown his private jet to Milton Point and rented a limo for the day. He hadn't come to negotiate a deal with insignificant Sage Tyler, but to track down his wayward stepson.

"I take it that Harlan didn't cotton to the idea of Hardtack marrying his mother," Pat said, rolling a matchstick to the other side of his mouth.

"Hardly," Lucky replied. "Apparently Harlan and his daddy were very close. When he came home from school—he was at Saint Edward's in San Antonio at the time—and they told him that their marriage was a done deal—"

"A *fait accompli,*" Marcie said.

"A what?"

"A done deal," Devon told her husband impatiently. "Get on with the story."

"Harlan accused them of carrying on behind his daddy's back *before* Daniel died. He made the same accusation today. That's when Mrs. Hardtack collapsed into a chair and started bawling something terrible. She kept saying, 'You're wrong, Harlan. You're wrong. I loved your father. How could you ever think I was unfaithful to him?' "

Laurie was automatically sympathetic. "I think Harlan was being too hard on her."

"He was fifteen years old!" Sage spun around and confronted them all. "Don't you realize how protective a fifteen-year-old boy feels toward his mother, especially if she loses her husband? Harlan's reaction was perfectly normal. He felt like Hardtack was usurping his position as head of the household."

Having had her say, she turned back around and began cutting up chili peppers, wielding the butcher knife with a vengeance. What weight did her opinion carry? None. She had made a fool of herself again, bragging about the contracts she was going to get for the company. Hardtack hadn't been interested in the merits of her sales technique.

Lucky continued. "Harlan probably was off-base, but, as Sage said, he was looking at it through the eyes of an adolescent."

"A child grieving for his lost parent and feeling betrayed and deserted by the other," Laurie said, ever fair and ever the sympathizer. "That was a no-win situation for them all, wasn't it? How tragic."

"Harlan resented Hardtack for trying to have everything that had belonged to Daniel Boyd. He judged his mother as a Jezebel. So he split," Lucky said. "He hasn't gone back since. Which brings us to today. When Sage showed Hardtack the drawings, he recognized Harlan's technique."

"How?" Devon asked.

"Unbeknownst to Harlan, Hardtack and Marian have been keeping track of him all this time, though they never interfered in his life. They'd seen his work before."

Chase said, "Hardtack admitted to having Sage followed after she left the drawings with him."

"Oh, my goodness," Laurie said.

The blade of the butcher knife hit the chopping block with a solid *thwack*. Sage was outraged at the thought of being followed and photographed by a private investigator. It seemed so sleazy. She didn't care how many zillions Hardtack was worth, he had his nerve!

"Hardtack pulls a lot of strings," Lucky said. "When he says jump, legions of folks ask how high. Anyway, he verified that Harlan was our draftsman, figured it was time to confront his prodigal stepson face-to-face, and brought Marian along for the showdown."

"He tricked her into coming? She didn't know?" Marcie was aghast at the thought.

"No, she knew. She was anxious to get a glimpse of her son, since she hadn't seen him in fourteen years."

"To his credit, Harlan treated his mother kindly," Chase told the group. "He let her paw him, his face, his hair. You know how mothers do when they haven't seen their kids for a while. They kissed each other and hugged for a long time. It was Hardtack he felt the animosity for."

"So his feelings haven't ameliorated with maturity?" Marcie asked.

"Apparently not," Lucky replied. "He accused Hardtack of taking it all—his partner's business, his partner's money, his partner's wife."

"Strong words," Pat remarked.

"Well, Hardtack was doing his share of shouting, too. He told Harlan that he could think anything he wanted to about him, but he staunchly took offense at Marian being accused of adultery. I got the impression that the tough old buzzard really loves her.

"He claimed that every penny belonging to Marian and Harlan is right where Daniel Boyd left it—in trust, earning interest at an astronomical rate. He said, 'Why don't you stop acting like a snot-nosed kid and claim your inheritance. It's time you assumed some responsibility.'

"Then Harlan said, 'I don't want my inheritance. Not if it could turn me into a money-grabber like you. Screw it and screw the ball and chain that go with it.' "

"Lucky!" Laurie remonstrated. "The children."

"Mother, I'm editing as I go. Harlan didn't say 'screw.' Then Hardtack said that Harlan had no sense of responsibility whatsoever and never would amount to anything except a bum and a drifter. That's when Sage piped in and told Hardtack that Harlan was the most responsible person she had ever met."

All eyes moved to her. "Sage, I commend you for defending our friend," Laurie said, "but it really wasn't your place to interfere."

She swung around. A piece of meat was skewered to the tip of the butcher knife. "It *was* my place. I have every right to stand up for Harlan. He's going to be my husband."

Their exclamations ranged from total disbelief to happy surprise.

"Does Harlan know that?" Lucky asked.

"He asked me to marry him last night."

Lucky came out of his chair. "When last night? Where was I?"

"You were sound asleep."

He looked hard at his wife. "Devon, I knew you were keeping something from me. Do you know something I should know?"

"Sit down, Lucky. You're upsetting Lauren."

"She's right, Lucky, sit down," Chase barked. "If you fly off the handle, you'll only make things worse."

"And if you fight him again, I'll break your arm myself this time," Sage declared.

"I thought you broke your arm when you tripped against a trailer hitch," Laurie exclaimed.

Lucky ducked his head sheepishly.

Chase sighed and said to Laurie, "He tripped and fell against a trailer hitch during a fistfight with Harlan over Sage's virtue. We were afraid she might be pregnant."

Laurie gasped and reached for Pat's hand. The sheriff's expression was thunderous. "Can't you young'uns ever behave yourselves? We leave town for a few weeks, and everything goes to hell in a handbasket."

"Is there more?" Laurie asked, looking pained.

"Not really," Lucky said. "Except that Hardtack didn't back out of his deal with us despite his shouting match with Harlan."

A door slammed upstairs.

"Shh, here he comes," Chase whispered.

In the sudden silence of the kitchen, Sage held her breath. No one had seen Harlan since his stepfather had called him a 'sniveling little sonofabitch,' whose damned stubborn pride was breaking his mother's heart. That's when Harlan had slung open the door of Tyler Drilling's office and stalked out.

Sage had plunged after him, but he was already out of sight by the time she reached her car. She had driven home through a blinding rain, hoping to see his pickup parked out front. She had sobbed with relief when she turned into the lane and saw it there.

But then she had lost her nerve. Instead of rushing upstairs, she and everyone else had allowed him privacy to sort through the upsetting events of the morning. After years of running from it, he had been forced to confront his unhappy youth. He would need space in which to grapple with it.

Now they could hear his boots on the stairs, then in the dining room as he made his way toward the kitchen. Everyone pretended to be occupied, but Lauren was the only one actually moving. She was blowing slobbery bubbles against her mother's cheek.

He stepped through the doorway, his eyes seeking out Sage immediately. She gave him a tentative smile, which collapsed the instant she spotted the duffel bag in his hand.

"I'll be leaving now. I cleared your room out. You can have it back."

The announcement left them stunned. Chase was the first to recover his speech. "You're leaving?"

Harlan stepped forward and shook hands with Chase. "I liked you the first time we met in Houston last year. I like you even better now that I've gotten to know you. Good luck."

He moved to Lucky and clasped his left hand. "Sorry again about your arm. I didn't mean to do it. You're a hell of a guy."

To them both he said, "Everything checked out this morning. With those new computers, the pumps'll work like a charm. You'll find all my drawings in the file cabinet in the garage. Using them as guidelines, your people shouldn't have any problems with the layout and assembly."

"We hate to see you go, Harlan," Chase said quietly.

"It's time I did." He glanced quickly at Sage. "Past time."

"But what about your commission? How'll we know where to send your checks? If some of these contracts that you and Sage worked on together pan out, you'll be due a lot of money."

He gave a dismissive shrug. "I've got enough cash to last a while. If I need the money, I'll contact you."

They knew he wouldn't. Even as he said it, he was backing out the door. "Devon, Marcie, take care of those sweet babies. I'm gonna miss them. Pat, look after Laurie. She's a darlin' lady."

Laurie stood up and extended her arms toward him in a maternal gesture. "Harlan, please."

"Bye, y'all." He pulled on his hat, ducked out the door and disappeared.

Sage gaped at the empty doorway for the space of several seconds, aware that everyone was trying desperately hard not to look at her with pity.

Before she had time to think about it, she dashed after him. Dodging furniture like an expert swordsman, she charged through the rooms of the house, bolted through the front door, ran across the porch, and leaped over the steps. Heedless of the cold, pelting rain, she caught up with him as he tossed his duffel bag into the cab of his pickup.

Grabbing hold of his sleeve, she spun him around. "Where the hell do you think you're going? You can't just walk out on me like this!"

"Get back inside. You're gonna get soaked."

"I don't care if I get wet anymore than I care if you're a Texas Donald Trump or as poor as Job's turkey. I want you, whether you come garbed in riches or standing buck-naked."

On her headlong flight from the kitchen, she had forgotten to discard the butcher knife. She shook the blade at the end of his nose. "I learned something about myself today. I'm a person to be reckoned with.

"At first, I thought that Hardtack had come here strictly to find you. Then about thirty seconds ago, it occurred to me that he didn't have to sign a contract with us to locate you. Once his investigator had sighted us together, he could have circumvented us and gone straight to you.

"So that means he *was* sold on me just as he said. I sold him on Tyler Drilling. I didn't get that contract because of you, but in spite of you.

"Oh!" she ground out. "You've been accusing me of avoiding the truth, when you've been living a lie for years. It's time you stopped avoiding who and what you are, Harlan. It's time you reconciled your differences with Hardtack, if not for your own benefit, then certainly for your brokenhearted mother's.

"And another thing, you can't make love to me and propose marriage and then hightail it out of here, Harlan Boyd. How dare you even try? How dare you embarrass me in front of my family right after I announced that you had asked me to marry you?

"This time I'm not going to swallow my pride and hide my hurt feelings like I did with Travis. This one counts. This time I'm going to kick and scream and pull temper tantrums and lie down in front of your truck and whatever else it takes to keep you.

"You boasted of never leaving a job unfinished. Well, last night you promised to remain faithful to me and make me happy. That's a job that's going to last for the rest of your life.

"You can't accuse me of wanting to marry you for your money either. Because when you asked me and I said yes, I didn't know you had a nickel. I loved you then as much as I do now. So haul that duffel bag out of that truck and march it right back upstairs. You're not going anywhere without me."

Rain was streaming down her face. Her clothing was plastered to her. Her hair clung to her face and neck in wet clumps. But she was impervious to it all.

In his adorable drawl, he asked, "Are you gonna poke me with that butcher knife if I don't?"

"I might. You're going to marry me if I have to kill you first."

Muttering curses and ruefully shaking his head, he gazed out over the sodden landscape. When his gaze came back to her, he laughed. Reaching out, he dug his hand into the waistband of her slacks and jerked her against him. Wresting the butcher knife from her hand, he tossed it away. It landed with a splash in the nearest puddle.

"I've got a lot of money," he said for starters.

"So what?"

"I'll never let it own me, Sage. Don't count on my changing my attitude toward it."

"The only thing I'll count on is your not changing your attitude toward me."

"What's my attitude toward you?"

"You love me. You adore me. You're addicted to me. You'd die without me in your life. I make you hot and hard and happy."

Laughing, he cupped his hands beneath her bottom and lifted her up. She wrapped her legs around his hips. He pivoted slowly while the rain fell on them. "You're crazy, but you're right."

"On which point?"

"All of the above."

"Then kiss me like you mean it."

When they finally broke apart, he glanced warily toward the front of the house. "Damn, Sage. If you don't quit kissing me like that, we'll have to start the honeymoon right here and now."

She bit his lower lip. "That's the general idea."

Epilogue

"Harlan, wake up. It's time."

He snuffled and buried his face in her hair. "I'd love to, baby, but I'm beat. Can you wait till morning?"

Sage laughed softly and removed his questing hand from her breast. "I don't mean it's time for *that*. It's time to go to the hospital."

He sat bolt upright in bed. "You mean the baby?"

"I've been having contractions for the past two hours."

"Two hours! Damn, Sage. Why didn't you wake me up?"

"As you said, you were beat. You really shouldn't have driven home from Louisiana tonight."

"If I hadn't, where would you be now, huh?" He shoved his legs into his jeans and stood up in one fluid motion.

He'd been in the neighboring state overseeing a rig Tyler Drilling had leased to a new oil company headed by his stepfather. When he had called at dusk to say he was coming home, she had discouraged him from making the trip that late in the day. Now she was glad he had insisted.

"I've been away from you too long, baby," he had said.

"It's only been two days."

"That's way too long."

Recalling the fervency behind his words made her smile as she reached for the nightstand telephone. "I'll call the doctor."

"Where's the damn suitcase?" he asked, plowing through the clothes hanging in the closet. "Good thing you already packed it. Where is it?"

"It's in the other closet." She asked the doctor's answering service to notify him that she was on her way to the hospital and hung up. "Harlan, calm down. We've got plenty of time. My water hasn't even— Uh-oh!"

"What?" His head popped out of the closet.

"My water just broke."

Cursing liberally, he wrapped her in a blanket and carried her out to the car. "Breathe," he commanded, even though his own breathing was unsteady. "Remember to breathe the way they taught us in class."

He tucked her into the passenger seat and ran around the hood, his open shirt flapping.

"Button your shirt," she told him as they pulled away from the house that Marcie had sold them, waiving her commission as a wedding gift.

"Why are you worrying about my shirt at a time like this?"

"I don't want all the nurses drooling over your hairy chest, that's why."

At a traffic light he stopped only long enough to hastily fasten the buttons, then sped through the red light. "You're going to get a ticket," she warned.

"I've got connections at city hall."

"Not for long. Pat's retirement party is next week. Oh, Harlan, I can't miss the party!"

Laurie had redecorated Pat's former bachelor pad from the foundation up, turning it into a dollhouse of a showplace. She loved living in town where she was close to all her friends and activities. For all practical purposes, they were still on their honeymoon. It was difficult to say which of them was more besotted.

"If necessary, they'll postpone the party," he assured her. Reaching across the car interior, he laid his hand on Sage's stomach. "He's early, isn't he? Why's he early? You don't think anything's wrong, do you?"

"Nothing's wrong. He's just anxious to meet you. I've told him so much about you," she said gently, covering his hand with her own.

The tires squealed when he pulled up to the emergency room. Not even waiting for a gurney, Harlan scooped her into his arms again and carried her inside.

Once they were officially checked in, a nurse said, "The doctor will need to see her alone for a few minutes, Mr. Boyd, then you can join her."

"Call everybody," Sage shouted over her shoulder as she was wheeled away.

By the time the family had been notified, he was able to join her in the labor room. He put on the scrub suit that was required.

"Definitely your shade of blue," Sage remarked once he was properly gowned.

"Always the smart aleck. Never knows when to keep her mouth shut." He bent over her, his eyes suddenly turning serious and misty. "Damn, Sage, I love you."

"I love you too." She gripped his hands. "I'm kind of scared."

"You?"

"Yes. And you know I wouldn't admit that to anyone except you. Stay with me, Harlan."

"Forever, baby. You can count on it."

Huffing and puffing and calling her OB a heartless, male chauvinist pig, she was wheeled into the delivery room. Minutes later, with Harlan's assistance, she gave birth to his son. The good-natured doctor lifted the squirming, squalling infant into the father's waiting arms.

"Congratulations, Mr. Boyd."

"Call me Harlan," he said absently as he laid his son on Sage's breast.

"Oh, he's beautiful," she whispered in awe. "Look, Harlan, at what a wonderful baby we made."

It was almost an hour later before they were finally left alone with their son. The nurse had warned them they couldn't keep him long before he needed to be returned to the nursery.

Sage fingered his cap of blond fuzz. "He's got your hairline, Harlan. Your nose."

"My penis."

"Oh!" she exclaimed. Then, giving him a sultry smile, she added, "Not hardly." They laughed together softly, then kissed. "Did you call everyone?"

"They'll descend on the nursery as soon as the hospital staff will let them in. The hospital ought to give us a family discount, as much business as we're giving them."

To everyone's delight, Marcie had announced that she was pregnant again, even though Jamie wasn't even a year old. Her biological clock was running out, she had said. Her business was prospering even though she only worked part-time, so she could indulge her maternal instincts. Chase and she were fabulously happy.

Devon's column had been syndicated to several out-of-state newspapers. Lucky and she were talking about having another child, although he swore he couldn't possibly sire another one as delightful as Lauren. In the same breath, he said he sure would have fun trying though.

Tyler Drilling almost had more business than it could accommodate. Between the two separate entities, they kept their trucks rolling from city to city. Until a few weeks ago, Sage had been at the helm of the irrigation business, coordinating schedules, soliciting new clients, and managing the office, which had been added onto and was now staffed with two secretaries.

"What about Marian and Grayson?" Sage asked her husband now. "Did you call them?"

"Mother flipped out. They're flying over in the morning."

Sage reached up and affectionately stroked his cheek. Thanks to her peace-making attempts, Grayson and Harlan were civil to each other. There was still some turbulence between them over Harlan's refusal to become Grayson's business partner. It was a point they constantly disagreed on, and always would. But mother and son had been reunited, and that was the most important thing.

Harlan had admitted to Sage that he had carried the wounds of adolescence into adulthood. He never really believed that his mother had been unfaithful before his father's death or that Grayson had done anything unscrupulous. It was simply easier to blame them for his father's death than to focus his anger on something he couldn't combat.

Grayson, with his brusque personality, was such a departure from the easygoing man who had fathered Harlan, that the boy couldn't accept him. Sage patiently explained to him that Grayson didn't treat Marian in the same manner he treated a business rival.

"I'm certain he loves your mother very much."

"I suppose he does. But after Mother married him, I started thinking of money as something evil," he had told her in an attempt to explain. "With enough money, someone could assume control of other people's lives. I wanted no part of it."

In the last few months, he had begun to dip into his inheritance, but only because he hated to see it lying in waste when so many people could use it. He was quietly philanthropic. The substantial donations he made to diverse organizations and charities never knew from whom the staggering contributions came.

"Why didn't you just give it away before?" Sage had once asked him. "For instance, when you saw Tyler Drilling was in trouble, why didn't you just give the money to Chase?"

"Because money alone wouldn't have solved the problem. Not in the long run. Besides, I liked getting involved and having to use my own resources to work out problems. Folks don't accept charity too well, but unless you're dealing with fools, they're usually open to fresh ideas. I left them with the satisfaction of knowing that they'd worked through their difficulties themselves. If I'd signed a check, they would have missed that personal gratification. So would I."

He still wore jeans older than most graduating high school seniors and drove a pickup that Sage threatened to shoot and put out of its misery if it broke down one more time. He claimed it still had some good miles left in it.

Now, gazing up at him with love, she said softly, "They asked me how to fill in his birth certificate. I told them his name is Daniel Tyler Boyd."

"Daniel," he repeated thickly, tears shimmering in his eyes. "Thanks, Sage. I like that." He swallowed hard and cleared his throat. "I can't get over how much he weighed. To be so premature, seven and a half pounds is a lot, isn't it?"

She moistened her lips and pulled her lower one through her teeth. "Actually, Harlan, he's not all that premature."

"You told me your due date was in early November."

"That's what I told you, yes. The fact is, Daniel's right on time."

"But this is the first of October. That would move his conception back to early January."

"Um-huh."

As clarity dawned, his eyes connected with hers. "Why you little liar. You were pregnant all along. It happened that day in the trailer, right? You lied and said there was no baby."

"I didn't exactly lie. When I said there was no baby, the jury was still out. I couldn't have you and my brothers at fisticuffs, could I? I certainly didn't want you to marry me out of obligation or pity. So, yes, I denied that there was a baby when, in fact, Daniel was already developing fingerprints."

Harlan stared at her for a moment, absolutely incredulous. Then he threw back his head and laughed. Daniel frowned against his mother's breast.

"Well, I'll be damned," Harlan whispered. He took the baby's tiny hand and rubbed it between his fingers. "Did you hear that, Daniel? Your mama really pulled one over on me this time."

Then he buried his free hand in Sage's hair and lowered his lips to hers. "You're the damnedest woman I ever met, Miss Sage. Kiss me like you mean it."